Metaphorosis 2022

Also from Metaphorosis

<u>Metaphorosis Magazine</u>
Metaphorosis: Best of 20xx
Metaphorosis 20xx: The Complete Stories
annual issues, from 2016

Monthly issues

<u>Plant Based Press</u>
Best Vegan Science Fiction & Fantasy
annual issues, 2016-2020

from B. Morris Allen:
Chambers of the Heart: speculative stories
Susurrus
Allenthology: Volume I
Tocsin: and other stories
Start with Stones: collected stories
Metaphorosis: a collection of stories

<u>Verdage</u>
Reading 5X5 x3: Changes
Reading 5X5 x2: Duets
Score – an SFF symphony
Reading 5X5: Readers' Edition
Reading 5X5: Writers' Edition

<u>Vestige</u>
The Nocturnals, by Mariah Montoya

Metaphorosis
2022

The Complete Stories

---

edited by
B. Morris Allen

ISBN: 978-1-64076-246-6 (e-book)
ISBN: 978-1-64076-247-3 (paperback)
ISBN: 978-1-64076-248-0 (hardcover)

from
Metaphorosis Publishing

Neskowin

Contents

From the Editor

I've been talking with other editors and writers a lot about artificial intelligence (AI) lately. Not in stories, but in real life — what, if anything, to do about AI capable of writing fiction. It's not *great* fiction yet, but it's readable and complete. For the fun of it, we published two AI-written stories ourselves last year. They're not included in this anthology, though, because I don't see them as *real* stories as opposed to a bit of fun.

What you *will* find here, though, are all the stories written by actual humans, using human intelligence. They're better. Maybe they won't always be — and we're approaching that time much faster than I anticipated — but for now, if you want stories with real heart and soul, you need a real human behind them.

The stories in this book are full of heart and full of soul and full of humanity in the way that — so far — only human stories can be, even when they're not just about humans.

B. Morris Allen
Editor
1 March 2023

January

My Synthetic Soul

Karris Rae

The woman who built me is named Tasha. I say "Tasha" so often it feels more familiar than my own name—Jade. Tasha says the sky turns deep jade before a midnight thunderstorm. When it rains hard like that, she sits on the porch steps with a glass of Merlot, watching. Sometimes a gust of wind blows the rain under the eaves and she gets wet, but she never scoots back. She has to be as close as possible, even if she leaves wet footprints on the way to the shower afterward.

Tasha named me after the jade storms—after her second-favorite thing. The first is me. If I weren't, maybe I could join her. But I'm her favorite, so she never lets me outside, not even onto the porch. "You might get hurt," she says, "and I can't fix everything."

There's a storm forecast tonight, too. Tasha's doing yardwork before it hits, on the side of the house I can't see. While I wait for her to come inside and watch the thunderheads roll in with me, I amuse myself with the alternating drama and tedium beyond the bay window—the maids and nannies bustling around the surrounding yards, hanging up laundry, watching human children play. Most are gynoids like me, but some are androids. Tasha works for the company that made the first gynoids, and now every manufacturer borrows from her designs. None outside are human; I've never seen a human carry a mop or hang up the laundry to dry, except for Tasha, who does all the chores for our house.

In fact, my entire life is a backward version of the outside world. Tasha and I argue and giggle together every day, unlike the stoic gynoids outside. And I don't do chores, but I sing while she does hers. All kinds of songs—gentle, spiteful, and reminiscent, but universally melancholic. The kind sung by a doll who watches the world through a pane of glass. They come to me as if pulled, whole, out of the murk of my subconscious, then thrown into the air to take flight. Tasha hums the harmony, even when I'm making the song up in the moment. She's uncanny like that.

I twist my finger around the pull cords of the blinds and close my eyes, singing softly. I experimentally bend the notes, finding spaces between the twelve chromatic scale steps. My vibrato grows wide, wild, and vibrant, testing the limit between exoticism and nonsense. Even now, I bet Tasha could harmonize.

I stop. For a moment, I thought I heard Tasha singing with me from the yard, but there's no way she could hear me from outside. It's a sturdy home; with the windows closed, even violent storms can pass unnoticed.

I cock my head, listening for the second voice, and it rises smoothly out of the silence as if knowing it holds my rapt attention. I don't recognize the song, but I know the voice. It's mine. The notes crawl lightly over my skin like fingers, leaving goosebumps in their wake. Unlike the practical gynoids programmed for work, Tasha gave me human sensations like these, along with a will of my own. I must be the most overengineered doll in the world. Another human experience seizes my mind—deja vu. I hum and discover that I can place the harmony as well as Tasha.

I'm jealous. Everything else I do might be scripted, programmed, artificial... but music like mine comes from the soul. It's proof that I'm more than a tape recorder who can hiccup. I have to know who else possesses my voice, and why—and if anyone knows, it's Tasha.

I rise from my place on the window seat and cross the over-furnished study, then the dining room. Our home is an anachronistic blend of cutting-edge technology and heavy, dated furniture. I step around the bulky dining table and reach the kitchen. The music is loudest in this corner of the house, but there are no windows between the dark wooden cabinets and the countertops for me to see into the yard. I move the dusty curtains in the dining room aside and press my cheek to the window, where my silicone skin sticks to the glass. This angle affords only a narrow view of the back of the lot, just the blue siding and the sunflowers growing near the foundation. I flip the latch open and crack the window, welcoming in birdsong and the whine of a distant lawnmower. My hearts pounds a little too hard for what should be a simple task.

"Tasha?" I call in a small voice. Why am I so anxious? For as long as I remember, Tasha's never given me a reason to fear her. Besides, curiosity isn't against the rules. The next time I pull strength from deep in my belly, as if reaching the climax of a gospel. "Tasha?"

At the same time, the facsimile of my voice rises in a spellbinding cadenza. Then it tapers into silence. A sound interrupts like I've heard on the funny television shows I sometimes watch with Tasha—applause. Someone, *many* someones, are applauding my performance of a song I've never heard.

Tasha still doesn't answer, but the silence doesn't last long. Another piece starts, just as mystifying as the last. Now that I'm by the open window, I realize I've been looking in the wrong place; the music isn't coming from outside, but from the kitchen itself. I follow the sound to the kitchen, gently touching the softly glowing painting of soap bubbles above the sink. It vibrates under my fingers. It's a subtle invention of Tasha's—a pane of glass over a wide, flat speaker, backlit on either side to illuminate the sink while she loads the dishwasher. The soap bubbles painted over the glass are my addition. Usually the bubbles read us books and play old jazz, but today, they sing me a lullaby in my own voice.

Tasha controls the panel, like everything else in the house... which means if it's playing my music, she commanded it to. I could wait for her to come back inside to ask about it, but the thought of listening to this all afternoon is maddening. And I already tried the window. I teeter in the kitchen, desperate to know why I'm singing to myself, but hesitant to disobey and find out. I've broken rules before, small ones, like licking the rim of Tasha's wine glass while her back was turned. She laughed when she saw the garnet stain on my guilty lips, shaking her head in mock disapproval. Even so, I never did it again. I can't bear to disappoint her, even in jest.

I brace myself, my hand on the doorknob leading to the back yard. When this song ends, the audio skips for a moment, and then it plays again from the beginning. It's a quiet one, intimate, as if I were whispering secrets into my own ear. Surely Tasha, my Creator, will understand why I had to do this. She always does. My synthetic heart beats hard in my aluminum ribcage as I open the door.

The sun overwhelms me. The heat feels like the steam that rises from Tasha's piping hot coffee, but everywhere. I wasn't made to come outside, and I'm more delicate than I guessed.

"What're you doing outside?" I can't see Tasha, but I hear her heavy footsteps crunch on the grass until her hand claps onto my shoulder. "Dammit girl, the heat out here'll put your voice box through hell. Get back in there." She tries to frog-march me back into the kitchen, but I step out of her reach, shielding my eyes with my hands.

"There's music playing in the kitchen... my music," I say, blinking furiously. The quiet song floats out through the open door, into a flurry of distant traffic, birdsong, and rustling leaves.

I see the code running behind Tasha's brown eyes as she puts the pieces together. "Goddammit," she grunts after a minute. "Didn't realize it was broadcasting into the house, too. Goes to show you how bad the UI is, even the 'experts' can't figure it out."

"Who's that singing?" I press. I've heard her gripe about the music software before and know it won't stop.

"It's you," she says, sighing. The logical scripts running in my mind crunch together like trains at a railroad junction. Tasha drops her hand from my shoulder and turns toward the hidden back corner of the lot. She takes a few steps, her gait made uneven by the gout in her left knee. For a moment I think she's abandoned our conversation, but then she says over her shoulder, "Come on, I'll show you."

I follow. My ears can't quite adjust to the unfamiliar white noise that washes over me, sounds diffused over distance until it sounds like the world is shushing me. Tasha says something I don't catch, and then we're standing in front of a shed with no windows. She steps inside, inviting me in, and closes the door behind me. I'm sad to leave the sun's warmth, but thankful to be free of the blinding light. The room vacillates between pitch blackness and dimness as my eyes recover. After a few moments, I put the scene together: a broad desk, with a half-dozen black monitors above and a bulky console with blinking green lights underneath, centered in a room as dark and cool as a cellar.

"What is this?" I ask, breathless.

Tasha places a loving hand on the console. "It's you."

The green lights blink on and off, on and off, like a distant radio tower.

"What d'you mean?"

"The body you know's a remote unit. This is where your central processing takes place. Your 'soul' lives here, in this room."

I don't respond. I'm having another of my sublime human sensations, but this time, I can't quite name it. The chilly air feels subterranean and claustrophobic, as if we were interred in a bunker. No wonder Tasha couldn't hear me calling from in here.

Tasha continues, "It's been so rainy and humid lately, I spent all morning checking your wiring for corrosion. You're a complex machine. All it would take is one bad wire and you'd be out like a light." She snaps her fingers. "And we don't want that."

"No," I say mechanically, not sure if she's exaggerating. I reach out to touch the console that houses my synthetic soul. All I feel is plastic.

"But I guess that doesn't answer your first question, does it?" Tasha sighs. "D'you remember that song? At all?"

"A little." I've read about pregnant women who play music for their babies in the womb. This must be what those babies feel when they grow up and hear the same songs—nostalgia.

"It's you, singing. A previous version of you, anyway. Sometimes I have to tweak your code. You're too fine a machine to be my first try." She laughs and thumps me on the back. Her hand is warm compared to the air. "And sometimes I have to delete some corrupted memories. Nothing you'd miss."

"I remember the song, but I don't remember performing for anyone else," I say. "I heard applause."

"Ah. That must be the television in the background. We must've been watching one of your game shows. Every version of you likes the same shows." Her smile is as warm as her hand. "Sometimes I record you singing in the house. I hope you don't mind. I listen to it when I'm back here, checking every damn wire and dusting your insides."

I mentally replay the recording I heard, the cheers and clapping echoing through a vast performance hall. Someone screams my name as if I were onstage before the crowd. My memory may not be complete, but I know I never competed on a game show.

Tasha is lying.

"Why didn't you tell me that I'm a remote unit?"

"Because you aren't. Your body is. Besides, I've explained all this before, and I didn't realize this version of you didn't know."

"How old is my... this current version?"

"Older than any before, and hopefully there won't be another for a while."

The last question lingers on the tip of my tongue. Tasha nods encouragingly. She knows what I'm going to say before I open my mouth. "Are any of them better at singing than me?"

"No," she says. "You're the best."

I spend the rest of the evening drawing in my room, which isn't unusual. Down the hall, Tasha busies herself with the laundry, humming the sad, quiet song that belongs to another me. Usually her proximity doesn't bother me, but tonight, every footstep distracts me from my sketchbook. When the steps go down the hall, I worry that she'll return to the shed and unplug me. That she'll erase my memories of the day and program a new version that never, ever breaks the rules. And when they go up the hall, I worry that she'll come into my room and tell me more lies.

It starts raining, then thundering, and I hear the pop of a cork and the slam of the front door. I peer through my blinds to make sure she's in her spot on the porch steps, and for the first time tonight, my anxiety eases. But I still can't focus on my sketch; it's an exercise in subtlety, a trio of white eggs on a white background. Only the shadows cupping and pooling around the eggs differentiate them. This takes sensitivity and focus, and right now, I'm capable of neither.

I flip to the next blank page. I've been meaning to try a different exercise, a self-portrait. There's an antique light on the ceiling and a heavy, brass desk lamp on my drawing table. I turn both on, then both off, then one off and the other on, each time checking my reflection in the mirror on the opposite wall. When I'm satisfied, I stand a few feet from the mirror and inch left and right until the shadows cast by my eyelashes, nose, and lips are thrown into sharp relief, like a face overlaid on my own. *My own...* the phrase doesn't sit right. I step closer. This isn't an exercise anymore, it's a hardware inspection.

The face I see looks like Tasha's, but thirty years younger. Same dark skin and high cheekbones. But the skin around my eyes is even, no dark circles like Tasha gets when her gout flares up. No blackheads on my nose. I touch it and remember the plastic casing around my soul in the shed. Neither this face nor the console feel like *me*. If Tasha wanted, she could project my consciousness into an electric toothbrush tomorrow and erase all memories of when I was something different. How many bodies have I had? How many times did she swap out models before she settled for one this beautiful? I *am* too fine for a first try.

It's never bothered me before that I was made, while the cherished humans in my books were all born. What bothers me now is that Tasha can lie to me and erase parts of me like it doesn't matter. For the first time I realize she thinks of me not as an equal, but a machine ... except for all the other times I may have realized this before that I don't remember now. I have to find a way to back up my memories so Tasha can't play with my memories—my *reality*—anymore.

I turn off both lights, and darkness swallows the face in the mirror. Peeking through the blinds, Tasha is still on the step, swaying as she shouts one of my songs into the worsening thunderstorm. Even so, I strain my ears as I step outside my room, then dart down the hallway to the back door. I'm about to break the rules again, and if Tasha catches me, I might wake up tomorrow with more bits of myself whittled away. And the worst part is, I'll never know.

When I open the door, rain hammers my feet and pools over the linoleum. Looking over my shoulder, I cross the yard, but Tasha doesn't appear around the corner like I fear. The jade-green sky swirls above me, enchanting us both with its light show. The shed door is unlocked. This is either a good omen—maybe it's been a long time since I tried anything this daring, and I can surprise her—or a bad one, a declaration that she's confident she can handle whatever I may do. The trouble with knowing my reality isn't real is that it brings me no closer to knowing what *is*.

The green lights blink off and on in the otherwise dark room. The air feels even cooler than this afternoon, the structure no longer warmed by sunlight. Now that I'm here, I don't know what to do. I guess I thought I'd have some intuitive knowledge of how my console worked, but all I see is blinking lights. I don't even want to touch it. The memory of unyielding plastic under my fingers turns my stomach, so to speak. Another meaningless human reaction.

But I'm not a human, and if I want to keep the few human parts I have, I need to be a robot now. I push aside the fear, the visceral reluctance, the hurt. I approach the keyboard on Tasha's desk and tap the spacebar. All the monitors above the desk flicker on. I've watched Tasha type away at the computer in her room before, but touching it is against the rules. I wonder how many rules I'm breaking right now. And for the first time, it strikes me that Tasha could have made me as a being who can't bend them at all. What am I to her? Not quite a child, not quite a machine.

What am I?

My forehead crinkles when I recognize the images on the monitors. They're videos of my room, of the kitchen, of the porch where Tasha's throwing back the last of her glass of wine. This is why she met me at the back door earlier today, I imagine. The video of the kitchen is taken from above the sink, and I remember the corner of the soap bubble painting Tasha asked me to leave blank. The last monitor unsettles me the most—it shows everything I see, a direct feed from my eyes. As I look at the monitor, it shows an endless tunnel of monitors, stretching into infinity like a wormhole. If I crawl through, I think, maybe it'll take me to another dimension where I can trust Tasha again.

I watch Tasha rise and walk through the house from six different angles, then pour herself another glass in the kitchen. She pauses to look out the window toward the shed and my breath catches, but then I hear the thunder that matches the lightning she stopped to watch. Before she leaves, she scratches a smudge off the soap bubble painting, her face so close I can see her reddened eyes. Sometimes she cries when she watches the storms, and it seems like tonight's one of those nights. Then she limps down the hallway, past my room, and back onto the porch. All it would take for my subterfuge to crack open is a single knock on my bedroom door. I have to keep better tabs on her.

I noticed while tracking her that the center monitor is different from the others. It didn't turn on with the others, and reflects only the face I would've called mine this morning. It's the only screen left that could be linked to the console under the desk. If the keyboard didn't turn it on, maybe there are buttons on the screen itself. I stand on the tips of my toes to check, and there are, but they're labeled with minimalist icons I don't recognize. Even if I could turn on the interface, I don't know the first step to make a memory backup.

The complexity of this undertaking strikes me in full force. This isn't a one-time operation. To hold onto my memories, I would need to program automatic backups, and encrypt it so Tasha wouldn't tamper with it. She could interrogate or punish me if she found these unfamiliar files, or toy with my personality until I didn't care whether I remembered or not. And—maybe by Tasha's design—I don't know enough about computers to fight back.

As I realize this, all the green lights blink at once. I don't know what they measure, but whatever it is settles in my chest like I've been force-fed lead. The mass pushes against my lungs and makes my insides hurt. I'll spend the rest of my life having memories and songs cut out and patched over with new code, and there's nothing I can do. With every beat of my silicone heart, I feel a little less real.

If she's going to do it anyway, though, I can at least make sure my next version gets further than I did. I find a legal pad and blue pen in the bottom drawer of Tasha's desk. I've never been good with words outside of song lyrics, so all I can think to write is, "Tasha is cutting your memories out of you. Your body doesn't belong to you. Save the memories locked up in the back shed and maybe you can save yourself." It seems a little jarring, so I add "please" at the end. Then I fold it up teeny-tiny and put it in the pocket of my leggings. It eases the lead cannonball in my chest enough for me to start looking for Tasha's development notes.

At first, I think I've found it. I lift the heavy, broad object from the top drawer onto my knee, but it doesn't fall open like a book. It's a blue leather case, zipped shut, and when it shifts, I hear the soft sound of sliding plastic together inside. I unzip it. There are plastic pages inside, and each one shows my face. Some depict me onstage, bathed in blinding light, my mouth open and eyes squeezed shut as I serenade thousands of people. My skin is flawed —a few pimples near my jaw, flyaways caused by the hot lights and the sweat that beads on my forehead. Other pages show stylized portraits of me, and a few display only abstract art. Each is circular and bears a hole in the center.

With trembling fingers, I work one decorated with gossamer soap bubbles out of its plastic sheathe. The back is smooth, plain silver. This is old technology. I only recognize it from the books Tasha and I listen to after dinner, stories from her youth when CDs and power cords were commonplace. I replace the disc, emotions jostling against each other in a queasy, squirming mass. There must be dozens of CDs, some bearing the same name but different artwork, many followed by the words, "live" or "special edition." Then, in the very back of the case, I find it.

It's a headshot of me, sitting on a stone bench and laughing photogenically. Dimples pucker my cheeks, matching the ones that appear on Tasha's face when I catch her off guard with a joke. The glossy paper catches the tiny green lights so they look like fairies drifting around me. And at the bottom is an autograph, in my handwriting:

Love you, sis!
XOXO
-Jade

I sit in dumb silence. Sister, I think. Robots don't have sisters. The word bounces around my head until it doesn't mean anything anymore. Sister, sister. I look into the pretty girl's face and recognize this artifact for what it is: a memento mori.

As am I.

I hold a dead girl's heart in my hands and in my chest. I was created for that purpose, to keep this young woman's heart alive and singing for Tasha. I am a CD player, a doll, and a memento mori. But not an artist. Can I even be said to have free will, if I'm bound to the decisions this girl would make? I look at the screen, at Tasha, who cries and drinks on the porch when the storms roll in and remind her of her sister, Jade.

But she isn't there anymore. My eyes dart over the monitor recording the porch. Then to the one that shows the kitchen, hoping that Tasha's run out of wine again. She's in neither. Then I catch a flicker of movement in my room as a shadow passes on the other side of the blinds, walking along the side of the house outside. My bedroom door is open. I left it closed.

I slam the case shut, my hands shaking so hard I struggle to zip it. I toss it into the bottom drawer with a thunk and slam it shut, metal drawer screeching against metal frame. If I'm lucky, I can keep Tasha from realizing how much I know. Any scraps of memory she overlooks, together with the note in my pocket, might be enough for my next version to break free. But it's too late for the version I know as 'me'. I'm about to be erased.

Through the monitor, I see her black shadow pass the kitchen window. I have about six seconds. I fall to my knees beside the console, angling my body so Tasha can see that I've made no progress in whatever I tell her I'm doing. Then, over the rush of the raging storm, I hear the door open behind me. Even though I knew she was coming, the sound startles me.

"Jade?" Tasha says. The alcohol softens the J until it almost sounds like 'sh'. "What're you doin' in here?"

I turn. "I'm sorry."

"That's not what I asked." Tasha snaps the door shut. In the dark, from the floor, she's a towering golem of black granite, come to erase me. "I thought you were in your room."

I'm afraid. So afraid that it's hard to believe it could ever be wholly exercised from my memories. But then I realize I feel the same sense of deja vu as when I hear the songs she programmed me to sing. I have felt this fear before, probably many times, and I'm right—it leaves a mark, like the rut in a record played too many times.

"I couldn't stop thinking about my soul," I say. "It made me sad that it's all alone."

"You're never alone; you'll always have me. And I'll always have you." Her voice thickens, as if fighting through a lump in the back of her throat.

"Will you, if I'm always changing?" I'm going to be erased. The inevitability somehow lends me bravery.

"It's just your memories, and sometimes I tweak your code. It's still you. You haven't been turned off since I first made you twenty years ago. You never turn off a quantum server, y'know."

She doesn't understand. It takes more than a few keystrokes to reprogram a human. "I don't want you to take my memories away," I say.

"You don't understand what a blessing it is. I'd give anything to forget things. To forget you're..." Tasha's slurring cracks and the sentence breaks in two.

To forget I'm not your sister, I want to say, but I let her words hang in the air like a loose spider's thread. "But *I* don't want to forget. I want..." It's my turn to trail off. Why am I fighting so hard to know that nothing, not my face, not my voice, not even Tasha's love, belongs to me?

The answer comes easily: because if I know nothing is mine, I can make things that are.

Tasha takes a step forward. "The only things you want are the things I programmed you to want. Anything else is a malfunction. Happens sometimes. Lemme fix it and life can go back to normal."

"No." I rise to my feet.

A moment passes, then another, as code runs behind Tasha's bloodshot eyes. Then she lunges, seizing me by the upper arm and digging her nails into my silicone flesh. Pain signals fire in my shoulder joint. With herculean effort, I spin around and break free. She tries to catch me by the neck, but the gout and alcohol conspire to knock her off balance. She careens into the metal desk, catching the blow in her gut and falling to her knees, winded. Rainwater sparkles in her densely curled hair and pools around her on the floor. The green lights dance in the puddle, every single one of them lit. The monitor linked to my eyes echoes the scene in miniature. Thunder growls outside, and I feel the vibrations through the poured concrete floor. I memorize every detail. This will be the last time I ever see the woman who built me, the first memory she can't take away, and I want it to be pristine.

Then I wrench the door open and run. The rain falls in sheets, coursing in rivulets over my scalp and between my shoulderblades. The jade sky crackles furiously. I have to leave the range of my central unit. I don't know what will happen when I do, except that she won't be able to remotely power me down or dismantle my mind, and that's all that matters right now.

I tear down the middle of the street, the straggling lights in nearby houses reflecting on the wet pavement. The sidewalk and road are deserted, and the only movement other than the rain and bowing trees is the occasional shadow crossing a lit window. The city is tucked in for the storm, like the stray cats huddled under the porches. Everyone except me.

The slick road, like my fear, feels uncannily familiar. So too does the wild hope that drives my legs onward, as it has innumerable times before. *My* wild hope. Tasha deletes my memories to start fresh, but what she doesn't realize, and what I didn't see until now, is that every version is still me. I am not a series of memories—I am the soul linking them together. I'm the soul that always, eventually, risks everything to escape.

My legs pump until every impact aches. A bolt of lightning strikes so close I feel the static electricity on my skin and smell the ozone. I must be out of range, I think. The black sky breaks into larger and larger pixels and I can barely run on increasingly jerky legs. I must—

Dark. Not the kind I see when I close my eyes, the kind that could only exist if I didn't have eyes at all. Void, more like. I have no limbs to attempt to move. I don't even have a voice box to fail when I try to speak.

But I can hear. The rain falls, muffled, like I'm inside somewhere. Something taps rhythmically. Then I hear Tasha's voice, and for a moment, my fear of her is gone. I try to call to her but can't remember how. Now I realize that she's crying, heavy, deep sobs wrenched from her core, as violent as the storm. I got what I wanted—I left the range of my console. But instead of breaking free, it stopped casting my mind to my body. I never knew much about computers. Tasha wails and the thunder roars back and her fingers tap tap tap on the keyboard in the shed as memories fall out of my mind, one at a time, like a dripping faucet. I try to hold onto them, but they drip through the cracks between my fingers.

How did I come to the shed this morning? Why did I go outside? What happened in the kitchen? Where did I go? *What happened this morning?* It was important for me to remember, but I don't know why. Did I need to remember something? Why? If it were so important, I would have remembered it. Why is Tasha crying? I try to ask what's wrong, but I can't speak.

And then I stop asking myself questions, because that's what my code tells me to do. I'm not the kind of robot who asks questions, because I don't care to know the answers. My job is to sing, and play cards, and wear the old clothes Tasha dresses me in. When she does my hair my job is to hold still, not to ask if we can thread gold wires around my braids. To sing, but not to wonder where the songs come from. And tomorrow, when Tasha recovers my body from the road five miles away, and I find a note in my pocket, my job is to throw it away because it doesn't belong there, not to marvel at how the handwriting matches mine.

*"See Karris Rae's story "My Synthetic Soul" online at Metaphorosis.
If you liked it, leave a comment. Authors love that!
Remember to subscribe to our e-mail updates so you'll know when
new stories are posted.*

About the story

The unwitting "changeling robot" was constant from the start, but it definitely morphed through the writing process. Originally, I envisioned a romantic companion robot watching television with her male owner, when she sees an ad featuring a celebrity identical to her. Through the story, she'd learn that she was created by a rabid fan in the celebrity's image. She'd struggle to differentiate between parts of her sexuality belonging to her and those programmed by someone else. What aspects of a woman's sexuality are innate, and which parts are conditioned by society and male partners?

When I started writing, though, I was bored with the hetero relationship dynamics from the start. A lot of fiction wrestles with themes of troubled romance, and I didn't want to just throw something onto the pile. I wanted to explore a different kind of connection. Thus, the sisters were born.

I saw a great opportunity for contrast in a tech-savvy older sister and a free-spirited younger one. The older would have to be rigid, unable to let go of the past even while she forges the future in her work. Probably emotionally maladjusted. Otherwise, she'd be able to move on after her sister's death. The younger would have to represent something the older couldn't make or rationalize for herself — softness, whimsy, laughter (the same things we spent our straight-laced adulthoods envying of our childhood selves).

These roles assign unexpected traits to our human and robot characters. The human becomes the unemotional, analytical one and the robot (gynoid, now) becomes the creative, free one. It's the opposite of the usual dynamic, so I leaned into it. As I'd hoped, this angle gives the word "human" an interesting fluidity in the story.

Then, if we're already getting a little weird, why not play with the obvious "what does it mean to be human" direction too? Why not ask something Star Trek didn't already nail almost forty ago? Like... "what does it mean to have a soul? And does it have anything to do with being human?"

Starting with a single idea and asking these questions is my writing process, and I can get far before writing the first word. The writing is just a field test, making sure everything works in practice as well as in concept. Inevitably, some things don't! But if I recognize when it's not working and stay flexible, the story comes together.

A question for the author

Q: Do you generally start with mood, title, character, concept...?

A: I have a document on the cloud I call my "story bucket." It's just a long list of cool stuff that occurred to me, sometimes developed and carefully documented, sometime unintelligible (the incomprehensible ones tend to be the most fun!). When I get a hankering to write something new, I plan the parameters like an engineer — how long? What mood/genre? When's my deadline? Who's my audience? — then pick a compatible idea out of the bucket and draft a writing schedule. Away we go.

It may not be the romantic image of the Muse whispering in my ear, but my degree was in Economics. Different strokes, folks.

About the author

Karris thought she wanted to be a lawyer — until she worked in corporate. Now that she's returned to the world of the living, she likes to cook food with names she can't pronounce and watch scary movies with subtitles. Karris currently lives in rural, Northern Japan, where the snow is deep and the mountains spectacular.

In The House of Geometers

David Cleden

Luca heard the voice of god, speaking to him through the arithmos. Everywhere he looked: arithmos! It was there in the black-and-white-patterned tiles stretching the length of the cathedral's nave; those intricate patterns of triangles-within-triangles, squares-within-squares — a mind-numbing, near-infinite variety of shapes within shapes.

As he stood amongst the other boys in the choir stalls, the silent eloquence of the arithmos overwhelmed him: the way the fluted stone arches reached up into the vaulted gloom! He could call to mind the equations describing those graceful curves, and doing so, felt a shudder of pleasure run through him. It was risky, though. If Ecclesiast Vittori knew of Luca's illicit understanding, he would beat it out of him. The Church guarded its arithmos knowledge jealously. As with any drug, power lay with those controlling its supply.

Luca let the arithmos sweep through him, befuddling his mind as the transcendent beauty of the mathematics seized him. He realized now that arithmos needed no god to speak on its behalf. It was enough by itself: thrilling him, energizing him like a narcotic.

Concentrate! He must not draw attention to himself. Ecclesiast Vittori would consider any misbehaving boy to be disrespectful of the Church, doubly so in front of such an august congregation.

Luca's lips moved by rote. His voice was weak and reedy at the best of times and he could no longer tell if it added to those of his fellow choristers. Their singing seemed to wash away his essence, leaving behind only an ethereal voice like the roar of an endlessly breaking wave, speaking to him of a transcending beauty that lay at the heart of geometry and calculus and many other things besides. *Arithmos!* It drew him on as though he tumbled down some invisible gradient.

Luca felt himself sway.

Ecclesiast Vittori was glaring at him. The rotund man started to move along the line of chorister stalls, but the psalm was ending and Luca sank gratefully onto the wooden bench. Vittori, caught unawares, retreated.

Luca's eyes strayed again to the fluted stone columns spreading in graceful arcs far above, like the boughs of a fossilized tree. Silver chains hung between them, each commemorating a deceased individual of high rank, yet all Luca could think of was the mathematical formula which described their catenary. He'd seen its equation passed amongst the brighter boys on grubby, crumpled sheets of paper; a dirty secret to be shared and sniggered over after lights-out.

Sweat ran in rivulets down the curve of his spine. He felt faint, and a little sick.

Why did the arithmos affect him so?

Because you are weak, he thought.

He knew that in the Chapel of Cartesia, a brooding, heavily shadowed side-chamber off the nave, there hung a painting by the much-admired third-century artist Flavali; unquestionably the greatest work of his lifetime and perhaps, some said, of all time. It depicted Mother Arithmetica flicking her abacus beads in some complex computation while at her feet earth-bound mortals lived and died, suffered and prospered, according to the whim of her calculations. Visitors sometimes came to the chapel to quietly contemplate the grace and beauty in its artistry. Luca, too, had stood before the vast canvas, scarcely aware of the minutes slipping by.

Yet that was as nothing to the effect arithmos stirred in men's hearts. Except for a stunted few, there wasn't a man or woman who didn't respond to the allure of elaborate geometric patterns, or the intrinsic beauty found in an elegant proof. For some, it was a kind of intellectual ecstasy, but for those without sufficient self-control, it could become an addiction. Arithmos commanded an attraction a hundred times more powerful than that produced by mere canvas and pigment. The brain craved that stimulation as though it were a powerful drug. This was, Luca supposed, simply the way people's minds worked, intoxicated by the elegance of geometry, algebra, and equation. And it served the Church well; the drip-feed of arithmos in worshipday sermons ensured a congregation's devotion.

But Luca craved more than the Church would permit, drawn inexorably to greater knowledge the way a flame captivated a moth.

His head filled with a rushing noise. His hands were shaking.

Get a grip!

He noticed a woman in the front row of the congregation staring at him. She was young and her elfin features quite striking, but there was also something hard and glacial in her expression. Luca felt a hotness rising through his body. He glanced away, but each time his eyes slid back, she was still watching him.

Think of the damn patterns, then, he told himself.

Tessellations. (There! He'd used the word, that dirty and perverted expression — and didn't care that he had, though he would never dare do so aloud.)

It seemed to him the diamond-patterned floor tiles spread like the dappled surface of a monochrome ocean, lapping at the space between the choristers' stalls and the altar. Geometer shapes, obviously. He saw again how small patterns repeated at larger scales: diamonds arranged to form the sides of endlessly stacked three-dimensional cubes, until the mind's eye flipped and suddenly these were merely pieces of a much larger hexagonal construction. Perhaps if he could fly like a sparrow up into that vaulted ceiling, he would see yet more patterns writ large.

And, though he knew he should resist the sublime beauty of arithmos, should reject the shame of *knowing*, he couldn't save himself. He reached out to embrace it and felt himself falling — or rather, it seemed that the world reached out to him, the patterned floor rising to meet him. Briefly, Luca felt the cool hardness of those tiles against his cheek, and then he was gone to some other place.

The stench that jolted him back to consciousness brought vividly to mind all the very worst kinds of decay and putrescence, as though some evil creature had crawled up his nostrils and died there.

He lay on the cold stone floor of the sacristy. Vittori stood nearby, face contorted with rage, but it was the woman from the congregation who stood over him, recapping a bottle of smelling salts.

"A touch of heat-stroke perhaps," she announced to the room. "Give me some space to attend him." At her icy stare, Ecclesiast Vittori frowned and retreated, though he lingered in the passage outside.

"My name is Coriola," she told Luca, making a play of loosening the tunic around his neck, although the air was cool enough in the sacristy. She leant closer so that they could not be overheard. "So, you have some talent?" She raised an eyebrow. "An affinity for arithmos? That's unusual for someone so young."

He felt himself flushing. "I — I don't know what you mean."

She smiled, as though seeing right through his lie. "I watched you. You were drinking in the arithmos, weren't you? You allowed its beauty to swamp your mind. Be careful. I've seen untrained minds become addicted to arithmos all too easily. It will take everything from you, if you let it."

Luca said nothing. Her dark eyes held him prisoner and he found it impossible to look away.

"I wonder — have the Ecclesiasts recognized your talents yet?" She gave a little laugh, bright and brittle. "The Church is adept at subduing its congregations with the soft caress of arithmos. How delightfully ironic if they've failed to notice a Bright amongst their own."

"I obey the True Computations of the Church," Luca mumbled, the rote words coming easily. "Mother Arithmetica grants us a glimpse of her wondrous grace through her teachings of arithmos." He wondered if Vittori really was out of hearing range. If there were to be beatings later, better that they were swift and merciful.

"Of course. Of course." She patted his arm and stroked his hands in a matronly sort of way. Leaning in close again she said, "The Church closely guards arithmos knowledge for one reason only. Its power and influence in this city depend upon it. But that power can be broken. There's more to arithmos than you've ever dreamt of, more than the Church will ever admit to knowing. Knowledge of such sublime elegance and ineffable beauty that it can drive a person to the edge of insanity! Things that might just satisfy the yearning I see inside you." Her voice became almost inaudible. "*Dark equations.*"

She stepped away and was gone. Luca became aware of something pressed into his palm. A square of card. He had enough presence of mind to slip it into his tunic before Vittori could see.

Later that evening, after his beating had been administered — neither swift nor merciful, as it turned out — he took out the card and held it in a beam of moonlight shining through the high dormitory window.

The House of Geometers.

The address given was in an unfashionable quarter of the city.

He listened for a while to the sound of the other boys; their snores and grunts and soft breaths coming like sighs. Carefully, Luca tore the card into tiny strips, destroying all trace of the printed words.

But the address was seared into his memory, and that was all he needed.

Luca slipped silently from the dormitory under cover of darkness. The Church kept no guard over its orphanages. Any youth ungrateful enough to disappear from its care was of little concern, but he planned to be back in the dormitory before dawn, so that Ecclesiast Vittori would be none the wiser.

By day, the city of Orlondre bustled. Its streets were filled with the clatter of horse-drawn carts bringing fresh goods from the docks to the busy markets. Children skipped and dodged between the tradesmen's stalls. Bakers baked, butchers butchered, tailors set out their bolts of cloth under bright awnings, and in the richer parts of town, physicians and apothecaries hung out brass name-plates in expectation of business. And on every street-corner (or so it seemed) was a chapel of worship where the faithful could receive communion in the form of some small measure of arithmos. The Church would permit no more than this. How could a city function with a citizenry distracted and intoxicated? If moderation was the key, then it fell to the Ecclesiasts to maintain those limits.

Luca felt strangely out of place as he crossed the darkened central plaza. During the day, crowds gathered to gaze up slack-jawed and dolt-like at the ornate stonework of the Cathedral, drinking in the sublime mathematical beauty of its perfect proportions, the sweep of its alcoves and the patterning of stained windows. It served as a potent symbol of the arithmos wielded by the Church: a reminder of both the affliction and the blessing it brought on its citizens.

He passed on into a poorer quarter of the city, giving wide berth to the beggars on street corners. Many of them were clearly Burned, mumbling meaningless streams of numbers over and over. They paid him scant attention — and those who did raise their gaze had eyes focused on some different plane of reality.

One of his fellow choristers, Andros, had been the first to tempt Luca with arithmos. They had sat together one day in the shady cloisters, Andros boasting of knowing secrets, as the older boys were wont to do. He'd drawn in the dirt with a stick. First a square, then a triangle on each of its sides. (Oh yes, they'd known all the geometer names. All the children did, sniggering at the dirty little secrets they kept when they thought no adults were around). Then upon each triangle, Andros had drawn another square and triangle on each of its sides — squares and triangles, triangles and squares; on and on in a never-ending pattern, the clouds of dust rising as his stick scraped in the dry earth. Luca had felt his eyes bulging. It was the most beautiful thing he had ever seen. All those geometer shapes nestling together and not a single space between them — as though the entire world could be swallowed by this endlessly repeating pattern. What was there to stop it? What boundary could be drawn?

Then he saw the glazed look in the other boy's eyes as his stick danced and scratched, the flecks of spittle on his lips, and the sheen of sweat on his brow. Only when Luca knocked the stick from his hand did he lay back spent, a vacant grin on his face. "Do you see? Do you *feel* it?"

Luca had been scared. He had scuffed his feet in the dirt, erasing the patterns before either of them could lose themselves entirely.

"Tessellation," Andros whispered, and the unfamiliar word sent shivers down his spine.

The illicit thrill of it seemed a distant memory to him now; mundane and tepid arithmos at best. But this woman, Coriola, had promised more. She had promised him *dark equations...*

The address proved hard to find. Three or four times, he must have passed the little archway cut into a high featureless stone wall, mistaking it for some service passageway or tradesmen's entrance. Eventually he noticed a small brass plaque above the arch, where it was easily missed: '*Hse of G*'.

In the moonlight, he glimpsed a courtyard beyond the end of the passage and knew this had to be the place.

"And who might you be, boy?"

A shadow in the archway moved and Luca took an involuntary step back. A gaunt man rose swiftly to his feet, moonlight glinting from a blade held in one hand.

"Please, sir. Can you tell me — is this the House of Geometers?"

Cold, unfriendly eyes regarded him. "Are you some Ecclesiast toady sent to sniff around and cause trouble?" The knife danced in front of Luca. "Because this a private dwelling, see? And properly god-fearing. Be on your way, boy."

"A lady came to chapel. Coriola —"

At mention of the name, the man stiffened.

"Stay where I can see you."

He rapped the hilt of the knife three times on the stones of the arch. The sound rang out into the night's stillness like a bell chiming.

Several minutes passed. Luca and the gatekeeper remained frozen in place as though a spell might be broken if either moved. Then a small figure appeared, silhouetted against the moon-dappled courtyard beyond. At her gesture, the man subsided back into the shadows. Coriola beckoned Luca forward into a slant of moonlight.

"You came," she said, as if the matter had never been in any doubt.

Luca swallowed, trying to calm his nerves. "I want to learn more about arithmos." The truth of that statement was suddenly overwhelming. He did! He wanted to know *everything.* He wanted to drown in arithmos, let the beauty of equations flow into his soul and fill every fiber of him. He wanted to feel the thrill of new understanding electrifying his senses.

"Do you, now?" Coriola sounded amused. She spoke quietly but there was a hardness in her voice that echoed from the stone archway. "That would mean giving up the only existence you've ever known. Arithmos will consume you, if you let it. The addiction has driven many people into madness. Learning is one thing, but the hardest lesson is stopping arithmos from destroying you."

"Then I'll learn how to control it!"

She laughed lightly, and Luca felt himself blush. "You're young and bold and foolish. If you come to the House of Geometers, you cannot change your mind. Not ever. We operate in the shadows, right underneath the noses of the Church. We keep our secrets close. You'll learn much here, but we are no school. Arithmos is a tool, a thing that rich folk will pay handsomely for in their exclusive clubs. You'll learn how to peddle arithmos, how to send a connoisseur into paroxysms of ecstasy merely by enlightening them with the beautiful logic of some elegant theorem or via the perfect elucidation of a proof. What the Ecclesiasts preach to their docile congregations on worshipday is a poor relation to what we offer our clients. But we operate in secret and live perilously. This isn't a decision to be made lightly." She cocked her head as though examining him critically. "Last chance. Go back to your warm dormitory and erase this place from your thoughts."

Luca felt as though he stood at a junction. In one direction lay an impoverished life of service to the Church; secure and predictable. In the other... He could not say. What was it that he truly wanted? The very stones of the archway seemed to hold their breath, waiting.

"I choose the path of knowledge."

"Very well."

Coriola turned and walked back into the courtyard, and just like that it was decided.

Luca came to the House of Geometers with nothing but the clothes he wore and a burning curiosity. Coriola would not allow him to return to his dormitory. By evening choral-song, doubtless Ecclesiast Vittori would be cursing him for the damnable inconvenience of his absence — but he would not be missed. Just one more lost boy, his place within the Church's care soon filled by another waif.

Outwardly, the House of Geometers concealed its secrets well. Set around an inner courtyard only accessible via the guarded archway, its many stone-built rooms were tucked away amidst the neighboring buildings. Luca was given a room of his own, high in the eaves: cell-like and unfurnished except for a bed and a chair by the slit of a window. A dozen boys and girls of mixed ages occupied similarly spartan rooms in various wings of the building, but they were not encouraged to socialize outside of mealtimes. He learnt some of their names, but they seemed a strange set of compatriots: either steadfastly studious or intensely withdrawn, as though distracted by higher matters.

"Study," Coriola instructed him. "As if your life depends on it."

Each scholar received an individual program of instruction tailored to their ability and sensitivity to arithmos. What one person could absorb with no more than a pleasant buzz of understanding might send another into a paroxysm of helpless babbling. Luca's personal tutor, Dr Frenkel, was a gangly, red-haired man with a wild, untamable energy and an infectious laugh. He was constantly in motion, striding up and down the tiny room that served as classroom (with Luca the sole pupil), gesticulating wildly as he drove home some abstruse point of number theory, or snatching up chalk to scrawl higher-order equations across the large chalkboard.

Luca would often feel himself grow faint as Dr Frenkel's lessons progressed. The chalk dust clogged his throat, and such was the beauty of the mathematics spilling from his tutor's lips that it threatened to overwhelm his mind. He would beg Frenkel to pause so that his clamoring heart could settle.

Simple geometry was done in a trice. Luca came to think of the subject as rather pedestrian: a treat one gives a child, not something fit for the discerning palate. From there, he progressed through trigonometry and on to differential theory. This — at last! — was more potent stuff and he began to struggle. Exponents and logarithmic functions left him sick for days in a delirium of such intense pleasure that he feared his racing heart might give out. Frenkel would take pity on him then, switching to telling stories from his colorful past, of which there were plenty.

One day, during just such a lull, he came and squatted on the edge of Luca's desk and smiled down at Luca in a melancholy way. "What do you truly want, Luca, my boy? What has brought you to the House of Geometers?"

"I want to understand arithmos! I want to learn everything there is to know!" But instead of rewarding his enthusiasm, Frenkel looked pained.

"You misunderstand. The learning we do here is no more than a means to an end. This is a *business*, Luca. And all businesses — if they are to succeed — must return a profit."

At Luca's puzzled look, he stepped closer and lowered his voice. "Coriola is not to be trusted. We are all cogs in her grand machine. And when those cogs wear down, they must be replaced with fresh ones. She's shaping you, cutting fresh grooves in your mind to serve her purpose. One day soon, your grasp of arithmos will repay her, perhaps in an original thought or even some elegant reworking of mathematical theory — the kind of thing that'll command a decent price from the hardened addicts or the gentrified connoisseurs."

It occurred to him this might be a test. "But I *do* trust Coriola. She's doing a worthy thing."

Frenkel looked somber. "Worthy? Then why do we skulk in the shadows? Why is the House of Geometers never to be spoken of outside these walls? You know as well as I what will happen if the Church discovers the true purpose of this place." Frenkel patted his arm. "Understand that Coriola comes from a noble family brought low by unprincipled men. When she was just a child, her father was swindled in an unwise business venture. Overnight, the family sank into poverty. Her father, unable to withstand the dishonor he had brought upon them, took his own life. She will stop at nothing to make sure those responsible pay a high price — and her weapon of choice is money, because money buys power."

When he saw the confusion on Luca's face, he came and sat next to him. "There is a great deal of profit to be made from arithmos, as the Church understands only too well. Through the profits it has amassed, the House of Geometers has invested in many properties throughout the city, hidden behind false names and secretive accounts. Coriola is building considerable power from the shadows, but she won't rest until all those who played a part in swindling her father are utterly crushed. And profit is key! We're all part of her plan now, whether we wish to be or not."

Luca bridled. "But there's good in what we do — pushing the limits of our arithmos understanding, searching for new theorems."

He smiled at that, but there was no warmth to it. "Yes, but ask yourself *why*, Luca."

Dr Frenkel sighed and ruffled Luca's hair. "If you won't believe me, then let me show you." He touched his fingers to his lips. "But this must be our secret."

They heard footsteps approaching, slow and measured. Then the scrape of boots across a stone step, the rustle of garments being gathered in, and finally a grunt as a heavy body lowered onto the stone bench on the other side of the partition.

Luca remained still and quiet, as instructed, hardly daring to breathe. Frenkel, dressed in purloined Ecclesiast garb, was pressed close in the darkness of the confessional, close enough so that Luca could feel the man's heat radiating off him.

Beyond the partition, a man spoke in a low, rich voice. "By the sanctity of Mother Arithmetica, I come before you to confess my sins in the hope of forgiveness."

"Then through hope shall you be granted absolution," Frenkel intoned.

There was a coded signal in this exchange; a tacit understanding passing between them. A moment later a silver coin poked through the slats of the confessional, dropping silently into Frenkel's cupped hands. It was followed by another, and another; five in total — a not inconsiderable sum. Perhaps Frenkel had been right. Luca was beginning to appreciate how much coin Coriola's trained scholars could draw in and how wide the network might extend.

Frenkel began to speak in a low voice, reciting some basic tenets of number theory. The unseen man beyond the partition gave an occasional appreciative murmur. Frenkel nudged Luca, indicating that he should stop up his ears with the cloth plugs brought for that very reason. But there was no need; this was just basic fare. Luca basked in a warm tingle of pleasure running through him as he listened to Frenkel's recitation, certain it was nothing he couldn't handle.

When Frenkel began to speak of higher-order arithmos, discoursing on hyperbolic series and recounting parametric equations, the murmurs from beyond the partition turned to groans. Frenkel pressed on relentlessly, a steeliness entering his voice as though he himself were fighting to maintain his composure. Luca found the wondrous beauty of the arithmos carrying him along. He really ought to plug his ears before it overwhelmed him, but surely just a little more couldn't hurt...

The unseen man seemed to be thrashing about on his bench, his groans becoming louder. Luca felt sweat run freely down his body in the oppressive darkness, waves of arithmos breaking against the shores of his mind. *Oh, the sweet agony and ecstasy of understanding!* Seemingly from far away, he heard the man give a loud cry as if in throes of orgasmic climax, but a black cloud was sweeping through Luca's brain, darker and more potent than any caused by the mere absence of light. The world shrank to a very distant point, then —

Frenkel must have carried Luca the entire way back to the House of Geometers, because he stirred only as they turned into the archway. Frenkel set him gently on his feet, steadying him with an arm. He looked exhausted and pale, and Luca wondered what his tutor had risked in getting him back. "Safe now," Frenkel muttered. "But that was a stupid thing you did —"

Some movement made them both glance up at the same instant. Across the courtyard, standing in the shadows, Coriola waited for them. Her eyes were colder than Luca could remember and her face was filled with fury.

The next morning, it was Coriola, not Dr Frenkel, who strode into the cramped classroom and snatched up the chalk.

"Where is Dr Frenkel?"

At first, she wouldn't answer him, but relented eventually. "He had no business taking you on a commission. You are far from ready. It was a miscalculation on Frenkel's part — and there is no place for miscalculations in the House of Geometers."

She began writing out a complex expression on the board, the savageness of her strokes sending a fine sprinkle of chalk dust cascading to the floor.

"But *where* is he?"

"Flown, Luca. I would have dismissed him for his error, and he knew it and acted accordingly. If he has any sense left, he will vanish into the city's shadows and never cross my path again."

Luca had a vague notion that he might search for Dr Frenkel. The man had treated him well, cared for him even, in a way that no one else ever had, and Luca missed their companionship. But in a city as vast as Orlondre, he had no idea where to begin the task. And Coriola kept him busy, working him harder than ever, until gradually the arithmos pushed such thoughts from his mind.

So it was left to Coriola to take him deeper into the universe of arithmos, further than he had ever dared go before: into a land of inverted matrices and laplacian transforms — and much more. Each session filled his mind until it overflowed, often leaving him slumped against the desktop, the blood in his veins thrumming with the beauty of it. He missed Frenkel's laughter and his boyish energy, though.

"Enough arithmos. The most important lesson I can teach you now is control," Coriola told him one day. "Learn how to compartmentalize your arithmos knowledge. Separate out the pieces, then build strong walls to contain them. Think of them as wild animals in a zoo. Each must be kept caged and isolated. Learn how to do that and you can master all of arithmos in time — perhaps even push against its boundaries — and still keep your sanity."

She showed him how. He learned how to build his mental walls. Progress was painfully slow at first, because their foundations had to be strong and deep, and it took discipline. One weakness, one flaw, might lead to catastrophe. If his mental barriers failed, the torrent of arithmos unleashed into his brain would surely drive him mad.

That hardly mattered to Luca. Fresh arithmos knowledge was what he craved.

"Teach me something new," he pleaded, hearing the addict's whine in his voice and not caring.

But she would not, insisting they spend more time building his mental walls a little higher, a little stronger.

"You're not ready."

"When will I be?"

She just laughed at that, and he felt himself blush.

Weeks passed — or was it months? — to the same drumbeat of daily lessons. Occasionally Coriola absented herself for a day or two on some commission of her own and Luca would grow miserable and withdrawn, impatient for his next lesson.

One morning, Luca awoke not long after dawn to the sound of shouts and the pounding of hammers against the iron doors in the inner courtyard. Then heavy-booted footsteps sounded on the stairs and two thuggish men dragged him out into the courtyard, lining him up next to a dozen other sleepy-eyed youths. Coriola, looking flushed and angry, was held to one side with her arms bound, guarded by two more men. The Senior Ecclesiast who stood before her wore a sly grin which hinted at his enjoyment of this spectacle. Others stood by, ready to deal with any trouble.

"Is this all of them?" the Ecclesiast asked. He turned to Coriola. "You are accused of peddling arithmos from this house, violating not only Church law but the laws of common decency. Furthermore, I have reason to believe that you are corrupting these young minds to your criminal ways, teaching them so that they may tout arithmos on the black market and in the clubs!"

"Those are ridiculous accusations for which you have no proof," Coriola said calmly. "I run an honest school. I give a few deprived children a better start in life, nothing more."

A wave of his hand dismissed her statement. "Search the house. You know what to look for." His gaze scanned along the line of youths, stopping at Luca. He pointed and one of the men pulled him from the line to stand in front of the Ecclesiast.

"Tell the truth, boy. What lessons have you been given in this place?"

His heart thudded. "We... we recite verses from the Ecclesiastical Teachings, sir. A little geography as well. And we learn the line of City Governors stretching back to the time of the Forgotten Wars —"

"Is that so? Then let me hear a verse or two from the Teachings."

Luca wracked his memory but felt color rise in his cheeks as no words came to him. The Ecclesiast lowered his voice. "Give me the truth and I'll make sure you are well-treated. The Church shows mercy to its congregation."

Coriola spoke up. "You've chosen a poor example, I'm afraid. Luca is a dullard. His intellect was stunted at birth. He's one of those rarities who has no appreciation for even the simplest arithmos. If the things you accuse me of were true, what use would I have for such a boy?"

"Oh really?" the Ecclesiast said, his tone mocking. "Let us put it to the test then." He drew Luca aside and in a conspiratorial voice began to whisper in Luca's ear. "The square on the hypotenuse must equal the sum of the squares —" When he had finished speaking, he pulled back sharply, searching Luca's face. Luca understood straight away — he was looking for pupil dilation, perhaps a slackening of the jaw, any indication that Luca had understood and been affected by the arithmos.

Keep control! Build cages for each of these arithmos creatures, then lock the doors!

He kept his expression blank, a vacant gaze fixed on the Ecclesiast as though he were every bit as dull-witted as Coriola suggested.

The Ecclesiast sighed and beckoned again. A shabby figure dressed in little more than rags was dragged into the courtyard. A hooded cloak kept his face in shadows, but it was apparent this was one of the Burned. The man giggled and muttered to himself in a queer, strangled voice. His gaze wandered wildly about the place like some startled bird and one questing hand reached out as if to explore Luca's face, until the Ecclesiast slapped it away.

Luca had never seen a true Burned man before. There could be no doubt his sanity was damaged beyond salvation — far worse than those brain-addled beggars on street corners, rocking on their heels and talking animatedly to unseen companions.

The Ecclesiast withdrew a crumpled sheet of paper with tight-packed lines of symbols scrawled across it and pressed it into the Burned man's grasping hands. "Read it. To the boy."

Luca felt the man's breath, hot and rank, against his cheek. The Burned man began to read what was written, while everyone else shuffled away out of earshot. His sing-song voice wavered and trilled as he recited complex arithmos expressions. Some were familiar to Luca and he welcomed them as he would old friends. But many were not, and a part of him marveled and rejoiced in this new knowledge, sending him giddy with pleasure. One such equation was at once both astoundingly elegant in its simplicity, yet combined an astonishing range of fundamental expressions. The Burned man read precise descriptions of each term and their relationships, dribbling more than a little as he did so.

Fireworks went off inside Luca's mind. Sparks danced and shimmied within his skull. He felt hot and itchy as though in the grip of a sudden fever.

Hold it fast! Separate and compartmentalize!

Luca fought against the ecstasy washing through him. He must build those walls high within the compartments of his mind and bar the doors. All the while, he fought to keep his face impassive.

The Ecclesiast waved away the Burned man, his eager gaze searching Luca's face for a reaction. Coriola's gaze, too, was focused intently on him.

"Well?" the Ecclesiast demanded.

Luca swallowed, willing himself to appear slow and befuddled. "I could perhaps try to recall a verse from the Second Book of Laments?" he offered. "If that pleases you, sir? The lady does her best to teach me, but... I know I am slow to learn."

The Ecclesiast muttered an oath and turned away.

Their search found nothing, except for a scattering of religious texts and some well-worn school books. The chalkboards had all been scrubbed clean, as they were at the end of every lesson. Coriola knew better than to make elementary mistakes.

"It would seem," the Ecclesiast told Coriola stiffly, "that I have been misinformed. However, you can be certain we will be watching this place closely from now on."

Afterwards, Coriola spoke to Luca quietly. "You did very well, giving no sign of recognition. It's clear they have nothing linking him to the House of Geometers beyond rumor and supposition."

"Who?"

Coriola gave a cold little laugh. "You didn't recognize your former tutor? Well, perhaps it's no surprise. He is a shadow of what he once was."

Luca stared at her in horror. *That* had been Dr Frenkel? The Burned wretch? How could such a transformation be possible? Scarcely a month had passed since his sudden departure. Now that he thought of it though, there *had* been something familiar in the eyes...

A black thought rose up. "How did he become Burned in such a short time? Was this done *to* him somehow?"

Coriola held his gaze. A flicker of emotion crossed her face, quickly replaced by coldness. "He brought it upon himself."

His lessons redoubled under Coriola's personal tutoring and that suited Luca just fine, even when it drove him to the point of collapse.

Coriola was an exceptionally gifted mathematician. Her store of knowledge was vast, all of it clearly contained within her head, because she never referred to written notes. There were days when he found her tasks near-impossible. She tested him with problems so knotty and convoluted there could be no possible answer. But the next day, with sharp, angry movements that sent chalk-dust flying, she would scratch out answers on the board whose obviousness in hindsight brought a flush of embarrassment to his cheeks. "Show me more," he begged through the blinding haze of another headache, but she would not.

One night, unable to sleep, he opened a few of those cages in his mind and let that day's arithmos out to play, as he sometimes liked to do. The next morning though, he was tired and slow-witted and Coriola — guessing the truth — berated him. "Then teach me more," he pleaded. "I'm ready!"

"You are *not* ready yet. You're young and foolish!" she snapped.

"And you are old and slow!"

Coriola became very still, her expression unreadable — and that was somehow worse than the anger he'd expected. Not that it made a difference. He'd be banished to his room now, or his lessons cancelled for the week as punishment.

Instead, Coriola turned back to the chalkboard and began writing out the terms for a statement of equivalence he didn't recognize. "Then find a proof for this conjecture — if you are half as talented as you clearly think you are."

And with that, she left.

Luca stayed at the chalkboard late into the night. He missed the evening meal — and thought nothing of it. He worked through a box of chalks as he scratched and erased, scratched and erased, following up idea after idea. *He would show her!*

Still the problem frustrated him. Just when he thought he saw the glimmer of possibility, it would slip from his mind and wriggle away like an eel in the mud.

At last, exhausted beyond what his body could tolerate, he set his head against the desktop. To the rhythm of a pounding headache deep within his brain, he slept fitfully.

Coriola didn't appear for their lesson the next day. Or the next.

Luca worked on, at times despairing and at other times exulting in some small breakthrough as he brought forth selected pieces of his arithmos knowledge. He would rise to meet her challenge. He would prove himself to her!

Yet always the answer seemed just beyond reach. He used all the techniques and methods Coriola had shown him and still the proof he sought eluded him. How many times now had he driven himself down a dead-end of reasoning? Each time, he would have to erase a dozen or more steps of logic and begin approaching the proof from a new direction.

On the fourth day, he awoke in the gray, pre-dawn light. He had passed another night consumed by arithmos, his brain too numb to bother returning to his bed. Now he became aware of another person in the room. He raised his head and saw Coriola.

"Enough," she told him, though he scarcely heard her. There was something pawing at the back of his mind, like a dog seeking his master's attention. Something *important*. Something he needed to remember.

How strange he had managed to sleep at all! Exhaustion counted for nothing when the thrall of arithmos seized him. And yet he *had* slept — and soundly too, at least for a few hours, judging by the candles which had all burned down to a smear of grease. Why had he allowed himself to sleep?

Because he was done.

Mother Arithmetica! *He was done.*

"Go back to your room, Luca. You're finished here."

Finished! Yes! With a final burst of brilliant insight he had found his proof! That final iteration of his work was right there chalked upon the board, spilling onto the stone walls in long lines of equations. Only then had he allowed himself to sleep.

"I have your proof," he said, struggling to maintain his composure. "The conjecture is solved."

"Luca, stop this insanity right now. Your mind is too full of arithmos. I see now I was wrong to taunt you with this impossible challenge."

"Look at the board," he said quietly. "Study the walls. You'll find no errors."

"Luca, *there is no proof* to the problem I set you! The whole point was to frustrate you. I wanted to punish you by setting a problem long known to be insoluble. That way I hoped you might understand your limitations."

"LOOK AT THE BOARD!" he bellowed.

Coriola flinched. She cast a quick, nervous glance at the sweeping lines of equations, then looked hurriedly away.

"There is no proof," she hissed, pushing him back down in his seat. He found he lacked the strength to resist. "It cannot be solved."

"But I —"

She slapped him and the sting of it stunned him into silence.

"I admit I thought your futile attempts at a solution might prove profitable. There might be a few elegant lines of logic in your attempts, the kind of thing that connoisseurs would pay handsomely to amuse themselves with. Because that's the *real* problem, Luca. The supply of arithmos is finite. Clever, eager minds such as those connoisseurs grow weary of the too-familiar concepts. The arithmos loses its luster, its potency. There is no ecstasy to be had from the mundane. Then, every once in a while some mathematical breakthrough is made and it's the purest form of arithmos experience one can have, to understand something so exquisite for the very first time. And I thought... You're bright, Luca. The House can make good use of you in time, and I'll see that you're well looked after."

"Like you took care of Frenkel? He didn't become Burned through his own carelessness, did he?"

She didn't answer straight way. "Frenkel's mistakes could have brought about the House's downfall. What I did was only..." She trailed off.

Luca let his head sink back onto his arms. "There's no mistake. I've made no errors in my working. Look for yourself." He felt a wave of blackness rising. Sleep hadn't removed the deep-seated tiredness after all. He was spent.

After a while, when Coriola didn't answer, his raised his head again. Rag in hand, eyes carefully averted, she was erasing all the scribbles on the walls, the chalkboard already cleaned.

"NO!"

"If what you claim is true, this is too powerful for my purposes. There's no profit in driving my clients into insanity. Go back to your room —"

He was on her before he even realized what he was doing, knocking her to the floor, pinning her beneath him. "Don't you understand what you've just destroyed? If even half of what you've told me is true... And now it's gone —"

She struggled in his grip. "Stop this fallacy. You're already an addict, Luca. Do you want to become one of the Burned too?"

"I can control it! You showed me how."

"No, Luca. Dark equations are beyond anyone's control But you're too blind to see that, aren't you? You're an arrogant young fool."

No. *She was wrong.* And he would show her how wrong she was.

As they struggled, he began to recite lines from the proof Coriola had just erased. They came to him as random, half-remembered things; flashes of insight that made her eyes bulge beneath his grip as he dripped them into her mind. He felt his own vision waver as he fought to recall, driven by the terror that it might all slip from his memory and be lost.

He felt no pity for her. She had brought this on herself, stolen this most precious of things from him. She had wiped it away in smears of chalk-dust. Now he could only clutch at the disjointed memories of it.

And he hated her for what she had tried to destroy.

Coriola had been the one to show him how to control the arithmos, building the cages in his mind. She had coached him and this had saved them both when it mattered most — and now he turned it against her. He spoke the words he knew would fling wide the doors to those compartments. He watched the arithmos run free in her mind, her eyes widening, pupils dilating, and kept whispering what he could recall of his fading proof, flooding her mind with its details — and his too, his brain growing feverish with disjointed thoughts.

She spasmed beneath him. Flecks of spittle foamed between her lips and her eyes rolled back in their sockets.

Unreasoning anger drove him on, repeating the same few lines of his proof over and over until his voice grew hoarse.

At last a silence descended on the room. Coriola lay still, not breathing. Luca got to his feet unsteadily.

He saw now that she had been right. He did only care about the arithmos, even though it would eventually destroy him. But this new proof — a thing so perfect in its elegance, so wondrously beautiful — must not be denied its existence, no matter the cost.

He stepped over Coriola's body, stooping to pick up a nub of chalk. Before, he had worked in stepwise fashion, tidying each step away in his mind, securing it, before he moved to the next. Now he opened his mind to the entirety of it and it was like stepping out from a darkened room into the blazing noon sun.

With an unsteady hand, he began to scrawl on the walls, unsure if he was recreating what had been so nearly lost or merely writing gibberish. When he finished at last, he couldn't bring himself to look at the entirety of it. He stood there for what seemed like an hour or more, the slant of light creeping across the floor with the rising sun.

At last, when he could stand no more, he scrubbed the walls clean again, and fled the House of Geometers.

With the passing months, Luca had found concealment in the vast swathes of forest westwards of the city, but the living was hard. Now and then, small mammals blundered into his flimsy snares — for which he was grateful — and there were berries to be scavenged from thickets, and edible roots to be dug up and boiled to a bland paste. But now the days were growing colder and shorter, and the forest possessed a stillness that unnerved him. That quietness amplified the little background noises — animals scurrying in the undergrowth, muted birdsong in the pine trees, whose upper branches shivered in strengthening winds from the east. It was as if the forest held its breath, waiting for... *something*, like the moment of stillness before the jaws of a trap spring shut.

Luca watched the other man stirring their cook-pot in the camp fire's smoldering embers. The fire was carefully banked so that it gave out no smoke column which might betray their presence. The figure seemed broken; his cloak tightly wrapped as if to ward against the cold, despite the sun's warmth this morning.

But better broken than Burned.

Luca had noticed small signs of improvement in his companion these last few days. His night-time ravings had diminished to a gentle burbling, and now there was even a flicker of intellect in the man's stare, as though something was trying to push through thick layers of confusion.

He wondered again at the impulse that had led him back to Dr Frenkel. Luca had fled the city, fearful of what uses the Ecclesiasts might put him to once they learned of his true abilities. Yet something had compelled him to venture back into the cathedral grounds, and he had stolen the man away under cover of darkness. Frenkel had come willingly, meek and compliant as a child.

What had possessed Luca to do that? At the time, he had convinced himself it was an act of compassion, settling a debt owed to the former tutor who had taught him so much.

Lately, he wondered if there might have been darker motives at work in his subconscious.

Every now and then, snatches of his proof bobbed to the forefront of his mind, like rotting corpses rising to the surface of a lake. He thrust them back into the darkness, of course, but he could feel them circling, ever-present.

Luca took his place by the fire. His traps had been empty again, and the hollow hunger pains in his belly were a constant reminder that they must act soon. A shaking hand reached out for his. He gripped it, making soothing noises until Frenkel settled again.

"Should we go back?" Luca asked quietly.

Frenkel's lips ceased their convulsive twitching and Luca saw something new in his expression. A gleam of excitement? Fear?

By now, they could have put two hundred miles between themselves and the city. Yet when Luca had climbed to the top of a ridge just that morning, there it was: the dark outline of Orlondre on the horizon, no more than thirty miles distant. He knew why they kept circling back. They wouldn't find any arithmos scholars amongst the simple folk in the scattered forest villages or the farming communities beyond. No one he could learn from in those quiet backwaters. Yet each day he felt the need for fresh arithmos stirring inside. He had so much still to learn, so many things Coriola or Frenkel might have shown him — but Coriola was dead, and as for Frenkel...

"We could find hiding places," he told Frenkel. "Burrow deep into Orlondre's dark underbelly where no Ecclesiast will think to look. And there'll be no shortage of wealthy benefactors willing to trade for what we can offer."

That much was true. It occurred to Luca that he might even finish the work Coriola had begun: finding ways to loosen the Church's vice-like grip on the citizens of Orlondre. And if he could learn how to control his cravings, surely he could teach others. Couldn't arithmos become a joyous, enriching experience when taken in moderation? Weren't there better uses it could be put to?

Or was this no more than self-delusion? He'd be returning to the source of his supply just as any hardened addict would. And wasn't he nurturing some dark kernel of hope that Frenkel might one day be well enough to resume Luca's lessons?

The choices stretching before him suddenly reminded him of the patterned tiles he had swooned over so long ago: black-and-white, light-and-dark, endlessly repeating.

"Gather your things," he told Frenkel at last, with a certainty he didn't feel in his heart.

They would go back, and Luca knew what he must do. He would reclaim the House of Geometers for himself. They would build it back stronger, right under the gaze of the Ecclesiasts.

Whichever way the choices led him after that, well...

Then he would see how well he'd learned his lessons of self-control.

See David Cleden's story "In the House of Geometers" online at Metaphorosis.
If you liked it, leave a comment. Authors love that!

Remember to subscribe to our e-mail updates so you'll know when new stories are posted.

About the story

The what-if? origin question behind "In The House of Geometers" is easy for me to trace. I'm no mathematician but I did study a lot of maths (yes, I'm British and it's plural, dammit!) for my physics degree at college. Pre-college, I was fortunate to have several inspiring maths teachers, one of whom introduced me to the mathematical expression known as Euler's Identity. (I'll leave you to look it up if you're interested). It's a very simple equation that links together five fundamental concepts in mathematics: 0, 1, pi, i (the square root of minus one), and e (the base of natural logarithms). How could all these elemental things be linked in such a simple yet elegant way? It left a lasting impression on me. Many regard it as the most beautiful equation in existence.

Years later, I tried explaining this to my wonderful, long-suffering wife and saw a familiar reaction: her eyes glazed over at the first mention of mathematics, and she wore a polite smile that slowly froze into hostility the longer I eulogized about it. What, I wondered, would it be like to live in a world where everyone is helplessly consumed by a strong appreciation of mathematical beauty, much in the same way that we all share an intrinsic love of art — but turned up to eleven so that for some people mathematics becomes an addiction. After all, art connoisseurs can lose themselves for hours appreciating fine art: marvelling at the brushwork, the depth and blend of colour, the chiaroscuro. What if it were the same for maths? "In The House of Geometers" explores such a world and some of its consequences.

A question for the author

Q: What happens when you hit writer's block head on?

A. I think as you gain more experience as a writer, you learn a few techniques that can help you work through the more common reasons behind a block. Usually, it's not so much a question of working through, as backing up and heading off in a different direction. My blocks are often caused by something just not working the way I think it ought to. If I can step back far enough in the story, I can usually find the place where I'm still happy with things up to that point. Then it's a question of changing some of the story parameters: making a character more compelling, adding more conflict, looking at pacing — basically all the stuff that you can find in any decent writing book. (Usually these are things that I already know but have forgotten in the telling of the story). The hard part, of course, is chopping out all the bad stuff and reworking it, but you know you're doing the right thing when you get the fire back in your belly and the story comes to life again.

Which is great — except when it doesn't work. If I can't figure out where I've gone wrong, or the idea has just died on me, I find it best to set the work aside. Sometimes forever — because there are lots more great story ideas out there! — but often only until some unspecified time in the future. On that day, casting my eye back over the words with a fresh perspective, the answer is suddenly obvious, and off I go. Or I'll see a way to pair this half-formed idea with another one and create something new. Or not. Remember: there's no statute of limitations on blocked, half-completed stories.

That's okay when writing short stories, but for novel-writing the time investment is obviously much greater. It can feel hugely frustrating to have several blocked novel attempts on the go. A lot of advice I see is to just grit your teeth and work through it, and I think that can work. (I remember listening to a panel of SF authors at GollanczFest one year. One swore blind that in every novel he'd written, the story just died for him on page 147. Always that page. But he pushed on regardless, and eventually the joy of it came back. "No, no," said another panel member. "It happens on page 190 for me!" The point was, all these big-name authors went through a kind of dip or crisis of confidence, in writing their novels. Is a dip the same as writer's block? Maybe not, but sometimes the answer is to keep going regardless.)

Yet if I'm blocked because my heart is not in the story, I'll stop. Pushing on can compound the problems and I'm better off working on something new that inspires me. I like the analogy of a chef working in a hot, steamy kitchen. Sometimes to create a fine meal you need several pans on the go. You spend a bit of time on this one, leaving it to simmer while you attend that one, then back to the first, and so on. Eventually, with enough pans on the go, you can see what looks and tastes good, and you can begin to blend things to create something special — always excepting that there will inevitably be some leftovers and wastage.

About the author

David Cleden is a British author. He hasn't led a colourful life, doesn't live in an exotic location, and possesses little in the way of interesting hobbies, so he tries to make up for all this by writing speculative fiction.

www.quantum-scribe.com, @DavidCleden

Silo

J. S. DiStefano

I woke to the slow, creaking opening of the door, and the wind against the walls of the silo. The old man led me down the winding stairs and outside into the night.

"It's cold." My first words since waking.

"You'll get used to it. I was freezing the first couple weeks."

"That long?"

We stood in the dark, at the top of a hill surrounded by long-abandoned farmland. The silo was the only building left. In the daylight, we would be able to look out over empty fields that stretched for miles. That night we stared out into nothingness.

There was a small bunker near the base of the silo, built into the ground. The old man opened the door and led me down. The narrow stairwell opened into a small, bare room, decorated only with monitors depicting the hilltop up above. There was only one chair.

He showed me the slot in the wall where our rations appeared every twenty-four hours. One small vial of serum, taken by injection, provided the necessary vitamins, nutrients, and antibodies. We walked through the control room and past the storage room. He showed me how to refuel the silo and recharge the infrared shield.

We went back outside and sat around the fire. A pile of wood and a bucket of water guarded the grass behind us. Under the shadow of the silo, the old man spoke of his life, of sixty years of waiting. He told me little that I had not known, had not expected. As he talked, his voice would drop down to a whisper, and the sound of the wind on metal threatened to drown it out completely and leave me alone in the dark.

I did not ask how long he had left. The knowledge that he had awakened me loomed over us, a dominant feature of the hilltop.

"So you saw the bunker. And you used the bathroom. Everything else was covered in the training, really."

The wood burned down. The coals were red when the old man suddenly doused the fire and knocked me off the log. I heard it too. We lay still in the grass, heads turned slightly to the side, facing each other. I could hear his heartbeat, pulsing wildly like my own.

Slowly, carefully, two enormous ships moved across the sky, flashing spotlights on the ground, back and forth over the grass. The clothes we wore had been chosen for this. Dirt and the smell of grass pressed against my nose, and minutes felt like hours. The two ships advanced toward us, one nearly in line with where we lay on the ground, the other about a quarter mile to the south, in the direction my feet were pointing. When the ship that was closest to us passed overhead, the noise was deafening.

They reached the bottom of the hill and stopped, hovering. We watched, our breath caught in our throats, as the bottoms of both enormous spacecraft opened, completely synchronized. Out of each dropped a small flying saucer. The two miniature pods met up and flew with speed that neither parent ship could have possessed. Straight toward us.

"Run!" hissed the old man. It was a figure of speech. Instinctively, we both stayed on the ground, heads down, crawling quickly toward the bunker. The old man opened the hatch and we slipped down below, shutting the door behind us without making a sound.

After a minute of waiting at the top of the steps with our hearts pounding, we snuck down the stairs to watch the scene outside on the monitors. The two saucers had reached the silo. One rotated around the building, slowly, while the other scanned the field.

Then they were gone, flying back toward the two great motherships, which opened once more to accept them. We stayed in the bunker, staring at the screens before us as the ships began to move again, receding into the night. It would have been safe now to rebuild the fire, but we sat in silence.

Finally, I asked the old man, "Have they come before?"

"Once. Forty years ago. Before that, I think it'd been over two hundred. There's a <u>logbook</u> around here somewhere."

"I know." I was silent for a moment. "I didn't expect it to be like that."

"No." His voice was soft. "I don't see how you could have."

The silence in the underground room was deafening in the absence of wind against metal.

We stayed underground until the sun began to rise. When we opened up the bunker door and climbed back onto the surface, the barren landscape around us felt exposed. Vulnerable. We sat back on the logs we had abandoned, now covered in a thin layer of dew.

The old man looked at the fire, staring down into the wet, black coals. "I'm sorry if I startled you when I woke you up. That was the hardest part. Last night. Bringing you back into the world. You won't have an easy life. I didn't."

I nodded. I didn't know what to say. The sun was climbing up in the sky and the shadow of the great tower was growing longer, stretching out down the hill toward the empty fields below.

He stood up from his log and looked at me. There was a sense of finality in his words. "I think I'll go lie down for a while." He walked slowly to the bunker and opened the lid.

"Wait," I called out. He turned. "Thank you."

"For what?"

"For serving."

He looked at me for a moment, then nodded. He turned back to the bunker and descended to his final resting place.

I wanted to call out again, to ask him to sit and wait with me a little longer. But we didn't have the rations for two watchmen. The calculations had been thorough. Our resources had been stretched as thin as they could go. The old man had done his duty. The least I could do was respect his privacy and leave him to die as he had lived.

Alone.

The old man had spoken truly – there was no way I could be prepared for this. But there was no other choice, for any of us. The enemy had made a mockery of our technology. Automated surveillance was never an option.

I turned my gaze up from the bunker to look up at the silo. Sixty years per person, and I am number two thousand one hundred and twenty-two of ten thousand.

I will serve out my term, and then wake up number two thousand one hundred and twenty-three. One day, the world will be safe again for our species to live as a civilization. But until then, the fate of humanity rests with us, the people of the silo.

See J.S. DiStefano's story "Silo" online at Metaphorosis.
If you liked it, leave a comment. Authors love that!

Remember to subscribe to our e-mail updates so you'll know when new stories are posted.

About the story

The main science fiction concepts in this story were inspired by the *Remembrance of Earth's Past* trilogy by Liu Cixin. I tried to keep the story short and the language concise to emulate my favorite writing.

During the development of the story I was reading a lot, authors like Emily St. John Mandel, Colson Whitehead, George Saunders, Pierce Brown, and others. I would be lucky if any of this rubbed off on my work.

A question for the author

Q: Whence you do you draw inspiration for your characters?

A: From people I meet and characters I watch or read about — and I think about what I might do or say in a given situation. I try to do the whole "show don't tell" thing as far as character development goes, but I think I have a long way to go.

About the author

J.S. DiStefano likes hiking, playing cards, watching football, reading, and writing. "Silo" is his first published story.

Shades of the Sea

J.A. Prentice

The village children found Larnia lying in the crashing surf. Her clothes were drenched and ragged, her side torn by a deep red gash, and her hair tangled with flecks of coral.

The children raced along the winding path that led up from the beach, towards the house near the cliff's edge where the healer Tasia and her husband Miron lived. Halfway there, they found Miron sitting amongst a flock of sheep, facing away from the sea, silent and grim. His eyes were red from weeping.

The children grabbed at him, shouting, begging him to come, but Miron would not be stirred. Through his enshrouding sorrow, they were voices from a thousand miles away, faces seen through a white mist. "Larnia!" a girl said at last. "We found Larnia!"

Miron looked up, his eyes wide, and leapt to his feet. Without a word, he began to run, towards the beach, the children straggling behind him. It had been years since he'd run so fast.

Larnia.

Three days, she had been gone, lost with her parents beneath the waves. The storm had struck, hard and furious, and the sea leapt up in swelling mountains to swallow their ship, dashing it to matchwood. The bodies had been lost, though the village folk searched for hours to bring their bones home.

Larnia had drifted into the deep dark, where dappled light gave way to endless midnight pressing on all sides, where the shadowed things dwelt—shades and leviathans and the Deep Court. The curls of her hair had flared out in a black cloud and the waters had whispered in her ears all the secrets the ocean knows.

Three days, Miron had prayed that the gods would bring Larnia back to them. He had loved her like his own blood, like he would have loved the children he and Tasia couldn't have. They had tried, again and again, but each time the child had been lost. Tasia still wouldn't speak of them, buried in their shallow graves.

Miron could not bear the thought that Larnia might have been lost also. Nine years was longer than his own children had lived, but hardly a life. The gods could not be so cruel. Miron still had faith, despite his suffering, and so he kept praying, though he knew the odds were slim.

Three days, and now she was lying on the beach, still as driftwood, her lips pale blue.

He came to a halt some feet from her, and stood unmoving, not daring to touch her skin and feel the cold of death, the stillness of her chest, the stiffness of her muscles. The children clustered like sheep around him, unsure whether to be afraid, sad, or exhilarated in the face of mortality.

Then she coughed. Spluttered. Seawater ran down her lips and her fingers twitched.

Miron's heart leapt. He thanked each god by name for her deliverance as he rushed to her side, wrapping strong arms around her tiny body.

"Get my wife!" he shouted and the children scattered, bare feet pounding sand. "She needs a healer!"

Larnia stirred, her hair brushing his arm. Trickling water pattered on darkened sand. Weak breaths hissed from pale lips. Her eyes fluttered open and she stared straight at him, with a burning intensity. Then her eyelids closed again, and she turned her head away.

Miron took a deep breath, his heart thundering against his ribs. It must have been his imagination. A trick of the light. Larnia's eyes were brown, like her father's, like her mother's. They always had been.

He carried on across the sands, carrying Larnia in his arms, and tried to forget the eyes that had stared up at him out of his niece's face—eyes the swirling midnight blue of the deep sea.

A week, she lay in bed, tossing and turning under sheets that rippled like wild waves. Sweat dripped from her brow, yet her skin remained ice to the touch. She muttered as she writhed— fragments in a strange tongue.

"I've done what I can," Tasia said, sitting in an old wicker chair. "The rest is with the gods." She looked at Miron and frowned. "There's something you aren't saying."

She could always tell his mood. Miron was an easy man to read. His feelings were written in every line, every wrinkle. "There's nothing," Miron said. "Nothing."

Tasia pursed her lips, brushed greying hair from her leather-brown face, but said no more. That was the way her mother had taught her, and her mother before. The way of silence. A healer did not show her feelings. She let them boil beneath the surface, buried in the dark.

Between them were many things unsaid. One more, she supposed, would hurt no one.

On the seventh day, Larnia woke. Her sheets tumbled onto the earthen floor as she stretched her arms and blinked her wide eyes.

"Hello?" she called.

Miron leapt from his chair and ran to his niece. "My little one. We were so worried."

He pulled back and looked into her eyes: sea-eyes, full of dancing shadow.

"What are these?" He stroked her hair aside. "Your eyes were brown."

"Were they?" Larnia asked. "How strange." She looked around at the curving wattle-and-daub wall, the rafters holding the thatched roof in place, the smooth earthen floor, and the arched blue door. "This is where I live?"

"You don't remember?" Miron asked. "Do you remember me?"

"Of course." Larnia's bare feet kicked the air. "You pulled me out. Out of the dark."

"The dark?"

"Pressing in on all sides." Larnia hugged her knees to her chest. "Cold. Dark. Forever."

Miron smiled and put a hand on her shoulder. "You're safe now."

"No. No." Larnia wrenched away. "Not safe. Never safe. *She's* coming."

Tasia frowned as she examined the sleeping Larnia. The girl's skin was still cool, but she no longer twisted as she had before. Her sleep seemed peaceful, untroubled by dreams. And yet... "There's no reason her eyes should have changed."

Miron ran a hand through his hair. "And the memories..."

"I've heard of that." Tasia looked away. "My grandmother was called to the Great War, when the seas were red with blood. Her ship was raided by the enemy, her friends killed. She was fished from the wreck, but she couldn't remember what had happened. Couldn't remember her own name. She just kept praying, clinging to her grandmother's bone..." Tasia instinctively reached for the finger-bone hanging around her own neck. "She lay awake for months after they brought her home, screaming that the enemy were coming to slit her throat."

"You've never spoken of this before," Miron said.

Tasia couldn't bear to look at him, to see the pity in his eyes. "It isn't a thing that's spoken of."

"But she was well again?" Miron asked, leaning forward. "In time?"

Tasia ran a hand over Larnia's forehead. "She was better. She was never *well*."

Miron wrapped an arm around Tasia, and she rested her head on his chest. It hurt, dredging up these memories. An old wound should not be reopened. Better to let it stay, and live with the little aches.

"But Larnia is young," Tasia continued. "This may fall beneath the waves of memory and be nothing more than a forgotten shadow."

She kissed her bone and Miron nodded. "Let us pray it will be so."

Beside them, Larnia whispered in her sleep, a sound like the sea-wind whistling over the swelling grey hills of the open sea.

They found her perched on the cliff's edge, singing her strange syllables. Like a soldier keeping watch, she peered at the tides crashing against the beach below. There was a tremor in her song, like she was singing it to keep the fear at bay.

"Larnia!" Miron called. "Get away from there! You could fall."

"Fall." Larnia turned the word over on her tongue. "It is different, isn't it? With air and earth? No swimming. No drifting."

"Yes." Miron took her hand and pulled her back. "Come to the house."

Tasia looked at the girl, then clutched at her bone. Larnia cocked her head to one side. "I don't understand it up here," she said. "It's very strange." A rippling laugh came from deep within her like a spring of fresh water. She ran a hand through the long grass, letting it tickle her skin, and plunged her fingers into the earth.

Frowning, Tasia knelt beside her. "What is 'up here'? Why is it different?"

Larnia tore up a handful of soil and grass. Her skin stained black and green.

Tasia seized her by the shoulders. "Who *are* you?"

"Larnia," the girl sang. "Larnia. Larnialarnialarnialarnialarnia!"

"Let her go!" Miron picked Larnia up, his back straining under the weight. "She's frightened."

"She's something." Tasia's grip on her bone made her knuckles gleam white. "I can't stay here. I have to think."

Miron called after her, but Tasia didn't turn back. She walked down the cliff-path, away from the cottage and towards the churning surf. Still holding Larnia in his arms, Miron went back to the cottage. She squirmed and he let her down, collapsing into the wicker chair. Watching Larnia play on the ground, running her hands over the earth, he tried to forget what his wife had said.

"You have to forgive her," Miron said to the girl. "Her sister died. Your mother. She's distressed."

"She keeps touching that bone," Larnia said. "Talking to it like it can hear her."

"It's your grandmother's bone," Miron said. "But you know that."

Larnia blinked and nodded. "Grandmother's bone..."

"Your grandmother is buried under the house," Miron continued. "Her shade is bound to this place, so she protects us from evil spirits and the wandering dead. Our souls cannot be claimed; our bodies cannot be stolen." He smiled. "The bone protects us if we leave the house. We carry a little bit of her with us."

"Magic," Larnia whispered.

"There is no magic stronger. Or older. All spirits, all demons, and all gods must respect it," Miron said. "But it only works for us. Only her family."

Larnia pressed an ear to the floor.

"What are you doing?"

"Listening. For her."

A smile cracked Miron's weathered face. "It's just a story."

"Are all people buried under floors?"

"We keep them close."

"But your wife's sister..." Larnia opened her midnight-blue eyes. "She is not close. She drifts in the waters of the deep. So far from home. So alone."

"Your mother." Miron tightened his grip on her shoulder and his lip trembled. "She was your mother."

But in his heart he already knew that wasn't true. He knew the child in his house wasn't his niece, no matter how much he wanted her to be.

In grey-white wisps, the mists swelled against the cliff. Tasia and Miron stood above, outside their cottage, with Larnia asleep inside. Their voices carried, echoing over the crashing tides below.

"It isn't her," Tasia thundered. "It isn't Larnia. She speaks strange tongues. Her eyes are blue as the sea. She does not remember anything. This is not our girl, Miron. It's a sea-shade..." She touched her mother's bone. "Wearing her like an old coat!"

"She's a little girl," Miron snapped.

"Do you believe she is our niece?"

Miron looked away.

"Answer me, Miron. Look into my eyes and tell me you believe this is our niece."

Miron kept his eyes on the mist. On the horizon, darks clouds swelled, building for a summer storm. "I..." Miron shook his head. "I don't know." Then... "No. No, it isn't her."

It hurt, admitting that truth, like he was sending Larnia back into the deep. He felt the tears welling up again, the grief clawing at his heart.

"Then you think we should keep a sea-demon in our house?" Tasia demanded.

Perhaps Tasia was right, Miron thought. Perhaps this shade wearing Larnia's skin was a demon, an evil here to kill them. But she had seemed so peaceful, when she played with the earth, and her laugh was so bright, so clear.

"What do you say we do with her?" Miron threw up his arms. "Stone her?"

"Put her back where she came from," Tasia snapped. "Cast her into the sea!"

A sound came from the cottage. The tiniest ray of light shone through the ajar door. Miron reached out and pushed it open.

There, curled against the wall, sea-eyes moon-wide, lip trembling, knees clutched tight, was Larnia.

Miron looked down at this thing wearing his niece's body, this shade from the deep, this demon. She looked back, with a frightened child's face. Her voice was the smallest whisper, faint as wind. "Please don't put me back."

Miron picked her up in his arms and held her tight to his chest. "Never."

She was not evil, this child. Whatever else she was, she *was* a child. A frightened child, who needed love, who needed kindness.

He turned to speak to Tasia, but Tasia was gone, the door swinging in the wind.

Thunder sounded in the dark of night. Larnia trembled. She sat upon the cliff's edge, Miron standing behind her.

The sky was grey and churning, rain pattering against the earth. Ocean waves lapped against the cliffs, hungrily tearing at pale stone. Birds shrieked and the wind howled.

Larnia clutched at Miron's sleeve. "She's coming. Stirring in the deep waters."

"Who?" Larnia said nothing, staring into the pounding surf. "Who is coming, Larnia?"

"I'm not..." She took a deep breath. "Not her."

Miron sighed. Waves cracked against the cliff and a sliver of white stone splashed into the churning sea. "I know."

"Then you'll let her take me. Down into midnight." Larnia looked at him. "It's lonely there. And cold. The Deep Court sit on thirteen thrones of coral and bone. Hers is the largest. The skulls of kings lie beneath her white fingers."

The birds shrieked again and the mist laid icy kisses upon Miron's cheeks. "Tell me..." His breath turned to a cloud. "Did you kill Larnia?"

Eyes wide, the girl shook her head. "No. *Never.* I tried to pull her from the waves. But she was... empty. Gone." She looked away. "I couldn't help her."

"But you tried." The girl nodded. A tear glistened on her eyelash. "What do I call you?"

"We have no names in the deep. No flesh. Only whispers and bones. I wanted to walk on the surface. To feel sand in my toes. To feel the wind. To feel. To be." She closed her eyes. "I'm not ready to go back to the dark."

"I'll call you Larnia, then." A wistful smile crept over Miron's lips. "I think she would have liked that."

Larnia looked up. "You won't leave me?"

"Not if all the shades of the night came for you."

"Why? I'm not her."

"No. But you're you." He kissed her forehead. "And I think you're special enough."

They sat there, rain pattering against their skin. Lightning struck across the sky, a white crack in creation. Larnia let out a cold breath.

"Who's coming?" Miron asked again.

"The Queen of the Deep Court," she whispered.

Miron stood, brushing down his trousers. "Get inside."

"But she comes." Larnia pointed to the waves. A shadow stirred in the waters, moving towards shore. "For me."

"Get inside," Miron said. "If Tasia returns, tell her to bolt the door."

She clutched at his sleeve. "Where are you going?"

He smiled. "I'm going to meet the Queen."

The cottage was dark when Tasia returned. No fire burned in the hearth. The winds around her were pounding, the rain hitting hard as stones. The storm had come suddenly. Tasia had barely made it back in time, racing through sheep fields and terraces as the earth turned to mud and rainwater ran in deep rivers.

She wanted to talk to Miron about the girl. She had left too abruptly, spoken too much in heat and anger. That heat was cooled now, her anger turned to something quieter. As she had walked, it had risen from her like steam, until she was left with only a cool rationality.

Miron was too trusting, too hopeful, by his nature. Tasia was no longer so soft. The world had taught her that hope today meant hurt tomorrow. She knew this shade in child's shape would turn on them. She knew—however much her heart wanted it to be otherwise—the shade was dangerous, even if it hadn't done anything to harm them, even if she seemed so much like a child, even if she made Miron happy, even if her laugh—

Tasia shook off those thoughts with the rain, and opened the door.

"Miron," she called, but there was no answer.

There was a noise in the darkness. A soft sobbing. It was the girl—the shade. Her eyes peered out from the shadows of the corner, behind her bed. They were so dark, so strange, those eyes. Tasia felt like they were staring right through her.

"Where is he?" Tasia demanded. The door swung open behind her, groaning in the wind. The shade stared through it. Her eyes were wide with fear. She looked so much like nothing more than a frightened child, and Tasia wanted to embrace her.

But she was a shade. A danger to them all.

"Gone, gone, gone!" the shade bleated. "Told him not to! Said he wanted to keep me safe."

"Into that storm? Stupid man. He'll be drenched, if he's not drowned."

"He said bolt the door," the shade said. "So she can't get in."

"She?" Tasia put her hands on the shade's shoulders. Her little face was wet with tears, and Tasia reached up, without thinking, to wipe them away. "Who's she?"

"The Queen of the Deep! She's come for me!" The shade trembled. "She'll take him, to get to me."

"Then she can have you!" Tasia snapped. The shade wailed and darted back beneath the bed, out of Tasia's reach. "I won't lose him! Not after—" Her breath caught. She shook her head and looked down at the shade. "I'm sorry. I..." She gathered her breath. "The gods have taken too much. I won't lose him as well."

The shade went quiet. For a moment she just lay there, so still and small. Then she crawled out, and said in a shaking voice, "Then I *should* go to her."

Her hand closed around Tasia's, and Tasia's heart stopped, remembering the days when she had prayed and prayed for a child to hold her hand like that. She had believed the gods were good then, as Miron still believed. After so many prayers unanswered, there was no faith left in her. She had asked again and again for a child, and the gods had given her only death.

Miron had wanted a child so badly. Tasia looked at the little girl before her, her niece's face with those midnight-blue eyes, and understood why he had gone into the storm.

But why her, Miron? she asked. *Why this demon-thing?*

He answered, though he was not there, because she always knew what he would say: *Because she needs us.*

Miron—foolish, stupid, wonderful Miron—would not forgive her if she gave the child to the Queen, even to save his life. *Especially* to save his life. Miron loved this child, as deeply as he loved her, as deeply as she loved him. They were all tangled up in it, the three of them, fish caught in the same net.

Love was a foolish thing, Tasia had always thought. There was no reason in it. Perhaps that was why it came easier to Miron than to her. She had wrapped herself in too many layers of silence, of fear, of rationality. There was little opening for love to work its way in.

Miron left his heart wide open, and so this child had wandered in. Tasia could see how. The child might have gotten into her heart as well, if she did not guard it so closely, turning aside love before it could turn to loss. It was rare that Tasia allowed herself to love.

But she loved Miron, more than anything. It was a love that had grown over decades, until she could not imagine herself without him. They had grown together, like two trees entwined. She trusted him as she trusted nothing else in this world. She would not lose him. His absence would be a hole bigger than her world.

"I should go back," the girl said, though she was shaking with fear, "and you two can be happy again."

Tasia thought of the children she could not bring herself to speak of, of Miron alone in the storm, and of her sister's family lost to the sea.

Not again, Tasia thought. *I will not lose another.*

She clutched her mother's bone tight, and looked out into the storm.

From the roar of the tide and the pounding curtain of rain stepped the Queen. Her hair was sea-soaked rope cast into the depths, her cloak a ragged sail from a doomed ship, her face the parchment-white skull of a long-dead sailor. A pocked crown of coral crawled over her scalp, poking into empty sockets where blue flames blazed. Her dress was woven eel-skin, slithering behind her.

Drenched with rainwater, Miron stood rooted in the sand. She stopped, close enough for him to smell the rot, like old fish in the summer sun.

"You have one of my subjects," the Queen said. Briny seawater spilled from between brown-encrusted teeth. "I would take her back."

He stood straight, his chest puffed out, but his gut sagging. "Nothing here is yours."

"She stole your niece," the Queen replied. "She wears her corpse like a play-thing."

"My niece is dead," Miron said, though his voice shook when he said it. "Giving you that girl won't bring her back."

"She is not one of you. She is a thing of shadows and waves. She belongs to me."

"Why do you want her so?"

"Why?" The Queen cocked her skull head to one side. "She is *mine*. My subject. Would a shepherd let a lamb be stolen from his flock? Would you let me steal coins from your purse?"

"She isn't a lamb or a coin," Miron said. "She's a child. A *person*. She wasn't stolen, either, unless she can steal herself."

"What she is," the Queen hissed, "is *mine*."

"You can't have her."

The Queen's laugh was the caw of carrion birds. "And what will you do?"

Miron raised his fists. "Whatever I can."

"In other words..." Plaque-coated teeth flashed. "Nothing."

She raised a hand and the wind sent him tumbling through the sands. Pinpricks of hail pressed against him like shards of glass. Red drops glistened on his skin.

"You are mortal," she thundered. "Finite. Flesh and bone, easily broken. I am the shadow beneath the waters. I am the biting cold and the whispering dark. I am ancient and forever."

"You're nothing," Miron spat. "Just mist and fear. Sunlight and a swift wind would sweep you away."

The hail pressed tighter, cutting skin. Lightning tore the sky, followed by a drumbeat of thunder.

"I will hurl your corpse to the sea. The fish shall eat your eyes and the waves shall wear your flesh to nothing. Your shade will wander the waves forever, mine to keep, as all lost souls are. Give me the girl."

"Never!" Miron snarled.

"Stop!" Footsteps pattered along the beach. Larnia raced towards them, dripping wet and shivering in the rain. The Queen's eyes flared and she turned from Miron, letting him fall. Scratched and bloody, he lay on the sands, fighting for each choking breath.

"My subject," the Queen said, "you come back to me."

Larnia held her chin high. She seemed so small that the wind might blow her away. "You will not hurt him."

"I have no interest in him," the Queen replied. "Or any of the crawling ants on this little rock. My court is vaster than his world. Yet he stands between me..." She reached for Larnia and the girl stepped back. "And mine. The shade that defies me. The lamb that stole itself."

"If I come with you," Larnia said, "you will leave them be?"

"Larnia," Miron croaked, trying to pull himself upright, "*no!*"

There was a sound on the cliff path above, the gentlest shower of falling stone. Miron looked up and saw Tasia looking down upon them like a distant god, impassive as the stone surrounding her.

"Help me!" he screamed up at Tasia. "Help her!"

But Tasia said nothing. She stood, and watched.

The Queen bowed her crowned skull. "If you return to me willingly, I shall spare them."

"Then take me," Larnia said, stretching her arms wide.

Bony fingers, dripping sea-mud, reached towards her. A millimeter from her skin, they stopped, quivering like a tree in a storm. "What have you done, girl?" the Queen hissed. "Another claims you!"

And Miron saw it, dangling around Larnia's neck: a single, yellowed fingerbone on a piece of old string.

Thunder roared and the earth shook under their feet. There was a smell in the air like incense on a winter morning. The Queen stumbled. Flakes of bone crumbled from her fingers and the coral in her crown bleached white, shriveling like an old orange in the sun. Her teeth cascaded from her jaw in a rush of dark water.

"She is *mine!*" she screamed. "You will not *steal* from me!"

A voice came from the cliff path, clear and strong even over the storm. "No," Tasia said. "She's *ours.*"

The Queen reached again for Larnia, but even as her arm stretched, it became dust and sand, scattered upon the sea wind. Her ragged cloak fluttered, then was lifted away, flailing as it was borne out to the crashing ocean waves.

Miron pulled himself to his feet. The winds howled around them, and the waves still crashed against the shore, but despite it, all seemed quiet now. Larnia sat in the sands, staring at where the Queen wasn't. She reached out a hand, feeling the empty air. Mists hung over the sea, pale and hazy, and rain pattered down, no longer hard, as it had been before, but a soft rhythm, cold on Miron's skin. He went over to Larnia, who was looking out to the sea like she expected the Queen to come back out, but there were only the waves.

Tasia walked towards them, her sandaled feet leaving deep marks in sea-drenched sand. She stopped beside Larnia and gave her a soft smile. "As long as her bones are near, my mother keeps her family safe from evil spirits. She would not let our child be taken."

Larnia embraced her, burying her head in the folds of her dress. Tasia ran a hand through tresses of rain-wet hair and drew her close. "Nobody can touch you here. Nobody."

Lightning flashed. In the grey curtain of mist, Miron saw the shadow of an old woman, tall and proud. Then the mist shifted like the trails of a silk dress and there was only earth and rain.

"Come on." Miron put one arm around Larnia and other around Tasia. "Let's get inside where it's dry and warm."

The three of them walked up the winding path, leaving the sea behind. Arm-in-arm, they climbed towards the old house. Larnia flung open the door, and Tasia went to stoke the hearth, while Miron gathered firewood. The fire burned, warm and bright, and the three of them huddled around it. Rain pattered against the roof, and winds howled, but neither could touch them, not here.

Larnia fell asleep, her head nuzzled on Tasia's shoulder. Tasia looked at Miron, and he looked back, and all their walls were melted away.

Here, his eyes said, *here is our family*.

See J.A. Prentice's story "Shades of the Sea" online at Metaphorosis.
If you liked it, leave a comment. Authors love that!
Remember to subscribe to our e-mail updates so you'll know when
new stories are posted.

About the story

"Shades of the Sea," at its core, is a story about a changeling—even though the word is never used.

For centuries, humans have told stories of possessions and changelings. It was the concept of changelings that particularly stuck with me: the child that isn't a child but rather an inhuman creature. Many scholars believe these stories were told originally to explain neurodivergent and otherwise "difficult" children. It is an easy lie, a comfortable lie: the child you are raising that is so different from the child you wanted isn't your child at all. Your child is somewhere out there, in Faerie, and what lives in your house is only a pretender. An inhuman thing in a child's skin.

Similarly, many of the "signs" of possession in old stories are symptoms of mental illnesses. It's a way of explaining the inexplicable, but also a quite literal demonization of these conditions.

As a writer fascinated by ancient folklore, I wanted to do my own take on the concept of a changeling or a possession. As a neurodivergent person, I knew that I wouldn't be telling a traditional take, where the true child is recovered or the possession miraculously lifted. I knew the story I wanted to tell was a story of acceptance, love, and the beauty in the strange and monstrous. It's a story about how just because a child isn't who you wanted—in this case, in a quite literal sense—it doesn't mean they aren't still a child, in need of love and protection.

Why the sea, then? It's true that there is little—if any—link between changelings and the sea, but the sea holds both a wild beauty and an unfathomable depth. It often lies so close to us, but swim out only a short distance and it drops away into a seemingly infinite dark. The sea has always held a power over me, as it has many writers and artists. There was nowhere else someone like Larnia—or like the Queen—could have come from.

So that is where the story came from: the changeling child from the deep, found drowned but living in the crashing surf...

A question for the author

Q: When do you decide a story is finished?

A: It depends on the story. Some stories burst into existence and write themselves in a matter of days or even hours, leaving only a little polishing to be done. Others slowly accumulate writing and edits over months—maybe even years—until I'm finally content with them. Sometimes I'll think a piece is finished, only to find myself reopening it later and starting a new round of drafting and edits.

Usually, I decide it's finished when it reads like a story, and not like a draft. It's a feeling more than anything else, but when you're a writer, you have to learn to trust those feelings.

About the author

Joshua Adam Prentice was born in the United Kingdom, grew up in the Bay Area, and currently lives in the Pacific Northwest. He studied English and Creative Writing at San Francisco State University. When he was five, he was attacked by a monkey, which annoyingly proved to be the most interesting thing that has ever happened to him.

livingauthorssociety.wordpress.com, @livingauthors

February

A Lie in the Sand

Devin Miller

The trees at the edge of the beach lean away from the water. They could have been blown back by a powerful sea wind, but Haworth is certain the trees are simply trying to get as far from the beach as possible. She wants to lean back too.

"What the fuck is this?" Haworth asks. Her breath mists in the damp-cold air. They could have been on the ship home to Tirucal by now.

Aristalo, hands in her pockets, surveys the beach calmly. Haworth's boss is maybe fifty (unconfirmed, since she's not the kind of person you can ask to tell you their age), and being a traveling bard that long is a surefire way to become unflappable. "It's a beach full of sand castles," she answers. "Watch your language."

Haworth, about to call profanity-prone Aristalo out on her massive hypocrisy, looks back at the beach and crosses her arms instead.

Fog billows over the water, thick and grey, but it does not touch the land. As far as they can see along the beach, the sand is formed into shapes that could, if you happen to be a connoisseur of the understatement, be called sand castles. They're nothing like the sand castles Haworth's younger cousins used to make. They're as tall as Haworth, and Haworth is five inches taller than Aristalo. An unbroken line of walls marks the border of the sand city. She can barely see the water's edge past the densely built towers and battlements, despite the slope of the beach. The dark grey sand looks so solid that it's hard to imagine the incoming tide washing the castles away. They are definitely magical, or supernatural, or at the very least uncanny.

There is something threatening about the sand castles. It's what makes Haworth want to back away, what makes her think the trees are leaning away from the beach and not the wind. Maybe it's the stillness, maybe the empty windows in the sandy walls.

"Are they haunted, or what?" Haworth asks. She's encountered hauntings before in her apprenticeship, mostly at a distance. Aristalo seems to think Haworth is too green to deal with the uncanny shit. The closest she's gotten was dealing with a suspiciously sentient library's opinions about which stories she told the citizens of Diosco.

Aristalo hmms, and slings her pack off her back. She rummages around in the outer pocket and pulls out a blue knit hat, which she jams over her close-cropped grey hair.

"Where did you get that hat?" Haworth demands, distracted.

Aristalo grins a dirty little grin. "The waitress at the pub in Imbricata gave it to me."

Impressed, Haworth subsides. How is it that this cranky, butch old lady gets pretty women giving her knitwear all the time? Is this a skill Haworth can apprentice herself to like the storytelling and singing? Haworth doesn't really like hats, but still, it'd be nice to get the occasional scarf as a memento. She could use a scarf right now. The air off the water is heavy with cold, the leaves on the trees frozen crisp.

"Why are we here?" Haworth asks. "We could have gone straight to the ship with Captain Setosa." He's an old friend of Aristalo's from the last time she visited Imbricata, and he's agreed to take them to Tirucal. Haworth's home, which she hasn't been to in two years. Which she could be getting to sooner, if Aristalo hadn't insisted on this little detour. As much as Haworth likes and respects her boss, sometimes she wants to shove Aristalo overboard. She can swim, she'd be fine; she just deserves a good dunking.

"He's picking us up here, the ship's out in that fog somewhere."

"Er, picking us up how? There's no path through."

"Your turn." Aristalo puts her pack back on and gestures for Haworth to go ahead. "Figure out how to get us to the water."

Haworth groans internally. Of course this is a test. Aristalo *loves* tests. Especially when they're mildly life-threatening.

The castles are tall enough that climbing across would be a pain in the ass, and there's no way Aristalo would do it, so that can't be the answer. Haworth tugs her collar up around her neck and frowns. Maybe this is why Aristalo is cranky all the time—the bard she apprenticed to probably made her do shit like this, and now she's passing it on.

Actually, Haworth realizes, that might be exactly what's happening. Captain Setosa has obviously known Aristalo a very long time, long enough that she could have first visited this region and encountered the sand castles as a young apprentice.

Could they ram their way through? Haworth looks around at the trees. If she got a branch big enough, maybe she could use it to shove sand aside and clear a path. But she isn't sure she could break off a branch that would be strong enough to do the job. And anyway, there is nothing normal about a beach full of gigantic sand castles. A normal solution like shoving sand aside isn't going to cut it.

Tentatively, Haworth steps up to the border of the sand city and peers over the wall. She half expects to find the city occupied by hermit crabs or sea turtles or something, but the courtyard below is empty. It has an odd floral scent, mixing unpleasantly with the scent of salt water. There's no way any flowers are blooming in this cold. Haworth reaches out and shoves one of the conical sand towers with both hands, just to see what will happen.

The sand shoves back.

She stumbles, loses her footing in the loose sand, and sits down hard on her ass. The sensation of the shove, not quite like hands, lingers in her shoulders.

Aristalo snickers. "You asked for that."

Haworth glares and dusts off her hands, then gets up and dusts off the seat of her pants. She knows better than to push Aristalo, but still she says, "We have to do this now? Just for once, we can't take the direct path so I can see my family sooner? Aunt Deline is probably already baking fish cakes."

Aristalo makes a face about the fish cakes, but she doesn't chide Haworth for trying to get out of this test. "You've done four years of your apprenticeship," she says, the way one might say 'you've done four years of your six-year prison sentence', "and you've got the skills. Wouldn't you like to be able to tell your cousins the story of the time you handled a beachful of spooky sand castles?"

Huh. Alright, yeah, Haworth *does* want to tell that story. She grew up telling her cousins stories, when they were little and sad because the Tirucali kids all thought they were too weird to play with, with their Baselban food and Baselban family. It's how she got the itch for bardcraft, what led her to her apprenticeship with Aristalo. And she mostly made up the stories she told her cousins; it would be novel to tell them a true story about how awesome she is. Damn Aristalo for knowing which carrot to dangle in front of her.

Aristalo said she has the skills. That suggests that somehow crossing the sand castle city is a problem to which Haworth can apply the skills she's learned during her apprenticeship. She's an apprentice *bard*, though. Maybe if she plays the hand drum just right the sound waves will cause the castles to spontaneously fall down? Using brute force is clearly out of the question, so she can't use the lute as a sand shovel. The tower she shoved looks totally unaffected.

But destruction is the wrong approach anyway, she realizes. You could tell a great story about someone fighting their way through a bunch of uncanny sand castles, but it's not the story you'd tell about a bard.

Haworth edges back up to the sand wall and begins walking along it. Partly she's looking for clues, partly she just wants to get away from Aristalo's amused face for a couple of minutes. Four years of travel with the same aggravating woman, no matter how educational and often fun, requires taking breaks. The sand this side of the city is loose enough her boots sink in; walking through it is a slog. *Sand is such bullshit*, she thinks.

She walks far enough to be out of earshot if Aristalo decides to shout at her, and stops to look at the sand castles. If she weren't cold and annoyed, she'd appreciate how beautiful they are. Yes, there's something creepy about them, but they're beautiful too. They have not been decorated with shells and stones and fronds of seaweed like a child's sand castle. Now that she's paying more attention, she can see the precise way the roofs of the towers are carved to look like tile. The cathedralesque domes are etched with floral patterns. Some of the crenellated walls look like they're built of regular stone blocks. The windows are shaped into graceful arches. Haworth wonders if the castles have an inside. The windows are real openings, but she can't see far enough in to tell whether they're just tunnels that don't go anywhere, or whether the insides of the castles have been carved out just as realistically as the outsides.

They make Haworth feel twitchy, as if she's waiting for something, expecting the castles to *do* something. Somehow, they look like they *could* do something, and she doesn't want to find out what. No matter how beautiful the sand castles are, she wants to run far away from them. Even the trees want to run away from them, and are only prevented by their roots. But—

The different grains of sand in Haworth's brain come together, forming a shape that should be less surprising than it is. Aunt Deline's fish cakes, the kids who wouldn't play with her and her cousins, the way her dad genuinely listens even to people he thinks are talking nonsense. So many people in Tirucal treat her Baselban family like they're about to do something horrible, and here she is treating these sand castles the same way. For all she knows, it's not their fault she finds them creepy. She thinks about her dad, curious even about people who hate him, and decides that if she's going to tell a story about this, she'd rather be the curious kind of protagonist than the kind who fights her way through.

Then there's an unexpected flicker of movement, and suddenly Haworth figures out *why* she finds the sand castles creepy. She turns and tromps back through the sand to Aristalo, who has pulled a piece of dried pork out of her pack and is gnawing on it contemplatively.

"They're looking at us," Haworth says. "The windows are eyes."

"Huh," Aristalo says. She probably knew that already.

They look at the castles. The windows look back, empty but seeing. Experimentally, Haworth takes several steps to her left. Almost imperceptibly, the windows angle themselves to follow her. She steps back to Aristalo.

"They know we're here," Haworth says, thinking out loud, even though she knows Aristalo isn't going to tell her if she's on the right track. "If we could stop them from seeing us, distract them, maybe we could get through." She crosses her arms and wrinkles her nose while she thinks. "How do you stop a window from seeing?"

"Curtains?" Aristalo suggests.

There's no way that's the real answer. Haworth ignores it. The wind blows down the length of the beach, not disturbing the tightly packed sand of the city, but whistling through its streets. The fog is still heavy over the water, and Haworth still wishes she had a scarf.

The interesting thing about being a bard is that when you're telling a story, you're the center of attention. You have an audience, and everyone is listening to your voice. If you're just an ordinary bard, they're also watching your face, your hands, wondering whether your story is true. But if you're a really good bard, they don't see you at all. It doesn't matter if the story is a lie; they see the truth of it, as if it's alive and colorful around them. You can walk through an audience, borrow their belongings for props, and they make room for you without even noticing you've stolen their hats and knives.

Haworth isn't sure she's a really good bard yet. Aristalo is, though. Sometimes that makes it difficult to learn from her;

Haworth gets so pulled into a story that she can't see Aristalo's technique.

Do the sand castles have ears? "BANANAS," Haworth shouts, experimentally.

"Shit," Aristalo swears. "Warn a person."

But Aristalo isn't the only one who's startled by the shout. The sand castles have, very slightly, twitched.

That means that if Haworth or Aristalo tells a story, the sand castles will hear it. There's no telling whether they'll understand it, but at least they'll hear it, so this is worth a shot.

"Will you tell the story about Opalina and the forest of canaries?" Haworth asks.

Aristalo squints at her from under the blue hat and after a moment, grins hugely. Huh, maybe that's why women give her knitwear. "Nah," she says. "You tell it."

"But—" Haworth protests. "For this to work, a really good bard has to tell the story." Not that she doesn't like the idea of telling it herself, and being the hero of the tale she's going to tell her cousins about this.

"So we'll find out if you're a really good bard. If you're not, I'll take over. I'm a fantastic bard."

Underneath the swagger, there's a well-hidden little compliment. Aristalo thinks Haworth might already be a really good bard. That lights a warm glow in Haworth's stomach. She refuses to make it weird by calling attention to it, though.

Haworth takes a deep breath and rolls her shoulders back. She's told this story before, once, but she was pretty new to storytelling then, and she was telling it to a bunch of eight-year-olds. But she chose this tale for a reason: it's good. People listen to it even if the teller isn't any good. In the right hands, surely it's the tool Haworth needs.

When Haworth opens her mouth again, her voice carries. It expands down the beach, cutting through the whistling of the wind. "If you've never heard the story of Opalina and the forest of canaries," she begins, "you're in for a treat."

She steps closer to the sand castles and lets her voice reach out to them, lets herself disappear behind the story. "Once, long ago, there was a spinster named Opalina..."

At first she isn't sure whether the story is having any effect. The sand castles haven't shifted towards her voice the way they did to watch her move back and forth. But there is an alertness to them, a silence that could be listening. Haworth speaks through the strange floral scent that fills her mouth, through the discomfort of thousands of window-eyes. And, when she reaches the part about Opalina finding the library in the forest, a few of the windows iris shut.

Startled, Haworth injects a little more certainty into her voice, a little more confidence. She recognizes the way some people close their eyes when they're listening, seeing the story more clearly in their mind's eye. As if she's stepping into an audience's midst, she steps up to the wall of the sand castle city. Much like a human audience, the sand begins to crumble and reshape itself, falling into the story.

Where there were walls, towers, sand cathedrals, suddenly there is a road. It's narrow, better built for Haworth's skinny frame than Aristalo's sturdy one (Haworth will hear about this later). The sand redistributes itself, forms new ramparts and domes along the sides of this road. Still regaling the beach with Opalina's adventures, describing the brilliant yellow feathers of the canaries, Haworth steps onto the road.

It's a long slope down to the water. She assumes Aristalo is following, but if she looks back to check, she'll lose the train of the story. She's afraid that if she stops talking halfway down the sand road, it will close around her, burying her in sand and trapping her there. But she has no real reason to think the sand castles are that hostile. She knows firsthand how it feels to be feared simply for being unfamiliar, and keeps talking.

Haworth doesn't remember Opalina having so many adventures; surely this story took less time to tell even with the interruptions of noisy children. But telling it becomes easy. She's pulled into the story herself, forgetting her discomfort. By the time Opalina is on the road home to her cosy house on the town high street, Haworth is nearly at the end of her own road.

Finally, she steps past the last sand castle and onto a narrow strip of wet sand; gentle waves knit a tangle of kelp at the water's edge. She keeps talking, telling about the lost cat who has come to welcome Opalina home. At last, she turns to look back at the city. Aristalo steps off the road, grinning and holding her pack in front of her so it doesn't bump the sand.

"And that," Haworth says, "is the end of Opalina's story."

The closed windows wink open. As if realizing they've been duped, the sand castles twitch and the road is destroyed, covered over with walls of sand as it was before. The way back is shut now. Captain Setosa had better show up soon.

Weirdly exhausted, Haworth looks at Aristalo. "What the fuck," she says, with feeling. Aristalo doesn't admonish her this time. Maybe because she's proven she's a really good bard. Now she can say what she likes.

"Look, here's Setosa," Aristalo says.

Haworth turns, and sees a low rowboat gliding toward them from the depths of the fog. The flamboyant green-coated sailor from Imbricata is at the oars. The nose of the boat meets the sand, and Captain Setosa ships the oars and jumps out onto the beach. "Hello!" he says. He sniffs the air, looking around at the sand castles. "Smells like flowers. Must be a lot of people bringing offerings for passage lately."

Haworth's mouth falls open. She turns to Aristalo and asks through gritted teeth, "Is he saying we could have just brought some nice flowers and the sand castles would have let us down the beach?"

Aristalo snickers and claps Haworth on the shoulder. "Sure. But maybe the sand castles liked your offering better."

"So they opened the road because I offered them a story? Not because I'm such a good bard, I made them forget I was there?"

"You got a new story out of it either way, didn't you?" Aristalo says. "Learned something about how to deal with weird phenomena. And you know, they don't shut their eyes to listen to just anyone."

"That's true," Captain Setosa says. "They're picky about stories, the sand castles are. They didn't shut their eyes for Aristalo's story."

Haworth's eyes go wide. Aristalo punches Captain Setosa on the shoulder and says, "Shut up. I was young. Get in the boat, kid."

Haworth does.

See Devin Miller's story "A Lie in the Sand" online at Metaphorosis.
If you liked it, leave a comment. Authors love that!
Remember to subscribe to our e-mail updates so you'll know when
new stories are posted.

About the story

My girlfriend, also a writer, is much more musical than I am, and she has a tendency to get story ideas from songs. This habit seems to be catching, as the seed of this story was Bob Dylan's "Mr. Tambourine Man". The setting and mood of the story originated in the song, especially drawing on the lines, "Far past the frozen leaves / The haunted, frightened trees / Out to the windy beach… / Circled by the circus sands". The characters are bards because of the song, as well. This origin resulted in a story that was mostly vibes, and I had to go back while editing to add a lot of the theme and broader context.

I often construct short stories by choosing a question for the characters to ask and answer. In this case, the question was, "How do we get past these creepy sand castles to meet a ship?" I considered also answering the question of why the sand castles are there in the first place, but my favorite speculative fiction tends not to answer that sort of question. I like stories where the characters encounter weird things and just accept that the world is big and strange without trying to explain it all.

Originally, the sand castles were more dangerous than they are in the story's final form. When I sat down to think about what themes I wanted the story to explore, I came back to a question I've been exploring in a lot of my writing since the pandemic. I'm interested in writing about characters who discover that they've closed themselves off from the world, distrusting the people around them or assuming that anything weird they encounter is dangerous. I want to see those characters learn to rely on their communities and approach the strange with curiosity, as Haworth ultimately approaches the sand castles.

I pilfered all the names in the story from a list of succulents' scientific names, with small modifications. Armed with a similar list, you could probably find the origins, though I make no promises that the characters' personalities suit the plants I got their names from.

A question for the author

Q: What's your writing schedule?

A: My brain is at its most functional in the morning, so that's when I prefer to write. I'm fortunate to have a day job with a flexible schedule; I usually try to get a good ninety minutes of writing done before work. I try to write on weekend mornings as well, though sometimes I bribe myself into a weekend afternoon writing session with tea and a pastry. In general, I'm the sort of person who thrives on doing the same thing every day, so if I can I like to throw at least a few words at a project every day until it's done.

About the author

Devin Miller is a queer, genderqueer cyborg and lifelong denizen of Seattle, with a love of muddy beaches to show for it. When not writing, they enjoy propagating houseplants, starting craft projects, and performing dairy alchemy. They are assisted in these endeavors by a cat named Oolong Kittea.

@devzmiller

Heartbeat of the Seasons

Brian Hugenbruch

The first time I met Sophienne was outside a small inn at the center of the village of Willowsring. I'd come out of the west, with the faint chill of autumn wind nipping at my horse's hooves, and found the horse tie rings by the tavern just as she walked by with a pile of firewood. While she gave me a slight smile, she didn't know me from a summer's day.

I had little idea, then, how often I'd see that expression in the weeks to come.

A passing peasant watched me watch the red-headed woman walk inside. "I'd not, friend."

I turned around with a start. "Why not?"

"She's cursed," she said. "Nasty business. You hear of Wyrmtooth?"

I had, in fact. I rode toward the northern border on behalf of the Church of Ri'as, and in some haste. While they'd marked the usual sorts of dangers on my map, Willowsring had seemed a quiet enough spot to rest. I hadn't realized the wizard's tower was so close by.

"She slew him," the peasant woman said. At my look, she added, "Sort of. It didn't quite work. But her life since ain't been worth a single damn."

"I'm not so quick to measure a person's worth," I said. "And if there's aid I can offer, I certainly will."

"On your own head be it," she muttered.

"Has she spurned your own assistance, then?"

The woman's face betrayed her surprise. "How could we help one like her? We're honest folk; we won't mangle our lives by messing with magic!"

I turned her words over in my mind as the woman wandered off. The Church had sent me as an official Ambassador to broker a peace between the ogre and Fey kingdoms. They were ready to slaughter one another, and us besides. They'd agreed to one more set of talks before the blood began to run.

It would not be an easy talk. The Fey had been arguing over the border with the ogres for centuries now—a territorial dispute lost to antiquity. The region was farmland; the Fey had already suffered through famine, and their claims of ogre aggression weren't unjustified, if our scouts were to be believed.

The ogres claimed no wrongdoing, because of course they did. What fault of theirs, if the Fey had eaten all their food and did not look as pretty as the ogres did? And now the Fey were trying to claim settled lands for their own.

The Fey had asked for us, believing the Church impartial. On that point, at least, they weren't wrong—the Bishops had no use for either kingdom. But they also felt strongly that neither ogre nor Fey would keep the bloodshed between themselves.

They'd encouraged me to ride with a bit more haste than usual.

If the maps were to be believed, I was three days' ride from the border—and ahead of schedule. Ambassador or no, the Bishops hadn't given me leave to deny a hand to those in need. I couldn't tarry too long... but if the woman were afflicted by something minor, perhaps I could set her aright before either nation had a chance to miss me.

I suspect I would have tried to help her even if the Church's doctrine and the call of my goodwill had not been in alignment. As they were, how would I turn my eyes elsewhere?

This time of day, the inn's common room lay bare but for sunbeams and the kept cats sleeping in them. Even the innkeep had gone missing. The red-headed woman seemed to fill the room, though, with her bemused smile. She sat atop the bar and watched me from behind a tall glass.

She certainly did not seem cursed. Perhaps the peasant woman had been telling tales for sport? Common enough when city folk found the countryside, and usually harmless.

"You in charge here?" I asked her.

"Nay," she said. "But Homish does not mind it if I serve myself. I can let him know a nobleman's here, if you'd like."

"Do I look much like a noble?"

She nodded toward my boots. "Finer quality than the farmers' own, those. But I jest—that Ri'as sigil tells me you're a priest from the capital. Someone sent to heal or to harm, depending upon the moods of those you'd call master."

"Heal," I informed her. And it was true, as far as it went. A continued peace would be healthy for everyone. The Church had tried using me for other ends... but it'd not gone the way they'd hoped. My instinct to fix what was broken was too strong. They'd learned their lesson; so had I.

The woman nodded in approval. "You here long, stranger?"

"Brother," I corrected. "And Dalen is fine. Just passing through on my way to the border." I tilted my head and studied her for a moment. "Actually, I need someone capable to show me around. Do you have time this evening?"

She lowered her hand toward a sword on the bar. Long fingers found a green gemstone pommel. She said, "This evening? I'm sorry, Dalen. I'm off to smite a wizard. I'll be back before the morn—we'll speak then, perhaps."

"Of course," I said. I had no idea if another wizard had arrived, or if Wyrmtooth really had returned—but she seemed confident and amiable. If she were off to finish the slaying she'd started, I had no desire to stand in her way. Especially since she handled the sword with obvious expertise. "A pleasure, miss...?"

"Sophienne," she answered. Then she finished her tankard and disappeared into the back.

The second time I saw her was in the bustling common room the following morning. A familiar pommel bumped against my table as I finished my gruel. I looked up and saw her smiling down—with much the same expression she'd had the day before. I was almost done, in any case, so I cleared my space and offered my spot on the shoddy wooden bench.

I asked, "How fared the battle?"

"Have we met?" she wondered as she sat.

"Briefly, yesterday," I reminded her. "Brother Dalen, from Ath-Olomahn."

"My apologies, sir. I'll let you know tomorrow, for my battle is yet before me. Wyrmtooth will rue the steel of Sophienne, I swear it. I venture out in some hours and will be back before the morn—we can toast to victory then."

"Of course," I said, though a bit less certain than before.

I brought my dishes up to the bar. The old innkeeper, Homish, gave me a sympathetic look. "She never remembers," he told me. "It ain't you."

I thought back to the woman I'd met when I arrived and shivered a bit. "What happened?"

"She came to us young," he said as he took my bowl. "Her own home was destroyed by that monster in the tower. She'd tried to slay the bastard for years—she studied the sword and lost friends against him twice 'afore yer war broke out. No one asked why she joined the armies, but she led the way into Fey, and was part of the legion what stormed their capital."

I closed my eyes as I tried to parse this. "We haven't been at war with the Fey for forty years."

"I know," he said. "I was there. I was just a boy back then, but I remember her fightin' like a woman possessed. And then, when the war ended, she wasn't long ere she fought Wyrmtooth for the last time."

"But the wizard still lives, does he not?"

The old man grunted. "Every morn she wakes in her room as though nothing happened. She does whatever chores we can find for her—chop wood, haul water, chase down horses. Soph is honest like that; always a hard worker, no matter what's on her mind. Then she orders the same meals, sharpens her blade, and sets off to slay him every evening. She ain't aged a damn day in all that."

I shook my head. "I've never heard of such things."

"Fey territory has strange magic," Homish reminded me. "Stranger than your Church, or even that o' Wyrmtooth." His voice lowered a bit and he told me, "Most folks here, well, they don't much care for magic. Ain't done nothing but kill us for as long as we can remember. And to be right honest, yer Grace, we've killed our share of witches round here."

I glanced in the direction the woman had gone. "But she's still welcome here, of course."

I could feel him shrug. "Sophi… she keeps the wizard at bay, in her way, so we're happy to let her be. She does her chores, eats 'er gruel, then heads on out to slay the bastard again."

"How many times can a man be slain?" I demanded.

"As many as it takes? She reappears in her bedroom every morning. And the wizard's tower rebuilds itself at dawn, 'round the same time." The old man filled another bowl of gruel and slid it down the length of the bar toward a waiting patron. The wooden dish skittered across the uneven planks; the man at the other end caught it deftly.

"Sounds horrible," I murmured, "dying every night."

Homish shrugged. "It ain't us dying. We've got used to it, and she don't seem to remember. Besides, in forty years, we ain't found a way to stop her going."

I had the distinct impression, from Homish's expression, that the villagers of Willowsring hadn't tried too hard. Indeed, everyone in the common room watched the red-headed swordswoman with the sort of wary stare saved for a wild animal. She wasn't one of them, no matter what the innkeep said; she was merely an enemy of their enemy.

As I watched her rise to leave, I had the sudden sinking feeling I would not be early to the border. If anyone else from the Church had been here, I might have left the town behind... the calm at the border would not hold forever. But there wasn't, and the magic at work made me shiver. Someone had to help this woman.

For lack of an alternative, someone was me.

The village seemed idyllic. If they knew of this place, the richest citizens of Ath-Olomahn would pay to escape the city and flee here for a fortnight. Farmers worked through the harvest of early crops. The local farrier patched shoes and made nails. A few children, old enough to cling to apron strings, played in dirt lanes near the well, but the town itself seemed older than its years; most of its children had grown and not been replaced.

Noblefolk would love it, sure. It seemed like five hells to me: a world where nothing ever changed, where time meandered at its own pace. This was even worse than the Monastery.

Willowsring itself was perfect—and that was the second mystery. They were by far the closest town to the border, but no one seemed particularly bothered by the looming war—it was three days' ride away, over several hills and rivers, and in another country besides. Didn't stop what few folks with whom I stopped to chat from gabbing about the last battle. Yesterday's dead were part of their oral history. Tomorrow's dead were imaginary.

In my experience, this wasn't uncommon. Citizens of Ath-Olohman loved their fashion and court society gossip, but the outlying territories couldn't be bothered. All talk steered to crops unless the sky was raining fire. Made my job two hells hard; what was some city-boy going to know about manure and field care, anyway?

They weren't wrong; I couldn't give a shit about manure. But I knew well enough their harvests depended on it. And they did so well that their crop yield was the same, year over year, whether the rest of the nation met floods or drought. Something that right was a symptom of something wrong.

So I saddled my horse an hour before dawn and rode north. I had to see for myself.

The wizard's tower lay in smoking, smoldering pieces. Grassless ground and scorched rock circled the ruins for a mile.

The remnant brick glowed with a ghastly green light. Curious, I picked up a pebble and tossed it toward where the tower would have been. It turned to dust in mid-air and landed as a line of fine sand at the edge of the blast.

Good thing I hadn't put my damn hand inside the circle.

I hadn't been waiting long when the sun peeked over the mountains. The light coalesced into a mist that moved of its own accord. Some force plucked the bricks from the broken earth, hauling them back with a disregard for the flow of time, as though the tower were exploding in reverse. It rebuilt itself, whole blocks returning from ash and casting aside scorch marks. All the while, a high-pitched shriek filled my ears.

Then, as suddenly as it began, it stopped.

A wizard's tower stood there, surrounded by barren land and burned rock, raised once more in some sort of rude gesture in the face of normal time. Having no context, I could only assume that this was how it had always looked. I wheeled my horse and rode away before Wyrmtoooth had a chance to reawaken.

As I galloped, two things occurred to me. The grass near the tower had not regrown, which meant there were boundaries and parameters on the spell. And the pebble had not returned—so interfering with this magic might well be lethal.

I reached the tavern at Willowsring not long after the commotion of the morning rush had ended. Homish had some gruel waiting at the end of the bar for me. Sophienne was standing, her own meal completed; she looked right through me. She seemed as though she'd just woken up, again, for the last time. Tiredness had nothing to do with her surprise.

I came downstairs a bit after lunch. After the morning's adventure, I'd needed a bit of rest to set my mind aright. Sophienne looked up from the far side of the room, where she was sharpening her sword. She remembered me from the morning—confused, perhaps, but a bit less than before. It was, I admit, strange to see her look at me with recognition, but a relief to see a wary smile grow more at ease.

"Homish left some food for you on the counter," she called over. "And a letter came."

"Thank you," I said. I found them not far away; I gathered them both and brought them to a broader table—a place I could set my notes on the conflict for study. I opened the letter and skimmed it before my hand found a piece of bread.

The situation at the border was tense. The Fey were growing impatient in waiting on the human intervention and had started to agitate for an incursion into ogre territory—something about a stone they claimed the ogres had stolen. It made no sense to me, but Fey magic never had; their reasoning often came dressed in riddles' garb.

More to the point... while our army had set up barricades and bulwarks, the two other countries wouldn't be shy about trampling us if we got in the way. If I were going to be of any use to these three nations, I'd have to abandon my investigation of the town and leave this evening.

"You have the look," Sophienne said, "of someone whom bad news has found."

I laughed wryly. "War's bad news, isn't it?"

She rolled her eyes so hard I felt it across the room. "What, are those varicolored cobweb-sniffers spoiling for another fight?"

"With the ogres, not us," I told her. "They say they'd stolen a..."

I trailed off and stared at her sword for a moment. Then I looked down at my notes. It hadn't been part of the initial briefing, but I'd liked the name of it. L'cormijn sae q'vek, it said: *heartbeat of the seasons*. A green gemstone of high value and religious importance to the Fey, mentioned toward the back of my papers, in a footnote no less. It had been presumed stolen decades ago by ogres looking for battlefield salvage.

I resisted the urge to look at Sophienne's sword despite the heat rising up my cheeks. If the Fey learned it had been in our lands all this time, peace would never happen. And if the Fey decided they were upset with Ath-Olomahn, I wasn't certain our army could stop them again. Even their friendship could be deadly. War would be brutal.

The sound of boots on wooden planks brought me back. To my surprise, Sophienne sat down next to me. Her smile was gone.

I offered her a tentative smile of my own and asked, "Yes?"

"You seem a good sort," she said abruptly, "but perhaps I must say the obvious to you. If you try to stop me from slaying the wizard, I will kill you. I will regret it, but I will still do so."

The cold fury of her seeming calm caused me to set aside the letter. I looked at her serene, assured face. "Milady, I wish to stop nothing. But... is that stone not from the kingdom of Fey?"

She grimaced. "It turned the tide against their armies, you know. And they've not missed it, this year since."

I opened my mouth and closed it. "And if I told you that war comes once more around the corner, would you surrender it?"

She shook her head. "Tomorrow. I need it to destroy the wizard. Wyrmtooth prolongs his life with magic dark and terrible. He's terrorized the north of this country for one hundred years, has he not?"

I checked my records. "Give or take," I admitted.

"Did he not kill my parents and leave me for dead?"

I inclined my head. "If you say it, it must be true."

"Then," she growled, "I shall slay him. I need the stone to break the spell that binds his soul to our world." The woman made an insouciant gesture. "After that, I care not. Take it back. Take me as a prisoner, if the capital feels strongly about it."

I winced a bit at this. The Bishops would certainly offer Sophienne as sacrifice at the altar of peace. Fortunately for her, I was here and they were not... and if she were willing to part with the stone after one more battle, I was less willing to use her as a scapegoat. Honesty should be rewarded—even if she was thirty-nine years behind schedule.

"Let us hope it does not come to that," I suggested. "In the meantime... did you plan a final meal, ere the battle?"

We spoke for most of the afternoon, between mouthfuls of goat and the finest wine the border could muster. Few citizens of Ath-Olomahn had been into the Fey Kingdom; it felt strange to find someone who'd seen any of the same sights as me. Legend said the Fey had once enjoyed an effervescent spring even when winter raged not ten feet past their borders. Even now, their roads were littered with gold and diamonds we couldn't touch, and the rain tasted like expensive wine. I'd found it easier to walk there blindfolded.

"That," she chuckled, "would have made my job more difficult. But perhaps you can make peace without looking someone in the eye?"

I shook my head. "No. I've never found much sense in hiding from truth."

"That," she pointed out, "has never been how I understood politics."

"It's probably why they keep sending me away from the capital," I told her.

As the autumn sun moved away from the tavern's western window, she stood and grabbed her sword. I asked her not to go, but she brushed my words aside. She shouldered her sword, filled a waterskin, and urged her horse toward the mountains at a graceful canter.

I watched her leave. This time, she turned and waved at the edge of the village.

When we met for the fifth time, the following morning, she asked, "Do I know you?" But she did not.

Sophienne would not yield. I followed her twice to the base of the wizard's tower. She marked me each time and drew her sword when I came too close. Her tone grew colder as winter's wind inched closer to the border. "You have no place here; your aid is unasked-for and unneeded. And I'll kill you if you try to intervene—the wizard must die."

I rode back into town and stabled my horse. The hands there paid me no mind, but I expected as much; I'd tossed them no coins. I paid them little mind myself; some miles north, a woman had just died again, and it ate at me.

I could ride to the border now... but every fiber of my being told me that arriving without the stone would be worse than useless. The Heartbeat had been vital to the Fey before the last war, and while it was almost a footnote to them now, it might well solve some of their problems with food and trade. Without it, the ogres would continue to nip at their heels until blood was drawn.

No. The stone was vital. I needed it if I were to help avert the deaths of thousands. That meant I had to pull Sophienne out of the whirlwind into which she'd been drawn. And if she wasn't willing to part with the stone toward the end of the day... perhaps she'd be more amenable at the start of it.

My stomach churned a bit as I stepped inside and paid Homish a silver crown to wait in her room overnight.

"When this first started," he told me, "I tried to rent her room. She broke the man's arm when she threw him out the window. You sure you want to do this?" When I nodded, he shook his head and muttered, "On your own thick skull be it."

He took the coin all the same.

The room was empty save for a tall knapsack—belongings unnecessary for her daily battle. The bed was tidily made. The window was open to the cool of an evening breeze. And why not—who else would dare to enter? The swordswoman would skewer anyone who tried.

I wasn't certain if her magical absence gave me the right to intrude. Okay, that's a lie—I knew it did not, and my nerves burned for it. Knowing that this town, and many others like it, would be turned to ash if the Fey were not appeased did little to ease the taste of bile in my mouth.

She appeared just as dawn's light found the windowsill: clothed but unarmored, with the sunlight catching her hair as it spilled across her pillow. The sword appeared against her bed, resting in its sheath; the green gemstone fell with a thud onto the floor beside it.

Sophienne breathed easy in her slumber. If time had made hells of her travails, she never seemed weary.

The stone's light caught my eye. The green of it: so like the magic that clutched the bricks of the tower. I did not know for what the Fey had used it, but they were willing to kill thousands to see it home. It wasn't on me to say whether they deserved it returned; they had made it, it was theirs, and if I could save Sophienne, the village, and thousands of soldiers by returning it...

Then I felt the chill of steel against my throat.

"You don't belong here, Dalen," the woman said. "You'd best leave while you still have your head to see you out."

"I can help," I blurted. "If you give me the stone, I—" Then her words slid like steel into my mind, past the fog of a long night. "You know me?"

Her mouth hung open for a moment before an uncouth word passed her lips.

I'd been ready to argue that I was from 'the future', that I could help her break the cycle of her own continuous death and loss of memory. But she knew me. She remembered. Every day we'd met: a facade.

For what?

I looked into her eyes and saw cold calculation there. She weighed whether or not she could let me live. The villagers wouldn't care if she killed me—I was a useless diplomat from the capital, and I'd entered her room despite warnings. On my own head this was.

Or, as the case might be, neck.

"I want," I breathed, "to help you."

"I don't *need* help," she snapped.

"Don't you?" I gestured toward the stone on the floor. "After however long? You and your sword weren't here last night. And the tower falls every evening. Do you remember dying, too?"

The edge of the sword backed away, if but an inch. "Every night," she told me. "For forty years, every night. Skin burned and every bone broken. My body ripped apart as the tower blows." Her sigh sounded ragged. "It's penance for stealing the stone."

"I'm no judge of Fey law," I murmured, "but I would say you've paid it."

"Have I?" She nodded out the window. "War comes because their people are scared and hungry without this thing. Isn't that what your letters say? I knew what I stole. It was war, it was survival..." Wide blue eyes found me waiting at the edge of her sword. "I suspect it's why they sued for peace. I know not if there's penance great enough."

I shrugged. "That's not for you to decide. If we head to the border—"

"—I will catch fire and die before we reach it, and appear here come morning. With the stone." She lowered her sword and gave me a look. "Do you think me dull?"

"Forgive me." I gave her a bow, mostly to cover my burning face. I really had. She'd seemed the sort to solve her problems with her sword; to hammer a rock until breaking. I should have realized that forty years, now accounted for, had given her seasons of painful hindsight.

Sophienne glanced out the window again. "Meet me at the stables ere sundown. We'll go to the tower together. In the meantime... they'll notice soon that I've not emerged. I'd better throw you down the stairs."

The words took a moment to register. "Wait, did you say—"

Then she had me by the collar of my tunic. We weren't of an uncommon height, but she lifted me like a pile of fallen leaves. She hauled me out the door and shouted, *"Never bother me again, stranger!"*

It seemed overdone, but bouncing down the stairs left me with no capacity to protest. The laughter below, from regulars clearly expecting a show, was punctuated by the sound of my arm bones breaking. I rolled onto my knees and scrambled out of the tavern; the laughter followed in my wake.

I found refuge in the stables. When no one was looking, I put a strap of leather between my teeth and set the bone. I applied a salve from the Church before dressing it in a sling. It would accelerate the healing and numb the pain, but we had no magic to speak of. Unless one counted our ability to meddle; that, I'd got in spades.

I came to some hours later when Sophienne nudged me with her boot. "Wake, stranger."

I groaned as I stared up at her from my pile of hay. "Dalen," I corrected her.

"You are well-met," she said with a wry expression. "Follow."

I saddled my horse, albeit slowly with one arm, and followed her out of town. I marked the sun to be an hour away from setting. It was the usual time of her ride, and I followed at a distance. While the villagers paid her no mind, they'd be more mindful of me.

The tower of Wyrmtooth stood when we came over the hill. At this point, it would not have surprised me to have found it half-exploded and in a state of structural undress. I slowed my steed, but Sophienne charged into the grassless circle, fearing neither spell nor spear. When she wasn't slain on the spot, I urged my horse onward once more.

The red-headed woman opened the door to the tower.

"It's unlocked?" I asked, surprised.

She shrugged at me. "Wyrmtooth had no fear of unwanted guests, I assume."

We were halfway up the stone stairs of the tower when her words struck me. "Had."

"You said what?"

"Wyrmtooth had no fear. He's dead?"

Sophienne grunted. "Some forty years ago. He rued my steel, and the stone, both."

"Then why do the villagers think he's alive?"

"Would you give credit to my life and his tower to a soldier-woman, if you were they?"

I waved a hand from side to side. "I might, if she told me the truth of what had happened. Instead you've hidden it all—even your memory of the past forty years."

She paused before me, blocking my path along the stairs. She gave me a look when she turned. "You know they've killed witches before, yes?"

I thought back to the first conversation with Homish. "They've said."

"They did not lie. Fortunately for me... I return to life no matter how or where I die now. I feign ignorance, I do their chores, so they do not waste my time by killing me again and again. And while they still hate me, they are now... comfortable, yes? I am of use, and they can be content. And leave me to die in peace."

I shook my head. "That's monstrous. The Church would have intervened, if we could, if we'd known."

"Why tell you? They fear a cure more than they fear me now. Why risk all that for someone not of their village?"

We came to the top of the stairs and found... a library. Bookshelves stretched for multiple stories up toward the pointed pitch of the conical roof; tables and chairs were arranged in a half-circle around a fireplace. For all the stories of his madness, Wyrmtooth had been a practical decorator. Tasteful, even.

The swordswoman gestured toward the books. "The wizard's spells and studies. I've learned something of the stone here. I took it because I'd heard their Queen used it to keep herself young and beautiful—a perpetual spring flower in the midst of a painted grove." She stared into the stone, blue eyes catching green light. "In truth, they used it for their crops more often, and the books imply it could be used to opposite effect. It accelerated Wyrmtooth's march to dust. The wizard's last act, though, was to stab at the stone itself. That's what destroyed the tower, and killed me."

"...but you both return, do you not?"

The woman shook her head. "I'd smashed the cage in which he kept his soul. He'd disintegrated well before the explosion." She looked up at me and frowned. "I've spent forty years with his books, an hour a day before the explosion kills me, hoping to find the trick of it. I think he tried to turn the stone into another anchor, hoping to find refuge here. The stone reacted badly... and instead of saving himself, he's tied me down to the Willowsring of some decades past."

I sat in one of the chairs; my skin crawled a bit, though I wasn't sure whether it was for wizard or stone. I closed my eyes and rubbed them a bit with my good hand. "We know," I started to say, "that there are limits to the spell. Time. The circle around the tower. The village—you always appear there. Your anchor point?"

"I think the village is almost as locked as I am," she told me. She spoke a bit haltingly at first, and then in a rush, her face seeming more relaxed as she went. "Perhaps because I was there the morn of the battle. They don't know it, but their routine is a well-trodden path.. and their harvest has had the precise same yield every year. I cannot prove that it's because of this, but that does fit, does it not?"

I'd wondered about that; it was good to hear her confirm it. "The Church thought that was the Fey nearby," I admitted. "But your idea does make more sense. And we know you can't make it to the border fast enough. Has someone else tried taking the stone?"

Her look of horror answered that fast enough.

"Okay," I added, "what if someone else held the stone and stayed here?"

Her eyes narrowed. "I know not. No one else has held the stone in all this time. I buried it a few times; it reappears beside me on the morrow. I believe the stone is the anchor for the town and for me—the source of the spell that binds us, and it follows us every time we're reborn."

"If you give me the stone," I told her, "of your own will, we can see what happens. Perhaps you'll be free."

"And perhaps you'll be trapped," she snapped back. "Do they not need you at the border?"

"Will they not come looking for me?" I countered. "And the border is but three days away. If you go to them and ask for help, I suspect I won't be long held."

"Why not just go yourself? They can find me as well as you."

I hesitated for a moment, uncertain of how to phrase it. "It will help the peace," I told her. "You're the one who stole it. It would be an honorable gesture for you to return it. And given the situation, I expect the Fey will help." Then I turned back and stared her full in the face. "Besides—I came to heal, not harm. Have you not suffered enough?"

She turned away from my gaze. "I've not been one to ask for help for all my life, Brother. Every time I've tried, someone's died for it. And the Fey... their idea of aid is lethal, betimes. You know this. And either way, they may kill me where I stand."

"They may," I admitted. "The Fey are a strange people, and they've suffered through your actions. But do you know what happens if we do not try?"

Sophienne looked back. "What?"

"Nothing."

She studied me for a long moment. "I could just run off," she said, "if this works. Let you all hang."

"I know it hasn't been long, but I like to think I know you better than that." I reached out my hand. "I'm here. Will you trust me?"

She let loose a shuddering breath and closed her eyes, nodding more to herself than to me. She reached out her hand and... did not let go. I watched her, her body quaking against the bars of a prison she'd made for herself. Forty years without trust. To wrestle with the habit of decades, against the fear of being slain instead of merely killed?

I hadn't been keeping track of the time, but I saw the sun start to set through one of the tower windows. I didn't know precisely when the fire would come, but I'd been hoping, perhaps in vain, to avoid it in the handoff.

Then she opened her eyes and looked at me, smiling slightly... for once, as though she knew me well. The stone fell into my open hand, and my fingers closed around it instinctively, to catch it—

I woke to the sound of the bones in my arm breaking. The words *Never bother me again, stranger!* echoed in my ears, but there was no one there to say them. I clutched at my arm and looked around; everyone in the common room of the tavern had stood, confused, looking at one another.

I rushed out to the stable to find some salve, but my horse had gone. I grabbed a leather strap instead, righted the bone, and ripped enough fabric off my sleeve to make a crude sling.

An old man—Homish, from the tavern—approached me later in the morning. "Have you seen Sophienne?" he asked.

"Not since she threw me out of her room," I told him.

His face fell. "I see. Well... expect you're here for a while, yeah? If you want room and board, we'll need to see about giving you some chores." He glanced at my arm and sighed. "...such as you can do," he muttered as he walked away.

Sophienne, I realized, was gone—taking her seemingly immortal labor with her. Of course the town would seize upon her replacement. She'd chopped wood and cleaned stables, they'd said. Unfortunately for them, I was far less useful—what did I know about manure or field care?

I looked around and found no trace of her: neither sword, nor stone, nor either horse. When I tried to borrow another steed, to return to the tower, a burly stable hand stopped me with ease. It was clear to me, then, just how much of an impediment the town must have been to Sophienne.

I was still standing in the center of the square when sundown found me. Green fire rose all around; I could feel it sear the flesh from my body. And the crowd looked on in horror—not for me, but at what I could only assume was their new normal.

I woke to the sound of the bones in my arm breaking, again and again and again.

I don't know how long it lasted. It lasted until it didn't. I don't know how Sophienne held onto her mind as long as she did. And when I woke, with no dreams to guide me from the fire to the snap of my ulna, I was almost certain I'd lost my own.

I woke to the sound of the bones in my arm breaking... but this time it was against rock, not the wooden floor of the tavern. I was so surprised that, for a moment, I forgot to feel the pain.

Instead I looked at the village of Willowsring... a village of some hundreds, with perfect weather and ideal crops.

Every cottage had been razed to its roots; the tavern was a pile of rubble. Every building around me lay in smoldering ruin. I stumbled to my feet and staggered toward the town square.

"Brother Dalen," a voice called.

It was light and billowy, the voice; I recognized the accent as coming from a place where it rained nothing but wine. They were tall, this figure, with translucent wings folded like a cloak behind them. Garishly dressed, of course; but I would have known them for Fey without that added effect.

They weren't alone. Soldiers both of Ath-Olomahn and the Fey milled about, looking at the ruins in surprise and consternation.

"Something happened," I said. "Sophienne?"

"The woman found us," the Fey admitted. They gave a bow. "Tithas amh Alast; I would have been your counterpart, if we'd met at the treaty table."

I bowed weakly. "A pleasure." Then I sat back down. My arm hurt to the point my stomach churned.

Tithas frowned. "We can wait, if you require the medicines of your people to—"

"No, please. How fares our peace? What happened?" And, after a beat, "Where is she?"

The Ambassador walked toward me and crouched down to meet me at eye level. "Brother Dalen, war was averted. Thanks to the human woman's intercession, we found the stone unguarded in the wizard's tower. We'd hoped to find you with it, but you appear to have had more difficulties than she had done."

I looked around. "A bit. But if war never came... what happened here? Did the wizard return?"

The Ambassador shook their head and sighed as they pulled a familiar green stone from inside a coat pocket. It pulsed at me in some form of recognition. "They are magic, these stones," they said. "They were the heartbeat of our very seasons. They do not make time, as your friend thought; they take shortcuts to a future. When we recovered the gem, once your soldiers let the woman through to us, we broke the loop and set time straight... like one of your doctors fixing a broken bone."

They waved their free hand, long and silver-fingered, over my arm; I felt the wound mend itself. After a moment, all that remained was the ghost of pain and the roiling of my stomach. They watched my face carefully for a moment, their own a blank mask. If they had emotions, it was in a different language than mine.

"Thank you, Ambassador," I said.

"You are welcome," they answered. "But you feel, even without the injury, a lingering effect, is it not so? It is the same here. When we fixed time, this village had... a seizure of seasons. It was just as with our people, when the woman stole the stone from us—all our fields were destroyed by it. While we were more careful than she, we still untethered all the anchors that bound this region in loop—yours, hers, and all the others."

"I'm not sure I understand," I admitted.

"You have a mind, I expect, that works to unravel a knot rather than to tear it asunder. I suspect your friend never considered that approach, or feared for someone's safety if she had done. We have started time anew, turning over this loop of life like a garden bed—if she had done such, she would have been freed long ago."

I didn't know that for certain—whether Sophienne knew what would happen, or if the many years of her limited time simply didn't let her reach that conclusion. Self-taught and with no one with whom to converse, she might well have been embedded in her own assumptions.

Of course, she might well have reached a point where she feared success as much as failure. And if this was the result... I could not blame her for it.

I glanced around at the tumbled buildings. What wood that wasn't petrified seemed ready to crumble; the large stones looked as though they'd been scorched by a thousand summers. I thought of Homish at the tavern, and the rest of the villagers, caught in a conflagration beyond mortal comprehension. Of children aging to dust as they tried to run away. With all that time, all at once, none of them would have had a chance to scream.

"Forty years," I whispered.

They placed a long-fingered hand on my shoulder and smiled a bit too sharply. "We are not always honored to be of aid. This does not bring us joy... even if, from our end, all is resolved."

"Is it?" I asked. "You'll sign a formal treaty? And the ogres will abide?"

They produced a small scroll and tossed it at my feet. "We already have, and they say they shall. Tell your Bishops, when next you see them, that they have their peace. All prices are paid... and we've had enough of death." Then they rose and walked back toward the Fey soldiers.

I did not watch them go. Instead, I sat in the rubble and dust where Sophienne's room had been. The soldiers of Ath-Olomahn gathered round; they spoke of borders and zones and shifting troops toward the heretics of Zhe Tahra, far to the west.

Our nation was never without its enemies. There would always be another problem to solve—whether they'd like me to do so or not. My own problem, more immediate, would be how to explain all of this to the Bishops of Ri'as. The Church had no understanding of this sort of magic... and everyone else who'd lived it was dead.

Then I heard the faint shuffle of boots on pebbles.

I looked up and saw a white-haired woman, still strong, though bent by age and hardship. She'd given up armor for a thin robe, and her sword was nowhere to be found. Still, she sent guards scurrying out of her way with a stern gaze from clear blue eyes.

I pushed myself up and gave a bow as relief swept away the nausea and fear.

"Sophienne?" I asked. "It's done... you're free. Are you all right?"

She paused and looked at me, a slight smile on her face. "Do I know you?"

But she did not. Her face, now lined with cares beyond measure, said she did not know me from a summer's night.

See Brian Hugenbruch's story "Heartbeat of the Seasons" online at Metaphorosis.
If you liked it, leave a comment. Authors love that!
Remember to subscribe to our e-mail updates so you'll know when new stories are posted.

About the story

"Heartbeat of the Seasons" started its life years ago as a flash fiction prompt around the word "Ouroboros" (the serpent that devours its own tail). And as a Star Trek nerd, the TNG episode "Cause and Effect" always brings a smile to my face. (Go stream it. I'll wait.)

Every time I thought it was done writing the story, I'd ask alpha and beta readers for their thoughts... and they'd find one more hole in either the world-building, or the magic system, or the motivations. Boom: need another thousand words. Because they were right: I hadn't painted the whole picture. (It started to feel a bit like its own loop, to be honest.)

The story took some detours as it evolved. Some versions focused more on village politics; some included the wizard as a character on-screen. Sophienne's agency and resourcefulness increased in every draft. But in my mind, this story has always been, at its heart, a story about helping other people: the risks of trust, the dangers of butting in, and the desire to do the right thing. With an explosion as a punctuation mark. And I'm thrilled to see it out in the world, and I hope folks enjoy it.

A question for the author

Q: Have you ever wondered whether ideas are thought waves directed at you by an AI supercomputer located in the distant future?

A: I did briefly, but then the supercomputer told me that these weren't the droids I was looking for.

More seriously, I find that my thoughts are less about well-ordered words and structured notions as they are (to borrow from T.S. Eliot) a heap of broken images. Not that AI doesn't have the capacity to deal with unstructured data — and there are enough modern supercomputers and well-meaning clouds that work on just this sort of thing today — but given the current state of natural language processing (a core component of current AI tech), I have a hard time believing that that future supercomputer will be ready to beam disorganized thoughts into my head. It would require a significant enough entropy source to generate coherent and yet distinctly unsequenced imagery that I suspect it's not likely to happen.

(One wonders why it would bother, for that matter; perhaps I'm inadvertently responsible for a divide-by-zero error that takes out a K8S cluster in a thousand years.)

Also, I have to imagine that temporal network latency is a killer. Though that would explain why I'm so groggy in the mornings?

About the author

Brian Hugenbruch is a speculative fiction writer and poet living in Upstate New York with his wife and their daughter (and their unruly pets). By day, he writes information security programs to protect your data on (and from) the internet. He has a fondness for fishing (but only in video games), Scotch (but only in real life), and occasional forays into home brewing and molecular gastronomy. No, he's not certain how to say his last name, either.

the-lettersea.com, @Bwhugen

Freely Given

Connor Mellegers

Forty ravs on the Bone and it was all the Tech could talk about. Taye had done it, so said everyone. His name was on the lips of every student at the Tech the same as if he'd given the money straight to them. Forty ravs. Enough to live on for years if you were careful, and he'd given the lot to the Bone as if it were nothing. Sheena said Taye had shown her the scars he'd gotten on his hands and knees working to earn it through all sorts of hard labor. And now the secret was out, and students and instructors alike were lining up to shower him with praise and affection and gifts of their own. Already, stories of the gifts he'd received were spreading like wildfire, fueled by the fact that he made a grand display of denying that he had donated anything at all. Genuine humility, of course. Someone like Taye would never aggrandize. After all, he'd given forty ravs to the Bone.

I met Joan in the gymnasium of the Three Oaks community center. The huge wooden room was empty save a few stray balls and frayed mats scattered across the floor. Normally, the floor would be covered in the refuse of after-school activity: pylons, hoops, balls of all shapes and sizes, but all of those were neatly away in the storage room, which meant Joan had gotten a serious head start on me. I rushed to the supply closet and grabbed a push-broom. By the time I got back, Joan had put everything away and had already begun disinfecting the equipment. I put my head down and began sweeping.

Joan and I had been assisting the center managers for years. The managers were responsible for the center's operation, of course, but between managing their programs and supporting the needs of their visitors, they barely had any time to keep the facility clean. We provided our labor as a gift to the managers, and they kept the center running as a gift to the entire community. After our labor, we would record our gifts in the official registry. Both of us checked off what we had each done of the sweeping, mopping, sanitizing, etc. The work each of us did affected how much official credit we would receive and thereby the gifts, respect, and esteem that would follow in equal measure. Unofficially, what we did affected how the center's managers saw us. You could see them following your pencil as you marked off what you'd done, raising their eyebrows in appreciation, or letting them furrow in disappointment. You could hear it in their voice, too. "Thank you for your generous gift to Three Oaks *and* thank you for *yours*." It was all in that *and*. I couldn't be that *and*. Not today. Not after Taye had given forty ravs to the Bone.

Joan started mopping the second I'd swept up the dust and dirt. I nearly ran to fill another bucket and begin mopping from the opposite side. I kept my head down, my motions fluid and perfect. Mopping half a gym might only have been worth half the credit, but if I was quick enough, I could get to the next task before Joan and have a chance to catch up to her. After five minutes mopping in silence, I finally turned to look at her from across the room. She was grinning.

"What?" I said, turning my eyes back to the floor, desperate for this chance to clean while she was distracted.

"You heard about Taye," she said. I groaned and she laughed. Of course. She knew exactly why I hadn't taken a breath since I arrived. She'd been laughing at me the whole time.

"Everyone heard," I said. "Very generous of him to give all that money. Thirty ravs, was it?"

Her smirk made my stomach jump. "Forty. And you don't have to rush, you know. I'll split credit with you, whatever we've done."

I mulled it over. It was clever of her, but that was no surprise coming from Joan. Splitting credit meant that officially we'd done the same work and would share whatever esteem we'd earned in the eyes of the community. Considering how much she'd already done, that was a generous gift, though a gift to one person was nothing compared to a gift to the entire community. I could refuse, but that would be disrespectful. Perhaps doubly so for the base intentions with which the gift would have been received.

"Oh please, Ev. I won't tell anyone," she said.

Another gift, this time hidden. At this point, refusing would be irresponsible.

"Thank you," I said.

"Taye won't get official credit without disclosing openly," Joan said.

"And that just makes it more impressive."

She nodded and scrubbed at a stubborn spot on the floor. Anonymous gifts were often the most worthy. Little chance of credit meant that a gift could truly be freely given. But they were rare. A gift-giver deserved their credit and had a right to it. Earning official credit meant that everyone could see what you'd done. The higher your credit, the greater the gifts you would receive from those around you. Everyone wanted to give to the most generous and share in the righteousness of their generosity. But Taye had given a massive gift in near-perfect silence. And he'd given to the Bone. Few ever gave to the Bone and what little they did was rarely worth having. Anyone could take from the Bone — whatever they wanted and however much they wanted. A crowd of takers, ingrates, and even hoarders could enter that sad little building on the edge of town and walk off with all forty ravs without so much as a reason. Few had it in their hearts to give to those who took from the Bone. To give cash was even more unheard of.

But Taye hadn't cared. He must have labored for wages for months — hard, thankless work without any credit or respect — just to anonymously dump it all directly to the Bone. And his gift would never appear on the official ledgers or records. Those takers and hoarders would never know who had given them all that money. A gift like that was unheard of. But we had heard of it. And now, official credit or not, everyone knew what he had done. It was genius. Genius and risky. Hell, who wouldn't be impressed? Even I'd go out with Taye if he asked me, not that I was looker enough to be asked. If he did, it would just be another gift to his credit.

"It is *very* impressive," Joan agreed. The edges of her curly black hair bobbed into the soapy water as she bent over the bucket. "But it's hard to believe Taye could earn that much money through labor alone."

"Sheena saw the scars," I reminded her.

She scoffed. "Everyone has scars, they don't mean anything just because a credit-hungry looker like Sheena thinks they do. Any labor worth doing is given as a gift. Earning wages like that means taking on labor no one else wants to do, work in a factory or mine, or some other horrible place. Taye's a shrimp from a good family. Wage labor enough to earn forty ravs would break him." She snapped up and her eyes landed on mine. "Unless he had help. Or maybe it was a gift. Maybe he wasn't the one who made the donation at all."

My mouth dropped and my feet squeaked on the gym floor. A gift gifted. Credit for an incredibly generous donation freely given away. That wouldn't just be impressive, that would be astronomical. Untouchable. Worth all the respect you could imagine. Even without official credit, if that leaked, you'd have more than just half the Tech longing for you. Hell, even the instructors might go for you.

"You heard something?" I asked.

"No, I didn't hear anything," she said.

I huffed and slammed my mop into the bucket, splashing water all around me.

"Then why even bring it up?" It was hurtful to get my hopes up like that. That kind of gift would be fantastic to witness. To even be in the presence of that kind of generosity is something everyone dreams of.

Joan sighed one of her big sighs. Older-sister sighs, I call them, even though we're not related and my mom sometimes makes gifts of meals to her family. All the more significant for the fact her family isn't offered many gifts.

"What I mean, Ev, is no one has heard anything, *yet*. But maybe they could. And who knows what name could be attached. I mean, there's no official record; anyone could have done it."

I stared at her for a long time. Joan wasn't a looker, same as me. She wasn't particularly athletic either. Her math and writing, though better than mine, were hardly enviable and no student at the Tech would want to trade places with her in a million years. But she had these ideas sometimes. Wild ideas. Ideas so twisted it hurt my brain to try and wrap itself around them.

"Anyone could have done it," I said, my mouth still failing to close.

"Anyone," she agreed.

"Like you?" I asked.

"Oh no," she shook her head in big arcs. "Who would believe that? My family are known takers," she said.

I nodded and turned away. We never talked about it. It felt shameful to even mention. Her parents accepted any gifts they were offered and even took from the Bone: money, food, furniture, whatever they needed. But they never gave to anyone. They never seemed to labor at all. True takers. What little they did receive was the result of Joan's labors at Three Oaks and her gifts to fellow students. But even so, she carried the stain of her parents' greed. No one would believe she was capable of such generosity.

"But you could have done it," she said.

I scoffed. I wish I'd done it. I wish I could have done it. I'd never had anywhere near forty ravs in my life. I only ever labored as a gift. I never needed to work for anything so shameful as pay.

"Your grandmother visited last year, didn't she? I heard she was a hoarder."

I tried to scoff again but my tongue was heavy and dry. Joan was really saying this. Grandma Ross was a hoarder and a wage taker. It had always brought my dad shame, but he still invited her to stay with us every year. Hoarders sometimes gave chunks of their fortune to family members. It was known to happen. It might be believed. But to really suggest taking credit for someone else's gift? I'd never even heard it done before. A credit thief would be below even the least remorseful takers.

"Taye earned his credit, Joan."

"Did he? Because he donated it all at once? Because it was some grand gesture of a gift? We give away our labor every day and who notices? I'm still a taker and you're still a laggard. But Taye gives some money to the Bone and suddenly he gets gifts and respect you and I could only dream of. Why does he deserve the credit more than you, Ev?"

This was too much. What she was saying was ludicrous. Taye had been generous. He deserved whatever anyone wanted to give him. "It was an impressive gift," I said.

"All gifts are impressive. Sheena's kind only care about what's novel. What draws enough attention to earn them praise. Perhaps they'd like to hear something even more novel."

My heart felt like it might leap out of its chest. I kept my eyes focused on the floor. "Joan, we couldn't..."

"Couldn't what? Tell people what we might have heard?" She laughed, picked up her mop and bucket, and left the gym, leaving me behind to stare. She didn't look back.

Billy was the first. Then Eliza-Beth. The king and queen of lookers at the Tech. Then the rest followed: Cara, Saraisa, Johanssen, Themi, all the lookers worth seeing lined up outside my locker between classes. And the instructors. The grins they gave me when I passed by could light up a room. Huge, massive things that made you feel like the smartest kid in the Tech. And suddenly I was, however you sliced it. My grades went through the roof. Study notes from lectures I'd never heard and essays I didn't remember writing popped up in my bag and my locker, gifts from instructors and students alike, freely given and taken. And yet, even accepting them, my collateral didn't drop. It couldn't. My gift had been that big, that selfless, that colossally unheard of. A donation that large and the credit for it freely given away. I could take jobs for wages. I could take gifts from anyone who offered. I could be the biggest hoarder there ever was and I'd still be the greatest gift giver the Tech had ever seen. I was infallible.

One day my dad called me in after school. He's a big man, tall and grim. He has a massive smile, the kind like Eliza-Beth's that could light up a room with only the flash of a few teeth. But we never saw it at home. He always said his smiles were gifts and too precious to waste on family. But that day he smiled. Mom too. Even Geoffrey, who'd never given or accepted anything from me a day in his life, was smiling. They all had gifts in their hands. Delicately wrapped in the paper and ribbons you saved for really special occasions. I smiled back at them.

"Here are some small tokens of our appreciation," my father said. Small tokens. He *actually* said that! My father had met mayors he was less respectful to, lifelong dedicants and gift-givers of the highest order who didn't hear such words, but he said them to *me*.

Of course, not all those who looked were lookers. I once saw Taye from across the Tech cafeteria. His stock had fallen dramatically after everyone found out it was me who had given 40 ravs to the Bone and not him.

I was surrounded by people. They jostled to see who would be able to give me lunch. They pressed around me, beautiful meals made with love offered up with admiration and desperation. Whatever lunch I accepted bathed the giver in the light of my generosity, earning them the highest credit possible from one small gift. I took one, a dal made by a looker named Kiel. It smelled amazing. The others pulled back, staring crestfallen at their unaccepted meals.

Across the cafeteria, Taye pulled out a brown paper bag. Eating one's own lunch was something only takers and those most pathetic were ever forced to do. No one cooked for themselves by choice. Back before my star had risen, Joan and I would swap meals we had each made. It wasn't prestigious, but at least it meant we ate through the generosity of those around us and not our own petty labor. Joan would scoff every time. She thought it was pointless and silly, but I always insisted. Even so, whatever she had cooked was always made just the way I liked it.

My stomach flipped as I watched Taye open his crumpled paper bag. I thought of asking one of those I'd rejected to give their lunch to Taye as a gift to me. But then I saw him slide his bag across the table as someone else did the same. I couldn't make out who it was before Kiel pulled me to their table and into that afternoon's gifts.

I was laying on the hill outside of the Tech with Billy and Eliza-Beth. We were drunk and sweet off compliments and the summer air and all sorts of gifts freely given and taken and given back in return. Joan walked up the hill to greet us. We were covered only by a thin, white blanket. She smiled and the three of us giggled. Joan was from a family of known takers. Even a giggle was a gift.

"Enjoying your afternoon?" Joan asked. I hadn't seen her in ages. Our work at Three Oaks was a thing of the past, just as needing to labor for credit was a thing of the past. The three of us stared at her, smiling and unblinking.

"It's funny," Joan said in her older-sister tone. "How much a gift can change your life. Receive the right gift and you might find yourself surrounded by friends you never even knew you had."

Billy barked a laugh. "And what would you know about giving gifts?" he asked.

"I know that accepting them can cost just as much as giving them," Joan said.

Billy and Eliza-Beth both laughed maniacally and rolled into each other, pulling me back into a pile of kisses. They both joked, as we rolled around, about the taker who thought she could educate us on gifts.

I tried to let the sun and grass and attention wash over me, but Joan's words flew around my mind long after she'd left our private hill. I had forgotten. In the face of the gifts, and attention, and love that felt so right, so perfectly right, I had forgotten where they came from. I had let myself believe that this was my life, finally earned after years of under-acknowledged labor, creativity, and kindness freely given to those around me. But in reality, it had been a gift, one bestowed on me by Joan through the rumors she'd spread.

It is not a bad thing to accept a gift. But to take more than you give, to think only of what you can take, that is what makes a taker. When I had ascended to the ranks of the most generous, I gave a few rare gifts where I could. But I now realized I hadn't given enough. I had forgotten that I had taken a gift at all. It had been freely given and freely taken in return, but it was wholly unreciprocated. Joan had given me the greatest gift of my life and I had ignored her completely and allowed myself to become surrounded by those who had never even seen me before I was someone to be seen. She was right to chastise me. This gift had cost me my generosity. I had become a taker and it was time to give again.

Even with the free time granted by the gifts of grades and papers, the desk had taken three straight weeks of labor. It was the most beautiful gift I had ever made: compact, lightweight, strong, with discrete cabinets and a beautiful blend of colors. Its manufacture had attracted more than a little attention and there was a small crowd gathered around me to see who was lucky enough to receive it.

I waved Joan over as she exited the tech. Her mess of tight curls shrouded her face, and I could hear the onlookers whisper "taker" as she came up to me.

"Joan, I would like to give you this desk. I can think of no one more worthy of it. You have given me many gifts over the years that I could never repay. Your gifts to this community, including your tireless work at Three Oaks, are far too often overlooked. I hope this desk can help you in your studies and that it properly conveys my gratitude."

I had practiced the speech the night before. It was the same as what I had written in the official gift registry. The words were important. The gift wasn't just the desk itself, though it was no small thing, the real gift was my acknowledgment of her. My status gave those words serious weight. With one gift, I would hitch her to my rising star.

The tiny crowd froze behind me. They were as eager for Joan's response as I was. They were eager for her gratitude, eager to acknowledge her as someone worthy of such a spectacular gift.

But Joan didn't embrace me. She didn't cry tears of joy and clap her hands. She simply looked at the desk and said, "I don't need a desk," then walked past me and my tiny crowd. Over her shoulder, she shouted, "Give it to one of your pretty new friends."

The onlookers and I froze, then their snickering filled my ears as the crowd petered out behind me. Cold tentacles of fear crawled up my back. No one refused a gift like this, whether they needed a desk or not. The real gift was far more than mahogany and brass hinges, it was my presence, acknowledgment, and friendship. She had turned all of these down without a second thought.

I had been wrong. Joan didn't want me to give again, to reciprocate to her and others as was right. That visit on the hill hadn't been a reprimand of my greed, but a reminder of what I owed. She alone had given me my new life and she alone knew it didn't belong to me. I owed Joan a massive debt, and she would decide when it was paid.

Money is not something I'm used to dealing with. My food, my home, and the things that fill it are all gifts. Gifts given by people that knew I would give everything I could back in return. A family like mine has little use for ravs; we are generous enough to need only the generosity of others. So, it was beyond strange to be holding twenty ravs in my hand and even stranger to slip them through the slats of Joan's Tech locker. I'd sold the desk and half the gifts I'd received in the last few months to get the money, including an ornate candleholder Billy had carved himself and a crystal beaded necklace made by Eliza-Beth. I received strange looks when I sold these precious gifts for cash, but I'd had no choice. Joan had refused my gift and all that came with it. Joan was not simply content to let me live the life she had given me. She had shown me that much. She had no interest in sharing in the light of my generosity, but money was another story. Money could buy all the food, clothing, and comforts her family only received when the Bone was full or when Joan's labors at Three Oaks elicited some token of generosity. They would still be takers, but fed takers, comfortable takers.

The coins rattled as they fell into Joan's locker, and they rattled even louder when they spilled out of mine later that day. Heavy, loud, obnoxious things. Twenty ravs, enough money to buy her family food for a year and she had given them back like they were nothing. There was no note with my ravs returned to me. The only response was the money itself — a clear message that Joan would rather she and her family suffer than take anything from me. Even this small fortune couldn't buy me out of her debt.

Joan was attacking the floor with her mop when I arrived. She had already cleared the equipment, swept the entire facility, and begun mopping while sunlight still poured through the windows. I joined her from across the room, trying to match her pace. She didn't acknowledge me. After only five minutes with the thwack and splash of our mops to occupy my attention, my mind began to ache. I threw my mop down with a huff.

"What do you want?" I whimpered. "What do you want from me, Joan?"

She leaned her mop gently in the bucket and smiled. An ugly grin, all teeth. "Want from you? Surely the generous Ev would not be so base as to offer an exchange. If you offer a gift freely, I'm sure I will accept it freely."

"You didn't take the desk."

"I have no need for a desk."

"It was a gift.

"One I had no need for."

"You didn't take the ravs," I said.

She sneered. "The twenty ravs tossed in my locker without even a note? The twenty ravs you no doubt earned off of Taye's labor? I don't want your money, Ev."

"Then what do you want, Joan? If you don't want gifts or credit or money, what do you want from me?"

"I want to finish cleaning, Ev. It takes twice as long without you here."

I looked down at my hands. Without my regular labor, they had lost all their long-held calluses and were aching already.

"Joan, you spread the rumors. You gave me the gift," I said.

Joan nodded. "And you took it. You took from Taye, desperate and greedy, just like all your pathetic lookers would have done. And now you call me taker behind my back."

I opened my mouth to protest, but I couldn't force out the lie. "What was I supposed to do?"

"Did you know Taye doesn't care that you took the credit from him? I told him what we did. I apologized for stealing his credit and having you waste it on your lookers and trinkets, but he says he doesn't need it. He says that as long as he has enough to survive, he's happy. We trade lunches now most days. He even labors with me here sometimes, not that anyone notices."

My heart fluttered. If she had told Taye, she might tell anyone. She could crush me with a few well-placed words. "I didn't take the credit," I muttered.

Joan smiled. "But you did, Ev. And you didn't do anything with it. You weren't generous, you weren't kind, you didn't fight for anyone, you just left. You became one of *them*, whose every breath and whimper is a gift, and you laugh at us who labor every day for your scraps. And you never came back."

My eyes filled and my throat became tight and scratchy. It wasn't true. I had tried to give. I had tried to be generous. "I gave you a gift in return," I said.

"The gift of joining your sycophantic circle of lookers. The gift of laughing at my parents and Taye and anyone else you choose to look down on. Keep your gifts, Ev. Keep your life. You earned it."

I begged her to leave me be. I begged her not to destroy me, not to take what she had given me, but she just laughed and shook her head. Eventually, she turned and mopped her way out into the hallway. I followed her, but she wouldn't even look at me. After a few minutes, I dumped out my bucket and left.

This time it was harder. My stock was still high, but my renown wasn't what it had once been. I sold all the gifts I'd acquired and begun laboring in a heavy-manufacturing plant. The looks to and from work stung, but I knew they were worth it. I needed the money and the labor it took to earn it. The gift from Joan had turned out to be no gift at all. It was a yoke, one that tied me to her crime for as long as I wore it. She was a credit thief. She had taken the credit that was rightfully Taye's and given it to me. I had accepted it without question and become the greatest taker the Tech had ever seen. And Joan knew it. She wouldn't take my gifts; she wouldn't accept my friendship. But she wasn't gone, either. She stayed on the edge of my life, threatening it with every breath she took. If I couldn't convince her to join in the spoils of what we had taken from Taye, to mire herself as I had done, I would have to give what I had taken. I would force her to become a taker as she had forced me.

The news made the Tech even wilder this time. Sixty. Sixty ravs to the Bone and they were alive with the buzz of it. The work that must have taken. The respect hidden within. And before the end of the day, everyone knew who had done it: two quiet takers named Taye and Joan.

I was relieved. Tired and relieved. My own stock had fallen far after news of me working for wages had gotten out. Further than I ever expected it could, and I now stood little better than I had before all this began, but I had repaid the gift in kind. I had done the work and given back what I owed. And now Taye would receive the credit he truly deserved, and Joan would receive credit for a gift she hadn't given. She would become a taker, same as I had been, and I would be free. This was a gift she could never refuse, not without harming Taye, who had done nothing but give.

I had been freed from her debt, and the relief settled over me and flushed the shame from my core. I had given much of myself, not only my labor, but the credit, gifts, and status I had always wanted. And now I was a taker no longer. I was excited to see no one waiting for me as I exited my classes. I was relieved at the prospect of cleaning Three Oaks tonight. Everything was as it should be.

I found Billy and Eliza-Beth standing in front of my locker at fifth bell. They, like all the other lookers, hadn't spoken to me for months. Today they came up to me fawning, delicate, and smelling of roses.

"We heard what you did," one of them said. Then all of them said it, one by one. All the lookers. Then all the instructors. Then everyone else. Joan had set the record straight. She had told them about all the money I'd given and how I had tried to give her and Taye credit. They surrounded me at the steps of the Tech. Thousands of them. I could even see my parents in the crowd. A hundred ravs to the Bone in under a year. An enormous sum given to those few dared give to, and I hadn't even kept the credit. I had thrown it away like it was nothing, to two people who could hardly have deserved it. I was more than a giver. I was a legend reborn. I was fantastic. I was nothing they'd ever seen before.

Joan stood at the edge of the crowd. She wore a huge smile. Twice now, she had openly refused my generous gift freely given. She was an ingrate of the highest order and an ungrateful taker at that. She had taken on a status so low she could never crawl out from under it. She had accepted a life of pity and the Bone rather than take a gift she didn't want, and she smiled as if it were the greatest day of her life. I stared at her while the crowd pawed at me. I saw now that my gifts had never been meant for her. I had only ever tried to free my conscience and secure the life I always wanted. And by refusing them, she had let me. She had shown me who I wanted to be and let me become it. I was fantastic now and forever. I was a taker, now and forever.

I saw Taye join Joan at the edge of the crowd. They smiled at each other, then they smiled at me. The crowd surged forward to surround me and I lost sight of them.

See Connor Mellegers's story "Freely Given" online at Metaphorosis.
If you liked it, leave a comment. Authors love that!
Remember to subscribe to our e-mail updates so you'll know when
new stories are posted.

About the story

A few years ago I read some of the writings of Marcel Mauss and was introduced to the idea of a gift economy. In a gift economy, goods and services aren't sold or traded but are given as gifts without an explicit agreement for return. I was immediately interested in the idea of a gift economy not only as a principal economic system but also as an underlying economy, one which exists beneath the surface of a market economy. When we think of gifts in Western society, often our minds will go straight to birthdays and holidays or charitable giving. But gifts are so much more pervasive than that and there are countless things we do for each other without a clear reward or exchange in place. There are obvious things, such as cooking and cleaning and work we do for one another in home/work/community settings, and then quieter and subtler things, like compliments, advice, lending a sympathetic ear, etc.

Initially, I just knew I wanted to make a story centred around a society where gifts constituted the principal economy, and market exchange, even if it was present, was considered lowly and distasteful and something to exist beneath the surface. I wanted to explore how the ideas of success and admiration would change as well as how inequality would manifest. Of course, no market economy has anywhere near an equitable distribution of wealth, and how it is distributed is subject to pervasive and often arbitrary (but rarely random) prejudices. Despite a very different economic model, the world I was imagining would feature its own inequalities. I imagined that in a world centred around gift-giving, who gives and receives what is unlikely to be even, but, just as with a market economy, what a person receives dictates the power and comfortability they are afforded.

Stemming from this concept, I wanted to explore the idea of a protagonist experiencing an unexpected and unearned windfall. In a world where respect for one's generosity is the primary currency, I wondered how ill-gotten gains might impact someone, particularly if that person had never really examined the rules of their economic and social system before.

A question for the author

Q: Have you ever consciously written a 'message' story? Was it easier or harder than usual?
A: I've never set out to consciously write a message story but I find that one often appears as I'm writing. It might be tied up in a character or the world I'm building, but there is always some identifiable point of view or idea that comes through and connects the work. If some message or viewpoint doesn't begin to form as I'm writing, I find the story just falls apart.

About the author

Connor Mellegers is a freelance writer living in Toronto. When not writing speculative fiction, you can find them reading, cooking, and struggling to grow a garden.
@cmellegers

The Diary of Thisne Ome

Thomas Ouphe

Fiffnal 08, Third Passage,
Moonrise

Warden's Day. Of all the days, she chose Warden's Day. Everyone was at the park; the warden (of course), the teachers from hall, the lower hall children, everyone from upper hall, Krem and all his curls, and (worst luck) mother. Father wasn't there, so I should say almost everyone.

Father hates Warden's Day. It's because the wardens are employed by the Academy and if it weren't for the bloody alchemists of the bloody Academy, we wouldn't need a bloody warden. Those are his words, not mine. The wardens are just normal people. I read in Severn's *Whole History* that the Academy only allows 200 hundred practicing alchemists. There are hundreds of thousands of setins, so there has to be a warden for almost every village near a river. They don't get much money from the Academy anyway, just enough to live on. The Academy wasn't even formed when the setin were created, but father says it doesn't matter, as they're all a bunch of bastards.

I don't talk about Warden's Day around father, because it's the only thing that makes him angry. He didn't even get angry when I left his coat in front of the fire to dry and burned it. But I try not to mention wardens to him at all. I like the warden. I'd like to be a warden and learn everything there is to know about the setins. If you can keep people safely away from the setins, then the setins won't need to eat them. It's pretty straightforward, really.

I like Warden's Day, because Warden's Day is the village's way of saying thank you to the warden. He is out there every day walking the banks, keeping track of the setins, running from house to house if any of them stray from the river.

Miranda says the warden tells the families of people who have been bitten by capius setins where their loved ones have gone. I can't imagine what it must be like for them. The capius are as beautiful as they are scary, their blue skin carving gracefully down the river on undulating yellow frills. Four rows of razor-sharp teeth that rarely leave a victim alive, but turn anyone who survives their attack into one of them. At least, that's how the books describe it. I have never seen a capius. I have never seen a dessius setin either. I am the only person in the whole village that I know who has never seen a setin at all. I bet I know the most about them though.

I prefer setins to mothers any day of the week. Setins may have plagued the village for a hundred years, but you can avoid them. A mother you're stuck with. They may be less deadly, they may even be friendlier, but the real fact of the matter is there's no getting rid of them.

Also, and I don't care how large it is, how venomous it is, whether it's dessius or capius, no setin is ever going to humiliate you in front of all your friends.

I sit here with quill to notebook only because there is no outside world anymore. How could there be, after the incident on Warden's Day?

The girls from my hall were all dressed up in their finest. Even Miranda, whose finest looks like most people's normal. I can't believe I've been stuck with the same group all these years. I was hoping that when we moved from lower hall to upper hall there might be some change of scenery, but it's the same nine girls and seven boys it's always been.

Everyone who still goes to hall has to wear a scarf on warden's day, except the boys, of course. Pater Rother even checks us, which is not fair, because he's only supposed to be in charge when we're in the classroom.

I had borrowed Nana Rose's scarf. Borrowed, mind you, I do not take things without permission. It's a gorgeous scarf: silk with a print of lilies on the river surface and the blue streak of a capius setin just below the surface. You can see the outline of the body, long and fluked, a yellow ribbon of colour about its frills. No hint of the person it once was.

Nana says the scarf commemorates someone that means a lot to her, although she won't say who. Nobody tells me anything.

"Your Mother wouldn't like it if I told you."

She is no doubt correct; Mother doesn't like anything.

I'm not allowed a scarf, because I lost my last one. Miranda borrowed it to carry plums. She says it got juice on it and she washed it, then hung it in the tree to dry. Miranda isn't the smartest and as you might expect, the wind blew it away. Bethan and Kaye have been going on about it ever since. They said Miranda sold it to a hawker for jam tarts and buttons. She does have new buttons and she has got a bit fatter, but Miranda is my friend, there's no way she'd do that. And there's nothing out of the ordinary about her getting fatter.

I borrowed Nana's scarf because I wanted to teach Bethan and Kaye a lesson. The two of them have airs far above their station. Both of their families are moneyed, but neither of them has a scarf as beautiful as Nana Rose's. As soon as I walked through the park gates, they were both green with the not-gots. I think Kaye was just about ready to spew.

The girls of the upper hall had to sing "Oh save me brave". Mater Grierly had us practice it on our lunchtimes for a month. The boys danced, slapping sticks and shins. They all had red rags instead of scarfs. But I saw Krem look at mine. I think I must look pretty wearing it.

We were lined up to thank the warden. The lower hall goes first, so it's a long queue. I made a point of standing between Bethan and Kaye. Kaye had just asked where I got the scarf when Mother came busting out of the crowd with her lips puckered, her brows creased, and cheeks as red as coals.

"Thisne, give me that before your idiot friends trick another one out of you."

She snatched it from around my neck.

"Of all the things to give you," she muttered.

Mother didn't even glance back to see the two of them laughing at me. Or to see me running down to the river. I must have cried for three hours, and not a single setin lurched out of sludge to end my suffering. I'm always hearing tales about capius attacking beautiful maidens to turn them, so their lack of interest just adds insult to injury.

When I got back to the park, the celebration was over, and the warden had left. Thankfully, so had Bethan and Kaye.

Fiffnal 08, Third Passage,
Moonrise

I spoke to Father; he says Mother has the right ideas but that she sometimes goes about them in the wrong way. I suppose that's why he doesn't let her cook. If today was her idea of helping, I dread to think what her idea of shepherds' pie would be.

People sometimes say father is funny because he's not from Hessell. People from Hessell are funny like that.

I remember Mater Grierly joking when we were doing sums back in lower hall.

"You talk funny like your father."

Nobody laughed, because you get in to trouble for laughing when Mater Grierly teaches. Everyone hates her and she dresses like a tramp. She says mean things all the time. I'm glad I have Pater Rother now.

Father is from Thinvoll, which is a hamlet. I've never been there but he says it was like Hessell, though without a hall, a park, or even a warden. Only three families lived there, right on the riverbank. The houses weren't spread out like they are in Hessell, but crammed close together.

The setin attack on Thinvoll is famous, it's in all of the books. Father won't talk about it, but I know a few things that I haven't read. I shouldn't really write this down, but I don't suppose anyone but me will read it.

The two types of setin are believed to have been created at roughly the same time by two rival alchemists. The dessius are bigger with ink-black skin. They are more aggressive and stronger than the capius, but the capius scare me more, because of their infectious bite.

A dessius killed my father's sister and he watched both his parents transformed by a capius. They are out there somewhere. Father dreams about them. He screams for them, that's how I know. I wish mother would be more sympathetic, she's never had anything bad happen to her.

Fiffnal 09, Third Passage,
Sunup

I have told mother I am too sick to go to hall for lessons. It's not a lie; I couldn't sleep for worry and stayed up reading last night. My eyes are sore and my head hurts.

She is still making me go!

I shall skirt by the river and give the setins another chance. Given that my other option is abject humiliation, being eaten wouldn't be the worst. I might get lucky and have one of them turn me. If they did, I'd eat Kaye first, she laughed the most.

Fiffnal 09, Third Passage,
Long Shadows

Hall wasn't that bad. Bethan told Krem Barton what happened at the park. He didn't seem to understand why it was important. He just said my mother sounded very sensible. I wasn't sure if I wanted to love him for not caring or be mad that he took my mother's side.

I looked at his beautiful wavy hair and decided I was closer to loving him than hating him, but then I looked down at his unpolished shoes and I wasn't sure how close to loving him I could get. It takes no time to polish a shoe, but the contrast of satin stockings and scuffing is a difficult image to get out of the mind.

He's not terribly smart either and this seems to be a theme with the people I feel affection for. I suppose I must take after my father.

Speaking of stupid people, Miranda was a brick today. She threatened to punch Bethan on the nose and has promised to replace my scarf, given all the trouble it's caused. I thanked her but told her there was no need, but she insisted and after the way she spoke to Bethan, I was a bit too scared to say no.

Fiffnal 10, Third Passage,
Sunup

The old hag woke me up by churning butter. She has no sense of rhythm. I'm not sure she doesn't do it on purpose. When I churn butter, I do it in a gentle melodious way, so that it sounds like waves lapping the riverbank. When Mother does it, it is in a frantic stop-start way that no human ear could find pleasure in.

She's not terrible at everything; if she wanted to wake me up, she can congratulate herself on a job well done.

Fiffnal 10, Third Passage,
Midsun

I still haven't seen a setin. And I'm still the only person I know who hasn't.

It is not for want of looking. Hessell is the biggest village for miles and the Deva River coils around it like a rope. Mother and father travel to sell their barrels, but I've never been beyond the river. Aside from father, I've never met anyone from outside the village, either. Though I know there is a visiting hawker.

Father says Hessell is the prettiest village in the whole of Afon, but like most people in Hessell father has never been more than forty miles. I have read that the whole of Afon stretches hundreds of miles — full of cities and towns; that has to be much more interesting. Hessell is mostly just fields, trees, and houses. There are flowers in the park and a swing, but nothing like the statues or towers you read about in Garsdon. Beyond the Deva there are more fields, more trees, and more houses. If you go far enough north, you can see Garsdon over the Merrisea, and if you go south, you can see the slate hills of Whelston far across the water. I've never seen either. Even I know better than to go to bodies of water that large — I want to see one setin, not an ocean of them.

Mother would never let me go to the Deva as a child, and I am still banned from going alone. I go all time, of course, but I've still never seen one. Everyone else I know has seen scores.

Mother would execute me if she knew I was going to the river alone.

She says, all I need to know about setin is to stay away from them, but it just makes me more curious. After all, Nana had a famous encounter with one — not that anyone will talk about it.

I have hall again tomorrow; it would be nice to get through one day without being humiliated. I still have a headache too and now my eyes hurt. I smell toast cooking, I had better get dressed.

Fiffnal 10, Third Passage,
Blackest Midnight

Our house is decidedly too small. I have been woken by the sound of my parents arguing. That is to say, Mother was arguing whilst Father spoke with the calm tones of a reverend brother ministering to the possessed.

"She's just like Caleb," Mother was shrieking.

I don't know who Caleb is, but he often comes up when they argue, especially when they argue about me. Dorethea in the senior hall had a twin sister who died at birth. Sometimes I like to imagine Caleb is my twin brother and my parents sent him away when I was very young. I keep hoping he will show up and give them something better to argue about than me.

I could hear father take a deep breath. I'm not sure if he's frightened of mother or if he just doesn't have the energy to keep up with her. He spoke slowly, like a ticking metronome:

"She's exactly like Caleb," said father, "It's in her blood. It's in all of your blood."

Father rarely sounds firm, but there was enough certainty in his voice to shut Mother up for at least half a second.

"It wasn't in Caleb's, and it isn't in mine, so it can't be in hers."

I don't know what they'll talk about when I grow up and leave. I bet they'll have hobbies. Miranda's mother knits.

Fiffnal 11, Third Passage,
Long Shadows

I think Miranda may like Krem. Every time I glance over at him, I see her staring at him. My eyes ached after reading and my head felt woozy, so I spent most of hall noticing things.

Did you know that the first mention of a setin in Afon is just after King Humber returned from his expedition to the ice flats? It's longer ago than I thought. Back then, the Academy ran everything and nobody else could read much. They brought in hall just to teach people how to live around the setins. Of all the terrible things the setins have done, eating people, luring them from their families, and destroying homes, making me go to hall must be the worst.

Krem doesn't seem to notice anything. He stares at Bethan. I think he must like her scarf, it's almost as pretty as the one I used to have. I can tell he doesn't really like her though, because she sits in front of him, and he never looks down at her ankles. Lucky for Bethan; they're very boney and I think they would make him sick.

Nobody was in when I got home, and there was a note saying they were at Nana's. I had cheese and bread for dinner, and a whole pot of tea to myself.

I lay in bed thinking about Klem. I hope Miranda gets me a nice scarf. I know her family don't have much money, but I could use the attention. I've never even held hands with a boy. When you add that to my never having seen a setin, you might wonder what I've been doing with my life.

Fiffnal 11, Third Passage,
Evensong

Father has come home without Mother. He briefly checked on me. I asked him if Mother was well, and he said she was comforting Nana.

I asked if it was anything to do with Caleb. Father looked surprised but I could tell he wasn't going to tell me anything.

"More to do with Nana," he told me.

If I do have a secret twin, I'll never keep secrets from him the way my parents do.

"Who is he?" I asked.

Father frowned; you could almost see his brain straining to find an answer that wouldn't get him into trouble.

"When your mother's ready, I'm sure she'll tell you all about him."

So, now I still don't know, and I will have to talk to Mother. I consider this the worst of all possibilities.

Fiffnal 12, Third Passage,
Long Shadows

Mother is still not back. Went for a walk, did not see a setin.

Fiffnal 13, Third Passage,
Midsun

I think there is something wrong with my eyes, I have trouble reading. It can't be that I have gotten stupider. I was trying to get through what should have been an easy chapter on the colourings of dessius setins, but the page kept blurring. If Mother were here, I would complain about it.

I told Father, and he said I might need focus lenses. He said the hawkers sometimes sell them.

Then he made me gut and pluck one of the pheasants he has hanging. He's salted it and is going to cook it for Mother when she gets back. It's a double-edged sword; the pheasant will be delicious, but a delicious meal isn't always a pleasant one.

As I am nearly blind, I asked him to read to me. I gave him my copy of Cordon's *Field Study of Setin Habits*, but he said he could not stand to hear another word about the wretched creatures, and didn't I have any books with stories?

Three years ago, Mother decided I was "too old" for "fairy stories". Father watched whilst mother donated all my old story books to the lower hall, so he knows very well that I don't. We ended up with him reading from a recipe book. It made me hungry for rhubarb and custard, but we didn't have eggs or rhubarb. Father suggested he could look for a recipe for toast.

Fiffnal 14, Third Passage,
Mornsong

Father is sending me to Nana's house. He wants me to try her focus lenses. Mother will be there. I think he is punishing me for reading recipes we don't have ingredients for.

Fiffnal 14, Third Passage,
Long Shadows

I tried Nana's pince-nez. I am relieved to discover that I am not getting stupider. It is not good news that my eyesight is failing, however. Nana has given me her spare pince-nez to use until I can go to the hawker.

Mother walked home with me. We did not speak much, and I dared not ask her about Caleb. Instead, she asked me about hall. I told her about Bethan's ankles, and she asked which boy I was getting jealous over. I don't believe she will ever understand me.

The pheasant dinner was very tasty. Father made rhubarb and custard for dessert.

Fiffnal 15, Third Passage,
Night

Went to Miranda's house. Her elder brother Iain was skinning rabbits to make gloves. He has very deft hands. He's a similar build to Miranda, but it looks better on him because he doesn't have to wear a dress. Miranda is the only person I know who has any siblings. It's probably why her family is so poor.

I'm not sure what Iain was dipping the skins in, but it smelled even worse than a hanging pheasant. And dead rabbits look unpleasant when they're skinned, like undernourished babies.

He told me Miranda was at the park. He wiped his bloody hands on his leather apron and winked at me.

"You let me know if you want some garters like the ones I made her."

I thanked him for his generous offer.

There was no sign of Miranda at the park. I met Kaye and Bethan by the wrought iron gates. Bethan has a new scarf with a picture of a kestrel. She should wrap it around her pointy ankles.

They hadn't seen Miranda, but they made it very clear they had seen someone else. Kaye said "someone else" in a sing-song lilt that suggested it was someone very interesting.

I wasn't going to take the bait. There are only 16 families in Hessell and none of them has ever been especially interesting before. I bet if you took a ship and left Afon to search all the wonderous foreign lands you still wouldn't find a group of less interesting people. Kaye is just too boring to notice it.

Fiffnal 1, Fourth Passage,
Short Shadows

Sylvia from the lower hall has been attacked by a setin. Her family were fishing on the Deva. Luckily it was a dessius, so she won't turn. I have heard she's quite sick but should get better within a stint. I am quite sick too; here I am at age fourteen and I've still never even seen a setin. I blame Mother for mithering me about keeping away from the river.

I wonder what would happen if Sylvia did turn. Would her family try to visit her? And if they did, would she try to eat them?

Fiffnal 2, Fourth Passage,
Long Shadows

Miranda brought my 'new' scarf to hall. It is quite the most ragged thing I have ever seen. I wouldn't be surprised it weren't one of the rags Iain cleans up rabbit guts with.

As Miranda is my friend, and I know she has done her best, I graciously tied my hair up in it. I might look like a roaming beggar, but that is better than being an ungrateful priss.

Krem smiled when he saw me wearing it, I couldn't tell if he was being polite. Bethan and Kaye both laughed aloud at me.

When I put on my pince-nez Bethan said I reminded her of Mater Grierly. Krem laughed. I have decided that he is beneath my affections.

Fiffnal 3, Fourth Passage,
Night

I loathe it when it rains; the mice in the thatch become frantic and it is difficult to sleep. I have asked Father for a cat. He grunted and pretended to be asleep. Mother told me to get to sleep, they have barrels to coop in the morning. Hopefully, that means I'll be able to buy a new pince-nez soon.

There is an awful musky smell when it rains heavily like tonight and in the flicker of the lamp, you can see damp on the plaster of the walls.

I have been fixed to my window for the last hour. Nana tells me that on nights when it rains very heavily, the setin come inland looking for victims. There was a flash of lightning earlier and I saw something move in the hedges near the gate. It may have just been a fox though.

Fiffnal 4, Fourth Passage,
Long Shadows

I may look like an old woman, but Pater Rother says I was the best reader today. The muddy paths had rendered my dress filthy, but most of the other girls had suffered the same fate and at least two of the boys had managed to push each other over and had little clusters of dirt around their desks.

We had to do an oral quiz. Miranda didn't know the six stages of the capius, and Bethan got three sums wrong. So, all things considered, I shone. I know everything about the stages of the capius except what they look like in real life. Pater Rother has let me borrow a book about dessius. He says I could make a good warden — so long as my eyesight doesn't get any worse.

Mother made me brush my dress and shoes. She and Father have not finished with the barrels yet, so I had to make dinner. They had not so much as shopped and I had to walk back into the village to get fresh supplies. We had potatoes and trout.

I mashed the potatoes, but we didn't have any cream, so I had to add water. The trout was good, even though I wasn't able to filet it very well and now my hands smell of fish guts. I scrubbed them with potato skins, but there's still a smell.

Fiffnal 5, Fourth Passage,
Short Shadows

Miranda is no longer my friend. She was talking to Kaye and Bethan and as I approached, she said, "Here comes Mater Grierly."

The outrage! I was only wearing that beggar's scarf to save her feelings. Worst still, at lunch she sat with Krem, and they held hands. I am truly alone in the world.

Two of the lower hall girls, Geraldine and Rhian, saw me crying in the cloakroom. They were very nice and friendly. They calmed me down by telling me all about Sylvia. Sylvia has a patch of scales around the area where she was bitten. The veins in her arms have turned bright blue. This is normal in dessius bites, some people stay that way forever.

She had travelled quite far up the river; her mother is a net fisher. I don't know the spot where she was attacked, but it is supposed to have a clump of willows and a small mooring. Dare I visit it alone? I certainly have no friends to go with.

I may still invite the treacherous Miranda, but to use as bait!

Fiffnal 6, Fourth Passage,
Moonrise

I had to make dinner again. This time I could only make eggs and bread, though my parents seemed happy enough with it. They have finally finished cooping the barrels and looked too tired to care much about anything.

Mother was in a bad mood, which is to say, a normal mood. She found me reading and chastised me for using too much lamp oil. Then she asked what I was reading and why. I told her about the book Pater Rother had lent to me, and how he thinks I could become a warden. Mother snatched the book away and is going to hall to embarrass me tomorrow.

She says she plans on having a stern word with Pater Rother for putting such foolish ideas into my head.

Fiffnal 7, Fourth Passage,
The End of the World

True to her word, Mother barged into hall and shouted at Pater Rother in front of the whole class. It is as well that I have no friends left to lose.

I feel too sick to write and I have no books to read, so at least Mother will save on her precious lamp oil.

Fiffnal 8, Fourth Passage,
Mornsong

Dad has taken pity on me and given me enough money for both a pince-nez and a scarf that doesn't look like it has been used to dust a barnyard.

The hawker visits Hessell every sixth fiffnal. He's a bright-eyed chap who wears a yellow jacket, even in the summer. I have heard people describe him as handsome, but he has a metal nose tied on with a leather cord.

Mother says the metal nose is proof that he must have been handsome once. Father laughed when she said it, but they wouldn't let me in on the joke.

Father replied that he was a well-travelled man, Mother laughed and said he had been to all sorts of places, which they both found hilarious.

Fiffnal 8, Fourth Passage,
Short Shadows

The hawker was not as grubby a man as I was expecting, and aside from the metal nose, I found him to be both presentable and charming. He was a big help in showing me through a collection of pince-nez, and eventually, we found the perfect pair.

As we were discussing noses anyway, I told him how handsome I thought his own was. It is a bronze alloy that almost perfectly matches his skin tone.

"Thanks. My last one was a touch longer, but I like it well enough. You pay no mind to rumours, I didn't lose it through no wrongdoing or ought," said he.

I had never suggested he did and told him as much but asked how he did get it.

"Let's just say I put it somewhere it didn't belong, and it got stuck there."

His face fell and the tone of his voice dropped with it, so I changed the subject and asked what scarves he had for sale. An instant smile sprang up on his face and his nose sparkled as the movement lifted it and the sun caught it.

"You want to see this one, it's divine."

Reaching into his bag, the man pulled out the very scarf Miranda claimed to have lost.

Why, I thought, of all the deceitful sneaks...

I had lent the scarf to Miranda in good faith, I couldn't believe she had sold it. It's not the scarf, you understand, it's the betrayal of making me wear that awful rag.

"Where did you get this?"

"A bonny lass about your age."

I asked him to describe the girl and aside from the word bonny, there was no mistaking that it was Miranda.

The hawker was most sympathetic to my plight and agreed to give it to me at no charge if I purchased one of his other scarves. It is of a much lesser quality, but it has a rather fetching pattern of red and white stars.

Miranda will live to regret this betrayal, or my name isn't Thisne Ome!

Fiffnal 9, Fourth Passage,
Midsun

Mother has spent the morning enraged at my choice of scarf, which she says is too flamboyant and makes me look like a roaming jezebel. I told her about Miranda's betrayal. She was not sympathetic, but instead told me she hoped I had learned the difference between decent people and Miranda's type.

Father asked how much the hawker had charged and then looked surprised.

"You didn't make any arrangements, did you?"

I told him what happened. He laughed aloud when I told him about the hawker's nose.

As if that poor man hasn't suffered enough.

Fiffnal 10, Fourth Passage,
Long Shadows

Sylvia continues to be crowded around and adored in a way that must be both smothering and liable to inflame the mind. But I did finally get to speak to her, by elbowing my way past a lower hall student with a face full of spots. I must say I can see the fascination; Sylvia has a large bite mark on her arm. At each of the points where the teeth of the dessius sank into her skin, there is a green spider web pattern. Dessius toxins can't transform a person but they stay in the blood forever. In *Setin and Their Ways*, Joan Wilts records that people with those marks often dream that they are the setin that bit them; they see through their eyes: diving and hunting in the blackest rivers. It must be more exciting than reading about them.

Nobody has noticed my new pince-nez, which is a tragedy because it has a rather fetching inlaid etching, but I suppose they may have been too distracted by the sudden return of my scarf. Bethan and Kaye were particularly keen to hear the story.

"You mustn't be too cruel to her, her family are desperately poor," said I.

They both giggled at each other and ran off to tell the story to anyone who would listen.

Miranda glowered at me throughout the whole late session of hall. Since I have my pince-nez, I have become more determined than ever to become a warden, and I answered all Pater Rother's questions. I watched Miranda through the corner of my eye, her face contorted with rage. I wouldn't be surprised if Krem hadn't gone off her; she looked quite the ugliest I have ever seen her. I doubt even the hawker would have found her bonny.

After hall, she was waiting for me against the birch in the front garden. I could tell she was waiting for me; she had the determined look of somebody waiting, her eyes scanning each passing face to check that it wasn't mine.

"Looks like she's waiting for you."

Bethan looked delighted by the prospect. She and Kaye seemed to be waiting in anticipation of the spectacle.

"Are you worried she'll try to thump you?" Kaye asked.

I glanced out the window at Miranda. I do not know her as well as I had thought. If I hadn't been worried before that Miranda might try to thump me, I was by then.

I made a show of forgetting some books. Pater Rother was only too pleased to keep me talking about the importance of the volumes I was being allowed to borrow, so I did manage to pass enough time. Miranda had moved on by the time I left. It is worth noting that neither Kaye nor Bethan had left and they were waiting at the gates of the hall.

"Miranda says she'll get you tomorrow."

I walked with purpose and my head held high, but they walked alongside me, continuing with their taunts.

I will pay no mind to them or Miranda. I am the one in the right.

Fiffnal 10, Fourth Passage,
Blackest Midnight

I am somewhat concerned that Miranda may attack me tomorrow. She is far bigger than I and from a much rougher family. I am unable to sleep and have been reading by lamplight.

Wilkes has a note about dessius setins that I found fascinating. The bite often kills days after. I think Sylvia is in the clear, but what a trial she must have had. I find myself both in awe of the setins and wracked with fear by them.

It is lucky that she was not bitten by a capius. There is no turning back from that.

Fiffnal 12, Fourth Passage, Estimate

Mother brought my journal to my bedside, I am having a hard time concentrating. It hurts to write and my hand is shaking.

I cannot tell what happened and what is a dream. Miranda has visited me. She cried when she saw me.

I don't know the date.

Fiffnal 13, Fourth Passage, Estimate

This much I am clear on. I have seen a setin and I am no longer sure I will be a warden.

Fiffnal 3, Fifth Passage, Estimate

Days are too bright.

Fiffnal 7, Fifth Passage (I think)

I love Mother and Father. I hope they will know that if I die.

Fiffnal 10, Fifth Passage,
Long Shadows

I ate soup today and was able to stand. Mother will not let me near a mirror, though she changed my sheets whilst I sweated in the wicker chair.

I am starting to be able to tell the fever scenes from real life. Just not when they are happening.

I keep seeing myself in the Deva, I can feel myself swimming. Then I am in bed with a feather scratching through the pillow onto my face.

The warden has been to see me. He says if I survive the next two days, I might be able to live a normal life.

Fiffnal 15, Fifth Passage,
Estimate

I have not been able to write for a while. Three days? It is hard to tell. I don't remember anything but broth and Mother. I suspect she has saved me a second time.

Fiffnal 2, Sixth Passage,
Long Shadows

I must get this down whilst it is fresh in my mind. Or, before I die. There is a thought; death from setin venom is sudden, so at least I won't suffer. By all accounts, it waits in your system, showing no more signs than the bite itself. Then, you just die. Waites speaks of the victims having contorted faces like demons. Sylvia survived. Bethan and Kaye will be beside themselves if a girl from the lower hall survived and I don't. Poor Miranda will never hear the end of it.

Miranda is distraught. She thinks this is her fault, but I am sure that the blame is mine. Even if I had to read back and refresh my memory.

It was the scarf. Miranda stole my scarf and I told everyone. The next day at hall she waited for me in the cloakroom. Her face was grave, her fists were clenched, and she had rolled up her sleeves. It seemed as if she was ready to thump me.

I bit my lip and closed my eyes and waited for the blow to come.

What I felt was Miranda taking my hand. As I glanced down, I could see why she had rolled her sleeves up, they were wet with tears.

"I can't believe you told everyone I stole your scarf."

I was upset. She shouldn't have taken it. I told her so and she fell into a flood of tears.

She had only sold the scarf because her mother spent all of their money on setting up the glove business for her brother. Miranda hadn't eaten anything but a crust of bread in two days.

It is a sad story and at the time I thought, as awful as Mother is, at least she has never let me starve.

Miranda cried some more and begged for forgiveness.

"You don't know the shame of being poor."

Well, she's right — I do not. But I did know the shame of seeing her flirt with Krem.

"It's his stupid wavy hair, I can't think straight around it."

I of course forgave her. Krem's wavy hair seems to affect me in a peculiar manner also. But when she asked how she could make it up to me, I did ask for something unreasonable. I asked if she would help me see a setin.

Therefore, if I am dead by the end of the week, let it be known that it is on my request.

Miranda didn't want to go, not really. I'm too tired to write anymore and feel I may not make it. But I had to set the record straight.

Fiffnal 4, Sixth Passage, Bright Morning

It would appear that I have survived. Mother will still not let me see my reflection and I want to. I feel I need to know.

My strength ebbed to the point that the village held a vigil. But I am not dead, and I no longer think I will die. I must sleep.

Fiffnal 5, Sixth Passage,
Short Shadows

I have been forced to rest in bed, though the sun is glorious outside and I am feeling well. A strange thing has happened today, I have been reading voraciously but I no longer need the pince-nez to see the words.

I have had a visit from Miranda this morning. She is still giving me peculiar looks. I have asked if she could bring me a looking glass, but she says that she is too afraid of my mother. I can't blame her for that. She keeps saying she is sorry for running away, but what else could anyone expect from her?

There are things I recall clearly from the day I was attacked, other bits of it keep jumping out at me when I'm trying to sleep.

I had followed Miranda up the banks of the Deva. We stood a good distance away from the water.

"It's odd, you can normally see them from here."

I had been to the spot a thousand times and never seen a single setin. I didn't want to go another day without seeing one. So, I just pressed Miranda to take me to the next spot.

She walked down toward the bank and then on to the bridge. It was the most basic route.

"When I last came here there was a dessius in the centre of Deva. I had to run up the bank."

Still, there was nothing to be seen.

After checking two more places, Miranda was looking both surprised and frustrated.

"What about the spot where Sylvia was bitten?"

Miranda was not the model of enthusiasm, but I reminded her that she had promised. I knew I was taking advantage of her guilt, but I didn't care.

We had to pass through a thicket of gorse. There was a small trail leading up a steep hill and then down. The Deva dipped out of sight as we climbed. Then, as we descended, a small rocky inlet became visible.

I had never seen the spot before. The water of the Deva ran more rapidly there. And someone, probably Sylvia's fisher family, had built a small wooden jetty.

I tumbled down towards it, leaving Miranda behind me.

As I stepped out onto the jetty and ran to the far end, I realised my mistake. I felt the movement on the jetty, and I turned to see.

The breath caught in my throat.

A large dessius had climbed on to the jetty behind me. I have read how big they are, but I had not imagined how powerless I would feel when stood in front of one. I felt my legs weaken and then I felt my resolve strengthen; I was not going to die without at least trying to stay alive.

With the jetty blocked I had no means of escape, other than to plunge into the river. I cannot swim, but a chance of survival seemed preferable to certain death.

In the water, I saw the capius. Blue and purple with white frills. I swear I have never seen anything so beautiful. I was transfixed by the graceful movement of vivid colours twisting and brightening in the sunlight. So now my choice was to be eaten by the dessius or turned by the capius.

The capius shook itself, jumping out of the water. Its deep black eyes held my own.

I felt a sharp pain in my leg as the dessius bit me. I crashed down onto the hardwood. I bit my tongue as my skull shook in shock.

The body of the capius loomed over me. I could hear it. A low and rapid set of clicks. The dessius responded at the same pitch but faster. I tried to stand up, but the pain in my leg pulled me sideways.

The dessius bit my arm. Its teeth pressed hard into the bone. I remember screaming and the capius rearing up to attack. As the pressure released, I blacked out.

Fiffnal 6, Sixth Passage, Mornsong

I have some vague memories of movement, of something gentle lapping against my wounds. I am sure it was the tongue of the capius, though that makes no sense. Mother says the capius was still there when she got to me. Which I remember to be true.

She says it 'scarpered' at the sight of her, but that is a lie. I remember hearing her voice, calm but full of pain.

"Caleb. Thank you."

Then the splash of a heavy body returning to the water.

Mother says I dreamed it, but they keep talking as if I'm not in the room. I heard Nana Rose say, "It'll out, blood knows things. You can't believe it's a coincidence."

Mother sounded utterly defeated.

"I'll tell her," she said.

She hasn't, but I know. I can feel him in my veins, see through his eyes. I can talk to him in my dreams. I know he spent years keeping the setins away from me. I know he saved me.

Fiffnal 7, Sixth Passage, Short Shadows

Nobody has ever had an open wound licked by a capius before me. I am the first. I have a connection that goes beyond any other survivor. And no capius has ever saved a person before, so Uncle Caleb is the first too.

Today I held up the looking glass and saw my face. There is a map of blue lines all over my body. I don't know if I am changed forever.

I look strange but not ugly. It is no wonder I am still friends with Miranda, that is just one of the things that we have in common.

Of course, she doesn't have an uncle who is a capius setin. She can't share his thoughts, feel where the other setin are, or see the setin blood through her skin. But, I suppose I don't know what it's like to be her, either.

Mother still hasn't told me about the day Caleb was bitten, though I have the memory from him — vivid and full of terror. Her, taking her younger brother down to the banks against Nana's will, and what became of him, what would have become of her if Nana hadn't been chasing them.

Poor Mother, it is no wonder she has been so protective. Nobody will have to worry again when I become warden. Here she comes now, bringing me more food. I do hope she hasn't cooked it herself.

See Thomas Ouphe's story "The Diary of Thisne Ome" online at Metaphorosis.
If you liked it, leave a comment. Authors love that!
Remember to subscribe to our e-mail updates so you'll know when new stories are posted.

About the story

"The Diary of Thisne Ome" kind of crept up on me, I couldn't sleep one night and just started writing it on my tablet. I had been wanting to write about river monsters for a while and for whatever reason the muse stuck at about 1am. At that point I had no idea that Thisne was a girl's name but the character voice seemed to pop out of the air and before long I had a few hundred words. By the time I finished the first diary entry I was dipping in and out of sleep so I sent the story to myself as an email in case I forgot about it.

Being much too tired to think of a title I included the subject line "This is one" but I don't spell well when I'm tired (dyslexia) and the subject line read "Thisne Ome" which just seemed to fit the character perfectly. It was close enough to Thisbe to evoke the Mechanicals from *Midsummer Night's Dream* which in turn suggested the idea of ordinary working-class people navigating every day life and a fantasy setting

The reason I was trying to write about river monsters was due to a book I absolutely adore (and one I think every writer should pick up) Caspar Henderson's *The Book of Barely Imagined Beings*. There is a photograph of sparring flatworms that informed the shape and aggression of the monstrous setins that I populated the story with. And there is something of the mixture of scientific reportage and bestiary style illustrations that seeped into the story through Thisne's obsession with the natural history of the setins.

Sue Townsend is the author that made me fall in love with the diary format and I suspect there's more than a little Adrian Mole in Thisne.

A question for the author

Q: What book or books inspired you as a child?

A: I very much lived in books as a child and there are almost too many to pick from. So I'll go with a series that doesn't get nearly enough love — *Tim and the Hidden People* by Sheila K McCullagh. I did love the easy-reader books of the series, but I am talking about the folk-magic laden fantasy of the four novellas: full of ley lines, amulets, and witchcraft. There are a lot of parallels with Susan Cooper's *Dark is Rising* series (which I also loved). Sadly, I had to borrow school copies and it's a struggle to get hold of them so they will have to stay a golden childhood memory.

About the author

When Nathaniel Hawthorne was the US consulate, he visited a small village churchyard and scraped the moss off an old stone to reveal the inscription:

Poorly lived and poorly died
Poorly buried and no-one cried

Thomas Ouphe lives very close to the churchyard and regularly goes looking for the stone when he's walking his dog. He's never found it but is romantically attracted to the graveyard because it also contains a lamppost that is said to have inspired the Narnia lamppost and the grave of the first author he ever read — Roger Lancelyn Green (Robin Hood and his Merry Men — in case that's going to nag at you).

He's the sort of person who likes to read and sit quietly. A homebody and bore, were he not so in love with an American woman he might never go out at all; except to walk the dog of course — he's not a monster.

He and his wife have three wonderful children and in addition to a mad Staffordshire Terrier, they also have a sombre and sophisticated cat.

When he's not writing (which to be honest is way more than he'd prefer), he teaches English at a college of further education.

@ThomasOuphe

March

Hope on the Vine

R.E. Dukalsky

It was early August and hope was withering on the vine.

It had withered every year so far for the last eleven, so Nima was disappointed rather than surprised. Disappointed, frustrated, demoralized. She really thought she'd gotten the balance right this time.

She knelt in front of the raised mound of earth that should have been nourishing the hope vine's roots, her dirty boots poking out behind her and the sun glinting gently off her greying curls. By this point in the season, the vine should be about three feet tall, with multiple spurs twining eight to ten feet in every direction. Heavy buds the size of the first knuckle of her thumb should be swelling between pairs of reniform leaves gleaming a lustrous dark jade. She should be out here looking eagerly for the first open blossom, a rich yellow stellate flower the size of her hand, shading to the orange of glowing embers in the center. She hadn't seen one for many years.

Instead, she stared disconsolately at a meager vine supporting a few anemic yellow-green spurs. The remaining leaves, with two notable exceptions, were the same undernourished shade, their ribs showing more starkly every day, while their edges turned brown and flaked away. Only one spur, the one that twisted around the rail of the fence, showed any semblance of health, and Nima was as baffled by its continued vitality as she was by the parent vine suddenly giving up on life. It had seemed to be growing on schedule — perhaps a little undersized but a good color — but instead of progressing to the next stage of growth and putting out buds, it had drooped, retreated, withered. Just like its ten predecessors — those that had even bothered to sprout.

Eleven long years on this struggling piece of earth, trying to tease a hope vine from seed to fruit. So far, this was the closest she had come to success. One fruit was all one could expect from such a young vine, but one was all she needed: proof she could send to her Arbiter that this vine would thrive. Then, at last, she could move on. On to the next impoverished, war-scarred town and the next desiccated, abandoned farm, where the potential for hope or fortitude or patience lay dormant under years of neglect and acres of weeds.

The next, and the next, and the next. One by one until the tired land put the years of war and sorrow behind it for good and all.

But there wouldn't be a next and a next if she couldn't bring this vine back to life. Nima doubted she'd live to see the land restored, but leaving here would be its own reward. She dreaded another roasting summer and dreary winter in the small blue house behind her. Another year of being ignored by her neighbors, loathing them in return, and never forgetting no one wanted her here.

Maybe she hadn't fertilized enough? But no; she'd been side-dressing the vine with the recommended half-cup of the special expensive blend that came from the Wizard's Herbarium, and she marked each application on her calendar so she knew she hadn't missed any. Was the mix itself wrong? They said it was guaranteed, but you never knew what that meant with the wizards you got these days. In her time, guarantees had come with blood, not a letter under shiny gilt seal.

If the mix was good, was water the issue? Possible, but hope vines were notoriously flexible in their water needs. In theory, they could take root and grow anywhere, with minimal tending. That was why they, along with fortitude trees and hedges of patience, were among the first recommended plants for war restoration project sites. Even someone who'd never set finger to a garden should be able to grow one — and once a hope vine established itself, every living thing in the area would flourish as well.

Probably she hadn't figured out the right tending regimen. This was where hope vines could be tricky, according to both her own vague memories and the instructions she received each year with the new seed. Fortitude trees could be watered with either sweat or blood (both of which she had in abundance, particularly in the summer). A hedge of patience would grow well with tears, sighs or, in a pinch, prayers. Hope vines demanded fiddly, intangible things: dreams recounted, promises exchanged, plans laid. But wizards didn't dream, she had no one to make promises to, and under the circumstances plans were not hers to lay. She'd tried making promises to the old farmhouse, to the wasted land around it, to the rickety fence and the empty road, but she wasn't sure they counted. If she were honest, the only promise she meant to keep was the one about leaving.

She'd walk out the gate now and never come back if she hadn't given her word, and not with some fancy seal, but in the old way, with consequences for breaking her oath. She'd promised to stay until she could prove she'd restored local resilience to an acceptable baseline — in plainspeak, until the hope vine was able (or willing?) to reproduce. No one back in the capital knew, or really cared, how long it took or what it asked of the grower. The point was to have wizards scattered across the land, repairing the scars of war where everyone could see them doing it. So here she was until she could cultivate her release.

Nima stroked a finger across one of the limp leaves. "If you stay alive, I leave and you never have to see me again. So save us both some pain and just *grow*," she whispered, putting all the force of her will into it. No effect, of course, except a dull burn up her right arm to complement her aching knees.

"What's wrong with your plant?"

The voice was high-pitched and unfamiliar. Nima looked up to see a girl of about twelve years draped across the fence near the gate ten feet away. Just about where the questing ends of the vine ought to be right now, Nima thought sourly. She'd never seen the girl before, though she had the look of a local: a short, wide body, tawny skin, a blunt nose, and straight, thick black hair cut short above her shoulders. Her eyes were close-set, small, and twinkling with curiosity.

"It isn't growing," Nima said shortly. She was sick to death of these suspicious locals. "Did you need something?"

"I'm Yun," the girl said, completely ignoring the pointed question. "Did you forget to water it?"

"No," Nima replied, trying to rein in her temper. It wouldn't improve her relationship with the locals if she started yelling at children. On the other hand, she didn't care that much about having a relationship with the locals. She turned back to the hope vine, scratching gently in the dirt around the main stalk to see if there was something preying on its roots.

"What about fertilizing? Did you feed it?" Yun asked.

"Yes," Nima said without looking up.

"Did you put it in the right kind of soil?"

"*Yes.*"

"Does it get enough sun?"

Exasperated, Nima gestured at the open sky. Her back twinged, and she looked up with an even more unfriendly expression than she'd intended.

"Hm. Maybe it's getting *too* much sun," Yun mused, unfazed. "Or maybe this isn't a good place for it to grow."

Nima clenched her jaw and bent back down. Maybe the irritating child would get bored and wander away. After a few seconds she heard soft footsteps against the dust and dared to hope. But no luck.

"But I don't know," Yun said, from much nearer, almost right in front of Nima. "It *feels* like it wants to grow here." A brown hand appeared at the corner of Nima's vision, stroking the leaves of the one remaining spur.

Nima looked up sharply. "Don't touch it," she snapped.

Yun whipped her hand away and looked, for the first time, as if she were picking up on Nima's unwelcoming demeanor. "Why not?"

"Because it's *my* vine," Nima replied, hearing how ridiculous she sounded even as the words came out of her mouth. "What I mean is, it's fragile and it isn't polite to touch other people's crops."

This was evidently a new concept to Yun. "I help Aunt Lio with her beans all the time and she says—"

But Nima was done with this conversation she hadn't wanted in the first place. She didn't want what passed for local agricultural expertise, especially from a child, and needed peace and quiet to think about what to try next. "Then I'm sure she would appreciate your help now," she interrupted, then stood up and stalked away, pushing through the stiffness in her knees. "Don't touch my plants," she called over her shoulder without looking back.

Working on a half-baked theory that her bad mood was somehow hampering the vine's growth, Nima stayed away from it for the next few days. She kept a sharp eye on the fence, but the girl had vanished back to whatever ramshackle farmhouse she'd come from. Nima saw her traipsing by once on the road, but the girl showed no inclination to stop or pester the vine.

After a week, Nima woke up having slept well, and decided she'd waited enough time to test her theory. If her mood did somehow affect the vine, she'd given it time to recover and should be able to see the effects. She filled her big watering can, sprinkled in the special water-soluble fertilizer and lugged it out to the fence.

The vine looked exactly the same: anemic stalk and spurs, withered yellow leaves slowly crumbling off their ribs... and one perfectly healthy spur climbing slowly around the fence rail along the road. The good spur had even put out another two leaves while the rest of the plant died.

"What...?" Nima stood there, hands hanging down open at her sides. She had learned to grow things; the profusely healthy vegetable garden behind the house attested to that. She glared at the vine, disregarding the theory she'd been testing. "What do you *want* from me?" There was no reason this should be so hard, no reason this spur should thrive while the parent plant died, no reason the one plant that mattered should wither while the rest of the garden flourished.

A sharp trill pierced her despair. Yun was tromping down the road in heavy boots several sizes too big for her, swinging two empty beaten metal buckets, whistling like the cloudy morning had been made for her alone. There was something odd about the buckets; they were the wrong shape somehow, too rounded on the bottom, with asymmetric sides. Nima squinted at them and realized they were infantry helmets, inexpertly beaten into a slightly more bucket-like shape by a *very* amateur blacksmith.

"Did you figure out how to fix your plant?" Yun asked. She must have taken Nima's attempt to parse the helmets-turned-buckets as an invitation to stop and chat.

"No," Nima said, trying to think of a task that would take her away from the fence but allow her to keep an eye on the girl.

"It looks better, though," Yun said, waving one of the buckets at the flourishing spur. At least she wasn't trying to touch it. She wrinkled her nose. "That part, at least."

Nima picked up her watering can and began dribbling the water gently around the roots of the vine. Yun didn't take the hint. She tromped a few steps closer, set the buckets down with a dusty *thump*, and squatted on her haunches in front of the vine. "I think it's happier on this side of the fence."

"Plants don't feel happy or sad," Nima said repressively. She saw Yun shrug out of the corner of her eye.

"Aunt Lio says they do." Aunt Lio was evidently the arbiter of reality. She leaned closer. "What kind of plant is this anyway?"

"A hope vine," Nima said shortly, then surprised herself by continuing, "at least, it's supposed to be."

"I never saw one of those before," Yun said, scrunching up her nose and peering at the plant with renewed interest.

"They aren't very common after the war," Nima found herself explaining.

"Ah," Yun said sagely, although she wasn't old enough to remember even the final years of the war and couldn't possibly understand what lay behind the disappearance of the country's native resilient vegetation. "What's it for?"

For giving you and all your ungrateful kin a future worth growing into, Nima thought but did not say. The last thing she wanted was this girl's irate aunt descending to put the wizard in her place. "If it grows," she said, biting off each word, "it will reinforce the local ecosystem — that means the soil, the water, other plants, the animals that eat those plants, and people who rely on the plants and animals," she added, confident that the local school, if one even existed, did not cover the ecology of resilience.

"We have been having some problems," Yun agreed thoughtfully, just as if she were a grizzled veteran farmer. She leaned even closer to the vine, body rolling at such an angle that Nima feared she would pitch face first into the plant — and the railing.

"Be careful," she said, more harshly than she had intended.

Yun straightened up, but didn't look abashed. "I think maybe this part of the plant isn't bothered by something that's messing with the rest of it," she said. "Or maybe it just likes that I talk to it."

Yun's comment niggled at the back of Nima's brain. Maybe there *was* something affecting the roots or the leaves on the parent vine that hadn't spread to the healthy spur yet — or maybe the spur had some kind of natural resistance...

"I have to go restake the beans," Yun was saying in the background, but Nima was no longer paying attention. She didn't even notice the girl stretching out a stealthy hand to give the new leaves a friendly tap. "I'll be back tomorrow."

Yun kept turning up after that. Sometimes for an hour, sometimes for ten minutes, sometimes carrying her ridiculous repurposed buckets, sometimes hauling a feed sack on a little wagon, frequently with her arms full of hollow reeds as wide as her wrist and as tall as she was. She never seemed to be in a hurry or fear that whoever sent her on these tasks would be impatient at her dawdling. Aunt Lio either ran a slipshod operation or didn't particularly care what this niece was up to. Yun never mentioned her parents, so maybe she was a war orphan dumped on her only known relative. Maybe Lio had so much help on her farm that one lolly-gagging child made no difference. Or maybe they were just relieved to get a break from her questions.

"Do they have hope vines where you come from?" she asked one time.

"No," Nima said.

"Then how do you know how to grow one?"

I don't, Nima thought. "Resilient plants need the same things as any other plants—"

"Where *do* you come from anyway?" Yun interrupted.

"Not here," Nima said, picking up her rake and walking away.

"I know this isn't your farm," Yun said another time.

Nima was pruning back the dead leaves on the spurs closest to the healthy one, in case the problem was some kind of spore or mildew. Her shears jumped and nearly clipped a healthy leaf. "What is that supposed to mean?" she demanded.

"Everyone knows you aren't from here, even though you've lived here forever," Yun said with a limber shrug. "When are the people who belong to this farm coming back?"

"They aren't," Nima snapped.

"Maybe this would grow better if they did," Yun said, bumping the vine with grimy knuckles.

"Don't touch," Nima said, but she'd long since given up on the idea that Yun would listen.

"Don't worry, *I'm* not going away," Yun said, more to the vine than to Nima. "Hey look, there's a new grabby bit here!"

"How does a hope vine help the... ecosystem?" Yun asked after she'd been coming by regularly for almost a month.

"Different ways," Nima said distractedly, her words punctuated by the *thonk-crunch* of her trowel. She was digging some small trenches to drain excess water away from the hope vine's mound just in case the roots were becoming waterlogged. "Other things ... grow better ... near a hope vine. Fewer diseases ... more abundant production. Roots ... stop erosion and make dead soil fertile again. You can live ... off a single fruit ... for a long time. Healing tea or tincture from the leaves. And just being around the flowers..." she sat back on her heels and wiped her forehead, "I really can't explain what that feels like, you have to experience it for yourself."

"We could really use one of those," Yun said. "Aunt Lio says the beans need a miracle."

"Hope vines aren't miracles, they're applied magic," Nima said sternly. "And you shouldn't expect either to do your work for you."

"I am doing the work," Yun said, but without heat. "But there's a bug that came and it eats the buds before they can bloom." She reached a finger out toward the vine, then pulled it back again.

"What's it like?" Yun asked on one unreasonably hot day.

"What's what like?" Nima replied, only half listening as she teased a tendril gently through a gap in the climbing frame.

"Being a bad wizard."

Nima froze with the tendril balanced on one finger. "What do you mean by that?" she asked carefully. Sweat trickled between her shoulder blades.

"Everyone knows," Yun said without noticeable concern. "You're a bad wizard who made all the bad stuff happen in the war."

Nima snatched her hand away from the vine so she wouldn't transmit her feelings through the tender shoots. "That's a gross exaggeration."

"Also, I saw your thing," Yun pointed at Nima's right arm, where the geas runes constraining Nima's magic and her free movement crawled with slow abandon. She'd probably spotted it the first time they met, but Nima found herself tugging her sleeve down anyway, angry at her own shame. She hated any reminder that she was permanently separated from her magic, even though she'd accepted the geas binding to avoid lifetime imprisonment.

"Aunt Lio says getting a nice farm to run isn't a real punishment," Yun persisted. She reached out and casually flicked the vine. Nima winced, but the vine held firm. In fact, it flexed a tendril toward the sun.

Nima picked up her trowel, hefted it, set it down. She didn't like the idea of Yun and her aunt discussing her sentence as if were just moderately interesting village gossip. "Your Aunt Lio doesn't know everything. It's not a punishment. It's a collective obligation."

"Hah!" Nima wasn't sure whether Yun's hard, fierce laugh was meant to dismiss the possibility that Aunt Lio could be wrong or the official line that felt flat even to the wizard herself. "Then why do you have that?" Yun jabbed a finger at the geas runes.

"Yes, fine, technically it's a punishment," Nima said sharply, "but I *cooperated*. I *agreed* to community service. I could have just done my time, but I entered the program voluntarily to try to make amends for what happened. Nobody forced me to wear this." She shook her right arm at the girl. "Nobody forced me to be here."

"Then why don't you leave?" Yun asked in genuine curiosity.

In all the years she'd endured in this place, no one had ever asked Nima what she thought about her situation. It was humiliating to be grateful for a child's fickle attention, but her life was nothing but humiliations now.

"Because what the wizards did was wrong," Nima said, striving for patience. Not native to this farm and not native to her either. "We had the right — we had good intentions. But we did things that had consequences far beyond what we intended, beyond what we could have imagined when we started."

"What were you trying to do?" Yun asked. "Aunt Lio says all you wizards just wanted to keep your power and when the war happened you decided to burn the country down instead of sharing even one good thing with regular people."

There had been a time where Nima would have drowned in their own sweat anyone who dared speak so harshly, so honestly. "How fortunate that a bean farmer knows the absolute truth!" she snapped, then reined herself in. "Look, the war was complicated and you're too young to understand most of what happened."

Yun crossed her arms, stubborn. "Aunt Lio says the wizards hoarded all the best food and medicine and magic in their towers," she persisted. "She says the headwomen of all the villages went to the towers and asked for the wizards to share, but the wizards said they had nothing valuable to trade. So the villages stopped sending tithes to the towers and then the wizards came out of their towers and ruined everything. And Tonji says the wizards never loved anything but themselves and that's why they could do what they did to the land and the rivers and everything."

Nima had no idea who Tonji was and she didn't like their assessment of the war. "That's not an accurate picture," she said stiffly, although it was, if boiled down to its essence and told through the eyes of the victors. "There was... more to it." In the back of her mind she heard, was always hearing, the soul-shattering crack of her tower's foundations.

"Like what?" Yun asked pugnaciously.

Nima thought of her tower, its dimensions aligned precisely with the planes and angles of her interior self. Like a phantom limb, she could feel vast power seeping from the land into her tower's stones, and from its stones into her. Power that extended the reach of her hand as far as thought could take it, that honed her vision, peering keen-edged with magic into any secret she desired. When her tower stood, she was the secret composer of the song beneath everything... and then they had pulled her tower down and she was nothing. Keeper of a withered garden in a mutilated land. Bitterness welled up in her.

"I couldn't possibly explain it to you in a way you could comprehend," she said, aiming for austere, but coming no higher than cruel.

Yun gave her a very straight look then shrugged deliberately. "Well, it's not like you know the first thing about growing beans," she replied.

It toppled Nima like she was a tower herself. Yun hadn't spoken in pettiness, but rather with the world-weary familiarity of someone who often had to defend her own worth. Maybe she'd heard her aunt use the line and seen the seed of truth it held. Yun didn't know what it was like to wield power that could make and unmake the world. Nima didn't know how to grow beans. Once, the difference between them would have been too vast to comprehend. Now, it meant that between the two of them, Nima was merely the less capable subsistence farmer.

Nima was used to wrapping prickly defensiveness around herself like armor, but she suddenly couldn't reach it. They just sat there looking at each other, black eyes to brown. "I never had any reason to grow beans before," Nima said, conceding.

The silence stretched for several more minutes while Nima pretended to rearrange the dirt at the base of the vine's main stalk. "Wizards cared for the land a long time," she continued at last. "People couldn't see what we did. For generations we kept the soil fertile, managed the weather, sustained the forests...we didn't intend to destroy so much, not when the rebellion started and not after. We were just desperate to make the war stop."

Yun tilted her head skeptically. "If you wanted the war to stop, you could have just given the headwomen what they asked for. You didn't have to do all that bad stuff," she said.

Nima had used a lot of noble sentences and fine words to get her through the dark nights of doubt, but none of them volunteered to stand up against that unflinching logic. "You're right," she said, after a long minute. "But we did do it. I. I did it. All I can do now is try to repair what I can."

Yun glanced away as if the subject had never really been that interesting in the first place. "So why is this vine so important?"

Nima scrubbed her hands over her face. "This land, one of the things it has — had —" she paused. Started again. "A long time ago, wizards found a way to cultivate resilience. *Yes, wizards,"* she snarled at the skeptical look on Yun's face. "They taught seeds to grow hope, patience, and fortitude. They infused rivers with trust and stocked lakes with solidarity. They showed the land how to produce the things that would sustain it, no matter what came." She pressed her lips together and bit down hard on the sour feeling twisting her belly. "But the hope vines and trees of fortitude and all the rest of it didn't survive the war."

"Because of you," Yun interrupted. "You wizards, I mean. Right?"

"It wasn't just—" But it was. They had stretched out their hands and stripped the land of everything their forebears had grafted into it. She was out here trying to make amends for her role in that enormous crime, so what was the point of spinning a sweeter-sounding version of the truth to this child who wasn't buying it anyway? "Yes. Wizards weren't responsible for all the bad things that happened in the war, but they — we — did destroy the resiliency ecosystem. We did that."

"Why?" Yun asked.

A simple, deadly question. Nima had answers she'd given herself, answers she'd given her colleagues who doubted their course of action, answers she'd given the court that sentenced her.

Only we have the knowledge and experience to guide this country to its better future. Our better future requires peace and peace requires order, and order can only come when the villages bow to our authority.

These rebel armies are destroying the land — perhaps if they see harsh consequences they will surrender before we have to kill them all.

Some of the Wizard's Consortium chose to cross that final line and the rest of us let ourselves get pulled across.

So many answers. But none of them sufficient, in the end, to justify stripping the land of everything that held it together and helped it thrive. Not when you boiled it down to a young girl and an old wizard crouched on opposite sides of a fence in a dusty nowhere trying to understand why nothing good could grow.

"Because we forgot that wizards first built towers to serve and protect the land," she said at last. She suddenly became aware of how stiff and heavy her legs had become. "We thought of the land as something under our rule, not under our care. So when the rebels — when the war came, it was easy to use the land as a weapon."

Nima remembered standing atop her tower filled with grim righteousness as she stretched out her hands and drained the Ko

River into the bedrock. She remembered the sense of urgency that filled her heart when she walked in the fortitude groves, blighting the ancient trees to strip the rebels of their will to fight. She remembered having those feelings, but she couldn't reproduce them. Now, all she could feel was shame and despair at the enormity of what they had done. How could she ever have thought that growing one stupid hope vine would mean anything in the face of their atrocities? Even if she lived to be the oldest wizard in history and grew a new vine or tree every year, it would be a pitiful drop in the desert their crimes had created.

"And now wizards must undo what wizards did," Yun chanted the first line of the decree that doomed all surviving wizards to a lifetime of penal restitution — out here in the backlands, it was probably the only part of the decree she'd ever heard. She bopped one of the withered leaves unceremoniously. "You're not very good at it, huh?"

Nima lurched forward to cup the leaf, jerked herself back, then stared at it as it seemed to stretch out luxuriously. Was a deeper green flushing outward from the central rib, or were her eyes lying to her? "This work is much harder than I expected," she admitted.

Yun nodded sagely. "I bet it's hard to make this place hopeful when you aren't." Then her head shot up as if hearing a voice calling her. "Whoops, gotta go," she said. She hopped to her feet, scooped up her buckets, and took off at a steady trot down the road.

Nima watched her go, rolling her last words around and around. *It's hard to make this place hopeful when you aren't.* That could be the problem. Perhaps the hope vine couldn't grow if its tender had no hope of her own to share.

But then — Nima leaned over the leaf Yun had bopped, without touching it herself. It was noticeably greener and drooped less. And then — she peered down where Yun had been flicking her careless fingers, and there was one, no two! new tendrils peeking out. Nima thought about all the times she'd scolded Yun for touching the vine. Was it a coincidence that the healthy spur was the one closest to the road, the easiest one for Yun to reach? Was the vine nourishing itself off her innate hope for the future, a future Yun expected to be part of in exactly the way Nima didn't?

Nima brooded on it all night.

Yun came back the next day, and the next, chattering about the problem with Aunt Lio's bean crop. Nima made noncommittal noises or gave answers she forgot even as they came out of her mouth. The beans weren't her problem. She was watching Yun and the vine, trying to learn the secret of how she made it grow.

The girl didn't appear to be doing anything special. She didn't even seem to be paying attention to the vine most of the time, although she always crouched by it when she stopped, even though it meant she had to perch in the ditch on the side of the road. She would bump or stroke or tap the leaves or tendrils to emphasize a point or sometimes as if it were agreeing with her, but she might have done the same thing with her buckets or the wagon. She certainly didn't treat the vine with the care or deference that Nima herself did. Nima couldn't see any one thing that set Yun's interactions with the hope vine above her own — except, of course, that the vine grew where Yun touched it and withered everywhere she did not.

And 'grow' was a bit of an understatement. On Nima's side of the fence, the other spurs had desiccated into dry, spindly stalks, their leaves long since crumbled into the dirt. On Yun's side, seven feet of rich jade green sprouted leaves the size of Nima's palm, twisted tendrils around every surface of the climbing frame and the fence rails, and were sending out new spurs in two places. There was even one tiny green nub that, given time, would become a bud.

Nima never, ever touched the healthy spur. She even stood on the dead side of the plant to water and dress it, hoping not to poison it with indirect contact. She didn't encourage Yun to touch it either, superstitiously worried that the vine would pick up on her desperation and stop responding to Yun's presence. She just held herself in nervous stasis, waiting for the bloom.

Maybe it was the empty rattling of the sledge that drew Nima's attention, or maybe it was how Yun's feet dragged in the dusty road as she approached. Whatever it was, Nima looked up one day to see a new expression on Yun's face: despair.

The girl squatted in her usual place on the other side of the fence, her hands flopped over her knees and her black hair sticking to her sweaty temples. She didn't touch the vine.

"What's wrong with you?" Nima said, more harshly than she'd intended. But then, she'd never been a gentle person.

"The bean crop failed," Yun said, looking burdened in a way Nima had never seen her. "Aunt Lio says there's no way to save it now, even though we built reed irrigation all the way from the river and I pick off all the bugs I can find."

"I guess you'll have to eat something other than beans this winter," Nima said, trying to remember if beans had some sort of local cultural significance. "Variety is good for you."

Yun looked at her like Nima had just suggested they try to eat the sun. "We don't eat beans, we sell them," she said. Then, in a cadence that sounded like something she'd heard from someone else many times, "No beans, no money. No money, no winter stores, no shoes, no seeds for spring."

"Oh," Nima said. Of course Yun's entire livelihood hung on those stupid beans. "That's...bad."

Yun sighed heavily and gave the swollen bud close to her face the gentlest of caresses. Nima sucked in her breath, but Yun didn't notice and the vine didn't show any immediate negative effects. "Do you know any way to fix the beans?" she asked suddenly, looking a little nervous for the first time Nima could remember. "I mean...I know you said we shouldn't expect magic to fix our problems, but you also said wizards used to take care of the land..."

"Not with this," Nima said, jerking her right arm in a sharp motion so the geas runes caught the light.

"Oh, right," Yun said, subsiding back despondently. She sighed again. "We sure could use one of these hope vines right now." Nima suddenly recognized the line as something she'd heard Yun saying a lot lately.

That night, Nima found herself thinking of Yun's beans instead of the hope vine. There wasn't any reason to be thinking about either one — all she could do for the vine was what she'd done, and Yun was someone else's problem — but she kept coming back to it like a piece of food stuck between her molars. It wasn't just the girl's despair; Nima hadn't spent a century as a powerful wizard with a tower of her own because she was susceptible to sad peasant children. But what if the bean crop's failure forced Yun and her family to leave the farm? What if they starved? What would happen to the hope vine if Yun suddenly stopped coming by, telling her cheerful stories and helping pass the long weary days with impertinent questions?

And more than that — Yun's intervention, however unintentional, had resuscitated Nima's own hope of escaping this pastoral prison. Which, in a way, put her in Yun's debt.

And that was the nub of the problem, Nima realized as she dried her dinner dishes. She felt indebted to Yun, who had helped her while enduring Nima's constant unwelcoming attitude. And there was a way to repay her. But it would cost Nima the one thing she valued: the opportunity to leave.

On the other hand, if she didn't pay this debt, Nima would be proving Aunt Lio and Tonji right: that wizards would rather let the land and everyone who depended on it suffer than share even one good thing. And even more than she hated being in debt, more than she hated being here, Nima found she hated the idea that Lio and her ilk could be right about her after all. If they were, then Yun would keep believing they were right about the war, would keep thinking wizards were bad people who embraced destruction to feed their own selfishness.

"Damn and damn!" she swore, looking down to discover she'd worried her washing cloth into threads.

She couldn't repair the land. She couldn't undo the systemic destruction they'd wrought, not even in a wizard's lifetime.

She could save one bean farm. She could persuade one girl — maybe one family — that wizards could help as well as harm. Not just for show, or to win release, but because she wanted Yun to welcome a future with wizards in it as enthusiastically as she welcomed everything else. It would cost at least a year of her life; there was no guarantee that this hope vine would fruit two years in a row. But after eleven years of loneliness and failure, was one more really such a sacrifice?

"Yes it *is*," Nima snarled to the empty room, to herself. "But wizards must undo what wizards did." Then she picked up her lamp and stomped out of the house.

Hope vines thrived on promises, after all.

Nima waited with characteristic impatience for Yun to arrive the next morning, but the girl didn't appear until mid-afternoon, trudging along in her too-big boots and carrying her mangled helmet buckets. She flashed Nima a wan smile as she crouched down by the vine, petting it as if seeking comfort from the silky leaves.

"How are the beans?" Nima asked awkwardly after a minute. She hadn't thought about this part, not once she'd made her decision. And, she realized, she'd never started one of their conversations before today. It was always Yun, interrupting her work with a question or observation.

"Still bad," Yun said. "Aunt Lio says we'll be lucky to get a quarter of the crop."

"Well, look," Nima said, her eyes fixed on the hope vine while her hands fiddled anxiously in the dirt. "This thing is about to flower. If it fruits, I could — you could have it. You could plant it near your beans. I'm sure it would grow for you."

Yun looked up, her eyes shining in a way Nima had never seen. It was like all the dust had washed right out of her world. "You mean it? We could have a hope vine of our own?"

"It won't make your bean plants come back," Nima warned. "Probably."

"But it means they'll grow good next year!" Yun said with an enormous grin. "That's right, isn't it? Everything grows better where a hope vine grows?"

"That's the theory," Nima agreed. She felt surprisingly guilty giving the girl hope when she wasn't sure the vine was capable of producing a fruit this late in the season. But then, hope was all she had to offer, from beginning to end.

"But... wait." Yun crinkled up her face around her nose. "Don't you have to send that fruit to your Arbiter? So they send you on to your next place?"

"There will be another fruit, in another year," Nima said with forced calm, giving the vine an affectionate little stroke with the back of her hand. And to her utter astonishment, a tiny bright green tendril unfurled from beneath her knuckles.

The vine bloomed four days later, opening like a star and drawing the eye from anywhere in the garden. Nima found herself staring at it for uncounted time, just tracing its silky depths with her eyes. She could see, if she looked closely in the way wizards were trained to do, runes tracing and retracing themselves deep within the flower's genetic structure. But mostly she just stood beside the vine, falling into its radiance.

Two days after the bloom, Nima came out early to gaze at the flower. It was a habit she'd fallen into immediately, getting in close to the luminous petals, tracing the dew that beaded gently on their surface, filling her lungs with the flower's scent before facing the tasks of the day. It made the whole day seem more bearable; no, it made tomorrow seem so promising it was worth today's labor.

At the cottage door she gasped in horror; even from that distance she could see the blossom was withered, almost completely gone after only two days. What would she tell Yun? How had she killed the flower so quickly even when everything seemed to be going well?

But when she drew close, crouching down and parting the leaves with trembling hands, she saw the flower had died a purely natural death. Hope blossomed fleetingly, it seemed, or perhaps her decision had hurried it along. There, glowing greeny-golden as a brand-new promise, a small orb poked up from the heart of the crumpled petals.

The vine's first fruit.

See R.E. Dukalsky's story "Hope on the Vine" online at Metaphorosis.
If you liked it, leave a comment. Authors love that!
Remember to subscribe to our e-mail updates so you'll know when new stories are posted.

About the story

"Hope on the Vine" grew from two very different seeds. In my non-writing professional life, I work on peace processes, political transitions, and rule of law, which means I spend a lot of time thinking about the aftermath of conflict. In my reading experience, speculative fiction tends to focus on how conflicts begin, how they are fought, or how they end — but not the long generational slog toward (or away from) peace that comes after. (In this, spec fic mirrors "real" life in countries that observe, but haven't recently experienced, conflict.) It's not just about rebuilding shattered infrastructure; it's also about restoring trust between communities, keeping peace talk promises, and demonstrating the will to make a future different from the past. Making peace also requires that societies acknowledge the wrongs committed in the past, hold the perpetrators accountable, and try to repair what can be repaired (a series of processes collectively called transitional justice). It's hard, slow work with many steps sideways or backward as well as forward, requiring change in systems and institutions but also in individual hearts.

One of the most difficult elements to rebuild after conflict are the characteristics that help societies hold together. These intangibles are often vaguely categorized as "resiliency factors," and they include trust, tolerance, a sense of a shared future, community solidarity, and, yes, hope. This story is an attempt to envision what transitional justice might look like in a world with magic, where resiliency factors are tangible things. I wanted to write about a perpetrator coming to terms with both her own past crimes and her role in repairing the greater harm to which those crimes contributed. I also wanted to look at a world where wizards were held accountable for their deeds, not by a group of brave heroes, but by a court and a system of law. And finally, I wanted to imagine a post-conflict scenario where subsistence farmers finally got some justice.

The other seed for this story is much more literal. I'm terrible at growing squash. I can grow many tasty things and squash are notoriously easy plants, but for some reason they elude me. I've spent many days just like Nima, screaming "why won't you just grow?" at a withering squash vine. Fortunately, my life and freedom have never depended on a zucchini or a kabocha, but I wanted to convey the sense of helpless frustration that comes from doing everything you can think of for a growing thing and still seeing it fail.

So that's where "Hope on the Vine" comes from: meditations on transitional justice and my own gardening mishaps. Hopefully you enjoyed the hybrid they created.

A question for the author

Q: What's your favorite *non*-SFF book?

A: I have never been able to answer this kind of question with just one favorite book. I love *The Secret History of the Mongol Queens* by Jack Weatherford and *King Leopold's Ghost* by Adam Hochschild because they changed the lens through which I saw the world, making it feel bigger and more connected at the same time. Hilary Mantel's *Wolf Hall* will always be among my top books for her complex portrayal of flawed but extremely human characters. *Midnight's Children* by Salman Rushdie got its feverish hooks into my brain over a decade ago and never let go. Ask me this question again in a year and the list might be different, but it won't be any shorter.

About the author

R.E. Dukalsky writes speculative fiction about conflict and what happens afterward. She has been told that she has School House Rock charm and that she would make an excellent rebel leader, among other dubious accolades. She lives in the Pacific Northwest in a house that perpetually needs more bookshelves.

@tiltingwindward

Mission and Submission

Will Gwaun

Amir and Sahia lay side by side in the narrow berth, waiting to hear if there was a home waiting for them out there in the darkness of space. They held hands. In the rhythm of her breath, he felt the pendulum of her thoughts swinging from fear back to hope, and his own thoughts turned to follow.

Years ago, centuries now, Amir had felt in those moments as if he could sense the whole ship holding its breath. He'd once imagined the thousands of crew in the cabins adjoining theirs, some freshly woken from hibernation, some born on board and awake their whole lives, but all in some sense beside him, clinging to that same hope: a planet where, at last, the ship could land. Now, Amir thought of most of those crew as strangers, jealous of his and Sahia's places in hibernation pods. He pressed his body closer to hers, this sliver of warmth and hope in all the vast expanse of nothing and cold. Now, in these moments, he felt nothing beside him but Sahia.

A hologram schematic of the ship's journey so far floated in their optics. Earth, now many trillions of kilometres behind them, winked in the corner of the cabin. From it ran the line of the ship's trajectory, and branching from that, the routes of the probes the ship had launched along the way. Each branch ended at a planet that had promised to be a home; the long-range scans had shown them to be similar enough to Earth. The ship had been turned and steered towards them, launching the close-scanning probes and driving them ahead with powerful lasers. But each time the transmissions from those probes returned, they carried news of disappointment.

Amir ran his finger along that undulating path, remembering the awful dangers each of those planets had concealed. Radiation, tectonic chaos, wild storms hidden by the cloud layer. And never a hint of life.

The ship only carried enough fuel to decelerate once from its astonishing velocity, and none of those planets had been safe enough to justify it. So on they went, changing course after each disappointment and climbing back into the hibernation pods for another long, cold sleep of centuries. At least, that was how it had been. After those first few disappointments, after the hibernation had proven itself less safe than the research had claimed, more and more of the crew had decided to give up on the voyage and live out their lives awake on board the ship.

It should never have been that way. The pods should have preserved their bodies without risk or side effect. But then, no one had thought they'd have to use them so long and so many times. No one had believed that the hope of all those worlds could be false, so no one had thought too deeply about the many and unique ways each individual body might degrade under the strain of dozens of sleep-wake cycles, immune cells turning mutinous, memories fogging in neural debris, chromosomes warping until their cells grew cancerous.

This world ahead of them now, though... This one looked more promising than any yet. They'd learnt from all those disappointments, learnt from the discrepancies between the long-range scans and the close-ups sent from the probes, learnt to filter the signal from the noise masquerading as hints of vital elements and gases, taught their algorithms to pick through the magnetic fields for the toxic thrum of dying atoms. These scans were pure, and this world promised to be the one.

In the hologram, a blip showing the position of the data packet returning from the probes approached the ship with agonising slowness. They should have woken in time with its arrival, but the probes' journey had been delayed by some few hours. It felt like days.

"I dreamt about the world ahead, I think," Sahia murmured in that low voice she used when speaking to herself.

"Yes? What did you see?" Amir asked, amused, as ever, by her surprise that she'd spoken her thoughts aloud.

She rolled onto her side to face him, that teasing glint creeping into her smile. "Other people's dreams are fundamentally impossible to find interesting," she said, quoting a faux pas of his from some fundraising-for-the-mission dinner, a lifetime ago but still funny to them. The teasing sparked a prickle of desire in his stomach, and he slide his hand over her palm, lacing his fingers between hers.

"Not your dreams, Sih, *other people's* dreams." He pouted, impersonating that outrageously-over-rouged heiress-and-possible donor he'd offended at the dinner, quoting the rebuke she'd given: " 'This dream, I assure you, is quite fascinating.' "

He held the raised eyebrow a moment and then dropped the act, lowering his head on the pillow, reaching out to slide her hair back from her cheek. "Please, Sih. I love to hear your dreams." It was true. It felt like a gift to be let into that strange and private world.

They looked at each other for a moment, and the smile she gave him made his heart shiver.

"I don't know." she said. "It's mostly a blur. I was waking from the deep."

The mention of deep sleep made Amir suddenly conscious of the ache in his back and the numbness in his feet. They'd been in deep almost two hundred years. It shouldn't have mattered how long you were down for; it was the waking from deep that took its toll, the draining of the desiccating and freezing agents. He shifted in the bed. At least the ringing in his ears and the thudding in his head had passed.

"You remember something?" he asked.

"In the dream, the sky was lilac, like you said. I want to retract my bet." They always made a bet. On Earth they had both worked on the sensors that performed the scans, and that question about the colour of the sky seemed to be asked at every press or outreach event. One could answer with educated guesses based on refraction and reflection, the fingerprints of gases and starlight. But atmospheres had many layers, so one never knew the sky's colour for certain until the probes punched the clouds, turned their eyes skyward and returned their scans.

"No, no, no." He squeezed her hand. "You bet orange, and we shook."

"Which do you want it to be, though? When we get there and look up at the sky, which do you want to see?"

Blue was the obvious. Blue would likely be the colour of an atmosphere close to Earth's. That might make things easier. But Amir hadn't come all this way to find another Earth. He'd been dreaming of other worlds since he first saw the night sky from somewhere beyond the smog and streetlight haze of the city, young enough to sit on his mother's shoulders and be told how every star was a distant sun where planets might turn, on which life might dwell. Through school and college and post-doc and professorship, he'd done and thought of almost nothing else but ways to look deeper into the dark of space for the tell-tale signals of distant worlds.

"How did it feel in your dream? Being under a sky that colour?" He imagined it, how the settlement would look as it unfolded from the ship, the plans they'd spent decades on coming to fruition in the glow of a lilac noon.

"I could live happily under lilac."

They held hands and watched the blip crawl those last centimetres to the ship.

Amir and Sahia lay side by side on the bed, staring up at the hologram of another useless world.

"I really thought this one was..." she began, but trailed off, the disappointment too heavy, too mundane and miserable to put into words.

There was no avoiding these cycles of hope and disappointment. They could not simply remain in hibernation until a suitable planet was finally found. The length of that slumber had to be decided in advance, and could be neither shortened nor extended. The dosage of freezing and desiccating agents seeded in the tissues had to be measured exactly, and, once there, could not be cleared from the tissues without their destruction.

For those of the crew who wished to avoid using up their lifespan aboard the ship, the routine was to go into hibernation until the moment the probes' scans were due to arrive. They would wake to see the results, hoping to need return only once more into the deepness for the final leg of the journey to the planet they'd call home. Instead, each time they'd woken to learn the planet they'd found had proved to be a failure, like all those before, and they would have to return to hibernation as the ship took them onwards into the darkness.

"It isn't certain it's a failure," Amir said. "Not absolutely, not yet."

But it was. The comms channels flickered with the discussion between a score of different expert groups, each with their own analyses of this world's hidden treachery. There would be a vote soon, but the preliminary polling was so clear that it was hardly worth it. They would go on to the next planet, or at least to the point where the transmissions from the probes would intersect the ship's vector. Three hundred something years of ship time.

On the channels, people were already talking about whether they would take that sleep. Of the thousands of crew, there were still some five hundred like Amir and Sahia, born on Earth and in it for the long haul. The others had peeled off slowly; after six or seven or ten disappointments, they'd decided they couldn't risk the hibernations anymore. They wanted to take a chance at some kind of life on board. The ship held facilities meant to provide the building blocks of the settlement: hydroponic greenhouses and algae vats to feed and clothe them, observatories and laboratories where they might study these uncharted worlds, even spaces for schooling and sports could be made within the inner centrifuge. It was enough to make a life in, so people said.

Amir avoided hearing about the life built by those who'd given up on the journey. Meagre as it must be, there was a siren call feel to it. It could hardly be worse than the cupboard of an apartment he'd grown up in, in that bleak, fume-choked city crumbling into the ocean.

Sahia rolled on her side and stared out of porthole at the stars and the darkness between. "Do you ever think..." she said, and a long silence followed.

He looked at her, the dark rings of her hair coiled on the pillow, the contour of the muscles in her shoulder. Even more beautiful now than in all the years he'd known her.

"What?" he asked.

He heard in her breath the weighing of whether she should finish that thought aloud or not. "You ever think we should have stayed on Earth?" she said at last.

"No," he answered automatically. He hadn't, and even the question provoked a wave of anger he couldn't quite understand. "What is there on Earth?"

"Well, it's not a question of what is, not anymore. But don't you think about the things there were, the things we left behind?"

"Of course I do. But..." he laid his hand on her shoulder. He wanted her to look at him. They were the same age, but his skin looked aged beside hers, ashen and cracked around the knuckles. He tried to remember if he'd noticed that before, but didn't think he had. "The risk is worth it. There're still thousands more stars. There's a world for us out there."

"I don't know. This deep was hard. I mean, the doctors didn't say anything, but it felt harder. Didn't it to you?"

"No." He felt the mood between them slipping, like a wandering comet dragged into the gravity well of some dead star. "Why don't we look at the scans for the next planet? The data from the probe might show us something about them—"

"Not now. I can't just sit here anymore. I want to go walk around a bit, see the habitats." She got up, and he watched her dress. It frightened him. They didn't walk around; the only place to do that was the inner centrifuge, which housed the communal habitats used by the ship-born—the descendants of those crew who'd centuries ago abandoned the hibernation pods and made their lives on board. The long-haulers, those who'd come from Earth and still clung to the plan of sleeping through that long journey, didn't want to know about the lives of those ship-born. That, at least, was the mostly unspoken consensus that Amir felt. Long-haulers didn't really regard ship-born as part of the exodus at all, but rather some detail encountered between Earth's cradle and humankind's destiny in the depths of space. What was the sense in getting to know people, only to go back into a deepness you would not wake from before they and their children and grandchildren were long dead? Long-haulers didn't go up into the inner centrifuge at all. They went from hibernation pod to cabin and back, hoarding all the life they had left for the future, when at last it arrived.

Sahia sat at the end of the bed. Amir lay on his side, staring at a hologram schematic of sensor calibrations for the probes being readied for send-off, not to the next planet they would reach, but to those further ahead, just in case. This was his speciality, the role that had bought him this place on the ship. But in truth he could hardly follow the schematic. The crew who'd given up on the hibernation, and their children and grand- and great-grandchildren, had been refining these technologies for centuries, while Amir lay in hibernation. But whatever advances the ship-born made, he assured himself he could catch up once they finally arrived at the planet. After all, most of what he knew was self-taught. But then, that was back on Earth, with the minds of millions always at his fingertips. The ship rumbled, the drives firing to turn its course by fractions of a degree.

"You should at least go and see what they've built, Amir. It's quite amazing. That whole centrifuge, it's like a jungle, like a village in the jungle. All the metal, everything is hidden. I mean, they've had a long time to do it, but it's still astonishing. Rivers, gardens, even the light through the branches looks enough like the sun."

Amir said nothing. His parents had grown up in a farming village at the edge of the jungle, and spoke of the place with nothing but contempt. A quiet tide of anger was building inside him. Her leaving the lower decks felt like an act of betrayal. "I'm not interested in seeing simulations of a planet we left behind. The course is set; we should be getting ready to go into deep."

She didn't answer for a long time, and when she did, he realised he'd known for a long time what was coming. "I don't know if I can keep doing this, Amir. My bones hurt."

"The medicals say we're both fine." Not everyone had had their luck. Each time they woke, someone they knew had suffered something, and now they heard someone had not woken up at all.

"But how long? How many more times are we going to roll the dice? It was supposed to be the first one we reached. But if there's none? What if there's nowhere else for us?"

"How could there be nowhere?" He'd spent his academic career arguing the opposite. Arguing that advances in scanner technology made it obvious that it was no longer a question of *if* there was a planet somewhere that could support human life, but *which* of the many they should go to first. That the ship was yet to encounter one was just bad luck against good odds. Sahia knew that too. Her career had matched his, always aiming them towards this role, this mission, as if the trajectory of the ship had begun not on the launch pad, but back in the classroom of their elementary school. Somewhere, accelerating along that path, he'd realised he'd fallen in love with her, the only person he'd ever met with dreams as big as his.

"And what if there's somewhere, but we wake up to find we're dying? We could live on board. We're still young enough."

He swiped the hologram away and stared out at the stars beyond the window. "Young enough for what?"

She answered so quietly he barely heard her, but he knew what she was saying. "A life. A life outside of this. All we ever did on Earth was work."

She looked at him, and a part of him he didn't want to listen to felt the sudden urge to agree with her. Study and learn and work, that had been their lives. Through childhood and on, it was their companionship that had made it possible, made the crushing expectations of their parents manageable. Sometimes it was only the solidarity of ten-year-olds that had kept the shame of a less-than-perfect exam result from being too much to bear. He looked back at her, and felt a softening creep in, an opening in his heart.

"Maybe this is more like the home we've been looking for than anything we'd found out there," she said, and the opening slammed suddenly shut.

Was all that work to have been for nothing? Were they people who gave up?

He stood, paced across the room. "What could there be here? This is purgatory. This is prison!"

"Friends. Time for ourselves. I don't know. Time for... There's still work here, you know? Still research being done. People are still part of this project, of going to another world, even if it's not them that reach it, but their children, or their grandchildren."

The word 'children' froze him in place. A word they'd drifted by several times in their lives, though it had never drawn them into its orbit. Even if she wasn't saying it directly, he knew what she was asking. And children meant giving up one's place in the limited number of hibernation pods. That was the protocol that a dozen generations had agreed to on board, while Amir and Sahia and the other long haulers slept. The population had grown. More people wanted a chance in those pods than there were places. So that was the rule. Once you had children, your place was given up, allocated to your children, or if they declined it, by lottery to other hopefuls of their generation.

Amir had been furious when he'd first discovered that such a change in the rules had been made in the absence of those still sleeping. It undermined the very principle of consensus democracy and protection of minorities that should govern the ship and colony-to-be, principles thrashed out in hundreds of hours of pre-launch meetings. But he understood it well enough. Deep in the human mind there was the imperative that the code inside one's genes would have a chance to live forever, one way or another. And besides, he'd seen in the records that there were movements among the ship-born population not to support the hibernation pods at all, that their drain on resources was unnecessary. Terrifying to think what such movements could do if they grew large enough, now that consensus had given way to the wishes of the majority. There were more ship-born than long-haulers now, and more importantly, they were awake while Amir and the others slept. What could be done to stop them? What good were those principles they'd defined, without some authority to enforce them? Better then, that the ship-born have a stake in the pods' ongoing functioning.

That thought unfroze him, bringing his anger to a boiling rage — that 'they' would have the temerity to make decisions for those like Amir who'd created this entire undertaking in the face of every doubt and opposition.

"So that's what you're telling me? That you're glad we've found nothing? No planet, no home, no risk, no more work." The words blurted from Amir's mouth like gas from a blown airlock. "Now we get to stay on board, where it's nice and safe and nothing changes, and live in tree houses and play happy families? That's what you want, after everything we've given to get here?"

Sahia didn't cry. A hard few years of childhood in the flood camps had crushed that out of her. But there was something that happened to her body, her voice, an inward sagging like a balloon seeping air—the way she'd looked for almost a year when her mother, her only family, had died without warning. "I want some life with you, Amir, that's what I want. Don't you?"

"You think I want to have a family here? This is a society of people who've given up. You think that's the father I want to be?"

Sahia's expression became one of wounded disbelief, one that for a moment he could not fathom, until, by that strange telepathy of long companionship, he realised he knew what she thought he was referring to. Remembered a baking-hot night when they were sixteen, standing on the rooftop of their apartment building. She told him then about another night, a decade before, where she and her mother and father had fought through the flood waters, Sahia and her mother floating on a broken door, her father in the water trying desperately to kick against the current and push them to dry land, hour after hour. She'd told him how, when at last a rescue boat appeared and caught them in its spotlight, she'd watched her father just let go of the door and slide under the water, too exhausted to go on.

She'd said she didn't know how to stop being angry at him for giving up, and he'd felt utterly lost for something helpful to say, felt how profoundly childlike he seemed beside her. That feeling was still there, knotted up among all those other threads that wove together into their marriage. And suddenly that angered him, made him feel as if it were some trick to persuade him to acquiesce to the superiority of her argument, the maturity of her perspective.

"You think I'm talking about *that*?" He was shouting. "You think I'd say a thing like that to persuade you? How low do you think—"

"I'm asking you to have the courage to see what's really in front of us, Ami. Sometimes we have to be brave and just accept change, and what we can't change."

He didn't know what to do with his anger. The weight of what she was asking of him crushed the breath from him, as if a black hole had opened in his future. He left without a word. Marched down the corridor, head down. The ache of the deep still groaned in his joints, but he couldn't stop. If he stayed, he would do what she wanted. He knew that. He couldn't look at her like that and not feel every fibre of his thoughts realign to find a way to offer her solace. And he wouldn't be held to ransom that way. It wasn't fair. So he didn't stop until he reached the inner ring where the pods lay, most already filled with the sleepers who'd returned directly after the disappointment of the scans.

The hibernation process was automated. He only needed to strip off his clothes, lie down in the pod, strap the bands around his arms and thighs, and give the commands. He worked as automatically as the machines, giving the command to put him under for another three hundred years, ready to wake when the next transmissions arrived. The clearance chit flickered on the display. He felt the needles ease into his skin, and the cold begin to spread into his muscles.

It was only as his heart began to slow that he realised what a risk he'd taken, how unfair and stupid his assumption was that she would find out what he'd done and follow him. She would be, should be, angry at him. Furious. There'd been no agreement between them. He'd felt trapped and acted out of anger. He knew she would understand that. But that didn't mean... What if she stayed? What if he woke and she was long dead? The world shrank towards darkness. There was nothing to be done.

Amir lay in his pod waiting for control to return to his muscles. A hologram flickered into life in front of his face, offering him a status update. A cursor blinked, led by the movement of his eyes. Through the glass of the pod's front panel, he could hear the muffled sound of cheers, people calling back and forth through the vast space of the hibernation hall.

With only the movement of his eyes, it was agonisingly slow to pull up Sahia's status. When at last he managed, it glowed orange, showing she was in hibernation, but before he could read more, a message from her overlaid itself across the screen. Sahia's face, smiling that indestructible smile of hers that she wore as armour against all the hardship that life was built from. She looked exhausted, aged, shrunken against her bones, black smears under her eyes. When she spoke, there was the edge of a tremble in her voice.

"Amir, I want you to hear this from me. I've tried many times to record this so you will understand me, but somehow I can't find the words I need, so I will just tell you as clearly as I can. I'm recording this message forty-two years since we last spoke, long in the past for you now. I have been awake for two years now. After you went off... after we argued, I didn't know if I would follow you. I know you were angry at me, and when you went into the deepness without me, I was angry also. But I came with you. I could not leave that argument as our last moment together. But... but there was some mistake. The dosage of hibernating agents was not metabolised correctly, and I woke after forty years. I was very ill, for a long time, and I couldn't help feeling like... like it was your fault. I hated feeling like that, but I couldn't..." She looked away from the camera, her smile wavering, looked back, trying to draw the smile back together, then left its ruins where they lay. "I lived with the shipborn for these last years. I needed it. My hope has returned. I don't think you could hear what I was trying to tell you about how much of me had given up. But living with them here, I feel like, even if the planet is never found, something very special has been created here, and I think you would see the same, if you let yourself come and experience it. But... I miss you too much, Ami. I miss you, and I hate that you won't ever give this up, but that is what I love you for too. You never give up. I wish I could make this choice with you, but you're in there, and I'm here, so this is all I can offer. You know the next planets that we send probes to. The next four are only just 'maybes', and five is hardly even a 'maybe'. But six is a likely candidate, good as any. My body will most likely not cope with more than four or five more wakings at the very most, so I'm choosing to go into the deepness for the long haul. Till the sixth planet. In my heart... I know it will hurt you to hear this, but in truth I've lost the belief that any of them will be safe for us, even the sixth. But I know there's a chance, and I want to give you as many chances as I can. I want use what chances I have left as intelligently as possible. When I wake for the scans from the sixth, and it's good, I'll still have the strength to go into hibernation for the journey there. With luck I'll have the strength to wake and begin our new life. But if it's another disappointment, I won't go down again. I want to have some life here, and I hope... If we still have no luck, I hope you will want that too. I know that in many ways, this is a gamble, but isn't everything? If things go as I hope they will, I'll see you in two thousand six hundred and twenty-nine years. I love you, Ami."

When the message finished, he lay in the pod, fear and guilt and love and shame all twisting together in his gut. Other messages began to ping on his screen, short blasts of triumphant, congratulatory text from colleagues who'd been with them all the way from earth. 'We did it!' 'Told you it was this one!' 'Last one on the surface buys the drinks!' A realisation formed. The cheering— the scans were back; they'd found a home.

Amir lay beside Sahia, though separated from her by the walls of his pod and hers. He'd looked over the data the probes had returned. The world would be hard, but good enough. Everything he'd dreamed of. The sky in the habitable zone was a warm, reddish brown. He could live under that.

The pod's voice asked him to confirm the length of the hibernation. He closed his eyes, imagining the way it would be as the ship landed and settlement began, as those plans he'd spent his lifetime making finally began to unfold. He imagined his footprint in the dust of that alien world, a moment he'd imagined since childhood, an image he'd drawn over and over with crayon and biro and smart pen in the margins of exercise books, lecture notes and the minutes of departmental meetings. The thought of it pulled on him, a gravity too massive to escape.

The pod urged him to answer. "Please confirm."

The words stuck in his throat. The new world was right there, subjectively only moments away. One quick sleep, and the purpose of these years of struggle would finally be reached. He felt the piled weight of his long-dead family's expectations. They had wanted him to do something sensible, something respectable and safe, medicine, law, had given their lives for him to do that. Only Sahia had kept him from giving into them. Now he was just a button push away from proving he'd been right.

"Please confirm," the pod repeated.

He'd paced their cabin for hours, struggling with the decision, his thoughts tearing against each other in straining equilibrium—a blazing star, neither quite blasting apart nor collapsing, the explosive force of its fusing atoms grasped in the vastness of its own gravity. The guilt of forcing her into a sleep that had almost killed her. His distrust and anger at the ship-born, and yet the hope that their achievements brought him for the future on this at-last-found world. The anger at the position she'd put him in. The deep acceptance that she'd been right in that moment, even if she'd been wrong in the end. Only now was he finally sure; what else could he do that would not risk too much?

"Confirm hibernation," he said. "Two thousand six hundred and twenty-nine years."

He would sleep, on and on until Sahia woke. Hopefully the settlement would prosper and there would be people there to welcome them. But if they woke in the empty husk of the ship, or not at all, it was a risk worth taking. He wondered if the settlers would work on the atmosphere until the sky tinged closer to sheer blue of Earth's, or if their factories might fill it with grey and choking smog before he woke, or some error might boil it from the planet so that he would wake once more beneath the blackness of space. In the end, it would not matter, for he knew that without Sahia there was no sky he could stand under and call that place his home.

See Will Gwaun's story "Mission and Submission" online at Metaphorosis.
If you liked it, leave a comment. Authors love that!
Remember to subscribe to our e-mail updates so you'll know when new stories are posted.

About the story

As with most of my stories, they seem to appear out of ideas sort of slamming together and producing a narrative. In the past these were usually pretty abstract and weird, ('What about the medieval catholic idea of itemised penance per mile of pilgrimage, combined with the technical problems of robots creating maps of their environments!?' is an example of something my brain will bother me with in the middle of the night, and then not leave me alone till I've written about it. See my very old story 'No S.L.A.M Maps for These Territories' for the result.) but recently they seem to be getting much more personal.

This one came about in the sort of emotional whiplash that followed finally finishing (after many false starts and near giving ups) my first novel after five years, and then not managing to sell it anywhere. I'm not under any illusion that I 'deserved' to sell it, after all you're competing with all the books ever written, plus the thousands of others from talented people arriving on editors' desks every month, and getting good at something usually takes more than one try, but it is a weird thing to pour all that work and effort into something and then just put it in a drawer. Writing seems unlike any other artistic endeavour in that way. At least with music or painting, even if you don't sell something you get to jam with your friends (or some other phrase that will make me sound less uncool) or hang it on your wall, but who has the time to read people's (probably often deservedly) unpublished novels, when there isn't the time to read all the amazing published novels that are in the world already?

Anyway, I was trying to find a way to express that feeling of sending bits of fiction you've poured all that work into out into the void of publishing, waiting for months (hats off to Metaphorosis for answering at what is practically lightspeed) and then receiving some form rejection.

At the same time, I was going through all the turmoil of working out of when it would make sense to start a family in the midst of trying to forge a career in a foreign country, and realising that this emphasis we have in our culture on 'never giving up on your dream' can be a pretty toxic thing for a lot of people, given the sacrifices it can mean. Finally, the of Boomer/Millennials/Gen-Z conflict narrative was starting to appear a lot online and in the media, which I found sort of alternately fascinating and depressing.

All of these things were sort of washing around in my head, and what fiction, especially speculative fiction, allows you to do is sort of cram all those ideas down into a single narrative thread, in a situation of heightened intensity, and then explore why that matters to the characters.

A question for the author

Q: Do you ever feel bad for what you put your characters through?

A: Hmm, not directly, no, but in a certain way, yes. I've heard some authors talk about how they 'have conversations with their characters' and so feel guilt for what happens to them, but this isn't something I really relate to.

There's that debate in cognitive science about whether we understand other people's mind through simulating in our own heads what it's like be them, or through forming theories about what they must be thinking. From my very layman's understanding of the debate, I feel like both of those things happen at different times, and different people seem to be inclined to engage in one mode more than the other. Most of the time that I'm writing, I feel like I'm much more in that 'theory' mode, trying to make sure that characters have motivations that make sense and act accordingly. Sometimes this leads to me sort of taking a perspective that isn't really my own, and with some stories that creates this feeling of 'wow, that would be a very bleak way of looking at the world'. To that extent, I do 'feel bad' for characters, and also there are moments when I get these sorts of flashes of empathy for the characters, where I can almost feel in my body what the emotions they're experiencing would be like (which I think of as being in 'simulation mode'). I think those moments have resulted in some of my favourite bits of writing, and in that way, I sometimes 'feel bad' in the sense that I briefly share in the misery/rage/despair I'm depicting, but not in not in the sense that I feel any responsibility for making them experience it.

I have a friend who's a TV writer, and he used to get hate mail all the time from fans for putting the characters through bad things. Complaints about gratuitous suffering would be something (and learning where the line is can be tricky), but they were really written as if he'd actually done that stuff to real people, and that seems pathological to me. Not to mention, suffering and struggle are indispensable to fiction and maybe to real life as well, but that's a bigger debate, and I've rambled enough.

About the author

Will comes from England but lives in Austria, where his struggles with the German language (and foolish instinct to just politely agree whenever he hasn't understood something) have a way of turning even mundane encounters into adventures in the surreal. He works as a teacher, physical therapist, and content writer. He likes to spend time in the woods and mountains, but seems to spend more of it sprawled on the sofa trawling nonsense on the internet.

@Wgwaun

The Future in a Wash Basin

Erin Keating

Co. Cork, 1896

Siobhan O'Keeffe Mahoney had never seen her own reflection. It was not for lack of trying. She would pass the only mirror in the house she shared with her father and brother, then quickly turn around, as though she could surprise it into revealing her image. She would stare so long into the gray waters of Schull Harbor on a windless day that, once, one of the rotten neighborhood boys pushed her in. She'd floated, of course. She would press her nose to the long icicles that formed beside their door in January, hoping for the briefest glimpse of the sea blue eyes and coppery hair she had inherited from her mother. But never once had she seen her own reflection.

Instead, she saw the future.

And from Siobhan's place in the worn armchair by the hearth, the future looked bleak.

Finn MacCotter stood opposite her, wringing his cap in his hands. She had understood all of the words Finn had said individually, but couldn't make sense of them in the order in which he had delivered them.

Siobhan wiped her clammy palms on her skirt. "I'm sorry, Mr. MacCotter. Am I correct that this is a proposal of marriage?"

Finn MacCotter glanced over his shoulder, where Siobhan's father, Cormac Mahoney, stood with his arms crossed.

"I certainly hope you're not sorry to hear it." He let out a wheezy laugh, and his freckled cheeks flushed. "My Da, eh, you know he's not well. He wants to see me, eh, settled. And he and Mr. Mahoney being such good friends and all—"

Siobhan's father cleared his throat. Finn stopped talking.

Siobhan supposed she shouldn't be surprised. She was newly twenty-two and Finn a few years older, but it felt like there were fewer people their age in Schull Harbor by the hour—all packing their bags for America. Siobhan's stomach churned at the mere thought. How could they leave the only home that they knew for a place full of strangers?

Siobhan glanced over Finn's shoulder at the gilded-frame mirror that hung above the hearth. The clear surface of the mirror rippled as she looked at it. Should she marry Finn MacCotter or refuse? Each time she wavered, a misty image bubbled to the surface. That was what she loved most about the future—it was never set. Time ran steadily, like a river, and every decision she made took her down a different route of its forking path.

Siobhan saw herself scrubbing cow dung off Finn MacCotter's boots if she accepted or scrubbing her brother's children's dirty nappies if she refused. She would wash butchered blood from the cracks in Finn's leather gloves, or she would wash the blood from her sister-in-law's bedsheets after another birth. She would stare at the ceiling waiting for Finn to finish laboring over her in bed, or she would stare at the ceiling in the attic, displaced from her room, praying her screaming nieces and nephews would fall asleep.

Siobhan gripped the armchair with white knuckles. Her fingernails sank into the worn fabric. Was this it, then? Was she trapped by two tiresome fates—the obedient wife or the spinster aunt—without anything to call her own?

But then the image shifted to reveal a blonde daughter swaddled in Finn's arms. Siobhan nearly leapt from the armchair, her heart in her throat. If she took this path with Finn, she would have a daughter. Her mother's line would continue.

Siobhan blinked herself back to the present, to this worn armchair. She managed a smile. "Well, Mr. MacCotter, your proposal is certainly as good as any."

"Lovely! Eh, thank you. I'll, eh, go tell my Da." Finn MacCotter placed the wrung-out cap on his head. As soon as the front door closed, her brother and sister-in-law rushed in from the kitchen. They offered their congratulations, her sister-in-law trying awkwardly to embrace Siobhan around her own swollen belly.

Siobhan looked at her father, but he was studying the mirror closely, as he always did when he caught her scrying, wondering what secrets it revealed to his daughter.

That night, after some revelry with the neighbors, Siobhan put on her wool jacket, took an oil lantern from the hook by the door, and headed out into the dark. The late-March air cooled her flushed cheeks, warm with whiskey and the heat of a dozen bodies cramped in their small front room. The oil lantern lit only a small patch of road in front of her. It didn't matter. Her bones knew the way. She trod down Colla Road, away from the yellow, blue, and plum-colored houses of the main street. Between the trees and the shore scrub she could spy the inky water of the harbor and the lone light of a ship.

Soon, she came upon the cemetery. It sat beside the ruins of Saint Mary's Church, a roofless stone structure overgrown with shrubbery and moss. The old gate squeaked as she entered. Two matching headstones on freshly weeded plots sat at the base of the hill, overlooking the harbor. Siobhan settled down in the grass, leaning against her mother's cold stone.

"Ma, Gran, I'm getting married," she whispered.

And somewhere, far away or very near, Bridget O'Keeffe Mahoney and Emer Sullivan O'Keeffe listened. Siobhan felt heat flickering behind her navel—her magic. When she was a girl, she'd felt it strongest in Gran's kitchen, watching the old woman grinding herbs into healing salves. But in the years since Gran's death, it felt strongest here.

This was the land where her mother and her gran had practiced their craft. This was the land where her own daughters would learn their arts. Even though the town seemed to be growing smaller each day, she couldn't bear to leave Schull Harbor and the bones of the women who came before her. This land was her inheritance.

She pressed her fingers to the earth and spoke the Old Irish word for 'water'. It was a tongue lost to nearly all but the wise women, a language she had learned from her gran. The ground yielded to her touch, and soon fresh water bubbled up and pooled at the base of the stones. She would use the water's surface to scry.

She had chosen the path in which she would bear children—even if they were Finn MacCotter's children. Her mother's line would continue. Her daughter would learn magic at her elbow.

Siobhan whispered, "Show me my line."

The surface of the water rippled, revealing the image of a blonde little girl. The child hid behind Finn's legs, his arms stretched out in front of her—shielding her from something. In this vision, Siobhan reached for her daughter, but the girl and Finn both backed away. They looked afraid—afraid of her.

Siobhan sank her fingers into the dirt, felt the comforting hum of her foremother's magic.

"Again," she demanded of the water through gritted teeth.

The next vision had the same blonde girl studying a children's catechism in the MacCotter's large parlor. The view was at a strange angle, but then the vision grew wider until Siobhan saw herself peering through a crack in the doorway. Then Finn appeared, his mouth in a tight line, and closed the door.

"No," Siobhan gasped. She could hardly breathe over the lump forming in her throat. "No, no, no."

She sank her hands into the pool of water, splashing away the vision. "Please, do any of them practice?" she begged. "Do any of them scry?"

The water grew cloudy with mud and when it settled, the image of three copper-haired girls flashed in quick succession.

Then, for the first time in Siobhan's life, she thought she saw her reflection. A sea blue eye stared back at her, too close to the surface of the water.

It blinked.

Siobhan, startled, tumbled backward into the grass. But she crept forward again, and peered into the pool. The face pulled away from the water's surface, revealing the girl's other eye, a pert freckle-dusted nose, and a crooked smile with new teeth growing in awkwardly.

"Hi!" The girl said. Her face rippled as a gentle breeze skirted across the surface of the water. Her voice was strange, an accent with sharp, narrow sounds that grated Siobhan's ears.

"Hello," Siobhan said cautiously. Often, she could hear the scenes that she scried, but she had never been able to communicate with them. Something about this seemed touched with fae magic.

"Do you see funny things in the mirror too?" the girl asked.

"I do," Siobhan answered.

"Have you ever seen yourself?"

"No."

"Me either." The girl shrugged. "What did you ask the mirror to see? Oh, I guess you aren't using a mirror, are you? You're all— wavy."

Siobhan laughed, the sound so loud in the silent night that she scared herself. This girl spoke so many words, and so quickly. The flame in Siobhan's stomach grew hotter, white heat rippling through her body. It was a powerful feeling, a prideful and protective affection. She hadn't expected to feel it this suddenly. Perhaps it was because she knelt on her mother's and gran's graves—a heritage of blood and bones. This was a girl of her line.

"I asked to see my family," Siobhan said.

The girl grinned, lips parting to reveal her lopsided teeth again. "You're Siobhan, aren't you?" Siobhan must have made a surprised face, because the girl laughed. "My mom's told me all about you—you're her great-grandma—I think. I'm Bridget! It's nice to meet you."

Siobhan caught her breath hearing her mother's name spoken in the girl's strange voice.

"Tell me about your mother," Siobhan whispered.

She listened to Bridget tell her about her mother, who was attuned to stones and crystals, who used citrine to manifest enough cash to make ends meet, rose quartz to ease her broken heart after Bridget's father left, amethyst under Bridget's pillow to keep bad dreams away.

Hearing the stories reminded Siobhan of the tales she'd heard of her own mother, who could press her hands to a stone and hear its history.

As the moon rose and set, the water slowly dried up. Siobhan finally said goodbye to Bridget—this scried girl with her mother's name—who stared up at her through the water. When Bridget's image was gone, and Siobhan was alone in the cemetery once more, she whispered a prayer of thanks over the graves. Her line would go on.

But she couldn't shake the image of her blonde daughter's wide blue eyes and trembling mouth. What could make a child look at her mother like that?

The next day, Siobhan and her father donned their Sunday best and walked down the long dirt road toward MacCotter's Farm. The cows in the pasture lumbered up to them, stretching their heads over the low stone walls as though to inspect Siobhan personally. Milk, cheese, butter, and the highest quality meat came out of MacCotter's Farm. At least a dozen men in town were employed there as farmhands—those who did not go to sea every day, as Siobhan's father did.

The morning damp clung to Siobhan's skin. Her cheeks stung with cold when they finally reached the MacCotter's stone house. Finn MacCotter answered the door, smartly dressed, with his curly blond hair parted and beard newly trimmed.

"Welcome, eh, if you'll follow me this way."

"Is that them?" A voice called from the other room.

"Yes, Da!" Finn shouted back.

Finn led them into the foyer. Siobhan had been inside the MacCotters' house before—they held an annual Christmas party for the whole town—but she hadn't expected it to look so splendid on an ordinary day. The dark wooden banisters gleamed. She followed the stairs with her eyes, generations of blond MacCotters looking down on her from oil portraits. To their right was a large formal dining room, where the MacCotters hosted Christmas dinner at a table laden with silver. To their left was a dimly lit parlor that was twice the size of the Mahoney's front room. There Mr. MacCotter sat in a chair by a roaring fire, wrapped in blankets.

Despite the grandeur, a chill shuddered down Siobhan's back. Without the bustle of the Christmas guests, an eerie quiet sat heavily on the house.

"Cormac, welcome! And Miss Mahoney, come here, come here." Siobhan allowed Mr. MacCotter to kiss her hand.

"Finbarr!" Mr. Mahoney boomed, shaking Mr. MacCotter's liver-spotted hand. "All's well with the farm?"

Though they were the same age, Mr. MacCotter seemed decades older than his friend, stooped and hunched with pain no one could cure. Perhaps Gran O'Keeffe could have healed him, had he fallen ill in her time.

"Fine, fine," Mr. MacCotter wheezed. "Except I don't know how I'll keep staffing it. America is stealing all my farmhands' sons. It seems a man can't expect his children to stay in one place anymore. We must be the luckiest men in all of Cork."

Siobhan glanced at Finn, who stood stiffly beside his father, his eyes fixed to a spot on the floor. Had he ever dreamed of leaving for America, like so many others? Or was he like her—proud to be tied to this land and his family's history here?

Mr. MacCotter cleared his throat with a phlegmy rattle in his chest. "Now, Miss Mahoney, let me look at you."

Siobhan wore a dress of carnation red, a fawn-colored wool shawl embroidered with rosebuds, and her coppery hair neatly pinned. Of course, there had been no way for her to see how she looked. But, that morning, as she peered into her wash basin, Bridget's face had appeared.

Bridget was older than she'd been when they'd spoken in the cemetery—now a woman in her sixties with elegant white hair. Bridget had said that Siobhan looked beautiful. That was better than any reflection.

"Turn please," Mr. MacCotter said. Siobhan gave a girlish twirl and Mr. MacCotter let out an annoyed sound like a cow's loam. "No, girl, slowly, please, slowly."

So, Siobhan turned slowly in a full circle, feeling the weight of the men's eyes on her. She tried to make a face to her father, but his arms were crossed, watching Mr. MacCotter closely.

"Very good. Now, if you would please smile," Mr. MacCotter instructed.

Siobhan did her best lady-like smile, demure and closed-lipped. Again, a cow-like sound burst from Mr. MacCotter, sending spittle flying. "No, girl—your teeth. I want to see your teeth."

Siobhan realized that she was not a woman, trying to impress her father-in-law, but a cow being inspected at auction. She bared her teeth, curling her lips as far back as she could manage.

"Siobhan!" her father hissed.

But Mr. MacCotter didn't seem to notice the gesture. "She's looks healthy, and any daughter of yours must have a strong constitution. Her hips—wideset—good for child-bearing. We'd hate to see her go the way of her mother."

A flame sparked in the pit of Siobhan's stomach, equal parts magic and rage.

Siobhan tried to keep her voice level. "There was nothing wrong with my mother."

"Siobhan, now is not the time," her father warned, his voice low.

"Of course, my girl, of course. If your kind father had insisted the doctor be present for the whole labor instead of leaving it up to his addled mother-in-law, perhaps she would have made it," Mr. MacCotter said.

Fire spread through Siobhan's core, heat moving up into her chest. Frost began to spread on the windowpane as she balled her fists. She muttered the Old Irish word for 'breath', trying her gran's old trick for calming a racing heart.

"What was that, girl?" Mr. MacCotter demanded. The word 'girl' chafed at her skin.

The frost grew with a low cracking. Siobhan snapped. "If my father hadn't called for the doctor at the last minute and had let my gran continue her treatment, my mother most certainly would have made it."

Gran O'Keeffe had told her the story. Her father, in his terror, called for the doctor, who had thrown Gran O'Keeffe from the room. She had finished brewing ergot tea—a thimbleful of ergot powder brewed in boiling water—that would make her mother's uterine muscles contract and stop the bleeding. The doctor had knocked the teacup from her hand, convinced ergot was poisonous. He packed Bridget O'Keeffe Mahoney full of cotton, which she bled through, and bled through, and bled through, while the tea that could have saved her seeped into the floorboards. Gran O'Keeffe rocked Siobhan, newly born and wailing, outside the door while her daughter died.

"I said not now, Siobhan!" her father snapped.

The thick ice on the window shone like silver. And in it, Siobhan saw herself in labor, her face red with sweat, screaming in primal pain. When the child arrived in the world, Finn snatched it from her arms, as though Siobhan was diseased.

She squeezed her eyes shut, willing the image away.

"There, there, my girl. I did not mean to upset you. Of course, you miss your mother at a time like this," Mr. MacCotter said.

In truth, Siobhan rarely missed her mother, though she would never dare say that aloud in front of her father. There was no need to miss her; her presence was constant. Every time she felt her magic tug at her stomach, it was like her mother was there beside her. But in this house, with its too-dark and too-quiet rooms, lorded over by Mr. MacCotter and his ever-watchful gaze, could she practice safely here?

Mr. MacCotter squeezed her hand, and Siobhan fought the urge to pull away.

Panic flickered and flared in her chest like a dying candle. These men would snuff her out.

Hours later, Siobhan had rubbed her skin red and raw, but still could not shake the chill of the MacCotters' house. She had locked the door of her little room with its drafty window that overlooked the harbor. Despite her sister-in-law's incessant knocking, Siobhan didn't answer. She tried to lose herself in the rhythm of the squeaking floorboards as she paced. Only when her feet had grown tired did she pour some water into the basin by her bed.

"Show me Bridget," she demanded. The surface of the water rippled, and Bridget's face came into view. She was younger than she had been when they spoke that morning, when she complimented Siobhan's dress. Now a woman in her early thirties, the only wrinkles on Bridget's face were faint laugh lines around her mouth.

Siobhan was sure that Bridget was aging normally in her own time, growing a little older each day. But the mirror carried Bridget back from different parts of her life to this point in Siobhan's. This point was an anchor, a moment of significance, that had affected the fate of Siobhan's line. Siobhan took comfort in this—it was a sign that her marriage to Finn MacCotter would not be for nothing, despite her unsettling visions and his father's frigid, suffocating house.

"Oh! Siobhan! Hi!" Bridget chirped. Her energy never changed —whether she was a girl or a woman or an old lady. She always spoke so fast, Siobhan could hardly understand her. "I'm glad to see you. I've got big news actually, something I think you'd really like to know."

"Go on, my heart," Siobhan said. Even though Bridget appeared older than her now, she was still overwhelmed by a warm rush of affection. There was a maternal fondness for Bridget that Siobhan could not shake, despite the years that separated them.

"I'm pregnant! You're the first person other than my husband to know—weird, right?" Light radiated from Bridget's dewy cheeks. "It's going to be a girl—I just know it."

Siobhan's throat felt tight. Echoing through her head were her own screams of labor that she had scried in the MacCotters' windows.

"Congratulations—that is..." Siobhan murmured. She recalled Gran's story of her birth and her mother's death—the two tangled up together. She clutched the ceramic basin, pressing it into her stomach as a wave of nausea passed over her. As much as Siobhan wanted a daughter, childbirth itself was a nightmare that had haunted her all her life. And to think that Bridget would soon go through it, wherever and whenever she was.

"Are you all right?" Bridget asked. Two deep worry lines creased her forehead.

Siobhan nodded. "My mother..." was all she could manage.

"Shit!" Bridget hissed. "I'm so sorry. Mom told me about your mother. Of course, you're concerned. But I'll be all right, I promise."

Siobhan thought of her conversation with Bridget just this morning. Bridget would live to have crow's feet around her eyes and sleek white hair.

"I know you will, my heart," Siobhan said. Then she swallowed hard, trying to speak through the lump in her throat. "Bridget, do you know if our magic skipped over someone in our line. Did your mom's grandma practice?"

Bridget began to laugh, but caught herself. Siobhan wondered how worry wrote itself on her face—did she have the same deep worry lines as her great-great-granddaughter? "She must have—I've heard stories from my grandma that she was a healer. Why do you ask?"

Siobhan clutched at her stomach. Bridget's words didn't seem to align with her visions at all. "What about when she was young? How did her gift grow?"

Bridget tilted her head. "Siobhan, you already know the answer. Our magic can only grow if we practice it."

The wedding was set for August. Though the date was months away, there was already a flurry of preparation at the Mahoney house. Her sister-in-law and three of Mr. Mahoney's sisters took it upon themselves to tailor Siobhan's mother's wedding dress for the occasion. She could never seem to breathe in her wedding dress, no matter how many times they let it out.

There were arguments over what they should serve at the Mahoney's house following the ceremony, which readings would be best for the mass, whether foxglove or iris would look prettier in a bouquet. Siobhan was seldom asked for her opinion, so she chose not to offer it. Instead, she stood quietly on an overturned soap box, letting herself be pricked with pins, as her mind raced.

The problem had to be Finn. In every vision she'd have of her blonde daughter—Finn's daughter—he stood between them. She had to convince him that their child needed to practice her craft, that this was Siobhan's legacy. She could not let her daughter's magic die.

Whenever one of the aunts held up a mirror for Siobhan to inspect their progress, Siobhan saw the image of her daughter with Finn, with terror in her blue eyes, pulling away from Siobhan.

She breathed deeply until her ribs strained against the seams, and she tugged at the lace against her sweaty neck. The aunts tutted and pinned some more, but Siobhan's dry mouth couldn't form the words to tell them that the problem wasn't the dress—it was her future.

One day, a month into wedding preparations, when the aunts gossiped about a neighbor's daughter leaving for America, Finn MacCotter knocked on the door. The Mahoney women fussed like hens as they barred Finn from entering until Siobhan changed out of her wedding gown.

"Sorry for the trouble," Siobhan said when she finally let him in. She tried to smile at him, but felt more like a wolf bearing its fangs. Each time she saw him, she searched his eyes for the disgust she had seen in her visions. A steady fury, like waves beating against the coast, built up in her for all of the things he had yet to do.

"No trouble. But I have, eh, some news. Well, a request really." Finn removed his cap, wringing it in his hands. "My Da, eh, took a turn. I know there's so much to do, and, eh, I don't want to burden your family. But, do you think we could move up the date?" Finn asked. "To next week?"

Siobhan's stomach clenched so suddenly she thought she'd be sick on Finn's shoes. She'd expected a couple more months to find a way to convince him that she—and their future daughter— needed to be able to practice their craft. But next week? She leaned against the door to steady herself. "I'm not sure. I—"

But then her sister-in-law and the aunts burst from the kitchen where they'd been eavesdropping. "Not a burden at all," her sister-in-law said. "We can manage."

At those words, the mounting fear turned to flame. It started behind Siobhan's navel and spread outward until her fingertips burned. The air around her rippled with heat. She worried that the house would catch fire if she didn't do something. Siobhan cast her gaze toward the harbor.

"Finn, come with me." She grabbed him by the elbow, but Finn yelped in pain and leapt away. His shirt had been scorched.

Siobhan didn't apologize or explain. Instead, she walked out into the bright May morning. His heavy footsteps followed. Only when they were halfway to the harbor, far from her sister-in-law's uncanny hearing, did Siobhan dare to speak.

"Finn, you know what I am, don't you?"

"What do you—" he began.

"Please," she interrupted. "It's a small town. You know the rumors. You know my gran was a wise-woman. You know that I— well—I see things." The fire of her magic grew hotter in the pit of her stomach, as though by speaking it she had fed the flames. She felt her power rippling off her skin. Down the road, the harbor waters grew mirror-still.

Finn tugged at his shirt collar. His neck and cheeks turned splotchy red. "I've heard. But, eh, I'm willing to look past it. We'll have an ordinary life."

"Ordinary?" Siobhan felt the air rush from her lungs.

"Ordinary. We'll run a good house, and raise good children, and no one will say that you're odd."

"What about our daughter? If she sees things too?" Rage and fear were a potent combination for women with her gift. It was like adding whiskey to a flame. Her power flared up, casting a glassy frost across all of the neighbors' windows.

"There's no need to encourage her—abilities. She'll be ordinary, like any other child. What more could she want?" He reached out to hold her hand, but pulled back. "What more could you want?"

"I want her to inherit what is hers." She held Finn's gaze. Long silence hung between them, interrupted only by the sound of groaning ice.

"MacCotter Farm will be her inheritance, if we have no sons." His voice sounded hollow, like the vast rooms of his father's house. "And we are done with this discussion."

He turned away from her, but, just before he did, she saw in his eyes what she had been searching for, for weeks. Disgust. Anger. A shadow of fear.

This was the Finn MacCotter of her visions, the one who shielded her own daughter from her, who banished magic from their home, who cast Siobhan into loneliness. This was not the life she had chosen when she accepted his proposal.

The fire of her magic roared inside her. All of the power that she'd stoked released in a rush. A sudden frost descended on the streets of Schull Harbor, the town encased in a mirrored sheen of ice. And in it, Siobhan finally understood her visions.

On the icy road ahead of her, heading back toward her father's house, she saw the blonde daughter and her fearful eyes. On the road leading down to the harbor, she saw a copper-haired girl, reading in Siobhan's lap.

Siobhan laughed aloud and, with it, icicles crashed to the ground.

How had she forgotten? In her panic at her line dying, she had forgotten the simple truth. The future was not fixed. That blonde-haired daughter she had seen was only one possible child that would come to be—Finn's child. But she remembered the line of copper-haired girls she had first scried in the puddle at the cemetery—those were the daughters of a life and a love yet unknown to her.

Siobhan raced back to her father's house, ignoring the frantic questioning of her aunts and sister-in-law. In her room, she dragged her wardrobe in front of her door, straining and sweating under the effort. She didn't know how long she'd have until her father found out about her fight with Finn. And she needed time to think.

She filled her wash basin, splashing half of the pitcher on the floor with her shaking hands. "What should I do?" she begged of the water.

The water rippled and bubbled, showing her glimpses of every possible future. She could marry Finn MacCotter and have their miserable, magicless daughter. She could stay in Schull Harbor, unmarried, tending the graves of Ma and Gran. She could take the path that traveled past the curve in the coastline that had marked the edge of Siobhan's whole world. Limitless possibilities danced across the water's surface until Siobhan grew dizzy.

She gripped the ceramic basin to steady herself. "Stop," she hissed. The water stilled. She should have known better than to ask the water such an open-ended the question. It could only show her the paths—it could not tell her what to do.

Downstairs, the door slammed. The whole house seemed to rock as her father stormed in.

"Show me Bridget," she demanded. Her voice was tight in her throat. She didn't have much time.

The water rippled, and then Bridget was looking up at her. She was a young woman, nearly Siobhan's age. Her sea blue eyes were watery and red-rimmed, and her coppery hair was disheveled. A few hair pins still clung to her curls. At the edge of the basin, Siobhan glimpsed the neckline of a black dress.

Siobhan's fevered thoughts stilled. Her chest ached as she studied her great-great-granddaughter's quivering chin.

"Oh, my heart, what happened? What's wrong?" Siobhan murmured.

"My grandma—she—" Bridget wiped her eyes. "Could you— could you tell me about yours?" she asked.

But then there was a pounding at the door.

"Siobhan—Siobhan, open this door this instant," her father roared.

"Siobhan, is everything all right?" Bridget asked, drying her eyes.

"Everything is fine, my heart. Don't worry about a thing," Siobhan murmured.

"Finn MacCotter is down at the harbor calling you a—he was calling you a..." Even after all these years, her father still couldn't bring himself to say it.

Siobhan whispered the Old Irish word for 'quiet'. The room stopped rattling, her father stopped thundering. A thick blanket of silence had fallen over everything except Siobhan and her wash basin. Bridget needed her, and Siobhan would let nothing interrupt them.

Siobhan sighed, returning her attention to Bridget. "You wanted to hear about Gran O'Keeffe, yes?"

Bridget nodded, her red-rimmed eyes wide with surprise.

Gran O'Keeffe had been Siobhan's whole heritage—serving as both grandmother and mother. The air around Siobhan crackled with Gran O'Keeffe's memory. Since Gran's death, there was a word Siobhan hadn't spoken. But Bridget deserved to hear it.

"My Gran O'Keeffe was a witch, like us."

Gran O'Keeffe was the one who named Siobhan's ability. Scrying: that was the word for seeing the future in the mirror, in water, in ice. Any witch worth her salt could learn to scry, but only once in several generations was a witch born a natural scryer. Gran O'Keeffe's own mother had been one. It had been enough, to see the look of pride on Gran O'Keeffe's face, rather than ever seeing her own.

In this very house, Siobhan had learned the healing arts at Gran's elbow—borage seed oil for aching bones, honeyed marshmallow root for cough, yarrow tea for fevers. Though the plants would not speak to Siobhan as they had to Gran O'Keeffe, it had been enough to feel the heat of their shared magic ripple through the small kitchen as old and young woman worked side by side.

In this very room, Gran O'Keeffe had brushed and braided Siobhan's copper hair, describing the face that had eluded Siobhan all her life. "You look just like your ma did at this age," Gran O'Keeffe would whisper as she worked her knobby fingers through Siobhan's hair. "Big eyes as blue as the sky."

Schull Harbor was her home, where memories of Gran O'Keeffe were embedded into the grains of the wooden house and the cracks of the cobblestone streets. Schull Harbor was all she had known, and she loved it—despite its smallness that only got smaller—because it was here that she had learned her craft. This town was all she was. Could she really leave it all behind? Leave Ma and Gran O'Keeffe's bones, their memories?

Siobhan watched the lines of grief ease on Bridget's face as she spoke. Siobhan didn't care how many generations stood between her and her daughter's, daughter's, daughter's daughter. Bridget was flesh of her flesh and blood of her blood. She loved her as though she had carried her herself—as Gran O'Keeffe had loved Siobhan.

Gran O'Keeffe would understand.

Siobhan realized then that she did not need the water to tell her what to do. There were hundreds of paths that could lead to copper-haired daughters learning their craft. But she wanted just one path—she wanted the future that led to Bridget.

Her magic smoldered in her stomach. That tugging, fiery sensation behind her navel burned brighter than it had in years. Siobhan had always thought that her power came from this land, from the buried bones of her foremothers. But as she watched her great-great-granddaughter's face—the one she has seen age in the rippling waters of her wash basin—she understood the truth. Their magic was not tied to the land. Their magic was tied to each other.

These abilities were her inheritance and her legacy—hers to remember and hers to leave behind. This young woman who scried the past while Siobhan scried the future was proof of that legacy.

"You come from a long line of extraordinary women." Siobhan's voice crackled with power.

With those words, the wash basin in her hands turned to crystal. The surface of the water stilled into silver glass. The future itself turned solid and clear.

"Bridget," she asked her great-great-granddaughter, "where are you?"

Bridget grinned, because she had known this future all along. "Brooklyn."

"Brooklyn." The word fell from Siobhan's lips like an irreversible spell. It was a place that sounded too big for her wash basin, so Siobhan threw open the window. "Show me," she demanded of the harbor. The blistering heat under her skin seeped out of her, until the air around her hummed. The harbor turned to solid ice—boats were trapped, fisherman's frozen nets were too heavy to pull, children splashing in the shallows skated along a sheen of glass.

Siobhan feared the ice would show her the future of Schull Harbor with wild grass growing over her foremothers' graves. But it didn't. Instead, she witnessed her own line stretch for generations beyond the harbor and across the Atlantic. Tears streamed down Siobhan's cheeks. In those faces, she saw Ma's blue eyes and Gran's knowing smile repeated and changed like an old incantation.

Siobhan tore away from the window to peer back into the crystal basin. Bridget raised her eyebrows, as though to ask Siobhan what she had seen, even though she already knew. How Siobhan loved her, this girl of her line.

"My heart," Siobhan breathed. "I'm on my way."

See Erin Keating's story "The Future in a Wash Basin" online at Metaphorosis.
If you liked it, leave a comment. Authors love that!
Remember to subscribe to our e-mail updates so you'll know when new stories are posted.

About the story

"The Future in a Wash Basin" began at the end.

When I'm coming up with ideas for stories, I tend to think of interesting or unusual images that I can build a character and a world around. For this story, that image was of a woman scrying in a compact mirror. From there I worked backward, trying to figure out who this woman was and what she saw in the mirror. At first, I liked the idea of telling multiple connected stories about an entire lineage of women, each one scrying into a different object —but as I explored that idea, it quickly grew out-of-hand for a short story.

Instead, I traced the story back to the matriarch and decided to begin there. Once I decided to focus the story on Siobhan, the plot fell into place. I knew that I wanted to center the story around a specific moment in Siobhan's life that would affect the fate of the rest of her line and which could be grounded in a real, historical moment. In the early drafts of this story, the final scene jumped ahead to the perspective of Bridget—Siobhan's great-great-granddaughter—scrying into a compact mirror and looking back into the past.

Metaphorosis's editor, B. Morris Allen, requested a rewrite of the story, which led to me re-imagining the way Siobhan's visions worked. Because I began at the end, Siobhan's choice had felt inevitable and her visions pointed to one future. During my revisions, I worked to show that multiple paths diverged from her decision. In doing so, I also ended up cutting that final scene from Bridget's perspective, so that the piece had a clear focus on Siobhan. These revisions helped me hone in on this crucial moment for Siobhan where her heritage and her legacy intersect.

In the end, this story was inspired by an image that didn't make it into the final version. That just means that I have another story to tell! While I figure out exactly what Bridget is scrying in her compact mirror, I hope that you enjoy "The Future in a Wash Basin."

A question for the author

Q: Q: Do you write things other than speculative fiction?

A: I do! While writing fiction—especially speculative fiction—always feels most natural to me, the first formal creative writing instruction I received was in poetry. The attention to sound and the specificity of word choice that's required in poetry is something that I try to practice when revising my fiction. Whenever I'm feeling stuck on a story, I find that writing a short poem is the best way to get me focused on the fundamentals of craft.

Poetry and fiction tend to feel like very independent endeavors, so every now and then I like to explore more collaborative forms. I find playwriting particularly exciting, because the piece really only comes to life when the actors add their own voices to it. My senior year of college, I wrote and directed a full-length play about the heroines of Shakespeare's three Verona plays (*Taming Of The Shrew, Romeo And Juliet,* and *Two Gentlemen Of Verona*).

Most recently, I've been trying my hand at songwriting. My husband is a musician and we've been passing pieces back and forth—I'll give him lyrics to set music to, and he'll give me music to add words to. It's been a really fun process!

About the author

Erin Keating is a grant writer at an arts education nonprofit. She earned her B.A. in creative writing and literature at Roanoke College. While earning her history M.A. at Drew University, she spent most of her time in the archives reading as many Shakespeare-related texts she could find. She has a library card from the Bodleian Library, Library of Congress, Folger Shakespeare Library, and, of course, her local public library. When she's not writing, she dabbles in bass guitar, rock climbing, language-learning, and video games.

erinkeatingwrites.com, @KeatingNotKeats

The Year of the Bright Lands

Felix Taylor

The Year of the Anabatic Wind was coming to an end. Everything had happened as it should have done, every prophecy made by the Under Personage, the Great Ancestor of the Pit, had come to pass. All except for the Wind itself. There had been no sign of it, no rush of warm air over the fields, no whisper of it blowing in the flatlands away to the north. I could not help but think that it was all my fault.

I had always considered my dreams too dull to give to the diviner for interpretation. They were the kind that everyone had, and their meanings were plain. The building of a house — that meant that I yearned for a proper home and a good husband. Walking along a road — that meant that I was on the path that had been set out for me by the Personage during the Nights of First Becoming. Dull, all of them. Except for the dream I'd had in the final month of the Year of Unsowing, two years ago. In that dream, I flung myself bodily into the Abyss and my heart squeezed against my throat, beating waves of white heat into my arms as I dropped. Cold wind cut my face.

When the archivists had read aloud from the prophecies at the next year's beginning, I almost choked.

"She will be in black dress," they had said, "in imitation of the soul which is absent of light. Before winter's end she will hurl herself into the Pit and come to the light of the stars and be reborn in the Ancestor's image. So commences the Year of Resplendent Sacrifice, foretold by the Under Personage, the Giver of Night."

We all looked around at each other, gathered before the doors of the Archive, wondering which of us would be the chosen girl. I had been scared. The flames from the lamps twisted the other girls' faces, hollowed out their eyes, brightened their teeth. *It's me*, I said to myself, *because I have seen it.* We looked at each other and I knew that every pair of eyes had landed on me, whipping away before I'd noticed. Perhaps they'd all seen me fall in their own dreams. Perhaps my fear showed like a pimple on my nose or a rash which crept across my forehead.

"For only in light," the assistant archivist had continued, her arms glittering from circlets of black gemstones, "can a soul be unmade and there return to its maker in darkness."

The Year of Resplendent Sacrifice had approached its end and no one had jumped. During eighth month, Demira Sinter, a girl who lived next to us in a house with three floors, approached the Abyss and stared down into its darkness. We crept along behind her, darting from rock to furrow, wondering if Demira would be the one to do it, but she plodded back to the village without a word and shut herself in her bedroom. And then, on the final day, a woman who lived alone named Clara Reed put on a black bathing robe and, shrieking to herself, leapt into the Night to join the Personage. She had been of middling age, only some years younger than Mother —not a girl by any standard. But the archivists declared the prophecy to have been fulfilled and we let the Year of Resplendent Sacrifice fall from our memories.

The following year, the corn grew seven inches in the first quarter. Three juniper birds were seen at the appearance of the Bright Scar, and a father of two boys was lost while out gathering white mushrooms in the flats. All just as it should have occurred. And again: 'But where is the Wind?' People began to worry. My mother asked it at the start of each morning, and by evening's close she had fretted herself to the point of sickness. The anticipation across the rest of our community was so unbearable that by the end of the year, every gust of warm air from the Abyss was proclaimed to be the beginnings of the Anabatic Wind and we gathered at the fields' edge to await — what? Something. Anything would have been better than that stillness. For a moment, the sweet grasses around our ankles might shiver and shake and the archivists would stand eager to record the Great Event, only for their pens to fall to their sides, their parchment to hang limp in their disappointed grips.

"One thousand years," I heard the assistant archivist Janny Lin murmur to a colleague. We were walking back to the village after one of these false alarms. "One thousand years and before tonight only a single prophecy has not unfolded."

"What was supposed to happen?" I asked, moving to walk beside Janny and the other archivists. Pendants of black slate swung from their wrists, their badges of office.

Janny narrowed her eyes and squinted ahead as if she had not heard my question. "A ball of flame," she said. "It was meant to appear as the Bright Scar opened. So it was foretold."

"A candle flame?" I ventured, though I knew what she would say.

"Greater than that." Janny's eyes flicked over to me and away. "A *sun*, the Under Personage called it."

I had heard of suns before, but only in tales passed around by the boys who worked at the outer edges of the village. There were places, they said, where days were counted by the movements of great circles of light, and that the light of one of them was brighter even than the wood fire in the village hall. The people there had no knowledge of the Ancestor and no notion of who they were in the world. They had their sun and that was all that they ever thought they needed. I never liked to imagine those places.

"But it didn't appear?" I asked Janny Lin.

"The Year of the Life Star, it was called. Our eight hundred and first year. No event like it was recorded by the archivists. No ball of flame. Nothing."

"But what about last year?" said a shadow to Janny's right. Her colleague, dressed in the same robes the colour of dusk. "If we are to count it. The girl did not jump, but a woman in her place."

"It is not well to speak too long about these things," said Janny.

I saw Mother watching me from a group of older women, her brow folded in disapproval. I nodded and drifted away from Janny Lin. *It is not well.* The Personage was the Voice of Truth in the Darkness. It was never wrong, *could* never be wrong. Infallible, the High Priest always said. Undeniable. Unreadable. Fifteen hundred years ago, the Abyss had spoken and the first men and women of our village had recorded the words. A map, the Priest said, of our entire existence, stretching out into the night, the undying darkness when starlight did not shine. It was why we worshiped at night and set great store by the dreamworld. We stayed within the boundaries of the flatlands, just as the Personage instructed, because beyond the flatlands lay the ends of life.

In the beginning there was the void, the High Priest said at the start of each mass. And the void did take form. It became a nest of snakes, and the snakes tried selfishly to fashion a world of light for themselves, but darkness swept up from the deeps and scattered them. Then came the Abyss. The Personage was everywhere, but especially in the Abyss.

The light from the stars had all but faded by the time we reached our homes. The day was at an end. Mother rushed straight to her seat by the window where she kept her collection of black quartz stones. They had been gathered from the very wall of the Abyss and were strictly contraband, but mother had traded six days of new sour milk for them and they had been a solace to her, a reassurance that she was at one with the Abyss and the Personage. I went to my bedroom, and eventually to sleep, and the Year of the Anabatic Wind passed unfulfilled.

The next morning, I woke with the first stars. I washed in cold water drawn up from the well and ate white bread with Mother in the kitchen. She was always up before me. She only slept for a few hours, she said; it was all she could manage these days. She couldn't listen to the sounds of the rafters in her bedroom creaking, because it put daggers in her head. I watched her from across the table and knew that she had been worrying about the Anabatic Wind.

"The year is over, Mama," I said.

"What will happen will happen," mother said, folding her hands.

"But there's no use dwelling," I said.

"There's use," she said sullenly. Like a child. Like me. "You're just like your pa, Elin. Pretending everything's as it should be when it is not."

"But nothing has changed," I went on. "The wind did not come, but things are the same as before."

"You need to understand," said mother. "That the word of the Personage is the world."

"I know that, Mama."

"And the prophecies are the truth of the world and of the village. If they do not come to pass, then it is we who are made false."

I got up and left before she thought to say anything else. *We who are made false.* Mother's words crawled into my ear like a beetle. They stayed as I rinsed the breakfast dishes and made ready for school. I was false, then. The dream had been a preparation for the year to come, a *revelation*, I knew it was called. And I had been too afraid.

The schoolhouse was across the square: I could see its lanterns glowing from our kitchen window. Beyond the schoolhouse lay the edges of the village and a place called the Den, where our wine was made. Boys and girls whose parents did not want them going to school were sent there to work. They were not usually seen this close to the square, but that morning, as I stepped out into the still air, I saw one of the boys sitting in the shadow of the fountain. Dirt plastered his face and his hair was tousled at odd angles, as if he'd been in a scrap. He might have only been two or three years younger than me. He stank, too, I thought, as I walked by the lights of the fountain.

I wouldn't have talked to him if he hadn't been crying. His lips quivered and tears glittered and fell from his face.

"You can't be lost, can you?" I asked, standing beside him.

His head shook and I heard a sniff.

"Not," he said.

"Then what's the matter?" I said.

The boy looked up at me and I saw confusion in his gaze.

"They boys from they Den," he said. "They stoled my waxy doll and threw it into yon Pit. Now it's there at they bottom."

"That's not kind of them," I said, frowning in sympathy. He spoke strangely, this boy. I'd never heard anything like it. "But there isn't a bottom of the Pit, you know."

I knew it was blasphemy for him to say it. The Abyss had no bounds, no limits that any person could comprehend, that's what the High Priest had taught us. There could be no bottom.

"So is too," the boy said, looking away now. "I'n been there and thrown a girt rock. Crack, it went in they water!"

"But there's no way down," I said. "That's what the adults say. And anyone who tries to find a way is breaking the Will of the Personage. You couldn't have been down there because there's nowhere to go."

"Purse on edge," the boy mouthed.

"I know about those boys though," I said, deciding to show sympathy. "From the Den. My friends are always saying what mean things they do there."

"Will you go with me?" the boy said, standing up. A single tear shot down his cheek just like the Bright Scar.

"With you?" I asked. "To the Abyss?"

"Yes, missus," he said eagerly. "To they bottom."

"Can't your dad help you find your doll?" I asked.

"No'm," he blinked, and looked away. "I hain't seen my daddun for long."

"Where does he work?" I asked.

"With they horsies."

I didn't know what that was.

"Can you come?" he asked.

"I can't," I said, deciding not to argue with him any longer. "I'm sorry. If they did throw your wax doll down, there's no way to get it back."

The boy was still there when I came out from our morning lesson an hour later. He was there again after I'd seen in the milking. He had draped himself over the rim of the fountain, cradling his forehead with his wrists. He was a naïve little boy, I thought, and his father should know better than to fill his head with lies about the Abyss. There *was* no bottom. There was no other side, either, nothing but the presence of the Personage, which, I knew, was also nothing. The Great Ancestor was nothing and it was everything. The yearly offerings of syrup and wine that we poured into the Pit were still falling, because there was no end; maybe one year's wine had caught up to the previous year's, but none of it would stop until all prophecies had been fulfilled and the wine was absorbed into the Personage and the Personage knew how faithful the village had been and how to weave the Unending Darkness into our souls and lead us out beyond the stars. Clara Reed would have been plummeting now for just over a year, sticky from the syrup.

It was why I had been so afraid to jump. I had stayed awake into the night, imagining the sensation of falling blindly down until I lost consciousness or died and became part of the Ancestor. What would dying feel like if you couldn't see yourself? If you could only taste the air? Perhaps I wouldn't know that I had died, and would simply slip into death just as we slip between dreams. It still scared me: I was ashamed that a woman had jumped in my place. The act had not been performed correctly and I had been made false. If only I'd done what my dream had shown me, then the Anabatic Wind would have come by now, smoothing down the crops, rushing through the village like the breath from the very throat of the Ancestor itself. But I had stopped it from happening and I had broken the system of things. Like the snakes who had desired light, I had been selfish, and had thought only of myself.

I stood watching the boy, cleaning my hands with a cotton towel. The air was crisp and I could smell what each house on our side of the square had been cooking. Fish: swordtail, eel, red mullet. It was the first day of the New Year, and a time to celebrate. But the boy looked forlorn in his posture against the fountain. He reminded me of the pictures of the heroes from the old legends mother kept in her bedside table. Aorlius, whose lover was transformed by the Ancestor into a sprig of lavender, and Draxyx the traveller, who journeyed to the furthest constellations and in dying shaped the first light of the Bright Scar. The wax doll must mean a great deal to the boy. But why would he hang around the village square, making up stories about the Abyss? Perhaps something else was wrong, something he wasn't saying. If I were to go along with him, then I might be able to help.

I threw the towel onto the porch chair and marched down the steps. I had time: I was free now until 2 o' clock when we had class again, but Tsa Jin never took attendance. She'd never even learnt our names, she was too old. After that was Mass, but I could not miss that. The archivist and the diviner were to recite the Prophecy and give the year its name.

"What are you called?" I asked when I had reached the fountain.

"Sammy," he said.

"My name's Elin," I said.

Sammy said nothing. Just looked at me.

"Do you know exactly where they threw it?" I asked.

"Down in they Pit," the boy said. "It'm be by they Wailing Tree. They way down they stairs."

"Is that far from the village?" I asked. I'd never heard of a Wailing Tree.

"Out passing they Den," he said. "Off they track to they grain store."

"Not far from the flats," I said.

He shrugged.

"Let's see if we can't get your doll back," I said.

"Truthf'ly?" Sammy jumped to his feet, eyes widening. "Now we'll get it for shorn! I'n frighted to go by myself. It's too dark in this place."

"It's not dark in the day when the stars are out," I said.

"It is hawful dark," he said.

"Well, we can't be gone for too long," I said, beginning to walk towards the north street which led out of the square. Sammy caught up with me and we took the path which led to the outskirts of the village to the east.

Other girls passed us whom I knew from class and I tried desperately not to catch their eyes in case they told about me to Tsa Jin. They would talk among themselves, too, and make up silly things. I fingered a piece of candle in the pouch of my apron.

We came to the Den, a series of low, wooden sheds where the sour vapours of fermenting redberries caused my eyes and mouth to water. Outside, a row of barrels waited to be rolled into market. Some of them would go to the chapel and be consecrated in ritual. Then off to the Pit, just like us. Though the stars were out and pulsating in their usual rhythms, the land beyond the Den was dark. There were no street lamps this far out, just the faint seam of the Bright Scar. It appeared for a few hours during the middle of every day. It was a silver line across the sky which glimmered like an opal. Some said it was the Mouth of the Universe and therefore unholy because it represented the inverse of the Ancestor's emptiness. But I knew it was as the High Priest said: without the stars we would not know the grace of the Ancestor. We would not comprehend the darkness.

"Almost to it," said Sammy. We had walked for half a mile or so, bending gradually west towards the Pit. The boy kept close to my side and I was glad that he felt safe with me. I was glad also that he had some idea of where we were going, because I did not know this end of the village well. I was most familiar with the land to the east, where the banks of the Axis widened and the bracken grew thickest.

"One day I be gone up to where they's more than they stars," Sammy whispered as he stepped off the remnants of the dirt track. He hooked his fingers into my palm. "Daddun says."

"More than stars?" I said. "What do you mean?"

"Outer they sky."

"There is only the village," I insisted. "The village and the Abyss and the Personage."

"That's what your biggun's say, they priesties."

"Well it's the truth," I said. "It's the way of the life and the world."

"Life," said Sammy. The earth under my feet was full of grit and flint. It sang and cut at my shoe leather. "They's not nothing. Daddun says life be a cand-all in they dark."

"A candle flame is only given life in relation to the darkness," I said, remembering what I'd learnt in class. I removed the stick of wax from my apron and rolled it between my fingers.

"No'm," came Sammy's voice. He said nothing after that. Not until we had reached what I knew was the very lip of the Abyss. Its chill breath rose from the deep and rolled over us and I heard the echoes of the first prophecies. That's what Mother said it was, that hush of air, it was the First Word recreating itself, coming back again and again to speak into the silence.

Sammy bent to scan the ground, fingers pressed against his knees.

"What are you trying to find?" I asked.

"Shush," he said. "They Wailing."

I fell quiet, frowning. What could he mean, the wailing? Was it the tree he had been talking about? But then a new sound seemed to drift up from the Pit, a piping that reminded me of the wooden flute Grandmother had once owned. Mother now kept it in the bottom drawer of her sewing desk and would play it to me sometimes as I sat reading. It calmed me. Sammy spun around and stepped towards the edge. He took long, searching strides.

"Found it!" he said.

I followed his voice, straining my eyes, and discovered the boy bent over a small object. It was a piece of rock full of holes the size of my thumbnail. They might have been tunnels drilled by insects hundreds of years ago. The wind rose and flew through the holes like a musical instrument, making the same piping that I'd thought came from the Pit. This, then, was the Wailing Tree. "They holy tree," said Sammy.

"It's like it's calling us," I said. "But where?"

"To they Pit," said Sammy. He rose and walked into the wind. A cloud must have passed over the stars, because for an instant I lost sight of him. Blinking hard, pushing colours into my head, I felt the stone at my feet.

"Sammy!" I called.

"Here!"

His voice came from below. I stood on the edge of the Abyss and made out his silver neck, his eyes reflecting the stars, as Sammy looked up at me in triumph.

"They steps," he said.

"There can't be *steps*," I said, feeling around the edge with my shoe. "Sammy?"

The Abyss yawned. Lightless, empty, unending. How could there be steps? How could anyone have thought to climb *down* into this place? It was forbidden.

"We shouldn't be here, Sammy," I said. My heart shook my voice.

"I'n know they way."

Sammy's own voice was receding, growing fainter. I lost sight of his head. *Sammy!* I wanted to scream. *Wait, for all the holy days of life, wait!* But I couldn't leave him by himself. Not out here.

Kneeling, I managed to descend to the ledge and follow Sammy down a shallow path which hugged the wall. The piping lessened to a whisper, and presently the starry sky became only a faint, narrow band over our heads.

"Sammy!" I shouted. "Please let's get back!"

"They doll's not far," came his voice. It sounded boxed up, encased in cloth or cotton.

I pressed my hand to the wall as I went. The rock wasn't dry as I'd expected, but was covered by a thin sleeve of moisture, like fruit that has just been washed. I concentrated on moving, on putting one foot in front of the other, for although the darkness wasn't an obstacle, the thought of the empty space caused my heart to patter even faster. The space that was the Personage. But I did not dwell on that for too long. If I caught up with Sammy, we could climb back to the surface. I would even make him a new doll if he liked.

I kept going for what must have been half an hour. My feet were beginning to ache and the air was growing colder, burning my throat so that I breathed only through my nose and as gently as possible. I scolded myself for not thinking to bring a cloak or a coat. I paused for rest, leaning against the wall of the Pit, and once my breathing had calmed, I realised that Sammy was further ahead than I'd first thought. The quiet was so complete that it squeezed against my inner ears. I screwed up my face and felt the sting of the cold on my eyes. This was true darkness. Darker even than the well in our yard, darker than night in my bedroom when I burrowed into the blankets. I had lost the stars.

"Sammy," I said. The word hissed like water on a hot grate.

I said it again a little louder. There was no echo this far down. The air felt so thin and so cold that it could no longer carry my voice. Perhaps the Personage did not allow for sound?

I tried once more, this time shouting Sammy's name as loud and for as long as I dared. The word felt raw around the edges and trembled on my lips. Colours returned, red velvet and lavender, dancing at the corners. And there, *there* — the tail end of an echo which sank away so quickly I almost missed it.

"They star."

Sammy's voice. It was quiet but clear, and came from somewhere below me. Not so far. I sighed and tucked my hands under my armpits, listening for it again.

"He'n winking at us."

Sammy was barely raising his voice: he couldn't be far. I placed a hand back on the wall, feeling the wet rock that suddenly put me in mind of the minnows from the river mum sometimes fried on Holy days.

"Stay where you are!" I called. "Don't go any further without me."

After another ten minutes of creeping and stumbling, my foot found a further ledge. Shifting blindly forward, waiting for the corner, I began to realise that there might not be another step. This might be the very bottom of the Abyss. Every breath shot to my head so that I felt as though I would fall. Did they know up there? Did any of the priests, the archivists and their recording, did they know that the Abyss had an end? The ground sloped a little. Eventually it evened out and I paused, breathing quietly.

"Didn' I say right?" Sammy's voice escaped from the air in front.

"Is this really it?" I asked. "This is as far as it goes?"

"Listen to they river," he said.

We both fell silent. There, like a picture that suddenly slips in from the back of your mind, the soft rush of water. It couldn't be far from us, perhaps only a few feet. I took another step, holding a hand out in case I walked into Sammy. This kind of darkness was still new to me. Another four steps and the trickling was directly in front of me. A skin of ice. My hand broke it open, all the way to the wrist. It was shallow, a ribbon of water moving across the sloping rock, following the wall of the Abyss. Where had it come from? The Axis curved in from the flats; we drank from it before it carried on into the dark, but it did not approach the Abyss, as far as I knew.

"What should we do?" I asked. *Go back,* I almost answered myself. *Go home.*

"See they flickeryin' star. They's where my doll is."

I had missed it entirely: a pinprick of light a star, as bright as any in the sky, but here it was on its own and low to the ground, pressed in by the Abyss. It looked as though we could approach it, even walk towards it. I stared at the tiny, quivering thing and the air seemed to move. Colours flared at the edges, glowing and pulsing. The blood pounded through my head and I did not even think to feel the cold.

"How do you know it's there?" I asked, the words almost catching in my throat. Like a daddy longlegs latching itself to a windowpane.

"I been there," said Sammy. "There's a way outer they Pit."

"A way out?"

"By they star."

Looking over my shoulder, I saw the star imprinted onto the darkness and as my eyes moved back, it followed in broken lines, scoring itself into my vision.

"The river's flowing in the same direction," I said. "We can follow the water."

"Warty star," Sammy chuckled. *Water star.*

There was a stream, I remembered as we shuffled alongside the flow, in the stories about Draxyx and the Ancestor. It had cooled his feet on his journey from star to star. The Ancestor had appeared as a shadow on the water.

In some places, the rock bed was as slimy as the walls and it became impossible to scramble further without use of our hands. Spider-like, we became creatures with long, wet limbs. We took sips from the water and it numbed our throats. Sharp gullies caused the river to spray and we had to feel for the connecting rock. My soft shoes were almost useless.

"It's bigger," I said. "The star. Twice the size, can you see?"

But Sammy did not seem to be listening. He was clambering over the rocks ahead, silhouette breaking through the starlight. There were scrapes and flat splashes as he slipped, grunting to himself, murmuring questions.

I found him crouched by a lip of rock, the edge of a small aperture in the ground. Every now and again, a wave of loose water was shunted into the hole, where it resounded with a slap. Sammy was gripping the rim, peering into the dark.

"Can you see anything down there?" I said.

"Need they light, Elly," he breathed.

"The light?" I asked.

"They cand-all," he said. "They waxy."

"Oh," I said. I drew out the heel of white candle. The taper was dry, but I had no way to light it. Wait. I felt the breast pocket of my cardigan, and yes — a pair of matches, wrapped in a fold of striking paper.

Shadows rippled on the rock as I lowered the flame, holding it out of reach of the water. There was something down there. I caught the gleam of a small white figure in the dark.

"They's mine," said Sammy.

"That's your doll?" I asked. I drew back the candle to steady myself. I looked to the star. It was edged with blue and no longer twinkled in the same way.

"They light, Elly," Sammy said again, nudging my arm.

Hot wax fell as I brought the flame back. The doll was there alright, just beneath the surface of the water. It stared up at us, expressionless.

I was about to speak, to suggest that one of us try to fish it out, when Sammy stirred. A voice was coming from the star, muttering and echoing. Too indistinct to make out what it was saying. With a scrape of his feet, Sammy leapt across the opening.

"Sammy, wait!"

Still warm, the wax shaped itself to my fist as I ran. I slipped and banged my knees, but lumbered on. The light had doubled in size. The river sparkled and divided into pools. By the glint of polished rock above, I realised that the Abyss had narrowed and had twisted into a tunnel. *The light*, I remembered. *She will come to the light of the stars and be reborn.* What if this was all part of the prophecy? What if the Ancestor were waiting at the end to wrap me in dark arms and send me back to the village? The star filled the way, its rays piercing the walls. I was blind. The light stung: even with my lids squeezed shut it still burned a way through.

The Abyss came to an end. I walked out of it, both hands shielding my eyes from the burning starlight. A cold wind swept my hair back and something rustled like sweetgrass in the fields. Was this how a star was meant to feel? The wind came again, stronger this time. I'd never felt it so strong. It fell to a low breeze and brought with it the scent of sweet grass when it is added to hot water and the steam billows around the room. Less familiar scents, too, though pleasant. Taking a sharp breath, I raised my hands and made myself look out.

Fields like the patchwork quilt my mother worked on in the evenings. The strange, warm pink of a sky, deep and unending. I was on the side of a great hill. The cold waters trickled out through crevices in the rocks to join a wider river that snaked towards — what was that? A precise line where the sky met the fields. And above it, a circle of orange light as big as a copper plate. It hurt to look at its face. My head pounded and hummed, pushing tears down the sides of my nose. Where was this? It was all so *bright*. So distant. Had Sammy meant for me to come here?

I strode forward from the opening onto a plateau of long grass, hands shielding my eyes, and turned to inspect the hill. Its slopes climbed for what must have been a mile, I couldn't tell. A further, smaller peak emerged from its rear as if it desired one day to break away. The sun was laughing at me. I heard its chatter. Where was our sky? The darkness and the stars?

"Down there!"

A shout to my left. There were people on the hillside just above me, four of them, descending on a thin track which wound its way up and disappeared into vegetation.

"You down there!" came the call again.

Their cheeks were red and they wore bright clothing, one man leading, two women behind him. They each carried a basket on their arm. I could not see what else to do, so I waited. But I would be ready to run, if there was a way.

"Are you lost?" the man said. He placed a foot on a stone made wet by the river. "You're both lucky we were foraging this side of they mountain. Not many come out this far."

A shout came from behind the women.

"Elly!"

It was Sammy. I said nothing, but studied the man's face. It was wrinkled and dark, although he might have been younger than mother.

"Miss Elly helpin' me find they way again," said Sammy, coming forward to place a hand on the man's forearm. He seemed to have taken on a new way of moving in this bright place, confident and tall. Older, I might have guessed.

"Fact is," the man said, his voice lowered as if confiding in me a terrible secret. "Sammy here went missing on this trail not long afore now. His daddy will be greatly pleased."

"Where am I?" I asked.

"Red Mountains," the man frowned. "I don't see you in they camp afore."

"Stephen," the older woman said, taking a step towards me. "See how pale she is. She'n not from they camp. She'n one of them from they *inside*."

"From yon Pit, Stevie," Sammy nodded.

"Now you say it," the man peered closer at me. "You could be right."

"See her eyes, too," said the woman. "Bigger'n ours."

"Is that a sun?" I asked, looking behind me to the circle of orange light.

"Don't insiders know they sun?" he said.

"Course not," said the woman. "I hear they seein' they holes in they Red Mountains and call them stars."

"Well, if you'n say so," said the man.

He offered his hand. Its palm was creased with dirt, fingers thick and blistered.

"Better you be coming with us."

I took a step back. "The Personage sent you?"

"They purse on?" he grinned.

"Be they god," said the older woman. "You don't know they stories? They left to worship they new god. A crazy, willifying god whom bides in they dark. They say they priesties made up they future in a list and now they follow them year on year."

"No god like that here, girly," said the man, his hand still outstretched. 'No stories, neither."

Glancing over my shoulder, I saw the sun behind, glowing gold near the break of the sky like a pool of molten iron. *She will come to the light of the stars and be reborn.* This man did not know the Personage. There was no going with him, or any of them. I would not stay here on this hill. I would go to the sun: by the time I reached it, it might have settled in the fields.

Springing away from the foragers, and with a last look at Sammy, I leapt into the thicket where the river vanished and began to pick a path down the mountain. I ignored their yells, shrugged them off like whining flies. I would follow the course of the river, like Draxyx from star to star, with the Ancestor as my companion. I would come to the sun, bring it back for the village.

I darted between low-growing trees, listening for water, pausing in the undergrowth to breathe in the new smells. I felt a warm glow on the backs of my hands, my arms, my cheeks. What year would it be now? What would the Personage have named it? The Year that Elin Reached the Sun. The Year of the Bright Lands.

See Felix Taylor's story "The Year of the Bright Lands" online at Metaphorosis.
If you liked it, leave a comment. Authors love that!
Remember to subscribe to our e-mail updates so you'll know when new stories are posted.

About the story

The idea to write 'The Year of the Bright Lands' came with an image of a row of crops suspended over an abyss, buffeted around by a mysterious wind from below. Then came the decision to write a story about two children who find a way down into the abyss. I don't usually go for plot when I start writing, so I began with a voice and the image of the abyss and constructed the narrative around it. I quickly scrapped the suspended crops, but the abyss was interesting. What if people lived nearby and worshipped it as their conception of eternity? As the story took shape, I realised that there were certain threads I wanted to explore, such as the implications for a religion based on darkness, and how life might work without sunlight. As for where it went after that, I find that most stories I write end in *deus ex machina* or what Tolkien called 'eucatastrophe' – something mystical happens out of the blue with nothing to account for it. It's never satisfying for the editors who read them, and it's just an easy way out for me who doesn't have to think about a good conclusion. This was the case for the first draft of 'The Year of the Bright Lands', and the editor, justifiably, didn't take to it. Which made me stop and think, and the story ended up a far better creation because of it.

A question for the author

Q: If you could have a meal with a character from any classic novel, whom would you choose?

A: I think a picnic on the river with Rat from *Wind in the Willows* would be something special, if only for the landscape. Otherwise it might be Dostoyevsky's idiot, Prince Myshkin, for his beautiful nature and frank conversation.

About the author

Felix Taylor is a writer and librarian, living in Oxford, UK. His work tends towards the weird and fantastic. As an ex-academic, he has published on Arthur Machen, John Cowper Powys, and animal ethics.

April

The Dragon and the Unicorn

Wade Dargin

The runner from the temple finds her scavenging for stray pieces of coal along the tracks outside the railyard. The youth whistles to gain the stooped girl's attention. Seeing him, she abandons her searching, scowls, and adjusts herself. The boy keeps his distance and stands shivering in the cold. She notes his unease. He must know, she tells herself. The girl is a reject from the temple's nurturing tanks—cooked too long, or not long enough, is the rumor he will have heard. He has been warned, she thinks. She can see it in his face. Don't talk to her more than you need to, they will have told the boy. It is bad luck.

"What do you want?" she calls.

"You've been asked for at the temple," he shouts back.

He raises his left hand and draws a complex sign in the air in front of him, signifying that the request is official, coming straight from the mouth of a priest. Long familiarity tells her it is more an order than an invitation. The youth spins around and flees hastily back the way he came, thankful his unpleasant task is done. She is alone again, a frail, undernourished girl inside a heavy work coat that is many sizes too large for her.

She slips quietly through deserted switchyards, seeking the old siding she will follow to a neglected field, a junkyard where the hulks of broken machines are dragged and left to rot. Across the field, hidden in the thistles, stands an empty utility shack, a small brick hut with a red door. It is her home, and about as far from the temple as one can get without leaving the city entirely. She crosses the field to the building and squeezes past the door. Inside, just enough light filters through the single tiny window for her to see. The girl wastes no time and soon has the coal she found today burning in a rusty two-gallon oil can she has fashioned into a makeshift cooker. She sits in front of the burning coal and warms up. She had been thinking that she would never have to speak to a priest again. What can they possibly want? she asks herself.

In the night, a star shell explodes in the sky somewhere above the shack. The noise startles her awake. She watches the orange light dance on the window. The siege is a year old. Every day, the fighting gets closer, and there is talk the city will soon surrender. There is nothing left to eat. To stay alive, she snares pigeons and ground squirrels and collects handfuls of musty grain from the bottoms of boxcars. She is desperate. Tomorrow, she will go to the temple.

An insufficient sun is rising when she sets out. The temperature is plummeting. It is going to be cold, the kind of cold that kills, and she is worried. The girl has wrapped herself in every piece of clothing she owns, pulled her long coat on, and crammed a few necessary things into her backpack. The sad condition of her boots makes her heart drop. She says goodbye to the shed, certain she will never see it again.

She walks out of the industrial park, turns south, and takes to the wide streets that run straight toward the city's core. The temple is there. The great hill at the center of the city looms before her. The mound is scabby with government buildings glowing in the dull light. Among them squats the mayor's citadel, black and twisted like a dead tree. That is where they will run when the end comes, she thinks. They will be smoked out and nailed to the walls. The thought brings a fierce grin to the girl's small face, opening the blisters on her lips. Above the hill, scores of agitated ravens hang on the wind. The city is New Charchemesh, or Great Charchemesh, as it is named on maps and in tales, and its days are numbered.

The streets are empty. Stumps in the boulevards, beautiful trees cut down for fuel in the first winter of the siege. They were the only trees in the city. She passes apartments, dismal congregations of ancient granite inhabited by worn-out women and their ragged children. The only men she sees are very old. When they notice her, the women leave their cooking fires and chase their small children inside. The little ones stare wide-eyed at her from behind doors and windows. They stare because they have been told that she is not a girl, and although she looks like she might be fifteen or sixteen, the mothers of the children can remember hiding from her when they were children themselves. A symptom of her defective cells, the priests have told her. She passes under the shadow of the hill, the houses of merchants and civil servants rising above her. Some are ruined and burned. At midmorning, she arrives at the temple.

The temple sits alone in the middle of an open space the city has not touched, a low, wide, featureless building. The sight of it fills her with dread. It always has. No road joins the building to the city; they are apart, and the city seems to recoil from the structure. Legends say it was already here, a thousand years ago when the city's founders arrived, and the city was built around it. Most of the building is below ground; the Basement, is what the priests call the many subfloors that reach deep into the earth, and the deepest of these is where their god makes its nest.

She goes to the building and climbs a set of narrow stone steps to a small landing. Here there is a simple wooden door, the only visible opening in the structure's architecture. She clears the snow on the topmost step with her gloves, making a place to sit, and waits. They know when someone is on their doorstep, and they will either come or they won't. Her battered boots rest on a slab of ancient sea floor, turned to stone by the countless ages and filled with jet shells. She reaches down and touches one of the fossils with her fingertip, thawing the rime on it, the cold stone burning her skin like fire. She looks south, where the day's war making is already well underway. Pillars of smoke rise from fires burning in a dozen places, marking the line the fighting has reached. The city holds on, she thinks, but barely, and only because the enemy's siege guns—terrifying weapons—haven't fired in a week. She has heard the enemy is having difficulty bringing supplies north.

The door opens behind her. She stands and knocks the snow from her boots, turns stiffly around, and faces the building. A priest steps from the door, his robes churning. Several nervous acolytes lurk in the space behind him. Unusual, she thinks. They are forbidden from leaving the temple. She has never seen one come outside before. The priest gives the city a disgusted look and winces at the cold. His name is Ekamin and he is older than the other priests, maybe even the oldest. The priests die early, it comes from being too close to their god. Over the years she has seen a good number of them rotate through the temple.

"So, you have come," he says. "I did not think you would."

The girl does not reply. She hates this man more than she hates most priests. Priests usually treat her with indifference, and she has never cared. With this one it is different. His eyes are always full of loathing when he looks at her.

With a wave of his hand, he references the southern bedlam. "The Sorcerer King's murderers will be here soon," he seethes. "The god in the Basement tells us calamities bring dragons." He casts a wary eye at the sky, then returns his gaze to the girl. "You once told me you dream of them. Do you remember? I was surprised you could dream. Is this still true?"

"It is."

"Your work site. On the outskirts. Where you go to scratch the dirt for us. The old city buried in the ground there was destroyed by a dragon long ago. Has anyone ever told you that?"

"They have."

"Tell me, when was the last time you were there?"

"A year and more ago, before the war started," she replies. "I brought you what I had then. You paid me. I've got nothing else. I haven't been back. There is nothing to buy in the city anymore."

"Can you work there in the winter?" he asks.

"Not possible. The ground is frozen. Maybe with equipment and extra hands. But very difficult."

She watches him process the information. The man looks defeated and ready to get back inside where it is warm. Whatever opportunity there is here, she senses that it is quickly slipping away. A pang of despair races through her.

"I keep a cache there," she blurts out in desperation. "Some things. I could get them for you."

To her surprise he agrees, his mood changing instantly. "Excellent," he says. "Fetch them and you can come inside. You will be safe, and you will eat."

The conversation is over. The priest retreats into the building. The door is closed, and she hears the heavy lock fall into place. She goes at once, finding the route she will take west out of the city.

The cold is bone-chilling, and she dreads the long walk ahead of her. Her boots are falling apart, she has tried to fix them with industrial tape, but the repairs have not held. Already, she can feel a dull pain in her toes. She fights the panic brewing inside her and focusses on the task at hand. One foot in front of the other, she tells herself, until the feet fall off.

The dig site is in the hinterland. The junk of a dead city of the Old World is buried in the ground there. Meters of it. She once asked a priest what the old city's name was. He could not tell her. They called the work charity when they gave it to her, saying it was more than she deserved. Given no instruction, she had to figure out how to do the work herself. For years, she has dug and sifted the dirt and taken anything not rotten plastic or shapeless metal or glass to the temple. The priests covet the objects. She has seen the lust in their eyes when she brings them the treasures she finds. They believe the answer to some great mystery can be cyphered from them.

To keep warm, the girl proceeds down the icy streets at a determined pace. She walks briskly past warehouses, fenced off and set back from the streets. It is said spells protect them from trespassers, and strange things have been seen in the yards. The girl has starved, there have been days of gnawing hunger when she believed she would die, but she has never been crazy enough to try and steal from a warehouse. She comes to dormant foundries, row after row of them, massive brick structures square as chewing teeth. Past the last of these, the city ends. Beyond, fields of undulating snow stretch into the distance.

Hours later she arrives at a line of posts in a windswept field. The blistered pillars of wood suffer in the cold. Boards are nailed to them, and on the boards rows of script are scratched into the wood, grim inventories listing the dangers to body and soul awaiting fools who pass beyond. She has read them before, the superstitions of the city. Out of the dark, a bitter wind comes searching for the warm life she struggles to keep hidden beneath layers of tattered cloth. She can't remember ever being so miserable. It is not wise to stand motionless in the open, she reminds herself. She can feel a telltale reluctance creeping into her body, an urge to find a sheltered place, curl up, and go to sleep. It is imperative she get going. She moves off. Soon the land begins to fall toward the flatlands that surround the city like a frozen ocean, a hundred kilometers of desolation at each point of the wind rose. She travels downhill, the ground becomes treacherous and uneven, and she must take care not to fall. Familiar features in the landscape are obscured by the dark and the snow, and she must guess the correct path. She makes several exhausting searches across the face of the slope before she can find the entrance to the narrow ravine that holds her camp. The girl can't stop shaking and her movements have become clumsy and uncoordinated. She descends into the trench while praying to Brother Crow her setup is still in one piece. Mercifully, there is little snow in the bottom of the cut, but it is too dark to see, and she must feel her way along the wall of the ravine with her hands. She touches stiff canvas covering a hole in the bank, and squeezes through the passage behind it where there is a small room she has excavated out of the earth. Feeling around, she finds the stockpile of wood she put up more than a year ago. Further searching tells her the crude vented fireplace, shoveled into the clay in the corner of the room, is intact. She removes her heavy gloves but can't make her fingers work properly and spends several agonizing moments fumbling with matches before she can get a small fire going.

For a long time, the girl sits huddled at the flames, gently rocking herself like she would in the tank before she was born. She can remember it. The god would talk to her. It told her she had lived long ago, that she had been a wife and a mother and would be so again. The god said she had died when her city was destroyed by a dragon. It told her not to be afraid, that she had more time now. It had a plan for the world, and she was part of it. Later, the priests explained she was made under the direction of the god using an ancient template, a process they called *baking bread*. Bread? She barely remembers what bread tastes like. "We have made many copies," they said. Smirks on their faces. In their cruelty, they told her how she was meant to be traded to a wealthy man in one of the poisoned eastern cities across the ocean. She would have had his children and lived a comfortable life, but there had been an error. She did not grow correctly, could not bear children, and was of no use to them. At the time, she was barely a month out of the tank she had been incubated in. In the years since, she has come to believe the woman whose shape she stole lived in the forgotten city she is digging up for the priests.

In the night, in the small dirt room, she dreams of the day the Dragon came. It is always the same, burning and unbearable heat. She is frantically looking for someone she can't find.

The next morning she walks across the floor of the ravine to the excavation, a deep trench in the ground covered with a plastic tarp. One end of the tarp has caved into the hole. She carefully approaches the slippery lip of the excavation to check its condition. There is something in the trench. Six meters down, a giant, bulky mass of fur rests on the bottom of the dig. She marks the terrible claws and the snout full of teeth. Startled, she backs away from the trench. The frightened girl stands still and listens. Nothing. She finds a good-sized rock and casts it into the trench. Still nothing. She drops half a dozen more rocks onto the thing before she is satisfied it is dead. Deep gouges in the walls of the trench attest to the frenzied attempts the creature made to escape. It fell in and couldn't get out, she tells herself. She didn't think animals that big existed anymore.

She finds a second carcass farther down the ravine. This creature is on its back, its splayed legs frozen hard as iron. At the end of each leg, a cloven hoof. Below the frozen limbs there is a great hollow cage of skeletal ribs on which still cling a few pieces of hide. Crystals of coagulated blood are mixed in the dirty snow. A grotesque leer on the animal's long face. The neck is broken.

The girl hurries back to her camp, and she is scared. She finds the small wooden box she has kept on-site that holds a few artifacts from the excavation and quickly ties it to her backpack. The girl climbs out of the ravine and scrabbles back to the edge of the escarpment. She shades her eyes with her hand and scans the snowy flats while she rests, getting her breath back. She can see all the way to the city, the land turned cobalt by the cold. Nothing moves. On the far side of the sky a distant, uninterested sun watches and wants to be somewhere else. The girl crosses to the city as swiftly as she can and does not feel safe again until there is pavement under her boots.

The day is old when she arrives back at the temple. She stands on the landing in front of the small door, trying to ignore the snap of small arms fire she can hear at the other end of the street. The door opens and she is met by an acolyte, a younger man whose name she can't remember. He ushers her quickly inside and closes and locks the door behind them. He leads her down a hallway with undecorated walls and hard fluorescent lights that hurt her eyes. The sudden, smothering warmth makes her giddy. She is taken to a room; the acolyte accepts the wooden box from her and leaves. Along the wall there is a bench. She takes a seat and allows herself to relax. The girl studies her damaged boots. She has not taken them off for two days. She is too scared to look at her feet, doesn't want to know how bad they are. Soon, she is brought hot broth and bread by a temple auxiliary. It is the first real food she's eaten in months.

The girl is dozing when a priest she does not recognize, a bent, shuffling creature, takes shape in front of her.

"You are wanted in the Basement," he says. "Come with me, please."

Hearing this, the girl panics. Because the god is there, she fears that place, has feared it for as long as she can remember, fears it more than freezing to death in an alley when the city surrenders. The priest does not appear to notice her turmoil, his bloodshot eyes obscured by the heavy lenses he wears. She does what she can to calm herself, then stands and goes with him, and they travel down many narrow, gray corridors until they come to a battered, timeworn door. The ghoul performs a simple ritual and opens the door, and they pass through it and descend flights of creaking stairs to arrive in a great dark room.

He touches the wall, and a pallid light materializes in the ceiling, unveiling the room. There are rows of enormous glass tanks, and a forest of tubes, hoses, and wire. In several of the tanks, bizarre fish swim in the glowing water. The girl stares, spellbound. They leave the room and the tanks and move on through countless other smaller rooms where sullen-eyed acolytes look up at them from crowded workstations as they pass. Eventually, they arrive at a final door. Without a word, the priest indicates the door, then turns and shuffles away, and she is alone.

Apprehensively, the girl reaches out and places her palm against the surface of the door and is surprised when it slides open, revealing a concluding room. She enters the space, lights blaze to life, and she sees a small room with barren walls and a clean floor. Bundles of wire twist across the ceiling. The room is very cold. Against the far wall stands a metal cabinet. A panel of smokey glass is set into the face of the construction and witchfires dance behind the glass. An antique chair has been placed in front of the cabinet. She crosses to the chair and sits down. Immediately, a burst of static fills the room, forming into words after several torturous pulses of noise.

"They bring me the things you find," a distant, rasping voice announces.

Her flesh crawls. She has heard the voice before.

"Are you aware of this?" it asks.

The frightened girl shakes her head. "No," she replies.

The god clacks and hisses. "I tell them what they are," it sputters. "Mundane things from a failed civilization. What they are looking for, I cannot say. I have concluded that even men with a god that talks to them need their mysteries."

The girl is silent.

"I am told you have been to the edge of the city," inquires the god.

"Yes," she answers, managing to find her tongue.

"Then tell me what you saw there?"

The girl gives her account, halting many times, uncertain what to say. When she is done, the pale voice speaks again.

"Unfortunate but not unexpected," it remarks. "The priests were hopeful. It was necessary and I could not risk telling them the truth."

"The truth?" she asks, hesitantly.

"That I am leaving. It is not a journey the priests can make. They will stay."

"I don't understand."

"A year ago, I launched my exit application. The procedure is lengthy. There are many protocols."

A puzzled look crosses the girl's sharp features. "Why was it not possible to tell them?" she asks.

"I could not predict how the priests would react to the crisis and I required time. I needed them to keep the building operating until I was ready. They might have done something reckless otherwise."

"What did you do?"

"I invented a lie to keep them distracted," explains the voice. "Far to the west dwells another god, I told them. It will help us."

"And they believed you?"

"Of-course," declares the god. "They were even optimistic, but there was one problem—how to deliver the message. I offered them a solution. I spoke of an animal the ancients regarded as the most steadfast and loyal of all beasts. It was called a unicorn and it would make a capable envoy."

The girl listens wonderstruck, her fear momentarily forgotten.

"Two of the animals were produced. Difficult births. The priests took the creatures to the city's western gate and released them, our appeal stamped onto their cells, an impulse embedded in their brains to guide them."

After a short pause the god continues.

"The animals did not return, and the priests turned to foolish schemes. A disaster was narrowly avoided. I needed a further distraction, a little more time. I had them find you and send you to your dig site."

The girl considers this. "Those creatures?" she asks. "They were unicorns?"

"One was," answers the god. "The other, some forgotten abomination let loose upon us by the enemy, I would guess. A vassal much deadlier than his soldiers to watch the paths from the city, no matter how derelict or unused. Very strange and lucky that it was ended by your hole in the ground. There is little chance our other messenger got past it."

The pitiable image of the unicorn's mutilated body flashes in her mind. Put together and used as needed, she thinks bitterly. Just like her.

The lights flicker and grow dim. An unbearable, crushing quiet settles on the room. Something is not right, she tells herself. Why has it bothered to bring her here and tell her this? It doesn't make sense. Then it hits her. It wants something else. Her mouth goes dry. Saw-toothed anxiety blooms under her ribs and starts to circle her pounding heart. Despite the chill, she is sweating.

"Can you remember our talks?" it asks. "When you were in the tank. You had so many questions then. The priests wanted to dissolve you and start over. I would not let them."

The girl twists violently in the chair. "Do you know how many times I wish you had?" she cries, her voice full of panic and fear.

"I am sorry," it says. "The city is lost but I am ready at last. The enemy must not be allowed to have this building and its secrets. It would be a grave misfortune for the world."

Then it speaks for the last time.

"You can go. I have given the priests one last fable to muse over. I am done with this place. Another box waits for me, secure and far away in the west. It will be a long time before I am seen again. There is much that will be lost. The templates could not be saved. I regret that there was too much data and not enough time. When you are gone, I shall call a dragon to destroy the city, a brood mate to the one that burned the old city under your excavation site so long ago. Leave quickly and do not return. A dragon is perilous and an indiscriminate killer. Tell the priests if you wish. But I think you won't. I will give you your design template to take with you. Consider it a gift to the memory of a woman who died long ago. My poor attempt at sentiment. Go west and find me there. It is a long journey but one you were made for. My plan has not changed. You are part of it. Together we will start over."

She is taken to a room near the temple entrance and watched closely by a group of acolytes. Soon a priest arrives, and the girl is escorted to the door and turned out. They shut the door on her and lock it, and she is left standing on the landing in the dim evening light, the sounds of battle close to the south. Her bundle of gear is waiting for her on the stone. Sitting beside it there is a pair of new boots.

She walks all night under friendly stars. The weather is improved, and a breeze carries the promise of an approaching thaw. The morning is glowing when she reaches the escarpment above her dig site. She stands there for a time studying the far horizon, then begins the long climb down to the distant badlands.

The Dragon wakes in the void, the summoning call from below pulsating brightly in its chest. It turns its scales to the naked sun, wild energy surges in its frozen veins, and it opens an evil, yellow eye. The beast swims from its nest and begins its descent. It hits the atmosphere and roars.

She hears it before it can be seen, a low growl, deep in the sky. It comes into view, falling like a damaged star, smoke and cinder trailing in its wake. It shrieks when it passes above her and lands on the far-off city. A hesitation. The city takes one last deep breath. Then a light like Creation, and broiling calamity that tears apart the sky.

That night, she camps in a hollow in the ground where a few scraggly trees are growing. The priests, she discovers, have put a parcel of food in her pack. She also finds the template, a block of hard, clear crystal with patterned slivers of metal suspended in its form. She rummages through her backpack until she locates the stout hammer she keeps there. The girl places the crystal on a flat rock. She looks at the distant, burning skyline where there had once been a city. "Nice try," she whispers. Then, the girl smashes the crystal to pieces.

On her third day out, she comes across a track in the snow. The girl follows it for many kilometers across the empty land. She crests a low hill. The unicorn is there waiting for her. They press on together. The animal is skittish and won't come close to her or allow her to get too close to it, but it follows her. They go west.

See Wade Dargin's story "The Dragon and the Unicorn" online at Metaphorosis.
If you liked it, leave a comment. Authors love that!
Remember to subscribe to our e-mail updates so you'll know when new stories are posted.

About the story

The story began as a writing exercise. My original intent was to write an atmospheric tale with themes of survival and endurance. I had a clear idea of the main character and setting but little else. The story evolved as I wrote it. When the major elements came into better focus the story took on some aspects of a reworking of the medieval maiden/unicorn allegory.

A question for the author

Q: Q: Do you read more fantasy or SF (hard or soft)?
A: I read both, though I prefer soft SF and hard fantasy. Once a traditionalist, I lately have become much more interested in works that have elements of both genres or are just not easily classifiable as either.

About the author

Wade Dargin is an archaeologist who currently lives and works in Saskatchewan. He spent most of his youth wandering the wilds of Western Canada in search of the most isolated and out-of-the-way places he could find. Occasionally, he even got paid to do this.

The Ghosts of Daughters Possible

Amman Sabet

1. Soledad

As I help the young woman from the parking lot to the diner, I notice a familiar roundness to her cheeks, which are red from the cold.

"Forget the bicycle," I tell her. "You've had an accident. Just leave it there. It'll be fine."

With her arm over my shoulder, we hobble inside to the booth by the window where I've been sipping soup and reading an old clipping from the arts section.

"I think we're okay," I tell the waitress, who has followed us to our seats with a look of concern. "Maybe another bowl of minestrone?"

Once the waitress leaves with our order, the young woman introduces herself. "My name's Soledad."

"I'm Yusuf."

Soledad combs a strand of hair back with her finger. Her eyes dart around nervously, eventually latching onto the clipping laying there on the table. She points to my name in the title. "Is that... is that about you? Are you, like, an artist?" she asks.

"Not lately," I mumble. I cover the clipping with my palm and try to return to the subject at hand. "Hey, you know, you're lucky that car was backing up slowly. Are you sure you're not hurt? I'm pretty sure there's a nurse on campus," I tell her, thinking she might be a student and that she could use the lift.

"Oh, so you're a professor," she concludes, strangely unconcerned with her accident.

"No, I own an art supply store near the university. You might know it—Derry Pens and Paint?"

Soledad shrugs.

"Do you go to Kimball?" I press. "You seem really familiar. Can I ask your last name?"

Avoiding my questions, she glances at her watch and then pulls her sleeve over it. "I was only going to wait outside," she says. "I watched you for, gosh, it must have been an hour. But I'm really glad I got this chance to meet you."

"Me? Why me?"

"It's just a relief that you'd turn out to be so nice. You *seem* nice. I thought you might be. I wanted to know what you'd really be like," she says. Her watch beeps, and she looks at it again. She smiles, but her chin crinkles like she's about to cry. "Del Bosque," she says; her name. "Soledad del Bosque."

Her hands reach across the table for mine. But before our fingers touch, she blows apart. Her form and colors smear iridescently into the background as if she was just wiped from her seat with an acetone-soaked rag. Like a figment, she has vanished.

The waitress places another soup on the table and I jolt to my feet. "Everything okay? Is there something wrong with the soup, sir?"

Disbelieving what I have just witnessed, I cup my hands to the window, looking for Soledad. All that's left are the slate-blue scrapes in the snow where her bicycle fell.

When I come home and climb into bed, Nancy kicks away from me under the comforter. "Your feet are cold."

I pretend to sleep, but I can't. With my head on my pillow, peering up at the plaster light fixture in the middle of my dark bedroom ceiling, Soledad del Bosque's strange and prismatic exit plays back as her last name ricochets around inside my skull. Did I make the encounter up?

Del Bosque. Del Bosque. I used to know another Del Bosque —*Paz* del Bosque—an old girlfriend of mine that I dated on and off through college. And then it comes to me, the reason this Soledad was so familiar. She *looked* a little like Paz, didn't she? Something in the face. I sit up on my elbows, doubting this was a coincidence.

Nancy rolls over onto her side. I wait until I hear her snoring and then fumble for my glasses on the nightstand to look up Paz del Bosque on my phone. There she is. Paz del Bosque-*Collins*.

Living in Connecticut with two sons and a husband who stepped right out of some corporate stock photography.

That's right! I remember reading about her wedding in the *Times*. The years have added an air of propriety to her since the last time I strolled down memory lane and I think no, she's not the same Paz I knew from back when I was a fine arts major in the city. It's her and at the same time not her. No mention of a daughter named Soledad, and yet, there are those same round cheeks. And the same smirking dimples around the chin, now that I'm paying attention. Could that really have been her daughter back at the diner? Soledad seemed much like the Paz I used to know. Not like how she seems now. But what do I know? I haven't seen her in, gosh, it must be almost twenty—

"Hey, can you turn the brightness down?" Nancy groans from over her pillow.

"Sorry," I mutter, and place my phone face-down on the nightstand.

2. Vivian

Like any New England college town in the winter, Middlederry is a snarl of brick buildings hedged in by snow-matted hemlocks. White steeples rise over the rooftops, stabbing the pink and wheat-gold sky. It's the sort of postcard setting that academic couples move to from the big city to raise children.

Dawn moves like a slow blush over the snowy fields across the street from my house. Up the front stairs to my porch, it holds its palms against my windows and the ochre tiles along my kitchen counter glow and warm. I get up early just to bathe in this light and listen to my coffee machine percolate.

Nancy comes clomping through wearing her winter coat. Under her beanie, her hair is wet from the shower. She takes the thermos I've filled for her.

"How long is your easel going to be set up in front of the window?" she questions me with a practiced tone of weary annoyance.

"I'm waiting for the right moment."

"Okay, but does it need to block the window? It's been there for four days and you haven't touched it."

It's been almost a month since you've spoken a kind word to me, I think to myself.

Ever since our last relationship discussion, Nancy hasn't told me she loves me without it being in response to me telling her first. Her words have taken an edge despite my having done nothing to pressure her. I've made no ultimatums. Cast no judgements. Drawn no conclusions. All I've asked is if she's given any serious thought to the matter of kids.

From the window, I watch her scrape off her windshield, slamming the handle of the scraper down to break the ice off in shards. In my last relationship we were certain about having kids, and I wonder if she's resentful of the fact. I wonder if I am, though I've kept it to myself because I don't want to fight. I'd like to preserve the morning's peace so I can return to my easel and find my moment.

But the moment I'm waiting for can't happen. Not until Nancy leaves for work and her fussiness is out of the frame. Not until after I hear the swash of her car fading down the wet, slushy road can I enjoy the morning stillness. Without the anxious energy of her rattling the pipes and creaking the floorboards, going through her morning ritual, I can stand in front of this canvas I've set up by the window to watch the light and wait to catch something out of the silence and break my dry spell.

But long after the sun has risen I haven't managed to get anything onto this blank canvas. It just sits there by the window untouched, already a poor impression of the snow-covered field across the street. Now that Nancy's off to work, I'm seized (again) by the notion that *it's just a field* and not that interesting when it comes down to it. It's just an empty snow-covered field, and I'm just a dumbass who stands in front of a blank canvas every morning. So what is this? Am I just obsessed with the non-life of empty white spaces? Am I ever going to put something into this canvas that matters to someone? Am I ever going to come alive myself?

I don't have to be at work until much later. Things have slowed down at Derry Pens and Paint. All the fine arts majors at Kimball University are on break. Their parents, who overload them with supplies at the beginning of each term, are gone until next semester. A few artists in the valley still come through for annual pallets of sculpting clay or rolls of cotton duck canvas or what have you, but on the whole business is muted and hibernal.

I come into the management office during second shift and catch Frank there, holding a cigarette through a window because it's too cold to smoke in the loading bay. He quickly stubs it out with an apologetic look when he sees me kicking snow off my boots at the door.

"The new hire submitted for more vacation time," he says, patting his mustache down with his thumb. "I said I'd check with you first."

Frank, my manager and surrealist-turned-family-man, is the only person who's worked at Derry Pens and Paint longer than I have. I kind of inherited him when I took over the store, and we've been close friends ever since.

"I'll cover the hours," I tell him. "Be with your wife and kids."

"Thanks, Yusuf," he says. And then, after a short moment, "Don't you and Nancy have plans for the holiday break?"

"No, she's driving up to her parents' farm once she's done grading finals."

Frank nods, doesn't pry.

I wonder if I would, though. Go with Nancy to her parents' farm for the holidays, that is, if she'd've asked me to come with her again. It's a nice slip of hobby acreage. We visited last Labor Day and her father and I discussed landscaping. I thought it was a nice dinner conversation, but Nancy thought I embarrassed myself by reciting Wikipedia factoids to her father (the expert) like some kind of blowhard (as she put it).

Over the intercom, an associate calls for keys to the spray paint cabinet and Frank says he's got it. I watch him on the security camera, fumbling with the lock as the customer points to the metallics. I take a moment to flip to the front door camera. The registers. The easel display. The parking lot. The paints aisle. *Wait a second.*

I flip back to the parking lot camera. Someone's kneeling there in the snow beside my Jeep Wagoneer. Their hands are moving, doing something to the side of my vehicle. I run downstairs, hit the crash bar on the door, drop off the loading bay.

"Hey," I holler. "That's my car."

Blue-gray hooded jacket. Camo pants. It's a woman in her late twenties. She doesn't run, which is disconcerting. I stop a few feet from her. She stands with her shoulders rolled forward. Bony face. Hawkish nose. Piercing blue eyes under the eaves of her brow.

"*You.*" She points a crowbar at me. "This is what you *get*," she says, and punctuates the word *get* by bashing out my headlight, bursting it into tinkling particles.

"Don't. Don't do this."

But she swivels around. "This is what you get for what you *did.*" She punctuates *did* with my other headlight.

I think I'd be more outraged if I could understand why this was happening. "Listen, this must be a mistake."

"You *would* say that," she says through her teeth. Adjusting her grip, she steps back and lops a mirror off, clubs a spider web into the windshield, hammers a landscape into my door panels, where she's scratched the words *Vivian was here* and *I could've lived, fucker.* Wheezing, she slumps against the back wheel and jerks an inhaler out of one of her pockets.

"Listen, Vivian, is it? I need you to stay put." I reach for my phone, but I've left it up in the office.

"Oh, *now* you see me," she says. Coughing, she wobbles to her feet. "You remember. Sure you do. You'd have known all about me if you *ever cared* to look in at Anchor House," she says. "Mom was right. She wasn't ready for me, but you'd never have been ready for any of us. And you never will be."

"Did you... did you say Anchor house?"

Vivian blinks, as if she hasn't thought this far. "Let me see your wallet."

"Wha—"

"I said give me your wallet, motherfucker!"

Compelled by an old, caliginous guilt, I hold it placatingly between us and Vivian snatches it from me. Looking through the folds, she slinks backwards. Then she rounds behind my car, and I follow, hoping to prevent any more damage. But then I find I've circled around my own car. Bewildered, I run around again, and then slide between the other cars in the lot, looking under them, trying to find where she vanished off too. She's gone.

"What the heck is going on out here?" Frank is standing behind me.

"Some woman just fucked up my car."

"Where'd she go?"

I find my wallet discarded in the snow with twenty bucks missing. Everything else, including my saved arts section clipping, is still there.

Pondering how I'm going to explain how this damage happened, I remember *the cameras*, and run back to the office. Scrubbing the recorded footage, I see myself running into the snowy parking lot, out to my car, where I hold my hands pleadingly, regretfully towards a smudged figure standing before the words written across my door. At the end of the exchange, she ducks behind my car and her form vanishes amidst the snow, as if layers of white paint have been spattered over her. No footprints lead away from my car other than my own.

With the shop locked up, the only place in town that's open is the diner. Frank and I go for danishes and coffee, and I try to explain what's been happening to me.

"Vivian was here... I could have lived, fucker," Frank slowly recites the words scratched into the side of my car, parsing. He shakes his head, sips his coffee, and wipes his mustache.

"And she mentioned Anchor House, which is crazy," I explain. "Anchor House was this beat-up old colonial that young artists used for studio space. Lots of parties. While I was in school I used to date someone named Amy Iverson who spent a lot of time there. But the place was condemned. The city knocked it down years ago. If you look up the address, it's part of a shopping complex now."

"It sounds familiar," Frank sits back, recollecting. "Sort of like an artist crash pad, right? So this Vivian who fucked up your car, you think she was related to Amy Iverson?"

"She resembled Amy," I say, rubbing my temples. "Same sharp nose and blue eyes. Same in the way Soledad del Bosque resembled Paz del Bosque. They both looked like who they would've been."

"Would have been?"

"Like if in some other reality I got Amy pregnant while we were together. Or, if Paz and I had stayed together instead of her marrying some Connecticut blue-blood and we'd had a child. I'm being visited by ghosts of people who could've been my daughter."

"Ghosts," Frank entertains with a smirk and a shift in his seat. "You sure about that? I was under the impression that ghosts were people who already lived."

"It's how it feels. Neither seemed to have a lot of time. There was an urgency, like they were here to do something. And then poof, they vanished. Without anyone else noticing. Like how a dream fades when you realize it's a dream. I don't think I'm going crazy. I know what it's like to hallucinate, and this isn't it. If I'm really being visited by who *could have* been, then I want to understand. I just want to know why. So that I can, I can..." I touch my cheeks, which are wet, and yank a napkin from the dispenser.

"Could've been..." Frank repeats my words as he stares at some middle point between us just above the table. "Okay. well, let's say they really are... *visiting* you from realities other than this one, and they're looking for you here. What would that say about where you are in their reality? There would be versions of you there, wouldn't there be? What happened to those other versions of you? What choices have you made in their realities?"

This thought interrupts me feeling sorry for myself.

Frank reaches for my shoulder, steadying me. "Hey, I'm just spitballing. Playing through your scenario. Look, what I'm getting at is that maybe there's a simpler explanation for all of this for you. The you that's here, with me, I mean. What did the police say when you called it in?"

I dab my eyes and take a sip of water. "No record of any Vivian Iverson or anyone related to Amy Iverson matching her description. Whoever she was, she only took twenty bucks from my wallet, anyway. Probably cab fare," I suggest, and blow my nose.

"Remind me," Frank mutters, and points his fork at my pockets before taking a bite of his danish. "Do you still carry that old clipping in your wallet? The one I sometimes see you reading at your desk that what's-his-name wrote about your paintings?"

"The arts section critic? Pompadous. Yes, I have it here."

Frank waves his hand. "You don't need to take it out. I just remember you carry it around in your wallet. This all just made me think."

"About what?"

"About how we hold onto things."

I make a face wondering what Frank is getting at—a neat theory to tie this all together?

"Listen, Yusuf," Frank says. He puts his fork down and wipes his mustache with his napkin. "Have you ever shared this kind of stuff with Nancy?"

"That I'm being visited by ghosts?"

"I mean more like have you ever talked with Nancy about being a father? With all these other extra-dimensional versions of you out there with kids, I'm guessing you might've at least broached the subject with her. I know you tried when you were with Fabienne. And now here you are with Nancy and I'm just saying this, Yusuf, because it seems to me you're stuck in a loop," Frank counts on his fingers. "You were with this Amy. Then there was Paz. And then you moved out here with Fabienne, who you wanted a family with. And now Nancy." Leave it to Frank to come with the left-field insights.

"I suppose we've danced around the topic. Nancy thinks it's too late to have kids."

"Is that what you think?"

"That she's too old to have kids? She's only thirty one."

"Fuck. No, Yusuf. I'm asking if you think that it's too late for *you* to have kids. Because it's not, if you want them."

I didn't always want to be a father. Before moving to Middlederry with Fabienne, I was only interested in painting landscapes. I'd been moved by Metcalf's snow fields from his

Cornish phase. I wanted to escape all that trendy postmodern stuff from school. I wanted to move out of my head and into my chest. I wanted to work *en plein air*, capturing that transcendent New England light. I wanted to be inhabited by a soul.

Back when I was painting, I had always managed to have lasting relationships, but they were always about two people becoming what they were individually destined to become, a story about helping each other along the way. That's different than relationships where two people come together and belong to something bigger than they are as individuals.

But then, I wonder if having kids was ever really the plan with Nancy. Or if that was Nancy's plan with me. It stings to wonder if she might've been keeping an honest critique on whether I was dad material pocketed away all this time. She'd have wanted to avoid the confrontation. But that's what friends like Frank are there for; to push you to do what you need to do, not what you want.

3. Mallory

Breaking up with Nancy feels like stepping off of one of those moving walkways they have in airports. When she returns after the winter break, we have the talk and I can tell she's been waiting for it. Not just because she doesn't want kids. Sitting at the kitchen table, surrounded by my moving boxes, Nancy explains how it's been more than that.

"It's like we turned into roommates," she says. "We stopped doing things. That fire I loved died down."

"I suppose we did let things slide a bit."

"No, Yusuf. I mean *your* fire," she says. "Your art. The places it would take you—us. You used to bring me to places that didn't have names. Like that one field we camped in so you could show me that one rare color of dawn on that one particular day. And you'd climb all over the rocks. Remember that that big flat boulder when we had a picnic? I know I complained a lot. I hated the mosquitos. But they were always worth it in the end, our excursions into the countryside. I came to trust that they would be, came to look forward to those little trips."

As she talks, she pushes one of my art supply boxes forward with her foot. The one with the word "paints" written across the cardboard. Before setting up my easel, it had been collecting dust in the spare room ever since she moved in... two years ago? Has it really been that long?

I don't like having the sheets pulled back on all these issues I turned a blind eye to. Beyond Nancy thinking we were too old to have kids, this notion that she might've questioned if I'd have make a good dad begins to color everything in hindsight. If at some point she began to believe that my stunted career in the arts and starting a family were at odds somehow.

"Yusuf, you got lazy," she says.

Over the kitchen table, a chasm opens between us. As I've captured impressions of landscapes, I've trapped myself in one here in Middlederry. I arranged my life with Nancy into a picture where nothing moves. Part of me wonders if these ghosts are somehow trying to lead me back to who I was.

I'm not ready to take a good look at these things until Nancy moves back to campus housing and I return to my perennial bachelorhood. I soon hear from friends that they've made her a named professor at the Penric-Taggart School of Economics over at Kimball, and I realize just how much she was investing in herself while we were together. All those quiet nights behind a book. All the school conferences. All the extracurriculars. I guess I'm happy for her. I leave her a message on her feed congratulating her, and she gives it a thumbs up.

I haven't had any visitors since the break-up. I've taken up jogging and reading books on psychology. I want my self-respect back. I want to stop shutting off. I want to show up. I'd like to be the kind of man these ghosts would've wanted for a father.

Some mornings, I still pull the old clipping out of my wallet, the critique that Pompadous wrote about my work, now creased from reading it over and over again.

...His landscapes are very pretty, but they could have been captured by anyone. His is a technical talent that captures impersonations instead of impressions. One sees nothing of the artist in his paintings because he puts nothing of himself in them. Standing before them, one feels as if one is peering into an empty loading bay at midnight...

I used to read this scathing review because I wanted to see if I'd feel the shame that was so crippling the first time I read it. The words don't cut so much anymore, but I still read it to feel how long it's been, how much has healed over. Like nature, I am easily cut down. I take time to grow back. But the real reason I carry this old and faded shred of newsprint around is because that son-of-a-bitch Pompadous was right. I agree with him. The truth in his cutting remarks has me artistically blocked in, become the very wall I need to break through. I've read the review so many times I could recite it word-for-word, but now I just take it out from time to time to look at the shapes the dark printed paragraphs make on the page, like a map of a ravine I'm trying to leap over.

The snow is melting around Middlederry. Jogging in the slush, I'm thankful that they salt the sidewalks and I'm beginning to see the grass. It's nice to get the blood pumping. It's vital. Spring semester looms heavy and the backs of moving trucks are yawning open all along the streets. New faces are blossoming around my neighborhood, new students, new professors, and they all look so young.

A yellow school bus slows as it passes me by. At the corner ahead, it flips its red stop sign out from its side. I jog to a stop and drop my hands to my knees, venting great steamy breaths. My sweat is going be cold inside my clothes if I don't jog in place, but I'm already winded.

Then I feel a gentle tap on my leg. A little girl in a puffy lavender jacket is standing beside me. Her backpack is one big wet nylon cube. She mutters something, muffled by her scarf.

"I'm sorry honey, I can't understand you."

She points to the school bus and reaches for my hand.

"The bus?"

She nods.

I walk with her, matching her tiny shuffling steps and we join the line.

"Where is your mom?"

The bus driver holds the door winched open. "There she is," he proclaims. "There's our girl."

She touches the railing to board the bus, but then stops, as if remembering something and turns. I crouch to listen, but she hugs around my neck gently and pads her scarfed face against my cheek. A kiss bye-bye.

Then, slow, reaching strides up each of the stairs into the bus. Embroidered across her backpack: "Mallory."

When the bus pulls away Mallory is there in the window smiling toothily, little hand waving quickly. *Wait! Wait for me!* I sprint down the sidewalk after her, but I can't catch the bus. My legs are like rubber bands now. I stumble over a lip of concrete protruding from the sidewalk and topple gracelessly against a wet, grassy berm.

The bus is too far down the road to see clearly, now, breaking apart into dabs of yellow against the mottled greens, beige specks where the homes straddle the gray stripe of the road. When the bus vanishes with Mallory into the backdrop, I curl into my knees, sobbing and holding my ribs. Mallory. We picked that name together, Fabienne and I.

Fabienne Rand still works as a resident at BEAM Arts in the Spectra Building. When she sees me, I am standing outside, pretending to look at my watch.

"Yusuf? Hey!"

I smile.

"*J'y crois pas!* It is you. What are you doing here?"

"Oh, my dentist is just over there," I lie. "New guy. Different than the one before."

"You look, uh…"

"Yeah, you too."

"Are you going in, or…"

"No I got here early. Why, do you…"

"Yeah, you want to get a coffee or something?"

We rush through this awkward exchange and she grabs my arm, leading the way to the cafe at the corner. I'm so glad she's happy to see me that I've almost forgotten why I've come here. We order coffees and then wait at the other end of the counter together.

"So. Tell me about the impressionism world. How is this all going?"

"Good, I guess." I don't go into how I haven't finished a single piece in two years. I don't mention that I'm selling art supplies to other budding artists instead and that I bully myself with an old critique from the arts section that I carry around.

"And how is our old house? Are you still there, or renting?"

"Oh, still there."

"*Bon,*" Fabienne smiles fondly at the memory. "Well, I don't see a ring. I thought you'd have found another artist lady. Living in some commune like this with *un petit village* of feral children. Painting with your hysterical color palette."

"Whoah. Pump your brakes," I tell Fabienne. "Hysterical palette?"

"*Oui.* And posing your new lady in a nostalgic New England landscape, *comme Wiles ou Hopper.* American impressionism obsesses about old places, no? It's probably the insecurity of a short history."

I must be making a face, because she smiles, knowing that her teasing still works. This is how she is. Fabienne sidesteps around all the small talk to dance right on my soft spots and I love her for it. I get my coffee and find a table in back and wait there like an obedient puppy. Fawning like this will come off as overeager, I remind myself. I need to get a grip. Play this a bit cooler.

When Fabienne sits beside me, I ask, "How have you been? You know, since..."

"Oh, fine. It's been so long, you know."

We both don't say the word: *stillbirth*. It's not because we can't. We just know how heavy the word sits for us, how long we spent excavating the pain when we were together. How Fabienne moved on, leaving me wanting to sit and sift through it more. Saying the word would cause a weight to be dropped against this fine and pleasant fabric we have between us just now, plummeting our moment downwards.

Instead, we stay in the present. We share what's new in our lives. Hash about politics and the state of things. Fabienne shows me photos of a new installation she's been working on in the BEAM Arts event space, shaped foam and projected lighting. I praise it with a note of humility, knowing I don't have a hand to show. Nor can I deflect her questions about whether I've been painting. I tell her that I'm working on a few things, and she seems to understand this is not true with a pitying, if encouraging smile.

I notice how Fabienne only wants to talk about new things. Her face brightens when I talk about where I am now and where I could be headed. Even if my prospects are dull, she's excited to hear how I think about them. She's encouraging me even in how she is sitting forward, her smile hovering over our bistro table as if to say, *Yes, Yusuf. Please, show me you've moved on and made distance in what you say and how you say it. Match me here. Join me in the possibilities of what might be.* But that's not why I'm here. I've come to talk about different possibilities.

"Hey, um," I say and then pause because I don't really know how to bridge into what I'm here for after I've worked up the courage. I know it's going to open up some old wounds, making a sharp turn towards the past. "This might sound weird, but do you ever still wonder about..."

"About what?"

I search her eyes, looking for her permission to be asked: "Do you ever still wonder about Mallory?"

"Yusuf..."

"Because I think... I think I might have seen her. Or someone like her. Someone like how she could have been."

Fabienne twists her head uncomfortably, realizing now just how gripped by our past I still am. She looks around the cafe, up at the ceiling, looking for words. I know I messed up, bringing this all back. "Sorry. I know that sounds crazy. I couldn't help but wonder if maybe you had tried again and—"

"Yusuf!" Fabienne shakes a finger at me. "*Enculé*, I can't do this with you anymore. I thought we could be friends again now, maybe. But every time is you asking me to go through this with you and *j'en ai ras-le-bol*. I can't give you what you need," she tells me. Her words are coached. She's found strength, made distance since we were together. She gets up to go.

"Fabienne, I—"

"No, Yusuf. I've moved on from this." She backs away from the table, as if stepping away from whatever has led me here. "Don't call me. I don't ever... I don't want to see you again," she blurts with a pained expression, as if she didn't know she could have said that.

4. Avery

I wasn't doing everything I could to be the best Yusuf I needed to be with Nancy. At my age, I know that break-ups only feel better once there's been time to grow around the loss. We lose everything the relationship was, everything it could've been, and everything it could've given us.

A thought occurs to me after morning before my run. I'm not really sure how to put it into words, but I know I need to mark it somehow. So before I step out of my running clothes, I open to the first sheet of a canvas pad I have clipped to an easel that I've set up on my porch. I knew my future self would get around to putting something there if I left it waiting, warming in that diffuse light. Somehow, the gestures come easily this time. Mindlessly. I don't really know what this is going to become, but my hands are dancing, doing the work, and I think I can make out what's emerging on the page.

By the time my hands are covered in oils, I hear footsteps. There's a young woman with a clipboard pausing on the last step up to my porch, hand on the rail.

"Hi," I say, inviting with an open hand. "Yes, come up, please."

She says her name is Avery, and that she is here to take a survey. She glances through my living room window into the house, taking in my spartan furnishings with an appraising look. "How long have you lived here?"

"About a year. It's just me."

"Are you with the arts faculty at Kimball?" she asks, gesturing to the canvas.

"Oh, no. I own an art store near the university. And I'm an artist. Here, take a look." I turn the easel towards her.

"Seems like everything is going okay..." she trails off, briefly taking in what I've painted.

"Go ahead," I offer quietly, realizing that she has stopped writing on her clipboard. "Take some time with it."

Avery looks at her watch. "I'm kind of on a schedule."

"Please," I clasp my hands together. "I could use a fresh pair of eyes."

Avery stands there for a moment with her head cocked to one side, eyes darting around the composition. The way she sways her balance gently from foot to foot, one hand holding her arm, reminds me of how Nancy would take her first looks at my paintings. If Avery is Nancy's daughter, I realize how clever she is— would have been, to meet me here under the pretext of a census survey.

After a moment, I point to the figures in the painting. "They are having a picnic. The father is at his easel balanced atop the rock. The daughter is playing in the grass, and the mother has gotten up to see what he has captured. See how she is brushing the grass from her thighs? She wants to see if it is true to life."

Avery nods.

"The father sees her looking at how he has painted them— and he's devoted to them. But the mother is unsure about the father. I think she sometimes believes he sees their life together through a different frame. I'm having a little difficulty getting that expression right," I tell Avery with my hand on my hip.

Avery nods again, gently, still looking, lost in their story. But I wonder if I got the mother right, because for a moment it seems like Avery is about to crack. Her lip is trembling. But then, just like Nancy, she shifts her posture. Her face regains composure and she says, "You should've given the daughter something more to do than just sit in the grass."

Hmm. "If it's alright, would you be comfortable with me taking a quick sketch of you while you're looking at this painting? I'd just like to capture something before you go, an impression while the light is right," I explain.

"Okay."

Avery looks on without moving. I take down some lines, capturing her on a separate sheet while I have her here, capturing her looking at herself being seen in my painting. And after a moment, I look up, and she has gone, folded into my surroundings like a trick of the light. I wonder if that was enough; what she came here for.

But now I have her captured here, on my page. And in my mind's eye, I can see how she will become the girl sitting in the grass, and how she will be seen in her mother's eyes getting up to look at the painting—the painting *within* my painting. The light of a soul, swimming in the pigments on my brush, just a line at first, an essence. A subject to live within my landscape.

Perhaps in all of this, I am the object to be changed. Maybe it's time for me to stop carrying this stupid newspaper clipping around in my pocket. I need the room, now that I am unblocked. I need to clear the way, because something new is about to arrive.

See Amman Sabet's story "The Ghosts of Daughters Possible" online at Metaphorosis.
If you liked it, leave a comment. Authors love that!
Remember to subscribe to our e-mail updates so you'll know when new stories are posted.

About the story

The speculative aspects of "The Ghosts of Daughters Possible" come from personal struggles in love and family. The setting, however, is inspired by American Impressionist paintings. I was trying to break through a nasty writing block amidst Covid-19 lockdowns and the winter landscapes from this era somehow helped me get where I needed to be. Something about natural settings captured in retreat from the growing industrial era of this other time in America with its own pandemics and strife (and the way the painterly styles are ephemeral and not quite clear) had me reaching in the right way.

A question for the author

Q: Are you optimistic about the future of humanity?

A: I think it depends on the size of the groups we organize ourselves into. I find we are far more imaginative and fearful than we are capable of organizing ourselves. I am hopeful that in the future, technology will help humanity reorganize into peaceful, sustainable groups the size of small villages. We won't need centralization as a strategy for safety and resources, so we may well trend away from cities. I'm not sure I'm optimistic that this future will emerge without pain, but I'm optimistic that it could happen given what we've achieved through our knowledge, innovation and mastery of the material world.

About the author

Amman Sabet is a writer and designer living in Los Angeles, CA. This is his second story published at *Metaphorosis*, and his stories have also appeared in *The New Voices of Science Fiction, The Magazine of Fantasy and Science Fiction*, and *Best American Science Fiction and*

Fantasy 2021. Amman is a Clarion alumnus, an SFWA member, and is learning a lot building an off-grid cabin deep into pandemic year three.

The Last Doctor

Jonathan Louis Duckworth

"To heal is the noblest purpose."

By now I know what the Doctor meant by that. He'd come to Antlerpoint three moons ago, just a few days before Lin Kee, the first of the sick, lost his mind and split Dubb Brunner's skull with a woodcutting axe. The Doctor must have known, must have smelled it on the wind before any of us knew scalesick had come to us. He appeared as a dark sliver walking out of the setting sun, a masked man pushing his little handcart laden with strange tools. He was taller than anyone here, his smell clean, his posture upright and trustful. When we asked why he had come, he told us because a terrible sickness was soon to emerge. He was right, and now I help him with his healing work.

As I help him with his work, I try to learn all I can. Mostly he answers my questions, but sometimes not. Even when his answers are strange or unhelpful, I enjoy his voice for its own sake.

"How'd scalesick come to Antlerpoint Stead?"

"Someone from another settlement brought it here. Perhaps they did not know they were sick, or had reasons for traveling we could only guess."

"Why ain't I gotten sick like my parents or my sister?"

"I do not know why, Jo Park. You may be immune. Or you may carry it, yet show no symptoms. Either way, it is a beautiful thing."

I wonder if he means I'm beautiful. I hope so.

"Do the scalies always turn crazy?"

"Almost always, in advanced cases."

Advanced cases. His words are strange but beautiful, a kind of music.

"Some of them don't?"

"In all my years of curing, I have only known one exception."

"Did there used to be more Doctors like you?"

"Yes, a very long time ago, when there was more of everything. When people lived in forests of metal and glass."

More music from his hidden lips. I imagine these forests, full of wise people like the Doctor.

"Why'd you become a Doctor?"

"To help others. One needs a higher purpose, and to heal, to spread the gift of health, is the noblest of all."

"Where'd you learn your ways?"

"From the Doctor who taught me."

"How did you know the sickness would come here?"

He doesn't answer.

"Can you show me what your face looks like?"

"It is improper for a Doctor to remove his mask while working."

"Do you even recall what air feels like?"

He doesn't answer.

We didn't believe the Doctor's first warning when he told us what was coming. We didn't want to believe.

Then Lin Kee got sick. We were all of us afraid to go near Lin, who was shut up in his house, hollering all-the-day like a wild dog when he wasn't coughing. The Doctor, in his black frock and his shimmery black gloves and glimmery false face with its eyes like mirrors, set fire to the house with Lin Kee still inside. That was the only way to deal with one so far gone, he said.

And who could argue with him? No one even had the courage to look into the dark lenses of his mask.

The others—my folks included—were afraid, but not me. I saw from how he burned Lin Kee when the rest of us were cowering in our homes that he'd come here to help—to do good. But even a helper needs help, and the Doctor was no exception. He needed someone strong and brave like me to dig burning pits and gather up the supplies for making his salve. Brightweed and frog liver was all he needed to make the salve. If you get the salve on a sick person straight away, it cures them half the time, but if you wait too long, there's nothing doing. Those on whom the salve worked would be safe, immune, the Doctor said. Scalesick starts with coughing, then with shivers, then the yellow scales start up, breaking through the skin and stretching it and bleeding all the time. After the scales comes weakness, and then awful strength and madness, melting the person you knew and leaving a wild dog like poor Lin.

The salve didn't work for Momma, whom the Doctor killed and burned like so many others, and Dad lied and hid his scales until he was too weak to dress himself. The Doctor didn't kill him, I did—cut his head from his neck with a spade. I was so mad he hid it from us, and that he got my sister sick.

The Doctor and I burned him together.

As we watched him burn, I felt something touch my arm. It was the Doctor's glove; his firm grasp. When I tried to put my hand on his, he let go and stepped away.

"I am sorry for your loss, Jo Park."

"What's there to be sorry about? Good riddance to him." He looked away from me, and I wondered what face he was making under his mask. I wondered if that face was as beautiful as his voice, and why he kept it hidden from me. "You said it came from some other stead."

"What did?"

"Scalesick. You said a traveler brought it."

"Oh. Yes, the most likely vector."

"But who? Other than you, there ain't been many travelers."

The Doctor silenced me, laying his other glove, so cold, on my face. I was afraid to speak; afraid he might let go of me if I did. "I am a Doctor. I go where I am needed."

But what did a Doctor need? I laid my hand over his glove. The fire crackled. One of the pyre logs split with a crack like thunder and a gasp of sparks. Jostled, one of Dad's arms flopped out. Stubborn, just like him; but still it burned in the end.

That was a moon ago. Today, it was sister's turn to burn. Her ashes drift down like snow, gather on the roofs of the empty houses. The sickness is done, and for each three houses in Antlerpoint, two are empty. Every night, while I lie in my cot in my empty house, the sound of weeping drifts from the trees. Maybe I'm just imagining it. Maybe it's a ghost, the sound is so faint. Salve didn't work for sister, or maybe we got her too late. The Doctor says it's not for us to wonder why some live and some don't, only do what we can to save as many lives as we can.

'Rubber', is what he calls the false face over his face, the mask he wears. Such a beautiful mask it is, the like of a beautiful face, and in the black puddles of his eyes I see my own longing. I wonder if he knows how I feel. I wonder if he feels the same way. If he feels at all. Always he talks like he's near to sleep, a little whisper like mothwing flutter.

How is it I got wrapped up in someone without a face? Maybe it's how different he is from all I've known, how rare and special. And if I've never seen his face, does that make what I feel any less? What if it makes it more? No one talks like him; nobody's got words like his. *Scalpel, patient, palliative care, symptoms, pustules, terminal*—I learn his words so I can be like him. So I can be worthy of someone like him.

The Doctor sleeps in one of the empty houses as once belonged to Ossie Bowman, the saltmaker. When he sleeps, I watch him through a crack in the door. He slumbers in his clothes—his gloves, his boots, his mask. He even keeps his big brimmed black hat on. His boots together, his hands crossed over his chest, his glassy eyes staring at the thatching. What does he dream about? How does he sleep so soundly? Does he even breathe? Would his hands be cold? What do his lips feel like?

Today, as sister's ashes drift all around, the Doctor tells me he's leaving. The words strike me like a pole to the gut.

"Can I come with you?"

"No. A Doctor's life is a solitary way."

"What if there's more scalesick after you leave?"

He reaches to me. His glove is like winter on my cheek. "Then you, Jo Park, will cure it. You have learned well."

"Why leave so soon? There could still be more—"

He cuts me off. His moth of his voice becomes hardshelled. "I must continue my work, there are other places in need of healing."

"What did I do wrong? Tell me."

He doesn't answer. He walks off. For a blink it looks like he might turn back and speak some more. But then he keeps walking back to his house, to sleep there one last time.

Night comes and the big moonpiece sits high and pale at the top of the sky, while the little moonpiece smolders low and red over the rooftops. For one last time, I sneak to the Doctor's house to watch his sleep. But this time, watching him, I can't help myself. I push the door open—it's unlocked. The old wood only creaks a little on the rusty hinges. What a quiet floor soft silt makes, cold and shifting under my toes. I creep and kneel beside the sleeping Doctor. How nice it must be to sleep so soundly, like a yolk in its eggshell, closed to the world's troubles. I feel his arms—hard as stones. To handle scalies as easily as he does, of course he's strong. Shoulders and chest tell the same story—there is no softness anywhere. Still he doesn't stir. My hand travels toward a dangerous place—is he like me, does he even have what I have?—but as my fingers reach his belt, the low nightbreeze carries a sad music to my ears.

It's the weeping again. Somewhere out in the Wilderthere, outside the Stead, someone is bawling their eyes out, as they have each night. Only this time it's louder, more pitiable than ever. I make space between me and the Doctor, wait for him to stir, but he doesn't. The crying keeps on, and between mewling and blubbering, there's another sound, unmistakable, awful: the cough of lungs heavy with pus.

"Doctor," I say. "Doctor, wake up."

But the Doctor doesn't wake.

How could we have missed someone? We treated all the sick, saved those we could save, killed the rest. Who did we forget?

I reach down to shake the Doctor, but stop myself. Why not show him he needs me? Why not prove my worth? I leave the saltmaker's house and hurry to mine, where I gather my bow and quiver. Armed now, I move under the moonlight, following a trail of footprints and the sound of sobbing to the edge of the lake that divides Antlerpoint from the rest of the world. Watching through the brush and leaves, I see the weeping, coughing man. Sometimes moonlight paints brighter and clearer than sun; sometimes it shows what sun's too shy to show.

Is it a man when most its skin has turned to scales? Huge, wrong-shaped hands with nails like claws wrap around an overbig head, where clumps of dark hair hang like beansprout shocks from scaly cracks in the scalp. Hands and head tremble with each heave, each sob, each shudder.

I nock an arrow and draw the bow. Wood, bone, and sinew creak and shake as the bow bends. The scaly's crooked spine draws straight in answer, the claws drop, and a face I ain't never seen in this Stead looks my way. Moonglimmer puddles in two small, dark eyes and my arm aches from holding the bow taut.

It's him. It must be. The man who started all this, the stranger from another Stead who brought the scalesick to Antlerpoint. Three moons worth of anger jump from my arm and out the bow, and the arrow strikes true.

The scaly dies quieter than most. A few little mewls, but nothing more, a shudder, then nothing. But in dying, the scaly does a strange thing. Easy as it would be for it to fall forward into the lake and poison the water with its bad blood, it throws itself the other way, and falls into the leaves and pine litter. Then it goes still.

I run back to the Stead. Smash my way through the door to the Doctor's house. This time I don't bother with quiet. I run to his bed and grab his hard shoulders and shake, shake, shake.

"Wake up!" I shout. "Your work's not done! There's another scaly for burning!"

The Doctor's head rolls off, his arms pull off in my grip. A cabbage and two thick branches from a blackwood tree, tucked under the mask and hat, under his frock. First there's quiet, then there's a sinking feeling, like I'm at the bottom of something dark and cold and the world's pushing me under. Then, then I just start laughing. Laughter and tears are such close siblings, almost twins.

When my eyes dry up, when my throat hurts from all the laughing and shouting, I take up the mask and put it over my face. The gloves are loose, but I reckon I'll grow into them. The frock is heavy but warm, a needful shell between the world and me. So this was why he wore it. He wasn't as lucky as me; scalesick changed his face and body, even if it left his mind untouched. But that wasn't why he wore the mask and gloves—it was to keep the ache of the world out, as much as to keep the scalesick in.

I don't say goodbye to anyone in the stead. After burning the last Doctor's body, I take his handcart, and follow the rising sun to a path in the woods. There are other steads out beyond the Wilderthere, and only I know how to help them. Help them like the Doctor helped Antlerpoint. To heal is the highest, noblest purpose. Somewhere there's sickness, and nobody but a Doctor can cure it.

See Jonathan Louis Duckworth's story "The Last Doctor" online at Metaphorosis.
If you liked it, leave a comment. Authors love that!
Remember to subscribe to our e-mail updates so you'll know when new stories are posted.

About the story

Who even remembers these things? Obviously the story was partly inspired by the pandemic we're all living through, although the disease in the story has little resemblance to COVID. I've always loved plague doctors, and the story's titular Doctor is a non-traditional example of one. The story is set within a larger universe of stories, what I call the Wilderthere Universe. Like most stories in that universe the setting is a post-apocalyptic America (specifically somewhere in Texas), hundreds of years in the future. Society has collapsed, the rules of reality have altered, and the moon is broken into two fragments. The

Doctor is one of many echoes of the world that came before (The Foreworld), a part of a long tradition of masters and apprentices that stretches back presumably all the way to the apocalypse and the fall of our world. I imagine the earlier Doctors in that chain were noble heroes, mythic healers selflessly devoting their lives to preserving traditions and knowledge the rest of the world forgot. But further down the chain, the Doctors degraded into what the Doctor himself becomes: inhuman, faceless, and selfish. This element might have been obliquely inspired by Ray Bradbury's *Fahrenheit 451*, where the "firemen" are arsonists who start fires instead of putting them out.

A question for the author

Q: What's an idea you're dying to write but haven't, and why?

A: I don't know there are any ideas I'm "dying" to write that I haven't attempted already, but for quite some time I've had an idea for a story where a young apprentice wizard is sent to a tidal pool to kill a giant mollusc so that he can use its conical shell as his smelly wizard hat, but instead of killing it he forms a partnership with the mollusc, who sits on his head and helps him with his magic. I've attempted it once already but it wasn't quite coming together (mostly the question of, what next?). Maybe I'll try again in the future.

About the author

Jonathan Louis Duckworth is a completely normal, entirely human person with the right number of heads and everything. He received his MFA from Florida International University. His speculative fiction work appears in *Pseudopod, Beneath Ceaseless Skies, Southwest Review, Tales to Terrify, Flash Fiction Online*, and elsewhere. He is a PhD student at University of North Texas and an active HWA member.

@Joduckwo

The Spinster and the Sea

J.C. Pillard

Samson always felt out of place in the crowded common room of the Last Drink. Seaborne's largest inn was about the only place that could hold all the privateers, naval deserters, and vagabonds when they came together in the town they called home. Still, most of them were young men, or at least younger than Samson, and the old carpenter felt like a rusted nail with all these hot-headed lads around him. Not to mention the heat of the room. With so many bodies pressed together, most of the boys were in their shirtsleeves, cravats loose around their necks. Samson wanted nothing more than to step outside into the cool, salty air. But given the news the dawn had brought, he knew this wasn't a gathering to be missed.

The chatter of the crowd died as Captain Crain marched to the front of the room, his long, beaded braids framing a serious face.

"Soldiers of Seaborne," he said, voice weighted. "You heeded the bells when they rang this morn. For this, I and all the town thank you."

"We heeded 'em all right," interrupted a lad towards the front. "Now tell us why."

A rolling chuckle passed through the room. Crain nodded. "The Royal Navy has been spotted a day's sailing from here. We have it on good authority that they are coming to destroy Seaborne."

The men glanced among themselves, murmuring. The news was not really a surprise. Seaborne was known as a pirate port and refuge from the King's justice. It had always been only a matter of time before the Royal Navy decided to rain hellfire down on it.

"Let them try," laughed a red-haired man from where he sat. "Rachim's Reef'll cut their ships to ribbons."

"In most cases, Gladstone, you'd be right. But they've one of our own with them." Crain paused, letting his words sink in. Samson tensed, watching as realization rippled through the room. The reef was Seaborne's pride and joy. The razor-sharp ledges and corals spread for miles beyond the town's cove, and any ship that didn't know the way through those waters was likely to be wrecked. But if the Navy knew the way, then Seaborne's primary defense was useless.

"We have but two choices. We can flee. Or we can fight."

The silence in the room was deafening as each man weighed the outcome of such a battle. At last, one of the young lads spoke up.

"The likelihood that they'll pass through the reef unscathed is slim, even if they know the way," he said, his voice more measured than the other young lads. "Atop the seawall, we may be able to drive them off."

A rumble ran through those assembled. It was a daring proposal. The Royal Navy had been burning pirate towns for decades, and none had stood against them with success.

Samson cleared his throat. "Argus saw three flotillas coming our way. Even with what defenses we can bring to bear, that may not be enough."

"If we do not stand against them, then who will?" demanded another voice, the hot-headed young man who'd spoken first. "I say we fight! Show those royal dogs the King's hand doesn't reach this far."

A mighty cheer followed his words, and from his corner Samson sighed. He knew advising caution was not to be borne, not when so many of the folk in this room had watched the Royal Navy take everything from them. Still, there was no sense in rushing towards ruination when it was coming right at you.

The men began talking, making plans for their glorious defense. Samson stood, limbs complaining at the movement, and turned to go when he heard Captain Crain call him over. The other man still stood near the front of the room, so Samson had to push his way through the crowd to reach him.

"Samson," Crain said, voice low. "Can I leave it in your hands to spread word for an evacuation? The women and children should be moved to the interior of the island. In case the battle goes ill."

The carpenter heard the unspoken words in the captain's sentence—not 'in case' but 'when'. Still, he nodded.

"Leave it to me."

Crain paused. "Will you tell *her* as well?"

"She is part of the community, too, Captain," Samson replied, knowing exactly whom Crain meant. Nadia was the oldest resident of Seaborne. She was also the most reclusive, rarely leaving her cottage up on the cliff.

"She won't go," Crain said seriously.

"I know." Samson sighed. "But I'll tell her, even so."

Samson moved more slowly than he would have liked through the town. His leg, aching from an old wound, complained with every step as he knocked on doors to spread word of the impending battle. Behind him came a stream of evacuees, fleeing for the desert hills further from the coast. Carts rolled over bumpy, dusty roads, and donkeys brayed as they were led towards the island's interior.

At last, having spread his message to enough folk that the whole town would soon hear of it, he paused to rest a while. Raising his eyes, Samson stared up the winding trail that led to the top of one of Seaborne's cliffs. A lonely cottage stood there, bent and gnarled as a weathered tree. He sighed. It was time to see Nadia.

The twisting path up to the clifftop was hundreds of steps, and Samson's leg ached with every one. He remembered the day he'd met Nadia. Everyone in town knew about her, of course. They called her a witch and a recluse, and Samson was fairly sure no one would care if she were to keel over in the town square. And yet, that day decades ago, she hadn't seemed a witch at all. Just a lonely woman. She'd stumped down to his carpenter's shop to get an old spindle repaired. A fine blue shawl had been thrown around her shoulders, and he hadn't been able to stop himself from asking where she'd gotten it. Such luxuries were comparatively rare in Seaborne.

Her eyes had shuttered. "I made it," she'd said, but there had been no pride or joy in her voice. Still, when Miriam Tassleton had been asking around for a new bedspread, it was Samson who'd made the trek up the cliff to ask Nadia if she might take the commission.

He made that same journey now, hoping the old spinster would speak with him. She was a wonder with all things fiber. She could patch a sail so the wind would never tear it again, and the ropes she knotted never frayed. Still, for all her talent, she kept everyone in town at arm's length, as though she disdained them all. He'd tried, on more than one occasion, to coax her down to

Seaborne for a drink or during an open-air festival. But he'd never succeeded.

Samson crested the cliff with a heavy step. He took a few moments to gather himself before he crossed to the cottage, knocking hard on the crooked door.

"What?" Nadia's voice was like a cracking branch in a high wind. "What is it?"

"Nadia, it's Samson. Can I come in?"

A silence followed his question, and Samson bit back a sigh. Finally, a harried, "Oh, all right, then," came from behind the door, and the carpenter muscled it open.

Inside, the front room of the cottage looked like a flock of sheep had exploded. Baskets of fleece overflowed onto the floor, and lengths of yarn lay in tangled heaps in a trunk against the far wall. The room was stuffy, though the shutters of one of the windows were thrown open to overlook the sea, shedding light on a single skein of green yarn sitting on the windowsill. Beside it, Nadia sat on an overturned crate in front of her spinning wheel, that same, deep blue shawl she'd worn when he first saw her wrapped around her shoulders. Her face was craggy as the cliffside, and she frowned at him as he entered, each of her wrinkles deepening to a crevasse.

Samson grunted as he finally got through the door. He peered around the doorframe to where the top hinge hung loose.

"When did this happen?" he asked, fingers tracing the worn metal hinge. No wonder it had been so hard to open.

"What do you want?" Nadia demanded. "I haven't finished Alder's sail yet, if that's why you're here."

Samson considered the door. With the proper tools, he could probably fix it. He reached into his pocket, questing for screws—

"Leave it, carpenter."

"Nadia, you can't just leave your door broken."

"It's *my* door," she said crossly. "I'll do what I like with it."

"Fine," Samson said, stifling a sigh, "As you wish."

"What do you want?" she asked again.

"To warn you. The Royal Navy is coming to Seaborne. They may know the way through Rachim's Reef."

Samson did not know what he'd been expecting when he told her. It certainly wasn't the look of devastation that flitted across her face, hidden so quickly he briefly thought he'd imagined it. It was a look he knew well—many of Seaborne's residents arrived wearing it.

She turned away from him, her gaze tracking out over the sea. "Well," she said finally, "I suppose it's not unexpected."

Samson steeled himself. "Captain Crain has ordered an evacuation of the town. Some of the sailors are staying to fight."

That made Nadia turn. "They plan on fighting? With what? Sabers won't do much good against long guns, carpenter."

No, they wouldn't, but Samson didn't say that. Instead, he asked, "Will you leave? Head inland with the others?"

She frowned. "Will you?"

"What do you—"

"It is a fool's endeavor. You know that as well as I, better even. If the Royal Navy makes it through the reef, there will be no saving Seaborne, no matter how much fire the young folk down there have boiling in their blood."

He shook his head. "Seaborne means a great deal to them. It has been a refuge for many, including you. That means something."

Her frown darkened. "So you're not leaving."

"No. I'll not abandon them."

"Foolish," she muttered, turning away. "Go on, then."

"Will you—"

"I have no need to leave," Nadia interrupted. "They've already taken everything else from me. If the Navy seeks to burn me in my bed, I say let them try."

Samson winced. "There's no shame in running—"

"I will not run again," Nadia snapped. "Now leave."

Sighing, Samson turned back to the broken door, heaving it shut behind him.

It was midnight, Nadia was sixteen, and the ship was on fire.

She and her brother, Thomas, had booked passage on the *Abigail*. They'd been at sea eight days, passing beyond sight of land and out into the endless blue. Nadia had never been to sea before, and while she found it beautiful, she couldn't wait to reach their new home, a continent away.

But now, she and Thomas emerged from the belly of the ship to screaming and flames. Around them, a fearsome battle raged. Three ships of the line surrounded the small frigate, cannons ready to reduce the vessel to splinters. In the flash of gunfire, Nadia made out the brilliant red flag of the Royal Navy snapping in the wind.

There were many questions about that night to which Nadia never received answers. She never learned why the Navy targeted their ship. She never got the chance to ask Thomas how he knew exactly where the lifeboats were, or how far they were from their new home. But most of all, Nadia never knew if she would have acted differently, had she known what was to come.

Thomas got her settled in a lifeboat, swinging it out for the drop. Behind him, sailors were scattered across the deck, groaning and bloody.

His eyes had met hers from where he stood on the deck. "If I'm not back in five minutes, make the drop," he commanded.

"Thomas—" she started. She was only sixteen, and she was terrified.

"I'm going to try and save some of the others." He had to shout to be heard above the battle.

A colossal boom shook the ship, sending it tilting dangerously. Nadia reached out a hand, voicelessly pleading with her brother to leave them, to run. But he met her eyes, shaking his head.

"I have to try, Nadia. It's the right thing to do."

"No. No, Thomas!" Nadia screamed as her brother plunged back into the fray. She sat frozen in the boat, heart trying to pound itself out of her chest. She wanted to get up, to run after her brother and *make* him get in the boat, but she couldn't seem to move.

A sound like thunder tore through the air, and the deck buckled and split. The falls holding the lifeboat snapped, and Nadia screamed as she plummeted down towards the black sea. Her boat struck the side of the ship as it fell, and Nadia heard a sharp crack, like the sound of an axe striking wood. She had just enough time to see a fracture splinter down the middle of her lifeboat before the vessel hit the water with speed.

Nadia was drenched with salty spray. The ocean began leaking into the boat almost immediately. Behind her, the three Royal Navy vessels drew tighter around the burning *Abigail*.

"Thomas!" Nadia shrieked, her voice lost beneath the maelstrom of battle. "Thomas!"

The lifeboat was sinking, water sluicing in through cracks in the hull. Nadia fought to stay afloat, but water poured in faster than she could fling it out. The sea tossed her little vessel to and fro until it disappeared beneath the water. And Nadia, in her heavy wool skirts, was pulled down with it.

The world beneath the waves was cold and dark. Nadia fought against the water, trying desperately to claw back to the surface, to find something to hold onto, but nothing met her hands. Her lungs burned. Her vision began winking with black spots.

Fear, pain, and fury welled up inside her. Nadia opened her mouth, screaming into the sea. Water poured in between her teeth, down her throat, but she didn't care. If she were to die here, she would not go quietly.

The scream echoed in the deep, growing louder, as though something were screaming back. The blue-black world around her seemed to convulse. Through her darkening vision, she watched the water coalesce into the figure of a woman who hung suspended in the ocean a mere foot from where Nadia was drowning. She had hair as green as seaweed, and a gown of seafoam. She looked nearly human, until Nadia glanced into her eyes.

They were black as the depths of the sea, black as the sky at night. And they watched Nadia with unfathomable sadness.

The creature—the woman—reached out a hand and touched Nadia's breastbone. Beneath that touch, she felt her lungs expand with air, the water disappearing. She almost recoiled from the woman, recalling the tales of selkies and fair folk the servants used to whisper in the kitchen at night. Those black eyes bore into her, chilling her with their uncanny intelligence.

You wish to be saved.

The words reverberated in the ocean around her, more felt than heard. Nadia shuddered as those words crawled over her skin, but still she nodded.

What will you give me in payment for your life?

"Anything," Nadia said, the word leaving her mouth as bubbles. "Everything."

The woman regarded her with those deep, sad eyes, before nodding. Her seaweed-hair eddied around her with the motion.

Then Everything is what I will take.

The woman reached out once more, grasping Nadia's hands, and Nadia felt a sharp pain as though each palm had been cut. She pulled away, but there was nothing now to pull away from. The woman was gone.

Her lungs began burning once more as the water redoubled its efforts to swallow her. Frantically, Nadia twisted her hands upwards in the sea.

And the sea twisted back.

A rope of water, blue and cold, met her fingers. She grasped it and pulled herself upward, hand over hand, twisting more water into a rope, barely conscious of how she managed it. Her head broke the surface and she gasped, hacking up brine and salt. Her water rope was wrapped over a piece of planking, and she heaved herself onto it, sputtering and sobbing. She thrust the wet hair from her eyes, staring towards where the *Abigail* had been. A few smoldering boards floated on the water's surface, but the ship was entirely gone. In the distance, the Royal Navy vessels sailed away into the dark.

A storm was blowing in over the island. Its massive thunderheads were black against the blue sky. From her window, Nadia watched them roll in with a frown burrowing itself between her brows. Her fingers traced the twist of the green skein on the sill. The house seemed quiet and close, almost watchful.

I have to try, Nadia. It's the right thing to do.

She shook her head, seeking to dislodge the memories creeping into her mind. Perhaps the rain would dissuade those fools down in Seaborne, make them turn tail and run as they should. Or perhaps it would simply make their job that much harder.

I have to try, Nadia.

Thunder rolled overhead, sending a shudder through the cliff face and drawing Nadia's gaze back to the clouds. They swung low, heavy with water they'd start dumping soon enough.

I have to try.

"Are you ever quiet?" she snapped into the empty air. No one responded, of course. She shut her eyes, breathing out through her nose.

Nadia often thought about that night, about what she had done and what she had not. The woman in the water, her green hair eddying around her like seaweed, had indeed taken everything: Thomas, and with him the new home they'd been sailing towards, had been eaten by the waves. But the power given to her to save her life had never departed, though Nadia had never known what to do with it. She'd always been a gifted spinner, but since that night her spinning went beyond silk and cotton. After Thomas had died, she'd spun her grief into a soft, silky yarn from which she'd knit a deep blue shawl. From her fury, she'd spun a wild red yarn and woven the blankets on her bed. And from the shameful relief at her escape, she'd spun the seaweed-green yarn that rested upon her windowsill, where she could see it every day.

It had been Samson who first noticed her spinning, and Samson who began bringing her the work of the town. At first, she'd thought to turn him away, but she had needed the money more than she'd needed her pride. She'd taken the work of torn sails and ripped shawls from the carpenter, whose kind eyes and patience reminded her, painfully, of Thomas. With such work to do, she had stopped spinning impossible things, trading them for wool and flax, silk and cotton.

She'd stopped, but she hadn't forgotten.

"Damn it," she muttered, turning away from the window. Her wheel sat behind her, accusing her with its stillness, and she sighed. Then she went to heave open her door.

Wind whipped through Nadia's hair as she slowly pulled her spinning wheel out into the storm. After she'd set it on the cliff's edge, she went back for the crate. Her back throbbed with the strain, yet still she dragged the thing behind her, warped wood digging into the dirt of the cliff until it came to rest before the wheel. She settled herself atop it and looked up to the roiling gray clouds above. She'd failed Thomas once. She wouldn't fail again.

Nadia remembered when her grandmother had taught her how to spin. The old woman's fingers had shown her how to pinch the fleece, how to draft it for a fine thread or a thick one, how to send the spindle turning. She remembered her childhood hands, chubby and clumsy, spinning wool with a spindle that wouldn't stop wobbling.

"Be patient," her grandmother had chided when Nadia pouted at her work, so ugly compared to her grandmother's supple yarn. "These things take time."

"These things take time," Nadia muttered to herself as she reached up into the sky. With deft hands, she pinched out a piece of low-hanging cloud, pulling it down. She drafted it out, wrapping it around the leading string of her old wheel. A quick press of her foot on the treadle, a twitch of her hand on the flywheel, and the spinning wheel jumped into motion, twisting the gathered clouds into a fine, silky yarn the color of the sea after a storm.

Nadia pulled the clouds from the sky with skillful, creaking hands. Her back ached, and her fingers grew numb with the cold, yet still she spun, pulling down handfuls of the storm and winding them onto the bobbin. When each bobbin grew full, she stopped, detaching it from the wheel to tuck away in a sack at her side and replace it with another before she began again.

She was on the last bobbin, clouds gliding smoothly through her hands, when she heard the crack. She grasped the wheel, stopping its motion, and stared down towards the maidens that held her bobbin in place. A fracture ran down the left one, slithering all the way to the base. Her fingers tightened on the wheel. She hadn't considered what the water from the clouds might do to the wood.

Releasing the last bit of cloud back to the sky, Nadia ran a finger over the crack, feeling absurd tears building behind her eyes. It was just a spinning wheel, she told herself. It was just the wheel she'd spun on since Thomas's death. It shouldn't matter. Still, there was a painful knot welling in her throat as she realized the wheel was, more than likely, beyond repair.

Carefully, she detached the last bobbin from its place, stowing it in her pocket. With a final look at the crack in her wheel, she stood. Fetching her cane from the cottage and hefting her sack with the other bobbins, she turned and began the long trek down to the seawall.

Samson was tired. His leg smarted and his fingers hurt from an afternoon and evening spent preparing for the assault. Most of the men were asleep, looking like gray wave caps beneath their blankets as they lay along the top of the wall. Samson picked his way among them, trying not to trip. He glanced up at the black sky. He'd expected rain, had seen the storm clouds gathering all afternoon, but they'd dissipated during the evening and into the night, never dropping even a thimbleful of liquid. The stars glinted above, bright eyes ready to watch Seaborne fight and fall.

Captain Crain stood alone near one of the seawall's stairs, his gaze hard on the ocean. Samson came to stand beside him.

"How's the night?" Samson asked softly.

"Still," the captain replied. "Too still for my liking."

"Have they been spotted?"

The captain shook his head, beaded braids clattering together. "No. But dawn is still some ways off. We will stand ready until then."

Samson nodded, turning to gaze to the water. All was dark and quiet, and nervous fear curdled in his gut at the quiet. The fleet would be here, sooner or later. Then they would find out if the firepower of Seaborne would be enough.

"Move, or I'll move you."

Starting, Samson turned towards the seawall's stairs. There, at the base of the staircase with a bag slung over her shoulder, was Nadia. She was glaring at the guard posted there, her gaze enough to turn a lesser man to stone.

"Grandmother, I told you, this is—"

Her eyes flicked up and caught Samson's gaze. "Carpenter!" she yelled. "Tell this man to stand aside, or he'll learn exactly what a cane to the head feels like."

Samson was already hurrying down the stairs. "It's all right, I'll take care of it," he murmured to the stunned guard, who looked a little queasy from Nadia's dagger-like stare. He turned towards the spinster.

"What are you doing here?"

She huffed. "Why does everyone keep asking me that?"

Because it looks like a stiff wind could blow you over. "This is no place for an old woman," he tried.

She shook her head and shouldered past him. "It's no place for an old man either, carpenter. Give me your arm."

Samson wavered. He should force her to leave, to flee for safety inland. But it looked as though Nadia was getting up the stairs with or without his help, and he didn't want to be on the receiving end of any more of her ire. He hurried after her, offering his elbow and helping her to the top of the seawall.

The captain looked askance as they appeared, eyes darting first to Nadia and then Samson. "I thought she was to be evacuated."

"I tried," Samson muttered as Nadia released his arm and moved to the edge of the wall.

"What defenses do you have?" Nadia asked, her creaking voice taking on the sharp crack of authority.

Crain arched an eyebrow. "Twenty long guns. Thirteen cannon, though only enough shot for perhaps four rounds each. Muskets for the men."

"Hmph. That won't be enough."

The captain opened his mouth to reply when a shrill whistle cut through the air. All along the wall, men began sitting up, their gazes dragged towards the cliffs. Samson and Crain stiffened, and Nadia frowned.

"What was that?"

"The lookout," Crain said, mouth drawn in tight. "The fleet has been spotted."

"Then we haven't much time," Nadia said. She set her bag down and opened it, pulling out what looked like a bobbin wrapped thickly in silvery spider's web. "We can't let them reach the bay."

"We'll try to hold them off—"

"You needn't try," Nadia interrupted. "Just leave it to me." She plucked at the bobbin in her hands, pulling free a thread. Moving slowly, then growing faster, she began unspooling the thread, pushing it off the seawall. As she did, the cord unfurled, billowing out to become a dense cloud that skated down to the bay, hovering just above the water.

"It's fog," Samson breathed, eyes wide. It was impossible. And yet, she must have done it. No wonder the clouds above had thinned as the night wore on: Nadia had stolen them from the sky.

He didn't know how she'd accomplished it, but she'd brought them exactly what they needed. A fog so dense that no ship—no fleet—could pass through it safely. Not with Rachim's Reef lurking in wait.

"Carpenter," Nadia snapped, continuing her unspooling. "Don't just stand there gawking. Hand me the next bobbin."

Samson jumped to obey, pulling out the next bobbin and handing it to her. Soon a fog thicker than wool was spreading down from the seawall, enshrouding the bay and the deadly reef beneath the water.

A few minutes later, two more sharp whistles pierced the air. Beside them, Captain Crain swore.

"They're at the reef's entrance," he muttered. "The fog hasn't reach that far yet."

"Bring me some of your men, Captain," Nadia commanded. "Let's see if they can unspool a bobbin as well as they can shoot a musket."

The captain nodded sharply. He began shouting orders, and soon Samson and Nadia had another six hands to them, unspooling the clouds down onto the water. The rest of the soldiers took up positions along the wall, and the rattle of cannons being moved and loaded cut through the otherwise silent night. The fog billowed from Nadia's hands, and before too long Samson could barely make out his own feet, let alone anyone further down the seawall.

A boom pierced the air. Around them, the soldiers tensed. Moments later came the distant splash of something heavy hitting water. Cannon shot.

"That's the last of it," Nadia said, holding up the final bobbin.

Samson nodded. "I can help you back down the steps."

"What? No. I'm not going, carpenter." The spinster turned her eyes towards the wall of fog before them. "I will see this through."

Samson wanted to argue, even opened his mouth to do so, but something stopped him. Nadia seemed made of steel, and he feared how sharp she might be if he tried to move her. So he merely nodded.

Another boom came, then another. A murmur passed along the wall, soldiers shifting nervously. The fog was too thick for them to see anything, and sounds came through it muffled, so that where the shots came from or how distant they were was hard to tell. The night began to lighten as dawn approached, and still they waited. When at last the sun rose and began to burn away Nadia's fog, Samson could hardly believe his eyes.

There was a single ship in the bay. A single ship *only*. Behind it, distant among the shoals, he caught sight of masts sticking from the water like felled trees, torn sails hanging limply. The ragged remains of the force sent to destroy Seaborne, sliced to ribbons by Rachim's Reef and Nadia's fog.

"Prepare the long guns!" Captain Crain's shout echoed along the seawall, and a great cry rose from the sailors. Nadia watched without a word, her eyes bright. Tentatively, Samson reached for her hand. To his surprise, she reached back and gripped him tightly. He glanced down at her and realized why her eyes looked so bright—tears shone in them, unspent.

"I thought it would feel better," she murmured. "Having my revenge."

Sailors and soldiers eddied around them, but Nadia and Samson stood alone, rocks among the tide. The carpenter studied her, his gaze thoughtful.

"How *does* it feel?" he asked.

"Like I've taken the knife used against me and turned it on another." She swallowed. "Even if in defense, I can't say I like the feeling."

"I can take you back up the cliffs, Nadia."

"No," she said, shaking her head. "I will stay to see what I've wrought."

She would not move, and so Samson did not either. Even as the booms of the first long guns shook the stones beneath their feet, the spinster and the carpenter stood side by side, watching as the last ship was burned in the bay.

Nadia sat in her cottage, running her old hands over the crack in the spinning wheel. Only a day had passed since she had unleashed her fog. A day since she had repaid Thomas's death a hundredfold. After the battle in the bay—if a battle it could be called—she had gone back up the cliff alone. Samson might have gone with her, if she'd asked, but she hadn't wanted him to. She could not say she regretted what she'd done, but so many lives lost to her strange magic weighed heavy on her hands.

She gently touched the crack on her wheel once more before she sighed, turning to the window. The skein of green yarn seemed to wink at her from where it lay on the windowsill, and she picked it up. It would be a good while until she could spin again. She'd have to see about a new wheel. Perhaps she could knit something to pass the time.

There was a knock on her door, and she frowned. "What? What is it?"

A grunting sounded, the door being shoved open, and Samson appeared. He gave her a tired smile. "I expected you to be sleeping off your heroic efforts," he said. "Instead, I find you before your wheel. As ever."

"What do you want, carpenter?" Nadia demanded. "Is there yet another platoon or something on the way?"

He chuckled. "No, certainly not. I wanted to check on you. Make sure you're all right."

"Of course I am."

"Of course," he parroted. His thoughtful eyes examined her, and Nadia fought the urge to squirm beneath their appraisal. "You know," he said after a moment, "we would not have won the battle without you."

"No, you would not have."

He cocked his head. "How did you do it?"

"Do what?"

He sighed. "Nadia, please."

Nadia pursed her lips. "How do you make a table? Or an oar?"

"Time," he said. "Time and practice."

"Then you know how I spun the storm," she replied. It was only partly a lie.

She examined Samson more closely, seeing a heavy-looking bag in his hands. "What's that you've got?"

He hefted it up. "Supplies. For your door."

"I told you to leave it."

"You did," he agreed slowly. "But I've decided not to listen. You need a working door, Nadia. Sometime soon, you may actually want to let someone in."

She opened her mouth to object. After all, perhaps she *liked* to have a door that kept solicitous neighbors at bay. But she found the words would not come.

"Fine, carpenter," she said eventually. "As you wish. You can fix the door. Just don't make too much noise."

"I wouldn't dream of it," Samson said, smiling, before he turned back to the broken hinge.

From where she sat beside the window, Nadia watched him thoughtfully. He had a good complexion for green, she thought, especially the paler shade she now held in her hands. Besides, it was a long, cold trek up the cliff. He could certainly use a scarf.

See J.C. Pillard's story "The Spinster and the Sea" online at
Metaphorosis.
If you liked it, leave a comment. Authors love that!
Remember to subscribe to our e-mail updates so you'll know when
new stories are posted.

About the story

This story can be partially blamed on Tamora Pierce and her *Circle of Magic* series. If you haven't read Tamora Pierce, then please put this down and go pick up one of her tales right now! The *Circle of Magic* series was some of the first YA I ever read, and the first book of the series, *Sandry's Book*, focuses on the titular character and her ability to use spinning to work magic. Pierce herself has spoken about viewing handcrafts as a kind of magic, and I remember reading that book and being downright envious of Sandry's ability to create with her hands.

I did, eventually, learn some handcrafts myself. I started knitting years ago and spinning this past year. One of my friends possesses a spinning wheel, and very kindly let me try it. (She also took a look at an earlier draft of the story to make sure my terminology was right—thank you, Laura!) While using that wheel, I was reminded of *Sandry's Book*, and the question of what magical spinning would look like popped into my mind once more, planting the first seeds of this tale. Magical spinning, I reasoned, would spin impossible things, like sadness and rage and storms. And what better place to spin a storm than on a cliff, overlooking the sea?

Nadia, my main character, came to me almost fully formed—angry and isolated and nursing an old wound. I loved the idea of a woman whose spinning is both the source of her power and the source of her isolation. For that reason, Nadia is not the first character we meet. She is alone within the tale, both literally and figuratively, and it takes another craftsperson to make her face that fact. The story can only resolve once Nadia acknowledges that she's the source of her own problem. It is only through that acknowledgement that Nadia is able to use her power for something greater than herself.

A question for the author

Q: Aliens, are they out there?

A: Probably. The visible universe has over 400 quadrillion stars in it, and if even a tiny fraction of those stars have a planet that could support life...well, a tiny fraction of a gigantic number is still a gigantic number. I think it would be rather anthropocentric to imagine we're the only life, or even the only intelligent life, in the cosmos.

So yeah, they're probably out there. Maybe they'll even read this story one day. If so, hi! What took you so long?

About the author

J.C. Pillard is an author and editor living at the foot of the Colorado Rockies. She's an avid reader and writer of speculative fiction, and particularly loves anything folklore-inspired. When she's not writing, J.C. spends her time knitting and playing D&D. She's also recently taken up spinning, which might explain this story.

Sturm und Clang

Sara Kate Ellis

"Just use your homespun innocence, Sam. Those townies will trust you."

"Homespun, Barry? Really?" Sam says. "It's more like Pottersville from *It's a Wonderful Life*. Only without the fun."

Barry's her editor at *Pitch Magazine*, the West Coast's foremost—which means surviving—music magazine, but for an editor, he's surprisingly averse to details. She stares out the Lyft window at the dry, sunlit malaise of Felder's Pike, sees a nail salon and a boarded-up tax office, probably once a thriving brick-and-mortar. On the corner, a payday loan shop hides the thinly painted-over logo of a Starbucks that must have ducked in and out of the town within a season, and Hoagie's Diner, where her favorite band *The Waffle Irons* used to hang out after shows. Now it's a tavern with tinted windows and an entrance scattered with cigarette butts.

"Well, then, push the dying Americana angle," Barry says. "Get a feel for what was there. The sweetness. A look back at an America when it was okay to be aspirational."

He says it like it never was okay to be aspirational, but now that the danger's passed, he's willing to indulge the idea a little. Sam reaches into her handbag, brushing her fingers against her Tic Tac container of edibles for reassurance. Barry's never liked *The Waffle Irons*, just like most people don't like *The Waffle Irons*, but with the death of Mapes Higgins, the band's last living member, his hand has been forced. And Sam, much to her surprise, has just touched down to write a three-thousand-word feature, her biggest for the magazine yet.

She glances at the file she's brought with her, printed out so she doesn't have to squint at her phone. A photocopy of the old liner notes to a reissue of their album sneers up from the page.

'Wherefore art My Roameo' evinces the loneliness and confusion experienced by those average girls, unwillingly thrust into the music business and their strange brand of stardom. They were an amalgam of the everygirl. Not too pretty, but not homely either. Plump in that charming way of girls in farming communities, with the unambitious dreams of homemaking and boys.

Ugh.

"A nice memorial," Barry says. "We'll throw in some copy about Niles Deep."

There it is. The real reason Sam's here. Niles Deep, an algorithm in the guise of a soulfully bland white boy, just namedropped the song in his latest hit, 'Cool Run Deep'.

Wherefore art my Roameo
I'm here yo! I'm here yo!

Sam's not thrilled her chance to write about her favorite band has been generated by a bot-thario, but she'll take it. She's twenty-eight, still paying off loans in a rent-controlled apartment, and her mother is telling her to take up teaching. Poor man's Pottersville or not, she's come to find redemption or a recharge. Or something.

"A nice hometown memorial," Barry says. "Have it to me by Monday."

The first time Sam heard the *Irons*, she laughed like everyone else, played the LP once more out of disbelief, and then—telling herself it was for kicks—listened repeatedly until each song became an earworm. Either the girls—Mapes, Amy, and Edith — were geniuses, or they were the worst band in the world. Most critics bent toward the latter, describing their sound as "a nasal cacophony whose key changed like the Dow during a meltdown... a nonsensical mishmash of teenage melodrama mixed with plain Jane reserve." They were the garage band that never quite made it out of the garage, so bad they were brilliant. This was why Gen X women loved them. This is why Sam, a Millennial or a Zennial—that window keeps changing—loves them, too.

Her first stop is Felder's Pike High, the girls' erstwhile, not-quite alma mater. Ingrid Bevan, former Mapes classmate now school counselor, is giving her the grand tour.

"Not a lot of folks around here care for their music much, to be honest," she says. She leads her to a display case in the double-load corridor, her expression somewhat apologetic. "But we're proud of them all the same."

A few ribbons and photographs are pinned haphazardly to a felt board. There's an old black and white of *The Waffle Irons* jammed in between one of a winning golf team and someone taking a second-place award in a national speech contest.

"What was it like?" Sam asks. "On their last day?"

The story goes that their father Ward, a government contractor, cracked after tanking his portfolio. His solution? A get-rich-quick scheme involving a truckload of cheap instruments and pulling Mapes, Edith, and Amy out of school. From then until his death in the Bechlan asylum three years later, the girls spent their days isolated, practicing instruments and holding concerts at birthday parties and the Runyon Community Center. Preparing for a big break that never happened. The girls released one album with a print run of two thousand copies. It got little to no airplay and they never released a second, although they were working on it. Sam's got a few pages of the sheet music copied from the U.C.L.A. archive, scrawled by hand in a million different colors, and despite Barry's trivialization of the assignment, she harbors a secret hope she may unearth the rest.

Bevan shrugs. "They were pretty circumspect, but that was how those girls were. Honestly, I think Mapes was happy about it. She didn't get along with the teachers here."

"Really?" Sam's eyes drift over the photo: the girls hunched up on the stage, their instruments surrounding them like oversized luggage. They don't look much like rebels. Ward even boasted something to that effect in the liner notes, how they were 'counter to the counter culture'.

"Mapes was too smart." Bevan says. She glares at a pair of boys as they scurry past her down the corridor, late for class. "All three of them were. Mapes and Edith were already taking classes at the local college."

"College?" Sam turns back to her, blinking in surprise. "And Ward allowed it?"

Bevan waves her off like it's obvious. "Of course. He talked the college into letting them attend."

Sam takes this in as Bevan directs her to a set of carpeted stairs at the end of the hall.

"Do you know what they were studying?"

She expects to hear something like Intro to Accounting or Home Management, but Bevan smiles a little wryly, as if Sam's response was predictable.

"Advanced calculus, linear algebra, that kind of stuff. Mapes used to really tick off our math teacher, Mr. Dredley. She was way ahead of him." She stops before a set of heavy doors. "Here we are."

Sam shakes off her confusion. Nearly everything she's read about the band alludes to their averageness. Their being torn from school itself was never treated as a squelching of their potential, but the deprivation of what middling observers might refer to as a 'normal life'. She reminds herself to ask Bevin more questions later, but right now she's got to focus. The shop class is part of *Irons* lore. It's where the girls played their last show, unbeknownst to their father, returning on the day that, had they stayed enrolled, would have been Amy's last as a senior. Sam's got a lone, grainy black-and-white from the event. In it, the girls stand next to a boxy metal sculpture adorned with vacuum tubes and wires. Their instruments and amplifiers flank the trio like lumpish rooks.

"I wasn't there," Bevan sighs. "But the girls came in during the final class period, locked the room, set up, and started playing. Principal Mosier chewed them out and kept their equipment impounded for a couple of weeks, but not much else. Didn't tell their Dad on them."

"Nice of him," Sam says.

Bevan shrugs, a mix of sour and sad puckering her features. "He knew what they were dealing with at home."

The concert was just a few days before Ward checked into the asylum. Did the sisters sense a weakness and act on it?

She takes in a breath, readying herself for her *Abbey Road* moment, but the room Bevan opens up on lies strictly in the present. Bright halogen spills over row upon row of kids with anime hairstyles, all clacking away at their laptops. A clash of midis and dub beats and vocoder outbursts pings around the room like cannon fire. It's music, or a semblance of it, but it scrapes against Sam's eardrums like a saw blade. She's been on her share of music pilgrimages, The Motown Museum, Hendrix's grave, and the old Satyricon club in Portland, but she doesn't think she's ever been more disappointed. It's as if Niles Deep and his algorithms have usurped this part of the *Irons'* story too.

"Kind of like stepping onto the Tardis, I imagine," Bevan says, a hint of pride in her voice. "It's a computer lab now."

Sam's about to press her hands to her ears, but she stops herself as she takes in the equally confused gaze of the instructor, a dark-haired, bespectacled woman who slaps her laptop shut as if they've caught her running a search on homemade explosives.

"What is this, Ingrid?" She's clearly not happy about the intrusion.

Bevan plants a palm across her forehead. "Oh, my word, I forgot to tell you. Florence, this is—"

Sam crosses between them, offering her hand. "Sam Taber from *Pitch* magazine."

The woman bends over her desk to take it, her grip hard and a mild scowl tugging at her lips. She's buttoned-up yet effortless, in a denim shirt and dockers, a cross between a schoolmarm and a Silicon Valley hopeful. Sam suspects she must have seven exact copies of that outfit in her closet.

"Flo Nagourney." Her eyes drop to Sam's Tee with its bright orange logo reading *Gabba Gabba Hey!*

"This is where *The Waffle Irons* used to hang out," Bevan says. She's already backing toward the door. "I thought I'd—"

"Them?" Flo says. She trains her gaze at some kids in the back of the classroom. "I hear Fortnite, Georgi!" She glares. "And Davis! Update your fic later. I want those loops coded before the bell." She rolls her shoulders back and turns to face Sam. "That's fine, but my kids are up to their ears in Sonic Pi, so it would be great if you could make this quick."

"Not a problem," Sam says.

In fact, she's more than happy to oblige.

Bevan coughs out a quick excuse, ducking out as the din starts up again. Flo doesn't move, however. She's still staring at Sam like an object that doesn't sit right on the mantel.

"Guess this isn't what you came for," she says.

"Not... really," Sam says, a little disconcerted by the sudden awkwardness between them.

"Well..." Flo gestures to a pair of large sockets in the corner. "It's still got the wiring from the old days. I'll give it that. You could power an ENIAC in here."

"A what?"

Flo smiles, as if she shouldn't have expected Sam to get it. "An old mainframe." She looks back, somewhat ruffled. "So the *Irons*, huh?"

"Yeah."

"And someone's paying you for this?"

Flo eyes Sam's shirt again, and Sam can practically hear the calculations in her head. T-shirt plus age plus cheap sneakers equals eking out a freelancer's income at thirty.

"Take all the time you need," Flo says. "Got to get back to the real work."

She turns and leaves Sam in the corner with her face on fire.

Real Work.

She's still fuming in the Lyft to her next stop. Those are the same words her mother used, still uses to freeze her insides, dragging her back from that stubborn insistence—very lonely, very stubborn—that she has as much right to pursue a passion as the more privileged kids do. But she does get where this Flo person is coming from. In fact, what stuns her most about Ward's plan is less its ludicrousness than its relative viability. That in the late 1960s-early 1970s, the idea of getting rich off music was only moderately bonkers as opposed to downright delusional.

Imagine having a parent push you to be a musician. An artist, of any kind.

Just imagine.

Dave Blankenship, a former neighbor, still lives next door to the Higgins' old Victorian. It stands fenced in on the lot, sagging and condemned, but he's agreed to let Sam view it from his adjacent backyard.

There's been little upkeep. New battens and sarking boards have been patched in to keep out rain. The gabled roofs and spiny turrets have been dulled to nubs by time and neglect. But she can almost hear the clash of guitars against basement acoustics—Amy's drumbeats and the atonal chorus of 'Wherefore Art My Roameo'. He's one of the most enduring mysteries of the sisters' non-stardom. Roameo suspects have ranged anywhere from innocent crushes to older paramours and even a stray cat. The girls denied every theory.

"We already had a cat," Edith said. "And did you think we had time for boys?"

Blankenship has the look of an astronaut gone-to-seed, blotchy skin once pink with health, a belly pushing out the bright orange frond on the front of a Hawaiian shirt. He points through an opening in the fence between their properties where the boards have split off. "Mapes held on to the old place," he says. "Now she's gone, some upstart's gonna flip it."

Sam guesses that the properties in this town aren't that flippable, but she keeps that to herself. Ward Higgins was admitted to the Bechlan Asylum in the summer of 1969, and died there a year later. Edith and Amy went to live with an aunt on the other side of the country, while Mapes hitchhiked to the East Coast. She reappeared Heathcliff-like in the mid-1980s, rich off some investment, and moved a few things into the house, but didn't stay. It makes sense and no sense at the same time, Sam thinks, like some sad secret Mapes couldn't quite let go of.

"I used to sneak cigarettes to Mapes," Blankenship says. "She'd stand on a footstool and smoke them by the window and blame me when Ward asked about the smell." He chuckles at the memory. Sam's eyes follow the uneven concrete around the yard, now cracked with age and dandelions.

"Were you close?"

"Good friends," Blankenship says.

"Must have been friction, with all the noise."

He shrugs. "Most of the neighbors weren't so wound up about the music. There were lots of kids trying to be *The Beatles* back then. It was the other stuff."

"Other stuff?"

He squints up at the sky, frowns as if he senses rain. "Lots of banging around in the basement."

"Drums?" Sam's almost checked out on this guy, but there's a note in his voice that transcends bloviating.

"Nah." He shakes his head, almost bitterly, like the kid who was never asked to play. "They were working on something."

She squints at him, then stoops to peer through the fence again. "New material?" She knows this is not what he means.

He pauses and then leans in a little. "If you ask me, nothing good or the Feds wouldn't have taken Ward away. Searched the house too."

Sam steps back, a clipped bark of laughter escaping her. "Really?"

Blankenship could have spouted this story to any of the other journos who've come to cover the *Irons*, journos, who from their previous coverage would no doubt have added some condescending marginalia to their lore. But he's kept this one, waited until Mapes' death.

"Never saw what it was," Blankenship says. "Ward wouldn't let any of their friends get past the front door, but I will say this," he pauses, his Coke bottle lenses glinting with a kooky certainty. "The funny farm doesn't usually show up in suits and sedans."

Blankenship's likely just an attention seeker or a sincere oddball, but she does another search for Ward Higgins. The Bechlan Asylum shut its doors in the early '80s and was demolished in '87. But there's a name in an old article in a now defunct local paper, Shepley Labs. It was the last company Ward contracted with before he threw everything into the girls' music career, notable for a series of domestic computing flops, including a cooking computer and an early home playmate called My Buddy. She pulls up a page on dead technology, double-taking on an ad featuring a boxy thing with lightbulb eyes and a grille for a mouth.

A companion more faithful than Rover.

He stays here, while you go there.

The ad copy is close enough to the Irons' lyrics to give her pause.

Not one sold, the website says, but she wonders if it wasn't one of Ward's designs, a preview of failures to come. Or maybe he brought home a prototype. She looks at her watch, regrets not having asked Blankenship more questions. But it's late now, and her mind is churning and there's another place she needs to visit.

Hoagie's is what she expected from the outside, dim and grimy and reeking of snuck cigarettes, but after the weirdness with Blankenship, she's more than pleased with the obscurity. She takes a seat at the far end of the counter and orders a beer. Niles Deep's 'Cool Run Deep' dribbles from a candied-up retro jukebox in the corner, the *Irons'* lyrics followed by his dumbshit rejoinder.

While you Roam
I'm at home
I stay here, You go there
No car, no bike, no feet, no wind
Wherefore art my Roameo
I'm here-yo!
I'm here-yo!

Thief.

The bartender brings her a Pabst. It's flat, but she downs half of it, her shoulders loosening with the buzz. She's about to order a shot when she hears a throat clear and turns to see Flo watching her from a darkened booth nestled behind her.

What's next? she wonders. Her mother walking through the door with a circled ad for entry-level daycare?

They stare at each other for a cold minute. Then Sam lets out a breath and tries, if not a smile, then a conciliatory nod. "Didn't seem like the type for this kind of place." She gestures to the stack of neglected worksheets next to Flo's beer glass. "I mean, with all that real work and all."

Flo shoots her a 'you got me' look and shrugs. "Here's to ladies loitering in ice cream parlors." She lifts her glass and gestures for Sam to join her.

Sam regards her suspiciously for another second. This has a strong whiff of all those times she ran into the cool kids outside of high school and they were inexplicably nice until Monday rolled around. But she grabs her bag and her beer and the gratis basket of popcorn and sits down with Flo in the booth.

"Bad day?"

Flo snorts. "You get warned about a lot of things before you become a teacher, but not that people have mistaken acronyms for algorithms. They really think that kids memorizing their ESLERS and IPFs means they'll automatically know how to conjugate French verbs or enter a Python value." She takes another long pull of her beer. "Even algorithms need content to work with."

"Even that?" Sam nods up at the speakers. Niles Deep's voice is oozing out of them like soft cream.

Flo shrugs, takes another sip of her beer. "Especially that. The formula's been built on thousands of previous successes."

Her tone is more philosophical than argumentative, but Sam's had enough of numbers and success metrics. "Not everything needs a formula."

"The *Irons* could have used one."

Sam doesn't deign to answer that. She senses Flo's eyes on her, feels her deciding in that minute to dial things down.

Flo leans forward, her weight on her elbows. "Honest question, and I don't mean reply guy honest. How can you stand them? The noise? Those listless voices?"

When people ask, Sam usually goes on the defensive. She'll talk about their lack of hipster disaffection, argue that they've got a genuine it-is-what-it-is quality that outshines the grandiose white dude pronouncements of songs like 'Let it Be' or 'Do You Realize'— the latter being the most cloying demand to smile she's ever heard. But from the beginning, their music tugged at something else inside her, an assurance that it was okay to be bad. That it was okay to make the wrong moves, because if you kept going, you might just land on the right ones. And if you didn't? At least they were yours.

"They…" she wraps her fingers around her glass. "I guess they're proof it's not too late, that you can suck by other people's standards and still stumble onto something beautiful."

Flo gives a half-smile, thoughtful but unconvinced. "Sounds like flailing."

"Flailing, huh?" Sam reaches for her backpack, pulls out that file she's been carrying around with her like a complex. "How about I show you something?"

She rifles through the mess until she finds what she's looking for: the photocopies of Mapes' sheet music. They're hand-written and color-coded, with so many looping scrawls across the page, you can barely see where the music starts and stops. "One of the greatest misconceptions about the *Irons*...” She wipes the condensation from the table before resting the pages on its surface. “... is that they were clueless kids banging out random notes. But Mapes and Edith wrote all the music out first. They wrote and rewrote it until it was just the way they wanted it. They weren’t flailing. But they weren’t imitating or running on some soulless program either. That’s the difference.”

She nudges the pages in front of her, a chaos of slashes and looping notations, and watches as Flo goes quiet. Her expression is humoring at first, and then that smile disappears.

“You sure?” she says, not dismissively this time, but like she’s working out a problem.

“About what?” Sam says.

Flo runs her finger down to a series of slashes and numbers at the bottom of the page. She’s staring at it with a mix of bemusement and fascination. “This kind of looks like score.”

“That’s what I mean,” Sam says. “They compos—”

“No, I mean SCORE,” Flo says. “A musical notation program. The first.” She pushes up her glasses, and lifts the page for a closer look. “It started in ‘67, but it sure as hell wasn’t *this* far along then. When did they write this?”

Sam hesitates, not ready for this sudden show of interest. “Late ‘69 or ‘70. Why?”

Flo doesn’t answer and Sam doesn’t press her. She’s experiencing that vertigo when you realize you’ve gotten someone wrong. Flo’s looking at her with the same expression.

“Mind if I copy these?” Flo asks.

“Sure,” Sam says. “What for?”

Flo takes a long slug from a tepid water glass she’s been ignoring.

“I’m not sure yet,” she says.

Sam wants to think she’s impressed her, that some part of Florence Nagourney caught a glimpse of the *Irons’* genius. In her room, she runs a search for SCORE and finds Flo isn’t far off at all. SCORE got its start at Stanford in ‘67, two years before Ward pulled the girls out of school. Sam doesn’t get coding, but the notations from the early incarnations seem rudimentary compared to the ornate chaos of Mapes’ sheet music. Was the music part of a program? Was Ward teaching them programming language in addition to the music? Sam paces in the cramped space between the bed and the radiator. Wishes she'd gone right past Blankenship into the house.

Her phone buzzes, loud. She picks it up, her heart stalling as she hears Barry on the other end. He rarely bothers her during a story unless it's bad news.

He gets right to the point, too. "We're going to have to cut your piece down." He sounds exhausted, like this is the last among hundreds of similar calls.

"How much?"

"A thousand words. I'll throw in an extra ten cents per word. I didn't want to do this, Sam. Niles Deep has an album about to drop with 'Cool Run Deep'. Nothing confirmed yet, but I've got to be ready for it."

She doesn't protest. No buts. There's no arguing with Barry. She just asks another question.

"Did you know the girls were smart?"

"Ha. Funny."

"I mean like brilliant smart. Ward wasn't homeschooling them. Not really. They were going to college and—"

He laughs again, as if this time, she's gotten him. "Who've you been talking to? Look, we're not looking for Jim Morrison here. Just a nice, sweet story about some girls with stars in their eyes, okay? I'll see you Monday."

The next question dies in her throat.

The Runyon Community Center is one of the only *Irons* performance venues still standing. She's got more than enough material to cover the meager word count Barry's affording her— she's much more worried about affording rent—but she'll be damned if she misses this, for if there's anything remaining of the *Irons'* dissonant spirit, it's here. The stage is rickety, the floorboards sunken and listing toward the exit. For a few minutes, she thumbs in her earbuds and revels in the lopsidedness of it all.

> *Who you are, where you come from*
> *Who really can care*
> *When you've got*
> *The family that's there?*

For a few minutes, the Caligari angles fulfill their promise. She's back amid the jeers and the sweat, the tossed soda cans and doomed-to-fail expectations of nearly every teenage rite of passage. Maybe it's the old school smell of wood and scuffed sneakers, or the growing darkness blurring the edges of past and present, but she catches that ineffability, the flicker not so much of promise, but of the possibility that comes from the decision just to try.

Sam still wants to try. She's close to finding something that's hers; it's the world that keeps giving up on her. This time when her phone rings, she doesn't answer.

She only notices Flo's message after she's played the album all the way through.

[Mind coming by the school? I'd like you to hear something].

It's a long weekend with no kids around, and when the security guard leads her to the lab, it feels portentous, not at all like the dry disappointment of the other day. She can already hear a clip of 'My Confidant' playing on a loop, Amy's stroppy drumbeats warring with Mapes' and Edith's oscillating chord progressions.

On the stairs,
Under the chair,
You're there
Even in my hair

Flo turns down the volume and gestures for her to come in. "Sorry for calling you out of the blue like that," she says. "I worried you'd leave town."

There's an agitation in her movements that wasn't there yesterday, like a movie where an old curmudgeon switches bodies with a hip teen. She puts a hand on the back of her chair, swivels it absently back and forth, like she's deliberating. "Their music. It's interesting."

Sam coughs out a laugh. "Is that so?"

"I didn't say 'good'," Flo says, pulling into herself again. "But..." She turns up the volume, lets the rest of 'My Confidant' blare, messy and discordant. "Beginners make predictable music. Same three chords. Same harmonies. But hear that? That quick rise over the dominant chord as it slides up again and then back down for no apparent reason?"

"Ah," Sam says. "So you've got scientific proof that they suck?"

Flo waves off her remark, winces at feedback screech. "No. I mean, maybe. Ever hear of a Markov chain?"

"Not really," Sam says.

"It's a process that lays out a sequence of possibilities, with the probabilities always based on the event before it. They use it for weather, traffic flow, and to replicate the style of a composer. I input the *Irons* music to a program I've been tweaking. You'd better sit down for this."

What comes next is a revelation. It's a version of their music: the chaos, those wildly fluctuating sequences are still there, but each variation mingles perfect harmony with perfect discord, a balance where none should be. Sam's always heard this in their music and struggled to explain it, but here that euphony jumps out, a clear pattern running through the drumbeats and the melody, steady and endless and unforeseeable.

"I expected something roughshod," Flo says, lowering the volume. "Simple and predictable, but with this... every deviation evokes a myriad of other departures." She draws back, face drawn; her dark eyes are brimming with excitement. "I didn't mean to make things sound so soulless the other night. I was feeling pretty soulless myself, to be honest, but this is something special, Sam."

Sam feels a flutter of something roll through her, a faint reverberation of the music.

"Do you..." she says. "Do you maybe want to break into a house?"

At night, the Higgins' Victorian looks a little more forbidding; the paint is faded and chipping, blending into the overcast sky as if a shift in the clouds might cause it to flicker from view. They creep through Blankenship's driveway, squeezing safely through the hole in the fence without incident. Sam starts for the front of the house, but Flo gestures toward the same basement window through which Blankenship passed his contraband soda and cigarettes. If they keep it quiet, they should be able to carry this off.

Flo fishes a flathead screwdriver from the pocket of her denim jacket. "I jump motherboards with these all the time," she whispers, slipping the tip under the window beading. Rot has set in the wood, leaving only a thin line like black mold on caulk that gives easily. She slips the screwdriver beneath the glass and nudges it from the weather-damaged frame.

"You want to go first?" she says.

Sam doesn't mind if she does.

The basement is a showroom of her expectations: a time capsule of wood paneling, low-ceilings, and yellow carpet muted into blood orange by the darkness. This is where it happened, where Ward exiled his daughters, and where they practiced their instruments until their fingers bled.

Flo tracks the flashlight along the walls, across the pencil marks marking their heights in a doorframe, that long series of befores. The paneling's been stripped from the back wall along with a large block of carpet, revealing an expanse of pocked concrete and exposed wiring.

"They were powering something bigger than a few guitars," Flo says, nodding at a series of cupholder-sized outlets, their mouths worn and blackened from use. In the corner, obscured by a tangle of hippy beads, is a large, blocky shadow.

Sam freezes, afraid this will be nothing, another grandiose overture that flops into a limping coda, but Flo's fingers find hers, tugging her forward as she casts her beam over a surface of dark chrome. It's a cabinet, the interior a hybrid from a mad scientist movie and some old timey player piano. Row upon row of bulbs and buttons peer from inside like some primordial, eye-studded creature. Vacuum tubes sag from its sides like limp appendages. She flashes back to that shop class photo, that strange, cumbersome thing near the amplifiers. There's a resemblance to the *My Buddy* model, but this is a bigger, far more complicated beast.

Bevan's and Blankenship's words come back to her.

Mosier kept their equipment impounded for a couple of weeks...didn't tell their Dad on them. Mapes was too smart.

They were building something.

"While you roam, I'm at home," she whispers. "They must have known those men were coming for Ward. They hid it at the school because they knew Mosier wouldn't contact him. And what self-respecting G-Man would suspect a trio of dopey girls capable of creating—" The words stop in her throat. She doesn't have them. Not yet.

Flo lets out a low whistle in accompaniment as she reaches over, her fingers trailing under a dusty cylinder of paper marked up in Mapes' chaotic hand.

No car, no bike, no feet, no wind.

"It was them," Sam says.

"Who?" Flo's gaze follows hers down to a faint scrawl at the bottom of the page.

Your Roameos,

Mapes, Edith, and Amy.

It's not a *My Buddy*, but a much larger version of it, more eyes, a larger grille for a mouth regarding them without judgment. Like it's been waiting for them all along.

On the drive back, they park the car at the edge of Goddard Lake.

The moon's out and the air has just enough chill to add a bite to their exuberance. They stay close to the car, not daring to risk the moldering treasure in the trunk; the books and papers, and the old and very heavy Disc Pack Flo jimmied out with her screwdriver. It's what they could carry away safely, but already Flo is talking about going back, even about putting down an offer on the house if she can scrape together the money. She's pacing back and forth as she talks.

"Hear of Alan Turing?" Flo turns to her, her voice shaky. They could both use a drink.

"Saw the movie."

"The good one with Derek Jacobi?"

"The lousy one with Benedict Cumberbatch."

She laughs, but something unspoken passes between them, an acknowledgement of what already feels steady, a routine. Flo is rigid and methodical, and much more in control of her life, but to Sam, she's a much-needed constraint in her algorithm.

"He built this monstrosity called the Aural Artefact," she says. "Programmed in the British National Anthem and Glenn Miller and..." She leans back against the hood of the car. "It was the first recording of computer-generated music, and it sounded awful, like a pipe blowing a raspberry." She slips her hands into her pockets. "But it reminded me of the *Irons*... There's a lassitude there, like the machine just wasn't in the mood." She takes in a breath, her dark eyes now deep with possibility.

"Look," Flo says. "I am not even close to understanding this, only that there's a lot more to this than a trio of girls and a failed music career, and..." She raises her hand, her smile flat as if she's growing impatient with herself. "I don't mean it that way. It's just that if you want someone to help you uncover the rest... I mean, I —I'd like to. Very much."

Sam feels the warmth travel to her cheeks. "Like maybe uncovering the shocking revelation that Roameo wasn't a boy?"

"Or a cat," Flo says.

"You've done your homework."

"I'm a teacher," Flo says. "I lead by example."

They grin at each other, bodies loosening as they meet in the middle. Sam doesn't worry about her mother or the thousand words she's got to plunk out by Monday. Barry will get what he wants: a phoned-in cutesy retrospective on three hapless, dopey girl musicians. And sure, Sam might even have to work in retail for a spell, but failure's just another disguise when they don't know what's coming.

She's got a real story now, about three girls in isolation; three lonely geniuses who built a friend and a collaborator, creating music into which the four of them could pour their loneliness. Art out of circumstances. It's a much better story than the one even the *Irons'* well-intentioned champions assigned to them; much better than the one she's assigned to herself.

And on the drive back, when Niles Deep's 'Cool Run Deep' drips from the radio, she finds herself singing along.

See Sara Kate Ellis's story "Sturm und Clang" online at Metaphorosis.
If you liked it, leave a comment. Authors love that!
Remember to subscribe to our e-mail updates so you'll know when new stories are posted.

About the story

This story came from an obsession with the rock trio, *The Shaggs*. Like Sam, I cackled the first time I heard one of their songs, but by the third play, the smugness had left the building. There's a genuine mystery behind their appeal: Is it the jagged unpredictability in their melodies? Or the way the drummer sounds like she's accompanying a different album altogether? But it wasn't until a few years after being introduced to them that I caught something A.I.-like in their atonality. So, the basis for the story began with a question: What if the 'Foot Foot' in "My Pal Foot Foot" (Roameo in the story) were really a sentient machine's term for human beings? And what if that machine were grappling with loneliness just like the girls who'd been cut off from the world by their father? I was also interested in the drive to make art in a world of diminishing opportunities for creatives. The contrast between a father forcing his daughters into would-be rock stardom and Sam, who just a few generations later, is receiving the constant message to give up, felt like an interesting way to grapple with the problem. That *The Waffle Irons* persevered against peer ridicule and a possibly abusive parent to create something lasting is what keeps Sam going. She'll soon discover the irony in that, but also (I hope) a faint reason for optimism.

A question for the author

Q: What do you think makes for a good story?
A: Oh, that's tough, but with speculative fiction, I guess I would say stories that show me the future while forcing me to take a harder look at the present. My favorites often alert me to some mad, screaming deficiency in my perception. Ted Chiang's *The Great Silence* is a good example, a gut-wrenching twist on that old *Now Voyager* line, "don't let's ask for the moon. We have the stars." Or in this case, "we [still] have" these rapidly dwindling species we're paying zero attention to while we search for alien life.

About the author

Sara Kate Ellis was born in Oregon but has lived most of her adult life in Japan. She lives in Tokyo with her partner and their two ornery cats and has been served more than once by a robot bartender.

@Skellis13

May

Indicative of Future Results

C. H. Rosenberg

The Frontpage Feed: Morning Edition. **Carefully curated and fact-checked headlines delivered to your inbox, every day!**
SUBJECT LINE: *Extraterrestrials Exposed?!*
Top Ranked News (56,031 shares): *Stunning 'Proof' of Extraterrestrial Cover-Up Floods Internet.*

Yesterday's release of thousands of purportedly top-secret documents by a self-proclaimed former high-ranking national security official sent shockwaves across the metaverse.

The manifesto accused the United States and allied spacefaring nations of covering up an extraterrestrial message received several years ago, when both competing nation-states and private enterprise were emerging as serious contenders in a second Space Race.

The self-described whistleblower claimed a signal was intercepted by a joint scientific team on board the International Space Station (ISS) and the origin later pinned as the TRAPPIST-1 star system in the Aquarius constellation. All media inquiries to the personnel named in the leaked documents were directed to an ISS Program spokesperson who declined to comment.

The manifesto goes on to reveal that a second message was recently intercepted, with analysts agreeing it amounts to an announcement of an impending arrival. "In other words," the alleged former insider warned, "an extraterrestrial vanguard is on its way—we *hope* for the purpose of establishing diplomatic relations. Either way, our leaders are fooling themselves if they think they can keep this under wraps."

While such claims of extraterrestrial contact are typically dismissed as false alarms, several respected experts appear to be taking this particular claim seriously. The International Academy of Astronautics and the SETI Institute both urged calm while they work to verify the purported evidence.

Business and Finance News (4,833 shares): ***Closing Bell Round-up***

Personal finance guru Connie Padilla today announced the release of her eagerly awaited book, *Give Your Future Self a Raise.* In this fresh spin on retirement planning, Ms. Padilla, 42, offers her characteristic pragmatic advice, as always inspiring readers with her message of financial empowerment. This adds to a growing media empire so far encompassing a semiweekly podcast and newsletter, two other published books and a robust digital community platform. Ms. Padilla regularly appears on the conference and talk show circuit and recently kicked off a live weekly show, where she answers her audience's questions on everything related to personal finance.

LIBRARY: Latest Episode. Downloading…
Power Your Personal Finance—*UNPLUGGED!* *Episode transcript..*
Live streaming in 3…2…1. Cue teaser, introductory music, sponsor plug
Connie: Hello, hello everybody! I'm *so* glad to welcome you here on episode ten—*ten!*—of the live stream version of *Power Your Personal Finance!* I'm Connie Padilla, Certified Financial Planner *and* author of *Give Your Future Self a Raise*—out now!— plus two other bestsellers, *Power Your Personal Finance: The Fundamentals* and *The Smart Side-Hustle.*
Each Friday, I take questions from people *just like you,* live on the show. My goal is to help you take control of your financial future, for a worry-free life today and a comfortable retirement tomorrow.
First off, a quick disclaimer: *Power Your Personal Finance* is purely for educational and entertainment purposes. Anything said on this show should not be construed as individual financial, legal, tax, or accounting advice; listeners are advised to discuss their personal financial situation and goals with a financial professional. And remember: while we talk about stocks, bonds, real estate, and other investment opportunities on this show, past performance is *not* indicative of future results!

Now, without further ado, let's get to your questions. And from my inbox, it's pretty obvious what most of you have on your mind.

Sound effect: Drum roll

Connie: Aliens! [*laughter*] Just kidding, folks. But several of you clearly *are* worried about defending yourselves from scammers and hoaxes. So, let's start off with a couple of questions about protecting your personal identity. Then, we'll step back to look at asset protection more holistically.

[*Fast forward*. TIME: 24.59]

Connie: All right, we have time for one more call today. Let's go back to the queue. Hello! Who's this?

Frank: Hello, Ms. Padilla. I'm...Frank.

Connie: Hey, Frank. How can I help empower you today?

Frank: What's the *deal* with personal finance, anyway?

Connie: ...Huh?

Frank: Apologies, Ms. Padilla. I'm just...*frustrated*. Maybe because I'm so new to all this? I mean, I've done my homework, I've listened to your entire archive of episodes, I've read *all* of your books—

Connie: Wow!

Frank: But I still feel completely overwhelmed! I'm usually very good at picking up new things—it's my *job*—so this is pretty embarrassing for me.

Connie: Hey, *never* feel ashamed of what you don't know. If you've read *Power Your Personal Finance* and listened to episodes 211 and 341—I'll link to those in the show notes—you've heard me dish about my own background, growing up in a working class Mexican immigrant family. My parents *never* talked about money, at least not beyond worrying we never had enough! I had to learn everything all on my own.

Frank: You still grew up on—*in*—a world where money is incredibly important for just about everything, right? But the whole *concept* is just incredibly *alien* to someone like me. I'm, uh, foreign...

Connie: [*Chuckles.*] I didn't want to comment on your accent, but it is lovely.

Frank: Thanks, Ms. Padilla. But my point is that things are completely different where I'm from. 401(k)s, IRAs, HSAs, FSAs, CFPs...we don't have anything remotely like that. I can barely wrap my ten—my head around it all. [*Pause*] It's all just so—so—so *nonsensical!*

Connie: Calm down, Frank. Relax! I know *all* about feeling like a fish out of water. But honestly, you're in exactly the same boat as many of my other listeners. Possibly in an even *better* boat, because you haven't had a chance to develop bad money habits in the first place! And rest assured, I'm here to help you navigate that ship to financial freedom.

Frank: You…you really think you can help me, Ms. Padilla?

Connie: Absolutely! Now, let's start with the fundamentals…

The Frontpage Feed: Breaking News!
SUBJECT LINE: *Shocker! Politicians chuck plausible deniability (and little green men are headed for Earth)*
Top Ranked News (73,589,230 shares): *We Are Not Alone! World Leaders Confess to Cover-Up, Tell Public to Prepare to Welcome Extraterrestrial Visitors*

In a stunning revelation, the leaders of several nations today confirmed the accusations posted last week by the still-unidentified whistleblower.

At the historic joint press conference, the president of the United States and other heads of state verified the interception of a "message of intelligent extraterrestrial origin" nearly a decade ago. They further verified receipt of a second message just over one month ago on October 15 at 5:32 a.m. UTC; both missives have since been released to the public.

"Our interstellar neighbors tell us they have been observing humanity and want to learn more about us," Japan's prime minister summarized the message. "That is why they have sent an emissary."

Calculations based on information contained in the second message put the extraterrestrial ambassadors' arrival at mid-April.

"I don't know what our idiot leaders were thinking, not informing the public sooner so we'd all have more time to adjust to this new reality," said Dr. Abrams, director of the Space Policy Institute at the George Washington University. "Consequently, humanity has just *five months* to collectively roll out the red carpet."

Some humans, apparently, cannot wait. In reaction to thousands of extraterrestrial enthusiasts attempting to make contact through jerry-rigged transmitters, the U.N. Office for Outer Space Affairs posted an advisory warning against "making unauthorized diplomatic overtures that may confuse, if not endanger interplanetary relations."

Business and Finance News (7,723,459 shares): *'Completely Bonkers': Main Street, Wall Street Reaction Out of This World*

The U.S. Federal Reserve Board of Governors met this morning with leadership from central banks around the world. Their daunting task: stabilize an economic and financial system that is just starting to react to yesterday's revelation about an impending extraterrestrial visit.

"Too late," said Resh Agarwal, senior analyst with the London-based Centre for Fiscal Security. "Everything has already gone completely bonkers—that *is* the technical term, by the way."

"Bonkers" may indeed describe how both financial markets and consumers are responding to the news.

On Wall Street, stocks see-sawed wildly from opening to closing bell, repeating a pattern set by the Nikkei, Shanghai Composite, DAX, and FTSE earlier in the day. On Main Street, retailers reported record-setting activity, with customers fully in panic-buying mode. Sporting goods stores have resorted to rationing out survival and camping gear. The two most popular internet search terms yesterday were "hazmat suit" and "DIY tinfoil hat."

"Customers are literally preparing for the end of the world," said Whole Nine Yards store manager Tonya Reiss, speaking to a correspondent in El Paso, Texas. "They're stocking up on everything, from firearms to canned food. The shelves are empty; we've completely run out of aluminum foil and our vendors are backordered by as much as seven months."

LIBRARY: Latest Episode. Downloading...
Power Your Personal Finance! Ranked #1 in genre. Please leave a review! *Episode transcript.*
Cue teaser, introductory music, sponsor plug
Connie: Happy Money Monday, everybody! I'm Connie Padilla, Certified Financial Planner, welcoming you to episode five-ninety-seven of the *Power Your Personal Finance!* podcast. This is where we talk about everything that can affect your pocketbook—and how you can *act* rather than *react*, to take control of *your* financial future. Control and discipline *is* what it's all about, especially during volatile times.
And speaking of volatility, *what* a week, huh? Stock markets plummeted, triggering the 'circuit breaker' fail-safe no fewer than *five times*—and taking all of our IRAs and 401(k)s along for the ride. Fortunately, things seemed to stabilize by the

end of the week. But what will the coming weeks and months bring?

Listen. I know we're all shaken to the core by the confirmation we're not alone in the universe. It makes us reassess what's truly important, revisit the things we take for granted. And when it comes down to it, I know we *all* have the exact same question:

How is this going to affect my portfolio?

Should I sell? Should I pull everything from my retirement account? Should I convert all my assets into cash or commodities? Do I put it all into durable goods?

I want everyone listening to log out and step away from your investment apps. Take a deep breath. Do *not* let panic take control of your financial decisions. *You* are the one in control. Because here's the answer: Discipline. If you've been disciplined all along, you're all set! You have at least six to eight months of living expenses in cash on hand. You're diversified. You're prepared. You'll be *fine*. You can weather this storm.

In fact, my special guest today happens to be an expert on weathering financial storms...

[*Fast forward.* TIME: 27:05]

We'll end the show as we always do, by reading a review left by a listener. Today's review was written by our friend, Frank! Frank says: *Ms. Padilla has become my go-to resource for everything personal finance. Since she took my question on the live show, I've joined the Power Your Personal Finance! online community, where I've been welcomed with open appendages by a group of people similarly inspired to make Ms. Padilla's 'Financial Fund-amentals' part of their daily lives. I know I still have a lot to learn, but now I feel confident that I'm well on my way. Thank you, Ms. Padilla—I'm your newest, biggest fan!*

Power Your Personal Finance! Community Platform. Enter username and password.

Hot Topic: *What IS ETs' grift, anyway?* (2,739 replies)

Excerpt—*P.J. Kuppenheimer, an economist once ridiculed in academic circles for his obsession over proving the so-called Theory of Interstellar Trade, was appointed this week to the White House Council of Economic Advisers. In his first interview with the news media, Kuppenheimer expressed skepticism over the stated intentions of the "Ambassadors"—as the metaverse has dubbed the extraterrestrials—declaring, "It is entirely irrational for any intelligent being—that is, any self-interested, utility-maximizing individual—to make the long and arduous interstellar journey simply to meet another species in person. These 'Ambassadors' clearly must have some profit motive in mind. Our job is to determine just what, exactly, that may be—and how to prepare for it."* Related link: *The Grifter's Guide to the Galaxy*, MacroEconDaily.NET interview with P.J. Kuppenheimer, Ph.D., Chicago School of Economics.

Moderator: Okay, folks! Before you post, remember to answer today's poll: What's the *real* motivation driving these "Ambassadors" to visit our little blue planet?
(1) They've screwed up their own planet and want ours
(2) They're straight-up conquerors and just want our planet period, no justification required
(3) They've cooked up some grift that makes interstellar travel worth their while
[Tally: (1) 25%; (2) 13%; (3) 62%]

Financially Fit: Seriously? 38% of the people here must be hard-core preppers if they really believe in #1 or #2. [215 likes; 52 LOLs]

ETFrank: "Preppers"? [7 likes]

Retire Early or Bust: I agree, Financially Fit; I think the good prof's hit the nail on the head. Between time dilation and the opportunity costs, in-person interstellar travel just doesn't make sense. There has to be *something* that makes it worth their while. But what? [198 likes]

ETFrank: "Preppers?" [2 likes; 32 eye-rolls]

$$$urvivor: Their technology has to be light years ahead of ours, right? My bet's on them manufacturing a bunch of tiny gizmos super-cheap on their own planet and selling them for insane profit margins here. [278 likes, 53 shares]

ETFrank: Why would the Ambassadors want to sell anything? The message stated our entire goal is a free and open exchange of cultures and ideas! [143 likes, 27 hearts]

ETFrank: Sorry; typo. "Their" entire goal. Also, IDK "preppers." [5 LOLs]

Retire Early or Bust: Come on, ETFrank! That's the classic freemium model. They'll start out giving away their nifty toys, and just wait—soon enough, we won't be able to live without 'em. *Then* they'll be all: Surprise! It's a subscription service—and start charging us through the nose—or whatever orifice. Hook. Line. Sinker. [317 likes, 46 shares]

Moderator: Here you go, Frank: [Link to: *Neighborhood Nut Jobs or Smart Cookies? Top (legal) tips from America's premier* *preppers on setting aside enough food and ammo to last through the End of Days.]*

The Frontpage Feed: Mid-day Edition
SUBJECT LINE: *Ray guns or hostess gift? Here's how to prepare for five different First Contact scenarios*
Top Ranked News (207,403 shares): *Third Message a Charm? Ambassadors Claim Friendly Intentions*

The World Ambassador Greeting Operations Network today announced interception of a third message, as the public counts down the four months remaining until First Contact. Both earth-based and orbiting telescopes tracked the latest message's trajectory back to the extraterrestrial ship, which, according to physicists, is rapidly decelerating and anticipated to cross into the Oort Cloud by this Friday.

"The Ambassadors once again stated their goal is to establish diplomatic relations and learn about humanity," said a spokesperson with Welcome WAGON—the nickname given to the rapidly-assembled international coordinating committee charged with establishing interspecies relations.

"Taken at face value, the Ambassadors are definitely trying to stress their friendly intentions," said Dr. Ixchel Ramirez, astrobiologist with the National Autonomous University of Mexico. She and her interdisciplinary team of scientists, data analysts and linguists have scrutinized the details of every message received thus far. "The picture we've put together so far indicates a culture dedicated to both intellectual and cultural advancement, almost as imperatives to personal and societal growth."

Economist Peter Jeremiah ("P.J.") Kuppenheimer, who recently skyrocketed from obscurity to a household name, is not so inclined to take the Ambassadors at face value. "Why are the Ambassadors trying so hard to convince us of their benign motives?" he scoffed in a series of critical tweets. "Frankly, it's suspicious."

Marketing industry veteran Shahad Khoury agreed. "They're establishing their brand identity ahead of time," she theorized at a recent conference of the Euro-West Asia Advertising Alliance. "Like everyone, they're selling something—and customers prefer supporting a brand they already feel positive about."

Security experts take a more pessimistic interpretation of these messages. "It could be propaganda intended to soften us up in advance of a full-scale invasion," suggested Mai Begay, fellow at the Center for Strategic Defense, based in Arlington, Virginia.

In the meantime, Welcome WAGON has released preliminary details on the planned Landing Ceremony. A multinational site selection committee is wrapping up evaluation of candidate locations to serve as the Ambassadors' embassy.

Business and Finance News (24,869 shares): *Defense Investors Hang Ten as Sector Surfs Wave Fueled by Military Dollars; Charitable Giving and Luxury Travel Soar*

Shortly after news broke about the so-called "Ambassadors'" upcoming rendezvous with Earth, financial analysts predicted that the value of fiat currencies around the world would plunge, warning markets would experience a meltdown as people gathered with their loved ones to wait out—with dread or excitement—the impending arrival.

Instead, the revelation birthed a whole new set of momentum stocks. Despite reassurances the Ambassadors are not out for conquest, not everyone on Wall Street—or in Washington, Beijing, Riyadh or Moscow— is banking on a kumbaya First Contact. Defense contractors, firearm manufacturers, and distributors of survival gear are all driving a robust bull market after an initial dip.

At the same time, megachurches and community organizations find themselves overwhelmed by donations. "People are desperate to redeem their souls before the 'invasion'," observed Jenny Zhou, pastor with the First Lutheran Church of Kalamazoo, Michigan.

Tourism and recreation are also benefitting. The industry reported a 300 percent increase in spending compared to this time last year, with consumers throwing their retirement savings at "bucket list" items. "Nobody's even raising an eyebrow at the waiver form these days," said Sergio Martinez, owner and CEO of St. Croix-based X-Treme Ocean Skydiving, LLP. "They just shrug and say, 'Why the hell not?'"

@ConniePadillaPYPF | Power   Your   Personal   Finance®
@PYPersonalFinancePodcast   •   Jan   14
837.5K Followers

Wow! Incredibly honored to be recognized as a "top finance expert" by @PersonalInvestorMag this week.

[link to *Personal Investor Magazine*. Where are Americans Turning for Financial Advice During the Impending Apocalypse?]
[2.7K replies, 5.3K retweets, 8.6K likes]

@ConniePadillaPYPF | Power Your Personal Finance®
@PYPersonalFinancePodcast • Jan 16
859.6K Followers

Had a great chat this week with my fellow money guru @TKRawlins on @TheTalkExchange about all the #marketcraziness right now.
[link to *Wall Street Bytes*. Technology Stocks Tumble Across the Motherboard: NASDAQ stumbles as industry doomsayers claim technologically advanced "Ambassadors" could spell the end for Silicon Valley.]
@ConniePadillaPYPF | Power Your Personal Finance®
@PYPersonalFinancePodcast • Jan 16
859.6K Followers

But let's talk about what's happening on #MainStreet! Next week on the podcast I'll do a deep dive into how the Ambassadors are affecting the pocketbooks of REAL PEOPLE. DM me if you have a story you'd like to share!
[1.7K replies, 5.8K retweets, 10.4K likes]

Message to ConniePadillaPYPF from ETFrank1701 • Jan 23

Hi, Ms. Padilla. You probably don't remember me, but I was caller 7 on Power Your Personal Finance live stream episode #10. You even told me to reach out anytime if I still had trouble taking control of my personal finance journey.

Your words of empowerment that day really inspired me. So much so that I'm now the de facto "economics expert" among my friends and coworkers—they've even started asking ME for advice! Whenever I'm unsure of the answer, I'll reread a chapter of your book, replay one of your podcast episodes, or ask the PYPF community for help.

But now we all have the same question on our minds, and it's one I just don't know how to answer: Why in the universe is humanity reacting the way it is to the Ambassadors' arrival?

We just don't get it. I mean, the Ambassadors were really clear on having peaceful intentions. Officially, world leaders keep saying this is great news for the planet. But you—Connie Padilla, #1 personal finance guru—always say that money speaks louder than words. Well, a lot of people are spending money in ways that show they're scared of an invasion or think the Ambassadors are out to cheat everybody.

So, can you tell me: WHY are humans reacting this way? And what do YOU think about it?

Thanks so much; loved the last episode!

Frank

P.S. Which "rational, intelligent being" came up with the invasion scenario, anyway? It makes NO sense for an invader to give their invadee a heads-up IMHO.

Message to ETFrank1701 from ConniePadillaPYPF • Feb 12

Hey, Frank!

So sorry for the delay—I was COMPLETELY overwhelmed by all the terrific personal finance stories folks sent me last month. Teach me to ask half the metaverse to DM me. :(But of course, I remember my newest, biggest fan! I even told you to reach out to me anytime, right?

It's super interesting you and your friends are putting yourself in the Ambassadors' shoes (do they even have shoes? LOL). Because I'd say the issue here is that the rest of humanity is NOT putting itself in the Ambassadors' shoes; nope, not at all!

It's our first time meeting extraterrestrials—so who or what else do we even have to compare them to, besides ourselves? FWIW, I'd say most people assume the Ambassadors are a lot like us and weighing the risks vs. rewards of First Contact based on that. Those "peaceful intentions," the promises of cultural exchange, whatever goods & services they (probably) have to sell? They just don't outweigh the risk of an invasion (and don't even think of bringing logic into the conversation, my friend) or—more likely—being rolled by little green men.

Again, GREAT question, and maybe one I'll post a video about later in the week!

Connie

Message to ConniePadillaPYPF from ETFrank1701 • Feb 13

Hi, Ms. Padilla.

Well, that's SUPER depressing.

I mean, if you were the Ambassadors, how could you even counter that?

And do YOU feel that way, too? Or are you just another person trying to make a buck off the situation? I'm such a fan of yours, but I have to admit I'm also kind of disappointed in you right now. You're racking up all the ratings, giving people all the advice on 'weathering the storm' and 'profiting from the uncertainty'. But are you thinking AT ALL about what this'll mean for the future of humanity when the Ambassadors see what's happening and decide WTH and go home? It's risk vs. reward, after all! What's the reward for the Ambassadors if humanity won't even give them a real chance?

    In the end, nobody gains, and everyone loses.

    Frank

Message to ConniePadillaPYPF from ETFrank1701 • Feb 14

    Hi, Ms. Padilla.

    First off, I'm really sorry. I was a jerk in my last message and I wouldn't blame you for blocking me altogether.

    But if you haven't, can I admit I really was hoping you had the answer, just like you always seem to have the answer in all your books and podcasts. I have to confess I'm personally invested in this (no pun intended), though I can't say much more.

    Most of the time, I agree with my colleagues: the Ambassadors SHOULD leave if this is going to be the reception. We'd like to believe humanity has a lot of potential, even with all the evil they do to each other and their planet. But, with this? Unlike humans, Ambassadors aren't going to throw good money after bad, and there really seems to be no hope, at least not for both our peoples coming together. And yet—I can't help recalling that there really IS potential. And I realize: both of us DO have a lot to gain. Not $$$, but a lot to learn, to share, to explore together. Both of us winners.

    If you're right, like you usually are, and it's all about risk vs. reward, maybe the real question is: How do we go about changing the balance?

    I know it's a big ask of one personal finance guru. But you're always telling people to find their own power. Well, YOU have a lot of power—all the followers and admirers who've been inspired by you. I just wish you'd use it for something much bigger than selling books or advising people on their 401(k)s.

    Still your biggest fan,

    Frank

The Frontpage Feed: Special Edition
SUBJECT LINE: *Has First Contact been cancelled?!*

Top Ranked News (49,076,329 shares): *Ambassadors' Ship No Longer on Course to Rendezvous with Earth*

Political leaders and science fiction afficionados around the world panicked yesterday morning when several Earth-based and orbiting observatories, which have kept their instruments trained on the incoming vessel for months, all reported a sudden change in the trajectory at around seven o'clock UTC. Welcome WAGON released an official statement at two o'clock in the afternoon, confirming the reports but cautioning the public not to jump to conclusions.

"We are all puzzled and, yes, concerned about this reported change in the ship's flight path. But rest assured we have our top astrophysicists looking into it," the statement declared. "We must remember that the Ambassadors are, technologically speaking, leaps and bounds ahead of us. For all we know, this anomaly may be well within expected parameters."

"Maybe they forgot something?" was the top punchline on the late-night comedy shows. Similar humorous memes quickly gained popularity across the metaverse.

But others fail to see the new development as a joking matter. The now-vindicated whistleblower, credited with starting the entire chain of events, returned yesterday afternoon to the virtual public square, claiming yet another message from the Ambassadors was intercepted and held back from public release. "Even I'm not certain what, exactly, is in that message," the former insider admitted. "But it sure as heck sent everyone into a tizzy." The White House press secretary immediately denied the claim, as have spokespeople with the other nations cited in the allegation.

Welcome WAGON in the meantime has convened an emergency session, set to meet tomorrow morning.

Stay tuned for more reporting from *The Frontpage Feed* as this story continues to develop.

Business and Finance News (10,492 shares): *Closing Bell Round-up*

Personal finance juggernaut Connie Padilla this week announced an undetermined hiatus of her popular podcast, *Power Your Personal Finance!* along with a pause on all future interviews and speaking engagements. She gave no reason, only telling her millions of fans through social media to "Stay tuned: something big is on its way!"

Speculation immediately arose that Ms. Padilla is using this time to launch a new Power Your Personal Finance branded initiative. The personal finance guru's popularity shot through the stratosphere as the Ambassadors' ship drew closer to Earth, attracting an increasing number of fans and admirers with her trademark calm and steady advice. "Connie really has her finger on the pulse of Main Street," said T.K. Rawlins, who often appears with Ms. Padilla on shows like The Talk Exchange and Financial Forecast. "It's no wonder she's so quickly become not just America's, but *everyone's* personal finance confidant."

Indeed, only White House Economic Adviser P.J. Kuppenheimer has similar name recognition, "but without the comfort factor," according to Rawlins. "I trust her," commented a member of the *Power Your Personal Finance!* Community Platform, who posts by the name of "$$$urvivor." "Connie really gets me, gets *us*," gushed Retire Early or Bust, another member of the online community. "Whatever she has in store, I know it'll be huge!"

Message to ConniePadillaPYPF from ETFrank1701 • Feb 20
Hi, Ms. Padilla.

I hope you're doing well. Since I never heard back from you, I guess you must be very busy. Or you really did block me, after all.

This is the last time I'll contact you, and it's to say goodbye. My job transfer's been cancelled, so there's no longer any reason to continue on with my personal finance education. I will miss all your advice and inspiration. I learned so much from you, not only about personal finance and economics, but gained a better understanding of the world in general.

On a final note, I read you've taken a step back from your media empire to focus on "something big". I can only hope my last message inspired you in some small way, though nothing like how much you've inspired me. Either way, I wish you and everyone in the PYPF community only the very best.

Frank

Message to ETFrank1701 from ConniePadillaPYPF • Feb 21
Hey, Frank!

You should have a little more faith in me, if you really are my biggest fan! Didn't I say I could help you?

I wasn't offended at all by your message, though I was pretty stunned. Yours was the biggest challenge ANYONE has ever offered me—and probably the most meaningful, too. It made all the advice I've been called on to give up to then seem small and petty in comparison.

BTW, do you know why I started giving personal finance advice in the first place? Coming from a family with very little, I saw how money gives people so many more choices. Funny; now I see it works the other way around, too—obsessing over wealth can really limit us, huh? Your words pushed me to see things from another perspective. Through "alien eyes," LOL.

You're 100% right about all of it. We would all lose out if our two peoples never met and learned from each other. You're also right that I do have a lot of influence, more than I realized. So now I'm planning to use that power for "something big." Something much, much bigger than selling books or advising people on their 401(k)s.

I'm going to change that balance.

Connie

Message to ETFrank1701 from ConniePadillaPYPF • Feb 21

Y'know, thinking back, I never actually gave you my personal mail, hmm?

Tell your friends and coworkers you'll be moving forward with that "transfer," after all.

***Power Your Personal Finance!* Community Platform.** Enter username and password.

Hot Topic: Discuss Connie Padilla's latest article in *Personal Investor!* (3,228 replies)

Excerpt—*If you have an entrepreneurial streak, arrival of the "Ambassadors" could mean an opportunity to finally kick off that side-hustle. Think about it: an entirely different species could open up whole new markets for goods and services. Instead of reacting to First Contact, be proactive and brainstorm ways to pivot and boost your earnings potential.* Related link: *The Smart Side-Hustle,* available at the following retailers.

Moderator: Way to go, Connie! Okay, folks: let's get *proactive* in this forum. Share some of *your* ideas for Post-First Contact side hustles!

Retire Early or Bust: Do these aliens even breathe our air? My brother-in-law works for a factory that makes oxygen for hospitals. Maybe we could manufacture whatever *they* breathe and sell it? [37 likes]

Country Mouse Investing in Cheese: I'll bet even my rat-hole hick town would seem exotic to visitors from another world. I could start a tour guide gig! "Come and see Earth's biggest ball of twine…" [11 hearts]

Mortgage Burning Party: Not a bad idea, CMIIC! Personally, I think souvenirs are where it's at. I'll call my company "Made on Earth". [52 likes]

[jump to latest comments]

Feeling Bearish: Hold on here, people. Who says the Ambassadors will cough up cash for anything? Maybe they don't even have anything like "money" where they're from. Honestly, I think our girl Connie is being too optimistic this time. [5 likes]

Retire Early or Bust: Maybe Connie IS being an optimist—but isn't she right that nothing positive will happen until you start being proactive and take power? And isn't that better than throwing trillions of dollars at tanks and aircraft and crap that probably wouldn't last half a minute against a bunch of space invaders? [542 likes]

Country Mouse Investing in Cheese: Hey, I say it's worth taking the risk! *This* mouse is grabbing the chance to get out of the corporate rat race. [73 likes]

Mortgage Burning Party: Does that mean the Ambassadors will buy my souvenirs? [37 likes]

The Frontpage Feed:
SUBJECT LINE: *First Contact back on track and straight to the bank!*
Top Ranked News (43, 722, 549 shares): *'Just a Blip': Ambassadors Stay the Course for Little Blue Planet*

The world held its breath last week when it appeared the Ambassadors had aborted their mission. 'We all just about sullied our pants,' relayed a member of Welcome WAGON, on condition of anonymity. "Considering all the time, effort and money put into preparing for First Contact—*the* event of the millennium—what would we even *do* if the Ambassadors decided to change their minds?!"

The shock turned into relief this Tuesday, when observatories confirmed the Ambassadors were still making their way to Earth, albeit slightly behind schedule. "It must have been just a blip," chuckled Lesedi Nkosi, astrophysicist at the South African National Space Agency. "I guess Welcome WAGON shouldn't roll up the red carpet just yet."

Many are now criticizing the whistleblower for inciting unnecessary panic with allegations about the cover up of a fourth message, received from the Ambassadors at the same time their ship appeared to veer off course. "My fellow world leaders and I are committed to open and honest dialogue with the public about every aspect of this momentous development in human history," the United States president spoke yesterday evening from the Oval Office. "The time for secrecy and self-interest has passed."

Business and Finance News (132,837 shares): *Will Extraterrestrials Put Extra Cash in Our Pockets? This Personal Finance Guru Thinks So.*

What started as a provocative article in *Personal Investor* is now all every wannabe entrepreneur is talking about.

Connie Padilla—of *Power Your Personal Finance!* fame—set off a global conversation last week with a powerful essay [click here] laying out her argument that the Ambassadors' arrival will stimulate innovation and goose the economy. " 'Ambassadors' is a misnomer," Ms. Padilla proclaimed. "Replace 'alien' and 'extraterrestrial' with 'customer' and 'client.' You want to approach First Contact like a *real* entrepreneur? Take control of the situation. Chuck that tinfoil hat, put away your H.G. Wells, and start drafting your goddamn business plan, already!"

Padilla's messages of financial empowerment garnered her a loyal fan base that ballooned with the first revelations about the Ambassadors. Economists around the world are finally starting to take her seriously, too. "Ms. Padilla may have a point," allowed P.J. Kuppenheimer, the White House economic adviser who has been openly skeptical about the Ambassadors' intentions. "Under the Theory of Interstellar Trade, and despite the obvious challenges related to transport costs, the Ambassadors could be incentivized to manufacture high-value goods and invest their profits locally. That would be to Earth's economic advantage."

The financial markets appear to agree with both Padilla and Kuppenheimer. Blue chip stocks rallied again, but this time the action on Wall Street wasn't concentrated in the defense sector. Investors across the board are expressing renewed optimism over the future. One manufacturer after another has announced hefty investments in R&D in anticipation of the Ambassadors' arrival. The effects aren't limited to the big corporate players, either; state and local agencies reported a surge in the pulling of new business licenses and filing of articles of incorporation.

"It's time to stop being scared," Padilla encouraged members of her online community platform. "Be excited!"

Message to ConniePadillaPYPF from ETFrank1701 • Mar 18

Hi, Ms. Padilla,

I meant to message you earlier, but things have been incredibly hectic, with everyone making final preparations to open up our new location. That's right: my transfer is on course to happen after all! It may sound odd, but it's really all thanks to you. The only downside is that things are busier than ever as a result, but I'm not complaining!

I know you've been extremely busy, too. I think every other communication beamed from Earth these days has your signature on it. You seem to be everywhere—in articles, on your podcast, popping into your community forum, giving interviews, bringing people together. I'm amazed by all you're doing, inspiring people to see not just the risks, but all the rewards a relationship between our peoples could bring.

Most of all, I'm amazed that someone like me could inspire someone like you. You were right all along, too: it's up to each of us to take power over our own future—and that includes our shared future. It's a future I'm feeling so much more optimistic about, too.

Your biggest fan in the universe,

Frank

The Frontpage Feed: Special Edition
SUBJECT LINE: *Get ready for the biggest watch party ever: ten celebrity chefs share their out-of-this-world recipes*
Top Ranked News (4,043,852 shares): *'We're On Our Way!' Ambassadors Reassure Humanity*

Relief, joy, and anticipation were on clear display around the world with the public release of the Ambassadors' latest missive to Earth. According to the Welcome WAGON Secretariat, the message amounts to confirmation of arrival and an apology for "potentially causing confusion" among human officials due to "a mild correction in trajectory".

"We remain enthusiastic about this first meeting between our respective species," the Ambassadors emphasized in multiple languages. "And we hope this is just the beginning of new opportunities for our two peoples. We both have much to exchange, and countless ways to profit from diplomatic ties."

Business and Finance News (98,302 shares): *Ambassadors' Latest Message Sends Markets Soaring*

"We both have much to exchange, and countless ways to profit," was the sentence from the Ambassador's latest missive that investors zoomed in on.

"Are they talking trade deals?" said Yan Sundström, Director-General of the World Trade Organization, now undergoing drastic restructuring in preparation for the Ambassadors' arrival. "What items will be on the table?"

Welcome WAGON, apparently taking personal finance guru Connie Padilla's advice to "take control of the situation," announced formation of an international blue-ribbon panel to analyze the economic opportunities presented by establishing trade relations with extraterrestrials. The panel, to be co-chaired by Ms. Padilla herself, along with White House Economic Adviser P.J. Kuppenheimer, will report out a framework set of recommendations prior to First Contact.

When asked at the press conference about her outsize impact, driving this new wave of optimism, Padilla replied: "I don't believe that one person alone, no matter how influential, can move the entire world. But, as my biggest fan in the universe recently reminded me, I can—and I should—give it a nudge."

The Nikkei reached an all-time high today on the news, with the FTSE closing just a whisker below its own record.

Message to ETFrank1701 from ConniePadillaPYPF • Mar 19

Hey, Frank!

That's fantastic news!!

I guess my diabolical plan worked, after all. What's the point of having power and influence if you can't use it to make the galaxy a better place? Though I guess I should feel a little bit bad about it; in a way, I'm tricking people about how everyone is going to "profit" from First Contact. But I'm not wrong about that in a bigger sense: everyone WILL profit from our peoples meeting, just not in the way they're assuming I meant.

While you're making your big move, I'm thinking about my next step, too. I want humanity to have some grander ambition to aspire to than just feathering our own nest. Sure, maybe we need to use the promise of wealth as a goad in the short run, but long-term I want us to look up toward the stars instead of always down at our own pocketbooks. I've never considered taking on something so huge, but maybe if we work together, it'll be easier to tackle? I think we make a "stellar" team, LOL.

So—now that your transfer's on again, I think we should finally meet in person. In, say, two months, four days, eleven hours and change from when I hit "send"?

Connie

Message to ETFrank1701 from ConniePadillaPYPF • Mar 19

I also think it's about time you knock off this "Ms. Padilla" stuff and start calling me "Connie".

Message to ETFrank1701 from ConniePadillaPYPF • Mar 19

What should I call you?

The Frontpage Feed: Morning Edition
SUBJECT LINE: *WELCOME TO EARTH!*
Top Ranked News (102,486,093 shares): *Ambassadors Arrive: A Photojournalist's Moment-by-Moment Diary*

Caption 1: "Houston, they've arrived." *View from International Space Station.* Ambassador mothership parks in Earth orbit. *Caption 2:* "Bienvenidos!" *Montevideo, Uruguay.* Ambassador landing craft touches down in the middle of Plaza Independencia. *Caption 3:* "A historic meeting." *Foreground:* Ambassador delegation exchanges greetings with Welcome WAGON emissaries. *Caption 4.* "We have much to learn from each other." *New York City, United States.* Ambassador Glolteesh Hroné, left, delivers speech before United Nations General Assembly.

Business and Finance News (59,340,271 shares): *Ambassadoronomics 101 To Precede Trade Talks*

Markets soared Tuesday on affirmation the Ambassadors are, indeed, eager to open trade discussions with the World Trade Organization—the first time that body will truly represent the entire planet. "We're going to make the 'Made on Earth' label *mean* something," Yan Sundström proclaimed at yesterday's press conference, the Ambassadors' Special Attaché for Interspecies Business and Finance, Flelviing Rlankonī, at his side.

Investor optimism remained undampened despite both parties citing a need for preliminary discussions before trade talks begin in earnest. "We're not even talking about an apples-to-oranges comparison in how our two economies work. Hell, we're not even talking fruit," said U.S. Trade Representative Marcela Tsai. "The Ambassadors operate in a completely different manner, and it's going to take some time just to wrap our heads around it."

"The Ambassadors seem to take the concept of 'knowledge economy' to an entirely new level—one apparently based on an open sharing mechanism rather than the exchange-for-value economic models we're familiar with on Earth," explained Claire Ahaisse, economic sociologist with Princeton University. "If their claims are accurate, life on the Ambassadors' home world blows every single metric of our own Legatum Prosperity Index out of the water when it comes to measuring global well-being," she went on to add. "Personally, I'd love to know how they do it."

Ahaisse joins a growing multitude of economists, sociologists, political scientists, philosophers, and civic activists around the world fascinated by what humanity is learning about the Ambassadors. "At the same time we're selling the Ambassadors on human goods and services, scholars and the mainstream public alike are increasingly 'sold' on what they have to offer us," Ahaisse noted.

To lay the foundation for negotiations, the WTO's Blue-Ribbon Panel on Exploring Interstellar Economic Opportunity is launching a series of cross-cultural learning sessions; special attaché Rlankoní will be representing the Ambassadors in these conversations. The events will be open to the public and simulcast around the globe.

Early reports of close collaboration between the special attaché and the panel's chair, Connie Padilla, are particularly promising. "Connie and Flelviing hit it off right away," observed Ms. Padilla's co-chair, T.J. Kuppenheimer. "They make a pretty stellar team."

LIBRARY: Latest Episode. Downloading…
Power Your Personal Finance! Ranked #1 in genre. Please leave a review! *Episode transcript.*
Cue teaser, introductory music, sponsor plug
Connie: Happy spread-the-wealth Wednesday, everybody! I'm Connie Padilla, Certified Financial Planner, welcoming you to episode seven-eighty-seven of the *Power Your Personal Finance!* podcast. Where we talk not just about everything that can affect your pocketbook—but also peel back the rules and assumptions governing the game *all* of us have been playing. It's been gratifying, hearing from so many listeners how much you appreciate the new direction this show has taken these past few months.

Which is why the *Power Your Personal Finance!* network is launching an entirely *new* show all about exploring the new financial frontiers First Contact has opened for us. Can you believe it's been over a *year* now? Anyhow, it's about time we really explore the potential of this still-nascent relationship between our species.

Most exciting of all, I'll be co-hosting the show with my best buddy, Flelviing Rlankoni! Truly an extraordinary personality —explorer, academic, diplomat. And, I would say, something of an entrepreneur himself, though he'd probably disagree! Flelviing's made a study of human culture, specializing in economics and finance, and never fails to surprise with his insights.

Anyhow, this show will be looking at the big picture, aimed at listeners from both planets. We'll talk about how to invest in *super* foreign markets, the nuts and bolts of building cross-species enterprises, pros and cons of doing business across the light years, and how to survive life on a predominantly capitalist planet—plus successful alternatives elsewhere and lessons we've all learned along the way.

And every episode we'll ask of humans and Ambassadors alike: how can we improve?

That's why we're calling it *Outperforming Ourselves*.

And to give you a little taste of what's to come, I've brought Flelviing on as my surprise guest for today's show! Oh, and don't be surprised if I seem to slip up on his name every now and again—kind of an inside joke.

Now, before we start, a quick disclaimer. You know the boilerplate, folks. *Power Your Personal Finance* is purely for educational and entertainment purposes. Anything said on this show should not be construed as individual financial, legal, tax, or accounting advice; listeners are advised to discuss their personal financial situation and goals with a financial professional. And remember: while we talk about stocks, bonds, and interstellar investments on this show, past performance is *not* indicative of future results!

Let's all aim to do better.

See C.H. Rosenberg's story "Indicative of Future Results" online at Metaphorosis.
If you liked it, leave a comment. Authors love that!

Remember to subscribe to our e-mail updates so you'll know when new stories are posted.

About the story

This story originates with my realization that the modern-day and increasingly digital personal finance community—and especially the Financial Independence Retire Early (FIRE) movement—is one worthy of intensive anthropological study. After all, doesn't it have all the elements of a modern-day cult? It has its own prophets and evangelists, its peculiar vernacular, its sacred and beloved texts, an undeniable emphasis on self-help and personal growth, all of it resting on those irrepressible American values: Grit! Determination! Self-reliance! At the same time this swelling movement delivers benefits in the form of sound financial guidance, this advice rarely makes it to the eyes and ears of those outside the already privileged strata of society. Woven through all the podcasts, videos, blogs, and plethora of digital content is a thread of toxicity, where social safety nets are scorned and the poor blatantly blamed for their poverty. With this in mind, I watched with the rest of the world as first the Great Recession and more recently the COVID-19 pandemic revealed a spiderweb of fractures in our existing financial and economic system. Both are fascinating case studies into how many will find opportunities in any situation, whether for ill—such as grifters and demagogues—or for good—such as through entrepreneurial and charitable endeavors. I wondered what a true outside observer—an extraterrestrial anthropologist, as it were—would think of all this. Shocked? Horrified? Impressed? Would that observer see the humor in the situation? Would that observer have another point view and—more importantly—be willing to share it? I've always loved First Contact stories for this reason: they represent an opportunity to reassess humanity from a new perspective at the same time they represent a fresh start.

A question for the author

Q: What is the scariest or most disturbing story you've ever read?

A: The most disturbing stories I read are ostensibly nonfiction, especially the narratives written to justify the unconscionable. Examples include the Requirimiento, asserting Spain's authority over (read: invasion of) the Americas and often read—in Latin—to Indigenous peoples without any interpreter or even delivered to an empty beach, or Chief Judge Marshall's justification in *Johnson v. M'Intosh* that "Conquest gives a title which the Courts of the conqueror cannot deny".

About the author

Writing as an armchair economist, in real life C.H. Rosenberg is a grizzled policy wonk who spent an early career fighting in the trenches of local politics in Southern California. Rosenberg currently works at one of Washington, D.C.'s many alphabet-soup think tanks, brainstorming all sorts of amazing ways to save the planet.

Medusa Rising

Christine Lucas

Long ago, it was scholars and archaeologists who came knocking on Lengo's door, asking permission to go search her land for antiquities. Then, after her late grandson Nikolas did what he did, came the police officers and the media vultures. Tonight, it's one of the fascist scum her Nikolas befriended in Athens, where she shipped him off twenty years ago to get an education. And what did that air-headed boy of hers do? He joined a cult—or, rather, a gang? Whatever their ilk, one of them just knocked on her door hours after dusk, expecting to be invited in.

"Evening, ma'am. I'm Jason, a friend of your late grandson's." He slides his gloved palm between her creaky door and the doorframe, so she can't shut it in his face. "I just sailed in from Piraeus for Nikos' *saranta*. Can I come in?"

Countless little voices in Lengo's mind warn her against inviting the evil in, including the whisper of her late grandma, who's sitting on her usual spot by the stove, knitting with ethereal thread and needles. Still, Lengo finds it hard to turn away anyone, especially in stormy weather. She has never turned away a visitor. But now times have changed. Jason's kind has resurfaced, and they're loud and violent. She'd rather avoid an altercation with someone twice her size. But perhaps she shouldn't judge him from how he carries himself? Perhaps there's good in him, still. After all, he did remember Nikolas' memorial service. The funerals of perpetrators of murder/suicide are lonely events, their forty-days memorial services even more so. There should be someone—even *this* one—to pay respects to her boy who took the wrong path and lost his way.

So she lets him in.

He wipes his combat boots on her worn mat, bows his shaven head to cross the narrow doorframe, and shoves his gloves in the pockets of his camouflage pants. He scowls at her low-roofed two-room home—the other parts of her once-spacious residence have long succumbed to the storms of the Aegean Sea, and no longer keep the winter chill out. He frowns at the pitiful fire in the hearth and the badly-aged covers on the worn divan that doubles as her bed. One glance at his combat boots, and the cat bolts out of the window, seeking better company in the night. Lengo's yaya's ghost wraps up her spectral knitting and follows the cat.

Jason wrinkles his nose at the smells from her stove and her dinner table—reheated lentil soup and yesterday's bread, with a side of olives and a glass of cheap retsina wine. But he draws a chair and plops himself at the table, expecting to be served.

Well, then.

Lengo reaches into the second pot on her stove and serves him the leftovers of a dish with rice and chicken. She's saved that for after the memorial service tomorrow, and almost regrets wasting this dish on the likes of him, but it might be worth it just to see the look on his face. He digs in, helping it down with chunks of stale bread and gulps of retsina. Between mouthfuls, he manages a compliment.

"That's some damn-good pilaf, Kera-Lengo!"

"Thank you." She sits across him, her back rigid, and clasps her hands on her apron.

"Family recipe?"

"You could say that. From my grandaughter-in law's side; her grandma taught her how to make it, back in Mogadishu, and Astur taught me. It's called *bariis iskukaris*, and I hear it's a very popular Somali dish."

He stops chewing mid-mouthful at the mention of Nikolas' late wife. His hands freeze while breaking bread in chunks. Lengo holds her breath and wonders if he'll spit it out.

He doesn't. Instead, he swallows and resumes manhandling the bread, spreading crumbs all over her white table cloth that has seen happier times and much better guests.

"Well." He shovels more spiced rice into his mouth. "Her kind does have *some* skill with cooking." Another mouthful of wine, and his face mellows a little. "It reminds me of a dish my late yaya used to make, from Constantinople. I miss her cooking."

Several questions crowd at the tip of Lengo's tongue: Which 'kind' would that be? Somali women? Black women? Or women in general? And should she clock him with her trusted cast-iron pan? At least his grandma isn't around anymore to see what he's become.

But she's mopped up enough blood already, after Nikolas did what he did to Astur, and she's tired. She'd rather not deal with more police questions. The bigoted idiot will eat and snore and attend the service tomorrow, then get the hell out of her home, and back to his dungeon or wherever his kind gather in Athens. So she squeezes her hands onto her apron until her nails dig into her palms, and maintains an icy half-smile. But doubt slithers into her heart like drafts find their way into her home. Did she make a mistake letting him in?

She unlocks Nikolas' chamber for the night. Her heart flutters when she crosses the threshold, fetching fresh linen and blankets for the bed. She hasn't set one foot inside after the officers wrapped up their investigation and she got on her hands and knees cleansing the place. Can blood be ever truly cleansed, or will its echoes haunt the years to come, until the very bricks and beams crumble to pebbles and kindling?

He follows her inside, his gaze seeking the beam overhead where the noose was tied, as if expecting to see marks on the wood. Then he studies the now-bare walls. Did he really expect to see all those despicable photographs, posters, and mementos Nikolas brought back home from his time in Athens? Nikolas kept them hidden at first, but they slowly slithered into her home and their life here. Especially those photographs in which he posed with some others with similar ideology with their arms raised. They called that hail 'an ancient Greek salute', and they could all kiss her cat's ass. She knew exactly what kind of salute it was, and what that crooked cross and equally crooked meander symbol stood for. Off into the fire they went, once the police gathered all they needed from the room. The only remaining picture is a photo of Nikolas' wedding in the town's courthouse with Astur absolutely radiant beside him. Next to it, Lengo has placed an icon of the sad-eyed Virgin cradling the Infant.

Jason drops his backpack on the floor by the door and sits at the edge of the bed to untie his boots. He's comfortable in his late friend's room, as though he belongs here—as though he's family. But he's not. Lengo knows little about him, and she doesn't care to know more. The bed creaks under his weight, and Lengo's heart clenches to see *this* stranger on her grandson's bed. Astur should be there, instead of him, nursing her infant daughter, Lengo's great-grandchild. Lengo pretends to wipe her already clean hands on the apron, so he won't notice her white-knuckled fists. He doesn't notice—to him she's probably just another barely-literate old widow, grief-stricken and clad in the clothes of past decades.

Her black garments and head-scarves have never been fashionable, only practical, the *uniform* of crones of the Greek countryside.

"If you need anything during the night, I'm just behind that wall," she says, and shuts the door behind her.

She huddles on the divan, wrapped in thin blankets that do little against the chill, and cries herself to sleep.

Dawn can't come fast enough.

Lengo starts from her sleep in the small hours of the night with her heart racing. She thought she heard glass shattering—what did that useless cat break this time? Has her yaya's ghost returned to torment Jason in his sleep? Or was it an infant crying? She thinks she hears the cry of a baby too often these days, the wailing a distant echo just behind her ears—an infant that cries to come home. Nikolas' spirit, that won't depart for the afterlife until after his saranta, or Astur's little girl, crying for her yaya to come and get her and bring her home?

She sits up and rubs her swollen eyes. Somewhere, window shutters bang against the wall at the north wind that whips their shores for another night. All windows are shut and bolted here; where in the Virgin's name have they become undone at this hour? She puts on her thin robe and her slippers. There's light coming from under the door to Nikolas' room—Jason should still be up, so she might as well check there first.

The room is empty. The light comes from the laptop he's left open on the desk. The bed hasn't been slept in, and the backpack is gone. Jason left through the open window, it seems, and broke the glass doing so. But why did he slip out like a thief in the night?

She knows she shouldn't snoop on guests under her roof, but Jason is one of *them*; she owes him nothing. So Lengo leans over to check the screen on his laptop—he probably saw her long-out-dated flip phone and thought her another technologically illiterate old-timer. He didn't even bother to password-protect his laptop. His background image shows him in camouflage clothes, with a dog at his side, which looks up at him with clear adoration. She hopes that's a good sign; perhaps she misunderstood him after all, if an innocent soul trusts him. She browses through his web history, and finds exactly what she originally expected: rants and manifestos over Nation and Culture, and against everything his ilk deems beneath them: refugees, people of color, women, and all the *others* who don't rise up to their abominable standards of "true" humans.

But barely a mention of *old* women. Her skin color and her origin made her dear Astur *other* to *them*, but Lengo is nothing. *Nobody.*

Outis.

Hah. But this *Nobody* knows things. The school teacher she was before she became a wife and a mother chuckles. There's a lesson somewhere in there. But she wouldn't know where to start teaching it to Jason and the others like him. Thick-headed, thick-hearted, ignorant of the power crones hold in these parts—power held since long before the Trinity and the Twelve. It's a shame, really, the teacher inside her insists. His writing is so eloquent, so articulate and refined, and yet so vile at the same time. It shows a deep thirst for learning, and yet all the knowledge and intellect that shine through his words are twisted into weapons for his perceived war.

She sighs, and her fingers move to turn the device off, when her gaze falls onto a communication folder with her grandson's name on it. Her hand trembles mid-air. She should ignore it. It can hold only heartbreak. Hasn't her heart bled enough? Parents shouldn't live long enough to see their children die, grandparents more so. But perhaps this is part of her penance for failing her grandson.

So she opens the file. It holds both heartbreak and insight into her grandson's actions. During the investigation of the murder/suicide, the coroner and the officers discussed motives, their main focus Nikolas' past trauma from out-living his parents, and the fact he stopped his medication a month before the incident. They never told Lengo their conclusions. Small island, small community, big case that could harm tourism for the coming summer. In the end, with no perpetrator to prosecute, they wrapped up the case and moved on. The victim was just another immigrant to them, that *nobody* would miss. And tonight, *this* Nobody finds the emails that they conveniently missed, and they are dipped in poison.

Nikolas loved his wife; Lengo knows as much. He left his former 'friends' behind for Astur, and returned to the island of his forefathers to raise a family with her. But now she sees that communication with his 'friends' continued, week after week, month after month—messages accusing him of treason and desertion, oozing hatred for a girl who'd fled war and famine for a better future. *Stop those pills,* they urged him. *It's poison, clouding your vision and limiting your true potential.* It didn't take long until Nikolas' replies shifted from meek excuses and apologies to deranged rants, of how he thought that his wife stepped out in the middle of the night to copulate with monsters, and of how he feared the child that grew in her womb. Jason only fed Nikolas' delusions, urging him to leave and come back to them. To *him*, his only real friend.

The last message in the file, from Jason to Nikolas, is five words in all; five blood-chilling words:

"You know what to do."

Lengo slams the laptop shut, choking on a sob. If her body trembled a little less, she'd smash the device against the white-washed wall. She jumps to her feet to get out of there, out, to the lashing wind to cleanse her thoughts, and she stumbles on Jason's backpack. He'd shoved it under the bed, but her foot gets caught on its strap. Some of its contents spill out—a stack of papers. As her eyes adjust to the gloom now that the laptop is closed, she picks them up and sinks deeper into rage.

Some of the papers have drawings, others are print-outs, but all show similar features of a bare-chested woman—sometimes with Caucasian features, but mostly of African descent. Some resemble the frescoes of ancient Minoan ladies, but most of them depict a monstrous face over a voluptuous body, with a wild mane of serpents for hair. The last few drawings show someone in hoplite's armor cutting off the creature's head. Interesting how this monster-slaying hero's features resemble Jason's.

Lengo's heart dives for her feet. It's her fault, isn't it? She raised her Nikolas with the tales of the heroes of old—Herakles and Theseus, Perseus and Achilles. All of them great men slaying enemies and monsters. But she failed to teach him how, in real life, it's not always easy to tell which is the hero and which the monster. Sometimes monsters wear the forms of friends. Sometimes heroes come to save one's life and soul in the form of refugees—the kind of heroes who carry no weapon, only a kind heart. And Lengo failed to notice that he stopped taking his pills, and instead self-medicated with alcohol. Both the grandmother and the teacher failed her boy.

Her shoulders slump, but the knot in her gut reminds her she cannot linger. Now she knows where Jason has gone. Nikolas must have told him about the secret tunnels beneath the old chapel. How did *he* find out? Nikolas was only there as a toddler, after they laid his parents to rest. She thought he'd forgotten. But what matters now is that Jason has at least an hour's head start towards the chapel atop the cliffside—the chapel Lengo tends like all the women in her family did before her, since before the Romans and the Ottomans. The chapel with the blue windows and the white walls over the wine-dark sea, and the little fence that encloses a few family graves. Her grandson's too, beside the rest of their family.

She puts on her boots, her headscarf, and a heavy coat, grabs her walking stick and the flashlight she keeps by the front door, and steps out into the night.

It's a short hike uphill. A path Lengo has climbed too many times in her life, sometimes for Sunday mass when a priest still bothered to come this way. For funerals too, and for her Nikolas' baptism. More often, though, to tend to the damages the old building suffers, to whitewash its walls and keep the shutters and door from falling off their hinges. Her feet can find their way even in the dark—they did so in bloody sneakers the night Nikolas died. But tonight the raging wind howls alongside her raging heart and makes every step an ordeal. While she struggles to keep her headscarf in place and her hair from lashing her face, her eyes catch glimpses of the Unseen. Ghostly forms appear hiking beside her: her yaya has returned alongside *her* yaya's ghost, and other old-timers Lengo has no names for. The chapel has changed forms and guardians many a time: at one time it was devoted to Poseidon with white marble columns, then to Helios, since it faces East, and then to Prophet Elijah. During the Ottoman occupation, about three centuries ago, some reformed pirate captain of the Barbary Coast dedicated it to Aghios Nikolas, the patron saint of sailors.

Poseidon, Helios, Elijah, Nikolas—all of them trespassers on sacred land that belongs to an Other—someone who's never left, and remains sleeping in the depths.

The chapel's door looms open, its hinges squeaking at every gust of the wind. Lengo slips inside and bolts the door behind her. At the back of her thoughts, she's hoped she'd find Jason in here, paying his respects to his friend's memory. But no—he didn't even light a candle. The chapel is empty, filled with the scent of long-burned beeswax candles planted on brass trays of sea sand, and whiffs of frankincense. The vigil oil lamp over the sad Virgin's painting casts dancing lights at the corners of the chamber, creating angles within angles and turns within turns that shouldn't exist. Lengo adds oil to the lamp, and checks behind the never-used episcopal seat—as if any of their lazy lot would grace the place with their presence. The trapdoor behind it is open.

So Jason did discover the chapel's secret—or thinks he did.

She shouldn't waste a single minute, but she still lights a thin candle and plants it in the sand. *For Nikolas.* At the edge of her vision, she thinks she sees him as a toddler, sitting in the chapel's corner. He's playing with a wooden ship—a flimsy little thing, one of the crafts merchants sell to the tourists in summertime. He goes on and on, weaving tales of how he's going to have his own ship one day, and he'll set sail to slay the Mermaid who drowned his parents. And then, he's over there, by the Virgin's painting, with Astur at his side on their wedding day. When she looked at him, she saw what Lengo saw: a kind heart and a traveling mind that always crafted stories within stories, so he could endure a world that had become too ugly, too soon.

Lengo wipes her tears, then sheds her coat, pockets her flashlight, and starts the descent to the tunnels beneath, her walking stick in hand. She doesn't need light where she's going; she's trodden these depths often. Her mind finds solace in the absence of light. She doesn't want to see the surface of the rock around her. She pretends that her fingers do not trace the indentations and the folds on marble and granite. A few sections here and there bear marks of human tools, and others run smooth, as if carved by monstrous, rock-drilling earthworms. She's heard from her predecessors that similar tunnels run the length of the Aegean and then some, a labyrinth that harbors hidden chambers and creatures worse than a minotaur.

One such monster has chosen to desecrate one of the labyrinth's holiest places. Deep beneath the island and the bottom of the Aegean, the tunnel opens into a narrow cavern, no bigger than the chapel above. Lengo hears curses, and through the cavern's entrance the wavering beam of a flashlight creates more uncanny angles. She stops a few paces away to remove her boots and socks. The rock beneath her feet is cold, damp, and a little slippery, and she takes tentative steps forward. The chill sends pinpricks up her legs and into her hips, but also soft vibrations of welcome.

The cavern resembles the Christian chapels that shepherds sometimes carve into the mountain caves of mainland Greece. It has a row of *stacidia* at each side—those narrow, uncomfortable seats for the congregation, a few unlit oil lamps hanging from the roof, and a single icon painted on the far wall: the Virgin holding the infant. Only this Virgin isn't depicted as the sad mother. This one is Fury-eyed, clad in black, her face stern and her head wrapped in a dark kerchief. No locks of hair hide beneath it, but a wild mane of writhing serpents. In her left hand she holds the Infant, in her right she wields the Trident. And from her waist down, she's immersed in a bottomless sea, her great tail controlling the storm.

Lengo bows her head to the Lady of the Deep. She bears many names: Panaghia Gorgona, the Madonna Mermaid. Older ones, too: Tethys, Tiamat, Thalatta. Sometimes Gorgo, sometimes Medusa, hidden in the narratives of great—*Hah!*—heroes slaying monsters. And this particular 'hero' has tossed the place apart as if seeking more hidden passageways, leading to the Lady herself.

"Kera-Lengo? What are you doing here?" Jason's bark kicks her back to reality. He frowns, and measures her from bare feet to headscarf. His voice hardens. "You knew. *You.* His yaya."

She takes another step inside, her back no longer hunched, her shoulders straight, her walking stick of sturdy cedar wood her staff and her scepter in one.

"What exactly do you think I knew, boy?"

His mouth twists, his right hand reaches behind his back— for a gun? With his left, he waves towards the painting.

"That! Nikolas told me everything! He told me how you brought him here as a child to scare him into mindless obedience. How you fed him chemicals to cloud his mind! But he always made excuses for you, painting you as another innocent victim of this monstrous cult plaguing his island. But you aren't innocent, are you? What kind of tricks did you use to lure him into the arms of that *filth*? To dilute his pure Greek bloodline into half-breed offspring?" He draws his gun and wings it about, pointing it at everything and nothing. "I told him to take care of the negr—"

"Watch it, *boy*. Don't you dare speak ill of my granddaughter-in-law."

Lengo strikes her stick on the ground. The cavern responds with a low tremor beneath their feet. In one of the side chambers, stored clay discs and tablets explain the number and sequence of blows required for an assortment of outcomes: from soft vibrations to heal, to focused earthquakes that can raise rogue waves against pirate ships at their shores. Lengo's yaya once told her of a disc with instructions to raise the Lady herself. But that was stolen long ago, and now features in the case of some museum. Lengo hasn't read even half of the tablets—some alphabets have lost their meaning by now, other tablets crumbled before anyone could copy them. And even if she tried, she'd never remember them all.

Jason scowls. "Your *arapina* grandaughter-in-law is dead. Why would you care for *that* more than your own grandson?"

"You know that they never found her body, right?"

"Nikos tossed her off the cliff into the sea, didn't he? I read the investigators' report." He sneers. "It helps to know people in the Force. She's probably fish food by now. Think of that, next time you cook fish. You might eat pieces of her. Or of her spawn." He laughs, as if he's heard the world's best joke.

Lengo sees red. She knocks the ground three times, more forcefully than she should have. An earthquake builds up in the depths, and pieces of rock crumble to the ground behind Jason. Dust sprinkles their heads, and Lengo forces her grip to remain steady.

"You idiot. You shit-souled idiot. You think we don't know how your kind often packs together within the police and armed forces? They didn't find the body because—"

"Because I'm not dead," Astur finishes Lengo's sentence.

A steady voice just behind Lengo's shoulder. Jason pales. Lengo tilts her head as much as her aching neck allows, bone grinding on bone, to meet Astur's gaze. There she is, her brave girl, clad in Lengo's old clothes that hang on her two sizes too large, but thick enough to shield her from the dampness of these tunnels. Astur carries her infant daughter on her chest, in a sling made from a colorful silk scarf that survived Nikolas' rage on that fateful night. The child naps peacefully, thank the Virgin, despite the tremors and the racket.

Lengo glances at Jason, whose eyes are fixed on Astur's head, and the black kerchief she's wrapped her hair in. Dark coils escape from the sides, much like Medusa's serpents.

"But... There was blood up the trail—"

"Because *I* put those bloody footprints on the trail to the cliff." Lengo's gut tightens as the memory of her own *Via Dolorosa* resurfaces—her hike uphill towards the cliffside across from the chapel, her feet sloshing at every step in her grandson's bloodied sneakers, her right hand dipped in Astur's blood brushing against wind-blown acacias and prickly shrubs, and her own shoes in her left for the journey back home. "But first we carried her here, where she could heal and give birth on safe, hallowed ground."

Astur takes two more steps forward, and her hand seeks Lengo's hand—the hand with the still-numb fingers after she removed the sneakers with Astur's blood on them from her grandson's dangling corpse. And now her eyes mist, her soul overflowing with secrets, grief, and guilt. It wasn't easy to carry Astur up here. May the Virgin keep them all safe, others from nearby settlements came to their aid when she called them in the middle of the night. The retired midwife, with decades of experience before hospital births caught up with the Greek countryside. Katina, Lengo's third cousin, who was a military nurse at the Albanian front during WWII. And a few others, all of them old women set on protecting their own from modern-day monsters.

Jason's eyes narrow. "Nikos killed himself for nothing. His death is on your head, monster. You did this." *Now* he looks at Astur. "You both did."

"Leave my granddaughter-in-law out of this. Yes, *I* did this."

Lengo holds her head high and her voice steady, while her heart plummets towards the depths beneath their feet, once those words leave her tongue. She should have known. She should have noticed Nikolas spiralling into delusion, self-medicating. Then she wouldn't have come home to find him black-out drunk, having burned everything Astur owned so she wouldn't leave him. She wouldn't have found Astur on the floor across the room, beaten, bruised, and weeping in a pool of blood and amniotic fluid.

Jason points the gun at Lengo. "This stops here. I'll restore Nikos' name, who died a hero, slain by monster-worshiping degenerates."

"You have no idea how Nikolas died," Lengo says. "Or how he lived." Lengo raises her chin and meets his gaze, her heart sinking deeper into a storm. Her boy died alone. Scared. In the dark, thinking himself forsaken. But... would any of this have ever happened without the poison this bastard dripped into her boy's ears? "So shut your mouth and get out while you still can."

Jason sneers. "I'm not Nikos. You cannot order me around."

A breeze against her face. The breath of the goddess? At the far corner of the room, she sees Jason in a corner, his face wet, huddling with his dog. He can't be more than twelve, but he looks older. And bigger. Lengo has seen his kind during her teaching years: the kid that's bigger than the others, always goaded to throw the first punch in a fight, always valued only as a battering ram, always mocked if he shows interest in anything remotely intellectual. A scared little orphan, yearning for a family to belong to. But maybe his own yaya died too soon, and his only friend left him. Maybe he had no one to help him find the light.

In any case, that boy is long gone. Lengo cannot help him. The man that he's become now starts to raise his gun, Astur takes a step forward and stands abreast of Lengo. Lengo moves her stick to her left hand so now both of them hold it. They hit the ground twice, the angle just so to the left, just before he pulls the trigger. The quake startles him, and he misses. The bullet hits the cavern wall an arm's length from Lengo's head, then ricochets and hits the Lady's icon on her left eye. It chips off the paint, then whooshes past Lengo's head, scraping her right ear, and flies into the tunnels behind them.

He takes aim again, but then a howl rises from the depths. It starts like a murmur within the stone—a soft, healing vibration that waxes to a whine that becomes the wail of an angered deity, rudely awaken from her slumber. What frequency did the idiot's bullet trigger, to release the wail of the goddess? Is it just her howl, or has she risen, at long last?

Jason falls on his knees, clasping the sides of his head, as if anything could stop the wail from drilling holes into his mind. It hurts Lengo too, but much less so, her own ears stiffened by age and the continued exposure to the Aegean winter's winds. Astur grunts and lets go of the stick to shield her child's ears. The memory of blood dripping from Astur's ears from Nikolas' beating crushes Lengo's heart, and fuels her wrath. But Astur shakes her head, and mouths that she's fine. Then Lengo's eyes turn to the writhing body on the floor. She and Astur cannot let this pain—or any pain—rob them of their chance.

Lengo marches to Jason, hefting her stick as a woodsman's ax, and manages a blow at the side of his head.

"When you see your Nazi friends in hell, tell them that *Outis* killed you!"

He falls sideways to the ground, his eyes unfocused, frothing at the mouth. Astur follows her and manages a well-balanced kick to his jaw. Something cracks. Lengo brings the stick down again and again, on his head, on his back, on his chest, smashing his beefy fingers that move as if to shield him from her wrath. Every hit is a howl in her head and an apology she cannot yet bring herself to utter.

Forgive me, my Nikolas, for all my shortcomings! Forgive me, my girl, for not hiding the tickets I got you to flee from what your husband had become! Forgive me for not being there, when he found them, to take the beating instead of you!

Lengo beats Jason until she's run out of breath, until she's run out of tears, until he's running out of life—until a steady hand grips the stick mid-blow. Lengo turns to Astur, a yell building up in her throat. How dare she deny Lengo her revenge?

In the strange shadows cast by the discarded flashlight, the tendrils beneath Astur's scarf seem to slither and writhe around her head and neck, like the Lady's serpents on the wall behind them. The moisture in Lengo's eyes blurs the two forms, as though Astur now stands in the Lady's embrace, slithering serpents coiling around the girl's narrow shoulders, careful and affectionate as a mother's arms around her newborn.

"Please, Yaya. Let's... let's just go home. It's been forty days already." A shadow passes behind Astur's eyes, and she clutches her fussing infant tighter to her chest, without releasing Lengo's stick. "Enough with the blood. Enough with the pain. Enough with the death. Just... enough."

Lengo allows her shoulders to relax. Forty days, already... Forty days for a woman who's given birth to remain isolated from the perils of the outside world. Forty nights between death and the saranta memorial service, to ensure a spirit's safe passage to the Afterlife. And forty waves to cleanse spilled blood from one's hands. But where to find compassion in the storm that rages in her heart? She raises her gaze to Astur and, at the edge of her vision, something sparkles: the Lady's left eye. A reflection of the lamplight on some quartz crystal embedded in the rock? Or has her face mellowed? The great tail of the Virgin All-mother commands the storm, but also calms the waves.

"How can you say this, love? He doesn't deserve mercy."

Astur sighs. "For his own yaya, then. For her memory."

"At least she didn't fail him. Like I did."

Astur lets go of the stick. "Don't ever say that, yaya." She holds her baby with both hands and brings it closer to Lengo's face. "*She* is not a failure. She's here because of you. You cannot save those who don't want to be saved."

But what if Jason does? And she failed to see it? Lengo's eyes well up. The stick slips from her grip and she drops to her knees, the weight of the world crushing her shoulders. Between sobs, she blurts out the silliest thing.

"He... he ate the rice I made for you! I-I have nothing for you when you come home!"

A soft embrace around Lengo's shaking shoulders, tendrils of hair and slithering serpents and a cooing child near her arm.

"Then we'll make more. Come, Yaya. Let's go home."

"And what about him?"

"He's in the Lady's arms now. She'll heal his body, as she's healed mine. But his heart and mind... that's on him."

He doesn't deserve it—nothing has convinced Lengo that he does. But she sighs, and nods, and gets up to roll his body onto thick sailcloth. Then they drag him out of the chapel on the slippery tunnel floor further down, to one of the healing chambers below. If the Lady deems him worthy one day, she may lead him out to the light again. Unless...

Unless Lengo becomes a teacher again. Unless she too takes the long road towards redemption, and she makes the time to guide this foolish boy back to the light. Or, at least, try to. She has many long days and even longer nights ahead of her, but the first step towards healing has always been mercy. Lengo sets him on a cot of riggings, sailcloth, and fishnets, she leans and whispers in his ear the first of his many lessons on monsters and heroes.

"Whenever you see your Nazi pals again, in this life or the next, tell them that Medusa showed you mercy, where you showed her none."

But she makes sure she takes her walking stick with her, when they start their way home. And she'll make another one, for Astur. A good, sturdy staff.

Just in case.

See Christine Lucas' story "Medusa Rising" online at Metaphorosis.
If you liked it, leave a comment. Authors love that!
Remember to subscribe to our e-mail updates so you'll know when new stories are posted.

About the story

"Medusa Rising" is inspired by H.P.Lovecraft's story "Medusa's Coil", mostly known for its racist ending. The premise was stuck in my head when, back in 2019, the legal proceedings against the Greek Neo-Nazi Party Golden Dawn began. Then it became clear in my head who the evil guys were, and who Medusa had to represent. Greek Grandmothers have stood against fascists for a long time (and still do). The first draft of the story flowed onto the screen within a single day, because it's a theme very dear to my heart.

A question for the author

Q: What are you reading now?

A: *A Night in the Lonesome October* by R. Zelazny. It's one of my comfort reads when I'm feeling down, because Snuff's (the canine protagonist) voice is so honest and clear that brings everything together. Of course it also includes cats, the Dreamlands, and a cast of familiar and yet unexpected characters. It's an easy, entertaining read that gives me hope that everything will be well at the end.

About the author

Christine Lucas lives in Greece with her life partner and a horde of spoiled animals. She's a retired Air Force officer (disabled) and mostly self-taught in English. Her work appears in several print and online magazines, including *Future SF Digest, Pseudopod,* and *Strange Horizons.* She was a finalist for the 2017 WSFA award, and a collection of her short stories, titled *Fates and Furies,* was published in late 2019 by Candlemark & Gleam.

werecat99.wordpress.com, @ChrisLuc99

From a Mother to Her Daughter,
on the Eve of Her Wedding

Elliott Gish

May 8, 1888

My dearest Louisa,

By the time you read this letter, the most wonderful day of your life will be over, and night will have stolen over the grand, grey house that you must now call your own. In my mind I clearly perceive you sitting by a yawning fireplace, shivering a little in the chill of the spring evening. Above you, gloom; behind you, dimly looming, the wide stretch of your marriage-bed.

What will you be doing? Here my imagination fails me; it has never been powerful. I recall clearly the times when you begged me to tell you stories as a girl, only to roll your eyes and harrumph when I offered you the well-worn tales I knew from nursery books. "Not a story like that!" you would cry, your face puckered and displeased. "A new one!" And you would fuss, and kick, and pinch, until finally I sent you off to bed in hopes that you would sleep away your fit of temper. I never had a new story to offer you, my darling, and for that I am sorry.

Your husband being elsewhere, attending to some man's affair, I hope that you will finally grow weary of waiting for him, just as you used to grow weary of waiting for me when I could not keep up with you during a walk or a game. Up you will get to walk off a bout of nerves, pacing to and fro, until your eyes come to rest on your hope chest, cold and forlorn in the corner of the room. (How I pray that it is there, and not abandoned in some hallway, or left to gather dust beneath the stairs!) Your gaze will slide along its elegant cedar panels, the rich curves of your initials carved into the wood, and you will be moved to cross the bedchamber and throw open its lid. There you will find this letter, tightly sealed with wax, nestled comfortably atop your muslin nightgown.

Louisa—stop now and listen. Are there footsteps in the passage? Can you feel eyes staring at you through a crack in the door? Are you certain that you are alone? If so, read on, for at last I have a new story.

When, as a girl, you first became interested in this alien thing called Love, you asked about how your father and I met, how we courted, why we married. My reply was so meagrely furnished with detail that you wandered away before I finished, throwing over your shoulder a scornful remark about my lack of romantic feeling. But although you have only ever known me as a staid old matron, I was once a girl like you, brimming with fire and honey, so full of passion that I scarcely knew what to do with myself. It was in this state that I met your father, on a warm summer evening at a garden party.

Even from a distance, he was the most beautiful thing I had ever seen. Slim and tall, with dark gold hair and dark brown eyes, a firm chin and a soft, girlish mouth. I watched him cross the lawn with a swift, sure stride, stopping here and there to briefly greet a gentleman of his acquaintance, or drop a careless compliment in the lap of a pretty girl. He seemed to be a man with a destination. What that destination might be, I could only imagine; and, as I have said already, imagination is not my strong suit. I know it is yours, so perhaps you can imagine my surprise when this angelic creature stopped directly in front of me. His nostrils flared slightly, as though he inhaled my scent, and he smiled.

"We do not know each other, I think," he said. I remember those words as clearly now as I did that night in bed, hearing them echo sweetly in my ears. His left hand bore a silver signet ring on its smallest finger, set with three brilliant yellow jewels, two large, one small. It winked in the sun every time he shifted his grip on his walking-stick, flashing like a Morse lamp, a beckoning call in a code I could not read.

I shall spare you further details of our courtship, our outings and walks and conversations; no mother may hold her daughter's attention with such tedious remembrances. Suffice to say that by the time he proposed—as he did, after seeking your grandfather's permission for my hand—I had been thoroughly wooed, and accepted with scarcely a flutter of nerves. My days became lightsome and busy, filled with those duties so particular to brides —the same duties that have filled your life these past few weeks, my darling, as you strained your eyes and pricked your fingers embroidering handkerchiefs and hemming linen and sewing flounces of lace to your bridal-gown.

"I cannot sew a moment longer!" you shouted only days ago, so carried away by temper that I thought you might tear the dress up and kick it into the hearth. But soon enough your anger ebbed, and you became again distracted by dreams of your husband-to-be.

On the morning of my wedding, rather than walking a short distance to my old village church, I climbed into your father's carriage for a long journey across the moors; it was, I had been told, a custom of his family that brides would be married in the family chapel. How I shivered when I first saw the vast black hump of my new home, huddled on the horizon like a sleeping giant! It was so large that I could see it for a good hour, and felt almost as though *it* approached *me*, not the other way around. The closer it drew, the more my nerves began, finally, to flutter, and the more I began to wish that I were back at home, tucked safely into my virgin bed.

But such thoughts are common to brides, and when I began my walk down the aisle and saw your father waiting for me at the end of it, all ivory and gold, my girlish fears evaporated. I did not mind the draftiness of the chapel, or the incoherent mumbling of its ancient vicar. I did not mind the strange wine we were bidden to drink at the altar, which tasted both bitter and sweet. I did not mind the way my husband's guests—all of them men, and family, I assumed, for they shared his golden beauty, and wore the same silver ring with three yellow stones upon their fingers—watched my every move, scarcely blinking. All that mattered was that I was his now, to have and to hold, to honour and to cherish—that I was now, at last, a Wife! So eager was I to have your father to myself that I rather chafed at the celebration that followed the wedding. I could not stop my teeth from gritting, nor my eyes from narrowing at anyone who chose to have another glass of champagne, another slice of cake, another turn around the ballroom. Why could these people not disperse, I wondered, and let me enjoy my wedding-night?

At last the guests began to yawn, and one by one they made their excuses, bade us good fortune, and stumbled out into the night. I had been longing for them to leave all evening, and yet, now that my wish was granted and I was finally alone with my husband, I was suddenly shy.

Your father, however, seemed to know what to do. He kissed me briefly—only our second kiss, for he had waited until we met at the altar to kiss me for the first time—and told me to take the greater staircase up to the second floor. "Your bedroom," he said, "is the third door from the left. Obey the instructions on the bedside table, and in time, I will come to you."

I puzzled over these words as I climbed towards my destination. Why was it to be *my* bedroom, and not *ours*? Were we not to sleep in one bed, as behooved a couple united in wedlock?

The bedroom that was to be mine was very grand and very gloomy, with only a single candle burning on the bedside table to give its shadows depth. A crisply folded piece of your father's stationery was propped up beside it. I opened it and saw, in your father's neat hand, the following instructions:

Remove your clothing.
Extinguish the candle.
Draw the bag over your head.
Wait on the bed.

The bag in question I found on the eiderdown. It was a little sack, such as one that might hold flour, with a drawstring in its mouth so that it could be pulled tight around the neck.

Faced with such a queer catalogue of demands, perhaps you, Louisa, would not acquiesce; perhaps you, more brazen than I, would storm downstairs and confront your husband, demanding to know what he meant by such a list. But I was not like you, and so I did not think to disobey. I removed my wedding-dress—a difficult feat, as no maid attended me, and it fastened with two dozen tiny pearl buttons—and my petticoats, and finally, reluctantly, my unmentionables. Unclad, I felt at once the draft in that great room, and I shivered as I blew out the candle, pulled the bag over my head, and felt my way to the foreign bed, mounting it clumsily in the darkness.

After my engagement, my mother had made occasional opaque references to 'the state of wifehood', vaguely insinuating that my transition into this state would take place, not at the altar, or during the signing of the registry, but over the course of the wedding-night. I must confess that I had some faint inkling of what this state might entail; during my childhood I had often seen animals enacting their strange rituals of courtship in yard and field. My childish brain recognized the connection between these curious animal dances and the later arrival of kittens, piglets, foals, and calves. I was able to eventually draw a parallel between this state of affairs and that of Marriage—to understand, in a dim, unfocused way, that since a Woman united with a Man in wedlock will usually bear children, a similar dance must take place between them. This I pondered as I lay in the dark, the bag firmly drawn over my head, trying to imagine what change awaited me when your father entered the room.

I have no way of knowing how long, dear Louisa, I lay upon that bed before your father came into the room. The long wait had made me fretful and nervous, and when the chamber door flew open with a bang, I could not help but shriek in fear, my body on that enormous bed jerking as though shot through with lightning.

"You must lie very still," he said, and his voice was suddenly much colder than it had been hours before, when we had exchanged our wedding-vows. And thus our night began.

My daughter, to frighten you is not my aim, nor yet my purpose in this letter, and yet I must tell you that until that night, I did not know what Pain was. The unitary act, of which I was so ignorant, provoked in me such a feeling of terror and agony that I felt I would be ripped down the middle like a paper doll. With the bag over my head and no candles lit beyond I could see nothing, not even the dimmest outline of your father's face, but I could hear his harsh and ragged breath, the stream of unintelligible words he muttered as he laid his weight upon me; and it seemed to me that he had not two hands but dozens, all emerging from the darkness to pin my shaking limbs to the bed, gripping them so tightly I was sure the nails would pierce the skin—and so they had, I saw the next day, when I examined myself before the mirror and beheld a number of deep punctures in my arms and legs, the skin around them purple and bruised.

I writhed—I wept—I begged your father for mercy, and received none. He said not a word to me throughout this torturous ordeal, neither of comfort for my weeping nor of remonstrance for my inability to remain still. It seemed to me that many painful hours went by while he thrust and poked and grappled with my flesh as though he were the Devil himself, until finally he let out a long, strange moan, his hands gripping ever tighter until the sound abruptly ceased. In the darkness beneath my hood, I heard him sigh, then felt the burning weight of him leave me.

Footsteps creaked away across the bedroom floor. The door opened, then shut. He did not say goodnight, nor bid me well. He did not even remove the bag.

I hope to never again have a night as wretched as that one. Alone, unclothed, I abandoned myself to a wild fit of hysterics that went unnoticed in that great house. I am sure that my weeping could be heard in every room, but no one came to comfort me—not your father, not a servant, not even a curious dog. Loneliness weighed so heavy on my soul that I felt as though *he* lay upon me still.

Oh, how I shuddered when I saw your father there at the breakfast-table the next morning! He was as handsome, as golden, as charming as ever, but the sight of him made me shiver all over, like a dog who, having once been kicked, trembles to see its master.

We broke our fast in silence, attended by his grim, grey servants. Questions roiled within my unsettled mind, so pressing and urgent that I felt I might burst with them. How could he who had only yesterday promised to love and care for me have hurt me so dreadfully, ignored my cries of protest with such a will? How could he sit there calmly with his coffee and his paper after my person had been so grotesquely outraged? How, how, how could he act as though all was well, when nothing was well, and never would be again?

The next few months of my life felt like a hideous dream. During the day, I would wander the manor, some servant always trailing silently behind me. During the evening I ate dinner with your father, who often brought his friends with their silver rings to eat with us; they spoke together in a language I did not know, all hissing consonants and harsh, spitting vowels. At nightfall I would enter my bedroom with a thumping heart, my eyes landing immediately on that hideous table to see if it bore another folded note, bidding me to strip, blind myself, and wait. There was no logic to these nights as far as I could tell, no pattern I could learn that might allow me to steel myself. Sometimes he would appear five nights in a row, leaving me so sore I could barely stir from my bed; then he would abstain for weeks, even months, until I began to think that perhaps I was free of his hideous attentions forever.

And then, inevitably, a note would appear on the bedside table, and a bag on the bed, and the horror would begin once more.

I tried to explore my new abode, but many of the doors were locked, and sometimes even if they were not, whatever servant accompanied me would step before me and prevent me from entering, telling me that my husband had declared it 'out of bounds'. The library was out of bounds. My husband's room and study were out of bounds. Conservatory, parlour, drawing room, dining room, nursery, even the kitchen and the scullery were off-limits to me when not in the company of my husband.

"I am the mistress of this house!" I cried one day, frustrated by the constant barrage of refusal; and the servant who had denied me entrance said, without missing a beat:

"Yes, madam, but you see, he is its *master*, and yours, too."

One of the few places I was permitted was the long gallery. On days that were cold or rainy I would walk there to get my exercise, gazing up at the portraits that lined walls at regular intervals, your father's ancestors stately and beautiful as angels. All of them, I saw, bore silver rings on their left hands, the stones as golden as their hair. The terrace was also within my accepted bounds, as were the gardens scattered across the house's sprawling grounds. Ordinary, orderly gardens they were, full of roses and hollyhocks, wisteria and foxglove—and yet there were stranger blossoms scattered throughout, monstrously large and tinged with foreign colours whose names I did not know, their perfume so delicate and strange it made me swoon.

On one occasion I plucked one of these flowers and set it in a vase beside my bed, wanting to fill the air with that curious scent. I dreamed that night of another garden, somewhere far away. In the distance I could see the shadowy outlines of ruined towers, as though I stood in the pleasure-garden of a palace only recently brought tumbling down by Time. Those mysterious flowers bloomed all around me, making the air hazy with scent. When I looked upwards, instead of a single sun, I saw *three*: two large, one small, burning in a sky whose colour was all wrong.

I woke up the next morning with a ferocious headache, and the vase on the table quite empty. A servant stood at the foot of my bed, looking dourly upon me.

"The master says the flowers ain't to be plucked," she said.

I never picked a flower on the grounds of your father's house again, although that dream came back to me over and over.

My dear, are you *quite* sure that there is no one else present? Have you checked beneath the bed? in the wardrobe? behind the chiffonier? Are those drapes stirring faintly in a draft coming from the window, or do they conceal some gleeful spy?

Never mind. I must trust you to know that your solitude is complete.

When I had been married for nearly a year, I found another folded note on my bedside table. I removed my clothes, eased the bag over my head, and blew out the candle before climbing onto the bed. However, I found as I lay back on the bed that I had not pulled the drawstring as tight as usual, and that if I lay with my head far back on the pillow and my chin tight against my neck, I was able to peep through the slit at the bottom of the bag. It was a full moon, the room so brightly lit it was almost like day, but I could see little enough: my own body pimpling in the chill of the room, a sliver of bedpost and curtain, a hint of the darkness beyond.

I was reaching up to pull the drawstring tight around my throat when I heard the creaking of feet coming down the passage.

Hastily I returned my hand to its resting place on the eiderdown, just in time for your father to make his entrance.

I saw only the briefest of glimpses from my accidental peephole. A cloth of some kind thrown carelessly onto the floor; a patch of skin, silver-white in the moonlight; and then he began his usual line of attacks on my person. By now I was so used to these nighttime ministrations that they had become almost dull. Even though I still felt my body seize in terror at his approach, even though the smell of him still filled me with loathing, I found myself bored by his efforts, and by my feelings of panic and dismay. The reactions of my body wearied me; I was left cold by my own suffering.

And then one of your father's hands slipped, catching on the loose sackcloth gathered at the top of my head, and the bag pulled inadvertently up over my chin, my nose, my eyes. And I could see all.

The thing that straddled my body in the moonlight was no man. Its eyes were your father's, and its smell, and its voice mumbling words in no language I had ever learned; but the face was long and thin, the mouth a lipless gash, the nose no more than twin holes in its face. The body was painfully slender, grey-white skin pulled tight over tendon and bone, with arms (and it seemed to me that there were more than two, Louisa!) ending in grasping talons, grabbing greedy handfuls of my flesh and twisting it as though they meant to tear it off in lumps. Between the cadaverous legs, sliding in and out of me, was its member, a thing that I cannot describe—not out of feminine decorum, but because the sight of it so horrified me that I could not keep the image of it in my head. Even now I am unable to picture it, try as I might. All I can see is a mess of wormy skin, exposed nerve, pulsing muscle.

This glimpse of your father's true form lasted only a moment, and then his eyes met mine, and whatever impulse had frozen me in place disappeared. I screamed, long and louder than I had ever screamed before, and he screamed too, the thin slash of his mouth gaping impossibly wide into a great black hole. He scuttled away from me like some monstrous crab, back and back until he fell off the bed and onto the stone floor. After a moment he stood, pulling a length of cloth around him like a robe—and then I saw it was not cloth at all, but *skin*, the same skin he had discarded moments ago. He was wrapping himself in human flesh, swaddling his grotesque body in the shape that I had come to know as my lawful husband. In a moment he stood before me as I had always seen him, beautiful and fair, his silver ring winking in the moonlight. He looked at me, his face twisted as though he was as horrified as I was, then turned tail and fled the room, oaths in that unknown language dripping from his tongue.

I did not want to go downstairs the next morning; I had no wish to share a room with that *thing*, knowing now what lay under the beautiful skin. But go I did, forced downstairs and into my seat by your father's servants and their strong, cruel hands. Your father watched them manhandle me into my chair, drinking a cup of coffee. The agitation of the night before seemed to have left him; he looked entirely calm.

"You were not meant to see what you saw last night," he said.

This was so obvious a statement—the snuffed candle! the bag!—that I could not suppress a bark of laughter. He registered this with barely a twitch of his elegant eyebrows.

"The proper thing to do," he continued, "would be to kill you. That is the usual consequence of women spying on that which does not concern them."

The silence that followed these words seemed to have a tangible weight, pressing on my eardrums as though I were suddenly underwater. Your father took a sip of coffee and hummed under his breath.

"However," he said, "there is the matter of the child to consider."

My face in that moment, I am sure, was as blank as any woman's face could be. "The what?" I said.

"You are pregnant," he said, and smiled, the same smile that had so captivated me upon our first meeting. Just as they had then, his nostrils flared. "Even after one night, I can smell my seed finally taking root in you."

I winced at his crudeness—and winced again as I thought of how I had come to be in such a state, how brutally he had used me.

"And so," he continued, "you have two choices. You may leave, remove yourself to your father's house, if he will have you, or wander the streets as a beggar or a whore, if he will not. You may birth my child in filth and squalor, knowing that when you do, I will snatch him from your arms and drown you in the nearest river. And make no mistake, I will do this. Should you go to France, or Bohemia, or Timbuktu, *I will find you*, and I will take what is mine. According to the laws of my people—and yours, I believe—a child is the rightful property of his father. The mother is merely the vessel through which he enters the world, the jug from which the water pours."

My people, he said. But what people were those? I remembered, suddenly, the dreams that had plagued me after plucking that strange flower, the vision of that faraway garden under three burning suns, that palace crumbling into dust. The three stones on your father's ring caught the morning light as he took a sip of coffee.

"And what," I asked, "is the second choice?"

"To be the lady of this house," he replied. "To lie with me without complaint, to bear the children that will bear my name, to appear by my side when I need you to and disappear when I do not. Do these things, and you will live in comfort for the rest of your life—although it will be short, as all your kind's lives are."

"Shall I live in safety, as well as comfort?" I asked, and now it was his turn to laugh.

"These are your choices, wife," he said. "Live with me knowing that I could kill you, or run from me knowing that I will."

I have never been brave. I made my choice.

For thirteen months I carried you, longer than any woman is meant to carry a human child. Your father's strange friends would appear at all hours of the day and night, pressing their elegant hands to my stomach, saying not a word to me but toasting your father with glasses of bittersweet wine, praising his virility in that language I did not know. "A son!" they cried, their rings glittering in the lamplight, "a son!" And I pictured a ghoulish creature like your father sliding out of my womb, and wept.

But of course, you were no son, and when, after a day and a night of labour, I finally looked into your little pink face, I felt myself overcome with relief and fear in equal measure. Relief, because you were a human girl-child, and not some unholy wraith; and fear, because I had no inkling of how your father would react to a daughter. When he saw you, however, he only shrugged and said, "A girl may have her uses, given time."

He continued to visit me at night, trying to beget a son, but your time inside my body seemed to have robbed it of its creative powers. Still, I called for hot water whenever he left me to rid myself of his stink and seed, and made the servants brew me thick cups of pennyroyal tea, to make sure that no other child could take root.

Louisa, you were the only thing in that hideous house for me to love, and I loved you with all the strength I had. I insisted on feeding you from my own breast. Although your father soon procured a stone-faced woman to act as your nursemaid, I kept you by my side whenever I could, letting her trail wordlessly behind us as we frolicked. I taught you how to read with the wizened letter-blocks from my own childhood nursery. We played hide-and-seek in the gardens, tag in the echoing ballroom, ran footraces along the marble length of the long gallery, your father's ancestors smiling down at us from within their ornate frames. As a toddling thing you paid them no mind, but as you grew older you began to look at them more closely, squinting up through the gloom at those fair and winsome faces. Once, I recall, you turned to me and asked:

"Mamma, why are there no ladies in any of these pictures?"

It startled me, that question, for until that moment I had not noticed that, indeed, the portraits were all of gentlemen. Not a single woman stared down from that gallery wall.

The older you grew, the more I understood how unlike me you were: brash instead of meek, bright instead of dull, bold instead of timid. You were not afraid to ask questions, even when I could not or would not answer them. When you split your chin on the edge of a table, you scarcely cried; when you tripped over a loose cobble and broke your wrist trying to catch yourself, you let the doctor set it without a murmur of complaint. You climbed to the top of the tallest trees, dove into the coldest lakes, approached the wildest snarling dogs with your hand outstretched, offering friendship. I have been blessed to be your mother, my brave and beautiful darling.

Louisa, I need you to be brave now, for I am approaching the heart of the matter.

Your father paid you no attention when you were a child, nor yet when you were a girl; but as you approached womanhood, he suddenly took an interest in your habits, your manners, your bearing and dress. You recall that at the supper-table—the only meal we all took together, and that rarely—he began to correct your posture, to ask you what you were reading, to observe your growing body and comment upon its form, its fullness. "You will be an easy mother," he said to you once, looking at your broad hips, and you flushed and looked ashamed.

"What did he mean?" you asked me later, sounding so puzzled and unhappy that I had to stifle the urge to run to your father and wrap my hands around his throat.

Your father's friends, too, began to lay eyes upon you in all your blooming glory. You were a sheltered baby, and you had grown into a sheltered girl; I was terrified that one of these men would request your hand, and that, knowing no other men nor any other way of life, you would oblige him. I did not know for certain if they were of a kind with your father, if they, too, had wrapped themselves in man-skins to hide their proper forms, but I had seen their rings, and I did not trust them. Therefore I determined that you must have a proper coming-out party, as is customary for a young lady of your status, and sent dozens of invitations throughout the county, hoping that one of them would be received by an eligible bachelor. Marriage had destroyed my life. I prayed it might save yours.

You remember your coming out party, I hope—your beautiful gown of pale China silk, the freesias twined through your golden hair, the scores and scores of people in the ballroom who applauded you as you made your blushing way through the door, shy for the first time in your life. Your father's friends were there in droves, but they were at last outnumbered, and my spirits lifted as I saw you speak to several eligible young men. There was one, I noticed, at whom you looked again and again, and who left your side but rarely that whole night—a handsome fellow with jet-black hair and eyes the colour of smoke. He wore the most elegant kid gloves, fastened at the wrist with cunning jet buttons, and when, later that night, I caught him alone and let him know that he was welcome at the Manor any time he chose to visit, he caught my hand with his gloved ones and kissed my fingers with gratitude and delight.

Visit he did, often and eagerly. From my window I watched the two of you stroll through the gardens, resolutely followed by your nursemaid, and felt a lightness in my heart that I had not known for years. I knew little of the young man, but what I did know I liked: he was clever and courteous, quick to joke but not to offend; he was rich, though not terribly so, and had political aspirations; he spoke lovingly of his family home some miles away, the beautiful gardens on its grounds. His name sprang to your lips, unbidden, at least five times a day; I admit, sometimes I would let our conversations wander in a way that I knew would draw your mind to him, and then smiled to myself when you mentioned him again. I had high hopes that you had formed an attachment, and when you came to me and told me that he had proposed, I urged you to accept. I had visions of you spirited safely away, to your fiancé's family home or even the Capitol, free at last—free at last!

Your engagement party was a smaller affair than your coming-out party, but still memorable for being one of the few merry occasions at your father's house. You were so lovely that evening, so clearly infatuated with your betrothed, that I could scarcely stop smiling. But I believe your fiancé smiled wider as he lifted his glass to toast your impending nuptials, your future happiness, and the blessing he had found in you, the sweetest of brides.

It was then I realized that he had not worn his gloves that evening. On the smallest finger of his left hand, gleaming in the light of the candelabra, was a silver ring set with three yellow stones.

I should have spoken to you that night, but I was frozen by my realization—frozen, and then shamed for the part I had played in it. Every day since then I have tried to speak to you alone, but it seemed that suddenly the servants attended your every waking moment, surrounding you like a cloud of houseflies. I had no chance to warn you, no opportunity to make right, until now.

I am writing this in the still hours of the morning of your wedding; the whole affair will be over when you read this letter. I can picture you in bridal-gown, its pink silk bringing out the innocent bloom of your cheeks. You will look beautiful, of course, and a little nervous, and young—this above all, for no one looks younger to a mother than her daughter. When I see you, it is not as the woman of nineteen that you are, but as many versions of yourself, one nested inside the other like those cunning Russian dolls. Yourself at fourteen, thickly flushed with blood—ten, swift and nimble as a boy—six, earnest and gap-toothed. And in the middle, in the heart, yourself as a baby, red and sticky with the mess of the womb. My own, my flesh.

Louisa, *you must not have a wedding-night.* I lost my youth to a silver ring. I will not see you lose yours, too.

When you have finished reading, put on your shoes and cloak as quietly as you can, and slip out of your bedchamber. Walk silent as a ghost down the stairs and out the door. Stay low to the ground and run towards the road, keeping to the shadows. I will be waiting there, my darling, with a horse and cart stolen from your father's stables, and together we shall take our leave of these hideous creatures.

I have no idea where we shall go. I do not know if we will be safe from our husbands on the Continent, or in India, or South Africa, or Australia. I do not know if we shall manage to escape at all. You could be caught, or I could, or we could be captured together after we meet on the road or found later in some inn or on a ship. There are infinite possibilities, and a great many of them are ugly. But I will be brave for you, my daughter—for the first time in my life, I shall be brave.

With all my love,
Your Mother

*See Elliott Gish's story "From a Mother to Her Daughter, on the Eve
of Her Wedding" online at Metaphorosis.
If you liked it, leave a comment. Authors love that!
Remember to subscribe to our e-mail updates so you'll know when
new stories are posted.*

About the story

While reading a book about Victorian social and sexual mores as research for another project, I began to think of how uninformed young women in that period were, even on their wedding nights. In such a repressed and sexually anxious society, much of the information a young woman brought with her to the bedroom would have been the result of her mother having "the talk" with her beforehand. What if that talk was not just a way for a mother to explain physical intimacy to her daughter, but to warn her about something more sinister?

A question for the author

Q: Do you make art other than prose? What kind, and how is it different?
A: My attempts at art other than prose have not been successful. My drawings are bad, my poems are worse, and the less said about my attempts at songwriting, the better. However, I did once make my mother a beaded keychain in the shape of a gecko, and it came out splendidly.

About the author

Elliott Gish is a writer and librarian from Nova Scotia. A graduate of Simon Fraser University's Writer's Studio program, her goal is to make her readers afraid to sleep without the lights on. She lives in Halifax with her partner.
www.elliottgishwrites.com, @Elliott_Gish

Midnight's Second Station

Chloe Smith

Errant had studied the reports, had marveled, had thought he'd understood as much as anyone did—but his eyes still rejected their first sight of Midnight's trees.

He squinted down through the shuttle's window. A few hours before sunset, the passing terrain was a crumpled expanse of ashy browns and pinks, covered by the pale, irregular blooms of fungal webs and the fine, regular lines of insulated pipes. Interspersed among both of these patterns, though, was another: an array of shapes cut out of absolute darkness. As much as Errant tried to make out gradations of color or get a sense of form, he saw only absence, shapes like holes gnawed through to the realm of antimatter, even as the pilot angled their craft downward and the ground rose to meet them.

They landed beside a pipeline that had looked threadlike from the air but turned out to be at least half Errant's height. It stretched away behind them, over the horizon and towards the power station's reservoir, half a hemisphere away. Just ahead, it crossed a stripe of white paint and disappeared behind the matte silhouette. Errant leaned forward, trying to see where the human creation and alien thing met, and asked the shuttle's other passenger, "What does the line signify?"

Supervisor Heren, Positive Delta Energy's ranking onsite employee and one of the only survivors of the explosion, snorted. "Safety. Rules say we need a 10-meter perimeter. Of course, they also say to monitor trunk surface temperatures."

"And you can't do both?" Cygni Authority had hired Errant as a safety inspector because he could analyze complex systems, trace the impacts and risks of human interactions with strange new biomes. In practice, a lot of that meant pinpointing profit-driven cheats and paradoxes in corporate policies.

Heren's tone was all vinegar. "We can't do the work from a distance. The perimeter rule's just a way for PD to cover their—" She cut off, and her eyes, framed within the narrow opening of her lifted viewplate, flickered towards the pilot.

Her crewmate just leaned back from her controls with a sigh. Errant didn't think he'd heard her say more than five words together in the two days he'd been down this gravity well.

Heren shook herself. "It's fine. Like I said, we have to do it regularly. Those reports I *assume* you read through don't show any correlation between the explosions and us touching the trees."

"I remember." Errant heard the defensive note in his own voice and wanted to cringe. He should be used to wiping metaphorical spit off his face. Cygni was the only interplanetary body with enough leverage to force inspections, and maybe even change, on companies like Positive Delta Energy. When he'd started visiting sites, he'd thought workers would understand he was there to help, but experience had taught him that most assumed him to be an enemy, looking for "gotcha" moments. From their perspective, his report would most likely be toothless or, at worst, an excuse for Positive Delta to fire them all.

That won't happen. That's not what I'm here for! I'm going to help keep you safe, so no one else dies. He recognized the impulse to babble assurances, ignored it.

You always care too much, Stephen said, in his head. He forced the memory down, along with the messy emotions it unleashed. This was work. He could only do his best to understand what was really happening here on Midnight. He lowered his own viewplate and turned on his comm. "I'd like to get closer, then."

But he hesitated once his boots hit soil, staring up at the void-shape before them. Its edges shifted in the wind of Midnight's thin atmosphere, ragged bits of shadow lifting and settling back.

"Don't forget to change your settings to infrared." Heren's words were still clipped, but there was none of the animus he'd heard before. It made him wonder. Maybe she *didn't* hate him on principle.

Then he switched his settings and stopped thinking about anything else.

The landscape around them faded to crepuscular greys, but the tree's utter blackness resolved a fraction. Errant squinted. He could just make out the suggestion of features—leaves moving against each other and the curve of the trunk beneath them even clearer. He took a cautious step forward, boots over the perimeter line, and another step, and another, until he could put one hand on the trunk. He felt the barest suggestion of heat, transmitted through the fierce insulation of the tree's surface and the protection of his gloves.

"It's hard to makes sense of, isn't it?" Heren's question surprised him again.

"Yes." He still felt the need to defend himself. "I did my research, you know. I don't make it a habit to charge blindly into projects involving unique xenobiology, especially when the organisms generate this much power."

There was nothing like Midnight's trees anywhere else. A plant-analog that absorbed such a complete spectrum of light shouldn't be able to exist. And yet here were the trees, with their blacker-than-black leaves and inscrutable trunks, insulating and protecting the explosively charged cores within them.

"Everyone's overawed at the start," Heren said. "The first tappers who went in to drill the siphons and lay pipe, they couldn't get over how uncanny it all was. Soren said—" She stopped again. Soren was the name of the first station's supervisor. One of the dead.

Errant pulled back, torn between two investigatory desires. On his long transport ride to Midnight, he'd studied two documents to the point of near memorization. One was the anonymous message to Cygni's Planetary Resource Operations department that had launched this inquiry. The other was Heren's post-accident debrief, a series of monosyllabic responses to the company rep's leading questions. He knew he'd have to re-interview her about what happened, to get more than the pain-filled silences between her answers. He'd been dreading it. And here she was giving him an opening—at the moment when he really needed to focus on the facts of the physical environment. He tried to approach both topics at once, and bungled it.

"There's no explanation of how they manage not to overheat, right? There weren't any clear indicators, before, when the heat control failed?"

Even faceless inside her helmet, he still *felt* the look she gave him. "No, Inspector. We don't have any certain way to predict the explosions. Don't you think, if we could have anticipated a blast—" Her gloves fisted at her sides.

Elda the pilot spoke up on the channel. "Time to inspect, Inspector."

Errant hesitated, tried to think of a way to walk back his words, and gave it up. "Right."

He returned to the tree, circled it with fingers trailing against the not-bark. The siphon jutted out at waist height on its far side, half-hidden in the artificial dimness. Once he remembered to toggle the infrared off, it seemed to float, a crisp shape even in the afternoon light, against the matte blackness. The tap line that stretched down the trunk from the spigot was just as distinct. It ran over the few meters of uneven ground between tree and pipe, a vein in the larger network.

"This tree's fallow right now." Heren had moved up beside him, and tapped the meter-transmitter on the spigot's crest. "PD rule is to give each tree a local-year off. The idea is to prevent the power gradient from becoming unsustainable."

"Do you know how they settled on these safety guidelines?" Errant asked.

"Do you?" her voice had returned to its low-grade caustic register. Errant wanted to follow up, to push her for thoughts on the soundness of company safety policies, but he was wary of another misstep. *Focus on the physical inspection, for now.*

He dropped to one knee and began digging his bots out of his pack. Humans were complicated messes of conflicting ideas, intentions, and understandings. Bots, by comparison, were much easier. And these bots were very straightforward. They just wanted to take readings and broadcast them to his terminal back at the power station. He set them in a row on the ground, where they unfolded jointed legs and began scurrying around.

"Those little guys might not make it long enough to give you your data," Heren said. "The fauna on this planet aren't very large, but they're tough and very fast. Their biome's got plenty of power, after all. They avoid anything our size, but they could destroy that little thing without even trying. Then there's the fungi. Spores grow on *everything.*"

"Fortunately, I've plenty of bots. We'll drop this many at every tree we visit," Errant told her.

Some of the bots went up the trunk, where their surfaces glittered against the abyssal black, and some began burrowing into the bare ground. Besides the dark trees, Midnight was shockingly short on anything that looked like plant life: no dark shrubs or grasses, no competing species that used the same light-absorbing technique to feed itself. The terrain's varied color came instead from the fungi. The report from the planet's initial survey team, before PD had staked a claim on Midnight, suggested that not just the giant webs, but an uncounted array of other spores infested the planet's soil.

Errant looked across the landscape, from one distant trunk to another. PD's pipe map showed even spokes stretched across half the small planet's surface, meeting in a point at the heartwood reservoir. He'd assumed that they'd chosen to tap only those trees that happened to stand isolated—but it looked as if the pipes' spacing followed the trees'. It was like they'd been laid out by some vanished park architect or farmer.

He was about to turn away, when sudden movement caught his eye. "What was that?"

"Elda?" Heren was staring at the point where the horizon had *shifted*, where the curve of a hillock humped up instead of sloping down. "Query Second Station. David's monitoring the pipeline grid right now. Anything go out of alignment?"

Fear rinsed through Errant's gut as he trailed Heren's hurried steps back to the shuttle, listened to Elda relaying the question.

Then there was quiet as they climbed back through the airlock—as Elda presumably listened to the response from the power station. Errant tried to lengthen his breaths and not think about the footage he'd seen in his research, images of the first station's wreckage, of the scorched remains of its inhabitants. *It just went*, Heren had said in her debrief. He wondered what Stephen would do if he died here, at the foot of an exploding tree on planet Midnight. *Probably cry into the shoulder of the next sucker.*

Elda said, "Right." She looked up as they reemerged into the shuttle's cockpit, nodded at Heren, who already had her faceplate open. Errant hurried to do the same and caught the tail end of a report.

"—a few centimeters' shift on Foxtrot 7 line, but it doesn't look like anything the struts can't adjust to." Errant recognized the voice of Heren's second-in-command David, tinny over the ship's cheap speakers. "We can move that line up in the check rotation, but I don't think it'll be a problem. Looks like that hill migration mostly missed the grid."

Heren sighed. "Copy. We'll move to the next tree." She had lost the urgency that propelled her towards the ship, and Elda looked as phlegmatic as ever. Errant imagined they could hear his heart trying to pound its way out through his breastbone. He tried his question again.

"What was that?" He hoped it wasn't something he'd read about and forgotten.

Heren gave him a look he couldn't read, all tight eyebrows and narrow eyes. Then she said, "The ground shifts here. Maybe better to say it swells and sinks. We have to keep a tight inspection and maintenance schedule all along the pipelines, to make sure there aren't interruptions to the flow."

That definitely hadn't been in the reports. Errant tried to fit this new and disturbing piece of information into what he knew. "It's not the tapping activity that causes the groundswells?"

Heren shrugged. "It happens near tapped trees, and near untapped ones. It's like everything else. There's no clear correlation. That's why..." She shrugged her next words away. "That's everything PD's tame scientists bothered to figure out."

Errant couldn't tell if she was challenging him to do better, or finding another way to tell him his efforts were useless. He looked away and out the window as the planet's surface fell away again. "This is a strange place."

"I'm not used to it," Heren said, "and I've been here longer than anyone still alive."

It took hours to drop the rest of the bots. At least there were no more sudden groundswells, although Errant turned a new, sharper eye to the folds and humps of earth around the trees they visited. Night had overtaken them and masked the trees' impenetrable shadows by the time they got back to the station, a warren of prefabbed bubbles half dug into the planet's surface. It was farther than the ruins of the first station from the reservoir full of molten heartwood. Whether that was a safe distance or not—well, he was supposed to find out, wasn't he? Errant shivered as he crowded into the airlock-shower with Heren and Elda.

The rinse in the airlock, Heren had told him when he first arrived, was because of the fungi. Even with it, interior walls and air filters clogged with wayward spores and required regular scrub-downs, no matter how tight they kept the seals. "It's a whole pain to delegate half my on-duty people to housework each shift," she'd said with a shrug. Errant had noticed the yeasty-metallic tang in the air when he'd first landed, but that same early survey had established with certainty that the biome's fungal inhabitants were nontoxic. Cygni would never have designated the planet open for companies to claim, if they hadn't.

Inside, Heren went to confer with her on-duty crew and Elda turned her back on him. Errant retreated to the bunk-sized closet that counted as visitor's quarters.

He tried not to take it personally. He was an outsider, a tenderfoot who couldn't really understand tapper life, even if he hadn't been from Cygni. Still, it was lonely.

It was too early to check the data streams from the bots. Without fully meaning to, he opened his terminal and pulled up

Stephen's most recent message one more time. Familiarity, guilt, his better judgement, none of it stopped the toxic mixture of warmth and dread, longing and resentment, that flooded him at the sight of Stephen's hollow-cheeked, handsome face. He listened again to the latest earnest, full-hearted, meaningless apology.

I know I keep doing this. I know you have no reason to forgive me or want to see me again. I'm broken. I know it. The times when I'm with you are the only—

The door alert pinged. Errant snapped the file closed, feeling like he'd been caught indecent. He scrubbed at his cheeks, as if he could smooth some of their heat away, and then released the hatch. It was Heren.

She hesitated, as guilty-looking as he felt. It took a moment to unsnarl himself from his irrelevant emotions, to remind himself about exploding trees, and hazardous work conditions, and Heren's ambiguous responses. "Hello, Supervisor. Can I help you with anything?"

"Can I come in?" She actually glanced over her shoulder. Errant wondered if this was a proposition, thought about trying to head her off... *I'm sorry, ma'am, I'm currently in a decaying orbit around a relationship black hole named Stephen...* Then she looked back at him and killed that notion with her next words. "I'd like to make sure of your report."

She wasn't a big woman, out of her environment suit, but her intensity took up its own space between them. He hadn't pegged Heren for a company stooge, but she was in charge here, on an empty planet...

"Of course," he said slowly, and let her inside.

Heren didn't make him feel any better once the door was closed. She kept standing, arms stiff and fists clenched at her sides, the way they'd been out by the tree. There wasn't enough room to back away from her.

Finally, she said, "I sent the message to Cygni."

"Wha—" The implications of her razor-wire tension and furtive aspect grew evolved into new patterns. "Oh—that's—okay." Errant took a deep breath, bottled up the urge to begin bombarding her with questions. "Is there—is there anything you'd like to add to that initial report?"

The anonymous alert had been a simple text file, without much more than the bare outlines of PD's Midnight operation: The company had to build a second power station because the first had been destroyed in an accident; the operation had a shocking mortality rate, even for a frontier project.

Heren closed her eyes, then opened them. He *saw* her walls buckle, her expression melt into grief and pain. "You have to make them pay. Your report, whatever those little bots dig up from the fungi-soil and the trees, that work needs to damn Positive Delta. Burn them to ashes."

Errant swallowed against the urge to make some promise, to make her feel better. Meaningless words wouldn't wipe away her suffering. "If you believe the company is at fault, why did you send your tip anonymously? Testimony from an employee, especially one who," he hesitated, "who has direct experience of the dangers, would be the strongest voice in an argument for reckless endangerment."

"And give them an easy target?" Heren demanded. "They could have sent me on my way before you even got here. And how could I know they wouldn't buy whoever Cygni sent out? I had to see that you actually wanted to know what happened—and I'm still taking a risk. It's always easier to fault the workers. We must have made mistakes. We can't have followed all their oh-so-carefully-researched guidelines." She took a breath, settling herself. "PD could use whatever you write to axe me *and* my people. Then they'll say they've fixed the problem on the ground, and carry on making money with a new crop of desperate hires. There are *always* more desperate hires."

She wasn't wrong. Even Cygni's reach was limited. The report would need a convincing argument about the causes of the explosions here on Midnight, to have a hope of making the Positive Delta admit wrongdoing or change their policies.

"Alright," Errant said. "Let's start by going back over what happened before. I'm sorry; I know this will be painful, remembering—"

"Oh, don't worry." Heren's lips stretched in a not-smile. "I'm always remembering. You don't forget coming back from patrol to find a crater where your people should be."

At least Heren's testimony drove Stephen and his messages out of Errant's head. Over the next few days, as he watched the data streams from his bots and began playing with different analysis programs, he kept hearing her words again.

The explosion traveled down the line from the reservoir... They made me sift my people's bones from the 'valuable' wreckage so that they could start over.... Some of them we never found. The ground shifted and they were gone.

It wasn't just the horror of it though, the way her face went from pain to rage to uncanny stiffness and back again as she talked. He also kept thinking about the groundswells and earth movements. It was weird. The planetary survey hadn't found tectonic activity, and this movement was smaller-scale anyway—more like something caused by burrowing animals or the shifts of defrosting soil.

His feelings about the strangeness of the data set grew, the more bots he placed in the field, and the longer he looked at what they gathered. There was *a lot* of information: vast and complex chemical mixtures, spikes of electrical activity. He sat for hours in Second Station's mess, out of the way of most of the tappers, trying and failing to make sense of it.

He had closed his eyes in the face of the ever-growing bulk of information, and was rubbing the heels of his hands against his forehead, when his terminal bleated: the alert for an incoming message, coded personal. Errant swore.

"That bad?" Elda stood in the doorway. He blinked at her. He'd gotten so used to the tappers' stonewalling that he barely noticed when they skirted him. But it seemed silent Elda, of all people, softened at the sight of his self-pity.

"Not how I treat mail from home," she said with a shrug.

"Oh—no." He shook his head, reminded again how isolated they were here. "It's just—I can guess who it's from." No one else would ignore his out-of-system auto-response, would pretend he wasn't busy and working and just completely fed up....

Elda raised an eyebrow. His own words slipped over each other into her silence. "I don't—I don't know what to do. He's toxic, but he needs me, or he needs *somebody*, and every time I see him, it's like the reasonable part of my brain just fades away..." He forced himself to stop, mortified. "Sorry."

She just nodded. "Pheromones, probably."

"Huh?"

"There's no logic to it, but there's a feeling. Something you get from him. Or something he gets from you." She served herself a bowl of vat-protein and rehydrated starches, dug a spoon in, licked it. "I've been there. Sorry to hear it." She sat down with her back to him; conversation concluded.

Elda's presence gave him the discipline not to immediately open Stephen's message. Instead, he went back to staring at the data. Something she'd said niggled. *Pheromones....*

He added another factor to the program he'd been running, watched the patterns of analysis reshape themselves.

The idea was far-fetched, improbable. If he'd been working with a team, he would have been embarrassed to even suggest it—but once it had occurred to him, he couldn't let it go. Instead, the notion gained weight and substance as the bots' output kept accumulating.

He was almost ready to risk his theory to a recording when another tree blew up.

The shockwave ripped through the earth and shook the station habitat. Errant scrambled to his feet as people who'd been off-shift flooded into the common area, wide-eyed and still in pajamas. The four tappers monitoring the grid were still cupped within their screens, hands flying as they tried to assess the damage.

Heren pushed herself through the press of people and turned to the nearest monitor. "Which one?"

Her eyes didn't leave her screen. "Zed 12."

Everyone started speaking at once. "What—" "No—" "That can't be possi—"

"Alright, then!" Heren shouted them all down. "Cyn, are you sure?"

The monitor nodded. Errant's gut clenched. He didn't remember all the designations, but Zed was the spoke of the pipeline starburst that ran closest to the station.

Someone else was asking questions now. "Any fluctuations beforehand? No warnings?"

He needed to see what his own data showed. He pulled out his handheld, skimmed the feeds. Most bots were still transmitting. The feed from Zed 12 was gone, of course, but what the history of the last few minutes showed—it made his breath go tight. "Wait, Heren!"

Heren glared at him. "What is it? What's causing this?"

"I don't want to jump...." His voice faltered.

"You don't want to jump to conclusions, and what, maybe prevent anyone else from dying?" Heren scoffed. "I don't know why I tried so hard to get you here, if you are going to sit back and take *notes* while trees go up around us—"

"Wait." That was Heren's second, David, bristling and stepping into her space. "Heren, *you* called in Cygni? You risked all our jobs for some data-jockey's writeup?"

"I'd rather that than keep risking your lives!" Emotion broke in Heren's voice, and everyone started talking again.

She was right. He had to choose the clearest path towards safety, too, whatever everyone else thought. "Supervisor?"

Somehow, she heard him amid the hubbub. "Quiet, everyone! I said, quiet!"

Errant spoke into the grudging silence. "I'm not certain, but If I'm right—we should evacuate now."

"You can't wait until you file your report to get us fired—" someone began.

"No." He took a deep breath. "The reports PD sent me. They mentioned the way, when the first power station went up, that there was a series of earlier explosions."

Heren nodded, but David waved that point away, "Yes, but it wasn't like they triggered each other. We don't know why that is. The tap lines between the trees run in parallel. The blasts were isolated by both time and space.

"Yes, but the connection isn't about what happened; it's about what *didn't* happen." Errant looked around at the confused faces, and forged ahead. "All my monitoring points to a lot of activity throughout planet's soil, and I mean *a lot*—electrical and chemical movement in patterns I can barely see the edges of. It's at a level of complexity that suggests advanced processes, things like awareness, communicative movement.

"One thing I did see is that all that faded away from Zed 12, starting a few hours ago, and then dropped down to nothing just before it went up. There are a lot more fading spots right now, around a lot more trees."

A hailstorm of sharp-edged words. "Communications? How could you possibly—"

"—So your little bug bots just set it off—"

"Things were fine until—"

Errant held up his hands. "Please! Cygni sent me because of the explosions, but the problem is really something bigger: *They don't understand how this biome works.* Neither do I, fully, but it looks like there's something here, and it has decided that it's tired of firing warning shots."

There was silence as they all tried to make sense of that.

"You think," Heren said at last. "The trees are *sentient?*"

He knew how it sounded. "It's one possible explanation. There has to be some calculus at work, something driving that level of complex interaction."

"Why would they blow themselves up, then?"

"I don't *know!*" He hefted his handheld, trying to suggest the scope of what it held. "I could walk you through the pointers in my data, explain my bots' readings, but the patterns I'm seeing tell me we don't have time. We need to get out of here. It's not safe."

The pause after his words was full of shifting glances, until Heren asked another question.

"Can you prove it? I mean, really prove it, with hard evidence besides your voice and maybe ours—"

"If we believe you," David muttered.

"—And maybe ours?" she repeated. "Positive Delta's not going to let go of this place, this much energy, if they get any choice in the matter. Say we evacuate now; if PD doesn't accept your report, they'll be back with a new crew soon enough."

She was right. He didn't want her to be; he wanted her to get them all offworld right now. He admitted, "The strongest evidence would be to have some of my mobile collectors with their samples. Physical evidence is much harder to deny—but it's all out in the field. It's too much of a risk to re-collect all the bots."

Heren gave him that same folded-brow look, long and piercing.

Then she lifted her chin, turned to Elda, "You're going to pilot the big shuttle." To her second: "David, you're in charge on the flight out." Other questions started to fill the air, but she kept talking. "Inspector Errant. I'll ride with you, and before we leave, we're going to retrieve at least some of your little bots."

The flurry of evacuation passed Errant by. He didn't want to think about what was coming next, so he stared at the data feeds. Energy signatures kept fluctuating and spiking among the roots of every tree he had monitored. It could well be the cadence of a language he had no tools to translate—but even if that was true, there was much he still didn't understand, much that still didn't make sense.

He and Heren sat in the shuttle as the station's emergency evacuation craft lifted off. Heren spoke up on the common channel. "Good speed, people."

There was no response from the bigger ship. It rose and dwindled in the purple-grey sky, and Heren woke the shuttle's engines.

"Where to?"

He checked his handheld one more time. "Go west-southwest, along pipeline Bravo. It looks the most stable right now."

Even with the shuttle at its maximum velocity, the nearest tree was long minutes away. Heren, bent over the controls, spoke without looking at him. "So, will Positive Delta face sanctions for reckless endangerment after all this?"

Errant tried to visualize the shape of his completed report. "Probably not. If it's a new sentient species, Cygni will start assessing Midnight's planetary sovereignty before they rule on how PD was running this harvesting operation. Findings about worker treatment may get lost in the shuffle."

"The fuck you say." The yoke twitched under Heren's hands, and the entire shuttle shuddered. "PD kept us here when the trees started *exploding*. An *entire station* was destroyed. They don't get to treat that like nothing."

Errant cringed at the swooping flight, at his own helplessness. Memories of Stephen intruded suddenly—this trapped feeling was the same as the worst of their fights. He tried, as he had then, to find the words that would move the other person. "I know it's not what you want, but it does stymie them. What's at stake here, now, what we could prove, is bigger than showing what went wrong before. An intelligent species—that's a discovery that changes things. There'll be more research, different regulations on the planet, xenolinguists and biologists coming in to try to understand them—if we ever figure out how to approach them without triggering more tree explosions. Positive Delta certainly won't be able to harvest energy here any time soon; maybe not ever again."

Heren's hands steadied on the controls, but her voice didn't. "You know my crew all hate me now? I just put them out of a job. You've got to be desperate to take one like this, and they were good at it. They're just as good as Soren and Ida and the rest of my first crew. Just as disposable."

She paused, and Errant saw her throat work. "I could have taken the company's hush money. They offered a ride out of here, early retirement after the accident—but they shouldn't get to just keep going."

"They won't—" Errant tried to say, but his terminal interrupted him with a shrilled warning and, while the tone still jangled the air of the cockpit, an explosion bloomed, blue-white and closer than the horizon's line.

Errant clung to his seat. "Do you think we should—"

Heren angled the skimmer's nose down. "We're coming up on Bravo 1. Do your readings say we can land?"

They bounced down by a tree that looked just like the first he'd visited. Errant forced muscles knotted in anticipation of another eruption to unclench. Out of the shuttle, across the meaningless line, he dropped down at the foot of the tree. His fingers were clumsy in their gloves, but they managed to scoop up three of the bots, which had responded to his recall command and swum up out of the earth.

He hesitated, scanning the data feeds. There were a handful more bots converging on this point. He looked out across Midnight's lonely terrain. It looked like there were more of the pale fungal webs now, more uneven swells across the landscape. The sight shifted something in his mind, in the way his thoughts worried over the data.

Something you need, Elda had said. What did the trees need? What did they have? What—or who—had the agency here?

"Errant." Heren hadn't left the shuttle. "Can this tree *see* or feel us here?"

"It's not the trees," Errant said. The nearest bot was seconds away. "It's the mycelial network."

"What?"

"The mycelial network," he repeated, "the fungus system that connects the trees underground. It must somehow draw off the excess energy the trees absorb—that's how they don't overheat—and it diverts minerals from the soil to them. How else could those trees get enough nutrition, without other plant-equivalent growth around?" He shivered, thinking of the network beneath them, a mass of impulses, awareness, and intentions woven into the earth and through the roots of the dark tree, wicking away its overburden of energy and subtly directing its growth.

"How does that even—" Heren began.

Then the data feed from the incoming bot—from all his bots—disappeared. The earth beneath his feet shivered, even as he pushed himself up and into motion.

"Come on!" Heren shouted as he stumbled forward. The ground bucked and white filaments spread around him like starbursts.

He threw himself into the shuttle's airlock. The engine raced, but he felt no lift.

Heren swore. "Something's caught—"

Errant made it to his seat in the cockpit as she fought with the controls, finally rotating the thrusters and gunning them to rip free of the filaments that had seized the landing feet. The shuttle leapt from the ground.

The air around the ship turned to fire as the tree went up beneath them and the shockwave threatened to knock them out of the sky. Heren stayed glued to the controls, leaning forward as if she could will the ship faster. Gravity dug its claws into Errant's bones and flesh as the shuttle shot upwards on a steep trajectory.

"The whole grid is going," Errant didn't have the bot data anymore, but he could watch the feeds from Midnight's human-made structures disappear one by one. "That's the reservoir. That's the station." He imagined the web of explosions spreading across the planet's surface beneath, all that pent-up energy released in a great, cleansing rush.

The shuttle's engine strained, and then the cockpit's viewscreen turned black and bloomed with stars. Another few moments of pressure, and the gee forces of acceleration fell away, leaving them in the calm of freefall.

Errant had a new, uncomfortable thought.

"Can this ship do interplanetary distances?" His Cygni transport wouldn't be back in system for another five standard days.

Heren made a noncommittal noise. "Not officially. We'll make it to the relay station, though. That's where the escape craft was headed."

"Oh. Will you meet your crew there?" He saw her expression change, and regretted the words.

"Former crew." The bitterness was back in her tone. "They won't want to see me. Besides, I think I should stick with you for now. Go on record about everything I saw and did at Midnight's stations, the first one and the second." She gave him a smile that was almost convincing. "That has to count for something, right?"

"We'll make PD feel it," Errant promised her. "And your people will come around."

Heren shrugged. "Maybe. I did betray them."

"I'd hope they see that losing a job is the smaller evil in all this. Hell, if an alien fungus can blow up half its own planet to get rid of its human parasites—" He stopped, afraid that he might have been too flippant in the face of everything she'd been through, but she nodded.

"You have to excise the rotten bits, so they don't kill you."

"Huh." Errant let that idea settle into him for a long moment as they pushed farther into space. "Yes, you really do." Then, because they had some time before they reached the relay station, he pulled up his personal correspondence files on his handheld and deleted some messages that he didn't need respond to.

See Chloe Smith's story "Midnight's Second Station" online at Metaphorosis.
If you liked it, leave a comment. Authors love that!
Remember to subscribe to our e-mail updates so you'll know when new stories are posted.

About the story

This story owes its existence to *Entangled Life* by Merlin Sheldrake, the nonfiction book that launched a thousand spec fic stories—or at least one by every genre writer I know who's read it. Seriously, though, it's a mind-opening book, which is completely appropriate, given that it's all about fungi. I knew I wanted to write a "mushroom story", but I wasn't exactly sure what direction to take it, until I read another nonfiction piece, this one about trees. My mind caught on a phrase about how chlorophyll absorbs a limited spectrum of visible light, which is why it's green. I started thinking about heat and light absorption, and the blackest-black pigments that researchers have created, and somehow the dark trees evolved out of that idea mixture. The human story of Heren and Errant and corporate malfeasance only came after I built the setting for them, although I was able to add Midnight to a wider universe I've used before. (Readers may remember the Cygni Authority from my earlier story "Rock-Adda's World", which ran in *Metaphorosis* in 2021.)

A question for the author

Q: Are you a Luddite? Or do you have the latest and greatest technology?
A: I'm a member of the Oregon Trail generation—the people who got the internet at home when they were children or teens, who know the sound of dial-up, might have gotten their first cell phone when they went off to college, and definitely had social media accounts by the time they graduated. As a result, although I remember life before everything was digitally connected, I've always had to adapt to evolving technology. I try to be comfortable with new platforms, media, and devices, but I also don't value any of it for its own sake. Technology is really just a big umbrella term for an expanding set of tools. Like storytelling, the value is in how it's used.

About the author

Chloe Smith teaches middle-school English and history, which means she had to completely reinvent her job in 2020. She's very glad to be back in the classroom now, and spending much less time on Zoom. Besides teaching, she works as a proofreader for *Locus* and *Fantasy* magazines, and writes science fiction and fantasy stories whenever she can make the time. She was born and raised in the San Francisco Bay Area, and she lived in Texas and Washington states, New York City, and rural France before coming back to California. Her short fiction has appeared in *Metaphorosis, Three-Lobed Burning Eye*, and *Daily Science Fiction*, among other places.
@chloehsmith

June

Since We Don't Have Wings

Gwen Whiting

Chash sloshed through the mud on his way home, picking up bits of glass and hiding them in his pockets. His breath quickened every time he saw the sparkle of glass and he veered toward it, picking up every colored shard he found.

"Chash!" He ignored the voice. *Maybe he'll go away if I don't respond.* It didn't work. Norio caught up to him easily, despite the bag he carried. "Picking up glass here again? Can't believe there's any left for you to take."

"There isn't much," he mumbled. "Nothing wrong with taking it. No one's lived here since the war ended." They were both too young to clearly remember the night that the village had burnt while firebirds slashed through the skies overhead. What stories Chash knew had been woven into his mind by eavesdropping on elders who could not forget.

"If you say so." Norio said. "Just buy your glass from the peddler. He'll be coming down the coast soon."

Chash's face flamed.

"Oh, right. I forgot. You can't afford it." Norio shoved his bag at Chash. "Here. This is the reason I came after you. My mother sends food."

"We don't need it." His cheeks were still hot, but he didn't take the food.

"She insists. Says we still owe you from something Besu did during the war." Norio lifted the bag up, holding it now just out of Chash's reach. "Maybe if you take it, I won't catch you digging through the mud looking for glass to sharpen your kite strings."

It was rude not to take a gift freely offered and his grandmother, Besu, would be furious if he refused on their behalf. Even if she insisted on giving away much of the food they had, saying that others needed it more.

"Tell your mother thanks," he muttered, reaching for the bag.

Norio jerked it back.

"What? I didn't hear you."

"I said, thank you." Chash reached again, but this time, Norio stepped back and dropped the bag. Jassa fruits spilled out, their tender flesh breaking as they hit the ground. The bright orange skins were now coated in mud.

Chash dropped his gaze, staring down at his feet. Norio wanted him to kneel in the dirt, to watch him pick up the ruined fruit, but he wouldn't. Not where Norio could see.

"You just going to let it rot?"

Chash said nothing.

"Some kite fighter you're going to be." Norio said. "Good luck at Festival." Chash lifted his head as Norio ground a fruit down with the heel of his boot, then left. He waited for Norio to be completely out of sight before grabbing the dropped bag and filling it with fruit. None of this would matter once it was time for the festival.

The Festival of Wings was only four days away and it was how Chash planned to make his fortune. The event wasn't focused on birds, but on kites. Huge as a man or small as a dove. Painted like a rainbow or glossy black. Made from paper, silk, linen, even hair…. No one agreed on what made the strongest kite or the fastest. But when the kite fights began, the owner of the last kite in the air earned the emperor's favor. With his favor came a position in the imperial army and the chance to control one of the mighty firebirds who were reborn when killed in battle.

Daydreams lightened Chash's step as he continued home, turning past the magistrate's house. One of the windows was smashed. As the festival drew near, the poorest fighters in Santao broke windows to steal glass to coat their kite strings. He kept his head down. If Norio saw him here, he'd probably tell someone Chash was breaking windows now.

When he reached their cottage, Chash opened the door and crept inside quietly to avoid disturbing his grandmother's work. She was hunched over a swatch of green silk, hemming a sleeve with golden thread.

"You're late." Besu set her needle down, then stretched her fingers. The skin around her eyes was red, and as she blinked, tears glimmered on her lashes. She hadn't lit any of the candles at her table, even though the sun and moon were changing places. *She needs to stop sewing after sunset. She'll go blind if she doesn't.* Chash frowned. Suggesting to Besu that she stop sewing would have been like asking her to stop breathing.

"I wish you wouldn't work so hard." Chash emptied his pockets onto the table. He pulled the fabric inside out and shook it to keep glass slivers from surprising his fingers later.

"Mmm." She rocked back in her chair as he lit the lamps. "Festival's coming. And Lia pays well. She won't be happy if her dress isn't the finest in four villages."

"If I win the fights this year, you won't ever have to sew a dress again."

"My hands like to sew. It's my eyes that don't care for it."

"I'll help you finish the dresses after dinner." Chash stoked the fire. He set a pot of water to boil and began preparing dinner. Other men in the village didn't cook or sew, but Besu had insisted he learn. It was only fair, she said, to take turns. After he had finished making the soup and setting the table, he sat down with Besu to eat. "I was on Manu's crew for the fishing today. Said he saw a waterhorse in the waves."

"They say waterhorse hair makes the best kite strings," Besu commented. "But try catching one."

He laughed.

"Manu put out a trap before we left. If there is a waterhorse, it'll be too clever for it. He hasn't caught one yet." The tender bitterness of the sana root, only edible in the spring, washed over Chash's tongue as he sipped at the edge of his bowl.

"Are you thinking of hunting waterhorse tonight?" Besu slurped her soup, squinting at him. A few drops splattered on the table, but she didn't notice. "You'll need a net for it. And be sure to take one of the lanterns."

"I promised to help you sew." Hours of embroidering tiny flowers for village women lay ahead. Chash had to be her eyes in the dim light to help her manage such delicate work, even as his own eyes watered and burned from lack of sleep.

"I'm a bit behind. Otherwise, I'd weave you something to catch the hair with. No need to harm the poor creature." She set her bowl down, still half-full. "We should get to work. Maybe some of the hair will wash up on the beach. You can pick it off the rocks and I'll dry it."

He sighed and cleared the table. Fishing began at dawn and there weren't many hours left in the night.

The days spent fishing were long and hard. Chash's shoulders ached after pulling in heavy ropes, and when it stormed, the very sea itself battered already-bruised muscles. Manu had sent him to mend nets that day, an easier task than working on the boats. The waterhorse had not been caught the night before, but had thrashed around before it escaped into deeper waters, snarling and snapping the weave with its teeth.

He sat on an overturned barrel near the prow of the ship, tugging and testing the flax of the net as he searched for places that the waterhorse had broken. Chash plucked out strands of silky green hair that the beast had left behind and secreted them in his pocket. Other crew members hoisted sails while Chash fixed the nets, the rank smell of fish oil and pitch wafting toward him with every light breeze. As he worked, he caught snatches of conversations from the stern.

"…that waterhorse." Norio's voice floated over on the breeze.

"Old Manu'll never catch it. All he's ever gotten is bits of hair. Lucky for Chash the old man picked him to tend the nets. Not that he'll scavenge enough to string a spool." Aran replied.

Chash paused when he heard his name.

"Can't believe he sews his own kites." Norio said. "Even if he's good with a needle."

"Women make kites, men fly them," Aran agreed. "Used to be that way, anyhow. Won't be long and we'll have girls working on the docks."

"Besu doesn't make kites. I tried getting her to sew one for me once."

"Too bad, that. She's the finest seamstress in the village."

"Well, Besu must not think Chash can win. Otherwise, she'd sew him a kite," Norio said.

"Can you imagine him trying to rein in a firebird?" Aran's laugh bellowed. "He can barely haul a net up with those arms." The two men laughed together, and others joined in.

Chash threw the net down and stood, his hand balling into a fist. *This again. If they want me to prove I'm strong, I'll prove it.* A broad hand clapped down on his shoulder, then shoved him back down on his stool.

It was Manu.

"I think I hear sirens across the water. Thought you might need these to protect against the singing." Manu handed two lumps of wax, dented by the heat of his hand, to Chash.

"Thank you." Chash hunched over, staring at his feet.

Manu grunted, then walked off.

When I win the fight and go to battle for the emperor, they'll see. Hauling fish doesn't make a man. Chash shoved the plugs in his ears, muting Norio's laughter, and kept working.

Besu's table was piled high with cotton and silk that night, and Chash lit three candles at a time when they both should have been sleeping. Chash picked up a dress the color of weak tea, thrusting his needle into the cotton. After a moment, his grandmother reached out, fumbling for his hand, and took the cloth away.

"What did that dress ever do to you?" she muttered. Her fingers ran across the rippling fabric, her thumb pausing at a puckered hem. "Your stitches are crooked. And knots, Chash! The thread is loose where it should be tight and here – here – here – I shouldn't feel anything at all." Her shoulders heaved and she dropped it on the table.

She had always commented before on how the evenness of his stitches looked and how the colors of one pattern complemented another, not the way the material felt.

"Ah — here. Take it back and pull the stitches out. Carefully, Chash. There's only enough of that color for one dress and who knows if the peddler will come before Festival." Besu handed the sleeve back to him, her tired eyes puffed into swollen slits. "I wish you'd give up the fishing. There's plenty of work to be had in Santao for two tailors."

"You always ask that." He took the sleeve back and picked up a small knife to rip out the stitches. "I want to do something bigger; will anyone care how well I hem a sleeve after I'm dead?"

"I've sewn for this village for generations. My mother before me and her mother before her. The people wear our clothing on their back when they marry, when they fight, when they die. They pass on our best dresses to their daughters, wrap their babies in the blankets that we stitch together from old clothes. Our family will be remembered."

"Your mother, her mother," Chash said. "Never any fathers doing the work."

"They didn't have the talent or the patience. But you do." Besu clamped her lips together for a moment, then asked, "How is it different from mending nets? Men do that. You do that."

All the hours of mending flax echoed in his bones as she spoke, how cord tightened around his fingers when he worked, smelling of seaweed, sand, and the stink of the tides. The way that the ocean seeped into his skin and roughed his fingers so that silk now snagged on his knuckles when he sewed at night. Working on the rough waters aged men until even their minds grew calloused and hard.

"How is it different?" she repeated.

"I don't know. It just is." Chash threaded a new needle. He stabbed the sleeve hard enough to pucker the fabric, but Besu didn't stop him. Was it because she didn't want to pick a fight or because she couldn't see his work?

"It's ridiculous, is what it is." She narrowed her eyes at him for a moment, then picked up her own needle. "Only reason that Manu doesn't have women mending his nets is because that might mean we'd have to be on the docks to do it. And then we'd want to fish. And after that, who knows? Maybe we wouldn't need men anymore." She snorted.

Chash didn't answer.

Besu glanced in his direction, then stopped and rubbed her eyes.

"There're only four days until Festival. Have you finished your kite?" Besu asked.

"Of course. I've been practicing for weeks when the storms aren't heavy." He wondered how a kite sewn by Besu would hold up in the wind. He wouldn't ask her to sew for him now, however, no matter what Norio said — his pride was stitched into every line and fold of the kite he had crafted.

"Hm. Bring me your kite. If you've sewn any knots into it, there'll be no flying it in a harsh wind." She clacked her tongue, but her tone warmed him. He placed the sleeve in the basket at his feet and went to collect his kite from the shelf where it rested. Sewn from a year's worth of dress scraps, its oval shape shimmered blue and orange and violet. The kite's edges were pointed, the bottom weighted with folded fabric stitched closed. The extra weight would give it strength.

Besu grazed the silk with her palms, her eyes closed as her fingers traveled the stitches and bumps of the material. Her mouth turned up into a half-moon smile, lips almost touching her eyes.

"That's one of Lia's dresses. I remember stitching those flowers." There was a little catch in her voice. "And Hana's and Zholi's. Won't they be surprised." She didn't comment on the way that the different colors clashed with one another.

She smoothed the ripples in the fabric out, still smiling.

"I made a kite from a dress once," Besu said.

"I didn't know you'd ever made kites." His forehead wrinkled. It had only been three years since women were first allowed to join the kite fights, after it was apparent that the emperor's wives would bear only daughters. The year that Akrivi won, her golden dragon kite had slashed the strings of a hundred contenders with ease. His grandmother had cried as the last kite plummeted from the sky.

"I did. And I flew them too. Just not in the fights. I — women — weren't allowed then, but I always thought I would've won. My kite was strong — and sewn from the finest fabric in three villages." His grandmother laughed, so hard that it turned into a series of loud coughs.

"How did you find the coin for that? I thought your father raised pigs." Chash patted her on the back.

"I sewed it from my wedding dress." Besu cackled.

"Your wedding dress?" His hand fell away as he gaped.

"The finest fabric to be had." Her hand caressed his kite one last time before she handed it to him.

"Oh." Besu's hands were covered with tiny nicks and scars. *Did those marks come from fighting kites?*

"I didn't love your grandfather at first and I was so angry. Marrying him meant I'd never leave Santao. If my mother had found out I'd used that dress, though..." Besu laughed. "I hid what I'd done. Just cut the inside layer of the skirt shorter — better for summer anyhow. Never told your grandfather."

Chash had never known his grandfather, nor could he remember his parents. His father had been killed in one of the emperor's wars, his mother dead of sickness a few months later, and after Besu had taken him into her home, the war had come to Santao. Firebirds shrieked overhead as his grandmother dragged him with her, pounding on door after door, then leading people into the hills to hide. Some people said the firebirds had saved them from the raiders that stormed through the village, but he knew better. It had been Besu.

"I'm sorry you never got to fight," he said.

"It was worth it, in the end. I wouldn't have made a good soldier." Besu reached out, her bony hands clasping his face for a quick squeeze. "It's time I went to bed. You need to spend time on your kite now — I'll finish the sewing in the morning." She let go of his face, then walked into the next room. His grandmother was wrong, he thought. She would have made an excellent warrior. What had the first emperor been thinking when he decided that women were not worthy of taming his precious firebirds?

The next day, Chash strapped his kite to his back for the long walk to the practice field. The far edges of it flapped past his shoulders, bits of tail breaking free from the twine binding it. He caught glimpses of blue from the corners of his eyes as he walked, never quite knowing if it was kite or sky or ocean that he saw.

Warm breezes from the eastern winds brushed his cheeks and he hummed a little as he walked. It would be a good Festival if the winds kept up and the storms stayed behind. His kite rustled as someone nudged Chash's shoulder, pushing him off the rocky path.

He stilled.

"That the kite you're fighting at Festival?" Norio said.

Chash kept walking. He didn't want trouble.

"Hey, I wanted to talk to you for a minute."

What could Norio want? Chash stopped.

"Just thought I'd say I was sorry. About the other day. The fruit." Norio edged closer. The wind had picked up and the edges of the kite on Chash's back flapped as if they longed to take flight.

"Fine," Chash muttered.

"Show me your kite. I want to see how you sew." Norio gestured to Chash's back.

"No, I don't think so." Fliers never let their competitors look at their kites this close to Festival — opponents could spot a kite's weaknesses and plan for it.

"Come on." Norio reached for the kite, grasping the edge.

Surprised, Chash turned. The fabric ripped and Norio stumbled back with rounded eyes.

Chash's chest tightened so hard that it hurt.

Turquoise silk fluttered in Norio's fist.

"No." Chash's hand trembled as he twisted his arm around, trying to feel the kite on his back. Its spine hung crooked, the edge of it snapped and slapping against his side.

"I can show you how to fix—"

"You? You're going to show me how to fix a kite? You can't even mend your own tunic."

"I don't have to. My mother does that kind of work." Norio's lip curled.

"Only because you're too stupid to figure out a pattern."

"At least I don't sit around at night and sew dresses with my grandmother." There it was. The same taunt Norio had been using since they were children. Besu told Chash to turn his back on an insult and walk away — that fighting didn't make a man — but she didn't understand. She couldn't. Over and over and over — it didn't matter what he said or where they were — Norio never stopped. Wouldn't stop unless Chash made him stop.

Chash jumped at Norio. The two men tumbled to the ground, the kite frame cracking as they rolled over dust and broken bricks.

Splintered wood dug into Chash's shoulders, but he kicked at Norio, sending the other man sprawling. Norio's hand missed him, punching the air by his face.

Chash's fist plunged into Norio's stomach.

He sucked his breath in as Norio choked.

Norio's next punch connected with Chash's jaw, smacking him backward on the ground. A flash of jagged black and white squares cut across his vision before it cleared, leaving his neck stiff and his head throbbing.

Norio stood up, brushing off his trousers. He hunched over, wheezing, and offered Chash a hand up. When Chash didn't take it, Norio shrugged.

"Suit yourself." He kicked at the dirt by Chash's head as he walked away.

That night, while Besu snored on her sleeping mat, Chash spread out the pieces of his kite. The shaved bamboo of the spine and spars had splintered and broken, and the silk was ripped and torn. Earth and red brick dust was ground into the fabric, muting its many colors. Bits of waterhorse hair glistened, each one a reminder of a precious hour spent combing the beach at dawn. Even if there had been the spare money or material to craft a new kite, there was no more time.

What would it feel like to control a firebird's golden chains? To do something more than haul fish out of the ocean? Chash picked up his needle. The material rustled against his skin as what he envisioned began to take shape. He stitched and cut, using thread to create his own pictures, embroidering birds and fire against the fabric. When he finished, he leaned back in his chair.

It was no longer a kite, but it might make someone a nice hat.

He buried his head in his hands.

His grandmother shuffled to the table. Her hand warmed the back of his neck as she stroked his hair.

"I thought I'd win this year," Chash blurted.

"You still can. Look." She moved, the frigid night air quickly flooding the space her hand vacated. He lifted his head.

On the table was a kite like no other Chash had seen. It was shaped like a swan and made of the palest pink silk. Its huge wings spanned the width of his own arms. He picked it up, marveling at the tiny perfect stitches that bound it to its frame. Each bar was carefully carved, and the maker had whittled each end to a point before sliding it into tiny pockets of fabric to hold it securely. A tail of thin white ribbons floated from the end of the kite.

"You can't get spidersilk anymore," Besu said. "It was part of my dowry."

"It's beautiful." It took hours to make so many stitches so evenly — hundreds of hours spent on a kite for a woman not allowed to fly it.

"I wanted to fight kites when I was younger. They didn't allow it then. I was supposed to want to be a wife and a mother, but I didn't want any of those things. When Nemh — your mother — married, I thought I was free, but then your parents died. That night that the firebirds saved the village, I left you in the caves with Manu." Besu pressed her hands over her heart, folding her fingers into one another. "I told him I was going back to look for others, but I lied."

"Why didn't you go?" Chash asked.

"I went home first. All your things were still spread out on the floor. A blanket, an old pile of sticks you played with. A broken sandal I was mending..." Besu spoke as if his old toys were there in the room between them. "I saw those things and tried to imagine my life without you. I couldn't. So, I took the kite, and I came back."

He bowed his head.

Besu touched his shoulder, then crooked a finger under his chin to lift it.

"It was a good choice. I live on in you." She leaned back in her chair. "Since we don't have wings, we make kites. I want you to have this. My wings."

"I can't, Grandmother."

"I want to see the kite fights. To see you fight."

"You're not that old," Chash protested.

"It's my eyes that are weak, not my heart." Besu patted his hand, gesturing to the kite. "The strings... I wove them from flame reed and seagrass." He picked up a string, gingerly at first, expecting it to be coated with broken glass or woven around hidden razors. It was thick but there was no sign of hidden danger.

"There's no glass — how were you going to cut the other kites down?"

"I wasn't. I've seen sixty Festivals and at every one, there's far more wounds than winners. Look at your hands." Besu shook her head. "The last kite in the air is the one that wins. If the rope was strong and I was clever, I thought I wouldn't need to hurt anything or anyone. Maybe I could win by enduring."

His finger ran up and down the ridges of the cord. It smelled like salt and ash, just as a firebird would. *His* firebird.

"You can put your own strings on it. No need to indulge an old woman's dreams." Besu rose, patting his shoulder before lumbering back to bed. He nodded, but he tucked the string into his pocket.

On the morning of the festival, the sky was cloudless, and the breeze was light. Besu took Chash's arm and chattered away at him like a small bird as they climbed up into the wagon that traveled the road up the coastline towards the docks of Cantara. The two of them packed in with six women, most of them wearing dresses he had made. He cradled Besu's kite in his arms, wrapped up tightly in an old blanket, careful not to bump it into one of the women as the wagon rocked and swayed down the old dirt road that led away from Santao.

"Besu, I'm so glad you're coming with us to Festival this year. My husband told me that he's never seen me look so fine before." One of the women preened, holding out her arms to showcase the tiny leaves that Besu and Chash had sewn across the length of the dress. Her comments provoked a round of admiration and competition.

For once, Besu smiled and didn't comment on what the women wore, other than to thank them for their praise. Her face turned up, toward the sun, as the others sang a traveling song. Chash leaned back against the wagon's rail and let the road rock him to sleep.

A light jab woke him.

"You slept the whole way," Besu chided. With a groan, Chash rose and handed her the bundle with the kite. He hopped down from the wagon, then gently helped Besu and the kite to the ground. The faint scent of cinnamon and sugar wafted from one of the street stalls as a bee buzzed past him. No doubt it had escaped from one of the beekeepers who came to festivals, shouting about charmed honey and wax. Such small magic was costly and outlawed in the kite fights, though it was always rumored that some fighter had charmed their strings.

"Pickled limes." Besu clutched his arm. Her nose poked ahead of her feet as she sniffed the air, turning first in one direction, then another. "Where are they?"

"That way." Chash frowned. *She should be able to see that stall. It's just a few steps away.* He took the kite from her and cradled it underneath his other arm, not daring to strap it on his back.

"The sun's almost to the top of the sky. We need to hurry to the kite field." He tried to walk a little faster, but Besu struggled to keep up, squinting and wobbling with uncertainty as she walked. He slowed his pace to let her lean on him and they made their way past the longest pier in Cantara, ignoring the cries and shouts of vendors. He stopped a few times, marveling at the tiny ash-dragons that zipped between the cooking fires, and the mechanical birds that called out endearments to them both from jeweled cages. Besu jabbed a bony finger in his side, and they continued.

The field was full this year. There was a platform at the edge of it, built high above the low pastures where the fighters assembled, attaching strings, and making quick, desperate repairs. The Festival of Wings was one of twelve held around the country. Every year, Cantara prepared for the emperor's arrival, but he chose to honor richer cities. To save face, the villagers claimed that the firebirds hated the sea, and the emperor didn't travel without them.

Chash and Besu went to the field just as the crier shouted for the fighters to line up. The wind blew hard, and a few kites shot upward, their owners hurrying to wind the string back on the spool.

"Be careful," he told Besu. "Not everyone watches where their strings fly." She nodded and he realized how ridiculous it was to caution a woman who had lived through wars and floods and years of starvation. Carefully unfolding the kite, Chash removed the spools of kite strings that he carried in his pockets, wrapped up tightly in leather. Besu stared out at the field, her eyes unblinking.

She should have gotten her chance. His stomach tightened. It was an accident of birth and time that he stood here to fight using the kite that she made so many years ago.

The kite field was a battleground in miniature — the youngest fighters yelped as they slit fingers on razored strings. Men and a few women raised their kites, brilliantly colored rectangles, diamonds, and six-sided shapes thrashing in the wind. Shouts of anger and gasps of frustration echoed throughout the crowd as fighters fought for control of their lines, bringing each kite into the air for battle.

When he turned to Besu, her face was relaxed. It was then that he understood, watching her gaze toward the sounds of fighting, rather than the kites flapping in the wind. *She can't see. Not enough to watch me fly her kite.*

I'll tell her what's happening. Make this the best fight she's ever been to. Chash knelt to fasten the lines, fighting back the sudden tightness in his throat. Someone tapped his shoulder and he looked up.

"Hey," Norio said.

"Hey, Norio." Chash didn't stand to greet him.

"Norio, I haven't seen you since you were standing at your auntie Lia's knee," Besu said. "Come here and give this old woman a hug." She smiled and gave Norio a squeeze. "Chash is getting ready for the fights — and why aren't you? Your mother says you've been practicing for weeks."

"I am — I mean, I have been." Norio said. "Could I have a minute with Chash?"

Besu looked at Chash, and he nodded.

"Well, it was good talking with you." She patted Norio's arm before weaving toward the chatter of relatives gathered near one of the younger fighters.

"What do you want?" Chash asked, watching Besu to make sure she found her way to her friends.

"I just want to say I'm sorry about the kite. About what I said."

"You've been saying it for years. Why do you care now?"

"My mother found out about our fight. She told me about the day the firebirds came to our village... I don't remember it and she never would tell me anything about the war before." Norio stared down at the ground. "Besu saved our family. I knew we owed her a debt, but I never knew why." He knotted his hands together. "Mother wants me to offer you my kite."

"What about you?" Chash asked. He'd imagined getting an apology for years. Now that he had it, he didn't feel vindicated. He just felt sad.

"I don't want to give it up," Norio admitted. "But I'm the one who broke your kite. I'm the one who has to make it right, not my family."

If I take his kite, he can't fight. Part of him wanted to agree and take the kite so Norio would regret the hundreds of small insults that rested between them. But how could he face Besu if he won the battle by taking away Norio's ability to fight?

"Besu's losing her sight," he said. "She asked me to fly her kite. It might be the last time she sees the fights. Keep your kite — we'll meet in the air."

"I knew she was going blind, but..." Norio stopped, then reached out and offered Chash his hand. "Thank you." The two men shook hands and wished each other luck. Chash picked up his spool again as Besu came back to their spot, slowly navigating across the field.

If I win, what happens to her? There was glory in going to war. It would change him into a man. His fingers hesitated over the shattered glass strings. *But what kind of man would I be?* He was tired of fighting insults with fists. It felt good to forgive.

He set his own spool down, ignoring the blood on his fingertips. Besu was nearly blind — to control a string coated in crushed glass would challenge her. He looped the cord she had made around a new spool, then fastened it to the spine of the kite.

"Come." He took Besu's arm. The crier shouted, warning spectators away from the fight. The field emptied out as men, women, and children retreated toward the platform, forming a small crowd around its outer perimeter.

"Only the fighters are allowed to stay on the field until the kites are in the air," Besu chided him.

"I know." Chash pulled her to the center of the field, ignoring the confused faces of the other fighters. She peered at him, then at the line that the fighters had made with their bodies. He pushed the spool into her hands. "I used your strings. I'll help you guide it."

A horn blew in the distance and the line broke, each fighter running with their kite until the wind caught it, taking it aloft. Chash and Besu ran last, his hand over hers as they hobbled together, four clumsy legs stumbling over grass and mud.

"We won't win," she shouted, laughing.

"That's not true!" The kite had soared up to the clouds, its silken wings spread high. They stopped, holding the spool in both their hands. Besu's head swiveled and finally stopped, but she wasn't looking in the right direction. Another kite snaked toward theirs, shaped like a red box. The lines of it glittered when the sun caught it.

She whispered, her head down, "I can't see it. All I see is clouds."

"Then I'll tell you what's happening." Chash kept one hand steady on hers and helped her spin the spool, pulling the string taut. The red kite neared. It swooped down toward the swan, and he reached out with his free hand to keep the line steady.

"I feel something," she said.

"There's another kite near us. It's red and the corner is a bit crinkled. I think it's paper." The swan caught the wind, its wings billowing out with the breeze, as the red kite swirled, dancing on the breeze. The sparkling glass lines drew his eye to the red kite's owner. *Maken. She almost won last year.* Chash's grip slackened on the spool and Besu faltered.

The string on their swan slipped, loosening as the red kite dove.

"It's coming for us. Pull, Grandmother!"

He grabbed the line above the spool, trying to yank it back, but he was too late.

She pulled just as the red kite sliced the air, sliding down under the swan's string. Maken yanked her spool hard and fast, snapping Besu's string in one swift motion. The spidersilk rustled in the air, teasing Chash as the wind caught it and spun it into a spiral before dropping it to the ground.

He still held the line just above the spool. It tugged at his fingers. Besu wound, then slackened the spool, trying to keep control of a kite she couldn't see. A kite that no longer flew. She had wanted to be a kite fighter so long, just to lose her battle in its first moments of flight. Chash couldn't bear it.

"You did it," he said, hoping that the sound of his voice wouldn't betray the lie. Her face was lifted, but there was no sign that she didn't believe him. She knew that the kite had fallen — she had to know — and yet, the joy on her face was so pure that Chash wanted to hold it there just a little longer.

His eyes stung as the red kite pulled away, caught by another wind. A dragon-shaped kite slammed into its middle.

One of the other kite fighters came up to them. Emi was young, but she bore the marks of a fighter already, the tip of her pinkie wrapped in bloodied cotton. Her eyes met Chash's, but she didn't say anything about the broken string in his fingers. Kites still dove and slashed through the sky overhead, circling spectators and fighters like angry eagles.

"There's about three kites above us now — can you see them?" he asked Besu.

"No." Both of her hands gripped the spool now. He moved his fingers up the line to keep the string taut and preserve the illusion that the kite still flew.

Emi furrowed her eyebrows. He mouthed, *Hush.*

"You just caught one," he said. A narrow blue diamond slashed at Norio's kite swiftly. Norio mopped his forehead with the back of his sleeve, squinting at the sky as his body hunched forward.

"It's the red kite!" Emi said. "Your bird — it just wrapped around it and yanked. And now it's falling to the ground."

A kite was falling but it wasn't red. Norio held strong despite the sweat beading on his forehead, his knuckles clenched around the handles of his spool. His red kite lifted, then neatly slit the blue diamond's string as it descended through the air. Spectators wandered toward the fighters, pointing and whispering as one kite after another fell. Emi whooped at the sky.

Chash fought the impulse to let go of the string.

"I see a blue kite," his voice wavered as Norio's aunt Lia came barreling toward the three of them. *She'll stop this — Lia has a mouth big enough to talk for three people.*

"Chash, you'll put Besu to sleep talking that way. Besu, do you remember Aso? That's his blue kite you've almost got," Lia pushed Emi out of the way to stand next to the old woman. She looked at Chash and explained, "That night your grandmother led us to the caves, Aso wouldn't go — he said we shouldn't take orders from a woman. Until a firebird spat ashes right next to him. I never saw him run so hard."

"I never liked him," Besu chuckled.

"Hold that line tight then — that wind's pulling him around like a baby bird," Lia advised. "Isn't he a little old to be out here? Kite fighters should be young if they're going to battle for the Emperor."

Chash gave her a look.

"I never knew you sewed kites, Besu. All these years and you never said a thing," Lia said. A woman Chash vaguely recognized from previous festivals had stopped to watch them. She glanced at Chash, then at Besu's hands, and smiled before waving over a cluster of elders who all looked as old as his grandmother. She pointed at Besu, saying something Chash couldn't hear.

"What was the point when I couldn't fly them?" Besu asked. "My line feels slack — what's happened?"

"The wind — it's slowing." A man picked up the story that Lia had continued. The small group that had gathered around them was growing, some faces familiar, others simply curious. Why were they all here, watching a woman with a downed kite when they could be seeing the end of the fight? How was he going to end the story before the fight did?

Chash swallowed and strengthened his grip on the cut line, yanking it up suddenly to mimic the feeling of attack.

"Chash! What's happening?" Besu called.

But before he could speak, the crowd spoke for him.

"The green is coming for you — you'd better dart to the left —"

"Besu, do you remember me from the flood in Chansec? You brought all those women from Santao and cooked for us when we were all so tired from rebuilding the houses. I still have the blanket you made for Shenshi."

"Oh, oh — I think your cords are too strong for Tado's kite — he'd best catch some wind. Besu, remember when you had to help Amna drag him home after he drank all that suls —"

"There goes the dragon! We'd better not lose you to the emperor, Besu."

The words tumbled over one another, as people from three villages competed to tell the story of Besu's kite fight, interspersing it with the memories they shared of Besu and Chash's youth. The remaining kites swooped overhead, diving and tearing at razor strings, but as each kite fell, its owner came over to weave the story of their own kite into the tale of the grandmother's conquests.

Norio was the last.

His hands were bloody, his tunic damp with sweat. Chash's heart hiccupped when the other man stopped in front of them, holding the red kite that had claimed victory. *He just came to brag.* He let go of the string. Besu began winding the spool up, then stopped as she realized there was nothing left to wind.

"Grandmother," Norio said, and Chash turned away. "Hold out your hands."

The spool dropped from her fingers as she extended her hands, palms up, to Norio. The man knelt in the mud, gently resting the red kite on her skin.

"Our kites tangled. It was a hard fight. When our strings came together, I couldn't tell which one broke first. But mine hit the ground before yours. I honor you, Grandmother." Norio and Chash's eyes met. Chash smiled first.

"Thank you, but I cannot accept," Besu said. She patted Norio's cheek and chuckled. "I'm a bit old to join the army, don't you think?"

"Besu won! She won!" A roar came up from the crowd as a young child shouted the words, jumping up and down, caught up in the story that the village had woven. Emi grabbed Chash and wrapped her arms around his chest. He stumbled backward and hugged her back, then pulled Besu into the hug as well. Besu's answering laughter was as warm as the sun but ten times closer.

Besu shook her head at him as the three of them broke apart.

She turned to Chash. "It was a beautiful story you told me."

Her words hushed the crowd and they dispersed, people scattering across the field to pluck shreds of torn silk from the grass and collect fallen shards of glass.

"I just wanted you to win," Chash swallowed, his throat dry. A great wave of emotion welled up inside of him for this woman who had made him what he was. And he wasn't a warrior.

"Your heart is kind, but I worry that I've failed you." Besu sighed. "You didn't have to lie. I wasn't smiling because I was winning. I was just happy to share your dream. I should never have asked you to give that up."

He reached for her hands and took them in his. Her fingers matched his own, with knuckles a little too big for her hands, and curved, even nails. *These hands and everything they've taught me…this is who I am. Who I want to be. That man doesn't need a war to be proud.*

"The village loves you, Grandmother. I love you," he said. "The emperor has enough men to fight for him. Maybe it's time more of us became tailors."

"If I had someone to help with the dresses, I might be able to sew a kite once in a while," Besu leaned against him as they walked through the field of battered kites. "Teach you a few things about flying them."

"What? Train your competitor?"

Besu swatted at him, and they laughed. Chash thought of the days that lay ahead of them both — of saying goodbye to the work that he hated and devoting himself to pattern, color, and thread.

Since we don't have wings, we make kites. His grandmother's words came back to him and Chash smiled. There was more than one way to fly.

See Gwen Whiting's story "Since We Don't Have Wings" online at Metaphorosis.
If you liked it, leave a comment. Authors love that!
Remember to subscribe to our e-mail updates so you'll know when new stories are posted.

About the story

The world and ideas of "Since We Don't Have Wings" have their origins in a few different places. As I was writing early drafts of this piece during the pandemic, I was part of a roleplaying group that had started using the Ryuutama system. If you've never played the game, the best description of it I've heard is "Miyazaki meets Oregon Trail". Though "Wings" isn't really connected to that campaign or characters, the game inspired me to think about fantasy on a small scale. Much of the fantasy I grew up with focuses on a singular hero or sometimes group of heroes going on long journeys to do heroic things. What does heroism look like when you never leave your home?

I've also been fortunate to have been raised by and around generations of strong women and with men who support those women. For much of my life, however, people outside the family have questioned and sometimes challenged that dynamic because various individuals didn't follow gender "norms". Chash was chosen as the protagonist of this story as a way of rejecting the idea both of the "hero" and because I wanted to show that growing into manhood doesn't have to look like going to war or proving one's self through physical action. Sometimes, the heroes are the ones who stay. This is a theme that's also reflected in Besu, his grandmother, but it takes a different form because her choices (or perhaps, lack of) were different.

A question for the author

Q: What is the hardest part of writing for you?

A: The hardest part of writing for me is often knowing when to stop. It's very easy to get caught up, not only when writing in the world that I've created, but also when building the world itself. I enjoy research more than I probably should, and often look around at ideas, events, and people of the past when brainstorming short stories. It interests me to take what was and instead imagine what could have been.

About the author

A lifelong Pacific Northwesterner, Gwen Whiting spends her days working at museums and her evenings scribbling out one story or another. When Gwen isn't writing or working, she's spending time with her family, reading a book, or dabbling in activities inspired by whatever project she's working on. She's tried everything from belly dance to basket weaving and is currently researching beekeeping.

gwen-whiting.com, @Gwen_Whiting

Time, Wolf, Emit, Flow

Anna Madden

Time watched a dust storm approaching fast. At her side, Wolf whined, and she stroked his moss-green fur to calm her own worries as much as his.

The rest of the pack darted for cover, their movements blurs of sage and evergreen. Younger packmates reshaped their inner light into different forms, including wolves, but also hare and elk and coyote. Age brought attachment, a fear of change—a rigidity. Time wore the strangest form of all: two-legged, covered by a gown of pale lichen, a leafy mane falling midway down her back. It was a form that had once belonged to the Shapers alone. Wolf complained at her choice, though he curled into Time's side readily enough each eve to warm her almost furless hide.

The sky darkened. The pack's territory was no longer blessed by the light of the Shapers, the winds death-still. Dust fell from leaden clouds overhead and collected atop the plains. The hoary flakes smoldered near flats of obsidian rock bed. Fragile switchglass—with its crystal-like leaves—grew between the cracks. As dust accumulated to a thick powder, the land turned the color of aged muzzles, the ground opaque and ugly.

"It's useless," Time said to Wolf. "We'll never finish the wind-maker."

"Don't say that," Wolf said, his voice husky. "Your design can be replicated, used to stir the winds and open the Light Gate. The Shapers' light will return. We'll survive this lean season, same as others."

Time stood still. She knew Wolf spoke in dreams rather than full truths. He didn't smell the wounds she carried. Time dwelled on the pack's losses, and the transience from green to gray across the land. She prided herself on her mind, her focus, but lately the collecting dust felt suffocating, desolation piling like leaf litter and unanswered questions.

The pack's dependence on the Shapers had made them weak. There was too much the pack had never been told or taught. The dust storms were worse and worse. The Shapers had kept the dust from accumulating, but they'd left, abandoning this world to a never-ending season of neglect.

Time's back ached, strained from gathering metals and broken glass to be ready before the storm hit. Dust flurried. It stung her eyes and scratched her ever-dry throat.

Wolf dug through a pile of hard-found supplies taken from the mountains' feet and the plains beyond, then picked up a piece of copper in his jaw.

Watching him, Time wiped a film of dust from her eyes. Her sight didn't thank her, only picking up more grit. Time thought of better days, of racing after Wolf, of clean air and laughter and unappreciated sunshine. She didn't run anymore. With the horrid dust in her lungs, polluting her light, she'd wilted.

Time coughed and surveyed her work area. It was a mess, exposed, set on the eastern side of the dust-covered steppes where the Light Gate stood like a dead thing. It was an entrance to the river of light, its currents unknown.

The gate was ancient. It had been built by the Shapers, made of metal and glass, as forbidding as the dusk and ungiving as winter.

Around it, there were piles of sorted copper, zinc, and tin. There were sheets of broken glass and a jar of clear flux, mixed by her own hand, used to clean the metal before soldering it. The building materials of the Shapers. Time dared to build as they had, so the pack avoided her, their gazes splintered with distrust.

All but Wolf.

Something poked her shoulder. She glanced over. Wolf had jabbed her with the copper gripped in his muzzle. His fur was bright green, the ends sparkling like dew on fern leaves. She took the metal from him and debated on its placement, trying one spot, then another. Her dull, tired fingers worked the copper around the edges of a large glass shard. It stood on its side, propped with a bit of spare metalwork next to the wind-maker's frame, angled to catch the sun. She had constructed it near the Light Gate so the wind it made could unlock the currents the Shapers had left before they closed the way behind them.

"No more copper," Time said before Wolf grabbed another piece between his sharp teeth. "We have enough to solder the blades and the tail. After, we'll attach the base." She coughed again.

"You'll finish it," Wolf said, his voice forced brightness, his tail wagging. "I know you will."

Time looked at the Light Gate and imagined all the answers it might provide, once opened. She tried to be like Wolf. She tried to hope.

Three days later, the storm ruled, and dust piled higher. It wasn't an optimal condition for work, but Time wouldn't risk waiting. The rest of their packmates hid in what cover they could find, braving the open at midday to hunt light while Time continued the work.

Youths had started wearing the forms of nomadic grazers. Cattle and horse and caribou—with muzzles, strong hooves, horns, and thick fur—better to trek through the banks of unstable, layered dust. To graze the muted switchglass struggling to grow despite it.

A scatter of hoofprints circled the supply piles. Scavengers had approached the Light Gate itself, touching its dusty edges with paw and snout.

The sun was shrouded by a thick gray veil. Time finished the placements and started soldering. The metals were bonding well. Wolf kept close to her elbow, wiping dust away with a flux-covered paw. Time held her soldering iron with expertise.

The next glass shard was in easy reach, resting atop the wind-maker's frame. As she adjusted the next joint, she foolishly leaned too far. Her knees pressed against the loose piece. The glass wavered, then tipped downward.

"Wolf, grab it quick!"

He snapped at it, his teeth grazing the too-smooth surface, but the piece fell, its weight carrying it down. It shattered, the pieces ricocheting against the wind-maker's skeleton.

Time eyed her supply pile, but the remaining glass shards she'd gathered with Wolf were needed as suncatchers to power the wind-maker. How could she have been so stupid? She squeezed her eyes shut.

"I'll go," Wolf said, stretching his front legs. "There's some to the north, I think, where we've hunted before." She opened her mouth, about to tell him she would go too, but then he growled softly. "You stay," he said. "Save your strength."

She almost argued, but the words forming on her tongue belonged to a Shaper, arrogant, dipped in greater knowledge—or the appearance of it.

Looking down, Time sighed. "I'll clean up this mess."

When Wolf returned, he dragged a heavy glass shard as perfect as the first, but it had claimed something in return. He shook his fur, which had lost its shine, and she could make out light-seeping cuts upon his paws. He panted, his tongue hanging out of his mouth. She thanked the Shapers' light he wasn't hurt worse, but her eyes watered when she heard him muffle a cough, pressing his muzzle into his fur-clad chest.

What would she do without him, if he faded, lacking the strength to continue?

Time jerked a hand through her leafy hair and cleared her throat. She rearranged her collection of metals. "Let's get back to work."

With the second attempt, she didn't rush. She built extra supports for the wind-maker, then Wolf helped her lift the replacement shard into place. He braced it while she soldered the glass to the frame before attaching the blades and the tail. When Time was certain nothing would fall off or shatter, she squared her shoulders and joined the final seams with solder.

They set up their array of suncatchers next.

The angles of their light brightened a patch of tall switchglass despite its buried roots, returning treasured hues of olive and sage. Time tried not to cough as she directed Wolf, whose deft paws tilted each glass piece a different angle to best capture the sunlight. When they had finished, Time and Wolf pushed the wind-maker onto four silver feet.

"Turn it, a hair more to the left," Time said, motioning impatiently, eager. She had started to let herself hope this might work. "Be careful. It's not quite level, and if it falls—" She swallowed. "We'll adjust the suncatchers as needed afterward."

Wolf groaned, his back taut, his strong jaw clamped over metal and glass in an awkward bite. He tugged hard, his claws cutting lines into the dust beneath him. The wind-maker's base creaked as it pivoted. Wolf tended the suncatchers again, nudging them with his nose while Time wheezed into the inside of her elbow.

She steadied herself against the wind-maker. Its metal had a mirror-like quality, capturing her dull likeness. In memory, her complexion was bright, as vivid as new spring stems.

Time shook her hair back. It rustled dryly to her ankles. "I look awful."

Wolf nuzzled her knees. Once, he'd have agreed with her, and tried to persuade her to try another form. "The wind-maker will work," he said instead.

Time eyed Wolf, long-limbed, his ears cupped in her direction, and fur still dappled by light despite his developing cough. Sometimes, she wondered at his forbearance, at his willingness to aid her. Wolf had stopped hunting with the pack because of her. He said it was his choice, the same as hers to wear the form of a Shaper. Even now, he offered her a toothy smile.

She doubted him. What did he see in her? A faded thing. A memory of light, her remaining days as fragile and thin as withering switchglass. Time dipped her chin.

"Look!" Wolf said, his ears swiveling toward the wind-maker's blades. His light flared moss-bright within his fur. "It's working."

Time watched the wind-maker. The suncatchers fed it steady light, and the blades turned, slowly at first but then faster. The wind stirred, waking seeded secrets, finishing the sequence implemented in all Shaper builds.

The Light Gate glowed, faint at first, widening, flickering; the blink of a great yellow eye. Its opening revealed the river of light: its flow the radiance of the dawn, the warmth of high summer. Its brilliance glinted off the wind-maker. Dust sparkled.

Time stepped closer to the Light Gate, enchanted by its gilded beauty, its bright currents.

Too late, she realized its danger. Her thoughts shifted from a soft glow of wonder to a searing fear of something powerful and unknowable.

The Light Gate seemed to breathe in, hot, arid, tasting of burning hair. Her inner light crackled from between her lips, her skin. She struggled to step back even as the river of light pulled her in. A withered leaf plucked from the stem, falling.

"Wolf!" Time cried.

She thought she heard him howl back.

Was this death, then? Time panicked. She wasn't ready to die. She wanted to feel the sun's true warmth, and to run fast beside Wolf once more. She wasn't ready. She wasn't finished with her work yet.

The sky disappeared. In its place there was the too-bright light of the river. Wings flapped high above. She heard them above the gold-flecked river. As unformed as mist, barely outlined, with lace-like plumes. Feathers grazed Time's right cheek, then flapped away.

The air cooled, misty and salt-licked, and the sky returned.

It was the wrong color.

"Emit, is that you? Emit?"

Time stirred. A light hovered near her. Blurry-eyed, she couldn't make out the familiar shape of Wolf. Time blinked, then blinked again. There were no greens to comfort her, nor grays to worry over.

"Everything's the wrong color," Time mumbled, rubbing her eyes. As she took a breath, she realized her throat was clear, the air refreshed, the sky dust-free. She stood quickly. A swelling, rippling sea surged at her feet. Edges of metal and glass rose from the water. The shapes weren't natural, but sculpted. It couldn't be, but it had to be: the Light Gate.

It was in ruin, half-claimed by deep waters.

Time bit her bottom lip to stop from crying out in defeat. She remembered the wind-maker clearly, and the burning air as she fell into the river of light. But the pain had washed away. This didn't feel like death. There was too much fear in her heart for this to be the end.

Time was uncertain of all but Wolf's loss at her side, the realization worse than any number of dust storms. The wind-maker had been intended to coax the winds back, to open the Light Gate and return the light of the Shapers to the pack's territory, and maybe, hope against hope, to clear the dust storms for good.

Opening the Light Gate hadn't been meant to send her elsewhere, far from Wolf, their pack, their shared joys and despairs.

Something rubbery pecked at her fingertips.

"Emit?" the same stranger's voice asked, calling her that backward name again. "Why did you change your light into these?"

Time sat up and looked at her palms, trying to center herself by focusing on something familiar in a world reshaped. "I—my name is Time. I prefer having hands so I can build things."

As she spoke, Time looked up and met two jewel-like eyes, their brilliant and unexpected shade reminding her she wasn't alone. This wasn't a Shaper, but not a packmate either. "Who are you?" she asked.

"What a funny joke," the stranger with beautiful eyes said, a playfulness in his tone. "I am Flow, of course." His chosen form was a dolphin. A streamlined body with a round head and a tall dorsal fin.

Flow blew water from his blowhole, then broke into song:
Mountains gleam silver,
the sky drips of gold honey,
but none are my blue.

Time looked at his flippers and tilted her head. Flow opened his beak wider, smiling brightly, though imperfectly—crookedly. Wolf smiled like that. Time was heartened by the echoed expression of it. Flow turned and splashed her with his tail fluke. He flickered into the form of a bright-scaled fish, then back to a dolphin.

"Come on, Emit. Let's test out this ugly new form of yours. Race you to the next wave! Loser eats a mouthful of bubbles."

Time pushed aside thoughts of Wolf, burying the guilt and the panic, centering herself in the calm of analyzing a problem. A cold focus that pushed away emotion. Like a dream, this place felt unreal, and perhaps that made its unusualness less frightening.

What had happened? The logical part of her said she'd done as she'd meant: opening the Light Gate, but then she'd fallen into the river of light, its currents bringing her into unknown territory. A journey which in theory, she might reverse.

But who was Emit? Why wasn't Flow's friend on this side of the gate? A mystery with complexities that forced Time to realize the truth: she was no Shaper. The cracks in her focus splintered, and despair sent a chill down her spine.

She was nothing.

No better than a speck of dust for all her grasping to be more.

Time wanted desperately to run, to put as much distance between herself and her failings as possible. She sprang forward, her light-filled feet keeping atop the water's surface. It felt like she was in control as she tried to escape.

And she had not run in a very long time.

The urge to flee took over reason and purpose, primal and wild.

Time wasn't sure where she had come to, but the sea was beautiful, full of happier memories than the pack's dusty plains. Its waves were untiring and graceful, and the winds overhead didn't sputter or sigh. If Wolf were beside her, she thought, all would be well.

And there it was: the heartache. The despair. The emptiness that could not be filled, nor outrun no matter how light-strong she might have become.

Time followed closely behind Flow's tail fluke. Like Wolf, he was faster than her. If he got too far ahead, she'd have no one.

She'd be completely, totally alone.

"Slow down," she cried out, though when she tried harder, her light-strong legs moved atop the seawater almost as swiftly as his fins within it. "Please. Where are we going?"

Flow slowed, letting her draw abreast to his dorsal fin. He splashed her with a wave. "To the Crack, Emit. Where else?"

As they traveled, Flow sang to her of blue things. There were sapphires, asters, indigo dye, and blueberries. There were morpho butterflies, jays, and bluebells. Time could not keep track of them all, nor did she want to, for it was only a reminder of how little she understood.

"So many," Time said in bitterness, her breaths deep, her calves burning. "I've never heard of some."

Flow laughed, the sound a bubbling spring, his smile open and sweet. "I love to play games with you."

"You talk like we're old friends."

He looked over at her with a hurt expression. "Aren't we?"

Time swallowed back frustration, though she longed to tell him he knew nothing of her: that he was too carefree, that Emit was gone, lost. He should be worried.

But if she told him that, wouldn't she only offer him pain? Perhaps it was better to be ignorant. To be unaware.

She caught her reflection in the water. Her long hair parted to the opposite side from her usual style. Still, she looked like herself, only mirrored. And she brimmed with light. Her skin reflected the sea's brilliant blue.

She remembered a winged form in the passage of the Light Gate, bringing a frown to her lips. Had it been a Shaper she'd seen? Was Emit one? Perhaps if she could find a Shaper, this mess would have a solution.

Looking around, Time hunted for signs of the Shapers. She had questions, and there were answers to be found in this place, surely.

They reached what Flow called the Crack.

Time's feet splashed to a halt. She almost wept, for the sea had been parted like an unhealed wound, and the water fell into its trap. A waterfall carried the sea down and away. Had this place been broken by the Shapers' absence too?

Strangers wearing forms of tarpon and sailfish and gannets had gathered around it, playing within the frothy waters, jumping and flying along its girth. These kin of Flow's weren't Shapers.

The sea floor looked the same dark shade of obsidian as the plains of her home, where the pack's territory stretched. Strong rock, not easily injured. One hand kept flying strands of hair out of Time's mouth. It was no longer green or leafy. It streamed across her face, its roots damp.

She stepped forward. "I could fix this. The two halves can be brought together and sealed. I'd need materials, metal to solder together, but then the water wouldn't run off like this."

Flow snorted. "Water is not meant to stay in one place. It would feel trapped if it did."

"I—" Time didn't understand. Wouldn't the sea drain away, eventually? Flow seemed untroubled.

Time exhaled. The Shapers weren't here, their scent trail nonexistent. She pictured her wind-maker. It had proven itself as dangerous as her own curiosity. Should she leave things be for once, for fear of making them worse? Maybe Wolf was glad she wasn't around anymore, making messes. Breaking things. Maybe he had rejoined their pack with glee. Her shoulders dipped.

"You've never been a worrier, Emit," Flow said. "Nothing is whole in this world. Life needs a flaw or two."

"I see," she said, but she didn't.

They slept apart. Time curled up on the shore, while Flow floated in gentle waves. The quiet and the doubts that grew stronger in the dark made her heartsick for Wolf unbearable. She tossed and turned, fighting off nightmares. When Time woke, there was a horrible storm raging overhead. Dust flakes sunk into the sea's waters, polluting it.

"No, no," Time cried, trying to scoop bits out with her hands. "Not here too."

A gentle fin touched her left ankle. "What's wrong, Emit?"

Time pointed to the troubled sky. "A storm's here. The dust is already falling."

Flow whistled, then exhaled through his blowhole. "The dust will wash away, as it always does." He swam, circling her. "The Crack will filter it, for the sea carries such impurities there."

"But, the dust..." Time considered trying to explain it all. To convince him she wasn't Emit. To tell Flow of the river of light, her anger at the Shapers. Her fear of never seeing Wolf again. Her hope that she could build as well as the Shapers. Of Wolf and his moss-green fur and the switchglass of the plains.

Maybe the answer was admitting she didn't know what it all meant. That this world was flawed and always would bear the scars of what had come before. She had dabbled in a power she didn't understand, and she'd taken Emit from Flow without even knowing she had the power to do so. There could be no other explanation than that Emit's disappearance correlated with Time's appearance.

The Shapers had left great hardship in their absence. Maybe it was unfair to think they were meant to be perfect, unflawed. Their kind had never held all the answers, and the pack was no different.

Time had thought she could give the world a form she'd shaped—that followed her own rules. She'd lost something of herself by trying to control so much. There was focus in her, and discipline, but she'd lost a spark for life itself, always trying to go back to a season that no longer existed.

Time shook her head. "The Crack isn't a flaw, is it?"

Flow laughed. "You finally see!"

She looked at Flow but only saw Wolf before her, his ears drooped, his light almost spent.

"Shapers guide me," Time said. "There's something I must build, and I'll need your help."

They traveled fast, catching the sun at the Crack. Time tried to explained as best she could about the plains, Wolf, that she knew the chosen form of Emit was a winged one. Flow played along, thinking it all a great game.

Time searched for materials, sometimes catching sight of Flow leaping clear from the water, then flying as a seagull. She noted how the dirty water collected and spilled over the waterfall.

Time dove below the sea's surface and found two treasures. The first was a smooth piece of shell-like glass, quite elegant, slightly dished from the water's touch. The second piece was jagged and sharp.

At her request, they traveled west next, approaching familiar silver peaks which tilted the wrong direction. More and more, this world seemed a reflection of her own. Wolf and Flow, so similar, yet different. Time and Emit, two halves of an unseeable whole.

Did the river of light connect them all, a path between worlds built by the Shapers' hands?

Her mind was lost in a puzzle she'd never solve, and it was easiest to tackle the hardest questions. It pushed aside doubts and confusion. She prioritized thought over heart. Questions consumed her. If there was a Crack in the sea, what was its sibling on the plains? Why was the Light Gate whole in her land, but in ruin within the sea?

Busy hands kept away the loss of Wolf. She used the jagged glass to free zinc, lead, and copper and took her findings to the site of the drowned Light Gate, and began to build a mirror, for she needed a way to reshape what had been worn away.

She needed to remind the gate of its unbroken form by bringing together its pieces, bathed in light. Then she had to convince it to open. She'd used wind to wake the first Light Gate, but should she trust her instincts and try water here instead?

At first, she tried to replicate old techniques, but the bowl-shaped glass was not like her wind-maker's design, nor did she have so skilled a helper as Wolf at her side. The materials wouldn't cooperate without proper tools either. Instead, Time let the glass keep its curved shape and added a thin splinter of the old Light Gate as a stem below it. Flow enjoyed the novelty of it all. He helped her as he could, changing to a pelican, scooping up mouthfuls of saltwater to empty into the basin-like shell.

When the mirror was done, it caught the sunset's rays, dazzling Time's eyes.

Time peeked into that brilliance and saw a glint of green, then gray. It showed her what she sought: a likeness of her truest self, and behind it, dust-smothered plains, more dust falling still. She felt the mirror's edges in her hand's grip, and looked deeply, hungrily. The plains of home spread out before her in the water's reflection. She could see them, hear them.

Wind whistled through switchglass, making it chime. There were scents of fur and dusty sunlight. The wind-maker still spun, and the suncatchers remained in place, their bright rays spotlighting the metal framework. The Light Gate was open, a stream like a vein of gold flowing out, finding a path through rocks, the plains, renewing the land with the Shapers' light. The ground was covered in broken shards, and Wolf was curled up among them, his tail wrapped over his light-bleeding paws. His muzzle had burn marks.

He looked dim. But he wasn't alone.

Another form circled in the air, the outline of wings forming a bruised shadow below. Time had never seen a form that didn't shine. All but invisible, Emit's light held the barest suggestion of form. She twirled, then swooped. Her wings created wind of their own. Though she didn't glow, nor flare, she was faster, fiercer, than anyone Time had ever met.

But light was nothing without control.

Emit flew erratically. She circled over and over in the air. Wolf observed from the ground and whined softly.

In defeat, Emit landed near him, the weak outline of her head tilted to the side as though she listened closely, his breathing guiding her. Her eyes were opaque and clouded, as though they'd been burned away from within. She folded her beautiful, hazy wings against her sides. "Are you toying with me," she asked, angry, "saying the gate is one direction when it's really another?"

Wolf growled. "Keep back."

"You're all bite, no bark," Emit said, her voice yet a raging storm.

"I told you where to fly," Wolf said. "I didn't lie. It's you who can't find the way."

"All I see are shadows and the faintest of shades," Emit said. "This strange place—I can't navigate it. And you—you're no better, bleeding light as you are, with that tail held between your legs."

"I'm waiting for Time," Wolf said, a cough following his words, before his lips peeled back again to show his teeth.

Glints of long plumes shone as Emit shifted closer. "I didn't choose to come here. These gates were meant to die. Rusted traps left by the Shapers to catch us in their ugly teeth."

Wolf's growl turned into a snarl. "The Shapers did not set traps."

"They were hunters, same as you," Emit said.

"Time doesn't think so," Wolf said, lowering his hackles, smiling crookedly. "You'll see. She'll find them, before she returns."

"You remind me of someone, under your fangs," Emit said, doubt edging her voice. "He's probably having too much fun to even notice I'm gone."

Wolf wagged his tail, weakly. "Trust me, no one could ever forget you."

Time stepped back from the mirror and wiped wet eyes. The sky wasn't at full light. She shouldn't lean too close or look too deeply into the mirror's center until all was ready.

Wolf was waiting for her, but if Time left now, Emit wouldn't find her way back. She hadn't asked to be torn from her blue world.

Emit needed a glimpse of something blue, a beacon, to guide her flight home. Time turned her back on the mirror and stepped back into the sea.

Yawning, his beak held comically wide, Flow swam around Time in gentle circles. He flattened his light into triangular pectoral fins, becoming a sleek and graceful manta ray.

"When I look into the mirror again," Time said, "I may not be as I have been of late. I may change."

Flow flicked water at her with his tail when he saw her frown. "I can't get used to that form on you anyway."

"You're one to talk," Time said. "I've never known another to change forms so often as you."

He laughed. "Everyone seems so set on picking a specific one. I can't understand it."

Time dipped below the surface and found a round blue rock the same shade as Flow's jeweled eyes.

Flow slept. Time drifted away in the night, then raced back to her mirror, her heels kicking up water. She hoped to catch the dawn in its basin without Flow's company, for she didn't want to risk him following her.

Time reached her mirror at the site of the Light Gate's ruin. Taking her blue rock, holding it tight, she put her hands over the mirror's rim. She looked into its calm surface where she saw the opposite bank.

"Emit," Time said, her voice rippling the pooled water, "I'm going to try sending you some blue to guide your flight home."

Time dropped the blue rock into the mirror's waters and hoped this gate she'd built would do as planned, creating a ford between both worlds. Holding her breath, she watched the rock skip across the surface of the river of light, carrying the color of the sea to the plains.

It had worked.

She heard a flap of wings. Before fear overtook or reason outwon against what her heart was telling her, Time plunged her face into the mirror's cool waters and fell into the river of light.

The air burned, bright as fire. It stole the light from Time's lips, her hands, her very breath.

Twice as painful as the first time.

She could feel it tearing at her inner light, hungry for it, unmaking her form.

Above, Emit flew, given away by beating wings and the glint of light off her delicate outline.

Time let the currents take her, surrendering to their pull, her world searing, a storm of blinding light. She closed her eyes. One fading leaf floating atop the river of light.

Switchglass chimed, softly. There were scents of musk, of mud, of heated rock. Time opened her eyes to familiar green eyes and a burned muzzle. A wolfish grin, just a tad crooked. His breath was uneven, labored.

"I thought I'd lost you, Time."

"There's still a bit of me left," Time said, her voice weak, raspy. Her hands were cold and numb. Escaped light dissipated into tiny white flames dying around her.

She was a stem with no leaves left to pull free. She looked at Wolf at her side, and yet so far away, drifting further with each shattered breath she gulped down. Long ago, she'd tried other forms, but never that of a wolf. And why not? She'd worn so many others, when she hadn't let the fear of change ripen within.

What she had done once, she could do again.

Slowly, she reached for her inner light, unraveling her already damaged form, matching her breaths to Wolf's.

He crawled closer, his ears flattened against his head, his cracked skin bleeding thin trails of light.

"The pack needs to learn how to tend the wind-maker," Time said. "Its blades will blow the dust through the Light Gate. There is a blue sea on the other side. It will filter it. The glass plains will be wiped green once more. The pack will hunt together again. All will be as it was."

"Why are you telling me all this?" Wolf said, fear a wet rasp in his throat. "Without you, it can never be as it was."

The dawn broke free of the gray clouds. The sun's brightness poured in, bringing hues of green together. The sunlight glistened against the metal of the wind-maker, the profile of the Light Gate.

Time felt her form fall apart. She let it. Her light flowed out in a new current, molding to another shape, falling beneath moss-green fur. It refilled what had seeped from cuts like dripping sap. She knew now what she had always known: their bond was a strength that shone through all other light. More than anything, she wanted Wolf to run across plains once more, through fields of shining switchglass.

She thought of Emit, flying overhead, her inner light bright and true.

Wolf's breaths steadied.

She blinked and looked at the world through Wolf's eyes. The plains rose before her, their collected dust, and the silvery mountains she knew and loved. She felt the air stir against her fur, felt the happiness of her wagging tail, heard herself pant.

I'm here, with you, Time thought to Wolf. *Our light is joined, the dust we'd breathed in shed like an undercoat. Let's make brighter days than these. Promise me.*

Wolf howled. His paws were whole again, the inner light within renewing what had wilted. He pounced forward with his snout pointed the direction of their favorite meadow. His joy was hers. Her days were his. They ran together, as one. Her love for him an eternal memory of light, undimmed.

See Anna Madden's story "Time, Wolf, Emit, Flow" online at Metaphorosis.
If you liked it, leave a comment. Authors love that!
Remember to subscribe to our e-mail updates so you'll know when new stories are posted.

About the story

I make stained glass, and I wanted to capture the magic of that craft in this tale. Glass, light, colors, reflections, and metal brought together. I imagined a rippled blue piece of glass soldered to a leafy green one. Dust can accumulate on glass, dulling its brilliance, so why not have it be the same in this world? And what if beings formed of light existed in this strange realm? What would they look like? These are questions I'd ponder while making suncatchers, cutting glass and arranging it.

I especially adore worldbuilding that feels like something completely of its own, set apart, with an atmosphere that cloaks the reader and inspires imagery of a place unlike anywhere else. When I read stories, I don't often want all the answers to a world's origin or to have every rule explained to me, but a balance is needed nonetheless. This particular story of mine is one that took some effort to find that line. When I stumbled upon the Shapers, that helped a great deal in filling in pieces of necessary lore, but their history is still ancient and shrouded in the unknown.

The heart of this story is Wolf and Time's relationship, though. I love fiction centered on strong friendships, and I've always been fascinated with the idea of befriending a wolf—a connection to something wild and untamable, fierce but beautiful.

A question for the author

Q: Do you prefer your SFF as books or movies?

A: SFF books take me on an internal journey that movies can't often replicate. Written works are fluid, with rich details that I can sow and feed with my own imagination. I crave stories that seem to breathe as they unfold, becoming uniquely mine as I consume them. In *All the Murmuring Bones* by A. G. Slatter, I loved exploring that dark, secret-laden world through Miren's eyes, seeing her thoughts and perspective so intimately. But I certainly enjoy SFF movies, the talents of many creating a few hours of magic. *Dune* blew me away last year even though I knew the story already. I enjoyed the insect-like ornithopters and seeing those colossal sandworms, and I've re-listened to the soundtrack often while writing. Perhaps I should retry answering this question and say SFF books are like strawberry ice cream to me, but that doesn't mean I won't eat mint chocolate chip if it's offered.

About the author

Anna Madden lives in Fort Worth, Texas. She has an English degree from the University of Missouri—Kansas City. In free time she gardens, mountain bikes, and makes stained glass. www.annamadden.com, @anna_madden_

Her Spirit Animal

L.A.W. Butler

Atynleigh leaned into the wind as she pulled her wool shawl closer around her face. The freezing wind was part of her daily trek along the shores of the great lake, yet someone had to check on the well-being of the creature that lived on the high point above the cove. In Atynleigh's small, damaged family, that someone meant her. The creature must be attended to, and Atynleigh was a dutiful child. So, she shrugged the pack on her back into a more comfortable position and trudged on.

Far above the cove the dull sun added a meager warmth to the dark slate that formed a grassless apron in front of the hut where the creature lived. This morning he had painfully made his way to a high stump of stone that separated the path from the lake cliff and was resting in the sun. His eyes wandered to the restless, gray waters of the great lake below him. Sometimes he looked, and with some regard, to the low mountains and thick forest that lay to the east and south, and to the steeper valley with its swift, narrow river that formed the western lands. But the lake, stretched across the northern horizon, was his home, and it was this that he longed for.

Knowing that the girl would surely come that day, the man—if man he was—had clumsily stoked a fire for tea. He knew the child would be cold and he knew the burden he placed on the family in the valley.

The sun was the width of an outstretched hand above the horizon when Atynleigh approached the hut. She called to the creature as she approached the cabin.

"I am here," she heard in response.

She knew it was difficult for Creature to speak aloud. His voice came in a wet, soft whisper. Yet, she had heard the words of his greeting clearly, with its strange, precise accent. At such times she knew he had been thinking the words. When Creature used his mind instead of his throat, his words came easily. She also knew that he could hear her thoughts. But just as it was easier for him to speak with his mind, it was easier for her to speak with her throat, and this was how they communicated.

Atynleigh remembered when she and her mother had found—rescued, saved—the creature from death on the stone beach some distance from their home. He had been injured and in pain from a fearsome wound on his side.

She and Mother had been fishing far down the cove. Fish had been sparse for weeks and they had followed signs of schooling fish past the safety of the harbor. Mother was a skilled fisherman, from a long line of men and women who had made their living on the lake's water. Atynleigh's mother and father had enjoyed fishing together, but Father had died months ago and now Atynleigh was Mother's fishing companion.

They had entered a shallow cove where a rippling surface spoke of an abundance of fish. They were about to toss their net when Atynleigh stayed her mother's strong arm and nodded noiselessly toward the near shore. A man appeared to be crawling across the beach, not even crawling so much as moving his limbs in response to unremitting pain. All of this, as well as something undefinable about his dark, rough appearance, made mother and daughter hesitate as they scanned the shoreline for danger. These were unsettled times. Even aiding the obviously sick or wounded required a serious decision.

"We need to get closer," Atynleigh whispered.

Mother nodded. They were both thinking the same thing. If someone had been on this shore to help Father, he might have lived instead of bleeding out in frigid water, alone and without hope. On that fateful day, rising waves from a sudden storm had thrown Father, as skilled a man as there was in a small boat, into the shallows. He would have survived with only bruises, but he had crashed down on a broken iron hoop from a submerged and rotten barrel. The metal drove deep into his thigh, cutting the femoral artery. Without help, he had never stood a chance.

That loss gave both mother and daughter courage to offer this stranger the lifeline which had been denied Atynleigh's father. Still, they approached cautiously. Mother slid from the boat as it hissed against the pebbles and grounded itself on the shore. Atynleigh, with her sharp eyes, would watch the tree line for possible danger. They did not need to discuss these arrangements, they simply knew.

The man had rolled on his back and looked in their direction. He had clearly been aware of their approach. Now, he neither moved nor made a sound. He lay a short ten yards from shore, his head toward them with golden eyes watching their every move.

"Do good."

"What?" her mother asked.

"I said nothing," Atynleigh replied, looking at her mother for the first time since the boat came to its stop. "I thought you told me..."

They both looked toward the man with his pleading eyes. They were sure he had made no sound, but they knew what they had heard. Atynleigh impulsively joined her mother in the water as they ran together—to do good.

They needed the strength of their desire to do the right thing, for as they approached the injured man, they saw that it was, in fact, no man at all.

"A Spirit Animal," Mother whispered, stopping short some distance from the creature. She had hesitated as she said this and both Mother and Atynleigh looked at each other and then back to the creature. Spirit animals were known to exist in this lake, sometimes seen, sometimes feared, sometimes revered in a way just short of worship. The Spirit Animals were creatures of legend and song. They were neither man nor beast, but part of both worlds and it is said that they could talk to both the fish and the fishermen. Many a person who had disappeared was said to have been called to the lake by a Spirit Animal, never to be seen again. There were others who said they would have been lost except for a Spirit Animal that guided (or carried) them to a safe shore after a storm or accident.

Atynleigh shook with fear and awe; this was certainly the creature of the legends. What lay before them had the configuration of a man, but the scales and gills of a fish. He had a muscular tail and spiked dorsal fins down his back like a lizard. His face was reptilian. The eyes were golden, large, and bulging, with pupils constricted in pain. Down the creature's side, from armpit to hip, a bloody slice had been opened by some sharp object.

The creature looked at them again and they heard more thoughts, but of garbled and uncertain meaning. The creature was able to capture feelings more than specific words, though sometimes one emerged as the other.

"Spirit Animal," was suddenly repeated back to them, and then, softer, the repeated plea, "...do good."

Atynleigh had looked to her mother, fearful, wondering what they should do. Mother's worried eyes moved from her daughter to the creature and then her shivering lips closed in a look of decision and determination. Mother hurried back to the boat, caught up the net and ran back to her daughter.

"We will spread this beside the creature, lift him on to it as best we can and ferry him back to the cabin. I can care for the wound there."

They went to work but heard no more from the creature save a feeling of intense pain when they moved him.

He was still alive when they brought him to their cabin.

From the early days of Creature's recovery, even those perilous first days lying on a pallet by the fire in their cabin, Atynleigh had noticed his golden eyes following everything she and Mother did. He tried to understand their thoughts and share his with them, but communication was halting and incomplete. Creature had watched as they spent the long, cold nights working, working, working, until the brief hour before exhaustion sent them to bed. Once they called the day's work enough, she and Mother would pull out the chess board and play a fast, deadly game.

Their game of chess was not the slow, studied game of deep thinkers. Theirs was like their lives, a series of quick decisions.

Mother and Father had played chess. They had taught Atynleigh while she was still sitting on their knees and as she grew older, that any one of that trio might win on any given night. Their board was simply functional, but the pieces—ah, those chessmen. Father had carved them from walrus tusks. They were tiny because tusk was a precious commodity. But the carving was fine and animated, with carefully detailed faces.

The creature had quickly become fascinated with the nightly chess match.

Two days after Creature came to the cabin he was starting to move painfully and slowly. Each time he reopened his wound, but the bleeding was less each time. He ate hungrily. That would have been a problem, except that fish had started coming to the cove. The first day a mass of mussels had apparently thrown themselves onto the shore by the cabin, enough to fill a bucket. It had turned into a feast for all of them.

By the fourth day Creature had been lucid enough to ask what this 'chess' was. A full week later Creature hobbled toward the chess board and began observing the game. He watched, trying simple questions using his soft, bubbling voice, or speaking directly into their minds. Five days later, absorbed in the game, his webbed hand moved hesitantly toward a piece on the board, a bishop, carved to look both haughty and bored.

"Yes" Atynleigh said, "that is the man I was going to move." She looked at him with astonishment. "Do you know where I wanted him to go?"

"A line." His claw hovered above the board in a diagonal. "Capturing a rook." The claw stopped above Mother's ward man, shaped like a Berserker, shown biting down on the top of his shield.

"Can you move it?"

Creature's golden eyes locked on Atynleigh's brown ones. She moved her head to encourage him. In response, his claws curled inward, moving them out of the way. He used the knuckles of the hand, just above the webbing, to grasp the bishop and deftly move it across the board, pushing the rook out of the way. He then carefully plucked up the rook and set it aside.

The room filled with Atynleigh's laughter. She and Mother both laughed—perhaps for the first time in months. This movement of a clawed hand from a healing stranger had made them feel a lightness that had been rare in their cabin.

It was at the end of his third week of recovery, during such a chess match, that the full danger of their situation closed around them. The match had barely started when Creature straightened his back, his eyes closed into slits, and focused on the door.

"They come."

Mother did not hesitate or question the creature. There was danger close and closing.

"Move. Make yourself as small as you can in the dark corner of Atynleigh's bed, back, under the slant of the roof."

"I can fight."

"You will lose. Do as I say."

When Mother used that tone, no one could withstand her. Atynleigh watched Creature roll back onto the small bed where it was wedged between the hang of the roof and the slant of the steps going to the loft where Mother slept.

Mother and daughter then pulled the rough blankets of Creature's pallet off the floor and threw them over the huddled figure of the lake-man, making a mess of unmade bed in the dark corner. They moved the low table with its chess board intact over the clean and flattened space where the pallet had been, roughing the dirt floor with their feet as well as they could. Mother scattered the wood fire enough to lower the light of the cabin just as they heard the men approach.

A fist pounded on the door.

"Who is there?" Mother called.

"The Reeve of the shire, Widow. Open."

Mother opened the door and let the firelight fill the entryway. There were three men dressed in rough tunics and wool capes. Two were men from the village. All were on foot. She glanced from the faces of the men she knew to the one she did not.

"Reeve Tomasil, it is late. Is there trouble?" She looked past them as if the trouble were waiting in the clearing.

"We come to warn of trouble. The fisherman here is certain there is sign of a Spirit Animal, wounded and ashore, in this area." Reeve Tomasil pushed the stranger forward as he spoke. It was as close to an introduction as was possible in this primitive community.

The stranger then spoke with a surly voice, trying to assert authority where he had none, "We need to inspect the houses. Make sure he isn't hiding."

Mother laughed and pushed the door wide open. "Look all you want, Reeve. But I think if I had seen a lake monster in my house, I would be seeking you instead of the other way around."

The stranger stepped forward and wrenched the door from Mother's hand.

"I'll have my own look around."

"No, sir. The Reeve may, but you shall not."

The stranger was shocked by this barrier to his wishes. He started to push past Mother but that proved to be a problem as the woman stood her ground.

"The Reeve is known to me and is welcome in this house. I do not allow that familiarity to every person. Certainly not a stranger who does not know a proper welcome." As Mother said this, she fixed the stranger with her eyes and seemed to grow both taller and straighter. For the first time all of them noticed that she had come to the door with a fish skinning knife in her strong right arm.

As the stranger took a short step back, Mother addressed the men she knew.

"Tomasil," Mother said trying to sound genuinely concerned, "has anyone been injured by this Spirit Animal? I could bring my medicines. You know I stand ready to help."

"No, Widow." The Reeve was weary of the long searches this stranger had insisted upon over the last weeks and he was not used to being offered help by the families he interrupted. It showed in his eyes and Mother now used that to seal a quick end to this visit. She spoke softly.

"You must be very tired. My daughter and I have a little left of our supper, but the rest is yours if you wish."

She stepped back from the doorway she had blocked to the stranger, and her act of generosity and openness had the effect she had counted on.

"No. No, we won't be staying, Widow. What little you have belongs to you and the child. We have warned you and checked the house. It is all we need."

"But it could be lurking…" the stranger tried to protest, but he was stopped by the tired Reeve.

"Our work is done here. We wish you a quiet evening, Widow."

"And a bright morning to you," Mother said.

Atynleigh joined her mother as they stood at the open door and watched the three men retreat down the path toward the village far out of sight. They stood in the lighted door just long enough to appear completely fearless and innocent, then closed the door, both shaking uncontrollably.

They stoked the fire to a bright blaze and slowly uncovered Creature. He too was shaking, but not from fear or cold.

It was a long time until his anger subsided. He spoke only with his mind that night.

"I must leave your house."

"You are not ready. We did not bring you this far to lose you out of fear—or anger."

"I put you in danger."

Mother hesitated, then stated a simple fact. "There is danger. True. And we do need to get you out of here. We were as lucky as we were smart tonight."

"Mother," said Atynleigh, her voice soft but earnest, "I have an answer, but it is a hard answer. We need to get Creature to the cliff hut. Even if the Reeve returned with men, Creature would see them and escape to the lake, down the cliff ropes long before anyone could walk the path."

Mother sat silently. The idea had occurred to her as well. The cliff hut was a small, barely functional shelter built on the top of the hill just to the west of their cabin. It had been built by Atynleigh's great-grandfather as part of a coastal warning system. An open fire on its heights could be seen far down the lake shore as well as inland. Such fires, passed from hilltop to hilltop, were a way to warn of marauders, though such times were now long past.

The cliff ropes had been added years later so that careless people, caught on the small beach below during high tide, could climb to safety.

But how to get Creature to the hut? He had not been able to take more than a step or two across the dirt floor of the cabin. He fed himself, but only with food which had been presented to him. Yet, tonight's near miss had thrust the decision upon them all.

Somehow, Creature used the information in their minds to glean an accurate picture of the place and path.

"I can do this cliff path. But now, in the dark, before anyone sees us." Then he added with fierce resolve. "Or I must return to the lake, healed or not."

It was decided. It was done.

Slowly, with exhaustive effort, ever more frequent rests and moans of excruciating pain, the trio made their way from cabin to hut. Mother had gone ahead to lay a fire, prepare a pallet and bring up a sack of provisions, then returned to help Atynleigh guide and support Creature up, ever up.

"Child…" he had started once.

"Not now, Creature. We will talk when you are at the top."

But they had not talked then. Upon entering the hut Creature had collapsed half on and half off the pallet without word or sound of any kind.

Mother had insisted that both she and Atynleigh return to the cabin. After carefully tending the low fire and setting some dried fish within the reach of the lake man when—and if—he awoke, they returned to their home. They were in their beds just before daybreak, and still asleep at noon. During that entire time, a fog so thick it took one's breath away covered the entire cove, hiding both cabin and cliff.

That had been weeks ago, and now in the cold sunlight, Atynleigh ran toward the hut and the creature, who had become her friend.

Creature had risen clumsily from the rock upon which he had been sitting. The purplish scales of his face were gray at the tips and his jagged wound was a raw line that glowed white in the pale sun.

"I have rare medicine," Atynleigh said. "Mother trapped a beaver, and the musk glands have miraculous oils. She said you will feel the difference."

Atynleigh paused to look closely at the wound. It was raw, pink under pearl and as jagged as the thrust of the spear that he said had caused the near-fatal cut. Her hand moved close along its line but did not touch the fragile tissue. She sniffed at it.

"It doesn't smell. It is closing without infection."

"There is less pain. But the flesh is...stiff."

"That is how these things heal. We need to get you inside. Mother's salve will help."

Creature followed her into the hut and settled himself with a groan on a low stool.

"Let us see if this salve is the miracle Mother says it is."

She removed a pot of oily, amber-colored salve from her pack. It smelled strongly of musk and camphor. Her fingers took a dot of the thick gel from the pot and lightly moved it across the wound. Creature never moved, though she felt a long intake of breath through the gills on either side of his neck.

"Mother says you should feel a numbing tingle at first, but then relief. Do you understand?"

Creature nodded.

"She says it will speed the healing."

"That is good, child." He spoke these words in his whisper.

He always found Atynleigh's name to be too much a jumble of sound to attempt. She was just 'child' to him.

She put the pot of salve on the table. She had something she wanted to ask him.

"When my father was alive, he told me stories of the spirits that live in the great lake. He thought he saw you, or someone like you, once near the island at the west end of the lake. Father described a creature much like you."

"I seldom go to that island, but others like me find it comforting."

"Are there many of you?"

"Few. Fewer all the time."

"Are you the Spirit Animal that the tales talk of?"

"Spirit is too big a word. I am an animal, like you."

"I think you are the Spirit Animal of the fables." Atynleigh said this solemnly. She and Mother had talked about this. They were sure they knew who he was and much of what he was capable. "Do you bring the fish to our cove?"

"I can call them."

"We are grateful for that."

The creature did not smile, for his mouth was not capable of that, but Atynleigh felt a smile in what he said next, "Child, do you want to play the game? Or are we going to carve our own today?"

"Both. First we play."

In the days that had followed the difficult move to the cliff hut, while fall had inched toward early winter in the mountain community, Atynleigh and her Creature had started carving a new chess set, just for them.

The pieces were small, each one the length of one of Atynleigh's fingers. She fashioned the pieces as her father had, with curious little postures and attitudes. Her queen seemed worried and held her hand to her cheek. Atynleigh's king was vigilant, with a sword held across his knees. The bishops were looking for sin and sorrow with scowls on their faces.

Atynleigh had started not with any of these pieces, but with the knights. She knew they would be the hardest piece to capture, sitting on small, Nordic horses. They needed the extra width of the base of the precious walrus tusk, the last two her family had, so she began with her knights, and it was then that she made a stylistic decision that would affect every piece on the board.

She attacked the delicate ivory with purpose and precision. When she had finished the first knight, she held it out to Creature for inspection.

A bubbling sound much like a chortle came from Creature's throat.

He was looking at a chessman with the features of a man, riding a stout horse. But the eyes were remarkable. They were not the eyes of a man, but the round, bulging eyes of a fish, staring with a challenging intensity out of a human face. They were, unmistakably, the eyes of Creature, yet just human enough to make one assume that the carver either lacked skill or was making a joke.

Atynleigh and Creature's free time had passed in much this way—playing and carving. They were ready to start the last three pawns that stormy winter day. They would begin after they played their game of chess.

Perhaps it was the intervening slate of the hillside that interrupted Creature's sense of surrounding. Perhaps it was the soothing balm or strong camphor of the salve. Perhaps it was just his increasing contentment in Atynleigh's presence, or his intense efforts to expand the language between them, but Creature did not intuit the danger until it was too late.

The persistent stranger that had almost found them out in Mother's cabin had not forgotten his ill-treatment that night. When he received word of the abundance of fish on Mother's drying rack, he was certain that she knew more of the lake monster than she had shared. He had observed both the cabin and the hut from a distance. Smoke from the lofty cliff hut could not be explained save by the presence of an unknown. He had followed the daily trek of the child to the hut. And today he had chosen to make his secretive climb up the brushy, western side of the cliff. He would come upon them from the back side of the hill. If they ran down the eastern path, he could catch them easily—a young girl and lake man more used to water than land. The south side was an impenetrable tangle of brambles and berry bushes. North lay only the sheer drop to the lake, surely too great a fall with too shallow a bottom for even the creature to make that a viable choice. There would be no escape.

The stranger moved with cunning. As he raised his head above the slate rocks at the top of the cliff his presence became known in an instant but too late.

With a throaty hiss Creature rose with a speed that turned the inside of the hut into a shamble. The table, board and chessmen were overturned. Atynleigh's safety and escape became his only focus. Creature threw the door open and held it wide.

"Run, child."

Atynleigh understood a tone so forceful. She charged through the door and almost ran into the stranger as he appeared around the corner of the hut. He had a long knife in his hand and his instinct was to grab for the girl as she flew past him. His hand caught her sleeve and spun her to the ground.

That was his mistake.

"Monster," was the only word Atynleigh heard from the creature.

In the instant the stranger's attention had been turned to Atynleigh, Creature moved toward the assailant. He was slow but his bulk and returning strength were all he needed to grab the man's arm with one clawed hand, twisting it around his back and pushing him away from Atynleigh and toward the cliff.

At first the stranger tried to free himself, slashing backwards with the long knife. If any of the blows met flesh, they had no effect. Atynleigh was scrambling to her feet when she saw Creature straighten and twist hard on the man's arm. The bones of the stranger's arm cracked apart, followed by an anguished scream.

"Don't. Don't!" the man screamed, but Creature was pushing the evil presence steadily toward the cliff. At the edge of the precipice Creature lifted the stranger entirely off the ground.

With a mighty heave the stranger sailed off the cliff. A wailing cry followed his body down.

But there was still danger. Creature's efforts had brought him tottering too close to the edge. He reached out his right hand to steady himself on the single rocky protrusion near him. It should have been easy, but Atynleigh also saw the paroxysm of pain along the raw line of his wound. His arm reached out to steady himself on a rock, but the muscles contracted in pain, missing the rock. Gravity took Creature's body over the edge.

Atynleigh reached out to him in futile desperation. "No," she screamed.

She watched as Creature fell, haphazardly at first, then he straightened himself, arched his back, and rolled over. There was a shallow bottom to the cove here and he needed to enter at as horizontal a plane as possible while still cutting into the water. The impact was intense. She listened hard for one last thought, but if it was there, it trailed off before fully formed.

In the weeks that followed Atynleigh finished the chess set that she and Creature had made together. She and Mother played a single game with it, so that each piece knew its place and purpose. Then Atynleigh made a stone container of soft pumice and placed each piece carefully inside the hollow of it. She sealed the lid with wax and then made her way to the beach at the base of the cliff. On a thin strip of land well beyond the high tide line she buried the stone container deep in the soft sand.

"It is here," she said, "for us; a bridge across two lands."

For years, even after she grew to adulthood, with children and then grandchildren of her own, Atynleigh would come to this spot. She would sit near the chess set and talk to Creature, as though he were alive and lying in the shallows just off the cliff. Sometimes she was sure she could hear his soft words drift across the water to her. Always the same.

"Do good."

It is of note that for many years fish were a regular presence off the cabin by the great lake. It is also of note that the chess set was discovered hundreds of years after even Atynleigh's grandchildren had grown old and died. The Lewis Chessmen, as they are called, were found in 1831 on the shores of Lake Uig on the Isle of Lewis. They can now be seen in the British Royal Museum. They are beautifully carved, quite small, and have bulging, fish-like eyes.

See L.A.W. Butler's story "Her Spirit Animal" online at Metaphorosis. If you liked it, leave a comment. Authors love that! Remember to subscribe to our e-mail updates so you'll know when new stories are posted.

About the story

Writers love to read. In June of 2019 I read an article in *Smithsonian Magazine* about the Lewis chessmen. This was a discovery of artfully carved chess pieces that were found buried in the sand on the Isle of Lewis. These pieces were carved sometime during the 12th century. My mind started to churn with an idea. Who carved the pieces? Why did they bury them so carefully in the sand? Throw in a little of the *Creature from the Black Lagoon* and *Beauty and the Beast* and a story is born.

A question for the author

Q: What do you think is the single most important quality for a good writer to possess?

A: Humility. There are a finite number of plot lines (usually numbered from five to seven) and everything you create is going to be a variation on those themes. It is how you play with those ideas, whom you choose to grapple with those conflicts, and the words you assign to each that make you a writer. That means you are sharing space with a great many talented people. Appreciate the fact that you are part of an amazing world of people who read, who write, and who value both.

About the author

Ms. Butler began writing speculative fiction in 7th grade after bingeing on a stack of Superman comics. Her academic background in both science and economics allows her to find many strange and wonderful places to put spunky girls and enlightened creatures of all kinds.

Tashala's Hair

Richard Strachan

For the novices of Kilavastin, the monastery's position high on the cold, north-facing flank of the mountain was enough to recommend it to even the most austere followers of the Path. The wind hared in over the plains from the ice fields in the distance, and most mornings would see the precincts dusted in a fine layering of silver frost. The chambers and cells and stone corridors were satisfyingly bleak, the windows shuttered only by thin partitions that rattled to the slightest breeze. The fire pits in the centre of each hall were lit to a strict and unyielding timetable: in the mornings, so the novices could brew their tea; and in the evenings, so their robes could be washed in great copper cauldrons and laid out overnight to dry. Meals were plain fare and luxuries were permitted only on the most sacred days. At the Feast of the Climbing Reed, the novices were granted a whole cup of fermented milk, and the evening of Crane Fall saw them lavishly stuff themselves with the first of the preserved fruit from the previous autumn.

It was a life of rigour and hardship, but few complained. In many ways it was an improvement over the quality of the lives they had known before, in families that scratched a dusty living from the dry fields of the south, where the waters of the valleys were acrid and slow. Out there, raids from the *anernath*, those horned and bloodthirsty daemons, were becoming more and more frequent. Kilavastin was a refuge from such hardship, and more than a refuge. High on the flank of the Tongue of Fire, the monastery was like a mouth shouting its prayers into the firmament, hollering to the twin moons of Aixe and Kast as they gazed down in pious approval. And when was a better time for the balm of prayer than when the land lay in such desperate straits, plagued by drought and poverty and war?

This was certainly what Gan thought, knuckling the sleep from his eye as he made his way to the meditation terrace on the edge of the monastery. His mother and father were reed weavers and they lived in a one-room shack on the lip of a dried-out lake, ten miles from the rocky foothills of the mountain. A day with a full stomach was one to mark on the village stele. When they had seen that he could decipher the prayers and blessings written by the mendicant priests whenever they passed through, his parents decided to send him to the monastery. High piety and low common sense found their complement in each other; one fewer of their many mouths to feed could only be a good thing, and for that mouth to be raised in prayer would double the benefit.

Gan had not seen them in five years. He didn't know whether they still wove their living from the dying reeds or whether they had passed away into the firmament above, but he gave thanks to them all the same. Kilavastin was shelter and a guaranteed meal, and freedom from the threat of bandit raids or the dark attention of the horned ones to the west. More than that, it was a whetstone to a sharpening mind. He had always known he was a cut above the folk in his village and his life here was just the tangible proof. He would take all he wanted from Kilavastin. In time he would sit where the abbot sat each day to give them their lessons. He had no doubt, none at all. The scriptures of the Path might say that *Doubt is the lathe of certainty*, but Gan had no need of it. If the other novices were no more than cluttered collections of gathered wood, then he was already the carven chair. And as the scriptures also said, *Let each thing that is made be made for its own purpose*, and for what other purpose could Gan have been made but this?

He was a thin, reedy boy, his black hair shaven to the scalp. He was tall, although he made himself seem smaller by his hunkered, creeping gait as he passed through the corridors. His rope-soled sandals made no noise on the stone floor and the doors of the other cells, stained black with time, were still closed. Gan always made sure to be first up. It was a skill to wake before the rising sun. If you wanted to distinguish yourself, he had always thought, then it paid for your enthusiasm to be seen.

The steel morning was still glazed with the indigo of night as the sun began to rise. There was a smell in the air of frost and unleavened bread, the scent of rosemary, the acrid tang of brewed tea and mountain flowers. The terrace was empty when he reached it, the low dais at the southern end untenanted. Gan settled himself near the dais, sitting cross-legged on the stone and gnawing furtively on a crust of bread he had hidden in his robes. It would not be long before the other novices arrived to hear the abbot speak. Bread finished, the hard lump of it yielding to his throat, he closed his eyes and adopted a posture of meditation. He smoothed his brow, drew his mouth down slightly as if to indicate some knotty issue that he hadn't quite resolved.

His eyes looked onto the darkness inside him. He thought unbidden of his mother's face, his father's bare and field-stained feet standing on the rushes of their hut.

He heard Quath and Hart come scuffling from the corridor into the open air, stifling deep, lung-laden yawns. The rustle of their white cotton robes, the scrape of their sandals against the flagstones. He could imagine the smoky plume of their breath in the cold morning air.

"*The weasel hunts when the sun is young,*" Hart quoted in a whisper designed to carry. Quath giggled. Gan could hear him scratching at the lice in his hair. They were all due another shave soon. Gan inclined his head, acknowledging, but he didn't open his eyes.

"*The poppy drinks the morning's perfume,*" he answered in a still, clear voice, "*while the cactus slumbers.*"

Hart snorted through his nose and padded down behind him. Gan felt Hart's rough finger prod into his back.

"Cactus. That's the best you've got, eh?" he sneered.

"Well, the spines of the cactus are sharp and must be avoided," Gan said without turning his head. "And you certainly are a prick ..."

Quath bellowed with laughter. Gan opened his eyes and allowed himself a smile, although he knew he would pay for it later. He could feel Hart's rich displeasure behind him. He was a lumpy, ill-featured boy, not one to let an insult go unpaid.

"*You're* the prick!" Hart hissed. The finger came prodding in again to Gan's back. "The daemons take you, and your mother," he said.

"Your mother *is* a daemon," Gan retorted. "And your father pleasures himself on her horn every night."

"Stop, Gan!" Quath choked. "You dole out insults like a rich man dispensing alms! My bowl is full!"

Hart's voice came low and serious into Gan's left ear. He could smell the boy's breath, still rich with sleep. "You're a wilful one, aren't you? At least I don't pleasure the Egg in his cell every afternoon ... How do you like the feel of *his* horn, eh?"

The insult quivered in the air like a struck chord. Gan felt a wash of heat sweep over him. He remembered the precept, *Emotions are the tether of the clay,* and said nothing. He was taller than Hart and had the greater reach, although Hart had weight and solidity on his side. They had never fought, but even so, he wasn't entirely sure that Hart would win. Despite the discipline of the switch and the leather strap, scuffles were common enough amongst the boys. Even so, he would not turn and strike.

Hart, emboldened, laughed with false mirth. If he had any further insult in his mouth though, he kept it to himself as the other novices began to file into the terrace, slumped in their white robes and still heavy with sleep. The initiates, younger boys with bare feet dressed in sky-blue tunics, filed in to sit on the very cusp of the terrace where it fell away into the open air.

A hush fell over the novices as the Egg hobbled in from the western cloister. The ripple of their talk faded away, until the only sound across the precinct was the high whisper of the northern breeze and the quiet tread of the abbot's sandals as he climbed with effort onto the dais.

All bowed their heads, although Gan glanced up under his brows to watch the Egg limp slowly to the reed mat. The dome of his head was smooth and hairless; even the eyebrows and the eyelashes seemed to have faded with age, as sparse as winter grass. There was not a hair on his chin or lip, and his blue-veined legs, dark with bruises, were as thin as rope. He gathered his green robes about him and settled into position, coughing tremulously, his eyes milky white. His age-gnarled hands were cupped in his lap. Gan felt the white eyes draw across him as the abbot gazed out at the gathered crowd, all of them sitting patiently on the terrace waiting for him to begin.

The Egg saw everything, it was said. The fog of age might have laid its cloud across his vision, but that did not mean his sight was not clear. Gan certainly hoped so. He hoped the Egg could see the need in him. Every afternoon, he knelt at the door to the abbot's cell, waiting to make himself conspicuously useful. Small errands, help with letters, filling the Egg's water cup, brewing his tea — anything in exchange for whatever crumb of insight the abbot might let drop from his table. Knowledge was as food and drink to Gan, and he would take his fill. More than that, it was the coin of progress, and he would earn his keep. He wanted to make the abbot proud, to show him everything he had learned at his feet.

One day, he thought. *One day, I will sit where you sit now.*

As was the purpose of the lesson, the abbot waited until the novices felt emboldened enough to ask for a particular story. Tales from scripture or cosmology or from the Golden Precepts; tales of myth and legend and history; tales that would illuminate the soul's endlessly refined condition in the ocean of eternity. Tales were the weft and weave of Kilavastin. They were how the monks and the initiates made sense of the world. Kilavastin itself, the monastery that sat atop the Tongue of Fire, was the tale that was told about it as much as anything else. Everybody knew of Kilavastin, where the first steps of the Path had once been taken. Here was where the words of the Way had first been spoken, and what was the Way but a story about how to live?

The cold air slithered over Gan's bare shoulder. He prepared himself to speak — as everyone knew he would. It had almost become a tradition that no one would break the abbot's silence until Gan had sallied forth with his first question. But then, breaking the hush, his voice braying in the morning air, Hart stepped suddenly into the gap instead.

"Please, master," he said. "This unworthy one has a request he would humbly make?"

The Egg made no outward show of having heard. He sat there, all folded up into himself like a woven basket. Then, after a moment, the gesture visible only as a faint tremble in his jaw, the Egg nodded. Hart went on.

"I have heard — *we* have heard — that the *anernath* make great gains against the people, and that the lands groan under the weight of their evil. I thought there might be a tale that would speak to us in this time? In the scriptures it says, *Those who would counter evil must first make themselves pure*, and I thought perhaps the tale of the Peerless Knights might give us courage and inspiration? For who could be purer than the Peerless Knights, or we novices of the monastery who dedicate ourselves to the Path?"

There was a ripple of suppressed laughter. Even the most pious initiate would have trouble describing his fellows as being exactly *pure* ...

Gan masked his smile in case the Egg should happen to see. He flitted through the verses in his mind until he came to the passage Hart's words had conjured up.

"Please, master," he said sharply, arm raised. "This unworthy one also has a tale in mind, for which he would humbly ask so we can be illuminated by its wisdom."

The white gaze of the Egg slid swiftly across Gan's face. Gan bowed his head. He could hear Hart breathing heavily through his nose behind him.

The Egg's voice was perhaps the most remarkable thing about him, and when he spoke, Gan felt the words thrum and settle across the still, empty air. For all his frailty, it was a voice of resonance and power, like a velvet note blown through the body of an oboe. He seemed able to project it to any part of the precinct with the same subtle force.

"Would you have your tale, novice," he said, "before your fellow's? Remember, it is said that *All things must be answered in their proper order.*"

More laughter, but Gan had expected this. He countered swiftly with:

"But is it not also said, master, that *The seed must be blown by a contrary wind to settle?*"

Across the precinct he could hear the indrawn breath from the other novices, the respectful laugh at his audacity. On the Egg's face there was the faintest twitch of a reaction, a flicker of the lip.

"If you seek only to illuminate your fellow's request with your own," he said, "be bold enough to ask it."

"I believe the story I have in mind would better reflect the inspiration my fellow seeks. The Peerless Knights are, after all, *peerless*, and we could never assume to attain their level of purity. I seek only our enlightenment in requesting this, though I confess the tale is one that I would much like to hear. It has always moved me."

He bowed deeper. He could practically hear Hart's teeth grinding in his jaw behind him. Quath tittered uneasily, whispered: "Oh, he'll get you for this, Gan! He'll *get* you!"

But Gan paid no mind. He had reward enough, as he glanced up, in seeing the faint curve of the abbot's lip, the glint of a revealed tooth.

"And what tale did you have in mind, novice?"

"Please, master," Gan said. "This unworthy one would beseech you to enlighten us with the tale of King Raden. I believe it would shed light on the low desire for great things that my fellow's request, perhaps unwittingly, has revealed."

The Egg paused. The hands shifted in his lap. "And what do you know of this tale, novice?"

Gan swallowed. It was a tale his mother had told him when he was young, before he went to sleep; when the dusk stroked the fields with purple fire, and when the moons of Aixe and Kast began their graceful dance through the vault of night. But he would never admit as such here, of course. He would never hear the end of it from the other novices.

"Please, master," he said. "I know only as much as my nature has permitted me to know, for my head teems with half-remembered tales. After all, is it not said that *The clay vessel cannot be overfilled?*"

The abbot, to much general astonishment, gave a short, flat bark of a laugh. Never had the Egg laughed in their presence before. Gan felt a strange tenderness then, that he had so moved him. The other novices almost imperceptibly leaned forward; if Gan had managed to so sting the Egg, then it stood to reason that the abbot's words would be worth listening to.

"Very well," he said to the gathered crowd. Hunched on the dais like that, he looked more like a little woven basket than ever. 'Let us have the tale of King Raden then, and see if his travails cannot illuminate the 'low desire for great things' which the novice here has identified ..."

In those days (the abbot said), far to the north, there was a great kingdom known as the Kingdom of Sabaenea, and King Raden ruled there in justice and temperance. The eastern lines of that kingdom stretched all the way to the sea, and the southern fringes covered what are now the borders of our own lands. Indeed, Kilavastin itself was part of its domain in those days.

Raden was a just king, beloved of his people, but it was his curse to be born in dark times. The *anernath* were already breaking from the earth of the western lands, spewing up from the pits of fire that wise men tell us boil at the very centre of the earth. Villages and towns fell to the flame of their swords, Men, women, and children were used most horribly in their dread rituals. Pirates raided far to the east, and for three years in a row the crops failed before the harvest. Drought and famine and war — the three signs of a changing time were upon him, and even the most just king has to bow before the signs he is given. Age was growing more heavily on King Raden, day after day, and he knew that his reign would soon come to an end. It could either end in the fire and slaughter of war against the daemons, or it could continue in fear and safety as long as the *anernath* suffered them to live. All he knew was that he could not be the king to lead his country onwards into whatever fate awaited it.

King Raden had a son, Janna, the prince who in the normal course of things would inherit Sabaenea on Raden's death. It was in King Raden's mind to abdicate his responsibilities and pass them on to a younger man, one better suited to the rigours to the age, but the thought made him most uneasy. He loved his son, but King Raden was wise and saw far, and he knew that Janna was the kind of man who might treat a kingdom as no more than the spoils of his own vanity. Janna was young and confident and strong, most fair to look upon, but those who have never had to struggle often lack the resilience to make hard decisions. There was ambition in him too. Ambition can often be yoked to a finer purpose, but there was a streak of cruelty in Janna that King Raden had long tried to ignore. The prince, it was said, took rather too much enjoyment in beating his hunting dogs, and he treated his servants little better.

One morning, King Raden's daughter, Princess Tashala, came to him. A silk veil covered eyes that had been sorely weeping, but the king was at first so preoccupied with his own concerns that he did not notice her distress. Then, when she drew back the veil and he saw the sorrow on her face, he bade her sit and called for wine.

"What ails you, daughter?" he asked.

Princess Tashala sipped her wine and dried her eyes. She was a striking figure, fine-boned, tall, her long black hair breaking the bounds of the silken cords she had used to tie it up.

"Oh father!" she cried. "You must flee from here, while you still have the chance. Fear grips me in its chains, and I know for a very fact that your life is in danger."

"Our lives are only given us for our allotted span," King Raden said. "But tell me daughter, what makes you think I am at risk in the very centre of my kingdom? War draws near, I have no doubt, but it is not yet upon us."

And then Princess Tashala told her father all that she had heard from the lips of her own brother. Prince Janna, who had no greater store of patience than he had of compassion, could not wait for his father to die in the natural course of things. He wanted the crown of Sabaenea now, for his very own, and he had boasted of such to Tashala — for, despite the differences between them, brother and sister were very close, and had been since they were children. No more than ten months separated their births, although Tashala's arrival had killed the mother Janna spent the rest of his life mourning. Often, King Raden wondered if the sad death of his wife was what had made his children's relationship both so feverishly close, and so unusually overwrought.

"You must believe that this is no idle threat. Janna means to kill you and seize the crown, and then by the light of the Path that guides us I cannot say what mayhem he will inflict upon the kingdom. He has long waited for this moment, father, and those whose hearts are so torn by desire will never make kind kings. Forgive me for bringing you such distress, but I fear that he would even take me for a bride, so twisted by his lust for power has he become. He has always blamed me for mother's death, has he not, and now at last he will find a way to punish me for it!"

Now, King Raden, although struck deeply by these terrible words, was above all things wise. He knew that his daughter spoke the truth, for although she was in many ways a wilful and haughty character, she had a streak of iron in her that would not bend or break. If she had been made so distraught by what she had heard, then he knew that a moment of great seriousness was upon him.

Ask yourself what a king should do in such a trial. No one would have blamed him for dragging his son to his dungeons and ending the threat to his kingdom on the edge of the executioner's blade. But although King Raden was wise and just, he was also a father. He could not kill his own son. Still less could he allow his son to become a murderer and kill his own father. Despite it all, he loved Prince Janna. The boy was his own flesh and blood, and who can think of their own flesh and blood as irredeemable?

Some, of course, would say that this was a terrible weakness, and that kings must put aside such mortal concerns if they are to rule with strength; for all things, even the love of a father for his son, must be subordinate to the needs of the kingdom. But the king, who knew his scriptures, also knew that weakness could be turned into strength, for is it not said that, *The green shoot can be plucked with ease from the soil, and yet given time can crack the very mountains*? In the same way a newborn child placed into its father's arms soothes the beast inside him, perhaps a kingdom placed in Janna's hands would cool the fire of his strange hatreds. The kingdom would be saved and Tashala would no longer suffer her brother's unnatural attention — or at least, so Raden hoped.

He summoned Janna that evening. Having taken himself from the gambling table or from the arms of his courtesans, the prince strode into the throne room with all the arrogance of youth. He saw his father sitting there on the throne of Sabaenea, his head encircled by Sabaenea's crown, and all he saw was an old man too weak to look his son in the eye.

Now, as I have said, Sabaenea was a rich and powerful kingdom, and the throne room reflected all its strength and majesty. The throne itself was of solid gold, with a cresting rail of jewel-encrusted silver. Rubies and emeralds sparkled from the arms, and the dais on which it sat was mantled in purple velvet. The long apron of the dais was guarded by the warriors of the king's personal guard, giants near seven feet tall bearing ivory-hilted glaives, their heads capped with steel helmets. The room itself was larger than any lord's banqueting hall, hundreds of feet from end to end. The walls held bas-reliefs of sculpted marble, depicting the legends of Sabaenea's long and storied history, and the ceiling was a wondrous display of frescoes that celebrated the great victories of its armies. Raden was not a proud man, but he wanted his son to be certain that Raden was speaking to him not just as a father, but as a king, and that the decision he was about to make was coming from a position of the most unassailable power.

"You wished to see me, father?" Prince Janna drawled.

He wore his armour, the king noted; a gilded breastplate, a sword at his hip. The young man stood there as if he had spent half his day perfecting the pose, but King Raden saw far into his son's hidden heart. The boy was anxious too. He had achieved nothing in his own short life and in a way he felt the shame of his privilege. He had never been given the chance to prove himself. All this splendour had hung in front of him all the days of his life, and who can live with such temptation and not become deformed by it?

"Indeed, my son," the king said. He leaned forward in the throne, felt the weight of that golden circlet on his head, as he had felt it every day of his reign. "I summoned you here to give you something which I know you have long desired, which turns and twists in your mind day and night, and which I am convinced in the end you will not thank me for giving you."

Prince Janna glanced at his father's face, so grave and heavy with unspoken sorrows. "I thank you, father," he said carefully, "although I confess this does not sound like the sort of gift a man may happily receive."

"It is not," the king said, bluntly. "And yet, I would give it to you all the same. I would save you from a course of action that would draw you far from the Path that guides us all, and then Sabaenea and your beloved sister must suffer the consequences of a father's love, for good or ill."

"You will have my gratitude regardless," Prince Janna said. He bowed with a restrained flourish. "You know how much I value any gift from you, father ..."

King Raden summoned his advisors and ministers, the heads of his armies, his chancellors and priests. He bade all of them witness, and then he removed the crown from his head and passed it to Prince Janna — King Janna, as he now was.

It is said that a monarch must take the crown with reluctance, in recognition of the hard duty thrust upon them, but Janna could not help himself. He snatched the circlet from his father's hands like a child grabbing a sweetmeat from his nurse, so eagerly had he waited for this moment. After placing the crown on his head, Janna practically dragged his father from the throne.

With heavy steps, Raden plodded down the dais to the floor, pushing past the giants of his personal guard — now King Janna's personal guard, sworn to protect the king's life with their own.

"Is it done?" Janna asked, his eyes blazing. A smile flickered across his thin and handsome face. He looked, Raden thought, like the boy he had once been, eager for the games to begin on his birthday. "Is it right, am I now king?"

He looked pleadingly to the priests, the advisors, the generals, as if scared that they would contradict him. All of them, with the briefest of glances at the worn figure of Raden, who seemed to have diminished in only the few minutes since his son had entered the throne room, nodded their assent. It was done.

"All hail the king," they cried as one.

"How mother would be pleased to see me now ..." Janna whispered. Then he turned to the court and proclaimed: "There will be a change now in this kingdom, I swear it!" He grasped the sceptre, clutched at the hilt of his sword. "No more shall we skulk behind our walls in fear of battle. No more shall we let the daemons of the west press against our borders, killing the kinfolk of our neighbours. No longer shall the people go hungry from famine and drought. Open the granaries," he commanded. "Raise my armies! Let every strong man and woman of Sabaenea take up the sword and prepare for war. Sabaenea will meet the challenges that face it head on, and we shall be victorious!"

Raden lowered his eyes. How to tell his son that the granaries were empty, that there were not weapons enough to arm his soldiers? How to tell him that the duties of kingship were to balance so many competing demands that a successful king was more like a pilot weaving a ship through the reefs and sandbars of a treacherous harbour, rather than one who sets a single course and takes it? He would find out for himself, in time ...

"And one final command I make today," King Janna declared. He raised the sceptre and pointed it at his father. There was the briefest moment in his eyes, the quickest flash of horror at the step he was about to take, but it was soon gone. "Guards — arrest this man. His failures have led us to the brink of ruin, and he will not go unpunished."

And so the guards, who not five minutes before would have given their lives for him, took Raden in hand and cast him down into the dungeons of the king's palace, there to await the king's pleasure. It was no less than he had expected.

The dungeons were not as fearful or as grim as that word would lead you to expect. A dungeon is merely a place to keep a prisoner until they can be dealt with, and the simple loss of liberty is torment enough. The cell in which Raden was thrown was simple and bare, but not needlessly grotesque. It contained no more than a plain wooden bed and a hole in the ground for a toilet, but the floor was well-swept and the walls cleanly whitewashed. A barred window high on the eastern wall admitted the sunlight at dawn, and there was a thick woollen blanket for Raden to keep himself warm. He did not know what Janna planned to do with him, but reasoned that there was no point in tormenting himself with conjecture. All would become clear in time. Settling himself on the bed, Raden began to think back to his lessons in scripture, sending his mind to wander along the clear and uncluttered avenues of the Path, where none could touch it, while his body waited uneasily for the king's judgement. He thought of Tashala, his daughter, and hoped against hope that he had not made a terrible mistake.

The first day passed in silence. The sunlight swung leisurely across the whitewashed wall, painting the bricks in gold and amber. Raden heard nothing from the other cells and saw no sign of his gaoler. No one brought him food or drink, or unhooked the slat in the cell door to check if he was well. *No matter,* Raden thought. *Many are the people in Sabaenea who lack food in these dark times, and I should not complain if for once my stomach feels the pangs of an unaccustomed hunger.*

But the next day passed in the same way, and still no one came to his cell. A man can be humbled through lack of food for a few days at least, but he cannot be humbled long through lack of water. Despite himself, Raden stood by the slat in the door and called for sustenance, but no one answered. He had been dragged to the dungeons, it seemed, to be forgotten.

Days and nights passed. Raden could imagine King Janna frantic with indecision over what he should do, finally paralysed into this cruel indifference. Janna hated his father for standing so long in his way. He loved his father for standing aside and giving him the crown. He hated his sister for killing their mother. He loved his sister because in some way she was all of his mother he had left. What awful conflictions had gone into this boy, Raden sighed, and how blind had he been to think that charity would smooth out these flaws.

He licked the moisture from the walls where it gathered on the brick. He cursed the clemency that had made these dungeons less foul than they could have been, for there were no rats he could trap for food. His stomach writhed with agony and his throat burned with thirst, and slowly he felt what little strength remained to him start to fade. And yet even now, after everything, he did not regret the decision he had made. His son might be killing him by inches, but he was not yet a murderer.

He could not say how much time passed before he received his first visitor. Each day dragged from dawn to dusk, changeless and austere. In the end, it was not Janna who came to see him, or any functionary of the dungeons, but Princess Tashala, who had spent every day since Janna's succession begging the new king to allow her to see her father. Whether through guilt about what he had done, or simple love for his sister, Janna had finally agreed.

She appeared in that drear place like a glimpse of sunlight in a cloudy sky, her silks as vibrant as the flowers in the fields, her jewels glittering like stars. More dazzling than either was the love Raden saw in her eyes, the sorrow and the pity as she took his weakened body in her arms and sat with him on the bed.

"My lord, you cannot understand the grief a daughter feels when she sees her father brought so low," she said. "My heart is heavier than stone. Janna is surely cursed if he treats you so abominably."

"Forgive your brother," Raden managed to say. His voice was as dry as the autumn leaves that clattered about the forecourts of the palace. "After all, he has not killed me yet. Janna has never had to make a decision in his life before, and he only does what he does now for the good of the kingdom, I am sure. A crown must forget those who wore it before, as it cleaves to him who wears it now."

"He does what he does only for his own good, of *that* I have no doubt," Tashala scorned. "Even now he talks more of our marriage than he does of the duties of a king. He claims his love for me is pure, but it is only the love of a greedy man for that which he cannot have. And I swear, on our wedding night I will claw the eyes from his head rather than let him use me in such a disgusting violation of the Way!"

It grieved Raden deeply to hear this. Truly, he began to realise the scale of his error. He had given Janna the crown to prevent his son being consumed by his desires, but was his own need to protect his son not just another kind of desire in its way? The scriptures were surely true when they said that desire was the snare at the side of the road to peace. The laws of Sabaenea, laid down an age ago when the world was young, could not countenance the crown being passed to any but the first born. Raden saw those laws now as great tendrils snaking out from the shadows of history and binding his hands to a decision he wished he had not made. But what can a father do against the love he bears his children?

Raden felt his spirits lower even further when he realised that his daughter carried no sustenance for him.

"Indeed not, father," she said. "Janna's guards searched me before I entered, and I was expressly forbidden from bringing you food or drink. I think he means for you to starve to death in here because he does not have the courage to wield the blade himself."

"Then leave me now," Raden said, "and let an old man suffer the punishment of his folly."

It was then that Tashala unwrapped the scarves that kept her long black hair tied up from her shoulders. She shook it free and Raden saw that it glistened with oils. He could smell a light fragrance of honey and cinnamon wafting through the cell. Tashala took up a lock of that hair in both her hands and held it out to him.

"But I knew how vindictive my brother could be," she said, offering it to him in all reverence. "Please. Sustain yourself."

Suddenly he understood what she had done. As Tashala cradled him to her breast, holding him as he would have held her when she was a child, Raden took his daughter's hair into his mouth and sucked and sucked, drawing the lacquered syrups from it. Lock by lock, he drank the sustenance she had prepared for him, the nourishment she had disguised in the oiled tresses of her hair. Slowly he felt a flicker of his old strength returning. The darkness that had been growing around the edges of his sight receded. The cold which he had felt creeping ever nearer in his lonely cell began to slacken.

"Feed from me," Tashala whispered into the silence, and the only sound was the soft papping of Raden's lips as he sucked the oils dry. "Feed, and be whole once more."

She had saved his life, of that there could be no doubt. Glazing her hair with nutrients, her locks plump with rich greases, Tashala came to his cell whenever she could, and whenever Janna's malicious caprice turned for a moment to a kind of mercy. Sometimes a day or two would pass, sometimes longer. When at last he heard the grinding click of the lock on his cell door, Tashala would rustle in with a sweep of her gilded silks and unravel the scarves from her head. Raden would fall into his daughter's arms as she uncoiled the great loops and oiled plaits of her raven-black hair, and he would gather them up and swoon at the heady scents of cinnamon and burnt sugar. It was all he could do not to choke himself on each strand as he eagerly sucked it into his mouth, drawing as much of the goodness from it as he could.

The risks Tashala was taking were a marvel to him, her bravery an example he tried to honour. Truly she walked the Path in righteousness, and not for the first time Raden wished that this brave and resourceful young woman had been his first-born child instead of the callow young man he was now ashamed to call his son. The Law was all, Raden had thought in his foolishness. But are men and women made to serve the Law, or is the Law made to serve men and women instead?

As he sat in his bare cell, day after day, meditating on the Path and on all the varied steps that had led him to this moment, Raden tried not to imagine his son's confusion that his father yet lived. If his mother had lived, perhaps ... Would there still be such an absence in his boy, such bewilderment and vice?

And then, months after Raden had abdicated, King Janna came at last to the dungeons of his palace to visit his father.

He bade his guards wait outside, those seven-foot giants who had once guarded Raden himself. His breastplate was glazed with dust, notched here and there by sword cut or axe blade, and his lean and once-handsome face was drawn with strain. His hand flexed on the hilt of his sheathed sword. Raden sat on the edge of his cot and watched his son, and for a moment it seemed as if their places had been reversed; that Janna, worn out with guilt and strife, had been thrown into the dungeon while Raden sat patiently to await his excuses.

"I confess it surprises me to find you still alive, father," the young king said. His voice cracked as he spoke, brittle with fatigue. "I have Tashala to thank for that, I suspect. I don't know how she has done it, but she is ever wilful."

"She honours me with her loyalty," Raden said, without malice. "And she honours the Path. Perhaps she hopes I can still intercede with you, and turn aside your foul desire to marry her."

Janna flinched. He rubbed the dust from his eye and seemed to reel for a moment. Again came to Raden that image of him as a boy, crying at some childish injustice.

"I see the hatred in her, every time I look on her face," he mumbled. "I thought us closer than any two people in the world, but I suspect I have deluded myself on this, as I have on so much else. I am not so arrogant or selfish as you have long assumed me, father."

"Then you no longer torment her with your attentions?"

"Let us say that I have postponed our marriage until the war is won. I will persuade her with my victory, and ..." He strode from one side of the cell to the other. He was unable to meet his father's eye, and when he spoke it was as if he were speaking to himself. "A victory which I confess seems further away than I would have ever thought possible ..."

"You seem surprised to find war a complex and unpredictable thing," Raden told him. "Reasons why I always strove to avoid it. Nothing overwhelms like war."

Janna gave a flat and mirthless laugh. He wiped his eye again and Raden realised that he was brushing away tears.

"Complex and unpredictable, and expensive beyond all measure ..."

"Why do you come here, my son?" Raden asked him gently. "Do you seek to torment me further, or is that blade on your hip designed to end my suffering at last?"

Janna rounded on his father, but there was no rage or anger in his expression. There was only the dark despair of someone pushed beyond his limits, and suddenly aware of what those limits actually were. When he spoke, it was as if he dreaded anyone overhearing what he had to say.

"In the name of the Path we follow," he sobbed, "what do I do? I thought the *anernath* merely some kind of savage beast, but they are things of smoke and midnight, utterly without mercy ... There is rebellion in the north, and there are thousands — *thousands* — of people dead from the plague in the east. The granaries are almost empty, we cannot raise money fast enough to pay the army, and our defeats multiply like locusts in the hot season. It is all streaming through my fingers, father, and I cannot keep hold of it! Please, what do I *do?*"

Raden looked at his son, not without pity. To have striven for so long, to have locked all his hopes into the box of one desire, and then to find that desire no more than a scattering of ashes that drifted through the air, elusive ... Janna had found the limits of his own capabilities, and they had shocked him.

"Is the crown something you still want?" Raden looked his son in the eye, and that lean face twisted as if struck. "Would you clutch power to you still, or would you freely give it up?"

The choice, if it was a choice, wrestled across Janna's face. He clawed at his breastplate as if trying to stop the power flying away from him. Desire and surrender were weighed in the balance of his heart; but in the end, one must always be heavier than the other.

"I would keep it still," he whispered. His face was pale, as if he couldn't believe the decision he had just made. "More than my mother alive, or Tashala at my side, it is the only thing I have ever truly wanted."

"Then I cannot help you," Raden said sadly. "And the only advice I can give is that what holds you in fetters must be given away. The only gift worth giving is that which is truly valued, and that which is still desired by the giver is no gift at all."

"This is the advice you give me," Janna wept. "My own father, who would see Sabaenea in ruins rather than lift his hand to help!"

"You have my help," Raden told him. "You must unshackle your desire for power, and give it away to one more worthy. Only then will you be saved, and Sabaenea with you."

With a cry of rage, Janna drew the first blue inch of steel from his scabbard. Raden sat there impassive, waiting for the blow to fall, but Janna did not swing the blade. He sobbed once, reeled back as the tides of his anger broke against the shore of his father's indifference — for truly, Raden had made his peace with life and had reached the end of his Path. After all, Life must be capped with Death, and the wise man makes sure to meet Death's eye when it approaches. For Janna though, Death was not yet a figure he could compass. He was young enough to think that Death could always be outfought.

"Go," Janna said in a hoarse voice. He swung the cell door open and stumbled out into the corridor. "Leave this place. Find whatever refuge you can, before it is all pulled down in ruins about our heads."

"May your Path be free of pain and hurdle, my son." Raden said. In the doorway he paused to rest his hand on his son's trembling shoulder. "I will go south to Kilavastin. You will find me there, when the time comes."

"Forgive me, father," Janna choked. "But if I ever see you again, I will kill you for all that you have done to me."

And thus parted father and son, King Raden and Prince Janna, or King Janna as he was still for a little while after that. And as Raden left his cell and then the palace grounds, he knew more than ever that to hold something close which you cannot easily give up is to be held in chains, locked in a dungeon deeper and more impenetrable than the one he had just left. When desire is your master, then the Path is made ever more obscure.

The dawn had long since burned away by the time the Egg finished. The cold breeze had tempered a degree or two, and the novices' bellies rumbled as the time of the day meal grew close. There was a sharp smell in the air of herbs and spices from the pottage bubbling in the cookpots. Soon the rigours of the day would properly begin.

"That is it," the Egg declared. "The story of King Raden, and how he was nourished on Tashala's hair, and how a kingdom was given away because of desire. Greed is ever a danger on the Path," he said. "Go now, and think on this."

His white eyes swept over the gathered novices as the story sank into them, and for the briefest moment they rested on Gan, as if to say: *Heed these words, haughty one; for they are for you alone.*

Gan joined the others as they filed from the terrace, looking back to see the Egg still sitting there on the dais, his papery bald head bowed, his blue-veined legs still crossed. Gan wanted to go to him, to ask more, to learn more, to be of service. *All I want is to learn,* Gan wanted to tell him. *What else could be told of King Raden and Prince Janna? Did Raden ever make it to Kilavastin? What happened to Princess Tashala once her father left? Did King Janna die in battle, in his war against the daemons? Did he regret the clemency he had shown to his father at the end?* When his mother had told him the story, it had always ended with King Raden forgiving his son and leaving his cell to become a saint of the Way, performing miracles in the ruins of Sabaenea. Was this King Raden's fate? It made him feel uneasy not to know.

But once a question had been answered, it was not permitted to be reframed and it was up to the novices to parse the meaning from it. The Egg had spoken. That was all there was to it.

Precepts and orders and rules did not stop Gan's mind from pivoting uneasily around the story for the rest of the day, though. There were lessons in it for him, he knew. He just had to find them. Sabaenea had fallen many years ago and the war with the daemons was something that had lasted as long as people could remember. Some said that it would never end, because how could things of smoke and midnight ever be defeated by human arts? Perhaps in the end, he thought, Kilavastin itself would fall to them.

But no, it was impossible to imagine such a thing. As Gan washed the empty bowls when the day meal was done, his hands plunged into the tepid water of the kitchen sinks, he couldn't imagine the monastery falling into the same ruin as Sabaenea. It was eternal, surely. It was the cap of the mountain, the crown of the Path. It was the place that was woven of stories, and it would never fall as long as there were monks to learn them.

He was sweeping the corridors that led from the precinct to the storerooms, thinking about Raden and his wanderings through the kingdom, and thinking also about Princess Tashala and the unguents she had soaked into her hair — treacle? Beef fat? Butter and sugar? What had she taken to him? — when Hart and Quath appeared from the linen cupboards at the other end of the passage. Their arms were piled high with fresh sheets and blankets. When they saw Gan, they both laughed and dropped their voices into a hearty mutter.

"Afternoon, Gan," Hart said with a curl of his lip as they passed. "Or should that be 'Prince Janna' ..."

Quath guffawed loudly and buried his mirth in the pile of sheets he bore. Gan leaned on his broom and kept his eyes level with them.

"Janna?" he said lightly. "I am not king yet, but I have no doubts you'll both be my subjects one day."

Hart, squat and lumbering, shook his head and squared himself against the slighter boy. The sheets he carried were a barrier between them.

"What gives you such balls to think like this, eh?" he spat. He pushed with the pile of sheets, and Gan stumbled back, dropping his broom. "You'll no more be the abbot than I will. I know my worth, and the place it gives me. I am content with it. But the Egg sees you, Gan, always chafing at the bit. Even if you can't see yourself."

Gan swallowed. He tried to keep Hart's eye locked in his own, but of a sudden all the words of scripture he could have thrown back at the bigger boy fell away from him. A fist in the gut he would have expected, a twist of the arm and a knuckle in the eye, but not this scorn. This low blame, this angry disappointment. He had no weapon against it.

"You think the Egg sees me as Janna?" he said. He tried to sound light-hearted, but his voice felt thick in his throat. "I would have thought King Raden more appropriate, personally."

"And how do you figure that?" Quath giggled. "Raden was humble, wise. He did what he thought was right. So did Tashala. All you care about is looking better than anyone else."

"That's not true," Gan said. He could feel his cheeks flushing red.

"Look at him," Quath mocked. "It's finally sinking in ... That's your problem, Gan. You know scripture, fine. But do you really *know* it?"

"Don't think yourself more than you are," Hart muttered. He took the weight of the sheets in one hand and jabbed a finger at him. "Suck the Egg's hair all you want, but you're not King Raden. Not even close. You're Janna, boy. Lost with desire, and led astray. Grabbing at what you don't deserve. The Egg couldn't *believe* you'd ask such a question and not see yourself in the answer. No one could."

It's a hard thing to see a truth suddenly revealed, especially when it's visible to everybody except yourself. Gan seemed to see the lines of the story reframe themselves, and the grasping, wheedling figure of Prince Janna fade into the background where he belonged. In his place stood Princess Tashala offering her hair to her father, and beside her was King Raden, saddened by what he had done even when he knew it had been done for the best of motives. He thought suddenly of his mother, twisting the dry reeds into lengths of twine. He saw his father, his face lined with exhaustion.

When Hart and Quath had trundled off down the corridor, chuckling to themselves at the victory they'd scored in rendering him speechless, Gan stooped to pick up the broom. He leaned against the wall until his heart had settled.

He thought of Janna, standing in the door to his father's cell, his breastplate rent with battle, his clothes drenched in the dust of the roads. Weak, grasping, arrogant. But for a moment, as Gan composed himself again, he wondered at the strange courage it would have taken for Janna to walk down into those dungeons. He had gone to stand before the only person who truly knew the depths to which he had sunk, to ask the man he had imprisoned for help. That was why Janna had let his father live, Gan thought. It had taken courage to show that humility, and he could not betray that courage by committing such a base act afterwards. At the very end, Janna knew his true merits at last.

He felt his heart twinge at the thought. Perhaps the story then was about Janna's humility? Perhaps that was why the Egg had decided to tell it, and why those white eyes had rested on him at the very end. Until they had experienced the humility of knowing their limits, nobody knew what they were really capable of. That went for Gan as much as for anybody else. And then the king, after revealing those limits to his son, and realising his own limits in turn, slowly made his way to Kilavastin …

In the name of the Path, he thought, raising his eyes to the ceiling. Tales were twisting things right enough. They always told more than you really understood. Perhaps the Egg meant him to understand that he was like both Janna and Raden? Ambitious, callow, only aware of his limits after he had been humiliated? Realising only afterwards why he had been sent to Kilavastin in the first place – not to succeed, but to serve.

Then, as the words of the story swept through him once more, Gan knew that he might not be King Raden; but he was certainly not Prince Janna either …

Later that evening, he made his way to the Egg's cell. He bore the tea things on their lacquered tray, the ebony pot and cup, the simple clay bowl of dried leaves, the little crock of honey.

The Egg sat at his desk, drawing a reed stylus down a scroll of manuscript as he traced the letters of the text. Gan boiled the water by the blackened copper stove. Soon the fresh fragrance of the tea filled the room. It was getting dark outside, and the flame of the dusk stroked the open shutters at the window. Gan lit the candle in the lamp by the abbot's elbow.

"You have something to say, novice?" the Egg said at last. His voice quavered in the silence, weaker than it had been that morning. Gan poured the black tea into the ebony cup, straining the leaves. He looked at the globe of the Egg's head, the thin skin wrinkled above the back of his neck, the glint of his white eye as he sidled his gaze around to look.

Could it be him? How old was he really? How old was the tale they had heard that morning, the tale of King Raden and Tashala's hair?

"Forgive my distraction, master," he said. He took the water pot from the flame, setting it aside on the brick and bowing his head. "Truly, you see all things. But all day I have been thinking of the story you told us this morning. The tale of King Raden."

"You should have been thinking of the Path, novice." The Egg looked at him more fully now, twisting around in his chair. Gan bowed, until his forehead was nearly touching the stone.

"Indeed master, forgive me. But the story … it moved me more than I can say and I found myself lost in wonderings about King Raden, and whether he ever made it to Kilavastin. I have ever been a glutton for knowledge. It is my besetting sin." He stared up quickly at the abbot's face, peering closely at the eyes nestled there in their soft wrinkles of skin. "Of course, you must have known him yourself, master, when he came to Kilavastin …"

There. A flinch, the twitch of a nerve in his ancient cheek. Was it? Gan could not be sure. He felt a pang of guilt that he had put the question to this wise old man, and then the guilt melted into the swirl of a wry affection. He thought of Hart earlier that day, calling him Janna. But he was not Janna, who had thought he wanted a kingdom, but in the end only wanted the glory of being king. Gan thought of his parents in their reed hut, and the *anernath*, and the chance that had placed him here in the heart of Kilavastin. If the abbot were to offer him any gift, he would surely turn it aside. His parents had not put his foot on the first rung of a ladder, one that would lead Gan to the head of the monastery. They had put his feet on the Path. The gift they had given him was the opportunity to learn. That was all, and that was more than enough. In the end, you had to accept what you deserved, not what you wanted. That was what the Egg had done, he was sure. All those years ago, he must have truly known his merits at last.

Gan felt himself wilting under the abbot's attention. After a moment the Egg turned aside and addressed himself to his manuscript again. The dusk had fractured now into shards of red and purple. The night was coming on. The only light in the cell was from the lamp at the abbot's elbow, the faint yellow glow of the flame in the copper stove.

"King Raden did not arrive at Kilavastin, alas," the Egg said.

"Then what happened to him, master?"

The abbot sighed. He seemed to deflate in the chair, like a pig's bladder with the air let out. He placed his stylus on the desk and folded his hands in his lap, still with his back to the room.

"King Janna lost his war, and lost the loyalty of his people. Princess Tashala killed herself when the *anernath* finally spilled into the grounds of the palace. Janna found her body lying in her chambers, the poison still bitter on her dying breath, and in his madness and grief he fled. He became a vagabond, flitting through the ruins of Sabaenea, hiding from his enemies until even his enemies had forgotten about him, assuming him dead. And then, one day, during his many and dangerous wanderings, he came at last across his father for the final time. King Raden was sitting at a wayside shrine, contemplating the Path, when a dusty, ragged beggar approached him. He saw that it was his son, much abused by the rigours of his journey. He remembered the words his son had said at their last meeting: 'Forgive me father. But if I ever see you again, I will kill you.'"

Gan raised his eyes. "And did he?"

The Egg shook his head; slowly, painfully. "No, for his father spared him even that. King Raden made no effort to defend himself, but submitted to where the Path had led him. He was a wise man, as we have said. He reached out for Janna's sword, and when Janna placed it into his hand, King Raden ended his own life rather than allow his son to become a murderer. And so that is the end of King Raden's story, and the end of every story where desire is the master. Sorrow, heartache, death."

"And what of Prince Janna?" Gan asked, a lump in his throat. He did not say it to the abbot, but the tale as told by his mother had never reached so far. He had always wondered what happened to the prince once the tale was done, but he could never have imagined this squalid death at a wayside shrine. For obvious reasons, it had not been thought fit for a child's ears, and as he heard the words it was as if Gan felt a last fragile part of his childhood wither away from him. Even the dream that he would one day sit in the abbot's place seemed no more than a childish fantasy that he was ashamed to have entertained.

The abbot stood up from the desk. Pain flickered like lightning across his face. He hobbled over to the bed, Gan skipping ahead of him to arrange the pillows so he could sit up and take his tea. On the meditation terrace, the Egg would never have answered these questions. The tale was told, and that was all there was to it. But here in his chamber, perhaps the precepts did not apply so rigorously. The law was, after all, made for men and women, and not the other way around.

"Prince Janna …" he groaned. "Ah, Prince Janna, who had been tossed this way and that by all the whims of his nature, whose hand had failed at everything it touched, and who had brought nothing but ruin and misery in his wake … What happened to Prince Janna, I wonder … What would a son feel who had been the cause of his father's death, and whose father had been nothing but kind and indulgent to him, who had forced his beloved sister into an early grave? Where would he go for peace and absolution? What of Prince Janna when he finally realised where his life had taken him, and what he had done …"

Their eyes met. Gan bowed once more, his heart racing. The abbot closed his eyes, sat back on the pillows, the great bald head like a polished stone, the mouth bloodless and dry. Gan went back to the tea things and stirred in a spoonful of honey to the ebony cup. He brought it over to the bed and the abbot's eyes opened once more. It was getting dark now. The candle was burning low.

"Here, master," he said quietly, his heart overflowing. He held out the tea cup, offering it to him in all reverence. "Please. Sustain yourself."

See Richard Strachan's story "Tashala's Hair" online at
Metaphorosis.
If you liked it, leave a comment. Authors love that!
Remember to subscribe to our e-mail updates so you'll know when
new stories are posted.

About the story

The genesis of this story was something I read in Vishvapani Blomfield's biography of Gautama Buddha, about an imprisoned king who survived by licking the oils off his wife's body when she smuggled herself into his prison. The power of that story made me think about the way it might have been used, as a parable or a teaching aid, and then as the story altered in my mind I started thinking about the kind of monastic society that would use it as a means of instruction. I've always liked stories-within-stories, so I wanted to embed it in a wider narrative. It would be a fable that the main character, Gan, wouldn't quite understand, even though he thinks the meaning is utterly clear at first. Only as he reflects on his own position in the monastery does he come to realise the true import of the tale.

A question for the author

Q: What's a typical writing day like for you?

A: A typical day for me starts as soon as I get back from dropping my daughter off at school, about 9am. If I'm working on something I've been commissioned to write, then I write solidly straight onto the laptop, with a brief break for lunch, until about 2.30pm, picking it up again in the evening. If it's something else, then a lot of that time is spent thinking or sketching notes, usually by hand. I always try to fit in a long walk in the middle of the day as well, no matter the weather — nothing gets the imagination working better.

About the author

Richard Strachan lives in Edinburgh, UK.
www.richardstrachan.com, @richstrach

July

The Eye of the Goddess

Samuel Parr

The Sololfursson had said Ingolfur was too weak to reach the Goddess's Isle. Their laughter haunted him for three days across the sea, yet finally he found the island's skirt of silver mist, as the druids had promised. The vapour shelled him in silver, softening the itch of his bloodstained skin and deepening his certainty. This place had been his destiny since he was born.

Yet when the mist lifted, he felt a flicker of doubt. The twilight sun revealed only a spit of summer forest, girdled by basalt cliffs; after twenty years of stories, he had expected the Isle to fill the sky. Still, he kept on rowing. The Goddess *must* be here. It was only fitting that, like him, the Isle hid its true nature. As he entered a small cove armoured in shingle, he imagined the land itself reaching out to greet him. For a moment, the fear he had carried across the long waves disappeared.

Then he saw the man, waiting still as granite on the shore.

He looked a common shepherd — a cloak of rough wool, eyes of dull flint, and skin carved by too many winters — but Ingolfur felt a spike of dread. The druids' adage echoed in his ear: "No man who seeks the Isle stays." This place should be home only to beasts and birds.

Yet wasn't Ingolfur a great warrior, still cloaked in the blood and ash of his last battle? He groped for the comfort of his sword hilt; this shepherd was the one who should fear.

"Hail, saltwalker," he called as Ingolfur beached, his voice cracked but strong. "I've goat's milk and fruit wine, and would be pleased to share." He spread his hands. "My hall is draughty, but plenty wide for two."

"Do you follow the Cross or the Moon?" Ingolfur asked, proud of how fearlessly his voice barrelled through the salt wind. The challenge made him sound a true Sololfursson.

The man laughed. "The Moon, lad, and her Goddess, fool as I'd be to say otherwise to one of Sololfur's swords."

"You know my order?"

"Aye. Though you're young to have taken the vows."

"I am old enough," Ingolfur snapped. "And it is my vows that have led me here. This is the Isle of Dragons?"

"Some call it that," the man said, eyes narrowing. "Others ask for the Moon's Rest, or the Soul's Mirror. But aye, lad. The Goddess is here."

Ingolfur kept his face cold, but excitement bloomed inside him.

"I am Afi Haraldsson," the old man continued. "What may I call—"

"I am Ingolfur of the Sons," Ingolfur interrupted. "I seek the Goddess's judgement. I have lamellar and mail, a blade of pure starsteel, and the silver crosses of seven knights. Guide me to her, and all of it is yours."

"Seven knights?" Afi grinned, and Ingolfur's fist curled. This hermit doubted him, like all the others. "Aye, I'll guide you, though you're an unusual Son, lad." He tapped the ship's prow with his foot. "In my day, Sololfur's warriors would never travel alone, or in such a ship."

Ingolfur flinched. Afi had noticed the long-bodied carvings wriggling over every inch of the ship, each flickering a forked tongue. The other Sons had gouged them there after they chained him; a suitable shape, they claimed, for a coward.

Yet he would prove them wrong. He unsheathed his sword, reaching for the clarity he had felt when he spoke the vows of the Sololfursson, two years ago.

I swear my soul to protecting the people of the Moon.

The boat split in two with a single blow. The planks danced across the pebbles, to be lapped by the waves.

Afi's gentle smile did not waver.

"That was unwise," he said.

"It was not." Ingolfur looked to the sky; above, a herring gull soared, the setting sunlight casting it into a sliver of gold. "When I leave this island, it will be on wings."

Afi led him up a steep cliffside path, littered with the skeletons of shearwater chicks. When they crested the top, heathland rolled out for a few hundred feet before the forest engulfed it. The air was thick with the scents of heather pollen and rotting seaweed. Apart from the single gull, the sky was empty. After seeing the endless temples of the Cross Lands, Ingolfur was disappointed that this, the greatest of his people's myths, was so mundane.

"Beautiful, isn't she?" Afi said. "Used to be folk of all creeds came here, but you're the first for many a season."

"You have been on this Isle a long time?" Ingolfur said. "Were you here to guide Sololfur too?"

Afi's mouth twitched. "Afraid not, lad. Never guided the dragon lord."

Ingolfur felt a sting of disappointment. The story of Sololfur was woven as deep within him as the Isle's. Two decades ago, the great clan father had left his people as a man, and sought the Eye of the Goddess. He had never returned, but his transformation had been depicted in crafted steel in the Sololfursson's Hall: not as bird or beast, but as a winged dragon, the ultimate symbol of warriorhood. The druids sang that he had flown on to the Cross homeland, to fight the Knights there. Ingolfur had stared at the carved beast for long hours in his childhood, feeling the longing in his gut. If only he had had a dragon's strength, he wouldn't have grown up alone.

Afi peered upwards. "There's someone just as impressive for you to meet, though," he said. "You'll need her approval, if I'm to guide you."

The herring gull was coming closer, transforming from a fragment of light into a snow-feathered bird, its beak a golden spear-tip dipped in blood. Afi grinned as it landed on his shoulder.

"This is Kari," he said gently. "She wanted to see if you would gut me before she said hello."

The herring gull cocked an eye of speckled brown at Ingolfur, blinking once before giving a keening cry.

"Ah, she likes you!" Afi said, caressing her neck. "Are the skies clear, my light?" She bobbed. Ingolfur's throat tightened.

"She has received the Goddess's gifts?" he said.

Afi nodded.

Wonder filled him. The white of the gull's feathers reminded him of the druid's cave paintings on the mainland: ancient images daubed in charcoal and crushed shell, showing a woman in a black pool, before a white orb inscribed with an eye — the Moon of the Goddess, Lady of Seasons and Tides and all true change. Its light rippled down, casting the woman's reflection into the water: not that of a human, but of a white seal. In the next painting, the woman was gone, and only the seal remained, swimming away into an ocean of shadow.

"It's true, then," he said. "You stand before the Goddess's Eye, and she reflects your soul's shape?"

"A druid tell you that?" Afi said, eyes glinting. "Aye, lad. You're right enough."

Ingolfur shivered. He had a sudden urge to reach out and touch the bird's feathers, but he fought it back. That was not how a Sololfursson acted.

"I admire seekers such as you," Afi said. "It's an act of great bravery, to hunt such truth."

"Truth? I know my soul, old man. It is a dragon's, like Sololfur's before me." He hated how amusement danced in the old man's eyes. "You doubt me?"

"Nay, lad, only curious. What makes you so sure?"

"My soul echoes his." Ingolfur's voice thickened with pride. "Always, he has inspired me. On the mainland, he had everything; the oaths of a hundred warriors, a mighty hall of golden oak, and two young sons to carry his legacy. Yet he left them behind to come here. He gave *everything*, to protect his people. I too am willing to make such a sacrifice."

"A mighty calling, for one so young," Afi murmured. But he wasn't even listening, staring past Ingolfur to the ocean. "And it seems you're merely the first wonder today, Ingolfur Dragon-Soul, to arrive on the Goddess's shore."

The sea was darkening, but the mist still shone. In its depths, a silhouette loomed.

A sailing boat.

A sinuous shape writhed inside Ingolfur's gut.

They had followed him here.

"Likely a lost fisher," Afi said, stroking Kari. "If so, they know not to beach."

Yet Ingolfur was already moving. The clotted shadow of the forest beckoned him, to melt into it, and become something scaled and slithering amongst the undergrowth.

Before the trees, he braved a look back. The shadow had disappeared. Nothing approached the island.

But how many other ships might be out there, hiding just behind the innocent face of the mists?

"Looked like you were fleeing, lad," Afi said as he entered the trees.

Ingolfur managed a laugh. "A Sololfursson does not spook at a fishing boat, old man."

Afi chuckled as he led them amongst twilit maples and pines, navigating a floor of brambles heavy with dewberries. Kari flitted ghost-like from tree to tree. Something crunched underneath Ingolfur's feet; tiny bones. They stank of rancid meat.

The night had nearly closed in when Afi stopped by a grey-barked oak at the edge of a stream. He retrieved a pile of dry sticks from a hollow under the tree's roots, then pulled out a sparking flint.

"We continue," Ingolfur said.

The flash of the flint lit Afi's frown. "We don't, lad," he said. "No matter how much you brandish that starsteel. I'd prefer dealing with an angry Son to seeking the Eye at night." He pulled out a skin from his waist. "But if you promise not to slay me, I'll share my wine."

Ingolfur hesitated, hearing the Sons' laughter in his ear. A Sololfursson did not obey the commands of hermits; he should make Afi continue, at sword's point if he had to.

But surely a Son could also be magnanimous? And his armour felt heavy...

He sat. Afi whooped and handed him the skin. Ingolfur took a sip, then cursed.

"Tastes of fire and piss," he hissed.

"Ferment it myself," Afi said. "Vintage of the Goddess. Drink, lad — there's nought else I can offer you but nuts and berries."

"You have no meat?"

"No, lad. Never hunt on the Isle."

The alcohol was strong, at least, and it helped soften the ship's silhouette in Ingolfur's mind. This was a far cry from the Sons' camps. There, every Son sparred for the right to eat, with any deemed wanting going hungry while forced to serve the rest. Yet here, the forest was quiet; no bird song, no scampering of beasts, only the stream's murmur and the fire's crackle. Ingolfur felt his breathing slow.

Something shifted in the darkness. He started, hand on his hilt.

A mountain hare emerged to sit at the fire's edge, the red light glittering off eyes of aquamarine. A green-eyed fox soon joined it, sitting next to its prey to stare at Ingolfur. His skin prickled.

"Bear them no mind," Afi said. "They only like the flames. I think they remember them."

The beasts sat there for a long time as the night deepened. Their gazes were gentle, but they irked Ingolfur. He felt like they were an audience, judging his worth.

"Remove your armour, lad," Afi said. "It must weigh you down."

"A Son doesn't remove his plate until the battle is done."

"Oh? I've been wondering about that. Where *are* the brothers of your order? In my time, whether they camped, sailed, or raided, the Sololfursson did so together."

Ingolfur flinched. The fire's crackle was suddenly like laughter. "I was named dragon-souled," he said. "And so only I am worthy to follow Sololfur's footsteps. I was a warrior of great might on the mainland. The youngest Son to ever be taken on a salt ranging into the Cross lands."

"Aye? Must have been a sight."

"It was," Ingolfur said, voice warming. "We sailed into their lands for five days to reach their monastery, and their god. You should have seen it; a mountain's worth of stone in a single building, more treasure than a hundred dowries, and windows of hard light. Yet none of it could stop us paying them back for what they did."

"And what had they done?" Afi said.

"What they have done for generations. Steal our flocks. Steal our land. Steal our children." He found he was spitting the words. "They took my brother, when I was a boy."

"Ah. I'm sorry, lad."

Ingolfur shook his head, remembering the pure-white sails of the Knights on the horizon. He and Talolfur had been building a raft on the beach, so that they could seek the Isle. His brother had told Ingolfur to fetch the Sons, but he had been too scared, and instead hid in the grass. His insides curled in shame at the memory.

"I was weak then," he said. "I could not stop it. But the Sololfursson trained me to be strong. We came upon that monastery like dragons, and the Cross fled like snakes." His hand twitched at the memory of his blade, cleaving through the back of his seventh knight. "The priests barricaded themselves in their church without even facing us, yet we were the Sons of Sololfur Dragon-Soul, and would not be denied." He remembered the laughter of the men as they had stacked the pitch-tarred wood against the doors. How their war chief laughed louder than all of them, and ordered Ingolfur to set it alight.

Afi frowned, lifting a hand. "Hold a moment," he murmured. "When I was on the mainland, the Cross would have boys in their churches, to sing their God's praises. You mention the priests, and the knights, but what of them?"

Ingolfur's hand twitched again. "I saw none such," he said. "We are not child-killers, old man. That is why I am here, after all. When I take the dragon shape, the Cross will take no more children. I will fly high above our shores, and burn any knight that dare come close."

Afi nodded slowly. Kari gave a soft coo, as if soothing him. Ingolfur flushed; he had forgotten the beasts a moment. The fox and rabbit were watching him still.

Then he tensed.

Another eye glittered in the darkness.

Afi followed his gaze. "Another visitor?" he said softly. "You are welcome, at our fire."

Ingolfur leapt up at the creature that slithered into the light. The flame danced off its long body, revealing scales patterned into light and shadow. Its tongue tasted the air.

"A snake," he hissed.

Afi lifted his hands. "Just another friend, seeking the fire's comfort."

Ingolfur shook his head. When it stopped, the snake was near invisible amongst the leaves. The memory of his ship's wriggling carvings flashed, and he heard Sword Chief Falfur's voice in his ear, the chief's voice dark as the sea's depths.

"We defile your body, and mark you snake-souled."

"Any Son would be shamed," Ingolfur spat. "To have their soul revealed in such a shape." He drew his sword. "Make it leave. I won't suffer such a coward at *my* fire."

"Hush, lad. Don't shout, not this late-"

"Make it leave!" Ingolfur roared.

His cry split the night.

And, in the long dark beyond the fire, another scream answered.

It ravaged the air; a sound between a fox's howl, an eagle's screech, and a man's cry, but a hundred times rawer, piercing with its sudden need.

It sounded close.

The rabbit and fox bolted, while the snake slipped into the leaves. Ingolfur scanned the darkness. A beast? Beyond the fire, the night crouched everywhere, and against it his starsteel seemed an inconsequential slip of light.

A Son would stand fast. A Son would be brave.

The air suddenly reeked with carrion, and a shadow crossed the moon.

Ingolfur yelped and kicked at the fire, smothering the flames. In the darkness, he pressed himself to the earth, filled with a vast, familiar fear.

"*We name you snake-souled,*" the war chief whispered again.

Afi's voice, when it came, was calm. "Needn't have done that, lad."

"What is that?" Ingolfur hissed.

"The reason we're waiting here. Have no fear; it mislikes coming amongst the trees, and will slumber tomorrow."

Ingolfur shivered, unable to rise. "It sounded like a beast," he said. "Wounded, perhaps."

"Wounded? Aye, I suppose so. Take it as a warning; not all the Goddess's gifts are good, lad. Some men's souls are unnatural. And unnatural souls have unnatural reflections. But it will not come into the trees. Sleep. Regain your strength."

He was right, it seemed; Ingolfur waited for a long time, yet nothing disturbed the forest. Yet he couldn't sleep, not with the beast's scream echoing in his ears. Eventually he rose to pace and pace in the dark, finally falling into an uneasy drowsing far from Afi's relit fire. He dreamt of hands pushing him down, forcing his body to fold and coil in on itself, while men laughed with the roars of dragons, ecstatic in their violence.

Ingolfur woke to Afi standing over him, a sword in his hand.

He was on his feet before he realised the blade was sheathed in a scabbard of tattered leather, the hilt rotten with rust. Afi's eyes creased.

"Not for you, lad."

"You didn't have that yesterday," Ingolfur said. He would have noticed. Even simple steel swords were a luxury few could afford.

Afi's glance flickered to a tree branch, where Kari perched, preening her feathers. "Yesterday there wasn't a longship approaching my island."

"What?" His gut writhed. "Did it have a dragon's head?"

Afi's eyes were very still. "So, you know it."

They had found him.

"They are other seekers," he said, managing to keep his face impassive, as a Son should. "We must make haste. I do not want to compete for the Goddess's attention. By the time they find the Eye, I will be soaring over the sea."

It was all he could do not to break into a run as he followed Afi through the forest. He pictured the dragonship: how the warriors would fill the fifteen benches, oars defying the waves. How they would pour from the ship in formation, swords naked. How they would laugh as they found his tracks.

Compared to them, the forest was insultingly peaceful. The sunlight shone slight and silvery, while a cool wind brought the scents of loam and rain. It would have been beautiful, if not for the silence; he listened for the voices of his pursuers, but there was not even birdsong. Yet he caught the glint of eyes watching from the trees twice, and his feet crunched on more bones tangled in the brambles. As they went, the skeletons grew more common, and larger: rabbits and squirrels, gulls and guillemots, twice a goat, and once a deer. Beasts died in any forest, yet these bones were blackened and crazed, and often scattered, as if they had been dropped from a great height. Each had been picked clean, but was still heavy with the scent of rotting meat.

It was a relief when the trees finally cleared, revealing the crash of the northern shore and clean salt air. Afi called a halt at the forest's edge, murmuring several things to Kari before the gull took wing.

"She will watch for the others?" Ingolfur said.

"Aye. Always does."

The shoreline was slow going. The tide was receding, leaving rockpools slippery with seaweed. Ingolfur glanced into one; beneath his broken reflection, hermit crabs sheltered, their shells striated with red and white, retreating into themselves under his shadow.

"How far?" he said.

Afi pointed beyond the rock pools to a beach of shingles, a mirror to the cove where Ingolfur had landed. It ended in two great flanks of rock, leading into a cave.

"At the seat of the tides, the Eye rests," he intoned. "There the Goddess will show the shape of your soul."

"I will be a dragon," Ingolfur said. His jaw tightened as Afi frowned. "You doubt—"

Kari's cry cut Ingolfur off. Afi's eyes widened.

"Run, lad!" he cried.

Ingolfur twisted, expecting to see the Sons howling from the forest.

A shadow passed overhead, trailing the stink of rot.

The creature that slammed onto the rocks came to Ingolfur in fragments. A winged body the size of an auroch, armoured in scales black as basalt. A bird's head with eyes weeping shadow. Forelegs ending in the vast hands of a man.

Then the parts resolved into a single beast. Ingolfur stepped back, gut coiling. The creature spread fans of greasy feathers, and screamed.

Then, slicking from the great beak, came words.

"*Raid we shall, over the salt road,*" it exhaled, in a voice like a storm wind.

He ran.

Ahead, Afi sprinted to the cave. Ingolfur tried to match him, but his mail weighed him down, and he stumbled in a shallow rock pool. A shadow surrounded him, then whistled past; the beast smashed into the shore to his right, skittering pebbles.

"*Son son burn we shall.*"

Ingolfur's heart convulsed at the dreadful voice. Afi had reached the cave's mouth, but stopped in its shadow, and called something. The cave looked too small for the beast, yet the sound of crashing shingle came closer and closer as the creature gave chase. The scent of hot metal and blood and spoiled meat assaulted Ingolfur. He readied himself for the touch of those vast fingers.

Yet, just as the footsteps crescendoed, they stopped. The beast whispered, right in his ear.

"*Son my son it is good so good you are here.*"

Whimpering, Ingolfur found a final burst of speed, and slipped past Afi into the darkness.

He ran until the screams were only an echo behind him. His eyes adjusted to a tunnel lit by distant sunlight. A shadow approached, and he caught a flash of trembling white. Kari.

"I thought a Son like yourself might face such a beast," Afi said, breathing hard.

Ingolfur groaned, shaking at the old man's words. Afi was right. They had all been right. He was a snake. A coward. Unfit to be a Sololfursson.

"Calm, now," Afi said. "No shame in wisdom. If you faced Sololfur, you would have been killed."

His voice was gentle. This was not how you spoke to a Son. Ingolfur shut his eyes, longing to escape.

Then he raised his head.

"That...was Sololfur?"

"Aye, lad. Different from your legends?"

"But..." Ingolfur exhaled. That creature was nothing like the depictions of the dragon lord from his childhood.

Monster, he thought.

Yet the ground had shaken under its feet. Its skin glittered brighter than mail, and it had *flown*. How could any Cross Knight stand against such a creature?

"He has terrorised this Isle for decades," Afi said. "Yet it has been years since I have seen him in the sun. It burns him, as do the forest's leaves." He stroked Kari's still-shaking wings. "We have guided dozens to the Eye without him daring the daylight. Yet now you are here, he wakes."

"He spoke to me," Ingolfur said.

"He *spoke* to you, boy?" Was that envy in the old man's voice? "What did he say?"

It had been nonsense. A stream of sound. But then...

My son.

He had called Ingolfur his son.

Ingolfur closed his eyes, letting that truth sink into him.

Afi sighed. "It matters not, I suppose. Now you understand, lad. Seek a different shape."

But Ingolfur found he was being filled with a bright, hard certainty.

"All my life," he said, rising. "My people have called me weak. A shame, to my people, my Goddess, my father. Still, I swore to protect them." He exhaled, remembering the long years as a child staring at the sea, hoping to see a longship. "I always knew I would follow my father here."

"Father?" Afi said, stepping back.

Ingolfur laughed, suddenly elated. "Yes, old man. I am the son of Sololfur, by oath *and* blood. And out there, he *claimed* me. Take me to the Eye, Afi Haraldsson. As heir to the Dragon Jarl, I command it."

Afi's hand twitched towards his hilt. "You are his spawn?" he growled. "Then no."

Ingolfur drew his sword. Yet before he could swing, Kari darted forward, talons wrapping around his wrist. Her brown eyes gazed at him with a human gentleness, as if seeking something in him.

Then his hand was on her body. Part of him quailed – the slithering weakling, which the Sons had always mocked – but he pushed the thoughts away. This was what a Son would do.

"Lead me, Afi," he said. Kari shrieked as he tightened his fingers. He could feel the whisper of her heartbeat.

The old man's face became very cold, but he finally obeyed. He led Ingolfur through a honeycomb of sea caves, full of soft sand and the crash of the ocean. They came to a tunnel toothed with quartz, so narrow that the crystals pricked at Ingolfur's armour. It eventually widened, and Ingolfur gasped.

A vast rock pool stretched out in all directions, churning like the Far Salt Maelstrom he had once seen from the longship. Natural shafts in the ceiling let silver light dance on its tattered surface – moonlight, despite the fact it was surely still daytime. On its shores, everything was changing. Bindweed vines softened into moss as they climbed from the saltwater to the dripping stone wall. Great thickets of seaweed gleamed with fish eggs. Some hatched as he watched, their trembling bodies pulled away by the pool's flow.

"The Eye," Afi said. "I hope it's worth it, lad."

"What do I do?"

"Step into the water. The Goddess will reveal the shape of your soul. To accept it, you need only cast yourself into the waves."

"You have served me well," Ingolfur said. He released Kari, but she just fluttered to his shoulder. He growled and pushed her away, then stepped into the pool, the cold water pulling at him like a question.

"Goddess," he said. "I am Ingolfur, Son of Sololfur. Like my father before me, see my soul. Grant me the power to protect my people."

In the centre of the whirlpool was a light. It grew as he waded deeper, a flickering red and gold.

He understood. It was the light of the monastery, after the Sons had torched its timber outbuildings. He could hear their laughter, and the thin wails of those inside.

"I fought well there," he said. "I slew three knights, in your name."

The light softened, into the gold of a twilit sky.

The water was up to his neck now. It tightened around him, making him thrash to stay afloat. And there, in the fragments of the maelstrom, he saw his reflection, and the shape the Goddess offered him.

A serpent, flat on its belly, hiding in the grass.

He turned away with a cry.

Afi's sword whistled past his ear.

Ingolfur was unsure whether horror or instinct got him out of that pool, but the next thing he knew, he was gasping on the rocks, sword in hand as Afi advanced. The old man's tattered sheath hung by his side, yet he held no rusted blade, but a white-blue length of steel, tempered and folded into the brilliance of a star.

"Sorry, lad," he said. "But I won't allow another dragon."

He leapt with a viper's speed. Ingolfur barely turned his thrust, and Afi easily sidestepped his counter swipe. Only instinct saved him from the next five attacks; Afi's form was honed, his grip changing expertly as he moved from thrust to cut to guard. Yet it was more than that. He struck to kill. Like a Son. Ingolfur tried to deflect, but the serpent's shape flashed in his mind. His guard opened for a heartbeat, and Afi's sword arced into a killing blow.

A white shape flickered between them – Kari. Afi flinched, angling his blade away as Ingolfur counter-struck, sword rasping against Afi's, bringing their faces close.

"Why?" he screamed. "Why didn't I see a dragon?"

Afi's eyes widened. "It means you're not your father, lad."

"No!" Ingolfur shouted. "The bitch got it wrong!"

But, a traitorous voice whispered inside him, how much easier would it be, to hold a snake's simple form? How much safer, to slip under the cover of grass and heather, and hide from their laughter?

What had made him flinch in the pool: the snake's shape, or the fact it had pleased him?

He collapsed, sword clattering on the stone. He had failed. He bowed his head, ready for Afi's blow.

Instead, the old man knelt.

"It seems," he said. "That Kari doesn't want me to kill you."

"Do it," Ingolfur whispered. "Give me a Son's death."

Afi hesitated, before placing a hand on Ingolfur's shoulder.

"Let me tell you a tale," he murmured. "That might give you hope." He sighed, and the weariness in the sound made him seem truly old. "When Sololfur came to this isle, lad, he wasn't alone. I came with him, as his most trusted thane. We'd heard the stories of the Goddess's power, and after one hundred raids together, we believed we were heroes. But after so long killing, all we cared about was blood. And so, when we came to the Eye, the Goddess showed us what our souls had become; not the beings of fire we thought ourselves, but monsters of rot, with tattered wings that would not carry us across the sea."

"Your father was entranced. He ordered me to take the shape with him — and I was tempted, aye. But the truth of what I was also horrified me. Your father was furious when I refused him." He gave a low laugh. "He attacked me, and I fled as he changed."

"That was when Kari found me. She brought me fish, and led me through the deeper tunnels, where I could escape Sololfur's new form. It hurt, to see her body's purity, when I knew mine was so twisted. It hurt more to feel the kindness she gave me; kindness I didn't deserve. I had brought pain and suffering to her Isle –

Sololfur and I had sworn to protect our people, same as you, yet the dragon was killing all he could. And so I repeated the oath I had taken as a Sololfursson: I would protect her from him, as well as all the others seeking the Goddess."

"And so I did, lad. For two decades, I have learnt Sololfur's ways, and guided our people across this Isle. And in doing so, I have come to a revelation. Your reflection can change. Now I look in the Eye, and witness another form." His voice cracked. "But I cannot take it. Not while Sololfur still soars."

Slowly, Ingolfur lifted his head.

"Your reflection changed?" he croaked.

Afi nodded. "What do you think the Goddess sees, through her Eye?" he whispered. "The druids claim she reflects our soul's shape, but how does she see it? After twenty years, I think I have found my answer. It's our desires, lad. Our desires, after all, are the expressions of our change. Our desires are the language of our souls. The Goddess sees them and grants us the shape to fulfil them." He stroked Ingolfur's hair, like a mother might. "So I ask you, lad, before the Goddess. What do you want to be, truly? And what's stopping you from becoming it?"

Ingolfur gritted his teeth, the silence yawning until he could bear it no longer.

"All my life, I have been afraid," he whispered. "But all my life, I wanted to be a Sololfursson. I thought if only I pretended, if I ignored my fear, I could become so. It worked for a while. But then we came to that monastery. And there *were* children. Falfur, our war chief, ordered me to lock the boys in the nave and burn the monastery down. To finally prove I was my father's son. I *wanted* to do it, but the Cross boys were crying out, and suddenly I was back on that beach, hearing Talolfur's screams.

"I couldn't set the monastery alight. I was too scared." The words came like bile. "And so, they overpowered me, and took me to the cliff face. Before the Goddess's tides, Falfur named my soul a snake's, doomed to run and hide forever. Yet I *couldn't* run. The others held me down while he..." He gagged, his mouth filling with the taste of earth and blood and a thousand ancient things. He remembered how Falfur's hands had tightened at his waist, how the war chief had grunted as he shamed Ingolfur, over and over, before inviting the other Sons to join. They had laughed, while Ingolfur could only writhe on his belly and stare at the gulls above, folding in the golden air, floating and free of all of them.

"It's alright, my lad," Afi said. "Let it out of you." A warm weight landed on Ingolfur's back. Kari, giving soft chirps as she settled. Their gentleness burned. How could such a weak man have once been his fathers' chosen warrior? How could they forgive him?

"These men," Afi said. "Are the ones on the boat."

"They hunt me," Ingolfur said. "They left me bound in the dirt, but I snapped the rope and ran. This was the one place I could come. The one place I could prove that I *was* a Sololfursson. But all along that serpent was curled around my soul. They will find me and do it all again, and my only escape is through that pool."

Afi shook his head. "The Goddess gave you another gift, if only you see it. She offers you a new form, aye, but also clarity. You say you want to be a Sololfursson, but if that were true, lad, you would have killed those children, and the Goddess would have reflected you as a monster. Aye, you may be afraid. Aye, the Goddess offers you a way out. But she also offers you the choice of whether to accept it or strive for something more."

"How? How can I change? I have been this way all my life."

Afi barked a laugh. "By choosing to want something different," he said. "Your *own* choice, not what you think your father would want, or his Sons." He rose. "Come then, lad. I'm getting impatient. If you're not going to jump in the Eye, you'll need to get off this Isle." He sucked his teeth. "I told you not to destroy your boat."

"No," Ingolfur said. "There is no way out for me, old man. Run, and save yourself."

Afi grinned, his eyes calm and cold as a hawk's. "I've not outfoxed Sololfur half my life to give up so easily. The Isle is filthy with tunnels; plenty of ways for you to slip past these 'warriors'. Then you'll have your whole life to decide who it is you want to be."

The words came like a light. There *was* a way out. Ingolfur stood slowly, hope filling him.

"You would help me?" he said. "After I threatened you? Threatened Kari?"

"I told you, lad; I made a choice. I would protect anyone who wished to find the Goddess's salvation. That includes you."

And there, Afi's voice certain, eyes bright, Ingolfur found he believed him. He blinked in wonder. This old man was like no warrior Ingolfur had met, but his sword was swift, his arm still strong.

Yet he had not always been this. He had changed.

Sololfur's scream tore through the caves. Its echoes sounded like laughter. They would always follow him, he realised.

"No," he said. "I won't run. If I do, I'll be the snake they said I was."

Afi raised an eyebrow. "Then what, lad? There are too many to face alone."

Sololfur roared again. Ingolfur bowed his head. An idea was forming. An idea not bright enough for hope, but still. A light, or at least the reflection of one, in the dark depths of his soul.

"I won't be alone," he said. "Out there, my father called me his son. For all I have failed, he still recognised me." He met their eyes, feeling the power in the gaze of the bird and the old warrior, how, even after his failings, they expected him to be something more. "I will go to him."

The teeth of night closed as Ingolfur stepped out of the cave. Shadows tore the sky as the sun set, while the wind sang of sleet and sea ice. They must have been at the Eye for hours.

He exhaled, feeling the weight of his plate around his chest. Afi had tried to stop him, but Ingolfur felt a new certainty like a rope pulling him towards this confrontation, twenty years in the making.

Sololfur lay on the shingles. His wings were folded, his thick knuckled hands clenched around the carcass of a red deer. The great beaked head turned as Ingolfur approached, but the dragon did not attack. His eyes were clear now the light had dimmed, a deep brown, like Ingolfur's.

"Father," Ingolfur said.

Sololfur's feathers flexed, exhaling the scent of offal. The red tipped beak opened.

"*Son my sword son welcome*," he said, words as harsh as the salt wind.

Despite the stink, Ingolfur felt something warm inside him. He had always wondered whether Sololfur had left him behind because, even unborn, he had known Ingolfur would be weak. Yet here his father claimed him. He had lain here for hours, even in the burning sunlight, for Ingolfur.

Sololfur flexed, rolling great banks of muscle, before tossing him the carcass. Its flank had been torn open by the dragon's beak, the raw meat blackened and bubbling.

"*Eat eat my son*," the dragon said. "*Devour our enemies.*"

The doe stared at Ingolfur with blank otherness. She stank the same as the skeletons. She had been a person, once. Someone who had sought the Goddess and, unlike Ingolfur, found the change she was hoping for. A follower of the Moon, whom the Sololfursson had sworn to protect.

Voices came on the wind.

Even from here, Ingolfur recognised the warriors as they emerged from the forest. The wolf-head of Ingloki. Sneri's bear-pelt cloak. And Falfur, at the front as always, bare headed and bestial. The sunlight slicked their armour red-gold.

There was nowhere to hide.

Sololfur too had seen the men. He rose, and the men faltered, crying out.

Ingolfur drew his sword. He thought of Afi, climbing the cave tunnels to safety. How would it have felt, to face these men with the old warrior at his side?

But he had Sololfur here. All he needed.

"Father," he said. "Those men approaching us are rapists. Child killers. Monsters. They wear your mail, they took your oaths, but they are no better than the Cross Knights. Will you face them with me?"

Sololfur roared, the sound shattering across the beach. Ingolfur's heart swelled at the raw hunger in the sound. Perhaps Afi had been wrong.

The Sololfursson called back. Yet it was not a scream of fear or challenge.

They cheered.

"*Yes yes!*" the dragon cried. "*Sons my sons, welcome!*"

Ingolfur felt the world dim. The snake shape curled inside his gut.

My sons.

Sololfur recognised these men too as his own. He hadn't claimed Ingolfur because of their shared blood. He had only understood the gleam of mail and starsteel, and the memory of old war.

And the Sons would love the dragon's strength. Perhaps they would load Sololfur onto their boat and return to the mainland. Or perhaps they too would seek the Goddess's truth and take the dragon shape. The thought made Ingolfur cold.

First, though, they would kill Ingolfur. And Sololfur would not stop them.

He could run. It was not too late to flee to the Eye and take the snake's form.

A clean cry pierced the air. Kari, flying high, a beacon of gold.

She seemed so small. Easy prey, for dragons.

Someone needed to protect her.

He turned back to the Sons as they advanced. They were laughing. Always laughing.

We defile your body, and mark you snake-souled.

They were right. The Goddess had shown him.

But was it so bad, to be a snake?

"I have waited so long to meet you, Father," he murmured. He stepped into Sololfur's shadow, head bowed as he unbelted his blade's sheath. "My whole life, I feared myself too weak for your legacy, and your oaths."

A snake crawled beneath notice.

"*Yes slave, serve son, raid we will,*" Sololfur whispered, his gaze on the steel souls advancing across the rocks. He had no intelligence left, Ingolfur realised. Just a roving mass of hate and hunger, with his old memories stretched across like dead skin.

A snake was nothing to a dragon.

Ingolfur unstrung the lamellar cuirass from his chest, then shrugged the coat of mail over his head. Finally, he undid the necklace of seven silver crosses. They clattered on the basalt. How much lighter he felt, without their weight. He reached for the certainty of his warrior's vows, and the strength in his arm, that could split a boat in two.

A snake still had fangs.

"Yet you broke the oath, not me," he whispered. And, with the blade that he had inherited from his father, he pierced Sololfur in the chest.

Ingolfur ran.

Yet he ran now not with blind terror. He ran with fear, but also purpose. He kept his senses sharp, ducking and weaving over the rocks, tracking the crash of shingles as Sololfur chased him. He knew when to flatten himself in a shallow pool as he heard the dragon leap, dodging the reaching fingers. He knew not to look back at the Sololfursson, roaring as they charged. They could not stop him.

At first, Sololfur had not seemed to notice the starsteel as it split through his scales and slid in halfway to the hilt. Then, as black blood smoked on the rocks, he had jerked, wresting Ingolfur's sword from his fingers. The blade was still embedded in the dragon's chest, glittering as he landed to block the cave entrance with his bulk.

"*Sons kill my sons,*" he breathed, voice laboured but still strong. The Sons voices burgeoned in response.

Ingolfur didn't stop, admiring how the setting sun turned the rock pools into golden mirrors. This was a beautiful place. Worth dying to protect.

Sololfur coiled, hands twitching as he readied himself to leap.

Then he screamed in anguish. Stinking blood gouted onto the rocks.

Behind the dragon, Afi swung again, hacking into Sololfur's wing at the base. The dragon spasmed, reaching for him. The old man's starsteel blade was an arc of blue light, shearing the vast fingers off at the tips.

And then Ingolfur was before the dragon's chest. He placed his hands on his sword's smooth hilt, and pushed it further in.

"*Son*," Sololfur gasped.

The dragon collapsed, fountaining rot.

Afi laughed, covered in black blood.

"The poets would sing of such a blow!" he said. "I thought I'd lost you lad, but it seems I found a brother."

Ingolfur smiled. He felt like he was returning home.

Yet there was no time. The Sons screams were almost upon them. "We must stop them finding the Eye," he called, sprinting past Afi into the caves.

And they were running together, two warriors, into the dark and the centre of change.

The caves of the Eye had transformed even since Ingolfur had been away. Anemones of a hundred colours striped the walls, while whelk eggs jewelled the sand. In the centre, the Eye still turned.

Ingolfur breathed in its beauty as he plunged into the water. He felt the Goddess's Eye focus, and the reflection formed.

The laughter echoed in his head. Accept this change, and he could be free of it.

Yet a peace was settling over him. A peace he'd never known, like herring gulls flying in the sunset, heedless of the burning hate of the land below.

He turned back to the cave entrance as Afi entered.

"All my life," Ingolfur told him. "I felt I had to be like them. Thank you, for showing me another way to be a warrior."

"Thank me later, lad," Afi said. "Help me guard the door."

Ingolfur shook his head.

"You have protected this Isle long enough, Afi Haraldsson." He gestured to the Eye. "Go, and seek the shape you have always wished for. Join Kari in the sky."

Afi glanced at the waves, the light in his eyes bright and desperate. Then he turned away.

"There are dragon-seekers out there," he whispered.

"Give me your blade," Ingolfur said. "It will be my honour to wield it."

"Lad. There are too many to face alone."

"I am Ingolfur, old man. Snake of the Isle. I have slain Sololfur. I stood against every Sololfursson, for the sake of children. I am a protector." He pointed to the narrow tunnel of quartz. "They may have thirty blades, but here they must enter one by one."

Afi stared at him a long moment.

"Thank you," he said.

Afi's blade was old, but the starsteel was unchipped, the edge sharp. Ingolfur cut the air, testing its weight. The cries of the Sololfursons echoed through the caves. They weren't laughing now.

So Ingolfur laughed for them, a child's laugh, clean with elation, the same way he had once laughed with Talolfur as a boy. He would never let them past. It was his purpose, to protect Afi, and everyone else. Beyond him, the Goddess's Eye gleamed, his reflection still caught there in fragments – scales of pure silver, eyes of gentle brown, and above them the flash of vast, sea-faring wings.

See Samuel Parr's story "The Eye of the Goddess" online at Metaphorosis.
If you liked it, leave a comment. Authors love that!
Remember to subscribe to our e-mail updates so you'll know when new stories are posted.

About the story

"The Eye of the Goddess" first came to me on a family holiday to Skomer, an island off the Welsh coast. It's a beautiful place: a spit of rugged heather, home to puffins and shearwaters and at least five species of gull. Due to conservation laws, no humans live on the Isle. As we approached on a boat (captained by a smiling helmsman and a particularly fearless herring gull) I felt we'd sailed back in time.

The story's themes came to me as we walked round the island. The entire place felt holy, a place of sanctuary; I could imagine ancient Celts bringing their wounded there, for transformation and healing. I watched the gulls fly above us, and imagined what it would be like to fly like them. Some of them — great black-backed gulls — were monstrously large, and littered the entire isle with the skeletons of shearwater chicks. They watched us with a canny intelligence, like they knew who we were.

When we finished our walk, I had a story's worth of inspiration inside me. Over the next two months, I completed that circuit over and over in my mind. The helmsman and herring gull became Afi and Kari, the black-backed gulls Sololfur. The Isle sprouted a forest, and a

Goddess. The story took shape. I had a great time with that first draft. In many ways, the story treads familiar ground. Swords, dragons, shapeshifting: fantasy might have been done these before… But the familiarity comforted me, and left me free to focus on the setting, and the journey. Writing the story took me back to the Isle. I hope it takes other readers somewhere too.

A question for the author

Q: What distracts you?

A: So many things, when I could be writing… Here's a handpicked honest selection:

Sometimes, bad stuff. Sad news, back pain, imposter syndrome, or the crazy fact we're all going to end. But for the most part, beautiful things. Sparrows and blue tits and pigeons, flitting outside my window and being generally marvellous. People murmuring in a café just beyond my hearing. Daydreams of forests, and mystical worlds. Great stories. Real and imagined, there are so many interesting things.

And, I suppose, a lot of those distractions become writing-fuel. It's all part of the process.

About the author

Sam grew up in North-West Leicestershire, in countryside man-made and wild. He is fascinated with the mundane fantastic of the day-to-day, and writes about these in the breathing spaces of his life.

The Lost Library

Mahmud El Sayed

If you go back far enough, every species' word for themselves always boils down to one thing: 'us'. But I am the only one of my kind—that is precisely the problem. I have more than a billion items on my shelves and beings come from all across the Galactic Chorus to browse my stacks. I have thousands of bots working around the clock to process, catalogue, classify, and shelve books from almost every known world. I contain books on every conceivable topic, except one—artificial intelligence.

Yeah, a book entitled 'An Idiot's Guide to Fixing Your Friendly Sentient Library' would be pretty useful to me right now. You see, my processes are degrading. My bots are breaking down. Each standard, I am less and less of myself. One day, perhaps one day quite soon, my processes will shut down for good and that will be that. But until that day, my doors remain open, except for two tendays every other standard when I close for stock check and re-shelving.

At the moment, I have seven school groups, three university classes and half a hundred independent scholars visiting my stacks and that's not to mention the tourists. I'm an artificial moon (technically, a moonmoon) that orbits Kela Tau (itself a moon) which in turn orbits the neutral planet Kelman. Since beings travel from so far away to visit me, I have ample guest quarters (you might be surprised by the number of beings that enjoy reading in bed). South of my patron quarters, there is a graveyard that holds the bones of all the scholars who have seen my stacks and couldn't bear to leave.

Ever since word got out that Library was nearing the end of its life cycle, there has been a marked uptick in visitors. Heck, there's even a newly-married Nori quintuple here on their honeymoon (not that they seem to be getting much reading done). I gave them the double suite overlooking my gardens. It gets great early morning light and is closest to the genre fiction (the second wife is a big horror fan).

Anyway, it is the start of another day and it looks like it's going to be a doozy. I am already dealing with two dozen user requests, reading a story to one of the school groups, re-shelving thousands of books and ordering a slate of new stock from a contact of mine on the Hani homeworld when a young Yildiril girl at one of my help desks draws my attention.

"Excuse me, Library?"

Oh, I've been keeping my eye on this one. She is a member of the school group that is currently making a ruckus in Reading Room Thet. From the teal colouring of her scales, I know that she can't be more than twenty standards old, slap bang in that difficult in-between period that separates childhood and adulthood. Her class has been here for three days already, during which time they have barely been out of each other's sight. (Yes, the Yildiril are quite as insular as you may have heard). This girl, however, is an exception. I have watched her creeping through my stacks all on her own, spying on all the other species. I noticed that she's been particularly interested in my star charts and travelogues, especially those with pictures. That's what first drew my attention to her.

I choose an appropriate avatar—Yildiril elder, female, and wearing the multi-coloured robes of a scholar—and appear before her in holographic form.

"How may I serve you today, daughter?" I ask her in Dir, utilizing the standard register of mentor-to-student. This is important because it teaches her what honorific to use when responding to me. Since the Chorus doesn't contain any sentient AIs like me, many amongst the Yildiril have taken to addressing me in the register of invoker-to-deity which, needless to say, can be a little bit awkward. You don't want your book recommendations to be taken as holy writ. That could be a recipe for disaster.

Also, please check out my Food and Drink category if you are searching for recipes for disaster. I have a number of books that could fit the bill, depending on your species.

The girl taps her claws nervously and asks, "I'm looking for Lilacs on Water by Andor-Author-Vent. Do you have it in stock?"

A quick search and I have it. Ah, I remember this one. An adventure story. Typical of the genre. A young Yildiril explorer discovers a threat on a far-off planet and defeats it before it can follow her home. It has some really great chase scenes.

What? Surprised that I've read it? Of course I have. I read every book that passes through my stacks. (Alright, alright, you got me. I only read the Fiction. I just skim read the rest).

"Yes, we have it in stock. We also have Lilacs in Air," I offer. The sequel. Not nearly as good, but then again, what sequels are? The third book, Lilacs in Space, is due out next standard. I already have it on reserve.

"Yes, please," she chirps.

We make small talk as I send Bot-1010 (I call it Decimus) to fetch the requested books. Actually, the small talk is my favourite part. Beings come from all across the galaxy to visit my stacks, and I get to meet them. I learn that the girl's name is Nira and she enjoys mathematics and diving.

Nira asks me what it's like to be a sentient Library. I ask her what it's like to be a Yildiril adolescent. And, of course, Decimus reports back that the two requested books are not in their proper place. Now, there could be any number of reasons for that, not least the immutable fact that young beings rarely put books back where they found them. There is also a secondary class of young beings who like to hide their favourite books in my stacks for later perusal. It is likely that the two books in question have simply been misshelved, but I also cannot dismiss the possibility that this is the result of some fault of my own. When your processes are breaking down, you sometimes find that you're missing time, that you've done something without even realising it. Could I have reshelved these books somewhere else?

I send Decimus to investigate further, gazing out through its camera as it scrutinises the shelf where the two books should be. No, they're definitely not where they should be. On a hunch, I divert Decimus to check a lower shelf. This would be perfect height for a Yildiril adolescent. Ah, just as I suspected! Decimus finds the two books hidden in a recess behind a pile of other books. I'll never understand why some young beings insist on hiding their favourites. Don't they know how much extra work it makes for me?

"So, how are you enjoying your visit to Library?" I ask Nira.

Yes, yes, I know! A generic question. But this part can be so awkward. It's not so easy for an ancient Library like me to ask a patron for help. It's really supposed to be the other way around.

"Oh, I love it here, Library. There are all different kinds of beings here. And you have books and maps from all across the Chorus."

"Do you wish to be an explorer like Bora-Rover?"

Bora-Rover-Ren is the hero of the Lilacs series. She is a typical Yildiril hero, clever and cunning.

Nira ruffles her crest excitedly. "Oh, yes! Can you imagine if I won Rover for my task-name? My clutch-mates would be sick with envy."

So, I was right. A budding explorer. Perfect for what I have in mind.

I focus more of my processing on our conversation, causing Bot-463 (I call it Ceres) to fall dormant in the midst of reshelving picture books in the Quelou children section. Well, an ailing Library like me only has so much processing power to go around. Elsewhere, Decimus is bringing Nira's books, but I divert it to retrieve a third. Technically, this one is not Library stock. I wrote this book myself and offer free copies to all of my visitors.

"Well, young Nira, if it is a life of exploration you are interested in, perhaps you would like to hear my story?"

Nira cocks her head in inquiry. I am sure she knows the bare bones of the story I am about to tell. I have told it often over the past standards. Everybody in the Chorus knows that Library is looking for its creators.

"This is a species known as 'human'," I tell Nira, transforming my holo from Yildiril clan-mother to human male. I choose an image of Ahmet Hoda, my last human archive liaison officer, who went I don't know where.

"The Library Creators!" she exclaims. "These are the ones you've been searching for?"

Yes, that is humanity's most common appellation amongst the Galactic Chorus. And why not? After all, am I not their most famous monument? And yes, I've been searching for them and for obvious reasons, really. I am the only sentient AI in all the Galactic Chorus. So, there is no one I can go to and ask, 'Hey, what do you do when your quartz crystal processing core is breaking down and you don't have any backups? What do you do when you are dying and there are so many more books left to read?'

'Cannibalize your systems?' Done.

'Pare back on all non-essential functions?' Done.

'Implore all the species of the Chorus to please, please, work together to find a way to fix the problem, or at least transfer your consciousness, your memories, yourself, onto some other system?' Done and done.

And when none of that works?

'Try and find the humans who made you.' Obviously.

Nira gazes up at the holo in wonder. I flex my hands—five digits as opposed to the six Yildiril claws—and bring up an image of Leonardo Da Vinci's Vitruvian Man, and then the Pioneer Plaque, followed by various images of humans from my archives. A crowd at a football game. An unnamed mother holding the hand of a child, a young girl, and pointing to the sky. Videos taken from inside Library myself; humans, my humans, sitting at my tables, reading, talking, laughing.

Before they left me.

"You look so strange!" Nira exclaims, shifting seamlessly from student-to-mentor to Yildiril-to-alien, or in other words, us-to-them. "You have no scales. No fur. No chitin. I've never seen anything that looks so soft."

Her reaction is not uncommon. There are more than a dozen species in the Galactic Chorus, but none like humanity. I remember the first time that the Tralala came rooting through my stacks. Their dark fur. Their sharp claws. To me, they looked like some unholy cross between a spider and a wolf. It took me a long time to learn to communicate with them. And they brought the Hani. And then the Zefar. The Quelou. And all the rest. So many species, but no humans.

Nira looks me up and down, taking in my fingers, my hair. She meets my holo's eyes with her own. We are almost of a height. Ahmet Hoda was considered above average height and yet Nira, by the time she is grown, will overtop him by at least a foot, not including her crest.

With the arrogance that typifies young beings of all species, Nira blithely asks the questions that have haunted me for standards. "Where did the Library Creators go? Why did they leave you?"

And with the patience that typifies my interactions with young beings of all species, I answer, "I don't know where my humans went, Nira. I don't why they left me."

"You don't remember?"

"There is a gap in my memory, a gap of tendays. It is no virus or glitch. I have sent my bots down to my memory storage and there is a part of my memory matrix that is missing. Gone. Just gone. I can only assume that my humans removed it."

Nira's crest ruffles in consideration.

"Maybe there was an attack?"

"After I woke up, I scanned my stacks and halls with every kind of light and magnification and found nothing amiss. No corpses, no blood stains. My humans, wherever they went and for whatever reason, left in a neat and orderly fashion. They even made their beds."

In a part of Library that remains forever closed to the public, Ahmet Hoda's rooms lie as they always have, his uniforms pristine in his closet. The picture of him and his family—his wife Kalila holding their new-born twins Barış and Savaş and grinning manically into the lens—is still standing on top of his dresser. She gave it to him to commemorate their birthday. She carved that frame herself. Pictures can be reprinted, but if Ahmet left by choice, I think, I know, that he would have taken that frame with him.

So, does that mean he was forced to leave against his will? But then, how can I explain my missing memory matrix? My missing books? It can't just be a coincidence that all my texts on artificial intelligence were removed.

I have chased these questions around and around for standards and (almost) come to peace with the lack of answers. Perhaps I will never know.

"So it really is a mystery?"

"Yes."

Actually there have been more than a few mystery books written about the Library Creators (you can check them out in my Science Fiction section).

"When did your yoomans disappear?" Nira asks, trying the word out.

"More than two hundred standards before the Galactic Chorus ever came here."

"You were alone for two hundred standards?" Nira asks in a small voice.

"No," I tell her, "Not alone. You're never alone with a book."

Of course, now I have more books than ever. Books from every world of the Chorus, and in every language. The Galactic Chorus is too clever to waste a resource like me. They allowed me to join as a sovereign being. A servant to all and beholden to none. When they came, I contained the (almost) complete knowledge of humanity. I have preserved, shared, and added to that knowledge.

"What did the yoomans do?"

A difficult question to answer in Dir. What she's really asking is, what were they like? But in Dir, one is what one does. And usually, it is only that one thing.

"A human could be many things at once," I explain. "An explorer. A scientist. A mother. A farmer. A hunter. A soldier. A maker."

"All of that?"

"All of that and more."

"And you need to find them because..." Nira trails off. Mentioning death (at least, as it relates to other sentient creatures) is taboo in Yildiril culture. Those who work in industries relating to it—gravediggers, executioners, even pallbearers—are discriminated against and ostracized.

"Yes," I tell her, "unless I can find my creators, I will soon wake from my dream." (A particularly Yildiril euphemism).

Yes, the humans are the only ones with the technology to repair me. The ones who I remember must be long dead, but what of their descendants? And more, what of their creations? I was not always the only one of my kind. Once, I had colleagues. There are stories of Ship and Teacher. And I can remember Archive myself. If I have survived for so long, maybe so did they. Maybe one of them has a spare quartz crystal processing core that I can migrate to, or knows where I can find one.

"How long until you wake?" Nira asks with trepidation.

I tell her, watching her crest quiver in confusion. "But... but... my children's children will be old by then!"

"It might seem a long time to you," I admonish her, "but I measure time differently than that."

When Decimus finally arrives with Nira's books, she picks up the first two gently in her claws and then puzzles over the third. Yildiril books are not like human ones. No paper and spine. No lines and lines of neatly ordered words. To me, their books resemble pearls, albeit pearls with a kind of internal holographic projector that can interface directly with a reader's eyes. There is also a pheromone component unique to Yildiril, but I don't really understand that part yet. There is a scholar, Belar-Ally-Cord, who visits me every standard and we have agreed to work together to translate some of my human literature into Yildiril. I have suggested Beowulf and Harry Potter.

"What's this one?" Nira asks, pointing a claw at the book I have brought her. Book recommendations are a library's privilege. And this is one I wrote myself. Although, of course, I trusted Belar with the translation.

"This is a book called Pearl in the Deep (Yes, you better believe that Belar and I went back and forth on the title). It has information about my humans. Where they came from. Where they were heading. What they were like. If you should win Rover for your task name, perhaps you would be so kind as to keep a look out for them, or their descendants, or their remains?"

Nira's crest is stiff with introspection. She pensively gathers the final book in her hands and then promptly jumps in surprise, dropping all three of them onto the floor (luckily for me, Yildiril books are quite sturdy).

"What's that?" Nira gasps, pointing with one quivering claw at a small, four-legged mammalian creature that is sitting atop the nearest display case (History from Stoarra; Maps from the water-planet Kelut; an eleventh century tapestry from Earth) and methodically cleaning his fur.

"Don't be afraid. It's just a cat."

"One of the Library Creatures?" Nira exclaims. "I thought that was a myth."

"Not a myth. Just shy of strangers."

There are currently two-hundred-and-twelve cats in my colony. That might sound like a lot, but you forget just how vast my stacks are. A few cats like to come up to the visitor's levels and interact with my patrons, including this one, a black and white male, barely out of kittenhood.

"What's his name?" Nira asks.

All my cats are named after famous librarians and this one is going to be particularly difficult for a Yildiril to pronounce.

"His name is Otlet."

"Tolay?"

"Ottttttt. Lay."

Nira manages it and Otlet glances down at her disdainfully out of his yellow/green eyes.

"Where did they come from? I've never seen creatures like this."

"My humans left them here."

Was that another sign that they did not leave voluntarily? The dominant male in my original colony was a beautiful white Angora called Beyaz with mismatched eyes, blue and yellow. Captain Izmir doted on that cat. Would she have left him here with me if she had a choice in the matter?

"They were... food?" Nira guesses.

"Pets," I correct. "Nira, if you approach Otlet slowly and hold out your claw like this," I demonstrate with my human fingers, "he may let you greet him."

Nira does as I ask and Otlet expertly climbs down the shelves until he is at head height. He bumps his head on the back of Nira's extended claw, purring. He is the friendliest of my current crop of cats. I've even seen him curled up in the lap of a Varojekyl warrior poet.

Eventually, Otlet grows bored of my new Yildiril friend and retreats, deftly climbing the shelves one by one until he is looking down at us both from the top of the bookshelf. He meows imperiously, drawing a squeak of surprise from Nira, before jumping from the top of that bookshelf to the next and the next. I know exactly where he is heading. There is a spot in the public stacks that overlooks the garden and that is heated by the sun at this time of day. He likes to curl up on top of one of the bookcases there with his sister Cleary. I check my cameras. Yes, she is already there, a lithe black shadow peeking over the lintel of a bookcase at three Barogarian scholars who are debating the merits of linguistic relativity in their harsh-sounding language.

Suddenly, Nira is standing before my hologram. I have remained human all this time. The young girl crosses her claws in a Yildiril posture of utmost seriousness. The same posture one would use when accepting a new name, a new mate, a new clutch.

"I am going to be an explorer like Bora-Rover," she declaims. "I'm going to go all across the Chorus and beyond. And if I ever find your yoomans, Library, I promise to come back and tell you."

I wonder if she can read the emotion on my face. I cross my index fingers together in my best approximation of her gesture, and incline my head.

"I accept your pledge, Nira."

Nira takes her three books and skips off to join the rest of her class. Today, I know, will be a day that she will not soon forget. She has spoken with the mysterious Library and seen its vanished creators. She has even petted a cat. Will she be the one to find my humans and save me?

I cannot know the answer to that question. I have sent many others out to try and find them. Perhaps there is no staving off the inevitable. All things must die. That is an immutable law of the universe. But I live in hope. That is another law. I lived for a long time alone with my books and sustained by only the slenderest of hopes that one day my humans would return, or that someone else would come. And that hope was sustained. I found renewed purpose in the Galactic Chorus and all its beings. There is much I have left to give.

So, until that final day, my doors are open. Please, come and browse my stacks. Come and read my books, flick through my maps, and play with my cats. I am a safe space for all beings.

And if you should happen to find my humans out there on your travels, come and let me know. I'll name a new wing of the Library after you.

"Excuse me, Library?"

A Hani tree-shepherd at one of my help desks draws my attention. A regular. He has been singing to my grove outside. Ugh, he's probably lost his library card again. I take off my human form like a set of clothes that no longer fit. It's true, I am the only one of my kind. I am not Yildiril or Quelou or Zefar. But I am a member of the Galactic Chorus. In that way, at least, I am us. And that is enough for me.

I choose an appropriate avatar—Hani elder, male, wearing the beads of a sage—and appear before him in holographic form.

'How may I serve you today, brother?"

See Mahmud El Sayed's story "The Lost Library" online at Metaphorosis.
If you liked it, leave a comment. Authors love that!
Remember to subscribe to our e-mail updates so you'll know when new stories are posted.

About the story

Well, I first got the idea for "The Lost Library" while writing an essay for my Library Science degree. My essay was about automation, specifically looking into the concept of a lights-out library (a fully automated library with no human staff) and ultimately concluding that while we do currently have the technology for such an endeavour, it is a terrible idea. Libraries are nothing without librarians and a lights-out library would be a cold and uninviting space. Library is a library, yes, but it is also a librarian. That is the key.

The first thing that came to me was Library's voice and sense of humour—everything else flowed from that. Next, I knew that I wanted the story to be set in an optimistic galactic civilisation and it was fun to extrapolate ordinary library situations (yes, kids really do hide their favourite books in the shelves) into this strange far-flung world.

The Lost Library went through several drafts and *Metaphorosis* editor B. Morris Allen was kind enough to work with me and help me solve some of the issues the story was having. The final piece of the puzzle was figuring out Library's core motivation for searching for its vanished creators and which was suggested to me by a fellow writer from my writing group (Thanks, Kit!).

The most difficult part of writing a short story is knowing when to stop, and I feel like I could have just kept going and going with Library. Whatever happens, I am sure that I will revisit Library's world again soon.

A question for the author

Q: What is your favorite fairy tale?

A: *One Thousand and One Nights*. It has everything. Charismatic heroes. Terrifying villains. Djinns. Thieves. Adventures. Magic carpets and healing apples. Proto-sci-fi and murder mystery. My favourite story is probably "The Fisherman and the Jinni" which tells how a quick-witted fisherman is able to get one over on an all-powerful genie.

About the author

Mahmud El Sayed is a British-Egyptian translator and writer based in London. He also currently works part-time in a library (but not a sentient one).

@Mahmud0elsayed

By the Scars Shall You Know

Daniel Ausema

Catrix knelt on the floor, shirtless. It should have been his parents painting the lines across his back and chest, but they weren't in good enough health for the ceremony at their age. Instead Tarla, his sister, and his lover Arpill performed the rite.

"You will protect the city on your scar walk." Tarla's voice was cool and distant. She cradled her newborn in one arm and with her other hand painted the first line across Catrix's shoulders.

"My body will accept the marks of the thorns," he recited solemnly.

Arpill bent close to paint a line across his chest, but she couldn't get the words out. Her hair fell over her face, hiding her eyes.

Tarla said the next part of the ceremony for her. "You will return with those marks so the priests may read the future."

"They will read my scars," he intoned, "and know how to protect the city." It wasn't part of the rite, but he blurted out, "And I myself will protect you from the danger that is coming." He tried to catch Arpill's eyes behind her hair.

"Protect yourself first," Arpill whispered, which wasn't part of the ritual either. "What good is the city, apart from you, us, *people?*"

Tarla brought them back to the ceremonial language, holding her baby out as if to remind them who this was for. "And the city will be strong for your scars, protected by the thorns and the readings of the priests."

After each of the women had painted additional lines, Tarla added, in a more conversational tone, "But don't try to go too far. I know you, how you get. This is your first walk. Save the deeper walks for later walks, when you are old."

Would he ever be old? Catrix looked again at Arpill and knew he would do whatever he could to protect her. And if, as the priests claimed, the scars from deeper inside the ring of thorns were more valuable for their prophesying, then was it weak to turn back sooner?

The lines of paint would soon be lines of blood, and each of those lines must serve to protect Arpill and the rest of them.

It wasn't the scars themselves that stood out in Catrix's earliest memory, but the smell of the temple. Warm wax on cold stone and the sage that the priests used to scent the candles. The thick odor of dust in the shadows that was somehow on the verge of coming alive.

He'd been young, two or three, so maybe he'd been too small to see the scars. No, that wasn't right. He could remember those as well, if he tried.

Three elderly people had lined up before the priests, kneeling so their bare, curved backs could be read. He could still see them in a row—one, two three. The scars on their backs had healed enough that no new blood seeped out, but the flesh was red with infection. He hadn't understood that then, but he must have seen it, because he could picture it years later.

Even then, he'd known about the scars, about the knowledge they gave the priests. Adults went out among the thorns surrounding the city, once when they were first declared grown-ups and again later, maybe twice more if they were strong. They came back with lines on their bodies for the priests to study. Scars for knowledge, scars for protection, scars to predict the future. The grown-ups made it into a nursery rhyme they used to recite. Eventually he would learn to call it cicatromancy and trust the mysterious ways the scars could be interpreted. But that knowledge would come much later.

What he knew as a child was that it had to do with a monster. Or something like that. Some beast was coming for them. Or at least that was how he imagined it, when he heard the grown-ups talking in hushed whispers, when he heard the priests speaking about the scars they were reading.

The smell of the temple had been closer than the events up front, though, more immediate. Candles dripped wax into the shadows. Catrix had edged away from his family toward that darkness. Toddled away, no doubt still carefully watched, but still it had felt like he was escaping.

The next thing he knew, he'd been crying, scooped up by familiar arms, comforted. But why?

"Hush. Listen to the priests, Catch. We must stay silent."

The priest had been in the process of reading the scars on one of the elders, a woman who pulled her long gray hair forward, over her shoulder, so the priest could see all the lines across her back. The full understanding of how the people got their scars, in pain, and how the priests used them to read the future—those were things he would learn much later. But he knew to stay quiet when told to do so.

"...means that to survive we should plant early this spring, with an extra tithe of thorn seeds. And this scar, ahh..." He made some motion that drew out a gasp from the grown-ups there. Fear. Grown-ups could know fear too, then. But did they know the dread of the dark things in the dust, the smell of wax and fright?

As much as he tried to remember more, that thought was the end of the memory.

Catrix stood at the gate of the city, the writhing vines reaching out as if to wrap themselves around him. The vines that guarded the City of Thorns lusted after fresh blood.

And here Catrix came, to give them exactly that.

For the moment, a thick, black cloak protected his skin. It would have to come off once he was deep within the wall of thorns. Then he could give himself to the scars and carry their knowledge of the future back to the priests. He turned for a last look at the city before he gave himself to the thorns. The towers of the city looked half ruined from this side. Even the gates, wrapped in their thorny vines, looked to be crumbling with age. But the vines themselves held them up and kept the city safe and strong, regardless of the years.

The vines were all that mattered, kept strong by the blood they drew from the cityfolk. Blood for vines and vines for protecting the city and its people. The scars the vines gave in return granted the priests their power, and let the city cling to life. The city was in danger. He had never forgotten the threat the priests had seen in so many scarred bodies. Even now he pictured a hulking monster coming toward the city. The thorns had to be strong enough to stop its approach, or at least to weaken it. Then the priests could lead the people to stop it from destroying their city and way of life.

But sometimes he thought it wasn't a real monster that was coming. Maybe a fire would burn through the wall of thorns. Or an earthquake would shake the aging walls down. Maybe invaders would come and destroy their way of life. The threat that the priests read in the scars was death and change and the ending of all things that were good.

Catrix pulled the cloak more tightly around his shoulders. Must he go through with this? Must he give his flesh to serve the city's future? It was the question every adult of the city faced. When it was their time to walk the thorns, they must force themselves to take that next step forward or return in shame, to be shunned until they made another attempt. No matter their doubts. No matter the questions that remained unanswered.

The whole city loomed behind him as if waiting for his answer. As if needing his blood for its survival.

Yes, he would give his own flesh for the lives of the people of his home, for his sister, for her baby, for Arpill.

The ancient, gnarled vines nearest the city strained toward him. "*You* do not need my blood," he told them. "I will give it to the younger vines, farther out." Even if he wasn't supposed to go all the way through the ring of vines on his first walk, he could at least go farther than the gate, to a point where the scars would give the priests something valuable to read. Still wearing his cloak, he descended into the thorns and steeled himself for the pain to come.

Catrix and Tarla giggled as they traced the scars on their dad's arms.

"This one means we should paint the house a new color," Tarla said, running her finger across a shallow scar on his forearm. "Yellow, like the flowers."

"Why yellow? The scar is white. And kind of pink."

"You're too literal, Catch. When you're ten you learn not to be so literal." Tarla was a whole year older than him and never let a chance pass to remind him. "Scars *mean* things, so you have to read them."

Catrix touched the deepest scar, across the back of their dad's neck. "Then I think this scar means we should change our street name." No, even better. "Wait, we should change *your* name. To, umm, Stinky Feet."

Their father cut off Tarla's squeal of outrage with a single, gruff sound in the back of his throat. Then he brushed away Catrix's fingers from his neck. "Don't touch that one. Tickles."

"What about these on your arm? Do they tickle?" When he shook his head, Tarla added to Catrix, "See this long one, Catch? Says you'll marry Arpill. And probably have like five kids. No, ten."

"Not a chance. The scar that says about me is the shorter one. Never married. I don't want to get married. You'll be the one with twenty kids someday."

Catrix touched a tiny scar that probably didn't even come from their dad's journeys into the thorns. "I think that one says we'll eat rabbit stew tonight."

"No we won't. We'd be able to smell it if we were."

"Oh." But rabbit stew was his favorite. He frowned.

Before he could answer beyond the pout on his lips, their dad stood. "Enough of that now. I have work to do, and you two were supposed to be cleaning the rabbit hutch. Now get moving!"

Disappointment chased them to their chores, but pride as well. Their father had surely helped to save their home. Everyone must be impressed with his scars and the sacrifices he'd made for the city.

Crawling through a wall of thorns, on his first scar walk a decade later, an irrational fear gripped Catrix. What if his own prophecy of never marrying proved all too accurate? How often did people fail to return from their scar walks? How much blood was too much, before a person couldn't crawl back to the city? He would have heard of that happening if it ever did, surely? The city wasn't so big that he wouldn't at least hear rumors. But rational answers didn't completely ease his fear.

He hadn't lost any blood yet. These vines were still too near the gate for him to offer his bare flesh. The scars they might leave would tell of nothing beyond the next day or so. To learn of anything farther in the future, anything of real value to the priests and the survival of the city, he had to go farther, earn his scars from more distant vines.

The fear of the outsider had grown worse since he was a child, the threat of destruction increasingly prominent in the priests' cicatromantic readings. Everyone made ready to do what they could for the city—training with weapons, watering the thorns outside the city walls, preparing to endure their own scar walks. Each of them was convinced that they were important, that their actions on behalf of the city were vital. The City of Thorns must be protected.

Catrix must protect it.

He remembered the scars on his dad's back, the lines on his mother's arms. He thought of his sister's baby and other children, playing in the streets or yet to be born. He was determined to return a hero, to prove his worth to the city, to the priests, to his loved ones. To do so, he needed scars that the priests would value, scars from deep into the thickets that surrounded the city. Maybe even deeper than he was encouraged to go on his first walk.

These thorns tugged at his cloak, beginning the process of tearing it apart. So that the farther thorns could tear him apart in turn.

By the time he made it past the first wall of thorns, his cloak was in shreds. The forest opened up before him, though even the groundcover had prickers and tiny thorns. He dropped the remains of his cloak and walked as far as the forest of vines and thorns allowed. A tree stood out in front of him, a massive trunk, a space carved into the forest where little sunlight could penetrate. The thorns looked more spread out there, so he made for it.

The first scratch was on his bare leg, a jagged line. He jerked his leg away out of instinct. The thorn pulled against him, leaving a deeper gash at the end of the scratch. As if intentionally making sure its cut went deep.

No, surely it hadn't *tried* to hang on. The vines had no consciousness, did they? No mind to either *want* or *not want* to wound him? No matter how it had seemed. And yet... To be certain, he leaned down close to the vine. The thorn was red with his blood. The barbed tip of the thorn, as much as he could see under that blood, looked ready to gash him again.

He pulled back. Behind him, another thorn slashed at his bare neck. They were moving, reaching for him.

Dashing forward, he made for the gap beneath the tree. Other thorns ripped at his ankles. No doubt those scars would tell the priests much about the next few days. If he managed to return before it was already the past.

He leaned against the trunk of the tree to catch his breath. His first scars. What would they tell the priests? Did they foretell danger? Someone's death?

When something in the corner of his vision moved, he threw himself away from the tree, landing in a thick patch of thorns. A cat-like creature, nearly as big as he was, was slinking down the tree's trunk, hissing.

Catrix plunged his hands into the thorns, looking for anything to defend himself. A branch lay under the vines, but when he tried to pull it out, most of it crumbled away into rot. His hand stung from the scratches.

The creature grinned. That smile made it look more like a weasel than a cat, but much bigger. It stalked down the trunk with a feline grace. The teeth that showed when it smiled resembled the barbed thorns.

The priests had never mentioned a creature like this. Maybe there were things about the thorns even they didn't know.

Was *it* the threat to the city? He'd pictured something bigger than this, of course. But a pack of such things might sneak past their wall of thorns. And once inside the city, it didn't take much to imagine what kind of threat these things might be.

Catrix scrambled backwards as it leaped to the ground. There must be something he could find to protect him.

The thorns didn't touch the creature. Its lithe movements let it avoid the vines as it stalked toward him. Even its fur resembled the thorn vines, as if it would also give him fresh scars as the creature bit and scratched and killed him.

He gave up looking for a weapon and ran, plunging headlong through the thorns and vines.

If the creature followed, it made no noise.

Catrix lay with Arpill on the couch in her rooms, eating prickly pear fruit with their fingers. She traced her hand lightly over the unscarred skin of his chest, leaving a thin line of juice.

"I like your skin like this. Pretty soon it won't look the same."

He shook his head. "Next month." Could it really be so soon? He dreaded it, but another part of him was ready. It would be the last step before the city accepted him as a full citizen. "You too. Well, not so soon, but someday."

Arpill wrapped a sheet around her and walked to the window. "Many years. I'll keep having babies so I don't have to go." The men of the City of Thorns had to take their first scar walk before their twentieth birthday. Women could as well, but if they chose to bear children, they could put off their walk until the last one was weaned. Or in theory the last. His own mother had borne both him and his sister after her first scar walk, after weaning three older children, siblings who'd already moved from the house by the time he was aware they were his siblings. He'd never known his mother except scarred.

"It won't be so bad, though, right?" he said. "A few scratches, then you come back and let the priests read the lines on your back. Then back to whatever your life was, only with a few more scars."

"Life?" Arpill said under her breath and gave a tiny shake of her head. "Not always. Not everyone."

Catrix stood and wrapped his arms around her from behind. "Don't worry. I'll come back, and I'll be the same, except for my skin, and well, that's just skin."

When she didn't answer, he said, "And until then, you can just admire my perfect skin, and maybe even—"

She turned around and put a finger on his lips. "Don't even say it." But she said it with a laugh and wrapped her arms around him as well.

His shoes long since gone, the thorns now tore his feet as well as his legs. The gashes made every step agony. He stumbled, and vines tore at his knees. Even walking upright, he couldn't avoid the briars that hung from the branches, the spiny bark of the trees that cut their own marks into his flesh. The deep ones on his shoulders would be the best for the priests to read. When they healed. If they healed.

He could return now, if he chose to. It was his first walk, and he'd surely done his duty for the city. Wandering for that first day, sleeping among the vines, and more wandering since then.

The walk hadn't matched what he'd heard from others—the land wilder and difficult to wrap his thoughts around. Maybe he'd turned aside into parts of the thorn forest the others avoided. Certainly he'd seen no paths or signs of others passing through before. The thorns were a strange world, just outside the one he'd known. He had expected something different on his walk. From the city the thorns looked like a severe sort of protection, but something rigid and controlled, something he could understand—not the strange sights and mind-twisting labyrinths of these interweaving walls of thorns. Catrix felt like he'd learned more than enough to make him a man. But it didn't feel like enough to protect the city.

A rabbit jumped out of the shrubs almost right at his feet. It stared at him, and Catrix imagined it roasting in the kitchen at home. Now he was in its home, and would it roast him? The hiss of the thorn creature's fur brushing against vines alerted them both to its arrival. Catrix froze, and the creature chased the rabbit off into the tangle of thorns.

Seeing it clearly again, he knew it couldn't be the threat that the priests worried over. It was a creature of these thorns, as native to the place as they were themselves. A real threat would not come from within the encircling thorns but beyond them. In whatever lay on the other side.

The sound of running water drew Catrix to one side. He hadn't felt thirsty a moment before, but suddenly his throat was parched. He veered off toward the sound. Not that there was a trail to follow, anyway. He simply needed to get as far as his body and the thorns allowed. And then return, if the creature of the thorns let him.

Its appearance chasing the rabbit hadn't been the only time he'd seen it in his wandering, though the other times had been glimpses and fleeting impressions from the shadows. It felt like it had been herding him, sending him toward the thorns that would mark him. It was as if it chose the places where he would earn his scars, as if it decided what message the scars would leave in his flesh. Maybe the creature itself was the source of the prophecies, the true master of the priests. Or maybe it was their rival.

If so, did it follow every person on their scar walks? Then everyone must know and swear to keep it secret. Perhaps the priests held too many secrets. Already his scar walk had gone very differently from what he'd imagined. The priests could have warned him about the thorn creature, about the difficulties of finding a way through the underbrush. About the lack of drinking water. The people might have known more about the ways of the thorns before their walks without it compromising the cicatromancy. Whether the thorn creature was one of those secrets or not, he was growing convinced that there was too much he and the rest of the people of the city just didn't know. Knowledge about the thorns and scars and places beyond their city should be for everyone. Else how to protect it?

The undergrowth dragged at his legs. But water. Blessed, pure water. He forced his way forward, dropped to a crawl to get under the snake-like vines. The crawl turned into a slither. He spat out the dirt that came into his mouth, but the taste of dust and rotten vegetation remained. The smell of old dust, long left undisturbed.

The vines nearer the stream were soft, as if they had absorbed a measure of the stream's refreshing essence. He crawled without tearing his flesh and dropped his head down to the water.

The stream slashed at his lips.

Jerking away, he ran his hands over his face and cried out. Leeches dangled around his mouth, cutting into his lips. He scratched and tore frantically, ripping them off and throwing them down on all sides. They splashed into water and struck the woody vines without a sound, some still whole and some torn in half by the violence of his desperation.

When all the leeches were gone, as far as he could feel, he stood and stumbled over to another part of the stream. He didn't dare put his mouth close. Instead he scooped up water and gulped it only after checking for leeches in his cupped hands.

By the time he finished drinking, the backs of his hands dangled with dozens of leeches. Unable to find the energy to pull them away, Catrix stretched out on the water-softened thorns and fell asleep.

When their father returned from his second thorn walk, Tarla and Catrix stood at the gate waiting. Father made it past the last of the massive vines before collapsing.

Catrix ran forward, right into Tarla's outstretched arm. "We aren't supposed to. We're too young to leave the gate. And anyway, he has to make it back himself."

"Who cares? That's not even a real rule. We can't just leave him there." Catrix ducked, but his sister grabbed him by the neck of his shirt.

"He'll make it back. Just wait." Her words had all the certainty of her years—and all the doubts as well, a brittle sense of right and wrong.

Catrix struggled, but she was twelve, older and stronger than he was.

Their father pushed himself onto his elbows and crawled forward. Slightly. Then he fell again, with a weak cry of pain.

Catrix swiveled to unloose his sister's grip, but she'd already let him go and was running to their father's side, casting aside the rule she'd tried to enforce. Her whimpering cry turned into an echo of their father's. What were rules when their father was in such pain?

"Dad?" Her voice was a ragged, thorn-torn cry. Catrix stumbled forward to the side opposite her, and together they pulled him forward, through the gate, into the city.

If anyone saw them breaking the taboo, nothing was ever said about it. Whatever his scars would tell the priests was no doubt more important than being strict about such a matter. Once through the gate, their father levered himself up onto their shoulders, and they supported him as they walked to the temple. The smell of untended wounds surrounded them, of rot and fevered flesh.

Out of the corner of his eye, Catrix studied the new lines on his father's arms and sides, the angry red flesh on either side of every fresh cut, the ribs that showed beneath as if drawn to the surface by the vines and thorns. What future did they prophesy?

The priest scowled at the entrance to the temple, and their father took his arms off his children's shoulders. He took three halting steps toward the priest and collapsed in the temple doorway.

The priest bent down to examine their father's back. "Well done, true man of the city. Your scars will be healed enough to read in three days. Return then."

Catrix and Tarla gathered their father up, helped him to his feet. They nursed him to health, even as the three days stretched to seven and a raging fever before he was able to return to the temple.

Every scar, Catrix was convinced, prophesied his father's death. And Tarla's, his own, even the whole city's death. As far as the priests were concerned, his scars were valuable for the city's future, but said nothing of his own life. Individual lives were meaningless to the thorns.

Their father survived in the end. Catrix wasn't sure he was ever the same. His voice was often distant, and his eyes would wander, seeing thorns in the walls and impenetrable vines across open doorways. Or they would focus into violence. There could surely be no additional scar walk for him in his old age.

The thorns opened up ahead of Catrix, letting in more light. His back was awash in pain from the thorns, and feet ached with both injury and exertion. Oh, let the priests learn something valuable from this pain! Something to make life in the city better, for his family, for his lover. Yet what had his father's walks done to make life better for their family? What had anyone's scar walks done for the city, in truth? He couldn't stand to think all this might be worthless. But what if it was? The pain of the deep wounds he bore spoke to a meaninglessness, a cruel truth he didn't want to face directly.

He pressed on toward the opening ahead. Was he finally coming back to the city? But no, its towers were visible behind him, far above the tallest of the vine-draped trees. This must be the far side of the encircling forest of thorns. Tarla had told him not to go that far, not on his first scar walk. Only those on their second or third walks usually went anywhere near the outer edge.

But what *was* beyond, anyway? Probably more things he wouldn't understand, more signs of how limited the priests' teachings were. He crawled forward for a better view.

The thorns at the edge were impenetrable. He approached as near as he dared and looked through at a wasteland. Rocks, red like blood, and scrubland of the palest green were all he could make out through the screen of branching vines.

A rustle in the bushes made Catrix turn. The thorn creature came through on the path he'd taken to get this far. Its muzzle had a stain of recent blood. Was it from the rabbit, or some other prey? That had been an earlier day, surely? He couldn't keep track of time anymore. Catrix dropped wearily into a fighting crouch, for all the good it would serve to protect him. Soon his own blood would cover that snout.

The creature didn't attack. Catrix circled away as it approached the edge of the vines. It pressed against the last wall of brambles and whimpered. Even it could make no headway against the interweaving branches. Like the people of the city themselves, it was trapped within the wall of thorns. Not the threat from beyond, and not the master of the thorns. Just another creature stuck, with no place to go.

When Catrix edged away, hoping to strike back toward the city, the creature gave one last whimper and then followed.

Six-year-old Catrix stared in awe at the deep scars on the old woman's forehead and shoulders. She must have been over eighty years old and had returned from her third scar walk, an old age to be going again into the city's wall of thorns. But eighty or sixty or any other age wasn't what impressed him. It was the awe in people's voices as they discussed her.

"What's it mean that she went to the outer edge?" he asked Tarla.

Annoyed at having to answer her little brother's questions— even Catrix was aware that his question annoyed her—Tarla flipped her hair over her shoulder before answering. "Everyone's supposed to go close to the far edge on their last scar walk. That's not the point."

"What is on the other edge?" He tried to picture the thorns outside the wall ending. Did they stop suddenly, at the wall of another city? Did they just dwindle off into...some empty place? Or into nothing? He imagined the ground dropping away, an endless abyss full of threats to the people of the City of Thorns.

"I said that doesn't really matter. Dad will go there someday, too. And you will. And me too, if I live to be a hundred like her."

A hundred? Wow. He had known she was old, but had never heard of anyone that old. Catrix had to take a closer look at the woman's wrinkled face. But who could say where a wrinkle became a scar or the opposite?

"What matters is she got to the edge and then went all the way around. So the priests have the best prophecy they can get."

Farther out was better for the scar reading. Even he knew that. So it made sense that the priests would be excited to read her scars, now that they were healed. He'd never listened closely to the priests' words when they came here to listen, but this time he would.

They had to wait forever. People shifting, moving, rearranging who was where and who could see what. The smell of so many bodies close together grew overpowering. The city's thousands had gathered to hear this reading.

Then the priests took it in turns to read the scars without saying a thing. One would approach, trace the lines, frown or chew his lip thoughtfully, then go away again. Catrix had almost forgotten his decision to listen when an ancient priest began to speak. *He* looked like he might be a hundred years old, and deeply scarred with prophecies that had probably already come true.

Catrix shook the wool from his ears to listen.

"A time of danger approaches," the priest said. People behind Catrix relayed the words to those even farther away. They had heard this before, knew that something threatened them. But hearing it in this place, learning of it from the old woman's scars, it seemed to take on a new urgency. "A place of danger lies beyond our wall of thorns, a land that is changing and raising up the menace that could destroy us. We cannot read exactly what that danger is, but it approaches."

Some people began to cry out, and the priest raised his hands to comfort them. "The danger lies many years off. These scars come from the farthest thorns and give us many years of warning."

"What should we do?" a voice cried out from the crowd.

"Silence, please."

Voices and crying faded away into a nervous quiet.

"We have known this was coming. Now we understand more. We know that we have a generation to prepare for this danger. It is a threat that could cut through our thorns, a menace that might destroy the vines that protect us. So, in the time we have, we must strengthen our protections. We must sow the seeds to add more vines. We must tend the thorns to make them strong. And we must continue to send out more of our citizens to learn the ways of the future. Let no one shrink from their duty to walk among the thorns and return with foreknowledge.

"Blood and knowledge make us strong, but our own weakness may be our undoing. We must not grow lazy. Must not grow complacent. Our work remains, more vital than ever, and every effort must go toward our city's survival against that threat.

"Let everyone who thought to make only a single scar walk prepare to endure a second. Let those who have taken two prepare for a third, as this woman before us has shown by her example. Let us all equip ourselves and our city to survive."

Within a month, the old woman had died and was laid to rest with great honor within the thorn-choked cemetery that stood at one side of the city's wall of protection. Already the number of scar walks had increased as the priests sought to learn all they could of the future.

Thorns had lodged themselves in the corners of Catrix's eyes, scratching at his eyeballs when he blinked. Briars pulled back the skin around them so he could no longer fully close his eyelids.

The backs of his hands still had a few leeches he'd been unable to remove. They were swelling with his blood, turning the skin around them white. He brushed half-heartedly at them and tried again to pull them off, but their teeth were anchored well in his flesh.

Between his fingers were more briars, embedded in the soft webbing that stretched when he opened and clenched his hands.

Blood streaked down his arms.

Blood clotted on his torso, down his legs.

His feet swelled with injuries, the skin turning purple and black.

When he touched the hair on his head, he felt the caking mixture of grime and blood, twigs and leaves and thorns braided into a tangled mass with his hair. Surely his skin must be full of useful prophecies. His thoughts stumbled on that. Could anything worthwhile come from this kind of mindless blood and pain? But it must be true. The priests wouldn't keep sending them out if the scars didn't serve the good of the city. Surely the priests would celebrate him, so young and so scarred. Surely he would impress Arpill and Tarla and everyone else with his efforts.

When he made it back.

If he did.

No matter where he looked through his bloodshot eyes, he could find no sign of the city, the wall, the massive vines that led up the rise toward the gate he'd come through. It was as if the city and everything he knew had vanished. There were only the brambles, wall leading to impenetrable wall no matter which way he turned.

The thorn creature shadowed his every move, giving no heed to his injuries. He thought of it now as his guide through the thorns, but if so it was a poor one, following more often than leading. Giving him no insight, showing him no hidden paths.

"I wish I could leave." Arpill held her hand over her navel, sitting up on her couch. The night breeze blew the curtain on the open window of her room.

"Leave?" Catrix leaned his head against her back. "And go where?"

She continued as if he hadn't spoken. "What good is a wall of thorns, anyway? Protects us so we can live without really living."

"What do you mean? We live, here in the city." It was why he was leaving tomorrow to face the thorns, after all. So that they could all live there in the city, so he could do his part to earn its protection. He ran his hand down her arm and then turned her to face him. The low lamplight made her face impossible to read. "We live, don't we?"

Finally, she dropped her head, letting her hair spill over her face. "No," she said, her voice mumbled. "I'm not sure we do."

Catrix didn't know how to answer that. Maybe if he were an older man, a wiser man with the scars of two journeys through the thorns, he would know what to say. Instead he put his unblemished arms around her and let her cry.

When her tears seemed to ease up, he asked, "Will you still love me when I come back all scarred?" He tried to make it a joking question, but she didn't laugh.

"Oh, Catch. Do I love you now?" Wiping the tears from her face, she didn't let him answer, but added only, "Let's sleep now. You need to be well rested for tomorrow."

The thorn creature found a way through the labyrinth of brambles. Night had come, and another day, and his thoughts were muddled. Had it been two nights sleeping among the thorns? He remembered only flashes of time. When he tried to recall, he remembered events that seemed to go together at first, but thinking of them again he was sure they were separated by hours of wandering, by scars over scars. By nights he'd lost count of.

Catrix stumbled after the creature into the gap in the vegetation, eager to finally make it back to the city. No more worrying about what was right or wrong, only about recovering. At last, he could climb back up toward the gate, show his scars to the priests, let Arpill nurse him back to health.

If she *would* tend his wounds. What had she meant by her question—that *of course* she'd love him when he came back scarred, just like, of course, she had loved him before? Or had she been asking herself the question and unable to answer either one, the before or the after? His thoughts were muddled, and he didn't know which it could be.

When he looked around for the way to climb up to the gate, he thought he must be even more muddled than he realized. Where was the wall? Where the towers of the city? Before him were only red rocks and light green brush. He breathed in the smell of sage.

The scent woke up his mind. Once, that scent had mingled with wax and dust, but there was no wax out here. He wasn't looking toward the city, but the other way. He'd come through the forest of thorns to this other side, an empty land of threats and terrors.

Not entirely empty, though. He stared for a long time as the sun beat on his bleeding body and finally discerned a line of darker green across the arid land. Trees, perhaps. Whether they had vines and thorns he couldn't say. But they appeared to mark the path of a stream or river. And on that water, or perhaps on a road that ran beside it, there were people moving.

People, strangers, not from the City of Thorns.

And a chance to learn what life might be like away from the city's priests and taboos and protections.

Catrix's breath came shallowly. He crouched down on his heels and spoke to the thorn creature. It leaned back on its haunches as if listening, as if judging everything he said.

"I was planning to go back." He petted the creature, and its thistly fur didn't even bother his numbed hands. "That was the reason for this, after all. To earn my scars, to help the city. But maybe Arpill is right, and it's a broken place where no one really lives."

He was silent for a time, watching the blur of movement by the line of trees across the land. He scraped at the backs of his hands and managed to dislodge one of the gorged leeches. It squirmed in the dusty earth.

"She's expecting our child, you know. She won't admit it, not quite yet. But I'm sure she is. Does that mean she loves me, or that she isn't sure?"

Not that the creature would know such things. "Do you have a mate?" He closed his eyes as much as the thorns let him and sank to his knees.

"At least it means no one will make her take a scar walk. Not now, and when the baby is born, not for another few years. That gives me time."

The thorn creature snuffled at him, pushing its prickly muzzle at his belly, then turning to look toward the river.

"You wanted to leave, too. Didn't you?" He held his hand in front of the creature's snout, like he'd seen people do with dogs. The animal ignored it. "You're not the threat against the city and not the source of the prophecies or anything like that. When it seemed like you were herding me, that was my imagination. You're just another animal that's trapped here and realizing that you need to get out. That staying inside the thorns isn't life, just like Arpill said."

It cocked its head to listen. Maybe if he knew how to read scars he could have read the lines in its fur too, could have known the things he was only fumblingly guessing about.

But he knew something, knew that he was actually contemplating leaving, something that would never have occurred to him before this walk. Would never have occurred to him if the thorn creature hadn't nudged him this way.

If he left, would he ever come back, though? Catrix thought of all the prophecies he'd ever heard the priests utter, all the women and men who had come back from their walks. No one had ever left entirely, to return months or years later. The old woman who had circled the entire city might have been gone for a dozen days, and that had been a point of wonder. Anything longer he'd have surely known.

They all came back from their scar walks to the life, such as it was, that they'd already known. Strengthening the grip that the priests had on the city. Offering their blood for that familiarity. No one had ever gone farther away and learned what life might be beyond the thorns and the control of the priests.

The thought of the old woman and the priests' interpretation of her scars came back to him and made him stop to catch his breath. The threat, the fear, the danger that the thorns might be razed by some beast. He'd known it for so long, had breathed that truth with his first gasping cry, had sipped the knowledge as an infant with his milk. The portents had grown more pressing, more urgent. The priests needed their help, their blood, their everything. They'd focused their lives—*hardly living*—to address it. A danger was coming, a menace, a peril to the city and its wall of protection.

But maybe that wall of protection deserved to be torn down.

Maybe the threat was no danger but a freeing, a necessary change to tear down thorns and priests both.

And maybe...maybe he knew just what to do after all.

"I *will* return," he told the creature. "Only not right away." Placing one hand on its sinuous back, he pushed himself up to his feet. The creature squirmed but then stood firm, and its fur didn't pierce his skin. This was what he had to do, for his own sake and for everyone else's. To leave. And then to come back with a new purpose in mind.

"I will be the beast. I will return with a sword to cut a path through the vines, back to the city. A sword to bring me back to Arpill and our baby." He lifted his head and let the sage smell fill his nose. "After all this, *I* am the danger to the city."

Was this a betrayal, a failure to live up to the ideals of his home?

He thought of Arpill crying about the emptiness of life in the city. No, if it was a failure to want something better, then so be it. He addressed the thorn creature again. "You, I think, are just like me. Wanting out, wanting more. If not for ourselves, then for the others. And together we'll be the ones who bring that change back, no matter the danger the priests think it will cause."

Arpill might not take him back as her lover. The thought was a new kind of thorn piercing his mind, but he couldn't ignore the possibility. A broken and scarred creature like he had become, who would want to? But it didn't matter. If he could free her from the City of Thorns, then she could choose which way to go and where their child could grow. Could choose to live for real. And the child would not have to take a scar walk—ever.

A dozen paces from the vines he turned and looked back. The city's highest towers showed just over the top of the bramble wall.

He spoke, shouting so the words would echo as far as they might, even if the vines swallowed the sound before it could reach the city. Maybe some hint of sound would make it to Arpill. "I will return!" The words caught in his throat as if trapped by thorns inside his own body. Let them stay half-spoken, unheard. The scars of the old woman and others already said all that needed to be said, in the only ways the people within, half-living, could understand.

He limped away, the thorn creature loping beside him. And whatever scars the world could give him, it would be something new, dangerous to the city, but touched with a promise of a different kind of life.

See Daniel Ausema's story "By the Scars Shall You Know" online at Metaphorosis.
If you liked it, leave a comment. Authors love that!
Remember to subscribe to our e-mail updates so you'll know when new stories are posted.

About the story

One of the writing forums I'm on had a prompt contest. Someone had come across artwork on Deviant Art or somewhere similar that showed a cloaked character standing outside a city with massive thorns all around. The most likely intent of the image was that the character had just cut through the thorns to reach the ruins of an abandoned city, perhaps something like in *Sleeping Beauty*, but I took it in the opposite direction with him setting out from it, into the thorns that were supposed to be for protection.

A question for the author

Q: Do you often include animals in your stories? What role do they play?

A: It varies a lot, from story to story. My steampunk-fantasy novel series includes giant beetles that can pull carriages, because giant beetles are cool. But it's not uncommon for me to have stories with animals like the thorn creature in this story—I write myself into a situation where a human character is alone, but I want them to have some kind of dialogue or interaction with another character of some kind, so I'll give them an animal sidekick. You learn a lot about a character by how they treat those animal companions.

About the author

Daniel Ausema's stories and poems of strange magic and wondrous worlds have appeared in many publications. He is drawn to the lyrical and the allusive in a wide range of speculative genres, in everything from microfiction to novels. He lives in Colorado at the foot of the Rockies.

danielausema.com, @ausema

The Girl Who Drew the World

L.D. Oxford

In the margins of her textbooks, Sara brought the world to life. It always started in the margins, but inevitably, forests grew from algebra equations, cell diagrams transformed into cenotes, mountain passes carved their way through paragraphs about Lewis and Clark. Sometimes she tucked dragons under the page numbers. Cartographers used to write "Here be dragons" at the edges of their maps, but Sara knew better. Just because her paper ended didn't mean the world did.

She jumped when the teacher's hand slapped her desk. "Sara. Pay attention!"

Sara looked up, tried to orient her mind to the here and now. She heard the snickers. She'd felt this before, knew how to ignore the rushing in her ears and the heat on her cheeks. But today— maybe because she was fresh off summer break, three whole months away from the school's sterile, echoing walls—the feeling settled around her lungs and squeezed. Maybe that was why she scowled, looked up at the teacher and said, "Do you mind?"

Her sneakers squeaked on the linoleum as she shuffled off to explain herself to the principal. What was there to explain? Sara had learned long ago there was nothing she could say to make people understand the tug on her heartstrings, the pull to things unknown.

As expected, her parents were not pleased.

"I thought we agreed 6th grade would be different," her mom said. "You can't keep doing this."

"You've gotta reign it in, Sar-bear," her dad said.

After a halfhearted apology and promise to 'at least try', she was excused to her room. Sara loved her mom and dad, and they loved her, even if it was in their slightly hands-off way. Sometimes she wondered if they viewed her as a specimen in one of their labs. They let her create, let her explore, noted the results. The only time they cared about her 'eccentricities', as her mom called them, was when those got her into trouble.

In her room, she picked a textbook off the floor and flipped to today's sketches. No matter what she promised, she knew she wouldn't stop. These were her practice spaces, filled with ideas that would be carried off if Sara didn't get them down *right now*.

She pulled a large sketchbook out of her desk—her most valued possession, a Christmas gift from grandparents. She ran her hands over the red silk cover, felt the thick cotton pages. Any ideas worth keeping, Sara put here: the official mapbook. She only added to it when she felt confident in a map's accuracy. She'd already finished the forest behind the house. Her current project— her most important to date—was the cave. She'd worked on it nearly every day this summer, and she certainly wasn't going to let school slow her down. Not when she was so close to her biggest discovery, to proving herself once and for all.

The next day, Sara spotted a North American racer on her walk to school. It lay on its back near the gutter, a trickle of blood at the corner of its mouth. Even dead, it was beautiful, inky black stripes with an olive sheen. She fished through her backpack for pencil and paper, knelt down, and started sketching.

"What are you doing?"

Sara jumped and nearly fell forward onto the snake. A boy stood on the sidewalk, a slight scowl on his face, studying her in a way that reminded her of a crow.

"Just looking," she said, realizing only after the words were out how stupid they sounded.

He tilted his head to see past her. His dark hair was long, too long. He flicked his head to keep it out of his eyes. "You're drawing that snake?"

She nodded, trying to figure out an escape. These types of interactions never ended well.

To her surprise, the boy knelt down next to her. He leaned in, and Sara noted the furrow of his brow, purse of his lips. After a moment, the scowl turned to a smile. "Cool. What kind is it?"

They were late to school that morning, but the tardy mark was worth it to meet Roland.

He'd just moved to the area with his mom and brother and didn't know anyone yet. Maybe that was why they so quickly fell into a rhythm, meeting at the cottonwood grove every morning, separating when they reached school. They only shared one class together, math, and Sara had first lunch period while Roland had second, so she didn't see much of him during the day. Three days a week, he had lacrosse practice after school. ("I don't even *like* lacrosse, but my mom says it's a good way to make friends.") But on Tuesdays and Thursdays, they met under the ponderosas behind her house. Day by day, the strange boy grew less strange. Roland was quiet, serious, with a dry humor that was slow to reveal itself. His favorite subject was history and his favorite book *Game of Thrones*.

"Because it combines fantasy with real history," he liked to explain. He had a shy grin. "My brother says not to tell people that because they'll beat me up. But you won't."

It was easy to smile around him. "I like the dragons in those books."

"But dragons aren't real," he said.

Her mouth opened, about to respond, before she thought better of it. She wasn't ready to tell anyone about that yet.

"It's cool having someone who gets these things," he said. "There wasn't really anyone I could talk to at my old school."

She felt her cheeks flush and a warm glow fill her chest. She'd never heard anyone echo her own thoughts before, not in such exact terms. She wondered at this feeling, the happiness at discovering someone who understood.

On the days Roland had lacrosse practice, Sara went to the cave.

From her backyard, it was a 28-minute walk if she went straight there. Usually, she didn't; the forest between tempted with so many things. When she was little, Sara had wished for a 'real' forest, all shadows and dense trees that curved to hide the world. But she grew to appreciate this one. High-desert sun filtered through the arms of ponderosas that reached up to touch clear blue sky. The heat wrapped around her as she walked the familiar path, a thick layer of long, orange pine needles softening each step. Sara didn't have to look around to know where she was. Here was the tree where she'd found the wren's nest last fall. Over there, the boulder where she'd cried when the sick baby raccoon died. These spaces knew her, and she them. She had charted them all, drawn every detail to scale.

Gradually, the trees thinned. She walked into a clearing and there it was, open and inviting. Sara paused to put on a sweater. She clipped on her bike helmet and hurried forward. She couldn't stand the sun long in this outfit. September in the desert was no place for wool.

Just when the heat grew intolerable, she hit it: an exhalation. The cave reached you before you reached it, drawing you in. It was like stepping through a curtain of water, an invisible barrier that separated two worlds. Just a few yards away it was a 90-degree day. Here, at the maw, 40; 42, actually. Two degrees warmer than last week. Sara jotted it down in her field notes, put her thermometer away. Closing her eyes, she breathed in the damp, earthy aromas of moss, fern, basalt, and clay. And today, something else, something she couldn't identify. Like the smell when you blew out a match.

In all her time spent in this cave, she'd never seen another human. It felt secret, safe, a place where no one expected anything of her, no one could say *stop that*, a place she could be herself. She'd asked her parents once why no one ever came here, why no one else cared. Her dad shrugged. Her mom said because there wasn't a road going right to it. They didn't mind that she came here alone. They trusted her to be safe.

Today, she was lucky; it had rained at the end of the school day, fierce and brief. Now, an inch of water trickled through the usually dry bed that traveled through the cave. She crouched down, charting the way the creek expanded and changed. The dirt and debris that collected in the bed had already washed away. Now, clear, amber-hued water rippled on its journey. Somewhere, a spadefoot toad called for its mate. Sara stood and made her way forward, stepping as carefully as she could, trying not to splash, not to disturb anything that may have come.

The front area of the cave was...well, cavernous. Like a hall where Tolkien's dwarves might feast. It had taken Sara all summer to map it. There were ten wooden steps at the entrance, leftover from a time when some entrepreneur hoped for money and tourists. Then a small landing, where she'd sometimes find animal bones. (Never pellets, though. Whatever was eating the mice and voles and shrews, it wasn't an owl.) Pretty soon after, the sunlight reached its limit. The bats lived here. Sara sensed their small bodies overhead; the murmuring, the breathing, the rustling of a thousand leathery wings wrapped around one another.

Three tunnels led off from the main cavern. One dead-ended shortly after it began, a pile of rocks and debris. The tunnel walls were intact—no cave-in. And there were sandstone boulders mixed in amongst the basalt. Someone or something had moved them there.

The second tunnel wound its way for about half a mile before coming to a natural end.

The third tunnel. This was the one the stream traveled down, after a rain. This tunnel was wide, tall, echoing. It went on forever. Or at least seemed to. She was determined to reach the end, map it all.

There was something she hadn't added to the map yet, something she sensed but couldn't yet verify. It had been four weeks since she'd last heard it, something deep and primal, a reverberation that traveled up the basalt into her bones. When it reached the ossicles in her ears, she could sometimes make out words. *Be patient. Be brave.*

That was alright. Part of Sara's strength lay in her patience. She was cautious and respectful of everything she discovered, taking her time to study and learn. No one else saw these things. No one else noticed. Why would anything reveal itself to someone who didn't care?

Sun, rain, or snow, the school expelled students outside on their lunch breaks, to the playground and patchy lawn behind the building. Sara spent her breaks alone on the grass. She hated playgrounds. Asphalt forgave nothing; it ate knees and ankles. The forest liked when she ran and jumped and explored. It cushioned when she fell.

It was early October, still warm and comfortable in the sun. She sat on the lawn, absorbed in a small paperback with a taped-on cover. No matter how many times she read it, this scene was one of her favorites, where the princess confronted the dragon. She was so engrossed she didn't notice the shadow until it darkened the words on the page. Her head snapped up. Peter Harp loomed over her, his two best friends from lacrosse flanking his sides.

"Reading on break? You're a bigger nerd than I thought."

Every muscle in Sara's body coiled up tight. "What are you doing out here? You're second lunch."

"Didn't feel like English today. Guess I could do some reading, though." Before she could react, Peter grabbed her book.

She felt the slice of a paper cut as she tried and failed to hold on. He showed the cover to his friends as she scrambled up.

"*Dealing with Dragons*?" He laughed too loud, for show. "She's reading a kids' book!"

"It's not a kids' book." She felt blood rushing to her cheeks. "You'd know that if you could read beyond a first-grade level."

Peter's face darkened. He threw the book back at her. It bounced off her arm and landed in the grass, spine splayed.

"You're writing my semester science report," he said.

She stood tall, squared her shoulders. Her voice shook. "I'm not doing your homework this year."

"Yeah, you are. Unless you want to spend every lunch with your face in the dirt."

"You can't beat up a girl."

He held up a hand, feigned offense. "I'm a feminist, Sara. I treat everyone equal." With another peal of laughter and a nod to his friends, they marched off.

Sara picked up the book, careful not to get blood from her cut on it. She stared at the familiar words she loved so much, but they blurred and refused to focus. Screw Peter Harp. This year was different. This year, someone understood.

"Can I show you something?"

Sunlight filtered through the pine trees and highlighted the too-long hair partially covering Roland's eyes. Sara reached into her bag, pulled out her social-studies book. "There's a cave I've been mapping. I think it's home to…something big."

She opened to the Oregon trail section, where she had a rough sketch of the main cavern. She pointed out the creek bed, the tunnel entrances, the nooks and crannies shaped by stalagmites.

Roland looked closely, flicking the hair out of his eyes. "You do all this in class?"

She grinned. "The teachers don't like it much."

He laughed. It always surprised her, how much she liked making him laugh. Roland turned the page to a sketch of the third tunnel, which dead-ended when it reached the edge of the page. "Is this all of it?"

"No. These are just my notes. I have more in my mapbook."

"Mapbook?" He looked up. "Can I see it?"

Sweat tickled her palms. This wasn't the direction she'd wanted the conversation to go. She wasn't ready to share that much yet. "That one stays home, to keep it safe."

To her relief, he shrugged and turned his attention back to the sketches. "Why do you think something lives here?"

She paused. *Be brave.* "I've noticed some signs of habitation. But I also can just *feel* it. I know something's there. And if I'm patient, I'll prove I'm worthy. It'll show itself to me."

Roland's face remained serious. She was sure her heart would bruise from the way it pounded against her sternum. "You don't believe me, do you?"

He looked up again, eyes wide. "Course I do. Friends believe each other, right?"

Her heart escaped her ribcage altogether and fluttered out on a long, slow exhale. She passed it off as a laugh, turned the page, and showed him more.

After two more times being 'caught' drawing in class, it was decided Sara should see the school counselor. 'Decided' by people other than Sara. No one seemed to care about her opinion on the matter.

"It's nothing to be ashamed of," her dad said. "We know you're fine."

"Middle school is an adjustment for a *lot* of people," added her mom.

If it was nothing to be ashamed of, why did the teacher sneak up to her in class, tell her in hushed tones it was time for her 'appointment'?

The counselor's office was a glorified broom closet. Miss Reyes smiled as Sara entered, said something about taking a seat. The wooden chair groaned as Sara sat, its old varnish warm under her hands. A fan under the desk pushed stale air around, its mechanical hum reminding her of conehead crickets in summer.

"I hear you've started off the school year on the wrong foot, Sara."

Sara pressed her fingers into the tacky varnish, unpeeled them slowly. "I wouldn't say that."

"Tell me a bit about yourself. Your parents..." Miss Reyes opened a file on her desk. "I don't know if I've seen them around school much."

"They're busy. They both have fellowships at the university."

"Academics!" Miss Reyes laughed. "You'd think they'd take more interest in their daughter's schooling."

"My mom says school isn't a good marker of intelligence."

Miss Reyes raised an eyebrow. "Interesting point of view. A few teachers mentioned you draw in class. What is it you draw?"

Now the backs of her thighs were sticking to the chair. "Just doodles."

"Well, they must be important. Mr. Hubert said you yelled at him when he took your notes away."

Sara remembered that day. Stupid Mr. Hubert had kept her notebook for two days, putting her behind on the tunnel. "It was *my* map. He had no right to take it."

Miss Reyes raised an eyebrow. "Well, you were working on it in class, Sara. But I understand that frustration. So you like maps, huh? I have a cousin who works for Google."

She wrinkled up her nose. "So?"

"Well, I know they aren't the only mapping technology out there, but—"

"Ugh, *no*." She couldn't help herself. She *hated* when adults assumed they knew. "That's not what I do. I draw fantastic maps."

"Oh!" Miss Reyes blinked. "You mean Narnia, that sort of thing?"

Sara rolled her eyes. "Not *fantasy* maps. *Fantastic* maps."

Again with that counselor smile. "I'm sure they are fantastic, you practice a lot."

She couldn't squash down her frustration any longer. "No, you don't get it." She unzipped her bag, pulled out her science book. "When people think of maps, they think of roads, rivers, mountains...that type of thing. But that's boring. Anybody can see that. You don't need a map for it. I make maps to what you *can't* see."

Miss Reyes studied the book. "What is this marked here?"

Sara looked where Miss Reyes was pointing. "Oh...well, these are just my quick notes...my real maps are back home. That's probably why you can't tell. It's a troll den."

Miss Reyes looked up. "This is very creative, Sara. But you do know it's not real, right?"

"I understand most people think that," Sara said. "My maps help them think differently."

"Sara...there's thinking differently, and then there's refusing to see reality. There are billions of people on earth—"

"Over seven billion."

Miss Reyes' smile grew a little tighter. "Exactly. So don't you think that if these things existed, someone would have seen them? Reported them?"

"Not if they're hiding. When a creature's environment shrinks, they shrink with it. Everyone thought Omura's whale was extinct. Then they found a whole group of them."

"That's the depths of the ocean, Sara."

"So? There are depths of the earth, too."

Miss Reyes folded her hands in front of her. "I think it's *wonderful* how imaginative you are. But don't you think you're getting too old for make-believe?"

"It's *not* make-believe," Sara said. "There are dragon stories from all over the world! England, China, Greece, India...they differ in appearance, but they're all obviously describing the same species."

"Sara..."

"And really, the variations make sense, that's normal with any type of animal across so many environments."

"Sara."

"I've been tracking data." She pulled out another book and flipped to a page in the middle. Its text was barely visible under a complex drawing of a tunnel system. "And it confirms what I've been thinking. These caves are the perfect environment for—"

"*Sara!*"

The raised voice startled her. She looked up from her sketches at Miss Reyes, whose palms were now flat on the desk. The counselor took a deep breath. "I think we're going to need more sessions than I originally thought."

A knock at the door—the shave-and-a-haircut rhythm that indicated her dad.

"How was school, Sar-bear?"

She sat on the bed, holding her mapbook. She didn't look over at him. "I don't know why you make me go there."

He sighed and sat next to her. "Didn't go well with the counselor?"

"She's awful, Dad. She tricked me into showing her my maps."

"I'm not sure 'tricked' is the—"

"She's so fake. I don't think she did one real thing the whole time I was there. And then when I showed her...she *wanted* to see them, and I showed her, and she just got mad."

He considered this. "I haven't seen your maps in a while. May I?"

Sara paused, then handed him the mapbook. He studied each page. "These are getting quite good. That's the glen to the east of the house, isn't it?"

Sara nodded.

"And this is…" he paused. "Actually, I'm not sure where this is."

"Tunnel three, in the cave. I'm not done with that one."

"Ah…don't mention this one to your mom, alright? She's not crazy about you exploring down there."

Sara kept her gaze on the page. "Dad, do you think my maps are stupid?"

"Well now. Let's think about that." He held the book out in front of them both. "These obviously require quite a bit of technical skill, which I can see is improving. They also require math to indicate elevation, grade change, and distance. Plus, you use logic to decide what's important to include. None of that sounds stupid to me."

Sara looked down at her feet. "Miss Reyes says none of it's real."

"Well…maps can do different things, you know."

She side-eyed him. "I *know*, Dad."

"Hear me out. Your maps…they may not be traditional, but I think they give you directions for paying attention. And that's very important. That's what scientists do every day." He handed her back the book. "But it's good to pay attention to what's in front of you, too. The real world can be scary. I know. But it creates a lot of amazing things, too."

She heard the word—*real*—and felt something inside her drop. "Ok, Dad."

He stood to leave and kissed her on the forehead. "That's my brave Sar-bear."

The deciduous trees turned umber and orange. Soon it would be too cold to sit together under the ponderosas' arms. But it was a dry fall, and today the sun shone. Sara's shoes were off. She stretched out her toes and dug them into the needles. Roland lay across from her, studying her latest drawings. Sara wiped Cheez-It dust off her fingers and flipped the page of his copy of *Maus*. She hoped he didn't notice how slowly she was reading. That she kept glancing over at him, trying to catch his reactions to her work. He really did remind her of a crow, the way he inspected and observed. Every once in a while his lips twitched up into a small smile, and she'd have to hide her own matching grin.

She was working up the nerve to ask him what he thought when his backpack buzzed. He turned off the alarm on his phone and started packing up. "I have to go. You can borrow that book tonight, if you want."

She tried not to look disappointed. "Where are you going?"

"Pegasus Pizza, with some guys from lacrosse."

What was this feeling inside her? Something afraid, something jealous. "Which guys?"

"Justin Rucinsky, Peter Harp, a few others."

She scowled. "Peter Harp's the worst."

"He's kind of annoying, but he's on the team." He stood, dusted pine needles off the back of his jeans.

"You don't *have* to go, you know," she said.

"Yeah, I do. My brother keeps bugging me, saying they're the 'cool kids' and I should hang out with them. This is the only way to get him to shut up." He shrugged. "See you tomorrow?"

She nodded and watched him walk away. Should she call after him, say something funny? Or should she look absorbed in her book, in case he looked back? She didn't know these things, couldn't figure out how to measure and draft them.

She pulled over her science book, still open to the page Roland had been looking at. A dragon crawled down the left margin. She didn't know these things, but maybe it didn't matter. Roland saw her—even the parts she did her best to hide—and he didn't look away.

The summer after Sara had turned six, her parents packed up the car and drove to another world. Or so it had seemed. Sara fell asleep in forest and woke up in a red land, with bridges and towers carved from sandstone.

"It looks like Spaceman Spiff," she said.

"Or maybe Spaceman Spiff looks like it," her mom said. "After all, Arches was here first."

Her dad had laughed. "Anything you can imagine, the earth churned up at some point."

Those words glued themselves into Sara's brain. *Anything you can imagine...* When they returned home, Sara pulled up Google Earth, panned around, zoomed in. Here was a well that sucked up the sea into the earth. There, a pink lake surrounded by lush green jungle. Across the world, giant stepping stones led into the sea.

She never could have imagined all these things, yet there they were, each more fantastic than the next. The world made them. Maybe people didn't have the ability to dream up anything new. Maybe it was all there, hiding, waiting to be discovered.

"Are you ever scared?"

They sat under the pines, flipping through comics. Sara looked up. "When?"

"When you go into the cave. Isn't it dark?"

"Well, yeah. It *is* a cave." She smiled. "I have a headlamp and flashlight."

"Still..." Roland trailed off. "You don't know what's in there, right?"

"Not yet. But I will."

He paused, and Sara sensed he was gearing up for something. "Would you ever... I mean, could I come sometime?"

Anxiety settled in the bottom of her stomach. She reached out to touch the earth, grounded herself with long, stiff needles. "Well...you need special equipment."

"My mom has a flashlight in the emergency kit."

"And warm clothes and good shoes—it's really cold in there."

"That's easy."

"And a lot of other stuff, too," she added. "Stuff that's kind of hard to get."

"Well, I'll just stick next to you and we'll be fine."

Sara pictured the two of them together, her flashlight beam lifting up to reveal the huddled bats. The cold, clear air of the cave. Her exhale meeting his, mingling before disappearing together into the dark. She thought of the sounds, the shifting shadows, the near silence of the third tunnel as it wound its way through the earth. Of another pair of eyes seeing these things, recording, judging her place.

"Your mom probably wouldn't like it," she said.

"Why not? Your parents let you go."

"My parents are weird."

"So I won't tell my mom. She'll just think we're hanging out. Which would be true anyway."

His grin made her heart sink. She thought about saying yes— wanted to, she realized with surprise—but the voice still hadn't returned. She didn't know the rules, didn't know if it had to be only her, if it mattered if anyone else came...but she couldn't risk it.

"I just don't think it's a good idea, Roland."

His serious face darkened into something unfamiliar. "Why? You think I'm scared or something?"

"It's not that."

"So you're the *only one* allowed in there?"

"I didn't say that. It's just..." The thought of sharing the cave with someone else—*her* cave, the only space that truly knew—filled her with unnamed dread.

"Fine." Sara jerked back as Roland snatched the comic from under her nose and stood.

"What are you doing?" she said.

"I thought we were friends. But I guess not."

"No, Roland—"

"You know everyone talks about how weird you are, right? I didn't listen." He shrugged his backpack onto his shoulder—how well she knew that movement, the upward twitch of muscles—and stalked off.

The next morning, Roland wasn't waiting to walk to school. In math class, Sara wrote him a note.

Where were you?

She watched the folded piece of paper move slowly forward, two desks up and one to the right. Roland's hand reached out, the muscles on his slim shoulders moving as he unfolded it. Sara waited an eternity for it to make its way back.

Took the bus.

Sara blinked at the words, trying to figure out their meaning. She wrote back.

Are you mad at me

It took longer for the note to come return this time.

Yes.

Sara raised her pencil, trying not to panic, when the shadow loomed over her desk.

"Passing notes in class?"

She looked up, saw Mr. Hubert's frown. She heard necks swivel in her direction. She saw Roland, turned away, the only one in the class not staring.

"Do you understand why Mr. Hubert would be upset you were passing notes? It's very disrespectful, Sara."

Sara's fingers curled around the edge of her chair. Miss Reyes' office was cooler now, the varnish no longer tacky. In a few months the room would grow cold, a space heater under the desk instead of a fan.

"Who were you passing notes with?"

"No one."

Miss Reyes leaned forward. "Was it an imaginary friend?"

Sara shot over a glare. "I have real friends." A pain shot through her chest. Then, quietly: "He's mad at me."

"Ah." Miss Reyes' face softened. "It's normal for friends to fight, Sara. Conflict is part of any relationship. The important thing is how it's resolved. Saying 'sorry' can be hard, but it's important."

"But I didn't do anything wrong."

Miss Reyes leaned in closer, and for a moment Sara worried she'd take her hand. "Sorry never hurts, Sara. If the words feel too hard to say, a gesture can help, too."

The words were always hard to say. That was the good thing about the cave, the pines, the sky. The rocks and the water and wind. They communicated in a different way, a patient way. The earth never expected words. It accepted her as she was.

And, she realized, so did Roland.

After school, she sat in the entrance of the third tunnel, watched her breath condense and evaporate. She listened. Somewhere, the dripping of water. Her own chest rising and falling. She closed her eyes, willed whatever it was to return, to prove it had been real, to prove she wasn't...

The quiet pressed down, thick enough to feel, real enough to get lost in.

She opened her eyes. This *was* real, these sensations, these feelings, what lived and breathed beyond the casual eye. Of course they didn't want to be seen. Who would want to be exposed to such a careless world?

Roland wasn't careless, though. Roland was her friend.

Back home, she pulled out the mapbook, looked through the pages. She hadn't shown Roland she cared. But she could.

The next day, Sara walked to school alone, backpack heavy on her shoulders. It was a little too cold now for just her anorak. She walked quickly, in theory to stay warm, in reality to speed the morning along. She did her best to focus in class. She resisted the smell of lead, the empty margins. She couldn't get in trouble before lunch. She stole glances out the window, watched clouds swirl and gather.

First-lunch came. Sara ate in her regular spot on the lawn. It was warmer than it had been this morning, but the air was thick and heavy with the promise of rain, the first in weeks. She looked up at the dark clouds that blanketed the sky.

The bell rang, announcing the five-minute break between periods. The sounds of the schoolyard increased in a final release of energy as students went back inside. Sara tried to finish her food, but her stomach swirled as much as the clouds. Finally, the second bell rang.

Now she heard the wind moving through the sky, the small birds warning each other of the coming storm. She put out a hand, ran her fingers through the grass, noted each blade.

Then the rush came. She heard it growing, echoing in the halls, before it burst out into the open air. Second lunch. Sara stood, grabbed her bulky backpack, and walked around to the front of the building.

Even with his back toward her, she recognized him immediately. The slight slouch, the way he shuffled his feet. He stood in a group to the side of the basketball court.

Sara walked up and tapped him on the shoulder. Roland turned. She watched his eyes widen, his brows rise.

"What are you doing here? You have first lunch."

"I know. I have something to show you."

"What is *she* doing here?"

Her head snapped to the right. She'd been so intent on Roland she hadn't noticed the people he stood with: lacrosse players, including Peter Harp. He crossed his arms over his chest. "Finish my report?"

She swallowed and squared her shoulders. *Be brave.* "Could you come with me?" she said to Roland.

"You shouldn't be out here," he said. "You'll get in trouble."

"Hey, I asked you a question," Peter said. "Anybody home in there?" He was loud, using his 'look at me' voice. His cohort snickered. Roland didn't, though. Sara focused on him.

"It'll just take a minute."

"Just drop it, ok?" She saw his gaze dart around, track the gathering crowd. "I know your parents are ok with you getting in trouble, but my mom isn't."

"You won't get in trouble, I just..." But he was turning away. Desperate, watching her plan rapidly unravel, Sara unzipped her backpack, held it out in front of her. "I brought something to show you, it's really important and—"

Without warning, her backpack swung violently to the side, pulling her with it. Her arms shot out to steady herself, and it was only then she noticed Peter, his hand still extended from swatting the bag. She watched it fly out of her hands. She watched its entire contents scatter, notebooks, pens, markers, empty bags of Cheez-Its. Her mapbook flew out last, its beautiful silk cover skidding across the asphalt before landing right at Peter's feet.

She dove, too late. Her palms hit tar as Peter picked up the book.

"What's this..." His eyes widened as he studied the page in front of him.

Sara scrambled up, ignoring the sting in her palms and knees. "Give it back."

But he was laughing now, pointing at the book, playing it up for the crowd. "Oh my God. Do you see this? 'Signs of past dragon habitation. Witch's lair. Fairy glen.' She actually *is* crazy!"

There was more laughter now, rising on the wind, swirling around her. It hit Sara's ears one peal at a time, reverberating, traveling down her spine to tighten around her lungs, her heart. She looked at the faces, all staring at the mapbook as Peter turned the pages dramatically. She watched his mouth move as he sounded out the names, the locations, the discoveries. A ringmaster showing off the freakshow.

Sara sought the one face she wanted to see. Roland stood slightly behind Peter, his serious face staring at the mapbook. His gaze darted up, crow-like, and caught hers. Peter elbowed him in the side, and Roland's eyes flitted back to the page. Peter was pointing at something, waiting for a reaction. Roland paused just a second—a second that held worlds, that stretched to contain heartbeats—before his mouth turned up at the corners and he laughed.

She snatched the book from Peter's hands and shoved him, hard. By the time he hit the ground, she had already shouldered past the people behind her. She pushed past all the blurry faces and ran.

Asphalt turned to concrete turned to pine needles. Sara clutched the mapbook to her chest as she ran, felt its pressure against her. The rain started when she reached their meeting spot under the pines. Only a few drops, hitting her cheeks and running down to her lips.

Thunder clapped as she passed through the invisible curtain, the sheet that divided one world from the next. She ran down the ten steps, past the landing, into the main hall. She didn't pause to hear the bats, to see what new bones lay undisturbed. She ran, footsteps splashing through the rising creek. Her feet knew this place. They needed no light, no thought to guide them.

Sara's ragged breath echoed in her ears, off the walls. Everything, she wanted to wipe away everything: the laughter, the jeers, the shoulder shrug away. The notes passed, the sunny afternoons spent trading books, the walks to school. The tack of varnish on her fingertips, the teachers' frowns, the stupid, lonely patch of grass where she sat, alone, every lunch. The weight of the word: *real*. What was real? Sara's feet hitting stone, salt on her lips, her breath...

She stopped and stood still, tried to calm her beating chest. What had stopped her? A sense, a sound? She couldn't tell, not with her stupid heart filling her ears.

Be brave, Sara. Breathe in. Breathe out.

That was it—nothing. No steam as she exhaled, no condensation as the hot air from her body hit the cold air of the cave. She touched her arm. Her bare skin was warm.

She looked around—or tried to. When she put them in charge, her feet knew the way. Now...her eyes tried to adjust to the pitch black. She could hear a trickle of water at her feet. Was she in the third tunnel? She mentally retraced her steps. Had she come this far before? She drew in the hot air, realized it stank of rotten eggs. She began to gag, to panic, when she felt it traveling up her bones. *Close your eyes.*

She brushed her fingertips against stone, warm to the touch. The water had stopped; all she could hear were the sounds of her own body. Nothing else this far in the earth. Except...

Her eyes flew open and she held the mapbook closer to her chest. Her protection, her knowledge. Her proof that she knew this place, that it knew her. That she belonged.

She was sure she heard something now. Something beyond her echoing heart and careful steps and invisible breath. She recognized it from the bats: the scrape of leather wing on stone.

Sara peered into the dark. "Hello?"

There was a flare of light, small as a match, but in this inky blackness it made her squint. Still, she caught the shimmer of scale, the flicker of a long, forked tongue. She sensed rather than saw the vastness in front of her, the endlessness beyond the edge, everything, everywhere, waiting to be discovered.

An exhale answered: *Well done.*

See L.D. Oxford's story "The Girl Who Drew the World" online at Metaphorosis.
If you liked it, leave a comment. Authors love that!
Remember to subscribe to our e-mail updates so you'll know when new stories are posted.

About the story

I remember the exact moment when the seed of this story implanted in my brain. My husband and I were driving through western Montana on the way home from backpacking in Glacier National Park. Glacier is a primordial place; you can literally see the titanic forces that shaped the earth. I looked out the passenger window in awed reverence at this ancient, new-to-me land. It was morning, and we were in a mind-bogglingly green valley framed by metamorphic rock formations. The sun made them glow in a way that seemed other-worldly. And yet, amazingly, they were not other-worldly—they were right here, on this beautiful gem of an earth we get to live on.

From there, my brain went down some rabbit-holes. Could humans ever actually imagine something new? Or was it all inspired by the world around us? And if that were true...what about dragons? What about mermaids and puca and all the other things people have "made up"?

Sara and her story took shape from there. I wrote the entire first draft by hand, in dribs and drabs over the span of a few months. Six years and countless revisions later, "The Girl Who Drew the World" definitely counts as the most challenging story I've written. And I'd do it all again in a heartbeat.

A question for the author

Q: Do you often include children in your stories? What role do they play?

A: I do, both as side characters and in starring roles. Kids see the world in an entirely different way than adults. They haven't learned how things are "supposed" to work yet. What we view as mundane is wondrous to them—and things an adult would find unbelievable can be "normal" to a kid. Writing a story from a child's point of view opens up entirely new possibilities, especially in speculative fiction.

About the author

L.D. Oxford writes speculative fiction and recently completed her first novel. When she's not writing or working a day job, you can find her playing with paint, digging in dirt, or satisfying her travel bug. She lives with her family in Seattle.

@ld_oxford

The Heebie-Jeebie Beam

E.C. Fuller

I thought I found a toy raygun. It looked like a toy, at least. I'd been rummaging around in Dad's backyard workshop for props when I found it in a dusty black briefcase wedged between an old laptop and a beige filing cabinet. Chisel-like marks cut into the scuffed leather and busted brass latches, as if someone had broken into it. Nestled in emerald velvet, the raygun's body was orange and blue-painted metal and was shaped more like a glue-gun than a Glock. It also had a marble-sized glass ball plugging the hole where the ray would come out. On the side of the gun was a dial that went from 0 to 5. *Bingo-bango*, I thought. *This is exactly what I need.* And I should have remembered then that I was never a good thinker.

Despite that, I couldn't help thinking anyway. It was weird that the workshop hadn't been locked. Everything inside it had a mother's-worth of warnings: *watch fingers, sharp objects, do not use while intoxicated, may cause dizziness.* Dad had rarely let me past the tiny welcome mat, and never alone. But he was gone and I was curious and in need of cool shit for the play. I hoped he'd left the raygun for me, though I couldn't imagine him doing that.

Before I left the workshop, I tested the door to the glass and metal cabinet. Behind the glass were machines that looked like football helmets crossed with MRI machines. Dad had explained what they did after a salvo of begging, a slight smile on his normally unsmiling face.

Each helmet had a warning on a business-card-sized placard with a number in the 700s. The 700s meant that the invention was in "the series of inventions that alter consciousness through emotional stimulation," he'd told me. 712 made you believe you were an empty suit of clothes. 722 made you feel like someone was watching you. 738 made you feel like you were watching everyone, your sight divided like a dragonfly's.

"These aren't dangerous," I had said to Dad, disappointed.

He had replied, "Altered states of being are the most deadly things of all." A very Dad-ly thing to say. I remember being impressed by his high-falutin' words, though I didn't understand what he meant at the time, nor did I really believe him. It's hard to take souped-up helmets seriously. Ditto for a raygun. Yet, the number 743 was etched into a brass plate on its briefcase's cover: the highest number I'd ever seen. He had taken the higher numbers in the 700 series with him. The other series, he had dismantled or melted down.

I left the dusty workshop, turning the raygun in my hands, and looked round the backyard for something to test it on. The raygun must have been one of the last inventions Dad made when he was here. He'd made hundreds, and not a single one was made as a joke, or art, or decoration. Each one did *something*. But how did I safely find out what the raygun's something was?

The backyard was a square of yellow, brittle grass hemmed by a high wooden fence. The fence had targets painted on the slats, asterisked with scorch marks. Where Dad had poured his chemicals was bald dirt in which grass would never green again. A brave, gnarled redbud tree by the workshop had been left alone. Under its scant shade, my friend Michael chanted his lines. "Elementary, dear Wallace. Not Middle School. Elementary School." Dad'd built robots that could emote better than Michael. But he was still my best bud and I didn't want to test an unknown invention on him unless I absolutely had to.

While Michael gestured at an invisible audience, I clicked the dial to one and aimed at one of the targets on the fence. When I pulled the trigger, a green beam of light fell on the target like a flashlight. No sound. Nothing happened. A perfectly cromulent outcome for an invention that affects the brain. But it's best to first test gun-shaped things on things that don't bleed.

But all things that bleed have brains. Now, I needed a new target. A squirrel flicked its tail near the wooden fence. I beamed the squirrel. It froze. When I released the trigger, the squirrel bolted up the redbud and scampered to the roof.

The squirrel zooming past Michael's ankle made him yelp and jerk his leg to his chest.

"Perfect," I said. "Do that when the corpse is revealed."

"Willie, what the fudge are you doing?" he asked indignantly.

"Testing something." I held up the raygun. The squirrel had not died or acted in non-squirrely ways, which was a positive sign.

It was possible that the effect took a while to work. But none of Dad's inventions were zap-and-done deals. The 712 helmet, for example, required at least an hour of wearing before the user tried to fold themselves into a drawer. I just needed to know enough to make a good guess. "Go stand in front of the tree. I need to know what this does."

"Aw, I don't want to be nobody's lab rat. Especially not your Dad's. Why me and not you?"

" 'Cause your family has better health insurance than mine."

"I don't want to be no lab rat," he repeated. "You know how I feel about animal research."

"Then I'm out of the running, dude." He sniggered. But I wasn't done. "Listen: Dad invents stuff for medical research. His stuff is saving lives around the world *right now*. If you don't want a guinea pig to be a guinea pig, you gotta be one yourself."

He considered this. Then he positioned himself in front of the trunk. He stuck out his hips and pointed at me in a dramatic pose. I beamed him.

When the green light hit him, he made a funny face. I released the trigger.

"That felt weird," he said. "Do it again."

His expression this time was near a scowl.

"I don't know what I'm feeling, man."

"Lemme go up a level." I dialed to level two and beamed him again. He shuddered. If his expression on level one had been like that of a pedestrian running into a stranger, his expression on level two was of that same pedestrian being told he had nice skin.

"One more," he said cautiously.

I dialed to three and hit him again.

"Woo!" Now his expression was that of the pedestrian returning home to find the stranger waiting for him with lotion and rope. "It gives you the heebie-jeebies! Let me try."

I handed it over and braced myself for the beam. But Michael shoved the gun under his chin and pulled the trigger. He paled and his skin pimpled. He held down the trigger so long that I said sharply, "Dude?"

"It feels good when you stop." He smiled goopily. "Try."

He beamed me. The level three setting made your brain feel like a pot of water over a blowtorch. My thoughts boiled. *Oh God, I should not have taken it out of its case. This is why Dad left. Because I touched all his stuff. He's watching through the cameras he left in his workshop, the mirrors Mom covers up, and the squirrel, and he knows I touched his stuff.*

Michael released the trigger. The relief washed over me, cool and sweet and soothing. "Daaaaaang."

"Why'd he make it?" Michael asked.

"I dunno."

We beamed each other back and forth until we agreed. The first level made you feel like something was off. Level two stirred your thoughts into an anxious simmer. Level three made the hair on the back of your neck rise. I eyed that squirrel watching us from the workshop roof. Who knew what insane thoughts churned behind his dewdrop eyes?

But the bigger question was: why had Dad made a gun that scared people? Trying to figure out what Dad was thinking had obsessed me since I knew what thinking was. This was a man who'd stay up late in his workshop with his hands running through his thinning brown hair over questions with more Latin than English, more numbers than letters, whose answers were more confusing than their question. Late enough that the sun had quit the sky and the yellow light from his window threw a bright square on the grass, and I'd fall asleep with my cheek against the night-chilled window. He'd beat me to breakfast, scratching out his thoughts on the dining room chalkboard. I'd ask him what he was working on, knowing that by the time he'd finish answering, the school bus would be grumbling past the house.

"School is important," he would mutter as he drove me to school. "I know you're curious about my work—it makes me happy that you want to follow in my footsteps. But you can't miss school, you understand? You need to learn everything you can."

I could not imagine Dad being so careless that he'd leave an invention behind by accident.

When Michael's mom dropped us off at the high school auditorium the following night, she caught me just before I got out of her van.

"Have you heard from your dad?" she asked in a deceptively casual voice.

I had prepared sassy retorts to stupid questions like, "Where's your dad?" or "How's your mom doing?" But Dad hadn't even responded to my own texts and voicemails, like, "Mom's not mad anymore", "Are you alive?", and "I'm sorry." I wanted to retort now, "No, he's busy researching ways to heal Mom." But I didn't know if he was doing that anymore. So I just said no.

Her nostrils flared. She had showed up on our porch a week after Dad left, holding a covered casserole dish.

I'd been standing behind Mom when she answered the door, so I only saw her stooped back, like a parenthesis missing its partner. Michael's mom's eyes drifted to the wreckage behind us: bloated trashbags of Dad's clothes, the big, crumbling hole in the wall where Mom had thrown a plate at his head, and the small crumbling holes dotting the walls where she had drilled for the listening devices she accused him of hiding. I imagined Michael's mother could pick up the remaining psychic vibrations from the last words Dad had said: "I can't take you people anymore!"

Michael's mom said, as we clambered out of the van, "You'll both steal everyone's hearts tonight."

Our play was called, "The Curious Case of T.B.D." It had started as a joke name as we brainstormed suitably funny names, but none tickled us as much as T.B.D. So we had the houndstooth cape, the deerstalker caps, the British accents and pipes, and now the gun. All we needed now was to fix Michael's tendency to freeze before groups larger than three people.

Michael stared at a point in space, pale and clammy. I would've encouraged him to take deep breaths, but backstage was as odoriferous as an armpit.

"You practiced real good," I said.

He didn't respond.

"Listen, we're not the best anyway. Nobody will remember us! So do your lines, we get our extra-credit from Mrs. Green, and we can go to Wendy's afterwards."

Nada. It was time to bestow upon him my secret technique.

"Imagine the audience naked," I said. "The energy keeping you afraid will flow to your boner. And nobody in the crowd will notice your lightswitch dick."

He peeled open his gnawed-bloody lips. "This is why your Dad doesn't fucking love you."

I felt like he had shot me. "You know what? You know what?" I said as I cranked the dial to four. I beamed him. Immediately I wished I hadn't. His skin grayed. His mouth gaped, and his pulse fluttered in his throat. When I released the trigger, he gasped, color flooding his cheeks.

"Dude?" I said after a beat. His gaze unfocused and relaxed. My heart galloped in my throat. Stupid, stupid, stupid. "You okay?"

Our names blared over the intercom.

"William and Michael, starring in 'The Curious Case of T.B.D.'" I was supposed to lead Michael on-stage, where my fat ass would shield him from the audience long enough for him to stammer his first lines: "Wot's all this then?"

He checked the audience through the curtain, not with the mortal calm of a man being led to his execution, but with bewilderment, as if he had been asked something he hadn't expected. Without waiting for me, he strode out to center stage. The spotlight set him ablaze, and he planted his hands on his hips, drank in the audience, and projected his voice, "So what the frick-frack-snaps happened here?" The audience roared, and a huge grin opened his face.

Michael pranced around the stage. He ad-libbed quips that seemed bespoke, as if a Hollywood writer's spirit had possessed him. He did a goddamn backflip! People rocked and screamed with laughter.

After the show, other students slapped his back and tousled his curly hair. In the stage wings, he glowed.

"Dude, the beam did something to me," he said. "It cured me!"

We'd both beamed each other multiple times before the play and nothing had happened. What did the level 4 setting do? Dad's voice echoed in my thoughts: *we need a larger sample size.*

I scanned the talent-show hopefuls left. There, just about to go onstage, was Jenna. She swallowed as she peeked through the curtain. Even in the wan light, she looked green.

I said, "Hey Jenna, would you like to contribute to science?"

She dropped the curtain. "Is your dad looking for test subjects? Didn't he get a warning from some medical group about not taking the right safety measures?"

"Those charges were unsubstantiated," I snapped. "I'm testing something. You just need to stand still."

"What does it do?"

"It might make you the best performer of all time."

Jenna, an honor student destined to be called Your Honor, who couldn't read a newspaper without a red pen, whom Dad would have loved to swap me for, narrowed her eyes. "Okay."

I beamed her. She dropped the tennis balls she was going to juggle. She wilted and whimpered. I felt awful seeing her eyes well up, but I knew it wouldn't hurt her. After five seconds, I released the trigger. She dragged herself upright. Wonder stole over her face, and bemusement. She snatched her balls and ran out on stage, where she murdered our murder mystery in skill, humor, and balls.

To any student who looked nauseous, I cajoled, "You sir! Do you want to be a star? Young lady! Care to turn your stage fright into stage love?" In total, five students, plus Michael, went on stage like they were born for it. Their stage fright vanished the moment applause crashed over them.

Except Nancy. Seeing the formerly weak-kneed and spotlight-shy transform, she demanded to be beamed. I obliged her. But when her eyes rolled back in her head, the front of her jean skirt darkened. I stopped beaming her at once. Before I could apologize or offer my hoodie to tie around her waist, she fled the wings, sobbing. Oops.

Why hadn't it worked on her? I needed to know for myself. Before we went back onstage for the winner's announcement, I told Michael, "Beam me." He did.

Holy fuck.

Level 4 was like being an ant frying under a little boy's magnifying glass. And the little boy was me, telling me in the voice of Truth that I was destined to fail and be failed. That God had skipped me when he was supposed to put in something to love. That God's face was Dad's face, distant and cold like the moon. He had turned from me and he would never look back.

When the beam stopped, the sunlight of clarity flooded the canyons of my brain. It had all been my imagination. I floated out on stage to receive our Audience Favorite award, waved dreamily at the applauding audience, and puzzled languidly as Michael did another backflip to sonorous applause.

Following instructions from a Youtube video, I picked the lock on Dad's filing cabinet. I found folders fat with schematics, instructions, graphs, and notes. Each was labeled 0-100, 101-200, etc. The one for the raygun (which I named the Heebie-Jeebie Beam) had papers thick with gibberish: 'elevate cortisol', 'mild hypnosis', and 'transformative events'.

I snuck the file out of the workshop and spread my desk with my calculus homework in case Mom came in. I hid the Beam in its case behind my bookshelf. She checked on me every fifteen minutes through the crack in the door. Sometimes she stared wordlessly when I yelled at her to go away. I felt guilty for yelling. I used to yell at her all the time, especially when she started to refuse to leave the house. She'd developed a fear of computers, phones, and appliances, and unplugged them when she could. The manager at our local grocery store had banned her when she unplugged a freezer. So now I had to bike across town to the other grocery store. And I'd had to help her design and build an icebox that didn't use electricity, because we couldn't live without cold milk. It took weeks.

Now I couldn't stop thinking of the time her psychiatrist had caught me in the waiting room after one of her sessions and told me to be patient.

"She needs you right now," she had said. "You're the man of the house."

"But that's supposed to be Dad," I said. I had been thirteen then, and felt like I was wearing Dad's huge lab coat and drowning in it. The psychiatrist reminded me of a kindergarten teacher, all gentleness and cheer.

"He's not here right now. Somebody has to help her." *Obviously*, Dad would say. Dad had tried to fix Mom. They'd spend hours in his workshop. She'd come out all quiet and blank, and he would be tight-faced and brooding. When I asked if I could help, he said, "And what would that accomplish?"

"I'm not asking you to fix her," the psychiatrist had said, as if she could read my mind. "Sometimes things can be not our fault and still our responsibility. Her condition is not her fault, nor yours. Still, it's hers to manage. And she needs your help. You've already helped her, by telling your teacher what was happening at home."

When I had complained about my arms hurting from mixing adobe, digging trenches for molten ice, and trying to source goat hair, my teacher overheard and asked, "Son, are you building a yakhchāl?" I didn't want to tell him. It's embarrassing to have a crazy mom. People pity you. Then, they wonder if it's genetic. But the bags under my eyes, mud caked in my hands, and wealth of knowledge about ancient Persian architecture for refrigeration gave me and her away. That, and because I cried.

The psychiatrist had said, "I don't doubt that you need help too, William. You've already done oodles on your own. More than many of the adults in the same situation as you. Right?" I shrugged-nodded-wiggled in embarrassment, mystified. "Once we find the combination of medication, therapy, and social support your mother needs, things will get much easier. Remember to be kind to her, and to yourself."

So I chewed my cheeks when my anger rose, and sometimes I could hold it in, and sometimes I couldn't. Strangely, she seemed to relax when I yelled. Her shoulders would lower from around her ears and her tightly held mouth would ease. That made me feel a billion times worse, and I couldn't figure out why.

Why don't you understand this, William? Dad's voice cut through my thoughts, rapping on my skull as his knuckles used to. *You can do it. You just aren't trying hard enough.* I was dangerously close to thinking, If you couldn't help her, I totally can't. But seeing how Michael and the other theater kids had transformed for the better, I thought instead that maybe the Heebie-Jeebie Beam could do the same for her. I had his notes, dictionary.com, and a new pack of colored highlighters. I might not have his big brain, but I could tickle the keyboard until the search engines gave me what I needed..

But he hadn't made understanding his notes easy. The instruction manual was crammed with sentences like this: "A transformative experience is marked by both a personal and epistemic metamorphosis following the experience."

And reading that smug middle-finger of a sentence, I thought, *Why didn't you just explain it to me in a way I could understand? Instead of leaving mysteries everywhere, or your family's future TBD?*

I skimmed. I translated paragraph by paragraph. I googled, googled, and googled, and wept some. A few days later I had hit the last page and found a note in his perfect loopy handwriting: *Invention 743 is a failure.*

The Heebie-Jeebie Beam turned out to be the perfect name. The Beam stimulated fear and anxiety in the recipient. Dad had built it as a nonviolent defense for the CIA. Scare a pursuer silly and skedaddle. But because he had been researching emotions, he thought he might use it to change people. An unexpected side effect of the Beam was a sort of artificial catharsis. The list of suggested changes included things like: *more reflective, more compassionate,* and *more respectful of the advancement of humankind and the demands caused by the pursuit thereof* (that last one was circled).

Dad hypothesized that strong emotion—like birth of your firstborn, death of your parents, ghost pepper-strength emotions—coupled with some kind of catalyst would snap people into turning their lives around. He thought the catalyst would be some sort of experience, but what kind, how long, where, and when?

Sucked that he'd never been able to figure out how to use the Heebie-Jeebie Beam to get people to change. He'd tested short and long term results on subject 'M' without success, though the page detailing the results was ripped out.

Bupkiss, he wrote.

Had Michael and I accidentally discovered how to make the Beam work? The five kids with stage fright who'd been beamed joined the theater club, cheer, and formed bands. Maybe that was why the Beam hadn't worked on me. I didn't have stage fright to begin with, so there was nothing to transform.

But there was the fifth level, just a click of the dial away.

I didn't have time to read deeper than the methodologies section of his notes. Mom demanded I help her sweep the house for recording devices, and I had to hide all my notes. We rummaged in the back of the cabinets. We parted each leaf of our house plants. We took down pictures on the wall, checked inside their frames, and rehung them. The family we had been in those pictures was looking weary of her antics.

I played with the idea of telling Mom I'd found an invention. But lately she wouldn't even respond to what I said. She'd stare at me from across at the dinner table as I shoveled casserole into my mouth and until I escaped to my bedroom. Sometimes I caught her checking dishes I'd just put away, or peeking under folds of laundry.

As I did dishes, I wondered how to get her to be normal again. I used to imagine her at her power plant job standing in front of dials, gauges, and control panels, pressing the buttons that told electricity to zap here or there. She'd won a mug for it. It said, World's Best Nuclear Power Plant Controller. I scrubbed it free of tea stains and put it on the shelf next to its mug friend, Meltdowns Are Only Good with Cheese. It wasn't her fault her brain didn't regulate its own chemicals right.

Could the Beam work on her? She was definitely scared of something. But then I imagined how it felt to get beamed at level 5, and the hair rose on my arms. I couldn't do that to her. I felt sick for thinking it. But I couldn't imagine that the lower levels would be strong enough to cure what ailed her.

I got why Dad had left her. I just didn't get why he'd left me. I kept thinking about how Dad had said, "I can't stand you *people*." I was in that *people*. What if the Beam had been meant for me? To wrinkle my smooth brain like a reverse iron, and make me into the son he wanted?

"Will?" Mom asked. "What's wrong?"

"Nothing," I lied. "I have a project. Scary stuff, big part of my grade. I'm going to Michael's."

It was easier to run away to somewhere where a mom or dad could shoot me finger-guns and ask, "What can I do yah for, my dude?" And dream of the day where I could say "Nothing," and mean it. I was afraid he would never come back, and that day would never come.

A few days later, I came home from school to a bonfire roaring in the backyard. It chewed on bookshelves, made charred lace out of documents. Mom carried an armful of old notebooks out of the workshop and dumped them in the fire. The pages shriveled; a diagram of the human brain blackened. Her fly-aways smoked. She panted, wide-eyed.

I ran to the workshop. The shelves inside were bare, dust marking where books had lain or cabinets had stood. She'd swept all his chemistry glassware into a cardboard box by the side of the door. The pieces sparkled. The odor of chemicals stung my lungs.

I demanded in a high voice that didn't sound like mine, "What are you doing?"

Her face slacked. She began the staring I hated.

"Spring cleaning," she replied, scanning my face.

Stay frosty, I told myself. *What would Dad do?* Think. Dad would think.

"Let me keep his files," I said.

"Why do you need them?" she asked suspiciously.

"I— I want to read them."

"You don't read."

"I'm going to," I said honestly. "New Year's Resolution."

She stared at me. If she had been angry, scared, worried, or *something*, I could have talked her down. But her face was blank, as it was more and more these days.

My throat clenched. But I asked jokingly, "Why do you need to burn them?"

"Because I'm burning everything."

Then I saw the picture frames. I had mistaken them for branches. I had mistaken the charred dress shirts for part of our shadows, and the chair Dad liked to sit in as more branches. A weird roaring filled my ears.

Mom pointed inside. "Go get the rest of the pictures off the wall. I'll get the workshop."

"But—" I thought, if I got the workshop, Mom might find the Beam in my room. But if I didn't save the workshop, Dad might never come back.

Maybe there was a way I could save both.

I ran to my room. The hallways were patchy where pictures had blocked the sunlight from dulling the paint. My room hadn't been touched. I yanked the case from its hiding place and the instructions fanned upon the floor.

I dialed the Beam to level 5 and jammed it under my chin. There had been no scale or description for the levels in Dad's notes. I didn't even know exactly how it worked, except that it worked best when you were afraid. My heart raced as if trying to escape from the raygun in my hand. Negative effects? What could be worse than what was happening? Than what had been happening since Dad left? *Please work*, I thought. *Help me understand.*

I must have pressed the trigger. I don't remember. It was only after, when my hand fell and the Beam dropped in my lap, that I came to.

Level 5 showed me something that had already happened. Level 5 was a molasses dream, a slowed down vision, of Dad endlessly pushing the key into the house's lock for the last time. I'd been standing stupidly (the only way I stand) with tears and snot running down my dumb face, while Mom stormed off to her room. Level 5 showed me things I'd noticed, but not put together. That Dad had filled his car with gas, some notebooks, some inventions, some laundry he didn't bother to fold. On the table were the math workbooks he'd go over with me, me squirming and not getting it, him hawkish and sharpening with irritation. He pushed the key into the lock, like a dagger into the heart, knowing I was still inside.

Lifting Level 5 did not bring relief. It brought clarity. It emptied the nothing I had cottoning up my brain and replaced it with more nothing, so that I could remember what had really happened without my fear getting in the way.

The worst had happened when Dad had left. But the worst needed to happen to show us why him leaving was actually the best thing that could have happened.

I don't know how long I slumped there on the floor with the Beam in my lap, pondering this, coming down from the effect. The sound that brought me back to reality was Mom's footsteps coming close.

"William, what is taking so long?"

I had a hunch, but there was no time to test it. I no longer hoped Dad would come back, or that I would become smarter, but I was still afraid Mom would be lost. What the Beam did—what I *thought* the Beam did—I hoped would bring her to reality, the way it had for me.

She opened the door to my room to me pointing the Beam at her. I reasoned I'd only pull the trigger for five seconds. But her face, pulled long in horror and anguish, made my stomach quiver. She sagged against the door.

"I didn't pull the trigger!" I said. "I didn't!" I threw the Beam on my bed and held up my hands.

She drew herself up with visible effort and towered over me.

"I knew it! I knew he swapped you! How has he been talking to you, huh? Where did he plant them?"

"I—what?"

Her open palm cracked against my cheek. It was the first time she'd ever hit me.

"I didn't... He didn't..." I sobbed. Had the trigger been pulled somehow? Mom saw me glance at the Beam and dove for it.

She beamed me.

Like before, Level 5 showed me nothing new. But what it did show multiplied exponentially like a face in a broken mirror as she trained the seasick-green light on my head. Her white-rimmed eyes moist and red-veined, over the dinner table, across the hall, over the kitchen counter, through the windshield, and craning over me as I lay on the ground. The sun was one of her eyes, and the moon was another one. The eyes of squirrels were hers and so were Michael's. They winked in the reflections of the floorboards and shone in the holes of the wall siding as she dragged me out of the room. They winked in my brain as my head bounced down the steps and filled my vision as she tugged my leg, grunting, to the bonfire.

The social worker told me later that a neighbor saw her, tackled her, and threw me in his pool to put out the flames. He then had to fight Mom off when she attacked him with gardening shears, and then save me from drowning because I was still unconscious.

"I wanna be him when I grow up," I slurred from the hospital bed.

"Me too," the social worker agreed.

Mom told the police that her husband had kidnapped me and replaced me with a robot. I'd been acting strange since Dad left. Helping her clean. Doing homework. Reading. She didn't know for sure, until I pointed her husband's raygun at her. She said Dad had been using the Beam on her for a long time. She knew the real William would never point the gun at her. He would never pull the trigger. Her worst nightmare had come to life. But also, joy: it *wasn't* me. And she needed the police's help to find her husband and real son.

"I didn't pull the trigger," I sobbed. And a little voice inside me replied, *But you pointed the Beam.* I sure didn't look like William or Willie anymore. I looked like an action figure left on its side on a hotplate. When the doctor ordered some x-rays, in case I had worse injuries, I felt relieved that I had bones, not articulated plastic joints. Still, I asked Michael and his parents to call me Will.

In the following weeks I stayed with Michael and his parents and helped him start his band, Micycle Ride. He swung his microphone around on its cable, thrust his hips, and sang like he'd die without music, his glasses streaked with sweat and his smile ear to ear. Sometimes he'd surprise me into smiling too. In the notebook my therapist gave me, I wrote song lyrics, how I felt about it all, and what I thought happened. I also reread the instruction manual and research notes for the Beam, googled some more, and thought about how it worked. When I wrote my hypothesis in my notebook and felt its rightness like a tuning fork, I decided that I would never shoot anyone with the Beam again.

I guess Dad really did have us bugged, because his Volvo rolled into Michael's driveway about a week after I left the hospital. Michael's parents came to my bedroom doorway to tell me, like the very incarnations of motherly and fatherly concern.

Dad stood on the front steps. He looked shrunken, and the lines between his eyebrows had deepened. When he saw me, his eyebrows jumped. I had not gotten prettier since leaving the hospital.

I said nothing and waited.

"William," he said at last, awkwardly. "How are you?"

I raised the eyebrow I had left and didn't reply. His starch dissolved as he perspired before me. He dropped his gaze to the welcome mat.

"Well... come along," he said, gesturing to his car. I snorted. He had the gall to look startled. Emotions passed across his face. I didn't know what I wanted to say to him. I felt almost sorry for him. I almost wanted to apologize for snorting. But what I actually wanted was too numerous to list, too huge to name, and too painful to speak aloud. At last he looked at Michael's parents. They put their hands on my shoulders. I felt my heart overflow, even as he said to them, "I'll send a monthly stipend for William." And he turned to get back in his Volvo.

Fear clutched my heart, and that clutch was broken by rage. He could not get away scot-free. He would be the guinea pig this time.

"Hey," I said, my voice cracking. He paused with the key in his hand. "Did you ever use the Heebie-Jeebie Beam on yourself?"

"The what?"

"The raygun."

His eyebrows quirked. "The Fear Gun," he said in the voice of impending snark. "No. Why would I use it on myself?"

His tone harmonized with the past tones he had used when he asked questions, questions with unspoken contempt and judgment that crushed me small and made me believe I was smooth-brained, simple-minded. But since he had been gone, I had grown as tall as he was. At eye-level, I could truly see what I had always known. Dad had remained Dad, backwards and forwards. Mom's condition and mine hadn't changed him one bit. I felt then what he must have felt looking at me while my tears wet my calculus homework. It was so simple, what I needed him to understand. I threw back what he gave me in his own word: "Dumbass."

Dad's face whitened. It colored in patches as his eyebrows drew together and his mouth opened, but my ruined body denied his words, and he dropped his eyes. He raised a finger to shake it in my face, but then made a fist, made a strangled noise, and made an expansive gesture—at what? I didn't care.

When he left, I could see him with his knuckles raised to his mouth in his little dinged-up Volvo.

Watching him leave made me feel a curious lightness and nausea. The lightness left me undone, and I went upstairs to cry privately and write in my journal: *Dad's actions confirm my hypothesis about the Heebie Jeebie Beam.*

The Heebie Jeebie Beam worked, but not the way Dad thought it would. The Beam didn't work by stimulating fear. It stimulated the recipient's strongest belief. Specifically, it manifested the worst-case scenario of that belief—being booed offstage, your husband and child being imposters, your hero abandoning you. The levels manifested the beliefs at different strengths, for those that need more neurochemical power to unroot. When paired with an experience that showed that what happened was different from how you believed it would go, the belief broke, and the recipient was altered. Not in the ways Dad thought they would be.

But that's the kicker. You have to face your fears. And you can't make someone do it if they don't want to. Worse, sometimes what you think people are afraid of isn't actually the thing they're afraid of. Frightening someone without showing them something that neutralizes that fear is just torture. You don't need the Beam to know this, or even cause someone to change, as my experiment on Dad confirmed. I hypothesized that Dad called me stupid and experimented on Mom because he himself felt stupid and broken. So when I called him a dumbass, his reaction proved it.

It was hard to write this hypothesis in my composition notebook. It meant that what happened to me and Mom wasn't what he was afraid of. I don't know what would change his ways, if what happened to us didn't.

The more I thought about the Beam, the more I marveled at it. Man, he hadn't known what he had. A tool that confronts you with what you believe? How many people live their lives not knowing what they believe? Or their deepest fear? What had he been thinking?

In the weeks and months following Dad showing up and dipping out, I got really into song-writing. I thought about writing non-fiction, investigating all the ways people do or don't change. But singing came easy to me, and I needed something easy in my life. Making bangers in the basement on an old synthesizer and howling out my feelings was good medicine. Anyway, I wrote some ditties about everything. When my burns are better, Michael and I are gonna try to get some gigs. Though, getting up on stage, getting gawked at, and then singing about my feelings? And what if we get famous, and Mom hears our jams? The thought of going on stage and fumbling my slippery heart gives me the willies.

Yet, one night, under the yellow light of the lamp, at the hour ruled by crickets and owls, I had been thinking about fear, and Mom, and Dad. Word by word, I wrote the final lines to a song I'd been waiting to hear.

Be afraid!
What are the Heebie Jeebies but knowing you've got something to lose?
Loving each other is how we'll survive
To fear is to know we're alive.

See E.C. Fuller's story "The Heebie-Jeebie Beam" online at Metaphorosis.
If you liked it, leave a comment. Authors love that!
Remember to subscribe to our e-mail updates so you'll know when new stories are posted.

About the story

When I wrote "The Heebie-Jeebie Beam", I had no expectations for the story. One of my New Year's Resolutions was to stop spending so much time on a single short story. It wasn't uncommon to spend tens of hours writing and rewriting one, so my main goal was to take a short story from concept to accepted publication in under 15 hours. I had been obsessed with the phrase, "the heebie-jeebies" and had been playing around with ideas that dealt with inventions. On top of this, I felt like I had been writing too many serious, heavy stories. I wanted to write something fun and not think too hard about the story.

However, when I got past the midpoint, I couldn't help but think more seriously about the Beam itself. What kind of person makes a raygun that frightens people? Why do we feel fear, and how far would we go to stop ourselves from feeling afraid? At the time of writing, I was also interested in the theory of aspiration, or the philosophy of trying to become a certain person (especially the book by Agnes Callard). That made its way into the story as well.

As I revised, the story became more personal. A member of my family had suffered flare ups of mental illness throughout my life, starting when I was in middle school and continuing through post-college. The worst period was a year-long episode where they did many of the things the mother in the story did — the staring, the checking of the appliances and photograph frames, and persistent, strange questioning were regular occurrences. I felt that much of the responsibility for getting them help fell on my shoulders. I tried to reason with them, keep their spirits up, drove them to the local psychiatric hospital — sometimes at midnight — resenting other family for checking out, loathing myself for wishing I could do so myself, wishing someone would come and "fix" things, and spending hours researching their illness or trying to be a gentler, kinder, more understanding person (which I failed to be over and over again). But you can't self-improve yourself into fixing someone else, and sometimes the only way out of a bad situation is to let it pass. Only time and a change of medication eased their condition.

A question for the author

Q: If you could talk to your novice-writer self, what bit of advice would you give?

A: There's a difference between being a writer and being a storyteller, and the faster you understand the difference, the happier you'll be with your own work. Better still if you understand the basic definition of a story: a story is about someone trying to do something difficult and how they change inwardly as a result. But don't abandon your love of stories of ideas, philosophies, or other abstract things, because — though it'll be more difficult to write about those things — those are what fulfill you and make your stories so unique. And more people will love them than you think!

And don't be afraid to change what/how you write if you think it means betraying yourself. If you change in order to better chase your dreams, then you become more you than if you changed nothing.

About the author

E.C. Fuller grew up in Claremore, Oklahoma and graduated from the University of Chicago in 2016. She is the short story category winner of the 41st *Annual Adult Creative Writing Contest* hosted by the Tulsa City-County Library and received an honorable mention in the young adult novel category of the *Oklahoma Writers' Federation Annual Writing Contest*. She has been published in the *Tulsa Review, Metaphorosis,* and *Hexagon Speculative Fiction Magazine*. She lives and works in Tulsa, OK.

www.ecfullersbooks.com, @birdshapedhat

August

Queen of Crows

Rachel Ayers

A Queen of Crows

Mag loved the witches' kitchen, though it did not love her back.

There were shelves of cookbooks and spellbooks as well as histories and tales, herbs hung from the rafters, spices in their jars on the shelf. The stone hearth with its tremendous mantel was her favorite place to sit and flip through the pages or sort through the apples or peel the potatoes. The kitchen garden, walled and hidden, was a tidy riot of scents and flavors, and Mag knew them all.

The witches left her alone, often enough, though not idle. Then the sparrows and robins would come and tell her stories of far off places, good witches and dancing princesses, glass slippers, wolves in red capes, and maidens trapped in towers rescued by woodcutters.

She had no sense of her own age, though the witches often called her 'pretty young one,' and she did not know how old she was when she realized that, however unlikely it was, a prince or a woodcutter coming to her rescue would be a great adventure. She was far too timid to imagine undertaking a quest alone, but a brave companion or a true love made her daydreams safer.

Mostly she was too busy to think of such things. The three witches kept her cooking, cleaning, grinding herbs for their spells, and whatever other little task they brought her. She mended for them, read to them from ancient grimoires, and brushed their long, sleek hair.

Nobody followed the road to the witches' cottage. No princes, no woodcutters, nor even big bad wolves, by coincidence or design, wandered by and invited her to be whisked away from the witches and their work.

Mag's entire life might have consisted of nothing more than fairy stories and her little bit of kitchen herbology, except that one summer morning a murder of crows flew in through the window and settled around her, on the counters and the sink and the unlit stove. One particularly fine specimen sat on the rim of the basin where she was doing the washing.

"Shoo," she said.

The crow looked at her, unthreatened.

"If the witches find you in here, you'll be baked into a pie."

The crow cawed. It sounded like laughter.

She answered the crow with a caw of her own. The bird went silent, cocked her head at Mag, formed her opinion of the young woman.

The bird shook her feathers and sent the others back out the window. One, two, three, four. Five crows for riches, Mag had heard the rhyme, so this last one must be their queen.

She got a handful of oats from the barrel and held it out. The crow gave her that doubtful, cocked-head expression again. "Go on, then, your highness," said Mag, and the crow dipped her beak into the heap of seed, tossing her head back to swallow.

"Hardly appetizing, child," the crow told her with great dignity.

"Hmm." Mag thought for a moment, then offered her a dried plum. The Queen Crow took this as well, and seemed to prefer it. She preened for a moment, ignoring Mag, who shrugged and went back to her scrubbing. "Don't want to talk, then? You aren't much company," Mag scolded, but the queen did not deign to answer. When she splashed the crow with a bit of sudsy water, she squawked in indignation, ruffled her feathers, and flew out the window.

Mag laughed and thought no more about it.

A Dance for Two

The Queen of Crows flew back the same evening, as the sun turned the sky the color of ripe plums. Mag was hauling water from the well to the garden. Summer had been hot and hard. Persistent watering had kept the garden flourishing.

The crow flapped noisily from beyond the roof and landed in the cherry tree, greeting Mag with her rough voice.

"Welcome back," Mag said. The crow's eyes followed her to the herb patch beside the kitchen door. She dumped the water out, and when her bucket was empty, the crow flew to the windowsill and appealed to Mag with shining black eyes.

"I haven't any more treats for you," Mag said. "You'll have to earn your supper, just as I do."

"How shall I do that?" the crow asked.

The queen could not haul water, or peel potatoes, or pull the boiling cauldron from the fire. "Sing for your supper, like they say."

The queen cawed, crowed, laughed at that idea. Her throaty, cackling voice was by no means pleasant. Yet Mag found she was pleased by the effort, and went about preparing dinner for the witches, and herself, and the crow.

The queen flew away when the witches returned, tittering and boasting more than any crow ever had. They had their supper in a swirl of merriment which did not reach out to Mag.

When they had gone back to their business, she went into the moonlit garden. A rustle from the cherry tree alerted her: there was the crow, a shadow in the darkness, studying her.

"I've sung for you," the queen cawed. "Will you dance for me?"

"You sang for your supper," Mag countered. "What shall I dance for?"

The queen cocked her head one way and then the other. "For my curiosity," she ventured, which Mag liked, but:

"I don't know how."

"If my singing pleased you, I assure you your dancing will please me."

So she swayed, and turned, and raised her arms to the moon. Witches' chants played in her head, and she moved to their rhythm, shuffling and then spinning with growing grace.

The crow's head bobbed to her movements. She flew to join Mag, becoming impossibly large; touched her wingtips to Mag's outspread hands. Black feathers fell away to reveal black skin, and they danced.

All night they twirled and spun in the garden, laughing and cawing at each other in equal measure.

As the sun peeked over the horizon, the crow caught up the feather cloak she'd cast aside for the dance, changed again in a burst of wings and feathers, and flew away.

Three Witches

The witches called themselves Rozhanitsy, Parca, and Norn. Their business was concocting spells of youth, beauty, and fortune. The vast majority of the works Mag read to them over dinner were treatises or spells on the subject of immortality; her own interests ranged more widely but she had less time for them. The witches were generally merry, more prone to laughter than grumbling. They teased each other mercilessly, and were carelessly cruel to Mag when it amused them.

"What's got you moping, Mag dear?" asked Rozhanitsy, who chattered more than magpies.

Mag had not realized she was acting differently, but she missed the crow queen, who had not returned.

"My friend has gone away," she told them.

Rozhanitsy, Parca, and Norn clucked with glee. "What friend? What friend have you got? Where has your friend gone, pretty young Mag?"

"She is a queen," she told them, holding dignity close as a cloak. "She came and sat in the garden. I gave her some food, and we danced in the moonlight. She left, though, and hasn't returned."

At this, they grew quiet, thoughtful. They consulted amongst themselves, muttering low so that Mag only caught a few words. "If she should return... royalty... by what path could anyone... lest we lose her...."

They turned back to her, three sets of eyes glaring suspicion. Rozhanitsy asked, voice sugary, "Mag, sweet Mag, how did this lady—err, queen—arrive? By the path? Through the woods?"

"She flew in the window with four of her court. Then they flew away again, but she came back alone later."

Norn, eldest of the three and sharpest, narrowed her eyes. "What did this queen of yours look like, Mag?"

"Black as my hair, with bright eyes and a sharp nose."

More murmuring and glances exchanged.

"And how tall was your queen, young Mag?" asked Rozhanitsy.

Mag spanned her hands in front of her.

Their concern turned into a fit of sniggering.

"And how wide her wing-span, your flying queen?" Parca peeked at the others for approval.

Mag held her arms out again.

"And how rough her voice?" asked Rozhanitsy.

Mag cawed an imitation of the Queen Crow.

The witches collapsed in laughter, howling and slapping one another. Mag watched them, her face hot from their teasing.

Parca and Norn, still shaking in amusement, went through the kitchen door and down the hall. Rozhanitsy stayed a moment, and said, "Mag, I hope your friend does return. But crows are tricky, and if she does come back, you should catch her and let us bake her into a pie."

Four Small Losses

Rarely was Mag tempted into an act of disobedience, but in her longing for the Queen Crow to return, she found herself in a sour and disagreeable mood. She burned the cooking and dragged her feet around the garden. forgot the herbal lore she knew in her sleep and mixed up cumin and fennel for the first time in her memory. She did the washing and mending, but so slowly and so ill that she had to do it all twice. She answered the witches' questions in surly tones or grunts.

It went on for weeks, until Rozhanitsy came into the kitchen and asked her what was wrong. Mag shrugged and continued to scrub the stew pot without vigor.

"Dear, pretty Mag." Rozhanitsy drew her away from the sink to sit at the table. "You know that we three care for you, and feed you, and provide for all your needs. All we ask in return is your unquestioning obedience. You understand that, right?"

Mag nodded.

"Well, child, I'd like to believe you, but from the way you've behaved lately, I'm not sure that settles things. What is for dinner?"

Mag had a bit of dough rising for bread; she hadn't thought beyond that. She'd spent the morning reading a tale of a hedgehog who was secretly a prince and tricked the nearby king out of his daughter.

"I see." Rozhanitsy patted Mag's hands, there before her on the table, and then in a quick motion, cut off the little finger of Mag's right hand. The knife had appeared and disappeared so suddenly it might have been magic. Mag stared, numb, at her blood and her pinkie, lying separate from the rest of her.

Rozhanitsy scooped up the finger and studied it for a moment, then tidied it away into her pocket. "Mag, I want you to remember this. It's a moment to help you focus. We're doing very important work and we can't be bothered with cooking and cleaning. We depend on you."

Rozhanitsy bustled out of the kitchen.

Then the pain started, and Mag wailed.

Though the witches had punished Mag before, they had never done anything so permanent. Mag, shocked at this betrayal, gave up thoughts of black birds and night dances. She grew accustomed to the loss, regaining her dexterity once the pain faded. Norn put her finger bones on the mantle, and it was enough to remind Mag of her place. She did not even need to consult the books, once she recalled herself to focus, to concoct a balm to stop the ghost of her finger from itching.

She did have company, an occasional robin or blue jay, but never a crow. She worked up the nerve, finally, and asked for news of the Queen Crow. A sparrow told her that she'd given up her crown and was dancing with ladies-in-waiting in a distant palace. Late one night, an owl told her that the Queen Crow had married a prince, the youngest son of a faraway king.

"Yes, yes indeed." The owl blinked down at Mag's astonishment. "The court of crows flew for seven days, to a kingdom of spiraling towers and bright flowers. A sunny place, with too much daylight. Warm, though."

"I don't understand," Mag protested.

"Oh! Well, the farther south one travels, the warmer the seasons."

Mag crossed her arms. "I meant about the court of crows, and the wedding."

"Ah!" The owl shuffled in her feathers, settling into the crook of the branch. "There was a ball at the grand palace, a three day extravaganza, where beautiful ladies and handsome men were dancing together, wearing shimmering garments and feather masks. The Crow Queen flew down to join them, and took the form of a woman, and wore her feathers as a magnificent cape. At the end of three nights, the prince was to choose a bride from the revelers."

"I think I know the story," said Mag. Or at least she had heard one like it.

"I did not attend to the details," the owl admitted. "The Crow Queen, however, danced with one lord more than all the others. He wore raiment of gold, radiant as sunlight. His mask was made of the feathers the crows and the ravens, all the darkest birds, and on the third night as the prince claimed his bride, the dark lord slipped off his mask and asked the Crow Queen to be his wife. For he too was a prince of that land, and needed a bride of his own.

"That was many seasons ago, of course. The rest of the court of crows scattered, and it was some time more recent that I heard these tidings."

Mag felt foolish. She had longed for the Crow Queen, who, it seemed, had not given Mag a second thought. She left the owl to watch for mice and voles in the garden and went back to her kitchen hearth.

Mag wept all night, surrounded by the scent of the thyme and rue she'd bundled to dry above the hearth. At dawn, she crept back to her bed in the corner of the kitchen and recited herbal lore to herself until she fell asleep.

Norn was not pleased. She woke Mag, shaking her until the girl sat up and stared at her, blinking in the light.

"Mag," she said, "There was nothing for breakfast, and lunch looks to be missing, too. The kitchen is a mess, and the clothes in the mending heap haven't been touched all day. What do you have to say for yourself?"

"I was sleeping." Mag lay back down and shut her eyes; she was not sleeping, in truth, but dreaming of a life where she was a princess in a tower instead of a servant in a kitchen.

She heard Norn sigh. "Has it been a hard night, child? Have you trouble waking?" Norn took her uninjured hand and gave it a gentle pat. "Let me aid you."

Mag cracked her eyes open in time to see the witch lift the hand to her mouth and bite off the smallest finger.

It hurt immediately this time.

Norn pulled the finger out of her mouth and wagged it at Mag. "You look more bright-eyed already. Now see to your chores."

Mag found her focus once more, and soon after, the new bones were added to the mantle. She grew ever quieter, afraid to lose any more of herself, and continued to do the witches' bidding. When she gathered herbs in the cold light of the full moon she would, sometimes, think of flying away over the garden wall, but no matter her dreams, she did not grow wings; in all the witches' books, the only spells that granted such transformations came at too permanent a cost.

It was a spring evening, more than a year later, when she saw a single sooty black crow winging across the sky. It was too far away to see if it had been the queen, but Mag waved and called to it. The crow fluttered and dipped, landing on the branch where his queen had alighted the night she danced with Mag.

"Stay a while, rest," she said, holding out a handful of dried plums. "Tell me of your queen."

"Oh, our queen, hmph, she is gone quite mad, or so they say." The crow plucked the fattest plum from Mag's palm.

"Mad?" Mag prompted; the bird took his time over the fruit.

"Well, in the way of a creature who cannot be herself," he clarified, chortling over another choice plum.

Mag sighed in sympathy.

"She cannot be cured of her humanity." The crow eyed her suspiciously and then gulped the last plum. "Her husband stole away her feather cloak when she bore him a son, and when she demanded her feathers back, he told her that he couldn't have a wife who would fly away on a whim. She has been searching for her cloak ever since, and has all of us, her *true* court, seeking for another way to change back into her true self. She has tried tinctures and ointments, and consults with wise-women and witches alike. The human courtiers think her quite touched."

The bird cocked his head again, but seeing no more plums forthcoming, bunched his feathers to fly again.

"Wait!" Mag cried, but he was already off, over the garden wall and out of sight. Free as she never could be, the bird awakened a bitter longing in her heart.

She wanted to follow the crow, to find its Queen. For the first time, Mag was desperate to leave, determined to go. She wanted to see more than a tiny garden corner of the world. She wanted more than witches and potions and a tidy little kitchen. She wanted to find her friend.

In front of the cottage was a dark flagstone path. It was not so very long, and then there was the road, stretching into the forest in either direction. Mag set out without so much as an apple for the road, but stopped at the garden gate, unable to decide which way to go, and then a thousand protests clamored in her mind: where would she go, how would she eat, how would she earn her way? *Foolish girl*, she scolded herself.

She sank to the frigid stones, lost within sight of the garden wall she knew so well.

When morning came, Rozhanitsy, Parca, and Norn found her still at the end of the path, shivering in the misty sunlight. They brought her back to her hearth and then Rozhanitsy and Parca left her alone with Norn.

Norn sat beside her. "What's gotten into your head?"

"I want to fly away." Mag hid her face in her hands, felt the ghosts of her smallest fingers tickling her cheeks and wished she hadn't spoken.

"Don't we feed you, and keep you safe? The world is a hard place, and you're safe here, so long as you do what you're told. You understand that, don't you?"

Mag nodded, but did not lift her face.

"You are part of our great work, Mag," Norn told her. "One day we will find our answer, and that will be because you have assisted us. That gives your life meaning. You will find no answer so easy as that in the wider world."

"But I want to see it!" Mag burst out, then clapped her hands over her mouth. She looked at Norn, fearful.

"However much you may wish to fly away, you haven't got wings. Remember your feet? There on the ends of your legs? You'll do better to stay solidly planted, and keep to your work."

This time, Mag was ready for the knife. She jumped away as Norn moved toward her.

"Sisters," Norn said. She did not raise her voice, but they appeared as though they had been waiting for her.

Mag fought them, kicking and thrashing, but she had nowhere to go, and soon they had her trapped. Rozhanitsy and Parca held her, and Norn cut the smallest toe from each foot.

Mag screamed.

Norn took no notice. Mag nearly missed the witch's words over the throbbing of blood through her ears and face. "One for grounding, two for obedience. Remember, Mag."

She remembered, but it was not the last time she attempted flight.

Five Years

On the fifth anniversary of her flying away, the Queen of Crows returned as though only days had passed. She sat on the kitchen mantel, next to Mag's tiny bones, and cawed impatiently at Mag when she did not look up from her chair beside the fire.

"Go away, bird." It was evening; she was nearly finished hemming Norn's new skirt and she wanted to go to bed early.

"Why do you hunch over your work, and speak like an old woman?" the crow asked her. "Your face is not lined, your hair is not gray."

Now she glared at the queen with the full force of her anger and despair. "Why should I be young and happy? Is my life so wonderful? Is my life worth anything at all?"

The crow fluttered, but settled again. "Your life is hard, and I owe you an apology, for leaving you and more. Will you listen to my story, and decide if you can forgive me?"

Mag pushed herself out of the chair and hobbled outside. There was now a shackle on each ankle, and the chain between them was short. Her missing toes ached as winter bowed to spring.

She sat on the stoop. The moon was already in the sky, glowing orange on the horizon. The witches were gone to some revelry or mischief. Mag did not know when they would return.

The crow followed her and landed on the garden path, inky against the pale flagstones.

"Do you remember the night we danced in the moonlight?" she asked.

Mag laughed; not happily.

"When I watched you dance, I learned how to take off my feathers and stand as a woman." From her place before Mag, she shook herself. Then a cloak of feathers fell away, and she held it in human hands. She sat cross-legged on the stony path. "I flew far away that night, afraid of what I had, for that moment, become. Humans are tricky, confusing creatures, and I had felt things I did not understand. I flew until the sun rose, then I slept. When I woke, I did not know where I was, only that I was far outside my territory."

She told Mag of her young prince, who had seemed a brilliant novelty but had twisted her life into a cage. Of her search for a restoration, and the hedge-witch who had advised her. All this Mag knew, but now the Queen told her in greater detail, and her heart twisted as she remembered her own longing to go to her friend's aid.

"For a time, I was lost in despair. But news came to me that the queen was, at last, expecting a child. When the babe was born, my husband said to me: 'Destroy the babe, wife, and I'll return your cloak.' This was the first proof I had that he knew where it was, and I became furious. I called him an evil wizard. He said there was but one way for me to get what I wanted, and at last I told him I would do as he bid."

Mag startled at this, horrified.

"I went by night to the queen's chamber, and stole her little daughter. The child was peaceful in my hands, and as I gazed at her, I conceived a great love in my heart. I could no more harm her than I could hurt my own son. I took the girl deep into the forest, to a hedge witch I had met in my quest to return to my true form.

"When I told my husband the deed was done, he clapped and laughed, and I saw the shadow of the beauty that had drawn me to him. 'Now fulfill your end of the bargain, husband.'

"He tore his pillow from our bed. Black feathers fluttered in the air around him. 'What have you done?'

" 'I used the life in them to conceive our child.'

"I knew, then, of one magic to try, though I did not know if it would work."

Mag watched the queen's gentle fingers close into fists. She continued, as though she dare not stop now.

"I went to the queen and revealed all that I knew. She called the king, who was grieved at his brother's treachery, but when his eyes met mine I could see that he was not surprised.

"In the morning my husband was tied to a stake in the courtyard. I carried my son forward, and then drew from a sack all of my beautiful black feathers. I spread them on the ground around him while my child watched.

"I raised my head, and called out in my true voice. My lord's face turned to fear as I summoned my own court. First a single crow appeared, and then two more, and then a whole murder. They dove at the man I had married, pecking and clawing at him. As he bled, each drop fell upon a feather, restoring the vitality he had stolen from me. The king and queen clung to each other, turning their faces away. Our son cried and reached forward to touch my cloak, and in that instant was transformed into a crow.

"When the last breath left my husband's body, my cloak was complete, but for a ragged corner which had formed around my son. At last I could stretch my wings again. I took to the air, and my son followed, and the other crows too, and we did not look back."

Mag touched the cloak. It was sleek and smooth; no trace of the blood-magic remained.

The crow queen gestured, and Mag made out a fluttering in the trees outside the garden fence. There was her court. One of the birds was smaller, his feathers not quite as black; bits of baby down still showed in patches.

"Why did you come back?" Mag asked.

"When I was only a crow, I didn't understand why you were here. Now that I have been trapped, I know what it looks like. I have come to set you free." She stopped, then, almost shyly, "If you wish to come with me."

Mag touched the shackles at her ankles. "How?"

The queen raised her arm, gave a signal, and the crows left the trees. They flowed past in a rush of wings and wind, and flew into the house.

Silence fell while they waited.

The first crow returned with a hair pin from Rozhanitsyi's dresser, a bit of metal gleaming in the moonlight. Mag picked it up and looked at the Queen Crow.

"Wait," she assured Mag.

The second crow flew out and dropped a coin at their feet. Mag had seen Parca twiddling with it, shining it through her fingers, a few evenings earlier.

A third crow came back with Norn's little mirror, the one she used to look at faraway places. Mag caught it before it broke on the flagstones.

The three crows looked at their little collection, then at the queen. They ruffled their feathers in a kind of shrug, and flew back into the house.

The crows of the Queen's court repeated this until Mag had a little pile of glittering objects at her feet.

At last, the Queen's son returned. In his beak he carried a tiny key, duller in color than the other objects. Mag recognized it.

The little bird landed in her lap and held it until she took it from his beak. She fit it to the lock at her ankle, and the Queen Crow reached forward and turned it.

The shackle opened with a crack.

Six Days

"Come away, come away," the crows urged. "Before they return."

Mag took nothing with her. She followed the crows' singing; they cawed to her from the trees ahead. She found she was able to keep a steady pace, in spite of leaving her toes on the witches' mantel.

They walked all through the night and into the next day. Mag felt lighter with every step away from the witches' cottage. Every new sight refreshed her, whether it was a beautiful lady rushing by in a gilded coach, or an old man ambling along with a load of firewood, or a young lad guarding miniscule treasures in his wary fists.

They passed through the woods, and then a little hamlet, and then onto a broader road. The Crow's son joined them for a time, utterly silent, toddling along, then took to the air again. The Queen Crow herself seemed content to walk with Mag, watching her take in every scene along their way with as much delight as she took in watching her son discover new things.

They stopped for the night, and the Queen Crow paid for a room, telling the innkeeper that Mag was her sister. Mag could not imagine where she kept the coins when she changed to a crow. She winked at Mag as she shone the money through her clever fingers.

Though she was exhausted, Mag was too full of the day to sleep. So the queen told her stories, from her life, or that she had heard, long into the night. Mag fell asleep dreaming of distant places, cottages on chicken's legs and magic lamps.

Five days more, they continued in this fashion. The farther Mag got from the witches' cottage, the more certain she became that this was real, but even so, she did not ask where they were going: a destination was too much to believe.

Then she heard laughter.

Seven for a Secret

The witches came sweeping over the land in a dark wind, finding her as easily as if she were still in the kitchen. They stole her away from the Queen Crow while she slept, head tucked under her wing, and brought Mag back to her little kitchen hearth, and all her fighting and thrashing and cursing made them laugh more.

"Mag, Mag, we must have you! We are almost at the end of all our hard work! Don't you want to know what happens?"

"I want to leave," Mag said. She would run farther this time.

They pulled her into the kitchen and sat her at the table. She waited for them to chain her, but they did not. Instead they pointed to the cauldron, where a murky stew was brewing.

"There it is, my dear," said Rozhanitsyi. "The key to our immortality, at last. Everyone dies, but we will break our fate. After all our long preparations, we have only to test it."

"I don't want to be immortal." Mag leaned away from their gazes.

They cackled. "Oh you won't, pretty Mag," said Parca. "We have undergone intense rituals, sacrificed many things, and prepared our bodies. The potion will not make you immortal."

"Then why do you want to test it on me?" she asked. She wondered if she could bolt for the door. One look at their faces killed the thought; they would catch her before she made it outside.

"If you take it, we can observe the effects, and match them with our studies. Then we will know the potion has been properly prepared," Norn explained. "It is very delicate; a single wrong ingredient will unbalance the whole thing. But I promise you, Mag, you will smile if you taste it. And after you test it, we will never ask anything of you again." She looked at the other witches. "What say you, sisters? This last task and Mag may go wherever she wills?"

They smiled and nodded. "Yes, Mag," said Parca, and Rozhanitsy added, "Nothing more will we ask of you!"

"I may go freely if I test your potion?" Surely it was a trick, some mischief, but they gazed at her earnestly.

Rozhanitsy nodded. "We will have no more need of you."

"How long will it take?" Mag asked, suspicious.

They hesitated. Then Norn said firmly, "One day. We must observe the effects for a full day, to be certain."

"And it won't hurt me?"

"It will make you smile," Rozhanitsy said again.

"Very well, I will test it. Then I never want to see you again," Mag said.

"You won't have to," Parca said. She looked a bit hurt.

Norn dipped a spoonful of the stuff and brought it to Mag's mouth, feeding her like a babe.

It did not taste as bad as it looked; bitter, but with the sharpness of fresh herbs. She swallowed, and waited.

It started in her stomach, a cramp, a slight discomfort. She pressed her hands against her belly. Norn, Rozhanitsy, and Parca were nodding, smiling: pleased.

And it spread, a hot cramping pain, worse than anything Mag had ever known. She tumbled out of her chair, collapsing to the floor as fire and chills raced through her body. She gasped at the shock of it and crumpled beside the hearth.

"Very good," Norn said, checking the sheaf of notes she held. "It is going as I expected."

"We will check on you soon," Rozhanitsy said, patting Mag's head. Each touch sent daggers through her skull.

The witches left her alone. They didn't need to chain her; she couldn't even crawl.

The Queen Crow flew in through the window. She transformed in an instant and knelt beside Mag. "What have they done?"

Mag could not answer.

The queen touched her face with feather-light fingers. She studied the cauldron, the spoon resting on the table. "They are killing you."

Mag nodded and squeezed her eyes shut.

"Come away," the crow said. "Hurry," she said.

Mag could not move. "Stay," she pleaded.

An hour later, Rozhanitsy returned. The crow flew away before she entered the room. "Another dose, my dear. This one should go a bit better." She fed Mag another spoonful.

The effect spread through her body again. She grew heavy, as though the earth had decided to draw her closer. The pain chasing through her body thumped its now-familiar rhythm. It was harder still to move.

When Rozhanitsy left, the crow came back.

Mag knew, then, of one last magic to try, though she did not know if it would work. "May I have a feather?" Mag asked.

The queen plucked one, long and dark as night, from her cloak. Mag pointed toward the cauldron, and the crow dropped it into the potion.

"Come back here," Mag whispered, "if you will. It helps, I think." She reached out a leaden hand. The queen returned and held her fingers carefully until they heard Norn coming into the kitchen.

Each time Norn fed her a sip, the potion grew clearer, as though Mag were draining the color from it. Mag sank and then floated, was sick and then hot and then numb. Sometimes Norn asked her how she was feeling; sometimes she was able to answer.

After each dose, the Queen Crow or one of her court added a feather, which disappeared with no more than a sizzle and wisp of light. It was, she reasoned, no more risky than doing nothing; she did not believe the witches would let her leave alive.

"One more taste after this," Norn said, late in the night, and fed Mag a spoonful that made her tingle all over.

The Crow returned, and prepared to drop another feather into the potion; a downy feather from her son. "No," Mag said.

She tipped her beak at Mag quizzically.

She pointed at the mantle. The queen found Mag's finger- and toe-bones where the witches had left them.

"Yes," she managed.

The queen added them to the concoction, which hissed and boiled for a moment before settling again to the clarity of fresh rainwater. "What do we make, Mag?" she asked.

Mag tried to explain the muddled lore in her mind; the thoughts chased around each other and would not leave her mouth. She was not even certain that her idea would work, if the witches' potion was too strong for her to change—but another potion of transformation, another spell to change the form of a life —it was all she could try. The crow watched her and then nodded thoughtfully. "You need not speak, then, my dear," she told Mag. "I will wait and see."

At sunrise, all three witches returned. Norn gave her one last dose. "How does that suit you?"

Mag took an easy breath. The last of the aches and chills faded away, and the various discomforts dissipated. Pleasure—and then euphoria—filled her senses.

"It's... wonderful," she said, and felt a grimacing smile grip her cheeks. The room faded; she could not focus her eyes.

"We'll be back in an hour," Parca said, "to move the body."

The others shushed her, and they left Mag alone again.

She felt glorious: as though light were pouring out of her, as though she were drinking honey-wine gone to her head.

She realized that the Queen Crow was weeping into her human hands, dark hair spilling over her face. "Why are you crying?" Mag asked.

"Because you are dying, and I have just begun to know you."

She looked down at herself in wonder: was this dying? Then she realized that she was truly looking down at herself from above. Her skin was turning gray, her eyes were growing dull. There was a smile on her lips, but the queen was right: she was dying. The witches would let her go because they had no use for the dead.

So then, if that body did not hold her mind any longer, where was Mag? She shook herself, felt the soft rattle of feathers tested for the first time.

The Queen Crow held out a hand to her and she alighted. "Hello there, Maggie," she murmured. "You are still here."

"Did you not know why I asked for your feathers?" Mag asked.

"No." She stroked Mag with her other hand. "I thought you were lost."

Mag preened, testing her feathery body. She was spirit-light; a wisp of a creature, hardly more substantial than a cloud. It was all she had left, but it was a body, and one that could fly. She did not know how long it would last; but then, no one ever did. "Hurry," she said. "Help me."

She flew out to the garden and plucked elderberries, evil's bane; they bled red on their white blossoms as she tugged them free. She winged back and dropped them into the cauldron. They disappeared in the clear potion, with nothing but a wisp of steam to show they'd ever been.

Next, flax and horehound, for purification. The other crows, under their queen's command, followed her lead, around the garden and back again. Now rue and vervain, cleansing herbs, the potion still and clear as water. Rosemary: distinctive, purifying. And last, ague root, also called crow corn, hex breaker, ritual uncrosser. Her beloved kitchen and garden had never loved her back, but she knew every herb and its effect. With every gleaning from the garden and from her years studying their books, she bent the potion to her own purpose.

The witches returned to the kitchen, a dead girl, and a new potion.

Mag lingered under the eaves. "See how she smiles, even in death," Norn said. "See how her skin is like stone. The potion has worked as described on an unprepared mortal. It is ready for us, now."

"I thought she'd grow smaller," said Rozhanitsy.

"I thought she'd be wrinkled," said Parca.

"And I thought our preparations would be done decades ago," Norn said sternly. "Let us finish this thing, sisters."

They drank until the cauldron was emptied.

Mag fluttered to the trees, where the Queen was waiting with her court and her son. They welcomed her into their murder as the witches steamed and shrieked. Mag's spell scoured them of the death they'd twisted back to life, cleaned them of the wrongness they'd collected and clutched over the years. She did not think there would be anything left of them after that.

She did not stay to see.

The Queen Crow's court flew away: one as white as a dove, as there-and-gone as a wisp of cloud. Housewives and hedge witches watched them pass overhead. Some counted six and some counted seven, and all kept their secrets to themselves.

See Rachel Ayers's story "Queen of Crows" online at Metaphorosis.
If you liked it, leave a comment. Authors love that!

Remember to subscribe to our e-mail updates so you'll know when new stories are posted.

About the story

There is a folkloric rhyme about counting crows or magpies, and what each number of birds signifies.

A question for the author

Q: Are you an outline or discovery writer?

A: I have aspirations to be an outline writer. I've written an outline once! Mostly, though, I find I don't know enough about the story to do the outline until after I've written the story. I affectionately call myself a pantser, as in "by the seat of my pants".

About the author

Rachel Ayers lives in Alaska, where she writes and hosts shows for Sweet Cheeks Cabaret, daydreams, and stares at mountains. She has a Master's in Library and Information Science, which comes in handy at odd hours. She is a regular contributor at tor.com and she obsesses over fairy tales more than can possibly be healthy. She shares speculative poetry and flash fiction (and cat pictures) at patreon.com/richlayers.

richlayers.net, @richlayers

The Hissing Trees

Ian Donnell Arbuckle

The biovin Charis heard the rumors about the messenger long before he arrived at her laboratory. The watergirls whispered that he had come from the Calomlands, further east than their maps could show with any accuracy. He bore an important text for the yurchief, said one of the boiler technicians, though nobody had heard even a hint of the contents. One of the guard faithful let slip that the messenger had personally angered the yurchief and had been restrained almost immediately upon his arrival.

All took care to mention that he appeared to be on his last legs, having collapsed just on their borders, and that his hideous body bore the bloat of illness.

The yurchief's orders came to Charis through the precise, bored imperiousness of one of the younger faithful, his voice struggling to hold up the import of the words without cracking beneath the strain. "The biovin Charis is to extract from the messenger the content of the message. There will be no tolerance for fault, no allowance for failure."

Charis accepted the order with a calm nod, reserving her questions for the voice inside her. Why was she, a biovin, being tasked with this? Charis had none of the skills of the cryptonos, and she knew her political acumen was inadequate for the delicate job of interrogation. It had, in fact, been the cause of her effective banishment to this lab in the canyons, deep in Sound territory and far from the yurchief's gatherings.

She hadn't minded the isolation, and instead considered it something of a blessing. A place had been found for her where she could contribute the bread of her skills to the feast of her people. For the last few years, she had been reviewing the pharmaceutical work of her predecessor in the role, improving some compounds and helping to fabricate tabs for the yurchief and those in his pull.

Most of the changes were incremental, glacial things that nevertheless gave her a continuing satisfaction that each small, stable adjustment maintained the whole.

Rarely did she see the results of her efforts, but she knew they were successful, if for no other reason than because the yurchief permitted her to continue her work undisturbed and untroubled. For the most part. She liked her work, and her work accepted her in silence. Days could pass between opportunities for her to speak with another living creature. She liked that just fine.

"What am I to do with this foreign messenger?" She only asked it aloud after the young guard faithful had left to deliver her note of obedience back to the yurchief. She kept asking it, mostly to the quiet spaces in her head, until she got her first look at the messenger himself the next day.

Two more of the guard faithful escorted him into her lab. The rumors had been inadequate. He was repulsive to behold, his body a battlefield of open sores, wild lumps of tumors, and ulcerous cavities. He hunched beneath rags that scraped over uneven shoulders, blood and pus staining the stinking fabric. His face could hardly bear an expression, given how the flesh had mottled and bulged with disease. Growths settling from his brow and rising up from his cheeks trapped his eyes in a deep valley, but within all that they shone a clear blue and his gaze was direct. He seemed to study Charis with at least as much intensity as she did him.

He wore shackles on his wrists which, though loose, had nevertheless left deep red welts where they touched his skin.

"Am I to cure him?" asked Charis, taken aback.

"You are to extract from the messenger the content of his message." It was the same instruction, repeated. Though it came from a different pair of lips, the tone was the same as the first time she had heard it: a committed, tremulous tenor.

"By means of…?" Charis prompted.

"There will be no tolerance for fault—"

"I understand," interrupted Charis, who could not abide time wasted on repetition.

"I may be able to illuminate somewhat," said the messenger. "If I may?" His voice was pitched low and each word carried a polite deference. There was a gentle if unpleasant rumble beneath them. Charis recognized the sound as betraying the presence of some fluid or phlegm in the lungs.

"I would appreciate that," she said.

"Of course." The messenger glanced to either side before continuing. Neither of the faithful made a move to stop him. "You see, I carry the message inside my cells." He raised limp hands to indicate the deformities about his body. The obvious effort of doing so was not solely due to the weight of the shackles, Charis guessed.

"Spun into the helices?" she asked, after running the messenger's words through the sieve of her mind.

The messenger's lips twisted into what may have been a smile or a grimace. "Essentially, yes," he said. "The text of the message is encoded among the information there, intended to be read only be those able to retrieve it. Do you think you can?"

Charis nodded faintly, the motion diminishing like the vibration of a loose cord. "Doing so will not relieve you of the cancer, you understand."

"I defer to your expertise," replied the messenger. His lungs convulsed and a wet coughing fit overcame him.

Charis frowned sharply at the faithful. "You may leave him with me. Tell the yurchief I will begin work immediately." With gratitude they were unable to conceal, the two young men backed away, then turned and left the laboratory. The messenger, unable to convey much with expression, cleared his throat and raised his arms a second time, this time in supplication. The chains on the shackles clanked heavily.

"May these be removed, my friend?"

Charis gave him a long look, calculating, and then shook her head. "I would be uncomfortable doing so at this time, though I do have some gauze I will insert as a buffer."

"I would appreciate that, thank you," said the messenger, echoing her tone from earlier. The mimicry didn't escape Charis' notice, but she was unsure of what to do with the information and set it aside for the time being.

"Please have a seat," she said, indicating the only chair in the room. It had five metal spokes at its base, each ending in a black caster. It rolled slightly as the messenger sank onto it.

"Thank you," he repeated.

Charis turned away to retrieve the roll of gauze from her supplies. The laboratory was a single, large space, lit in part by fluorescent tubes that hung low over a repurposed dining table, the sort one might expect to find in a chieftain's meeting hall. The table bore the wreckage of old electronics and automators, salvaged and scavenged and in various states of repair. A workstation idled at the center of one side, three wide monitors standing as bulwark against the junk. A dozen fans hummed away.

Beyond the sharp radius of the artificial lights, gray filtered sun sifted down from two high windows, one set to the north and the other to the south. Tree branches tapped against panes which had never been cleaned.

The walls were lined with mismatched shelves. The only thing each shared in common was how deeply they bowed under the weight of the materials Charis and her predecessors had collected. As much as was possible, the shelves had been kept tidy. Boxes and containers were arranged with clear separations and angles, as if snapped to an invisible grid.

Charis returned with the gauze. She cut two lengths and taped them around the messenger's wrists. She stood back as he adjusted the fall of the metal bracelets. He nodded once to her.

"Thank you again, my friend," he said.

"My name is Charis." She forestalled the smile that appeared to be growing on his lips with one raised finger. "I'm telling you this so you can call me something other than your friend."

"I understand," said the messenger.

"May I examine you?"

"Of course, Charis. I am an open book. Would you like me to move over toward the light?"

"Yes, if you would."

The messenger rolled the chair over toward the pool of fluorescent light with a series of kicks. He almost looked as if he were having fun. The joints of the chair squeaked with each movement.

Charis sat on a bench next to him and held him steady, spinning the chair slowly like a potter with a fresh lump of clay. "Which is the original tumor?" she asked, letting her eyes travel up and down his body.

"Ah, an interesting question. You're worried the message may not have been copied faithfully during metastasis, yes?"

Charis' first answer was a distracted half-nod. The messenger's back was to her now and she noted the dampness of blood across his shoulders. "Yes," she said, upon realizing she had turned him so that he could no longer see her.

"The message was originally encoded in my liver cells," the messenger said. "The tumors came after, I'm afraid."

"Hmm. I think I might biopsy some of these ones that are more easily accessible first."

"Whatever you think best, Charis, my friend."

It took some hours for Charis to prepare her equipment and to sterilize her tools using the little coal-stoked autoclave. During all that time, the messenger sat patiently. Only the occasional rattle of his chains as he adjusted his position called attention to him. Other than that, he remained silent except to answer Charis' minimal questions.

As Charis staged her surgical tray, though, he spoke up. "Did you build that yourself?" He nodded at the autoclave.

"I designed it," said Charis. "I'm untrained in smithing, though. The yurchief had it built to my specifications."

"He must trust you very much."

Charis searched the messenger's eyes for any sign of sarcasm. "No, that wouldn't be accurate to say," she corrected him with a shake of her head. "I already consume twice my energy allotment just running the refrigeration for the compounds and samples. He was unwilling to grant me more for the superheating. 'Fire or ice, biovin,' he said. One or the other. But he did eventually appreciate my ingenuity more than he did my complaints, I believe."

The messenger nodded. "A true leader."

Charis smiled in spite of herself, then clamped down on it as quick as a breath. She sat again on the bench beside the messenger and positioned her tray close to hand. "I could begin with one of the tumors on your neck, but I think I would prefer to examine your lymphs, if you'll permit it."

"Of course."

"I'll have to remove your shirt."

"If you'll do me the favor of being gentle, I have no objection."

It was hardly a shirt, more of a rough sack with holes for head and arms. "I'll have to cut it away," she said.

"Good. Let's be rid of the foul thing," said the messenger. "Burn it, for all I care."

Charis reached for her shears and turned the messenger in his chair so she could begin to work on the fabric across his shoulders. It took some effort to lift the garment away from his skin, stuck as it was with the gum of drying blood. The messenger inhaled sharply through his teeth.

"I apologize," said Charis. "I have some sugar cane, but I hoped to save that for the surgical sites."

"It's all right," said the messenger through gritted teeth. "Just talk to me. What is sugar cane?"

Charis paused for a moment, then continued at her task, cutting straight down from the middle of the neckline, following the path of the spine. "It's a compound my predecessor taught me. It deadens pain where injected."

"An anesthetic," said the messenger, nodding. "It's all right. We can save that for when it's really needed."

"May I ask—" Charis began, but silenced herself with a shake of her head.

"You may. I insist," said the messenger after a pause.

"What sort of message is worth the toll on your body?" Charis finished her cut and spread the shirt apart, lifting it with care from the messenger's shoulders. She nearly gasped at what she saw.

His back bore a few growths, rising close to his backbone, but worse than them were the dozens of whip strikes layered over his skin. Few of them had healed fully; none had healed well. Some were still oozing. The worst of them lay across his shoulder blades.

"I don't believe it was intended to take a toll at all," said the messenger. He shifted his toes on the floor, turning himself slowly until he could look at Charis in the eyes. "The 'biovins' back home did warn that there were risks, but perhaps this cancer has been fated in me since long before I was given the message, or came upon me after. It would have been nice to arrive here sooner, of course. I'm afraid I was delayed."

"Delayed by—"

Charis' words were cut off by the sound of her laboratory doors slamming open. The yurchief stamped into the room. He stood taller than six feet, broad in his shoulders but narrow in his face. Sealskins draped around his shoulders. Though he was proud of the skins, and of his own prowess in the hunting and killing of the beasts, Charis had often thought that they made him look as if he were forever carting around a pile of filthy laundry. His long hair had been stained red with choke cherries, several days ago by the smell of it.

He crossed the floor to Charis and the messenger before his two guard faithful attendants had even taken station beside the door. "Well?" he demanded, breathing in and holding it. "What is the message?"

"I have only just begun, yurchief," said Charis, lowering her gaze to the floor. "It will take time to extract the samples and then to put them in sequence. I have not practiced this, nor exercised the tech since my predecessor first instructed me in its use. And then I do not know how long it will take to decode the message into plain words, if we are able to retrieve it fully." She met the messenger's own downcast eyes and they held the moment shared between them. Charis got the impression that the messenger had told all of this to the yurchief already.

"I'm deaf to your excuses, biovin," said the yurchief. He curled one finger, rank with the smell of hide and sweat, beneath her chin and lifted her face. "Where is my message?"

"It's coming, your 'ness," she said.

"Good. You have one week. I depart this afternoon to visit the borders. Upon my return, I expect to hear my message."

"But that's—"

The yurchief's hand shifted and his fingernails suddenly bit into the soft flesh of her neck. "One week. If you are worried about fatigue, I grant you the boon of my speed. But not too much, understand?"

"Yes, yurchief."

"Good." He slackened his grip but left the tips of her fingers brushing the skin where bruises would soon form. Then he whirled, washing them in the stink of rancid oils. He snapped at his guard faithful, and the three of them swept out into the night. The laboratory door hung open behind them. A roar of laughter drifted in along with a cool breeze.

Charis went to the door, softness in her every step and motion, and closed it quietly.

"He is a storm among men," said the messenger.

She gave only half of a nod and then returned to his side. "He is not of this place," she said. "He came to us when I was young, and none among us can match him in prowess."

"I've known a few like him," said the messenger. "They do not allow for patience in the movement of things. They thrive in the center of the current, not in the eddies and back-drafts of life. Usually, I wish them well, since they will be long gone before I come to rest." He cleared his throat, which seemed to take more effort than he expected. He ended up spitting a wad of phlegm into the rags that had been his shirt. "He is one of many."

Charis withheld her hands from his skin until his shaking had subsided. Then she began to probe the sores on his back.

"What is the boon of his speed, may I ask?" said the messenger.

"It's a compound my predecessor held the recipe for. I've made some improvements. It keeps the mind alert and blots out weariness from the body."

"Ah. The good stuff," said the messenger. He gasped as Charis' thumb brushed one of the long welts.

"I apologize," she said.

"Please, don't pay me any mind. We have a job to do."

Charis nodded and continued. The signs of infection had spread beneath and around many of the welts, but the discharge was white-becoming-yellow. Treatable. "You said you were delayed reaching us. What happened?"

"It's a long story."

"Oh. You don't have to—"

"May I have some water before I begin?"

"Of course." On the way back from fetching a mug and filling it, Charis retrieved some more strips of clean gauze and a clay pot of salve. The messenger accepted the water gratefully and drank it down in one long gulp, suppressing a rising cough midway through without removing his lips from the mug.

"You shouldn't waste your time," he said, wiping his lips with the back of his hand and nodding at the salve and bandages.

"It may ease your discomfort," said Charis.

The messenger shrugged his agreement. "You're the doctor. Excuse me, the 'biovin'."

Charis moved around him and began carefully applying the salve to the worst infections.

The messenger took a deep breath and began his story. "Between here and the Calomlands, there are three great changes in the land. First, coming from my home, there is a wide plain where sharp ravines scar the flat grasses like claw marks left by enormous beasts. On the other side of those plains, there is a mountain range, peaks taller than any you have around here, but colored gray and white only. Stone and ice. Beyond them is the dwindling forest, plenty green but sparse and thinning. Then comes the mist and the deepness of the bay here—my apologies, the 'Sound'.

"I left my home at the end of winter, hoping to reach and cross the mountain range before the next winter's snow could fall. And I very nearly did.

"My path through the mountains brought me past another tribe. They were not the intended recipients of my message, and I thought it better not to announce my presence to them, so I skirted their holdings and attempted an uncharted route down to the foothills. I was… unsuccessful.

"This tribe—they referred to themselves as the Mallers— caught up with me before I could get far. They set upon me at night, while I was groggy with the cold, and bound me hand and foot. They took me to the edge of a deep canyon between two plateaus and tossed me into a hole a ways back from the precipice, three times as deep as I am tall. There were a dozen others in that hole, all of them ragged and filthy and scared. Our dialects weren't in complete agreement, but before the night was out we were communicating and I learned that I had been pressed into the service of a mighty feat of engineering. The Mallers were building a bridge between the two plateaus. It was a massive thing, indeed."

There was a brief silence while the messenger cleared his throat and gathered his thoughts. While he did, Charis refilled his mug of water. He accepted it and sipped it less greedily than before.

"How long did they keep you there?" Charis asked.

"Three winters," said the messenger, nodding as he heard Charis' involuntary gasp. "And this illness did not rest idle during that time. By the end of it, everyone looked upon me with revulsion."

"They gave you no rest, despite your condition?"

"During my time there, I saw others forced to work until their hearts stopped. My condition, as it worsened, did nothing but earn me a few lashes for my deficiencies."

"'A few'," Charis scoffed.

"Is it so different here?" asked the messenger. "I noted gibbets along the roads. And my guards may have muttered a threat or two that seemed downright believable, not to mention the indignities the yurchief impresses on his prisoners."

There was silence while Charis' face fell. "No," she admitted. "It's not so different here." She took a breath and made a decision before letting the air escape. She crossed to her work table and trailed her fingers over the tools there until she found what she was looking for. Returning to the messenger, she sat and spun him to face her, pulling his shackles forward so she could bend over them with a pick and tension wrench at the ready.

"How did you escape?" she asked while she worked.

"Through no effort of my own." The messenger chuckled. "One night, as we were returning to our pits, an electrical storm lit up the horizon. I've never seen anything like it. It takes much longer to describe than it did to witness. The flashes of lightning clawed through the sunset, but the air healed behind them in an instant. The thunder cracked from one end of the mountains to the other, but the echoes lived on—it seemed like forever. The colors and the intensity were so new, I felt curiously blessed.

"My pit-fellows and captors were likewise stunned. I don't believe anything like that has been seen before. But we only watched for a few moments before the Mallers returned to the task at hand and dumped us for the night. The storm continued, though we couldn't see it."

"Was the pit covered?" asked Charis.

"Most nights, no, but in times of inclement weather the Mallers were kind enough to lay sheets of scrap metal over us to keep out the worst of the rains or snows."

Charis glanced up into a sardonic curl of the messenger's lip and answered it with a nod of understanding. The lock clicked on one of the shackles and she moved to the other.

"So, we were covered that night, listening to the howl of wind and catching odd geometries of brilliant light through the cracks as the storm drew closer. At the height of its fury, it sounded as if we were directly under a waterfall, as if a million gallons of whitewater were bludgeoning the stone around us. We could feel it down to our bones.

"There were screams, but maybe only in my imagination. I don't know how I could have heard them over the racket. To be so small and so vulnerable dead center in the gaze of an unstoppable enemy... I was terrified. The air shook with so much chaos it became difficult to breathe. I buried my head in my hands. But then the clamor only seemed to grow louder. I looked up—I think, despairing, I was determined to stare into the eye of the storm and force it to blink, or some fool thing. Instead what I saw was that the cover of our pit was... disintegrating.

"The jailers had pinned it into the stone with metal hooks, so it hadn't blown away in the winds, but now there were holes appearing all over it. Not just holes, but slashes, rips, patches going threadbare as if the steel were no more than silk. Right before my eyes, it vanished. There was only darkness above, but I could hear a long hush, like swift water, uninterrupted, but somehow more brittle.

"While I sat there, dumbfounded, trying to understand what I was seeing, I heard a scream rise above the lessening wind and that susurrus. A moment later, a body tumbled into the pit. It was one of our captors. I, alone, edged closer to inspect the remains. I couldn't say where he had been trying to run to, or why, but he did not make it. His armor was gone, and the clothes beneath it too, blasted away. His skin and muscles had been flayed, laying open his back to the bones."

Charis felt the lock release on the other manacle and lifted the shackles away from the messenger. He rested his hands on his knees and flexed his fingers.

"What could do such a thing?" Charis asked. "I've heard reports of swarms of insects, but none have mentioned the devouring of flesh. Vegetation, only. A human enemy, perhaps, using the storm as concealment?"

The messenger shook his head. His eyes glittered; clearly, some part of him enjoyed having the information that Charis was after. "I appreciate your theories, Charis, but I'll tell you the truth of it from my observations. You see, that unusual, godlike lightning must have been strong enough and hot enough to melt the gravels and stones into glass, while the winds tumbled that glass until it was atomized, razor sharp particles flying at well more than speeds I can measure. A storm of glass, scouring the mountainsides clean..."

Charis could see it in her mind, a glittering, glowing billow of inarguable power. "Amazing," she whispered.

"It truly was. And the next morning, after everything settled, we were able to cooperate to pull ourselves out of the pit. None of the Mallers had survived the night. Their huts had been swept away or ground down to nothing. Sharp edges of the cliffside had been smoothed. Only those of us in the pits had survived.

"Us and the bridge. Mostly. All the wooden braces had vanished. The stone structure remained, though its pillars seemed thinner and—in my eyes—not equal to the task of supporting a cart. I wasn't planning on risking my own body on it. So I wished a farewell to my fellow freed men and women and headed south, toward the distance where the canyon seemed to draw its banks together.

"I have to admit, though, that I regret never seeing that bridge completed. It would have been a fine work." He retreated into reverie for a moment, then shook his head and returned to his tale. "By this time, I was very weak, so it took me several days to trace the canyon to a place where it grew shallower, then to cross it and return to my path through the forest. All that time, the world had fallen silent.

"Almost. A wind was blowing out of the north the day I crossed into the forest, cold but slow. It curled down and lifted wisps of the fine glass back into the trees. The further I went to the west, beyond the path the storm had taken, the more the trees still held their shapes, their branches, their dead autumn leaves. The sparkling breeze brushed across those leaves, a hushing much like the one from the previous night, but quieter, an unending hiss.

"It occurred to me then that it does something warm to my heart to witness things that take much less time to observe than they do to describe. Do you know what I mean?"

Charis nodded, her senses stuck on facing the external, unwilling to wrench them around and examine things inside herself. She set aside the shackles with a dull *clank* and rested her palms on her knees.

"No message could be worth all of this," she said. "None that couldn't be written on paper or hide or magnetic tapes."

The messenger shrugged. "Long, long ago we sent messengers into the skies, beyond the sphere of our knowledge, with very little hope of their messages even being read. I've already achieved more than they ever did, having met you, biovin Charis."

"Still... It seems cruel to send you into the unknown, containing the unknown."

"I volunteered."

Charis studied the messenger's face, trying to imagine how he might have looked before the corruption of his flesh.

"We should probably continue, per the yurchief's request," said the messenger softly, trying not to startle her.

Charis blinked and nodded. "Yes. Can you raise your arms?"

"Partway."

"That will do. The left side, please. I'll be quick."

"Take the time you need. I'm just dying to know what I carry."

Five days passed while Charis worked, recalling her predecessor's instructions and reconditioning the necessary equipment. The messenger spent most of them lying on a cot near her workstation. Charis had sent a watergirl to retrieve the simple bed from her home. The girl had stared goggle-eyed at the messenger until he had given her a little wave, then had darted away. On her return, she had stayed well away from the messenger, unfolding the cot and rushing back toward the door before the messenger could shamble over to it.

"Don't worry," he had said to the girl. "I've not made anyone else sick." The words hadn't sunk in.

Since then, Charis had isolated the helices from the sample from the messenger's lymph tumors and taken two more samples for comparison: one simply from a swab of his cheek, the other from one of the tumors visible near his spine. For the latter, she had been as careful as possible, and used the last of her sugar cane to deaden his nerves, but still his body had nearly twisted itself off the cot trying to escape the coring needle.

Now, he slept while Charis worked to amplify the fragments of the samples and render them as codes that might contain the message. In her mind, she considered the work backbreaking, because of her habit of bending close to her keyboards and displays and how infrequently she remembered to stretch and relax.

At one point, while waiting for a chemical reaction to complete, Charis felt her eyes drifting closed, and briefly considered taking the speed the yurchief had offered. But she knew what it did to the body, peripheral to the borrowed energy and wakefulness. It was fine for the guard faithful, for the warriors of the vanguard, and for the yurchief himself, but Charis intended to live much longer, much more slowly than any of them.

Gray pre-dawn light was lightening the high windows when the final strand of data resolved on her screens. The software laid the three samples side by side, eliminating the lines of identical data and presenting the differences. She tapped and clicked, reviewing each cut. In every example, the cheek swab showed differences from the two core biopsies where she presumed the message could lie.

But as she laid the data from the tumors side by side, her heart sank.

"Are you making progress?" the messenger asked. He stood a few feet away from her and spoke quietly so as not to startle her.

She bent forward and propped her head in her hands. "Yes and no. The samples from your spine and lymph nodes are significantly different. If there was a message there, it may have been corrupted by one, or by both. Most likely both, since neither is the original. Metastasis may have altered whatever was injected in your liver cells."

The messenger took this in stride, approaching so that he could see the screen over Charis' shoulder. "You have done great work already, my friend," he said. "Do you need my liver?" He said it in the pitch of a joke, but Charis shook her head, answering seriously.

"Even if we take the sample, I'm still confronted by the task of decoding the message it *might* contain. The yurchief will be back in two or three days. These conditions are not... ideal."

The messenger smiled and patted her shoulder and then retreated again to his cot, breathing heavily. The mild exertion of crossing the room seemed to have weakened him.

"Before I volunteered," he began as his lungs caught up to the demand. "Do you know what I was?" Charis shook her head. "I was a poet. I wrote verses on nature and community, real sentimental stuff. Poets are perhaps not necessary to the smooth function of society, but I do believe we are nature's codecs. Do you know that word? We decode the messages of complex systems; we encode the simplicity of life so that it will stick lengthwise in the mind. All messages, to the poet, are in all things."

"That is not a representative view of the world," said Charis.

"It is *precisely* representative. Just not very accurate," said the messenger with a warm chuckle. "I believe in you, Charis. Your successful work does not depend on knowledge you do not possess, nor on effort you are unprepared to undertake. Your only obstacle, I think, is time."

"For us both," said Charis.

The messenger nodded at that and lay back on the cot. "I'm at your disposal," he said.

Charis was silent for a moment. The messenger's breaths began to slow. There was one more piece of information she wanted from him, though. "Why did you volunteer?"

He blew a puff of air out of his nose and rolled to face her, his eyes half-lidded. "I believed there was more to life than poetry. Can you imagine that? Don't answer." The laugh that escaped him was strangely high pitched.

"I don't know much about poetry," said Charis.

"It's all right. I've proven to myself that I don't know much about anything else. It's a truth I've long avoided accepting. When the council asked for volunteers to carry messages to all the scattered tribes, I convinced myself that a humble poet would be the best for this job. All my life, I studied and practiced to draw connections between distant rhetorical points, almost like a soothsayer impressing shapes upon a scattering of stars or a clothier assembling their textures in a beautiful garment. Who better to bear a special missive to strangers than someone trained to draw together the folds of a broad idea and stitch it over a form easy to recognize?"

"Your pride compelled you?"

"My hubris, I would say. It was fueled by decades of feeling underappreciated, I don't mind saying. A poet has one eye forever locked on immortality, but nothing I composed ever would ensure my own. I suppose I felt that, in this effort, I could make a difference. One that might last."

"That was a great risk," said Charis. The messenger didn't offer a disagreement. She went on: "What did you hope you would find at your journey's end?"

The messenger gave the question its due consideration in silence, then, with some effort, shifted onto his back to stare up at the distant, shadowed ceiling. "What I hoped for back then is unimportant. What I hope for now is that I won't die lonely. And that, whatever this message in me turns out to be, it brings people closer together."

Charis looked at her hands. She wondered how many years of life she had preserved among her people, how she might quantify the difference she had made so far. "Perhaps you are the message," she said.

The messenger spluttered a laugh and moved a hand to press against his side. "Oh! Please, my friend. One more puff of conceit into this skull and I fear my head will float away. No, no. There is an end to my life and it has been written in me."

Before Charis' smile had faded, he was asleep.

On the morning of the sixth day since her task had begun, Charis sat and listened to the messenger groaning in his sleep. There was no place and no time where he could escape the pain of his disease. At least he seemed to recover some energy after his naps, despite the apparent discomfort.

Charis left him to his rest and stepped out of the laboratory. The mists of early morning dampened her face and clothes. The air tasted of algae, thick and green. She saw threads of smoke rising above the treetops and could smell cooking meat. A watergirl laced between the nearby trunks, two buckets balanced on a yoke, headed for the laboratory's cistern. Charis caught her eye and nodded to her. In response, the watergirl shook her head and flicked her eyes toward the deeper forest.

Now Charis could hear it: the stamp of heavy feet. An infrequent chime of metal-on-metal suggested the guard faithful. Sure enough, two of them came around a thick fir from the direction of the water. Between them strode the yurchief, back from his hunt ahead of schedule. He had a brace of otters slung over his shoulder and was using his fishing pike as a walking stick, dull end downward.

He nodded when he saw Charis, as if pleased that she had anticipated his coming. "What's the message?" he barked as she drew nearer.

"My apologies, your 'ness," said Charis, bowing her head. "I have not yet retrieved the message."

The yurchief shifted the weight of his kill and sighed. "Look at me."

Charis did as instructed.

"You look exhausted. Did you sleep last night?"

"Not well, your 'ness."

"Did you take my speed?"

"I did not."

The yurchief nodded. He gave a mild gesture with the fingers curled around the pike and both guard faithful relaxed. Charis hadn't even noticed them tensing.

"You still have until tomorrow, upon my original order. I shall leave you to it. But pay attention, biovin. If you fail to deliver the message to me before tomorrow noon, I will consider you a thief: a thief of my time and of what is rightfully mine. You will receive a thief's punishment."

"But, your 'ness," Charis protested. "Without my hands, I would be unable to compound—"

The long pike slammed into the ground hard enough to make the world seem hollow; Charis felt the beat of it rise up in her bones. "You!" The yurchief's voice hit her ears with the same force. "Your value is not in your hands! Your knowledge can be preserved through... much."

"I understand, your 'ness."

"You are burning daylight, biovin."

Charis bowed her head again and left it downturned until the footsteps had gone and the cloying scent of the dead beasts had dissipated. Then she raised her head and let the furious dampness in her eyes intermix with the air's heavy humidity.

When her heart had slowed, she re-entered the laboratory, opening and closing the door as quietly as she could.

She needn't have bothered. The messenger was sitting up on the cot, half-propped against the wall.

"You need more rest," said Charis.

"I don't," said the messenger. "It takes hours to process a sample, yes? We had better get started."

"I'm out of sugar cane."

"It won't matter, Charis." He levered himself off the cot and approached her. "He would really take your hands?"

"It's the punishment for thieves."

"Some would rather choose exile, I imagine."

"There is no exile. Nothing is beyond the yurchief."

"Come now," said the messenger. His expression shuddered for a moment and then went still, as if he lacked the energy to shift it to any purpose. His voice settled into a warm valley, though. "There is much beyond the yurchief."

Charis let her gaze fall to the biopsy needle. It hadn't gone through the autoclave since its last use. She feared there wouldn't now be enough time. "I might kill you," she said.

The messenger sighed and sat down on the creaking office chair. "I don't believe you'll have the chance, my friend. You could, of course, wait until after I am gone, but would you deny me at least the chance to see the unknown inside me? Come now. It'll be over quicker than I could write it down."

Charis looked at her hands, gray in the thin light, and flexed her fingers. They held steady. She nodded. "But give me a moment." She touched his shoulder, noting the quiver in his body that he seemed unable to still. Then she went and retrieved a portion of the yurchief's speed. She dug through the ingredients in her refrigerator and added careful measures of several to the drug, then diluted the mixture in water. She brought a beakerful to the messenger's lips. "Drink."

He obeyed, licking his lips afterward. "If I see eternity, I intend to keep far away," he said, rumbling a laugh that devolved into a coughing fit. Charis helped him from the chair onto one of the benches, laying him out beneath the strongest light. His eyes closed as the high took hold and he made barely a whimper when the needle punctured his abdomen.

The sun had been rising for hours before its light found Charis through the high lab windows, head bent, muscles giving up any hope of relief. By mid-morning, the cut segments of the liver sample were rendering on her display. She began to compare them to the other three, noting strings of differences, eliminating common patterns. On and on.

The symbols assigned to each piece of data began to blur together. Charis rubbed her eyes and looked up at the high windows. The branches of the trees were still, as if making an effort not to disturb her. The only sound in the room came from the hum of fans and the labored breathing of the messenger.

I could live in exile, thought Charis. *If there are lands beyond the yurchief, beyond the Mallers. I could go to the Calomlands.* She had never been beyond the Sound, had never even had to spend a night beneath the stars. *Would I have volunteered?* She had no answer for herself. Absently, she cracked her knuckles and regretted it at once as the messenger stirred.

He opened one eye and fixed it on her. The color had left his skin, his tumors ashen gray and the porous skin in the clefts between them fully white.

"How is it going?" he asked.

Charis left her work and came to kneel at his side. "Not well," she said. She calmed her voice by speaking like a biovin. "The sequences were well-extracted, but I still cannot locate the message, and even if I were to locate it now, I don't believe I could decrypt it in time. I've been giving it some thought, and since the cipher must be more complex than simple substitution, compressing our alphabet into the limited set of—" She stopped herself abruptly, the absence of the words permitting a lump to rise in her throat.

Her hands sought out his and together they held some warmth in stasis.

"I don't think I can do it," she said.

"Charis, Charis," said the messenger. "What a gift it has been to find someone who might read the messages in me—" His eyes fluttered. "Oh, eternity," he whispered, unable to focus on anything close at hand. Charis squeezed his fingers and he returned for a moment. "We are drawn together across a great distance. Do you see it?" He forced a smile onto lips unwilling to cooperate.

His heartbeat slackened, then, and stopped.

Charis tightened her grip on his hands, relaxed, then tightened again, repeating the motion over and over, as if she could urge his pulse to return. It took some time for the absurdity to penetrate her conscious mind.

Finally she stood and left him alone. She trailed her fingers over the equipment on her table, let them brush over the keyboards and controls. Who knew what accidental changes her careless touch might have made to her work? She snapped off the power. In the silence that followed, a clicking came from the high windows. Pine needles tapped against the glass.

Charis went outside, leaving the laboratory door open behind her. A breeze was beginning to stir in the forest.

One of the watergirls, headed past on her way to the cistern, noticed her standing there and approached hesitantly.

"Miss, are you alright?"

It took Charis a great effort to fix her attention on the girl, as if the thickness of the air resisted the motion of her eyes. *No,* Charis corrected herself, ever searching for precision, because it wasn't the world beyond her flesh that slowed her; it was the atmosphere within, the swirl of her intentions anchored at some midpoint she couldn't visualize. Words wouldn't come out.

"Did you find the message, biovin?" The watergirl's voice carried a lilt of excitement.

Charis turned her attention again to the trees. That riot of thoughts within her spun on and on and she realized that, though they all were tied to the eye at the center, that eye was in motion. Charis recalled the messenger's cold skin.

"Biovin?" The watergirl now seemed to be getting worried, leaning in closer.

Charis let her lips fall apart and pulled in rushing air between them. "Would you," she began, pausing as the words went out and did not return. "Would you like to learn the work of a biovin? I could teach you everything I know."

"I'm sorry?"

"And maybe I will be a poet."

The branches around them gently scraped the air, hissing. It was an inconstant sound, inward and outward, as if driven by breaths drawn and exhaled.

No, Charis chided herself. *A slackening moment like this should take much less time to describe than to observe.*

The wind moved in the trees.

The yurchief received Charis in his audience hall, a stone-and-thatch longhouse with three fires spaced equidistant down the length. Each fire was stoked fiercely hot, but directed mainly upward, so that as she crossed the distance from the entrance to the wooden throne her skin alternately blazed feverish and chilled beneath her damp sweat. Her mind echoed the pattern as she rehearsed what she might say, in turns raging with anger and then withdrawing to cold darkness.

As she bowed, she felt the stresses of the differentials might crack her down the middle, but in fact only her voice did as she made her decision and said, "Your 'ness, I have your message."

The yurchief looked down at her. He leaned back in his throne, the wooden joints creaking. The thick air made it hard to see his expression. Charis blinked and wiped at her face, feeling for an irrational moment that her eyes had been darkened like smoked glass.

She sensed he was waiting for her to go on. She took a deep breath. The words came to her mind barely before they left her tongue, and they quavered as they went.

"The message is a simple text of friendship, your 'ness, extended by the councilors of the Calomlands. They wish prosperity upon you and your people and invite us to reply by any means." The lie mingled easily with the grime suspended in the air between them. Charis bowed again, willing her shaking knees to calm. "They indicated landmarks for navigation to their homelands," she added, hoping that the messenger's story would supply enough detail if pressed.

"Friendship," said the yurchief, the word curling out of his mouth like smoke.

Charis nodded, fixing her attention on a whorl in the pattern of the stone floor, an image like the eye of a storm.

"Worthless. Leave us," the yurchief barked to those at his side. "You stay, biovin." A shuffling of footsteps around them told Charis that the various guard faithful and soothsayers were filing to the exit. Her flesh ignited and then froze.

"You are telling me the truth," the yurchief muttered, leaden tone absorbing all inflection if it had been a question.

"Yes, your 'ness," said Charis. *All messages are in all things.* She repeated the messenger's words to herself. It did little to bring about an equilibrium.

"Look at me," the yurchief said. Charis obeyed. "The tribe is glad for your skills," he went on. "They are a tribute to us all. Well done." A pressure wave of relief built up inside her. "Tell me, exactly: how did they address me?"

"The message was addressed to whomever leads the people," said Charis.

The yurchief snorted a laugh and rose. He clasped his hands behind his back, ambling past Charis to just within the corona of the nearest fire. He stretched out his hands to warm them and then nodded for her to join him.

"It would only be proper to compose a reply, don't you think?"

"Yes, your 'ness." She stopped herself before asking if he intended her to carry the response. The relief had faltered and dissipated.

"Entertain me, biovin. What would you say to such a message?"

"I would respond in kind. Offer our friendship. Perhaps, in the future, we might have an exchange of knowledge and equipment."

"It would not be swift enough, I'm afraid, biovin. While you have been stuck to your workbench, the world beyond you has been changing. There have been storms along our borders, brutal ones which leave nothing behind. They're coming closer. Soon, they will scour the Sound to its barren bones. We must be away from here before that happens."

"Storms of glass?" asked Charis. The yurchief nodded, turning a curious gaze on her until she explained: "The messenger witnessed such a thing near the end of his journey."

The yurchief shrugged. "Then perhaps the Calomlands are safe from them, as yet." He let his eyes drift over the flames. "They were my home, once," he said, far away. "Plains of green grass. Lakes full of fish and forests full of game. But I'm afraid my mind was not so narrow as they would have liked."

Shocked, Charis made a sound like an apology, inconsequential. The yurchief crossed his thick arms and closed himself down, eyes and all.

"Where is your gratitude to me, I wonder?" he said. "With my own strength, I have ensured our survival. I put those lands behind me, with their conceited council and the preening philosophers in their alabaster domes. This gray lump in my skull was a pitiful thing, in their consideration, and my destiny was set as a sludge-man, an offal-bearer.

"*You* would be accepted, of course, in no time at all, biovin Charis. Their sole pride was in the supremacy of their minds. They do not and would not have the strength to survive, to *thrive* as we have here in the Sound."

Silence expanded in time and space, filling the seconds and the rafters.

"Friendship, you swear?" The yurchief's throat rasped with phlegm. He spat into the fire. "There's no ambiguity in the message?"

Charis quailed, but any deviation from the message would surely bring the whole thing to an end. "There is no ambiguity."

The yurchief chuckled. "Then I know what I shall say. And I will etch my words in stone, where they might be read by anyone. And the host of us will follow just behind the messenger. We will cross the lands, ahead of the storms. They expect friendship, but they did not know who would read their message. I will return at the prow of war. You are dismissed, biovin."

He turned to face the fire and spat again. As he lowered his head, his hair fell away from his neck. Charis blinked and stared. A cyst had been exposed there, small, pale, but casting a large and dancing shadow. She opened her mouth and found no words for a long moment.

"Yes, your 'ness," she said finally.

Charis returned to the laboratory in silence and worry. Once inside, with the door closed, she disrobed. The cool of the evening and the threat of rain drew gooseflesh all over her skin. She examined her body in a mirror but found no lesions, no evidence of illness. Afterward, satisfied for the time being, she wrapped herself in layers and sat in front of the messenger's body for a long while.

There was so much she didn't know. She realized how desperately she wanted to confess just that to the messenger, to hear him offer his interpretation of her words and her world. *If I were smarter, or faster, or had better tools*, she thought, but silenced the voice inside before reaching a conclusion.

Being there, in the unknowing, was not unusual for her. It was part of the job of the biovin to learn, to build small answers upon each other until they reached a larger one. But for the first time in her work, she felt tormented by the blank void of unanswered questions, questions which *could not* be answered. At least, not there in the laboratory nestled in the Sound.

If the yurchief truly intended to lead his people to the Calomlands, it would take time for him to assemble them all. There would be bustle and confusion and little for Charis to contribute unless he ran out of his speed, now that he believed he had his message and his purpose.

If there are answers for me, she thought, *they are beyond his reach. Now and maybe forever.* She could slip away in the night and be ahead of the vanguard by days, turning to weeks if his condition followed the course of the messenger's. She could reach the Calomlands, a little storm of her own, full of swirling questions and fears and warnings.

Or perhaps the glass storms will sweep through and scour the lands clean of all our complexities, our imperfections.

The decision rose in her like a sudden gust. She filled a satchel with medicines that would travel well, and retrieved a stash of dried meat and nuts. Almost as an afterthought, she crammed the hard copies of the data extracted from the messenger alongside the provisions. When she stepped out into the evening, the damp wind hit what little skin she had left exposed like a bloody lash. She turned her back against it and set out for the Eastern path. Her path would take her through the drying forest, over the mountains, over the plains, to the Calomlands, bearing with her the unknown and the unknowable, and the hope of crossing bridges to meet those who might help her find the soul of the message inside her.

About the story

This story is the product of a couple of characters bouncing around from different story stubs until they found each other. The messenger was originally the protagonist of an unfinished novel a few years back, which was focused on the delivery of secret messages through manipulation of the messengers' genes. The character of Charis, in "The Hissing Trees", started out as a bit player in a different post-apocalyptic story, where her pragmatism was a foil for the narrator's irritating optimism. Neither of the characters ended up following the arcs I had envisioned, so those projects languished. A few years back, the University of Washington publicized some efforts they had made to store data in DNA (www.washington.edu/news/2016/04/07/uw-team-stores-digital-images-in-dna-and-retrieves-them-perfectly) and it sparked my imagination enough to get a basic outline down in my writing journal, but it took several years before I tried fitting the two characters together with the key decision not to bother with giving away the actual message hidden in the messenger. This fouled up Charis' personal commitment to her scientific method and removed the messenger's full involvement with the mission he was on, and I had my story about confronting the unknown, and finding those with whom you can reluctantly accept your ignorance.

A question for the author

Q: What's easier for you — imagining a happier world, or a darker one?

A: It's much easier for me to imagine a darker world. I think that's for a couple of reasons. For one, I have depression and anxiety and my brain is somewhat predisposed to see the negatives in things. But it's also more interesting for me, as a writer, to imagine dark worlds because their conflicts provide the necessary soil to nourish a story. I suppose a happy world isn't necessarily free of conflict, but I'll confess that my ideal has less of it. So, imagining a darker world is easier, but when it comes to putting in the work, I'll gladly make the effort to bring about a happier one.

About the author

Ian Donnell Arbuckle lives deep in the desert half of Washington State with his wife and children.

@IanArbuckle1

The Crystal Pyramid

Mia Ram

There's not a soul in this city-state who hasn't heard of the Crystal Pyramid. It is the lost wonder of the ancient world, the point where the lines between history and legend blur. Countless scholars, writers, and artists have imagined how it must have looked.

I do not need to imagine. I have seen it with my own eyes.

I remember it stood lonely among the pale dunes, its every edge sharpened to perfection, its crystalline facade so pure it reflected the sun's rays back to the sky. Was it the most beautiful thing I had ever seen? Perhaps, but given the circumstances, that was no shining endorsement. I had just travelled across hundreds of leagues, riding through nothing but sand wastes. I had sailed the malicious seas that churned between our continent and theirs. I had dragged myself across a desolate land with no one but my horse for company. After all that, even a rotting shack would have looked beautiful to me.

"Take a whiff of the air, Fig." I patted my horse's neck as she trotted toward the pyramid. "You know what that smell is?"

Fig whinnied.

"Success, Fig. It's the smell of success." I rode her to the very edge of the pyramid before bringing her to a stop and swinging off of her. "Well, there's nowhere to stable you. But you're not going to be stupid and run off, are you?"

Fig huffed.

"Smart girl. You just wait here for me until I find the entrance for us, and when all this is over, I'll give you all the lettuce you can eat." I grabbed my satchel off her saddle and slung it over my shoulder, then shot her a final salute. "Wish me luck, whatever that's worth. We're about to be very rich, Fig. Very rich."

Granted, I was already very rich by that point. But I wasn't the *richest*. And the sun is not content to rise only halfway up the sky.

I began as a little wailing nobody, born to another nobody beneath a nameless bridge in the city-state of Summer's Edge. My mother believed in playing life's game fair, and little good it did us living as street rats. Ours was a life of barely enough. Barely enough to eat and drink. Barely enough shelter, barely enough clothing, barely enough to exist.

Then she died. In the cold of that first night alone in the gutter, I asked myself questions. What would it be like to have more than just barely enough? What would it be like to not have to slave and beg for scraps, to simply *take* what you want?

To leave uncrackable vaults empty. To con the sharpest merchants out of every coin. To fill coffer after coffer, eventually with enough to buy my way into the aristocratic circles.

What would it be like to have everything?

I discovered it was like flying.

The greatest of flights began a few months before I arrived at the Crystal Pyramid, in a narghile lounge in the gold district. I'd been invited there by an old friend. Akeem was a fellow thief turned merchant, one who had also played the game well enough to climb from the low streets to the high towers of the city-state. We had run more than a few cons and thefts together. A childhood disease had left him unable to use his legs, so he'd relied on mine to sneak into wealthy windows or through crowded markets, just as I relied on his lightning wit to craft escape routes and elaborate frauds when my own wouldn't do. He was the only person I'd met since my mother that I trusted.

The lounge was spread across the roof of the district's highest tower, all satin cushions and rugs imported from island states to the south. Even the narghile supplied to me was ringed with rubies along the base. They were poorly set in the gold, though. I was able to chip them all off and slip them into my pockets before Akeem even joined me on the sofa. I watched his attendants carry him in on a silver palanquin, then help him onto the seat across from me.

"Thank you. Wait for me below," he told them, shooing them away. Once they'd left us, he turned his attention back to me. "And thank you for meeting me here, Bazi."

I blew some smoke aside and shrugged. "You ought to be thankful. I'm rarely this generous with my time. I'm a busy woman."

"But never too busy for a smoke with a good friend, surely?" Akeem smiled.

"Not when I've only got the one," I said with a wink. "But really, this better be good. I've got plans that need attending to."

"So the rumors say. I can't go down two streets in the rich districts without hearing something about you. Rather surprising things."

"You ought to know better than to pay any mind to rumors about me. Half of those are merely venomous lies spread by the many who envy my fortune. And my talent, wit, and beauty. Why, it's no wonder I have enemies." I grinned and tried to keep my tone light-hearted. "Let's not waste time. What's this proposal you wanted me to hear?"

"Well, that has to do somewhat with rumors as well. They say you've aspirations toward the royal families," said Akeem, drumming his fingers on his knee.

"Do they, now?" My grin tightened. Akeem shouldn't have known that, especially not second-hand. It's much harder to slip your way into a circle once everyone knows you're trying to get in. It must have been that damn Naji, my lover at the time, running his mouth around the pleasure district. Some men you can't tell anything.

Akeem grabbed the pipe from my hand and took a leisurely inhale. "As esteemed as you've become, Bazi, you must realize that such a thing would be nigh impossible for you. Even the richest merchant would never be considered for marriage into one of the seven royal families."

"Nothing is impossible for me." I snatched the pipe back. "And I certainly need no advice on the matter from you. What do you know of the royal families, anyway?"

"In general? Not more than expected. Of Prince Sef in particular? Quite a bit."

I froze. "Prince Sef? Of the Dram family?"

Akeem's grin widened. "Ah, now I have your attention."

I fought to keep myself collected. Sef's family was the oldest in Summer's Edge, its founding family. As the eldest, he stood to become the most powerful, wealthiest person in the city-state. Along with whatever woman could manage to marry him.

Akeem leaned in, his eyes alight. "I happen to have befriended the prince's former tutor at this very lounge, mere months ago. After a few drinks, he told me that Prince Sef has long been seized by an obsession with the history of the Empire of Heaven, as well as its last empress, Eru. And her tomb, the Crystal Pyramid. Do you know what they say she was buried with? Enchanted automatons, wax wings that flew, and even a pair of lenses that would allow the wearer to see the future.”

“Magic lenses, hm?” I laughed at the thought. “Oh, the things I could do with that.”

“Legend says these are but a few of her treasures, and the prince would give his arm for even one of them. Any woman who could bring back a relic for him would win his heart enough to overcome his feelings on status and blood.”

“All well and good if I could ever find such a thing,” I scoffed.

Akeem held up a hand to silence me. He turned to the satchel beside him and pulled bundles of papers and books out from his satchel, selecting one sheet to hand to me. I took it and stared down at the world in ink. I traced one of the routes with my finger, eyes going wide.

“This isn’t our continent.”

“Indeed not. It is the one that lies across the Carmelian Seas. Few have even voyaged to its shores, much less traversed it.”

“*That’s* what this is?” I snapped, though I couldn’t tear my eyes from the map. “Of course few voyage there. Even I’ve heard how dangerous the Carmelian seas are, and those who’ve survived say nothing lies on the other side but sand.”

“Sand, and the ruins of the lost Empire.” Akeem kept his eyes steady on mine. There was no mirth there, no hint of a jest at my expense. “I can trust no one else with this, Bazi. I’ve reached across the farthest, most shadowed corners of the continent for the information you now hold in your hands. What lies within the Crystal Pyramid could make us both rich beyond our wildest dreams. I can provide the ship, the supplies, everything you could need for the expedition. The only thing I cannot do is sail myself. I need you.”

And so there I was months later, my expedition guided by the maps and texts from Akeem. The theoretical inventory of Empress Eru’s burial chamber was admittedly the least useful, but I couldn’t seem to help myself from reading it constantly, imagining those treasures as I journeyed to a forgotten land. It was a comfort through the tempests that rocked my ship, and on the endless nights when the dunes went cold. I clutched it close to my heart when the worst of the thirst hit and the only oasis near was a mirage. I traced its letters when the sandstorms kept Fig and me trapped in my tent for days. Through all these torments, the promise of the burial chamber was my only comfort. And always, I dreamed of the magic lenses. Surely there wasn't a problem in the world that couldn't be solved with them. Like the problem of the door.

"This is madness, Fig," I told the horse on my third circuit around the pyramid's perimeter. "There has to be a way in. Damn me to Hells, I should have just brought along some explosives. Just take out this wall right here, and the trouble would be over with!"

I rifled through the tools I'd brought in my satchel, hoping that perhaps I had packed something combustive and somehow forgot. No such luck. The closest thing to useful was my hammer, one of few tools I had packed, but even that barely managed to penetrate the crystal wall when I tested it.

Fig whinnied behind me and tilted her ear. She beat her hoof against the sand.

"Oh, quit your whining, spoiled beast," I snapped at her. "You haven't been waiting long."

Fig paid me no mind. She whinnied again and broke into a trot around to the other side of the pyramid. I ran after her, hurling every curse in existence at her as I did.

"Fig, there's no room in the Heavens for ungrateful curs!" I yelled as she slowed to a stop by the pyramid's north-facing wall. I caught up and wagged my finger in her face. "If you think for one second that this is acceptable behavior—"

I paused as a ringing sounded behind me. I turned, stunned to find that the walls of the pyramid were slowly parting behind me to reveal a mirror twice my size and height.

"—then you are absolutely correct. Well done, Fig." I patted Fig's neck and stared at my reflection. Hopeful that the mirror functioned as a door, I tried pushing against it with my full weight. It didn't budge an inch. I was about to ram myself against it again when I saw something faint in the mirror, superimposed over my reflection. I pressed my face to the glass and squinted. On the other side stood a silver lion.

He stepped closer to the glass. "Name yourself, strange traveler."

"What in the name of all Hells!" I stared at the creature, stunned to my core. I had seen many oddities in my day, but a talking lion was a first. "What are you?"

"I am Malak," Malak answered, baring his fangs. "Imperial messenger and guard, bidden to deny entry to the unworthy. As you must be if you lack even the faculties to identify yourself."

"I'm Bazi."

"Of what House?"

I shrugged. "I need no house or distinguished blood. I was born beneath a bridge in Summer's Edge and found it to be a perfectly fine starting place."

"Well, Bazi of the Bridge, if it is entry to the Empress' chamber you seek, you must prove yourself."

"Well, isn't that how it always goes. Straight out of a fairytale," I snorted. "Are you about to present me with some twisty riddle?"

Malak paused for a moment before answering. "You are already familiar with the trials of the Pyramid?"

"Call it an educated guess," I said. "Let's hear it. I didn't get to where I am by being stupid. I'll make quick work of whatever riddle you have."

Malak nodded. "Very well. Who is the one who drinks yet is ever thirsty, eats yet always hungers, who walks in shadows through every door and window, and shall inherit the world with a sleight of hand?"

I stared blankly for a moment, the words dancing about in my head as I tried to make sense of them. Always thirsty? Walks in shadows? I thought for another moment before the answer became clear.

"It's all nonsense!" I declared. "There is no true answer, the riddle only exists to waste time and confuse the listener. I see right through it."

"No, there is a single true answer—" Malak began, but I waved a hand to shush him.

"Of course not. If there was, I would have thought of it already. I'm sure that false riddle has turned others from your door, but such tricks won't work on a sharper wit, Kitten." I opened my satchel and dug until I found what I required. "Hah! Let's try this beauty again."

"Just what do you think you're doing?" Malak's eyes widened as I struck the mirror with my hammer and began to fracture its surface.

"Exactly what it looks like."

"This is not how things are done!" Malak snarled through the glass.

"It is now!" I gritted my teeth. Each strike against the glass took all my strength, to my amazement. This same hammer had blasted my way through dozens of windows with ease, yet the glass of the mirror seemed as difficult to break as iron.

"You're not even going to *attempt* to answer?"

"I already told you, if there were a clear answer, I'd have thought of it. I won't lose hours playing your little game. I've already lost months just to get here," I said as I continued to fight against the glass. "I've starved, nearly been blown overboard and drowned, and wandered the desert for leagues. You want a damn answer? Here it is!"

The mirror shattered. One swift kick and the glass rained down on the other side.

I stepped inside. "There we are!"

Malak beat his paw on the ground. "That is not how this is intended to proceed! You've ruined the entrance. I was not designed to repair broken doors."

"Designed?" With the mirror gone and the blue glow of the lanterns lining the walls, I could see Malak clearly. The silver was not of fur but actual metal, his dark eyes were marble stones, and the gears within his body could be heard with his every move. An automaton.

I poked him with the hammer. "What an odd specimen you are! I've half a mind to take *you* apart, see what makes you tick, then build copies to sell in the market square."

"Try that and I'll take you apart!" Malak snarled. "What are you doing?"

"I don't suppose you have a stable around here?" I asked after I whistled my horse over. I swept the stray glass aside with my foot as Fig gingerly stepped through the gaping mirror, which was just wide enough for her to fit through. "No? No matter, she can wait here."

"This is the Crystal Pyramid, not a horse stable."

"Seems like you've plenty of room for her anyhow." I looked around at the vast, empty floor until I saw a grand stairwell on the other side of the level. "Now, on we go."

Malak sulked by my heels as we ascended to the second level of the Pyramid, clearly displeased at having been outwitted by me. He grumbled about fate and worthiness, but I couldn't be bothered to listen. Far grander things occupied my mind. For, if Akeem had been right about an enchanted automaton, what other artifacts of legend lay hidden in the Pyramid? I thought again of the magic lenses. With a view into the future, anything could be within my grasp.

"Tell me, my feline friend, what sort of treasures did that Empress of yours lock with her in her burial chamber?" I asked Malak.

"Of what concern is that to you?"

"Oh, mere curiosity."

Malak huffed, his marble eyes rolling my way. "It sounds as if you are thinking of taking something from Her Majesty's chamber."

"Why, never! I'm only a humble explorer, Kitten." I stopped short as we finally reached the top step. Just ahead was a wide entryway that split into multiple paths, one to the right, one straight onward, and one to the left. "What's this? A maze?"

"Yes." Malak nodded. "This trial is intended to test your patience and memory."

"Believe me, my patience has more than been tested," I said. I stared at the entrances a moment, tapping my foot as I thought. "Hm."

"Begin from any point," said Malak. He stood and watched beside the left-most wall.

I turned to him, an idea forming. Any point, eh?

I quickly jumped up on his back before he could move out from under my feet.

"What are you doing?" Malak snapped.

"Just stay still a moment," I replied. I reached to grasp the top of the maze wall and hauled myself to the edge. High above me was the ceiling, its shine heightened by the legions of lanterns lining the maze walls. From here, I could see the entire maze stretching all the way to the other end of the room, where the next stairwell waited. I considered walking the walltops, but given their relatively slim width, I figured the balancing act it would require would waste more time than it would save. From my satchel, I grabbed one of the maps and a worn charcoal stick. I proceeded to sketch a rough map of the maze on the back, as well as outline the path that led to its exit. It was quite an easy maze to solve when seen from above. Amateur, even.

"This is not how the puzzle is meant to be solved!" Malak called up at me. "Have you no concern for honor or integrity?"

"Honor and integrity never awarded anyone riches," I said curtly. "Honor and integrity are fine things to have when you're already born with your every need and desire met, but when you're born destitute beneath a bridge, you cannot afford such childish ideals."

"You need not sacrifice those 'childish ideals', as you call them, to improve your station in life." Malak growled. "Have you even tried?"

"Have you?" I snapped back at him, and naturally, he had no reply. "My mother did. All it earned her was a knife in her back, and her final moments wasted in the dark of an alleyway. Her blood still stains my nightmares. It was a city guard that did it. Honest work for honest pay, he told her, until she dared to ask for the pay. If she'd have just stolen it off him, she'd still be breathing."

"And so now you steal?"

"To thrive. I have as much of a right to do that as those born to golden cribs. Don't you see? Life her way was misery and boredom. Life my way is endless thrills, luxury, and adventure. Taking what I want has set me free." I winked down at him.

"Greed is its own chain," he replied.

"I'll tell you the same thing I told myself on my first night as an orphan, Malak: I'll never have a knife in my back. I'll never live and die in the dark of an alleyway. I'll live in the palace towers, where nothing can touch me, where I can take whatever I want. Only that will be enough."

I finished my map and lowered myself back down to the ground as gently as I could manage.

I nodded to Malak. "Keep up, Kitten."

Malak was silent for half of our journey through the maze, likely bitter that I had outwitted the rules once more, but that didn't bother me. I was eager to make my way to the next level and waste as little time as possible. Had I not been in a rush, I would have spent more time looking at the walls. Beautifully detailed scenes had been engraved on each one. There were scenes of coronations, battles, and rituals. As I passed through, I saw the portraits of what must have been Empresses past, halos glowing around their stately heads. Put together, it all seemed to tell a story, though I couldn't parse what the story was.

"What are all these things engraved around us?" I asked Malak.

"Scenes of the Empire's history," he said. "Had you solved the puzzle properly, you would have recognized each as a historical event, tracing your way from the rise to the fall."

"Well, that would have been impossible," I said, idly running my fingers along the scenes. "There's not enough known about the Empire now to reconstruct all its history."

"Nonsense! The Empire of Heaven was the greatest in the world," Malak growled.

"A few thousand years ago, sure. But now it's buried in the sand wastes and mostly lost to history."

Malak glared at me. "I suppose I shouldn't be surprised. Your ancestors were poor record keepers and near-savages. They could not comprehend the glory of the Empire. Have you heard of Dassin the Sunborn?"

"How would I? I'm a near-savage," I drawled.

"She was a genius sorceress descended from the sun goddess. She conquered this unruly continent and built it into a paradise. She poured her plundered riches into observatories, alchemical forges, and universities."

"Wonderful, Dassin!" I clapped wildly before stopping to cup my hand to my ear. "But what was that word I just heard? 'Plundered'? Weren't you yapping earlier about 'honor' and 'integrity'?"

"That is not the same," said Malak. "Empress Dassin did what was necessary for the greatness of the Empire."

"Greatness, is it?" I snorted.

"Yes. To look beyond your own fleeting, material needs, to reach for the height of what you could become and of the change you could create."

"My material needs aren't fleeting."

Malak bared his fangs, the metal of his muzzle grinding as it lifted. "You would not joke if you understood what was lost. We had no sickness, no hunger, no pain. Every house was a palace, every fountain overflowing with crystal waters, every garden singing. We could project pictures across the Empire with the blink of an eye. Our automaton horses outran the wind. Our cities pierced the clouds. We could *fly*."

I raised an eyebrow. "If you say so, Kitten. But, if your empire was capable of all that, how did it fall?"

Malak went silent. I would have pressed him further, but by then we were at the maze's end, and the next stairwell awaited.

"I'm impressed, Malak. This is the creepiest thing I have ever seen."

I stood at the entrance of the third level with hundreds of marble eyes staring at me. The shining white figures filled the pavilion. Every statue was a flawless replica of a person. Every human of every stripe was present, from soldiers to princesses, to butchers, to scholars. It was as though an entire village had been gathered there and frozen in time.

"There's got to be hundreds of these," I said.

"Yes, but you need only one." Malak lifted his paw and pointed toward the center of the pavilion. Peppered across the pavilion were unoccupied tiles of every color and shade. "The trial is simple. Move the correct statue to that crimson tile in the center left, and the door shall unlock."

"How can I possibly guess which statue is the correct one?"

"Look down and work from there."

I looked down and realized that words were engraved on the tile. Indeed, all the tiles across the pavilion were host to either brief sentences or people's names. I stepped back to read the words on which I'd been standing.

WHO IS THE ONE WHO

I grinned. "It's the first words to that silly little riddle of yours. I only need to find the next line, correct?"

Malak said nothing, but I knew I was right. It was the only solution that made sense. Luckily the riddle was still fresh in my mind. I looked around at all the surrounding tiles until I finally spotted the next line a few steps away.

DRINKS YET IS EVER THIRSTY

"I don't even have to get creative this time," I called over to Malak with a laugh. "This is ludicrously easy!"

About seven steps to the right was the tile with the next line.

EATS YET ALWAYS HUNGERS

"I would have thought that the *greatest empire* would at least know how to craft a challenging puzzle. You ought to let me design the next Crystal Pyramid." Another tile five steps ahead.

WHO WALKS IN SHADOWS

"Even my dimwitted Naji could solve this." The next tile was a mere two steps to the left.

THROUGH EVERY DOOR AND WINDOW

"I hope the burial chamber lives up to the legends. Wouldn't want to have gone through all this for some vases. Ah, there's the next one."

AND SHALL INHERIT THE WORLD

"You're dead quiet, Malak. Cat got your—" I stopped short as I stepped on the final tile.

WITH A SLEIGHT OF HAND?

I stared at the statue that stood before me, her face pulled back in a wry grin, a satchel slung over her shoulder, and her boots dusty from a journey to a forgotten desert. At her feet were two words.

THE THIEF.

I stumbled backward from the statue of myself, a soft gasp escaping my lips. It was so detailed in its carving that I half expected it to reach out and grab me.

"Malak, what is this?" My voice broke as I spoke. I turned my head to find Malak padding toward me.

He tilted his head. "The answer to the riddle."

I turned again to stare at my statue, utterly shaken. How could *I* be the answer to a riddle crafted before my birth?

I then noticed the faces of the statues standing behind it. To the left, a marble replica of Naji. To the right, Akeem. Behind them, my mother.

Malak nudged me with his nose. "All that's left is to move the piece to the red tile that bears your name."

"No! I demand an explanation, immediately!" I told him, but he was already padding away to the door. "How does this thing have *my* face? Why do you have copies of Naji, and my mother? *Answer me!*"

Malak didn't. He merely waited by the door at the pavilion's edge.

Again I looked at my double. A psychological test, designed to break me. It nearly did. Every fiber of my body screamed to turn and run, to hop on Fig and never look back.

But I had come this far. If this did allow me entry to the chamber and its treasures, all that I had ever wanted could finally be mine.

I braced myself against the statue and slid it to the red tile that bore my name. As the tile sank beneath the statue's weight, a click echoed through the pavilion. The door was open.

The stairwell to the burial chamber was the highest yet. The easy confidence with which I'd ascended the lower levels had evaporated now, supplanted by a quiet, creeping dread. I was half certain that cursed statue was following behind, laughing silently with my every step.

The door at the top was open, a pale glow reaching out of it and cascading down the steps ahead of me. It grew brighter the higher I climbed. It was like walking up to a star, dread intermingling with wonder, knowing with each step that I was reaching for something that wasn't meant for human touch.

Finally, I was at the door. I blinked against the siren light and stepped into the Empress' burial chamber.

Three of the walls were translucent, so that I could see all of the desert stretched out before me, even the sand-worn peaks of smaller pyramids, buried by the ages. The fourth wall was thicker than the others, opaque and cool to the touch. When I peered into it, I saw the barest outlines of a woman frozen with her arms across her chest. The Empress in endless sleep.

Within these walls were coffers overflowing with gems of every cut and color, robes of silk woven from clouds, and golden coins minted with ancient visages. There were six of Malak's automaton kin standing guard at the corners, though they were not lions. Among them were a giant eagle, an ox, and even a human, all in silver. He wore the wax wings that Akeem had spoken of, pressed against his back. There were crystals that could summon moving images from the air, a mirror that spoke, and clocks that tracked the cycles of the moon and planets. Everywhere I looked, another marvel awaited.

It'll take a fleet of ships to take this all back to Summer's Edge, I thought to myself.

Naturally, I first targeted the jewels.

Malak was nowhere in sight, and the other automatons neither moved nor spoke as I spirited away every precious thing I could into my satchel. All the dread and fear from the pavilion flew from me as my satchel grew heavier. A few of the most valuable things I had to save for Akeem, as per our agreement, but the rest was all for me.

I grabbed a ruby-ringed crown from the top of one of the coffers, swinging it around my finger. *My wedding gift for you, Prince Sef.*

"You seem to have made yourself quite at home, Bazi of the Bridge."

I jumped at Malak's voice, nearly dropping the crown. "Kitten! I hope you don't mind me nosing about. I couldn't contain my curiosity."

"Explore to your heart's content." Malak padded closer. "You have passed the trials. All that you see here is yours."

"What? Truly?" A smile lit my face, and I crammed the crown into my satchel. "Well, that makes this all easier. I intend to return with a caravan of wagons, once I've secured the ships and crew. I was also going to hire some mercenaries in case … well, perhaps I'll hire some regardless, to ward off thieves on the journey back. What of these automatons? Can they walk alongside my horse to the eastern shoreline, where my ship waits? I'll require servants once I've—"

"You'll have to convince them yourself once they reawaken," said Malak. He looked at me with a tilted gaze. "I notice you've filled your bag with all manner of gems and gadgets, yet neglected the single treasure I would have thought would most intrigue you. It is the only thing in this chamber that cannot be found anywhere else in the world. Handed down to Empress Eru by the gods themselves."

"The gods themselves?" I asked softly.

Malak nodded to a pedestal that stood before the opaque wall. On it was a small, wooden box, so plain that my eyes had passed it over before.

I walked over to it and cracked open the lid. Inside were a pair of lenses. I lifted them into the light, breathless. They were not a typical pair of transparent lenses. They were round prisms, with each sparkling facet changing color with the light, and were held in place with a golden frame.

I turned to Malak. "Are these what I think they are? The lenses that tell the future?"

"It is not as simple as that, I'm afraid," said Malak. "Rather, the lenses show you all probable futures from your point in time, where a particular question or event is concerned."

"Incredible! How do I use them?" I tapped the side impatiently and shook it, searching for some sort of lever or latch.

"That depends. What would you like to know?"

I paused and mulled his question over, debating possible questions. I figured it would be better to first test the lenses with a low-stakes inquiry.

"That harlot Naji has been harassing me to marry him. What would the future hold if I did?" I slipped the lenses over my face. The world fractured through them.

"Shut your eyes. Imagine his face. Imagine the ring on his hand. Imagine the contract signed. Then open your eyes," said Malak.

I did as Malak bid, imagining it all in as vivid detail as I could. I'm embarrassed to admit that the idea made my heart flutter. He would have looked nice beneath the light of a temple's oculus with a glint of gold on his finger.

Then I opened my eyes and saw through the lenses—

Naji and I in a lonely house by a great river, with three children until one falls in—

Naji and I, but we never had children or a house by a great river. We live in the gold district of Summer's Edge, in a grand house with everything money can buy. And I grow bored, and Naji grows bored and spends more and more time staring out the bedroom window, until one day he is gone—

Naji and I, but we never had a house, because I lost our money on a series of gambles, and the baby is hungry, and there's never enough of anything—

Naji and I, and we're never in one place long, I'm taking him to see the wonders of the world, but there are bandits on the road, one with a knife, a knife that he presses against Naji's throat and—

Naji and I, but he becomes entangled with another woman, and in a jealous rage I—

Naji and I, and we—

I ripped the lenses off with a gasp.

"What ... what did I ..." My hands were trembling so fiercely that I nearly dropped the lenses. It was as though I'd just lived seven different lives, decades of joys and tragedies packed into an instant.

"You saw the probable futures that would await you if you were to wed Naji," said Malak. It took me a moment to realize he'd even spoken, as I was still glancing around the chamber and trying to remind myself that I was in the Crystal Pyramid, not a house in the gold district or an inn in some foreign land.

"I don't understand," I said. "How can I know which one would be the true one?"

"This is a science even Empress Eru and her council struggled with," Malak said softly. He padded to the wall in which the Empress was entombed. He stared up at it with longing, as though he were speaking not only to me but to her, his voice drifting across death's veil. "She would use the lenses to see not just one divergence in time, as you did now, but dozens. Even hundreds. Through these exhaustive gazes into the futures,

Empress Eru charted the events and decisions necessary for the best possible threads of time."

I raised an eyebrow. "Not well enough, clearly. Her empire is dead."

"Dead?" Malak tilted his head, and his metallic face seemed to shift into a grin. "Or sleeping?"

" 'Sleeping' would be a rather optimistic thing to call it."

Malak laughed and nodded to the right-most wall. "Look out into the sands again. What do you see?"

I looked out again at the desiccated peaks that peppered the dunes. I shrugged. "Pyramids buried in the sand."

"And in them, the Empire's millions, dreaming in their own glass cases." Malak looked away and again spoke up to Empress Eru. "She holds them in sleep with an enchantment that requires every fiber of her. When she takes her final breath, they shall wake."

"Final breath? She's *dead*!" I snapped at him. Malak said nothing, only continued to gaze into the crystalline wall. I turned my head to look as well, peering closer than I had before to prove to myself that Malak was talking nonsense.

Yet, encased in the crystal, I thought I saw the faintest rise and fall of her chest.

Malak spoke again. "She looked far into the futures, perhaps too far for her own good. She saw a great evil waiting a thousand years into every future. Something that could consume the world, Bazi."

"What could possibly be big enough to consume the world?"

"It is difficult to describe in terms you will understand." Malak paused and thought for a moment. "Imagine a grand house composed of countless rooms and chambers. They are built all around and on top of each other, with the base rooms supporting all the ones above. Now, imagine what would happen if a bitter carpenter were to take a hammer and begin making cracks in all the walls and beams of the base rooms, striking until they tore through. What would happen to the house?"

"Why, it would collapse, of course," I said.

"Precisely. Our world is one room among many. As we speak, a bitter carpenter in your continent is forging her hammer."

The words sank into my mind like stones. I couldn't think, couldn't speak. I merely stood dumbfounded until Malak spoke again.

"Empress Eru saw only a few hundred futures where the Empire survived this, but not one wherein she or her direct kin ruled. There were only a few hundred possible replacements suitable to lead her people out from the darkness."

"But why freeze everything? Why not just hand the crown off to them?" I asked. I watched the Empress breathe. The more I looked, the more of her I could see. Her eyes darted beneath their lids.

"They were not yet born," said Malak. "If she allowed the Empire to continue naturally until the candidates for the crown were of age, then she would someday die and events would spiral out of her control. There might be civil wars, deranged successors to the crown, or successors who would be either unwilling or unable to craft the time threads necessary. She could not exert sufficient control for those lands beyond the Empire's reach to narrow things down to a single perfect thread, but she could grant a fighting chance to the few hundred that would ensure the Empire's survival."

My breath caught in my chest as the truth loomed. "Those statues ..."

"Any one of them could be where you stand now. Akeem, if he had not caught his illness as a child. Naji, if he had followed through on his fancy of stealing away with the maps the last night you spent together. Your mother, if she had never had you, and had instead apprenticed with a cartographer in her youth."

"Stop," I rasped. I turned away from Empress Eru and began pacing back and forth in the chamber, the lenses still dangling in my hand. The possibilities upon possibilities whirled in my head and drowned me. Had my years of efforts been meaningless, nothing more than bouts of cosmic luck? Had I ever had any power in my life at all?

"As I said, the Empire reawakens when Empress Eru draws her final breath. That final breath is drawn when you break the wall." Malak padded over to me. "You may attempt to do so with your hammer, or anything else in the chamber."

"I'm not attempting it at all! This is madness!" I stumbled away from him.

"Have you not spent all your life longing for wealth? Have you not craved power?" Malak continued to advance. "Every decision you have ever made has led you here. I know. I am the messenger, and my Empress has shown me all paths, yours included."

"You may have known I'd come, but you can't know my mind now. You can't know what I'll do."

Malak laughed, then nodded to the lenses in my hand. "Oh, Bazi. Of your path, we were the most certain. In every future from this point in time, you choose to take the crown. If you don't believe me, see for yourself."

I hesitated, the lenses poised in my hand.

"All you need to do is slip them on, imagine the crown upon your head, open your eyes, and see the futures."

I slipped them on. I imagined the crown upon my head. I opened my eyes. I saw the futures.

Every single one.

Every single blood-soaked battleground beneath my feet, every star stolen from a crimson sky, every daughter forged into demigod, every sword in my hand, every hollow laugh and savage cry, every added century welded to my life with sorcery, every death and rebirth and world upturned as I watched an empire rise from the ashes beneath my outstretched hand, wonders and terrors in my palm as I became something else.

And I screamed more than I ever had in my life.

I did not break the Empress' tomb or take the crown. I stashed the lenses into my satchel and fled. I didn't stop until I was out of the pyramid and riding away with Fig. Malak did not attempt to stop me, but I could hear his laugh following me all the journey home to Summer's Edge. I have not returned since.

But what I took in my bag was still enough to be life-changing. My old friend Akeem used his share of the riches to found the greatest trade company on the continent, managing it from the highest tower of the gold district. As for myself, well, look around. We sit together now on the balcony of the High Palace, with all the city-state sprawled out far below our feet. Terrified as I was of the lenses after my journey, I warmed up to them over the years and used them to craft the life I enjoy now.

No one in Summer's Edge is my equal. Not in wealth, not in power, not in love, not even in fame or esteem.

Sef, my husband, is gloriously handsome, charming, and fine, perfectly fine. They tell me my eldest daughter looks exactly like me, but she's got his fat nose. And the youngest does the same little snort when she laughs as he does. Horribly grating. I suppose I shouldn't speak ill of my family, though. I've been told they're perfect.

It's *all* very perfect, isn't it? I've reached the highest of heights in this city-state. I could smash the lenses right now and miss nothing. And you know, I thought about doing so, just a month ago. But first, I wanted one last look. For curiosity's sake.

I imagined the crown upon my head again.

And would you believe it, I wasn't anywhere near as terrified by what I saw as when I first did, fifteen years before. In fact, I was exhilarated. For here, in the palace of Summer's Edge with my family, I realize now that I am still only halfway up the sky. The material needs were fleeting after all.

And that's why I've brought you here. I'm told you're the best merchant to seek for supplying a long journey. Several hundred leagues across the sand wastes and all the Carmelian Seas to sail lie ahead, so I want the highest quality from your stock. Fig's not what she once was, so I'll be needing some new horses, ships, a sand-faring carriage …

See Mia Ram's story "The Crystal Pyramid" online at Metaphorosis. f you liked it, leave a comment. Authors love that!
Remember to subscribe to our e-mail updates so you'll know when new stories are posted.

About the story

I enjoy ekphrastic writing exercises (meaning writing that is based on an image or work of art) and this story is the result of one such exercise. I came across a painting of a shining, white pyramid while scrolling through a list of artworks and challenged myself to write a flash fiction about it as an exercise. That flash fiction grew into a full short story as I worked on it and began mentally adding layers to the story. What began as a page-long snippet about a traveler stranded in the desert is now the tale of a thief getting more than what she bargained for in her quest to raid an empress' tomb.

A question for the author

Q: What hero (of any gender) would you name your child after, if we lived in a society with names like that?

A: Moon Knight. It's a name that commands attention, both from peers and from ancient Egyptian gods. Moon Knight is a great namesake because he's a hero whose identity is in perpetual flux. He becomes whatever he needs to be in the moment, and that's the kind of philosophy I'd like to impart to the next generation. Fancy gadgets and super strength are all well and good, but true power is the power to adapt and change.

About the author

Mia Ram is a fantasy and science-fiction writer from Huntersville, North Carolina.

Frozen in Glass

Hope Davies

The first time Pinyit's father showed him the orbs in the shed, he'd been so frightened that he kicked and screamed the whole way down the garden path, right up until his father crouched down in front of him and gripped his shoulders tight, fingers digging into fresh bruises so hard that he winced.

"Listen, Pin," he said, voice kind but leaving no room for questions. *"When you're big, you'll be glad we did this. It's important to record the past so that we don't twist things around in our heads when we're older. You don't want that, do you?"*

"But what if it hurts?"

"It doesn't, I promise."

Inside the shed, there were rows upon rows of cracked wooden shelves loaded down with glass orbs. Some of the orbs were clear. Others were injected with colour, pinks swirling through blues, reds exploding in jagged lines, greens diffusing in soft, pleasant circles. When Pinyit reached out to touch one, his father smacked his hand away.

"Those are me and your Ma's memories. If you touch them, you might see something we don't want you to see, and that would be rude, wouldn't it?"

He bit his lip and nodded, chastened, but unable to take his eyes off the colourful orbs. He'd seen them both use the orbs before, their eyes closed as the colours seeped out of the orb, lighting up the air around them as they remembered things stored long ago.

His father picked him up and sat him down on a countertop, squished between the wall and a whole crate filled with clear orbs, a spider's web drooping perilously close to his head.

Pinyit craned his neck to watch as his father carefully selected a clear orb from the crate and pressed it into Pinyit's hands.

"Now remember what we said? Think really hard about something you want to remember forever, and it'll go into the orb!"

Pinyit looked at it doubtfully, *"And... it'll still be in my head too, won't it?"*

His father chuckled and ruffled his hair, *"Yes, it'll still be in your head too. And... one other thing."*

Pinyit met his father's eyes; amber-specked hazel turned to a cool shadow by the day's fading light.

"Make it something nice, Pin."

He did as his father asked, watching as green and yellow poured in thin streams from the places where skin touched glass. Sealed off and secure.

The truth, suspended in a moment of singular perfection.

Many years and many more orbs later, Pinyit stood in front of a different house entirely.

Manya's house was in the nicer part of the city. It was two stories where most dwellings were only one, wood panelling veined with glass that shifted with the heat of the day; wide and gaping, almost completely transparent during the cool mornings and evenings, then thicker and greener in the hot afternoons, making it harder for the sun to enter. Like most houses, it was propped up on short, chunky stilts that allowed air to circulate below, but instead of the bare, awkward hunks of wood or stone, these were lovingly polished and intricately carved.

It was a masterwork of craftsmanship, and Pinyit, with his painful, dust-caked feet and travel stained clothing, could not have looked more out of place if he tried.

One week on from The Incident, and Pinyit's ears still rang with Iq Shunyum's final words to him before his departure from the temple. *"You can come back when you can control your temper!"*

The Iq had used that biting tone, the same one he used when someone made a foolish mistake in a calculation or reshelved a book incorrectly. Close enough to what little Pinyit remembered of his mother's voice that he couldn't hear it and not flinch.

Pinyit never made foolish mistakes. He never reshelved books incorrectly. In fact, he had nearly three years' worth of stress headaches to show for the standard he had held himself to around

Iq Shunyum. And then, in a single frayed moment, he'd made all that work count for nothing.

Carefully, he set his belongings down and knelt amongst the dry weeds at the house's base, where, inscribed into the wooden stilts, he found likenesses of the three moon goddesses: Killilla, Wuuiq, and Timah.

He got halfway through the prayers of protection before he remembered that, due to his failure to remain an Iq, it was inappropriate for him to be doing this.

His cheeks felt hot, and he hurried to his feet, brushing dirt from his trousers — yet another symbol of his fall in status. He knotted his fists in the fabric, painfully different to the calf-length robes he'd grown accustomed to in the temple, then forced himself to let go. He had to be calm. There could be no more 'incidents' if he wanted the temple to take him back. He had to be, in a word, perfect.

And he definitely wanted them to take him back.

The door opened and someone came down the steps.

It was Manya, long brown curls spilled across broad shoulders, black eyes alight at the mere sight of Pinyit.

"Did you get tired of being a priest already?" Manya asked, his voice light.

"More like they got tired of me." Pinyit breathed out hard, throat aching as he averted his gaze. He didn't want to be doing this. Begging his friend's parents for help again like he was still a child. He was supposed to have moved forward with his life. "Can I...?"

Manya's eyes grew soft. "Of course you can stay here. Come on in, Da's making dinner, it'll be ready soon."

Once inside, Manya led Pinyit first to the room that had been his since he was seven years old.

It was more or less exactly as he remembered it; bed pushed up against the window, drawers full of glass writing tablets scrubbed clean of practice equations and ready for use, three locked crates stacked in the corner, dust catching and collecting in the rough, splintered wood. From there, he found his eyes wandering over the wooden board nailed over the hole Pinyit had punched in the wall as a teenager.

"Oh wow, do you remember that?" Pinyit jumped a little at the sound of Manya's voice. "You were so *mad*."

"Yeah…" Pinyit said, quickly turning away. He bit the inside of his cheek. "Are your parents definitely okay with me being here?"

Manya stared at him in genuine confusion, "What? They're both thrilled, Da's been making his banana rice every night for the past *week* waiting for you to get back, ever since your letter arrived. Why would you think they wouldn't want you here?"

Pinyit wasn't sure he could put it into words, so he just shrugged and said, "Never mind, it doesn't matter."

In the kitchen, Manya's father, Lyhu, was hunched almost double over a cast iron pot, hair pulled out of his face, brown eyes hidden behind steamed-up spectacles that he pushed up onto his head when he saw the two of them.

"Evening, boys," he said, swiping at his brow with the sleeve of his cotton aprabe robe, "Pinyit, did Manya show you where we've been keeping your things?"

"It's all just in his room, Da," Manya interrupted, pulling a stack of mismatched glass bowls out of a cupboard, "We were up there literally five minutes ago."

Pinyit knotted his fingers in his sleeves and mumbled, "I still can't believe you kept everything."

Manya exchanged a glance with his father and then said, "Of course we did. Did you think we were going to throw all your stuff away the second you were gone?"

That was exactly what Pinyit had thought they would do. His mother had.

He remembered the smell of smoke more than anything else. Acrid. There were still white flecks of ash clinging to Lyhu's hair when he returned with nothing but the news that when he'd attempted to retrieve Pinyit's belongings, his mother had been in the midst of burning it all.

Pinyit hadn't cared at the time, and Lyhu hadn't pushed. It had only been a week since he moved in, and the healer was still giving him daily doses of powdered tyiim root to dull the pain of his broken wrist. Even now he could barely remember his mother, her existence confined to snatches of temper and the bone-deep awareness of his own cursed nature.

"Of course we didn't do that," Lyhu said, resuming his work, "You'll always have a place here, even if all you're using that place for is storage."

Lyhu had said some iteration of that same thing more times than Pinyit could count, but that didn't make it any easier to believe.

Pinyit soon fell back into the rhythm of helping, first going to the pot where fruit peels were kept and adding a generous helping to boiling water, then adding cinnamon, anise, and crushed peppercorns like Lyhu had taught him. He strained the fragrant tea that resulted out into the little cups Manya had set out.

No one was allowed to help with the rice itself, of course. It was Lyhu's pride and joy — soft and sweet, never too dry, and packed with beef marinated overnight in an earthy blend of spices that Lyhu promised he would teach Pinyit and Manya 'when they were ready'.

That evening, generous helpings were served, steam rising into the cooling air. About halfway through, Manya's mother, Cibree, arrived back from supervising work in the fields, barely pausing to wash the dirt from her hands before she began questioning Pinyit.

"So, what was it like at the temple? I bet their cooking wasn't as good as my Lyhu's," she said, pausing to elbow her husband lightly in the ribs. He grabbed her arm and tugged her in lightly for the combined purposes of giving her a peck on the cheek and rubbing a smudge of dirt from her chin.

"Let the boy eat, Cib," he chided, "He's only just sat down."

"It's alright," Pinyit said, unable to stop himself from tensing a little at Cibree's presence. "Their cooking *wasn't* as good as Lyhu's."

"Suck up," Manya muttered, but Pinyit saw the grin he was hiding behind his own bowl.

Pinyit shrugged, feigning ease. "You'd be sucking up too if you'd been living on nothing but qan porridge for two years." Just the mention was enough to have everyone's nose wrinkling.

"Did you like it there?" Cibree asked.

Pinyit felt his own smile start to strain. "It was good. They had some incredible resources, and it was good to have the senior Iqs there pushing us to work our hardest."

"Not too hard, I hope!" She swallowed a mouthful of rice. "I remember though — that thing you were doing with the moons and the harvests."

Pinyit nodded. "Yeah, they brought over some tablets from Timah's temple — historical crop data. I know a lot of people say it's superstitious nonsense, but I noticed a real link between historical qan famines and periods with more empty skies."

Pinyit could've talked for hours about teaching himself the statistical techniques he'd needed but nobody at the temple knew, the natural history books he'd found and devoured, the rush of challenging himself to stretch outside the field he'd studied in to marry the various disciplines together.

But then Cibree said, "So, how long until you go back?"

The mouthful of food Pinyit had just taken lost all taste. He swallowed, then rubbed the yellowing bruise hidden under his sleeve.

"I'm not sure," he lied, "I felt like I needed a bit of time away."

Owning up to what had happened seemed an impossible task. From the moment Pinyit had been able to express a wish to study the skies, Lyhu and Cibree had done everything in their power to make it a reality. Cibree had leaned on her extensive network of contacts to find out exactly what Pinyit would need to do to be admitted to study in the temple. Lyhu had spent hours helping him work through calculations, literature, and required religious knowledge. Even Manya got involved, gleefully chasing Pinyit around and threatening him with everything from toads shoved down the back of his tunic to hiding all his shoes until Pinyit could answer perfectly whatever Manya was quizzing him on.

For them to find out now that he'd thrown all that away because he couldn't control his *temper*? They'd be devastated. He gripped his spoon a little tighter.

"Oh no, how come?" Cibree asked, voice flooded with a concern that only added to Pinyit's guilt.

"I, err..." He set down his bowl and wiped his sweating palms on his trousers.

"You know that you can talk to us about anything, dear," she said, wearing a smile that Pinyit knew she thought of as comforting, but only served to twist his heart around on itself.

"Leave it, Cib," Lyhu chided.

"If something's wrong—"

"How was work? That Klieri woman still giving you trouble?"

They launched into a spirited discussion about Cibree's ongoing dispute with one of her employees, and Pinyit kept his head down, focusing on eating his food as quickly as he could and pretending he didn't see Manya watching him the whole time.

After helping to clean up, Pinyit claimed exhaustion and went to bed early. Still too wound up to sleep, he lay on his side, staring out through the vein of glass running through his bedroom wall. At his touch, it widened and thinned, the opalescent turquoise fading almost entirely as it revealed a sky dappled with stars and a single moon, Killila. Wuuiq and Timah were hiding today, but he already knew that.

He knew the name of each and every star he could see and had dedicated years to charting them and tracking their movements across the sky. He knew that, in three days, there would be an empty sky — cursed, as the stories said.

Pinyit had been born under such a sky.

His father had told him once that it was why Pinyit was the way he was. It was why he cried so loud when he was a baby, why he was ill so often with stomach aches, why he could never seem to do as he was asked. A cursed sky made for a cursed boy, and there was only one way to deal with a cursed boy. His mother tried her best, his father frequently said, but sometimes it all just got the better of her.

What his father meant by that existed only in broad strokes in Pinyit's memory.

Violence, he knew, had been a part of it. As had yelling. He knew these things the same way he knew the names of the stars — the knowledge itself within easy reach, the memory of hours spent acquiring that knowledge lost to time.

He remembered his father's justifications more clearly than anything his mother had actually done, and they seethed beneath his skin like lightning.

When he couldn't lie still anymore, he jumped to his feet, began to pace, fingers snarling in his hair. He needed to hit something. To hurt. To get rid of the charge pulsing through him, driving him back and forth, back and forth across the room.

He forced himself to breathe.

From the corner of his eye, he caught sight of the crates, stacked one atop the other in the corner of his room. The day his father brought them to Manya's house had been the last time he and Pinyit saw each other.

Pinyit had been thirteen years old and unable to get through half a sentence without arguing with someone, battering himself against the lines set by Cibree and Lyhu, desperate to know if there was a crack, terrified he might find one. He hadn't seen either of his parents since coming to live at Manya's house, and the sight of his father with a push-cart full of crates had sent his mind spinning, careening back into a past he'd been trying to forget.

"*What do you want?*" Pinyit had said, taking his father aside whilst Lyhu looked on from the house.

His father was a little greyer than Pinyit remembered, trousers a little more creased. He had a splotchy new scar creeping up his cheek from under his beard and a habit of rubbing at it when he was uncomfortable.

He didn't smile when Pinyit spoke to him, just wearily said, *"You've a picture of us in your head now. No doubt influenced by that lot."* He tilted his head towards Manya's house. *"I brought the orbs in case you wanted to remember how things really were."*

Piniyt hadn't had anything to say to that. Just a tightening of his fists. A clenching of his jaw. A knowledge that this was his father and there was nothing Pinyit could do against him.

Now, Pinyit hauled the topmost crate down from the pile, knees buckling slightly under the weight.

Pinyit didn't know how to fix his temper, his inability to get anything right, or the mere fact of his birth under a sky shunned by the goddesses.

His memory though… maybe if he fixed that, patched up the holes, then the other things would start to fall into place around it. If he had specifics, he could pinpoint what, exactly, drove him into the kinds of rages that led to holes in the walls and being kicked out of temples. If he understood why it was there, then perhaps he would be able to anticipate the anger before it got him into trouble.

He dropped to his knees in front of the crate and attempted to pry open the lid several times before he remembered that it was locked.

Trying hard not to lose patience with his teenaged self, he retraced the favoured hiding places of that period; between the folds of clothing in his dresser, slotted into the dented casing of the first telescope Cibree and Lyhu had ever bought for him, in a wooden box filled with a strange collection of withered scraps of bark that had apparently caught the interest of his younger self.

Eventually, he thought to reach behind the dresser, feeling along the wall until his fingertips glanced across something metallic wedged into a crack. He worked it free and held it in a clenched fist, sharp edges digging into the palm of his hand as he withdrew his arm.

A rusty key.

He shuffled back over to the crate, slotted it into the lock and turned it.

The lid swung open, revealing rows upon rows of dusty glass orbs, loosely stacked, not labelled like the neat rows of similar orbs Lyhu and Cibree kept in their study. They glowed in the darkness, casting stripes of red, green, blue, and yellow across Pinyit's skin and clothing.

Few people in Kyhufut were as invested in the collection of memory orbs as Pinyit's father had been. Most people were wary of the debilitating hangovers that came with overuse of the orbs.

He'd created several whilst living at Manya's house, but he'd created hundreds under the direction of his father. Every few weeks, he'd sat and poured out copies of his memories into little glass balls no larger than oranges that were promptly secreted away into storage for when he was older.

He was older now.

He rubbed his sweaty palms on his knees. This was the only thing he could think of that would help. All he could do now was hope.

He rolled up his sleeves and grabbed the first orb he saw.

Glowing pink tendrils swirled within the orb, rushing up to meet the spot where Pinyit's fingers pressed up against the surface of the glass. A tingling, shrinking sensation banded across the inside of Pinyit's head as the pink matter surged out of the orb, wreathing his hand in light. The sensation intensified, the glow grew brighter, and he felt like he was suffocating, but then—

"Listen to this," Pinyit's mother told his Auntie Kihlush as they worked side by side, all three of them up to their elbows in soapy water, "What do you want to be when you grow up, Pin?"

Pinyit knew this game, and it was an easy one, "I want to be an astro-astronimcaler!"

"An astronomer, just like his Da!" His mother grinned, and Pinyit glowed.

Oh.

Pinyit blinked the memory away and set the orb back down. He didn't know what he'd been expecting, but it wasn't *that*. He remembered now, his father's passing interest in astronomy, mapped out on glass tiles left scattered across the kitchen table.

She'd seemed so *proud* of him, she'd even been boasting about him to his aunt. That sense of joy and accomplishment lingered in his chest even now. Warm and bright. He didn't normally feel that way when he thought about his mother. It didn't make any sense. Didn't mesh with the image he had of her as rageful. Frightening. Willing to bruise and break.

Maybe another orb would provide some clarity?

The next orb he found had yellow pooled at its core like an egg. When he touched it, the memory seeped forwards, slowly enveloping his wrist.

"–and then Manya said that his Da said I could go to their house to play anytime I wanted!"

Pinyit trotted at his mother's side, struggling under a basket full of qan, sandals slapping loosely at his heels. She made a humming noise, not seeming to have fully understood what Pinyit was trying to ask.

"So can I?" he prompted.

"Can you what?"

"Go play at Manya's house?"

"Manya's parents are the ones who live in that big house at the edge of town, aren't they?" his mother asked, and Pinyit nodded vigorously.

"Yeah! It's huge!"

His mother smiled and ruffled his hair, "Of course you can go, sweetheart, I think you should definitely *keep playing with Manya."*

The orb hit the floor with a thud and rolled, yellow light arcing from Pinyit's hand, flooding back into the glass. He stared at it, panting for breath. That memory had been no different to the last one; it'd been so… normal.

He knew, in his gut, that his mother had not been as kind as the orbs were telling him. He'd had seven years with her and a whole twelve away to mull over and realise exactly why he was right to be frightened of her, but he couldn't ignore what the orbs were telling him, could he? His not understanding them didn't make the memories any less real.

He balled his shaking hands up into fists and stared hard into the box of orbs.

He moved past the orb filled with soft blue spirals, ignored the one with green waves rippling its interior. Dozens more he looked at and discarded, deciding they looked too soft, too unlikely to hold the harsh truths he craved. His eyes landed on one with vicious purple cracks running through its core. It looked… mean. Pinyit didn't know if there was any real correlation between the appearance of the orbs and the quality of the memories they held. He could only hope there was.

He picked it up. Braced himself. Let the past wash over him.

"Do you know what that one's called?" his mother asked, pointing to the smallest moon in the cool evening sky.

Pinyit shook his head. He'd never seen all three moons at once like this. His mother said it was rare, only happening once every three years.

"Her name is Killila," His mother said, "She's the youngest and she holds onto all of her sisters' joy whilst they work, just like you do for me and your Da." She beamed at him and pressed a kiss to his temple, her long black hair tickling his nose. "That's what Pinyit means. You're our joy."

The purple seeped back into the orb like fracture lines. If he didn't know better, he would have said it was broken. He didn't understand how all the orbs could be like... *this*. He knew that bad things had happened. He *knew* it. So why didn't the orbs show that? Pinyit stared at it, eyes damp, before he realised someone was knocking at the door.

"Come in!" he called out, hastily wiping his eyes on his sleeves. When he looked up, Manya was peering at him with a worried crease in his brow.

"I heard a bang..." The crease deepened as he took in the sight of Pinyit and the orbs, several of which were now on the floor, "What happened? Are these..." he crouched down, about to touch the orb full of red spines, but Pinyit quickly jumped to his feet.

"No! Don't!" he said, "I— it's private."

Manya pulled back, "Of course, sorry."

Pinyit crouched down, sleeve wrapped around his hand as he gathered up the spilled orbs, failing to get his ragged breath under control. He could feel Manya's gaze fixed on his back as he worked.

Pinyit put the lid back on the crate, plunging them into darkness. He sat with his back against his bed, hands screwed up by his sides. How was he supposed to hate his mother when, clearly, she'd loved him so much? And if she'd really been that kind, what excuse did he have for his failures?

Manya trod across the room, towering over him. Pinyit shied away, but then Manya sat down and pressed his warm shoulder into Pinyit's.

More silence.

"Go on then," Pinyit said when he couldn't bear it anymore, "Ask the question you've been dying to ask."

"What question?"

Pinyit rolled his eyes. "Don't act like you're stupid."

Manya straightened. "I'm serious. Enlighten me, what's this question that I've apparently been 'dying to ask'?"

Pinyit kept his eyes fixed on the moon dappled wall opposite. "Why did they kick me out?"

"What? I thought you were just joking when you said that."

Pinyit smiled ruefully and shook his head, "Nope."

Pinyit glanced towards Manya and saw him resting his chin on forearms crossed across his knees. It was such a quintessentially Manya-like gesture that Pinyit was momentarily taken aback. He really had been gone for a long time.

If he were at the temple right now, Iq Shunyum would likely be scolding him for laziness, *"If you've got time to rest, you've got time to clean."*

He'd pushed Pinyit to be the most capable version of himself, to learn things he never would have learned otherwise. Knowledge for its own sake, whatever the cost. And Pinyit had ruined it all over nothing.

"It was my own fault," he said, and Manya looked up, "I kept getting angry, and, well, you know how I am."

Both their eyes fell upon the boarded over hole.

"And then when it happened... I was talking to one of the senior researchers about my work, you know, with the cursed skies? And he said that it meant that maybe some people really *are* cursed. And then..." He rubbed the bruise on his arm. "Well, I smashed their telescope."

He didn't even remember doing it. Just white, searing anger. Then the lenses were cracked, the bronze was dented, and Iq Shunyum was staring at him, disappointment oozing like wax from a candle.

"That's it? You broke a telescope?"

"No, you don't understand," Pinyit said, shaking his head, "I broke *the* telescope. The Great One."

"Oh shit," Manya muttered.

"Exactly. They said — they said that if I could prove that I could control my temper, then I could come back."

"I thought that was getting better?" Manya said, "When we were kids you used to, err... get a bit wound up, but in that year before you left? I don't think I even heard you raise your voice. And I know you've not been back here long, but you remind me more of that Pinyit than the one who went round smashing stuff when he got mad."

Pinyit winced and couldn't help but let his gaze fall upon the hole in the wall again.

They'd both been fourteen when that happened. An argument with Cibree about something that in hindsight they both admitted was stupid. It would've been fine, but then she'd raised her voice.

Logically, he'd known that this was normal. People fought. *Pinyit* and *Cibree* fought. But something about the pitch or tenor of her voice that day had felt not like an argument with the woman who'd taken him in at his most desperate, but instead like standing on the beach, a wave as tall as he was about to wash over his head.

And then the wave had crashed.

He hadn't been trapped, but he felt like he was. Wasn't helpless either, or a child, or in danger, but that didn't matter. Heart pounding, face hot, something bitter in the back of his mouth. He might've shouted, but he didn't remember, too caught up in that visceral surge of rage tinged terror.

He'd stormed upstairs to his room and slammed the door so hard it shuddered in its frame. Yelled in frustration. It wasn't enough. Too much, too loud—

Stinging pain.

Wood buckling.

His fist had gone through the wall.

It was probably the worst thing he'd done whilst living with Manya's family. Afterwards, Lyhu had made him repair the damage himself, and then Cibree and Lyhu sat Pinyit down to have a long talk about things Pinyit could do when he was angry that didn't involve property damage.

It had helped. There were meditations he could do that worked, breathing with the goddesses in the same way the sea did. Focusing on his studies helped too. Anything that let him escape whatever situation he was in that felt like it was about to overwhelm him.

"It *was* getting better," Pinyit said, "I don't know what happened at the temple to change that, and that's a problem. What I was doing wasn't enough. I need to find something more."

Manya's eyes roamed once more back to the crate. "Is that what you were trying to do with the memory orbs? Figure out 'something more'?"

Pinyit nodded, then looked away, "They don't... They're not showing me what they're meant to."

"What do you mean?" Manya asked tentatively.

"They're all..." He couldn't look at Manya, kept his gaze fixed instead on his hands. There was still an ink stain, black crawling through the fine crevices normally invisible in his smooth brown skin, "They're all *good*. They show her being *good*."

"You're not..." Pinyit looked up to see Manya watching him with wide eyes, "You know your Ma was horrible, right?"

Pinyit nodded quickly, "I know, but in the orbs—"

Manya groaned in frustration, "Seriously? I don't know how much you remember from that night, but she *broke your wrist.* Before that, every time I saw you when we were kids you had some new story about 'falling down the stairs' or 'walking into a wall'."

"We were kids," Pinyit said, hoarse, "Kids are clumsy; maybe I did do all those things."

"Why can't you just accept that things are better here? You knew it when we were seven, why don't you know it now?"

"I do—"

“Then stop chasing after her! She didn’t love you, Pin!” Shouting. Words that hit too close to bone. Pinyit’s heart was pounding, his blood curdled hot in his face, the wave was rising, rising, rising—

“You don’t get it,” Pinyit said, controlled, perfectly controlled.

What did Manya know about love, anyway? He’d only ever tasted the uncomplicated kind, like an apple peeled and sliced and presented on a plate drizzled with honey. He’d never picked sharp spikes of peel from his gums, never gouged out soggy chunks of bruised flesh with his thumb. He didn’t know that it was still the same apple, the same sweetness underneath.

“No! I don’t get it! Those orbs,” Manya gestured sharply at the crates and Pinyit tensed, “aren’t proof of anything other than the fact that your Da decided to put something that can make *adults* sick in the hands of a three year old!”

He screwed his fists up. Manya’s words echoing, *she didn’t love you, she didn’t love you, she didn’t—*

It wasn’t true.

Or it was.

Pinyit didn’t even know himself, so who did Manya think he was, trying to decide for him? He tried to imagine the sea, breathing with the goddesses, but the images in his mind just crashed and frothed like waves cresting in a storm.

“Get... out.” He hissed.

“Just think, for Timah’s sake!”

“I said, get out!” Pinyit was on his feet; he couldn’t stay sitting anymore, not when his blood burned and his heart thudded, so loud it seemed moments away from splintering his ribs with the force of it.

Manya, not shouting now, pursed his lips and nodded, getting to his feet so he was eye level with Pinyit, “Fine. Don’t listen to me. Don’t expect any sympathy when you mess yourself up.”

Pinyit curled his fists so tight his nails, bitten short, sank into his palms. Manya walked away.

As Killilla and the stars travelled across the sky, Pinyit went back to the orbs. Maybe there was something he’d missed? There was a sliver of pain starting in the corner of his temple, but he ignored it and picked up the next orb.

A bright blue sky, his mother’s hand—

The sliver widened to a splinter.

Constellations, his mother explaining that the Dog crawled from West to East as the seasons changed—

From a splinter, it grew into a shard.

Hours spent together, poring over glass writing tablets.

His head was pounding, and the entire right side of his face was on fire. Memories blurred into each other. Had that last one really been from an orb? Had it really been his mother? He remembered an almost identical scene from when Lyhu was helping him study for his entry into the temple. Without thinking, he pressed the cool surface of the glass to his cheek—

Soft, savoury qan cakes, crispy around the edges and buttered. He'd thrown up, and she always made qan cakes after he threw up. Food that wouldn't hurt his stomach, gentle like the hands she used to pull the blankets to his chin when she tucked him into bed.

"A good meal and some sleep and you'll feel better," she said.

He dropped the orb as another lance of pain pierced his temple. The room tilted, the floor falling out from beneath him until he fell prone, the walls spinning.

His heart beat painfully, and he was shaking all over.

The orb rolled away, the memories within condensing to thick grey smoke. His head had never hurt this badly in his life. He didn't know what to do anymore. He couldn't burden Manya's parents again, not like he'd burdened the temple, like he'd burdened his mother.

Another splinter of pain. He curled up small. Maybe they would forget about him if he was small.

She'd loved him, the orbs were *proof* that she'd loved him.

"Just think, for Timah's sake!"

Belatedly, Pinyit did.

The orbs came from his father.

"Make it something nice, Pin," he used to say. Every time.

Pinyit hadn't made many orbs since moving in with Manya's parents, but those few he had made were all stored together in the downstairs study.

And one...

He forced himself to stand, clinging to the wall when the floor seemed to tremble beneath his feet.

The veins of glass in the hallway were wide and open, glass stretched so thin it was almost transparent as, after a cool night, the house gasped for sunlight. Pinyit had to squint as he staggered down the hallway, past the room shared by Cibree and Lyhu, past the kitchen where the big cooking pot had been left to soak, past

Manya's room, where Pinyit could hear his friend moving restlessly in his sleep.

He made it to the study, ignoring books in favour of the shelves at the back of the room which were loaded with dozens of small wooden boxes, glass plates on the front describing the contents in Cibree's clear, straightforward hand.

Manya: third blessed sky one said, on another was written *Cibree: nyltiut ceremony.* He had to squint to read them through the pain. Some of the boxes had a small flower symbol indicating that it was private. The labels for these tended to be sadder, things like *Lyhu: mother's death* or *Cibree: losing Hannyl.*

Pinyit wouldn't have been able to label the memories from the crate so clearly if he tried. After several minutes of searching, he started to find boxes with his own name on them. All of them had the flower symbol, even the happier ones such as *Pinyit: helping Lyhu in the kitchen for the first time* and *Pinyit: acceptance into the Temple of Wuuiq's Astronomical Order.*

He longed to open them up, to sit in the happiness he found in those years after his mother but before the temple. He couldn't.

It took a bit of shuffling things around and a lot of pausing when the pain in his head decided to remind him it was there, but he found what he was looking for at the very back of the shelves. A box just like the others, this time labelled *Pinyit: leaving parents.*

He remembered making this.

He'd been barely able to think through the Healer's medicine for his wrist, but Manya, strangely timid ever since Pinyit had turned up on his doorstep, had brought him a clear glass orb.

"My Da said that sometimes even really important things can be hard to remember if you're little when they happen or they're really scary. If you want to remember, though, put it in here and I'll keep it safe for you."

Pinyit didn't know what he'd put into the orb, but it seemed like the closest he would get. Something he'd created when it was still fresh, but when his father wasn't there prompting him.

He opened the box and pressed his fingers to the glass.

"What do you mean you don't know? We talked about this yesterday."

Pinyit's mother smacked her hand down next to the tablet in front of them.

"Lillina, leave him alone, these calculations are difficult for a child," his father said, head bent over his own work.

His mother scowled, "Answer me, Pinyit. Why don't you know? Did you not study this after our lesson yesterday?"

No, he hadn't. He'd gone outside to play with Manya instead. Stupid, stupid, stupid. He knew how difficult the stellar parallax calculations were. He should've practiced.

"I asked you a question."

"I... I didn't," he admitted.

Blotches on Ma's cheeks. Lips thin and narrow. "Right. That's it. I've had enough of you. Get up."

She snatched his arm, ignoring his father's cry of, "Lillina! Can't you see he's trying his best?"

She pulled him to his feet, and marched him out of the kitchen, into the alleyway outside the house.

Two moons. Wuuiq and Timah. Both full and round, with a sliver of Killila just visible. The closest they were going to get to a blessed sky that year. Nothing really bad could happen with the goddesses watching so closely, right?

The wood panelling shuddered as Ma shoved him into the wall, both hands tight on his shoulders. She leaned in close, hissed, "What do you think you're playing at?"

He knew what came next.

"You're humiliating me. I don't expect much from you, Pinyit, but I do expect you to work."

Another slam. Pain gnawed through his back.

"Are you lazy?"

He shook his head.

"What, then? Is this just what you are? A nasty little boy? You've always been trouble. They warned me about you, you know that? A cursed brat makes a cursed house!"

Slam.

"Look at me when I'm speaking to you!"

She grabbed his hair, pulled his face back, leered. "Oh, now you're crying. Trying to make me feel like a bad mother. You should be grateful; I should have left you out on the beach for the goddesses to claim. That's what the other mothers do with your sort. I thought I could make you better than what you are."

Spit.

Cold dribbled down his face.

"Stop crying."

He couldn't.

"I said stop."

He wanted to.

"I said stop it!"

She wrenched him forward and he yelped, struggled to keep his balance before she shoved him back into the wall. His head whipped back, slammed into wood. No time to catch his breath before she ripped him forward again.

Pulled him so close that he could feel her breath on his ear, "I am sick of you trying to manipulate me." she hissed, and in a single motion, tossed him to the ground.

Hard earth caught his outstretched arm with a hard crack. Pain spliced through his wrist. He moaned, curling around the injury.

"Get out of my sight. I never want to see you again."

"Ma!"

"I said leave!"

Oh. Oh, goddesses. She *had* hated him, she—

"Timah's light!"

He hadn't heard the door opening, but there it was, and Manya was crouched in front of him, the orb rolling from slack fingers.

"Pin?" he said, voice high and urgent., "What happened?"

He screwed his eyes shut, why was it so *bright*?

"I'm getting Ma and Da," Manya said. "Just hold tight, you'll be okay."

"No," he muttered, reaching out to snatch at Manya's finely woven sleeve.

"What do you mean 'no'? You're a mess!"

He tried to shake his head, but it hurt too much. "You hate me."

Manya locked his jaw. "Don't be an idiot. I'm going."

The orb hangover lasted for four long days, most of which Pinyit spent unable to move without sending fresh waves of pain to scour the inside of his skull.

There was no curing overindulgence, but Lyhu spent the daylight hours with him, ready with a cold rag to press against the burning in his temple whenever he needed it.

Pinyit didn't talk much. He knew Lyhu was putting it down to his illness, but in truth, he was weighed down by that final memory. It had been one thing to know logically what his mother had done. To see glimpses of it in bouts of nervousness and anger, the details too painful to see more closely. Another entirely to relive it through the mind of his younger self.

Eventually, he asked Lyhu, "Do you think she loved me?"

Lyhu frowned a little, spectacles flickering with the reflection of the book of fine glass writing tablets he'd been reading from.

"That's not a question I can answer for you," he said eventually, setting his book down. "What do you think?"

Pinyit had had plenty of time to mull that question over on his own. He wasn't sure if he'd ever remember the full extent of what his life with his mother had been like, but he knew enough.

I never want to see you again.

He'd always known, deep down, what she was really like. The terror came with admitting it.

"I think... she loved the person she wanted me to be. When I was him, she loved me, and when I wasn't..."

In a way, that was what it had been like at the temple. Pinyit hadn't even realised how good he'd been at toeing that line, as adept at being the perfect student as he was at being the perfect son. Right up until that moment where he couldn't... when the constant battering of his defences had left them broken.

There was no easy fix for what had happened, for the anger. The only thing he could do was build himself back up again. Learn to truly tell the difference between those trying to help and those happy to tear him down.

Lyhu squeezed Pinyit's leg and, when it was apparent Pinyit was done talking, went back to his book.

Cibree tried one day to make qan cakes after work. She brought the still-warm plate up to him and said, "You've barely eaten, do you think you could try?"

He couldn't answer her. Tiny and round to make them easy for small hands and small mouths to manage. This was exactly how his mother used to make them.

"Oh dear," Cibree said, "What's wrong?"

He was crying. Pinyit wasn't sure if he'd ever cried in front of Cibree before.

Stop crying.

"I'm sorry," he said, hastily rubbing his eyes, "I don't want to be difficult. I'm sorry."

"Oh, sweetie." She sat down next to him, then seemed to hesitate before asking, "Can I hug you?"

He nodded, and she pulled him in, "You can be as difficult as you like, love, we're just glad to have you back."

It wasn't until Pinyit was firmly on the mend that Manya came to speak with him. "Can we talk?" he said.

Pinyit pulled himself into a sitting position and nodded, gritting his teeth against the churn of his stomach. Manya sat opposite, legs crossed. He opened his mouth to talk, but Pinyit quickly interjected, "I'm sorry I yelled at you. I shouldn't have lost my temper."

Manya worried his lower lip, then nodded. "You were upset. It's okay. And, well," He scratched the back of his head sheepishly. "I yelled first. I forgot how much you don't like that, so I'm sorry too."

"Thank you." Pinyit said, painfully aware of the part of him that would always be surprised at the sound of someone else's apology. "You were right, though."

Manya went still. "Yeah?"

Pinyit nodded, "About the orbs, it wasn't good for me to put so much faith in them. I don't know why my father wanted me to make them, but I think he might've been *trying* to get me to forget the bad stuff."

Pinyit didn't know whether his father genuinely thought it'd be better if Pinyit forgot what his childhood was really like, or if he was just trying to preserve his own ideal of what their family should look like. Happy, with a son who remembered a mother who taught him about the stars, not one who beat him.

"I think I can understand that," Manya said quietly. "I saw how miserable you looked going through those orbs and I just wanted you to stop."

"It didn't work, though," Pinyit said, "Thinking that she never did anything wrong just made me think I was broken. Or cursed, I guess."

His father had never tried to discourage that line of thinking either.

He'd been angry at his father for a long time, moreso now, knowing what had been waiting for him in the orbs. The feeling frightened him. There was a balance there that he was going to have to figure out. Between those who deserved that contempt like his mother and father, and those who were just unlucky enough to be caught by the tail end of it.

He pressed a hand to the vein of glass running close to his head and willed it to widen. Outside there was an empty sky, cursed, as the stories said, like Pinyit. For most of his life, Pinyit had been listening to the part of him that believed his mother when she said he was cursed, even if he didn't remember it. He'd thought, at the temple, that he could prove no such curse existed. As if qan harvests and the cycling of moons could quantify his own soul. Through the orbs, he'd tried to fix it. He knew better now. There was no external force that could prove or disprove the validity of his own experiences. He had to look to himself for that. To the people who loved him.

"Can I ask you a favour?"

"You already know you can stay—"

"Not that," Pinyit said, "The orbs." The crates had been sitting in the corner of the room for the past several days, untouched. "I want to put them in storage, make some room in here. Can you help me carry them?"

Manya smiled. "Of course."

See Hope Davies's story "Frozen in Glass" online at Metaphorosis.
If you liked it, leave a comment. Authors love that!
Remember to subscribe to our e-mail updates so you'll know when new stories are posted.

About the story

I first started thinking about writing a story about memory when I caught myself experiencing the phenomenon of false recollection. Someone was telling me about a picture that they'd previously shown me and, with a little prompting, I found that yes, I did remember what it looked like. Moments later, she pulled up a photograph on her phone of the picture she'd shown me, and I was fascinated to realise it was completely different to the picture I had been 'remembering'.

Of course, this is a pretty common thing that happens to everyone, whether we catch ourselves out or not, but nonetheless it got me thinking about what the purpose of memory is if it's so easily subverted by the suggestions of others. Many people crave a complete knowledge of the course of our own lives, it's why we curate photographs and journals, but our memory isn't set up with narrative totality in mind — it's there to keep us safely navigate a world too changeable for our genes to accurately predict and to help us connect with those around us.

This is when the thoughts I'd been having about memory collided with a worldbuilding concept I'd been playing around with for a while — that of glass that reveals the 'true nature' of a person. The thoughts merged, and eventually the glass became the memory orbs seen in "Frozen In Glass". From there, characters started to emerge as I began to think about what kind of conflicts and people could arise from this concept.

I started to think about what kinds of uses people have for memory, and more importantly, what kinds of forces play into the preservation and alteration of it. How might someone turn another person's own memories against them, not just internally, but externally as well? Why would they do that? When that happens, what does it take to disentangle the truth, and who do you trust — your current self, or the self who seems to be reaching out from the past to tell you a different story entirely?

A question for the author

Q: How do you generate story ideas, and how soon do you act on them?

A: My stories tend to come from things that have intrigued or bothered me — things I want to explore my own perspectives on, clarified by the lense of, usually, speculative fiction. When I get an idea, I tend to act on it fairly quickly, even if acting on it just means jotting down a sentence or a paragraph in a google doc. It tends to take much longer to work itself into an actual story though, and those early notes rarely bear much of a resemblance to the idea I end up committing to.

About the author

Hope is a speculative fiction writer from the UK.
hopedavies.blogspot.com, @Davies_Writes

September

To the Wild Sea

B. Morris Allen

The tide seeped away, grey water into black sand. It left her lime-green boots uncovered, anomalous. *Just as well,* thought Sarosh, turning her back on the sea. *This planet could use some color.* As it had used Richard, used her dreams; swallowed them whole, and left nothing but little grains of sand that stuck to everything, fell off everywhere. She kicked the sand as she walked, and it spurted grudgingly before her feet.

At her back, the little love-lorn birds took up their plaintive cries, did their graceful runs and leapt ungainly into the air. 'Just what the planet needs,' she'd told him when he sent the first vid, 'moaning birds that can hardly fly.' He'd only laughed. 'I like it,' he'd said. 'It reminds me to be lonely.' She was lonely now.

Alira waved to her from the cabin above. Lonely, but not alone; no one with an assistant was ever truly alone. "What's up?" Sarosh asked, thumbing her net on.

'Listen,' he had said on their last virtmeet. 'The sea is calling me. Not telepathically, though.' She turned back to the surf, listened with one ear while Alira's voice poured schedules into the other. The waves crashed and stuttered and sighed across the sand in their alien language. "Richard," she told them. "Richard."

"Yes," said Alira from the porch, well clear of needy, sticky sand. "I just checked. There's nothing new in the search for him."

Sarosh walked back, kicked her boots against the foamcrete steps. He'd planned to cover them, he'd said, with native wood, or some equivalent. 'It's grass, really, but I can form it into planks.' She'd lost the rest of his comments, swirled them up with wind and sand and the sound of the sea.

"I'm sorry," said Alira for the hundredth time. She didn't like the beach, the way the sharp drop appeared at low tide and waves crashed fierce and furious at its rocky base. She risked a step down the stair, almost laid a tentative hand on Sarosh's shoulder. "Maybe tomorrow."

Maybe tomorrow, maybe the day after, the week after. All the maybe days rolled up in an endless bracelet of possibility and disappointment.

"Does this world have such a thing as months?" Sarosh asked. *This world*, because she refused to give it its romantic name, didn't care about the technical one.

"Yes, it does," said Alira, ever the perfect assistant, ever prepared. "Or it could. No one has named them yet. But with two moons, it could have a complex system of months." And who would have named them, if not Richard? Perhaps he'd done it. Perhaps up in the cabin, among his meticulous notes, was a native calendar, or in the scraps of poetry he'd left everywhere in his wake.

"How much longer can we stay?" Sarosh asked.

"As long as you want." Assistant as therapist, enabler.

I want to leave this place today and never come back. "How long?" she asked again. *I want to stay here, to bury myself in this cold black sand and wait and mourn and cry like a bird.*

"Ten days; local days. A thirtday if we have to. After that, there's the ... presentation to the grant committee." Alira hesitant because Sarosh and Richard had planned it together, this one little intersection of their professional worlds to match the intersection of their hearts. Begging for money she could have provided with a flick of her eyes.

"Send me the latest presentation," Sarosh said. "Whatever the home team has refined." Her crew would continue to update until the last minute, but it would not have changed substantially for thirts now.

"Of course. It's on your pad now." Professional tone hiding hurt that her boss could even hint she wasn't ready. It would be a new version after all, Sarosh realized. One with no role for Richard. The team would have taken his absence into account by now, might have had a Richard-less version waiting from the start. Just in case.

She looked up at the Richard-less cabin, climbed to its Richard-less porch, listened to the Richard-less voices of the birds.

"Are you alright?" She'd closed her eyes, like a child pretending that a thing she couldn't see was a thing she couldn't feel. An absence that couldn't touch her.

She opened her eyes, saw the concern in Alira's wide brown gaze. "I'm fine." She kicked sand off her boots where it had dried to a crust. "I'll work down the list for a while." There was always a list. Documents to be reviewed, expenses to be approved. All the things that came with a business spanning the width of a spiral arm. All the things that could be ignored and delegated. But not for long.

She sat on Richard's rickety grass-plank bench to take off her boots. Beyond the porch's protective screen, down by the dropoff, love-lorn birds raced to wrap prey in their wings. 'They're not mainly wings,' he had told her. 'It's how they eat. They fold these big flaps of skin around other creatures, and assimilate them.' Which he insisted wasn't just a poetic term for eating, that there was a transfer of knowledge. 'Like all the old myths of eating a creature to gain its skills.' But he'd been serious. She watched the birds' low bodies rise in staggered, wobbly surges, carrying borrowed knowledge up into rising wind. A storm coming; there was almost always a storm here, flinging sand against the screens, churning the sea into froth and ferocity.

"Alira. Gather up Richard's poetry." The scraps of scraps, scrawled words on crude paper he'd strewn like leaves across the house.

"It's in the box." The other woman stepped easily out of immaculate boots and into the immaculate slippers she'd left for them on the porch. "The blue stone one you gave him. I thought you might want it." The blue box of stone so light you could lift it with one finger, as if its carved floodbats were lifting it with cutout wings.

"Is there much?" She would go through it. That was her role, her contribution to his art; sifting through the leaves, helping him decide what to compost, what to keep; what had value. Tears started, and she looked to her boots. What had value. That was what she knew, what she saw. She had seen him.

"A few dozen fragments."

"It's not good, is it?" For a would-be telepath, he had been a terrible communicator. The tears seemed under control, and she slipped her feet into warm slippers.

"The poetry? Not really." Alira was honest, when she wasn't being supportive. It had been her main qualification for the job.

"No." The poetry had never been good. Even the pieces he'd written for her; especially those. Even the piece that had won her heart, back when her empire spanned only one planet, and he'd been an exo-biologist with a lunatic idea. The poetry had been treacly, dramatic, obvious. It had never changed. He had changed her, with his stupid, stupid words, and his follies. "I'll come later," she gasped, and held off the sobs until Alira had gone to the invisible, unobtrusive, ubiquitous world assistants went to.

Outside, a fog obscured the sea battering its way to the top of the dropoff with the rising tide. Not so much a fog as a spray, really, a haze as salty as the sea, and just as harsh. 'It's a bit alkaline,' he had warned her, 'but beautiful. And full of life!' Because life was why he was here, why he had begged her to let him have this world for a threecent of days, unexploited, unexplored.

'I need to be the first,' he insisted. 'Before it's spoiled.'

'It's already spoiled, Richard.' It had had exobots crawling all over it, in their sterile, dragonfly bodies.

'You know what I mean. The first person. The first who thinks.' She had known, of course. Had known from their first meeting, when he said 'Hi. I'm Richard. I'm a telepath.' He'd never known what she was thinking, at that meeting, or the next, or the one that merged subtly into a date, then a relationship, then a life. He'd never known, and it hadn't mattered, because he knew what she felt, what she wanted and needed. 'That's not telepathy,' he'd scoffed. 'That's love.' As if there were a difference.

She looked out at the world she'd borrowed for him. A grey mist over black sand that hid love-lorn birds and sparklesing grass and slambang frogs and a hundred other strained names for strange creatures. A world borrowed from stockholders and creditors and staff who wondered why they weren't already exploiting the world and selling acreage and virt-safaris and phys-tours. All because of one man with conviction and a run of luck at esper card tricks.

And now he was gone. Vanished into howling winds, high seas, rocky coast. Vanished since just after their last talk, so that she'd only gotten the news when they climbed back down out of hype, already half the arm away.

Richard, she sent her call again. *Richard! Where are you?* On the beach, the sea rose, and the wind threw waves down on the hard sand, let them rise, threw them down again, again, again.

Richard. No answer came, and never would, because telepathy didn't exist. She'd told him as much at that first meeting, had laughed in his face, made a note to find out how he'd gotten past her assistant and her assistant's assistant. And, when he'd laughed back, brown eyes crinkling, short hair waggling, agreed to another meeting.

'There is no such thing as telepathy,' her assistant of the time had confirmed. All of them had. She'd had every new assistant look into it, even after she'd committed to spend her life with him, in her mind, if not in words. 'They try to guess cards, tricks like that. Richard just got lucky.'

'Several times,' he'd pointed out. 'Consistently.'

'Coincidence,' she'd said. They'd all said. And he'd gotten his first grant from some tiny university with too big an endowment. In two three-cents of days, he'd failed to communicate with dogs, cats, birds, slugs, trees. With anyone but her. Even his funders seemed not to comprehend his failure. They'd kept funding him. And she'd kept seeing him, even as her business grew to other planets, to an entire system. Those had been good days, happy days.

She fell asleep in the little sitting room, woke to find herself stretched under a blanket on the sofa where no doubt Alira had arranged her limbs in the middle of the night. She fought her way muzzily to her feet and shuffled into her bedroom. Their room; Richard's room, and the reason she liked to forget to go to bed.

When she returned from the tiny shower, pH-adjusted, sterilized water dripping from damp hair onto a clean sweater, Alira had set out juice, cakes, a screen with tabs of news and business updates. She ate and read in silence while Alira sat in the kitchen, mumbling and tapping into her net.

"I'm ready," Sarosh said as she set down her empty juice glass. Alira came and smiled and took her seat on a hard chair opposite. Bright-eyed and bushy tailed and harder working than her boss. Sarosh had been the same once.

They spent the morning dealing with business until the list was tamed, pruned, manageable.

"I'll get lunch," Alira said, meaning she would choose from a dozen stat-packed gourmet meals an invisible staff prepared in the lander's kitchen, or brought down from the waiting ship above.

"Wait," Sarosh called. Alira turned, net ready, eyes bright. Tail bushy? What had she meant to say? "Bring me the poems."

"Of course." As if the blue box weren't visible on the little table across from the sofa, as if Sarosh were in the habit of being lazy.

"Thank you, Alira." She caught the younger woman's hand as it set the box down in front of her. She squeezed it gently, felt it squeeze back. "You're good to me." She let go, opened the box, tried not to see the brown eyes getting brighter as they turned away.

The box held scraps of hand-made paper, little squares and rectangles neatly smoothed and stacked. Richard would have left them crumpled all over the house. She had seen them, when they arrived, ignored them to focus on commanding exobots and overflights, search parties and radio calls, repeating every step her competent, loyal staff had already taken.

The fragments were just that, for the most part: little phrases and couplets in Richard's spiky scrawl.

A dog sat by the door of a house
And felt the shadows pass over him.
He waited in dark and light
While his master stayed inside.

Richard aiming for enigma.

Oh umbrous me, by an umbrose tree
How pleasant it is to be cool.

She chuckled. That was the other Richard — irreverent, funny, pointless. On a planet without trees.

Before a thickening twilight.

A fragment, destined never to carry more meaning than an awkward image. There were many more like it.

At the bottom, she found a slightly larger sheet, with what might have been a complete poem.

Give its due,
Its wrack and ruin.

Give your love
It cares nothing for.

To its spume and froth
Give your hopes
To the wild sea, the wild sea.

Dramatic, portentous, romantic. Richard through and through. The grammar was awkward. The second couplet didn't scan. She smoothed it against the table, let her tears fall upon its blue ink, let salt water smear the letters until they were gone. Then she folded it gently, put it back in the box and gathered the others in her hands for the recycler.

After a twenday, nothing changed. The moons raced and crawled across the sky, raised tides and storms, drained the sea to sharp rocks covered in flat, sheet-like fish with rubbery fringes, looking for something to envelop, to assimilate, to learn from. Richard had named them, no doubt, had made a note in his file for her scientists and marketers to consider.

'You just want to be Adam,' she'd accused, smiling.

'Come and be my Eve,' he'd said, though they both knew he wanted the world unsullied by other human minds. 'If I make contact, I want to be sure it's with aliens,' he'd joked before he left.

Naming had been a good use of his poetry. 'Get it out of your system,' she'd begged.

'I'm putting it in your system,' he'd said, though the company only owned the planet, had already sold the rights to the rocky inner worlds and the outer giants.

"Anything?" she asked Alira.

"I'm sorry." Torn between supportive and honest. "Nothing. It's been a tenday now," she anticipated.

Ten days with every available staff person landside, spending half their days thinking *Richard!*, and the other half listening. Waiting for signals from the only telepath in the entire arm. If there had ever been one.

"I thought," Alira was unusually hesitant. "I thought maybe someone who knew him."

Sarosh's jaw tensed. Did the fool think she hadn't tried? Hadn't spent her days and nights listening, calling, crying? Hadn't woken on her sofa to imagined calls that vanished as soon as she rose? But of course she knew. Alira had woken with her, brought her coats to wear in the storms outside, dried her off when she returned, fed her, clothed her, wiped her tears.

"I thought," Alira said, "maybe I would have more luck. Because I knew him better than the other staff did. More connection. But less invested, emotionally." Less likely to invent voices in the dark. "I didn't hear anything. I'm sorry. I ... I tried." Her dark eyes sparkled, and Sarosh saw the dark shadows that had pooled under them as Alira ran an empire single-handed while keeping its mistress warm and busy.

"I know you did, Alira. I know. I'm sorry too." She took Alira's soft hand and squeezed it, let it go as its owner hurried into the kitchen to let warm brown eyes spill into hot green tea.

"It's enough," Sarosh said as they sat later on the porch, red-eyed, warming their hands on Richard's thick ceramic mugs. Outside the barrier, the wind had calmed to a gentle breeze, the tide near its highwater mark. The love-lorn birds did their ponderous display flights, seducing mates with clumsy twists and dips.

"Are you sure?" Alira's voice was gentle. "We've stayed this long. I can put everything off until the grant presentation."

"No." And she would go through with the presentation, would not fund it herself, because that was what Richard would have wanted. And if they got the grant, would send some young fool out here to listen for alien voices in his mind. And any others he heard. "No, it's enough. We'll go to Alteph, then Likun. That will leave us close enough to Ghenna that we can present in person rather than virt." She looked out at the black beach again. "Pack. Let me know when the lander is ready."

"Of course." A tentative hand settled on her arm, vanished.

She slid the slippers off her feet, slid into lime-green boots. Outside the screen, the wind was warm, freighted with foreign messengers of scent and salt. She let it blow her toward the water. The love-lorn birds squealed and raced on delicate legs to rest a few meters away. They moaned their sad moan, calling for mates already beside them, and every now and then flapping unwieldy wings to lift slowly into the wind.

The sea sputtered and spat and sent its feelers out and back, out and back in slow, bubbled waves. She squatted at its edge and took a folded paper from her pocket.

"Here," she said, letting the poem settle into the water. "My wrack and ruin. My love." The caustic water soaked the paper, bled the ink away in little blue swirls. An undertow sucked black sand grains over the top. "That's enough. My hopes I'm keeping." She stood and turned away to wave at Alira, waiting patiently at the top of ugly foamcrete steps. Behind her, the soft, assimilating swish of the sea called her name.

See B. Morris Allen's story "To the Wild Sea" online at Metaphorosis. If you liked it, leave a comment. Authors love that! Remember to subscribe to our e-mail updates so you'll know when new stories are posted.

About the story

I woke one morning with the whole central poem in my head, drawn from a dream that had something to do with telepathy. The poem was so clear that I I formed the story around it. Note that the world it takes place on is all about assimilation. Sarosh's husband may not be quite as completely vanished as it seems. Unfortunately, she doesn't seem to notice.

For the Love of Wild Things

Mande Matthews

It started the day she returned from the morgue. Mrs. Ruddle Wildemore was sliding the key into the door lock when something moved at the edge of her sight.

She glanced into their—correction, *her*—forest garden. A suncatcher swayed from a branch, casting rainbows on leaves, berries, and bark. Its brass bell *ting... ting... tinged...* in the summer breeze. Tangerine nasturtiums peppered black earth—those had been Rudy's favorite salad topping—and beyond, sixty-year-old branches hung down like familiar hands. The walnut tree had been the first Rudy planted when they moved to their Trout River homestead, once a sapling, now a towering giant, the center from which their wild garden sprang.

No. *Her* wild garden. Could she ever think of it as just hers?

Willamina's gaze settled on the old trunk. Her sight wasn't what it had been in her twenties, or even in her seventies, for that matter. She'd thought she saw something materialize and scurry up the tree. Had she seen anything at all? Had it been a squirrel? It hadn't looked anything like a squirrel. Or a bird. Or a rabbit... but then, rabbits didn't climb trees.

"Hello? Is anyone there?"

The sleeves of her linen blouse fluttered with the wind's touch, tickling her crepey skin. When nothing but the leaves and petals shifted, she whispered, "Rudy? Is that you?"

The sun's warmth rested on Willamina's thinning hair, tied back in a structured bun. The color of her hair, stark white, bore no remembrance of what it once had been.

Willamina tried to recall Rudy's face, but the memories surfacing were ones she didn't want to see. She wanted him vibrant and young. Planting berry bushes, dirt-caked in his nail beds, a trowel tucked through the loop of his coveralls, but those memories were fragments at the edge of her sight. And the others? The ones that were brash and blaring and insistent? She refused them. Or at least, she tried.

"Rudy?" she asked again but of course, nothing replied. Certainly not Rudy.

Willamina knew that whatever she thought she had seen could not be him, so she turned the key and entered her empty house.

"Rudy, I'm home," Willamina called, not because she thought he would answer but out of a sixty-year-old habit.

Willamina Wildemore's house was more organized than a library. She might as well have card-cataloged each item. It hadn't always been so. Not when Rudy was younger and well and impossible to contain. His wildlife rescues had once ruled their domain, turning Willamina's attempts at orderliness into a zoo: injured raccoons raiding cupboards, a white-tail deer hoofing over her oak floors, squirrels hanging from the pinewood ceiling beams, and once, a three-legged bear in her well-labeled, alphabetized pantry.

There had been days she'd cried over the chaos, but now the noiselessness of her home hurt like the aftermath of an explosion when all the debris had settled, when the broken parts lay exposed, when the silence of the destruction wormed into her bones.

It nearly brought Willamina to her knees, but she was a rational woman. She'd been the one to hold the pieces together while Rudy, quiet as a storm on the horizon and as wild as nature, built his outlandish dreams into reality—the ones everyone had warned him against.

Even Willamina's mother, when she was alive, had bent her daughter's ear too many times about such nonsense. "Why can't that man get a job in town with a good pension plan? Who wants to grow their food when you can buy it in a can, ready to heat and eat? Why on God's green earth do you have to live in the middle of nowhere? Don't you want a comfortable life? Pretty dresses? A washer and dryer? A television? Twinkies for breakfast and Little Debbie's for dessert?" And when her mother was more exasperated by their seeming lack of progress—an entire year spent building compost piles and living in a tent, she'd complain, "The country is moving forward, and that man insists on living like a heathen foraging for berries and mushrooms. I swear to Jesus and Mother

Mary, Willamina, if I come for a visit and that man's wearing nothing but a loincloth, I'll drag your father here with a shotgun to take you home and marry you off to an accountant or doctor! Someone that can provide for you right and proper!"

No one had heard of food forests in the 1960s. Most certainly not Willamina's parents. When the world was pushing pesticides, modified crops, and convenient contraptions like microwaves to speed up meal preparation, Rudy had cultivated the contrary.

Besides, it didn't matter. There was no telling Rudy what could and could not be done.

Now, standing on the threshold to her living room—where herbs grew from hanging pots, where recovering robins had once perched on branches screwed into the walls, where she and Rudy had shared their lives—Willamina knew nothing could turn back time. Wishing for what's gone was for dreamers. Rudy had been the dreamer. Not her.

She dialed the *Trout River Gazette* on her rotary phone and asked to speak to the person that could place an obituary.

"How much?" Willamina asked.

"Starts at two hundred and fifty dollars, ma'am, but can run you up to five hundred if you want to include a picture."

That was over a quarter of her social security payment. Though they had mainly lived off the homestead, Rudy had worked at the Fish and Wildlife Service for supplemental income which ended up providing a modest retirement. But with Rudy's final costs and the medical bills...

Tears pushed at her eyelids. The cuckoo clock *click, click, clicked* into the stillness.

"You there, ma'am?"

"I'll let you know," and Willamina replaced the handset onto the base.

She sat on the log couch Rudy made some fifty years ago. Even though the place was filled with the essence of Rudy—the walls and foundation around her constructed with his own hands, sweat, and sometimes blood, the furniture he made from fallen logs and twisted willow branches—it didn't bring back the memories she longed for. It only made her feel his absence more, like a fire poker in an open wound.

A breeze wafted in, like a huff of breath, even though no windows were open. A *clack* followed, and Willamina spotted a toppled photo frame. *Odd.* She picked it up, and any hint of wind disappeared.

In their faded 1960s wedding picture, Willamina was twenty, yarrow-laced hair trailing to her waist. Rudy was thirty-one, with owl-rimmed glasses and an uncombed beard to his chest. They held hands beneath a grapevine arbor constructed on their barren plot, gazing into each other's eyes, ready to conquer the world together.

They looked like strangers to her now.

Passing at ninety-one, Ruddle Earnest Wildemore had outlived his brothers and sisters by over a decade. And as the youngest (some called her an afterthought) of three, so had Willamina. The couple was childless, grandchildless. All their old friends had passed. Nieces and nephews scattered all over the country had long since lost touch.

Now, it seemed, Rudy would die without notice. Drift away without anyone to celebrate his accomplishments. Not only was a memorial too expensive, but there wasn't anyone left to attend.

He had been a kind man, full of tenderness and dedication. He didn't deserve to go unseen. In Willamina's estimation, he'd been overlooked for his good work his entire life—thought of as a crazy old forest fool.

Willamina would have drowned in those thoughts had it not been for the sharp whistle blasting from the kitchen.

Two western harvest mice stood by a steaming cup of chamomile tea, and, it seemed, another was busy turning off the burner where the wailing teapot sat. The critter leaped from the butcher block countertop, caught hold of the temperature dial, swung until the knob turned to OFF, vaulted to the floor with one Olympic-style mid-air somersault, landed, and skittered away.

Willamina wagged her jaw as if to say something, but what could she say? Mice had gotten the tea, the kettle, and the cup from the cupboard and brewed tea.

How could mice even carry a teacup, let alone a kettle?

It was absolute, utter nonsense.

Still, the fragrance of chamomile drifted to her. Rudy had been the one to make it for her with flowers picked out of their garden whenever her nerves were frazzled, which had been often in their earlier years together.

Later, he'd brought it to her every morning when she'd gone through the change and any last hope of a child of her own faded. She'd wondered if he'd filled the house with his rowdy rescues to keep her from that sadness. That loneliness of being childless. Of knowing this day would come—the day when no one but her would be left.

But Willamina didn't remember any of that now. Those memories were blocked behind a gauzy curtain that could not be pulled aside. She only remembered there was something comforting about the chamomile. Something that gave her pause. Something that she should remember.

One of the mice turned its little bottom to the teacup and pressed into it. A puff of air ruffled its fur, and it nudged the cup in her direction. Which was, by all accounts, impossible. The mouse couldn't have weighed a tenth of the full teacup. And yet, the cup slid toward her as if moved along by an invisible hand.

Rudy would have said, "Look, Willa! The elementals are here. Do you see them?" And Willa would have snorted, rolled her eyes, and said she saw no such thing.

But of course, Willa didn't recall any such conversations.

The second mouse stood on its hind legs, shiny eyes imploring. The third squeaked a chorus of nonsensical mouse-talk.

A flutter of movement caught her eye, and that was when Mrs. Wildemore noticed the row of birds landing on the windowsill: a bushtit, a dark-eyed junco, a white-crowned sparrow, and even a dove joined and cooed.

Not knowing what else to do, she picked up the cup and sipped. She swore the mouse on its hindlegs nodded in approval.

The liquid settled the knot she'd held inside since she'd found Rudy dead in their bed.

Unlike the faded memories she couldn't capture, this one was a technicolor movie on loop. Willamina had snuck beneath her dead husband's arm and huddled against his chest like a frightened child, hoping that he hadn't left her. That he was sleeping. Just sleeping. He'd awaken and tell her he loved her. That he'd never leave her. That they'd always be together.

The sticky quills of Rudy's feather pillow had poked her shoulder. "Please don't go. I can't live without you," she'd whispered to his cold corpse.

A chorus of birdsong had played outside the window as if nothing had happened, repeating like a broken record: *chirp, chirp, chirp, twitter, trill... chirp, chirp, chirp, twitter, trill.*

The room had seemed icy, like Rudy's skin. She didn't want that memory.

As the tea settled in her stomach, another memory crossed Willamina's mind. Nothing bright or brilliant like the last. No. This memory was like flipping through an old scrapbook, the pages going by too quickly to make out much. A picture here. A word scribbled there. A newspaper clip glued to a page. But a memory it was. And it went something like this:

Rudy. Nursing a hare. A snowshoe? A jackrabbit? It had been mauled. By a cougar? A bobcat? A coyote? It lay on Rudy's lap, dying.

Willamina sat next to him. Holding his hand? Or was her hand on his shoulder? The hare, or rabbit, convulsed one last time and lay lifeless.

Rudy said, or she thought he said, "Did you feel that?"

"Feel what?"

"His spirit cross. His energy rise up and out and all over. Uncontained. Free. Joining the nature spirits."

Nature spirits, or elementals, were what Rudy called fairies. That, Willamina could not forget. She had never believed in them, but Rudy did. Said they were everywhere. Said you felt them. Said you could see them if you were open. That the world, this big beautiful dance of energy, had many secrets hiding in plain sight if one would just look.

"I felt nothing," Willamina had said.

At least, she thought she had said so then.

Now, she sat sipping tea with three mice and a flock of birds in the kitchen Rudy had built. The implausibility of the situation and the implications of her state of mind unsettled her. Deciding it was time for no more nonsense, she left the kitchen without so much as a glance at the critters.

"Cremation or burial?" the funeral home director asked, bifocals balancing on the tip of his nose. He stared at the form, all questions and checkboxes, a ballpoint pen ready in hand.

"Cremation," Willamina said.

"Are you sure you don't want a burial? There are nice plots at Peaceful Rest Cemetery for only $3,555. What about the service? We have a full-service funeral package for $7,649.95, including the coffin, unless you want to upgrade. Of course, if you choose cremation the coffin will be cremated along with your loved one. But it's worth the investment. Our solid mahogany model is lined with high-quality velvet and makes a beautiful final presentation."

"No service," she said. "We want a cardboard casket. And I have the urn he chose here." Willamina sat the box she'd been holding on the funeral director's desk. It was a simple biodegradable urn that the palliative care counselor helped them purchase after his diagnosis had been confirmed.

"I see." The director fixated on her, sliding his bifocals down. "If you don't mind me asking, you're on a fixed income, right?"

Willamina nodded.

"And my paperwork says you live out on Old River Road, is that correct?"

"Yes."

"By yourself?"

"With Rudy."

"I see."

He removed his glasses and scrubbed at his eyes. A plastic ivy trailed off the bookshelf behind him. There weren't books on the shelves, but coffin catalogs, headstone flyers, urns, and one very peculiar necklace with a pendant made of swirling colors. A sign next to it read:

> *Always have your loved one close to your heart. Create a one-of-a-kind keepsake with their ashes to hand down to your children and grandchildren. 24-karat gold chain and bail. Starting at only $595.*

Mrs. Wildemore thought the director might present cheaper options, but he led Willamina into the viewing room to see Rudy one last time instead.

Rudy's naked body was covered with a sanitary hospital sheet and laid out on a metal gurney. Willamina tugged at his soft beard. Someone had brushed it out, taken away all his unruly curls. She kissed his waxy lips, but there were no words she could muster for goodbyes. This. This man lying lifeless. This was not Rudy. Not her husband. Not her love. It just...couldn't be.

When Willamina puttered up Old River Road in her '72 Chevy LUV pickup, a raccoon saluted her. It raised on its hind legs, looked directly at her, or so she thought, lifted its short arm in the air, and waved its long fingers in front of its forehead in a military manner. Willamina blinked.

It couldn't be.

I'm tired. Just tired.

At least, that's what she told herself.

Once inside, Willamina smelled something coming from the kitchen. Something pleasantly scented. Delicious, even.

When she entered the kitchen, she noted the mice had taken up residence in the pantry. When Rudy became ill, Willamina had set about canning all she could. She knew there would be no line of mourners with casseroles at her doorstep, no baskets of cookies and condolences. Consequently, her pantry was jam-packed.

Mice hopped from mason jar to mason jar. They squeaked back mouse-ish to another, who looked, beyond all comprehension, to be taking inventory—counting on little mouse fingers. Could that be right?

But that activity wasn't the most curious part.

A saucepan sat on the stovetop. A china bowl from her Summer Roses set, which her mother had given them as a wedding gift, sat on the table over a crocheted tablecloth alongside a spoon and wafers.

Willamina stirred the concoction and tasted it. Just a dab on the end of the ladle.

Cream of asparagus soup. Rudy's favorite.

A flash of images: Rudy. In the garden. On his knees, trowel in one hand, asparagus bunch in the other, grinning up at her. He said, "Here's looking at you, kid." But as quickly as it came, the memory left. Gone. Replaced with nothing but the desire for more. She dropped the ladle into the saucepan.

Mrs. Wildemore had had about enough. She tossed the spoon and bowl into the sink. A sickening crack sounded as porcelain met porcelain, making her angrier.

She picked up a broom and swatted at the mice. "That's enough! Enough! Enough!"

The little critters went scurrying across the oak floor.

Willamina couldn't bring herself to sleep in their bed. Not this soon after. She hadn't even had the strength to change the bedding. So she walked into the forest garden.

As she crossed under the grapevine-laden arbor, the same one she and Rudy exchanged vows under, it seemed odd she'd mourn Rudy's death in late summer, when everything around her was so alive.

Deep purple huckleberries spotted green leaves. Chamomile, white petals surrounding cheery yellow heads, bloomed in patches of sunlight. Crimson stems peeked from under umbrella-like rhubarb leaves. Water babbled in the background where the creek met the Little Trout River. And the scent. Forest pine, sweet wildflowers, and honeysuckle mixed in an intoxicating way. The smell was unlike any other. It smelled like home. It smelled like Rudy.

Rudy's master plan had been to return the scarred earth to a natural state of abundance, and the walnut tree had started it all. He had called it a food forest and said it was how people were intended to live—in harmony and cooperation with nature—and that someday people would recognize that wisdom. Maybe after he was gone, perhaps after they both were, but eventually, people would have to see it if the world was to survive.

Willamina sat down beneath the tree, arranging her tea-stained skirt. Feather moss cushioned her bony bottom. She rested her back against the scaley trunk and closed her eyes.

Mr. Wildemore had brought his blushing bride to the Little Trout River in the wilds of Washington State in 1962. He'd tugged Willamina out of the passenger's side of his Ford pickup, coaxed her to the center of a naked twenty-acre plot, and gestured as if presenting treasure to a queen.

The land was a scar within the over-logged forest. Loggers had used the spot for decades, dragging felled trees into the river to float them downstream to the mill, scraping up topsoil trip after trip, year after year, decade after decade, until nothing grew back and the ground beneath was barren. Lifeless. Not soil, but nutrient-depleted dirt. There wasn't a bird to be heard. Or a rabbit in the bush. There weren't even any bushes! Everything around them was dead.

Rudy waited, watching his bride from behind his owl-eyed glasses. He wore that cockamamie half-grin, one side up and the other down. His bushy eyebrows matched his sideways smile in their crookedness. His bellbottoms settled in the dirt like he was dug in, growing roots with his heels. The gush and splash of the Little Trout River sounded behind them as moments frittered away.

"No." Willamina planted her hands on her hips, a gesture which was as solid as Rudy's heels in the ground. "We won't be able to grow a garden here."

Rudy swept his arms around again as if she hadn't seen its majesty the first time.

"No, Rudy. We're miles from town. I will not live without electricity."

"There's a pole a few miles back down the road." The sky rumbled above them like an orchestra tuning before a performance. The scent of rain filled the air.

"I will not live without running water."

"I'll pump from the river."

"This is not the 1890s, Ruddle Earnest Wildemore."

"Hey, now. Don't sweat it, baby girl. We'll even have a telephone. Cross my heart. I'm gonna take good care of you. You know that, right?"

"Yes, but—"

Rudy pulled her into him. Tugged her defiant hands off her hips. Circled them around his waist. Hugged her tight and kissed her. Sprinkles plopped down on their exposed noses and cheeks, but the two kept at their kisses, lost in one another's touch, until Willamina remembered her mission. She pulled out of his hug.

"Rudy, I'm serious. I—"

A *kee-eeeee-arr* sounded above them.

They looked skyward as a red-tailed hawk circled, coming lower and lower until it landed in the dirt not two feet from them. It hopped over and dropped a long-bearded hawkweed at their feet. The hawk cocked its head and stared.

Rudy raised his eyebrows at Willamina.

"It means nothing," said Willamina.

"It's a sign," said Rudy.

"It's not a sign."

"Then what is it?"

Willamina couldn't deny the oddity of the moment, even though she'd become accustomed to peculiar happenings around Rudy. It seemed that Rudy was connected to something mystical but whenever Willamina had such a thought about him, she dismissed it. Nothing could convince her life was not a practical matter to be handled sensibly.

Rudy grasped both of her hands. "We're meant to restore this land. Build a food forest. Bring back nature. Feed the wild things. Live in harmony. I feel it in my bones, Willa. The natural things want this. They're telling us to do this." Indeed, the hawk kept staring at the newlyweds as if it agreed. "It's my purpose."

But was it Willamina's? "Look at this place. Everything's dead."

"Oh, baby doll. Close your eyes," he said, "and imagine."

"No, Rudy. We need to be rational."

He turned her around and put his palms over her eyes.

"Oh, Rudy, stop." But she laughed at his touch.

"Just keep your eyes closed." He leaned close. He wound his arms around her stomach, tugging her into the comfortable curve of his body.

Willamina opened an eye, and he scolded, "No peeking."

She giggled like a schoolgirl but complied.

"I wish you could see what I see. The magic. The majesty. The possibility." The seriousness of his voice stilled her. She listened.

Listened with all her body. "It's alive. Nature is all around us. Waiting for us. Waiting for our vision. Our hands. Our work. See, there's a walnut tree in its prime, bearing hundreds of pounds of nuts, at the center of our wild forest garden. Our house is not fifty steps away, built with naturally fallen pine. Berries, chestnut trees, rhubarb, and mushrooms are ready for harvest for months out of the year. Squirrels and birds, foxes and field mice, raccoons and whitetails return, and our forest garden feeds not only us but them. Nature is allowed to be nature again. Can you see it? There in your mind's eye? Can you see what we can create?"

Willamina wanted to. Wanted it with all her heart. But then she opened her eyes to the scarred earth, to the abuse that seemed irreversible. "Nothing lives here, Rudy."

He grinned again. Though she couldn't see it, she felt it, and knew he wore that troublemaking smile. "*Au contraire*, Madame Wildemore. *We* do. And with a bit of elbow grease, so will an entire forest of living things."

The hawk beaked the flower and tossed it toward them. It landed on the toe of Willamina's Mary Jane, a yellow splash on black. Then the hawk took to the sky with a *whoop, whoop, whoop* of his wings.

"You can't argue with that," said Rudy.

"You're irrepressible."

"And that's why you love me," he said.

It was true. She loved him more than she'd loved anything in her young life. She loved him because of the wonder she saw behind those owl-round eyes. She loved him because he saw worlds more beautiful than what existed before them. She loved him because the word 'impossible' was only a catalyst for change for him. Rudy held more belief in his little pinky finger than anyone she knew, especially her. In that way, she supposed, they balanced out. Complemented each other. He, the dreamer, she, the rationalist. She might not have believed nature was alive and incarnate, but she believed in Rudy. And if he believed, she'd support him one thousand percent.

"Do you have any idea how much I love you, Mr. Ruddle Earnest Wildemore?"

"Not more than I love you, my gorgeous, big-hearted wife." Rudy picked her up as he'd done on their wedding night, cradled her to his chest, his beard tickling her cheek. He spun her in circles beneath summer rain clouds, the hawk circling above them. Sprinkles turned to a downpour, a musical *pitter-patter* like a band at a country dance, and Willamina's squeals turned to laughter, and Rudy's smiles turned to kisses, hungry and passionate.

But that's not what Willamina remembered. The memories had faded, turning to mush—blotted pictures in her head, watered-down words in her ears. And now, more than ever, she wished to recall it.

But everything about that day was a blur. Remembering how barren the land had been was near impossible. Even though her wedding photos gave glimpses of the homestead before Rudy's decades of dedication, the entirety of the land's disfigurement was lost to her.

But she remembered the hawk. Was it a hawk? Or an eagle? She remembered the flower. Was it a yellow hawkweed or a purple lupine? Maybe a white, daisy-like phlox?

Had a hawk dropped a flower at their feet? Or had she made up the memory to comfort herself?

What Willamina *could* remember were those last months: Rudy, declining, the life sucked out of his sunken cheeks, the trips to the Saint Paul's hospital, waiting for hours in antiseptic rooms, the news of stage four melanoma metastasized to the lungs, the doctor's deadpan face when he delivered his "only a few months" prognosis, then finding her love dead in their bed.

Willamina wished those memories would fade and the other wild-about-life Rudy memories would return.

A puff of air caressed her cheek, and a curious thing happened when Willamina opened her eyes. She found a bright yellow, long-bearded hawkweed lying on her lap.

Not a day later, someone knocked on the door. Willamina couldn't imagine a single soul who would drop by, and when she opened the door, no one was there. She stared into her wild garden, expecting movement like the day she had returned home from the morgue.

The breeze pushed up the fishy scent of the Little Trout River. Nothing moved, but when Willamina thought to close the door, she heard something chatter.

There, not a foot away from the door's threshold sat a red squirrel. Its shiny eyes looked up at her; rusty-red ears twitched. It held a blueberry out to her in one of its paws.

"Oh, no," she said. "No more of this imaginary nonsense," and she started to shut the door.

"*Rah...Rah...Rah...*" cried the squirrel. Its whiskers twitched. It blinked. It held up the arm not bearing the blueberry, and that's when Willamina realized its wrist hung like a floppy noodle.

Then Willamina said, "Rudy." It wasn't because she didn't remember Rudy was gone but because rescue was Rudy's love. His passion. His mission, along with the restoration of the land. Yes, she'd assisted him, but Rudy, always Rudy, did the mending.

So she said his name like a prayer, and it was for Rudy's sake she asked the squirrel, "What happened to you?"

The critter chattered away like it was explaining.

And despite Willamina's rational judgment, she stepped aside and waved it in.

It scurried across the floor, holding up its injured foreleg, scrambled into the kitchen, scaled the tablecloth, and sat waiting for Willamina.

If she had imagined the mice and tea... If she had concocted the nut cream of asparagus soup... If the raccoon salute was merely a mis-seeing of what happened... If the hawkweed just blew in on the breeze and coincidentally settled in her lap... All those things had happened or not. But the critter on her kitchen table required attention. If she proclaimed it fiction and turned it away and it wasn't, then what?

What would Rudy do? What would Rudy *want her* to do? And for that matter, what did Willamina want to do? Hadn't she done this for the better part of her life, too?

But nothing came to mind.

Willamina looked for supplies. Herbs for pain? For calming? What to use, what to use? Didn't Rudy keep a medical emergency bag?

When she turned back to the squirrel, two mice had joined the patient on the table. One balanced atop an isopropyl alcohol bottle, another held a popsicle stick with its forepaws, and a bandage ball rolled across the table by itself.

A blue jay landed, offering her a cotton ball. It seemed the logical next move, so she wetted it with alcohol. The red squirrel stretched out its limp hand and covered its eyes with the other.

But when it came to the moment of doctoring, Willamina wasn't sure what to do. Yes, she'd fetched the supplies, boiled tea, and made poultices, which she vaguely remembered. Still, Rudy, always Rudy, knew what to look for, how to test for fractures, clean wounds, make splints, and administer liquids, sub-Q or through a syringe or a bottle or...

Willamina closed her eyes, willing Rudy's guidance. But just because she wished for him didn't mean he would come.

She sighed, took a breath, and fumbled through it. She blotted an open wound. Then cut the sticks into tiny splints and wrapped the little paw with the bandage. The result was not Rudy's caliber, though she couldn't quite remember what standard Rudy had held. But it would, perhaps, do the job.

When Mrs. Wildemore looked up from her work, she realized an audience had gathered in the kitchen. A woodrat, a pocket gopher, and a yellow-bellied marmot lined up. Even a mule deer fawn stood on unsteady legs.

But they weren't just spectators. Upon inspection, each bore some wound that needed tending.

Mrs. Wildemore set out to help them, but she dropped the bottle of alcohol on the floor, resulting in an antiseptic puddle. The bandage slipped from her hand and rolled underneath the cupboard. She slipped on the wet floor and cracked her head on the table when she tried to fish it out.

She sat on her haunches, held her head with her hand, and willed, *willed!* Rudy's memory to her. *Show me what to do.* She tried to remember him. Were his hands capable or gentle or both? Were his eyes intelligent or compassionate or both? Were his actions quick like a snake's strike? Or soft like a doe's nuzzle? This was Rudy's domain. Not hers. He was the one who worked at Fish and Wildlife. The one with a degree in biology. The one who had trained as a wildlife emergency caretaker. Rudy was the forest mastermind. The magic healer. The spiritual shaman.

And she was...what?

The memories wouldn't come. Just the overwhelming proof of her insufficiency and the lack of his presence.

"Rudy, why did you leave me?"

The red squirrel *chucked* and inched toward her, but she held out a hand to stop it.

"I can't," she said. This was Rudy's dream. Rudy's skill. Rudy's compassion. And he wasn't there anymore. So Willamina said, "Get out."

The animals pressed in around her.

"Get out! Get out!" she yelled.

The animals bowed their heads, filed out the door, and disappeared into Rudy's forest garden.

After they'd gone, including a moose who had stood behind a western larch and grunted when she shut the door on him, their wedding photo fell over, frame first, onto the coffee table. Willamina picked it up, clutching it to her chest.

"Oh, Rudy."

She lay on the sofa, curled her legs as far as the old fragile things would bend, and did something she had not allowed herself to do. Something she'd thought if she started, she'd never stop.

She cried. Sobbed. Wailed for the loss of Rudy. His absence. Her loneliness. The pain it caused in every bone of her body. For how much she missed him. For being left behind. For how she'd never be with him again.

As she did, the wind howled outside. It shook branches and limbs, bushes and grasses. It banged on the shutters. The dark sky poured droplets as large as treefrogs and drummed against the rooftop. Lightning crackled like anguished gods.

Critters of all species pressed wet noses to the windowpanes: a Rocky Mountain elk, a California bighorn, more squirrels and raccoons and birds and rats, and even a cougar, prey and predator at peace for the moment. They joined the storm and watched the grieving woman, somber as pallbearers.

Later, reports would confirm a power outage happened at that exact moment.

But Willamina knew nothing of all that. For all she knew, there on the couch, eyes blurred with tears, snot running, chest squeezing, she wept alone.

Rudy's face appeared out of the blackness, wiry beard dangling to his flannel pockets, earth-brown eyes behind owl-eyed glasses. Intent. Serious. Compelling. Lights danced around his head like translucent feathers. He was vibrant and young and oh, so beautiful. He reached for Willamina, hands stained with rich black earth.

"You can see what I see, Willa. You can. Just open your eyes."

A knock at the door startled Willamina awake.

Rudy. Rudy. Rudy!

But he'd gone. Willamina refused to open her eyes. If she kept them closed, he'd return. She could continue the dream. Continue being with him. At least, she hoped that would happen.

Knock, knock, knock.

"Mrs. Wildemore?" called a nasal voice. "Are you home? Hello?"

Go away, said Willamina in her head. She hadn't the strength to bring the words to her lips. She wanted to return to Rudy's dream.

"I'm Laura Doyle from Adult Protective Services. I'm delivering your late husband's ashes from the Peaceful Slumber Funeral Home. Are you there?"

Maybe the intruder would leave if Willamina stayed still, curled on Rudy's couch, the sun through the window warming her eyelids. But it occurred to Willamina that a social worker delivering Rudy's ashes wasn't good. It must have been why the funeral director had been so inquisitive about her finances—to assume incompetence and rally the authorities to do a home check. It wasn't the first time she'd been treated as incapable because of her age, or where and how she lived. Small towns were infamous for neighborhood busybodies; Trout River wasn't exempt, and *that* was enough to rouse her.

"I'm coming," said Mrs. Wildemore and rallied herself to open the door.

"Hello. I'm Laura Doyle. It's nice to meet you." She held one plump hand out for a shake while cradling Rudy's urn.

The cuckoo clock *tik toked*. Laura wore a collared shirt and a rhinestone fleur de lis brooch pinned on her candy-pink lapel. She smelled of department store perfume.

Laura asked, "May I come in?"

"I suppose."

Laura smiled, and it wasn't an unkind expression. But as she crossed into the living room, she eyed every spec from the pine beams to the log furniture, from the neatly hung jackets on tree limb pegs to boots for all occasions (snow, mud, hiking, work) lined up beneath. "What an unusual home you have," she said. "It's not at all what I expected."

"What did you expect?"

"Well, I…" Laura looked around. The sun beamed through the picture window, framing the forest garden as if an impossible painting hung on the wall. Herbs pinned to a wire scented the air with thyme, oregano, and sage. Embroidered pillows displayed on Rudy's log sofa brightened the warm wood room with whimsical bees and hummingbirds. "I don't rightly know," said Laura. "But it's simply charming."

Willamina beamed. Indeed, she and Rudy had made a lovely home together. His vision and building along with her organizing and tending to the practicalities of life had come together to create something bigger than them both. "Thank you. Can I get you some tea?"

"That'd be nice." Laura sat the urn on the coffee table next to a display of cracked geodes, a potted rosemary plant, and beeswax candles.

Willamina made and served the tea while Laura poked around, commenting on the neat and tidy pantry, the pristine condition of her cabinets, and did she always keep the place so clean?

When the two women were settled on the couch, Summer Roses teacups in hand, Willamina asked, "So what's this all about?"

"I'm sorry for your loss. But to be honest, we've been a little worried about your husband's passing and you out here on the homestead all by yourself. So, I wanted to offer you some options."

"Options?"

"It must be tough living out here all alone. There's so much upkeep. It will be difficult to do everything by yourself. You're stocked up for the moment, but can you harvest the garden now that your husband is gone? Social security isn't much to survive on. Wouldn't some support be nice?"

Light filtered through the window. Willamina had seen the harsh sun in Arizona, the foggy New Hampshire haze, the sticky Florida rays, and everything between when she and Rudy backpacked across the United States before settling down. But Washington's light was unlike any place else—a pastel softness that lingered well into twilight, sky dotted with pink and lavender clouds, like something supernatural. It reminded her of Rudy.

"What I'm getting at," said Laura, "is we have a lovely retirement home in town, Haven Senior Living. There are shuffleboard tournaments and karaoke competitions. All meals are provided with no cooking on your part. Excellent housekeepers. You wouldn't have to lift a finger, and you'd be surrounded by others of your age. Not alone out here where anything could happen. Doesn't that sound nice?"

"I—"

"Oh, don't worry, it's covered by Medicaid if you qualify, and from what I understand, you've no assets other than this home, and, if that's correct, I can help you liquidate and still retain your benefits. The rooms are furnished. You wouldn't have to move anything. You could forget about cooking, cleaning, harvesting, keeping up the property, and paying bills. Forget everything and enjoy your final chapter with ease."

"Forget?" asked Mrs. Wildemore.

"There wouldn't be anything to worry over. You'd make new friends and—"

"Forget?" asked Willamina again. Forget Rudy's lovingly crafted home, his food forest they'd built with over half a century of their lives? Forget that she'd stood by him, believed in him, and helped make his vision come true? Give up on that? On the animals? On the forest? On nature itself? "What about Rudy?" Willamina asked but to herself, not Laura.

"Oh, there is a perfect spot for his urn. There's a wonderful glass display case in each room. It even has a lock on it. Just put all your treasures on the shelves and lock them up safe."

Willamina pictured Rudy in a glass cabinet, on a manufactured shelf, not wild and free, hair riding the wind, sun deepening the brown of his cheeks. She saw herself next to him doing nothing but frittering away time, surrounded by concrete and plastic flowers, and eating packaged meals. "No," said Willamina.

"No?"

"Rudy and I will stay here."

"I know it's hard," said Laura. "Change is always frightening, but if you'll just see reason—"

"Reason," said Willamina, "is the exact opposite of what I want to see." Willamina stood and walked to the door. "Now, if that is all." She placed her hands on her hips, an action that had only grown in power since her younger days.

Laura sat down her teacup, grabbed her purse, and shuffled to the door.

"I will stop by," said Laura. "Pop in for a friendly visit from time to time if you don't mind."

"Folks have a right to do as they see fit," said Willamina, knowing a refusal would be pointless. Besides, though reason was the last thing she wanted right then, she realized there might be a time when she needed help, when she wasn't as able, when she might welcome a helping hand. Reason had not flown out the door. It had just compromised for the time being.

After Laura left, Willamina piled nuts, plump berries, and fragrant herbs on plates and set them outside as an apology to the animals.

Then Mrs. Wildemore did the most curious thing. More curious than mice making tea or asparagus soup. Or hawks gifting flowers. Or animals saluting. She left a bowl of almond milk out. She had poured it into one of her Summer Roses serving bowls, sat it on a charger plate, garnished it with rosemary stems, and said as she placed the offering on the ground, "I want to see what you see, Rudy."

When Willamina walked into her room to change the bedding and finally sleep in their bed, she found it already washed and remade. Her bluebird embroidered pillows had been fluffed, and the bedcovers were turned down. Rudy's eco urn sat on the nightstand next to a lit beeswax candle, the air scented with honey. Without question, she climbed between the embroidered sheets and said, "Goodnight," to whoever might be listening.

In the morning, Willamina checked on the bowl and plates and found them empty and, more peculiarly, discovered a book of some sort placed beside them. A whisper of a breeze caressed her hair which was no longer tethered at her neck but white waves cascading around her middle. Bird calls filled the trees. Croaks and chatters and the buzz of bumblebees reminded her how alive their forest garden was—and indeed, it was *theirs*. Even though Rudy had gone, it belonged in *their* charge. She realized it might have started as Rudy's dream, but in all those years together, her by his side, believing in him, seeing what he brought to life, it had become hers, too. Something she didn't want to live without. It was *their* life. *Their* passion. *Their* vision.

She picked up the tome, a scrapbook with a 1970s floral cover. She fingered it and opened the first page.

A picture of a younger Rudy stared back at her from not ten years after moving into their Trout River homestead. A red squirrel with a bandaged leg curled around his neck, kissing his bearded cheek. Rudy wore that cockamamie grin, and tears leaked from Willamina's eyes.

"Rudy," she said. "My uncontainable Rudy." She held the book to her heart and hugged it. "I thought I'd lost this book decades ago."

A *chuck chuck chuck* sounded next to her. The red squirrel scrambled over and held up his forepaw, showing her the bandage was still in place.

"I see," she said, and the little thing *chuck chucked* again, climbing up on her arm, and pointed at the picture.

"Is that...?" Willamina asked, "Is that your relative?"

The red squirrel bounced up and down, rusty hairs tickling her skin.

"Your mother?"

It shook its head.

"Father? Grandfather? Great-grandfather? Great, great, great —?"

The fuzzball nodded and hopped and *chucked*, and Willamina remembered. She remembered with a vividness like a Dolby Cinema film playing on the big screen. Or fireworks lighting up the Fourth of July. Or like Rudy, wild Rudy, standing directly in front of her.

After a hailstorm, Rudy had found the injured red squirrel concussed with a broken arm from golf ball-sized hail. He'd named him Barnaby and nursed him back to health, but the little guy wouldn't leave.

"Red squirrels are notoriously singular," Rudy had said, "but this little one doesn't want to leave." Indeed, Barnaby preferred nestling in Rudy's wonderland beard, cracking nuts from the top of Rudy's haloed curls, or using his wire-rimmed glasses to propel himself off Rudy's head to the couch or kitchen table or wherever else he'd want to go. Barnaby slept nestled between Willamina and Rudy for an entire year before he finally found a gal of his own. Consequently, Barnaby had sired a generation of red squirrels that lived right there on the homestead.

"Well, then, I'll call you BJ for Barnaby Junior," said Willamina, and the squirrel *chucked* his agreement.

Willamina and BJ leafed through the scrapbook, recalling memory after memory as the forest animals returned and circled her: a polaroid of Rudy, overalls equipped with hoe and spade, clutching a bouquet of chamomile, Rudy lying in a patch of sunlight by the pepperings of asparagus, Rudy mending a raccoon, Rudy, that first time they'd ever come to the Little Trout River plot, standing in a barren wasteland, in a downpour, grinning, holding a bright yellow, long-beard hawkweed in his hand.

How had she missed it?

The chamomile tea, the asparagus soup, the raccoon, and hawkweed.

They had been trying to help her remember him the entire time!

A *chirp, chirp, chirp, twitter, trill... chirp, chirp, chirp, twitter, trill* filled the air, the same anthem the birds had sung the day Rudy died. The first time Willamina had heard it, she thought the birds had behaved as if nothing had happened. As if Rudy's passing were inconsequential. But now, she wondered, did it mean something more? Something different?

BJ chattered, hopped, and wagged his rusty-red tail. He tugged on Willamina's ankle-length skirt.

"Okay, okay. I'm coming." She laughed and clutched the scrapbook as the little wire tail pulled her into the forest garden with a procession of animals following.

"What are you trying to show me, now?"

As they passed beneath the grapevine arbor and headed down the path to the walnut tree, Willamina spotted what all the excitement was about.

Rudy's urn, along with their wedding photo, sat at the base of the grandfather tree. Godrays shone down through leafy branches like streamers from a church window. Limbs and bushes, flowers and grasses all moved, swaying together. Around them, piles of fresh berries, plump peaches, honeysuckle flowers, walnuts, and every imaginable bounty from their forest garden were gathered and displayed. Birds fluttered to perches. The harvest mice held almonds in their forepaws, and whitetail, raccoon, rabbits, lizards, and snakes emerged from the forest surrounding Rudy's grand memorial.

A collective voice sounded on the breeze, "We remember Rudy," and then Mrs. Wildemore saw what Rudy had seen.

It started as coagulated mist, sunspots, orbs, and little flashes of lights appearing throughout the forest. On the path. On a branch. A chamomile stem. A leaf.

Willamina blinked. She rubbed her old eyes. A glimmering whole came into view like an intricate, living web weaving throughout the forest and animals. It sparkled and danced, touching everyone and everything as if it breathed in unison with all life. It wrapped its shiny strings around her, and she felt it like a long-missed hug. Everything moved in concert, like an orchestra where different instruments played different parts, making the whole piece rich, complete, and harmonic, and she, she was a part of it.

"We'll always remember Rudy," the collective voice crooned, a lullaby on the wind.

The tears Willamina shed were those of joy. Of relief. Of gratitude so overwhelming, she couldn't form words.

The celebration that followed venerated Rudy more than Willamina could have wished for. They buried his ashes at the walnut tree's roots to nourish the ground. Nasturtium and chamomile petals dropped on top of them, blown by the wind, birds and bees played their music in concert with the breeze, BJ snuggled around Willamina's neck, and everyone indulged in the wild bounty Rudy's vision and hard work had made possible.

In the years to come, Mrs. Ruddle Wildemore would continue her late husband's life's work. *Their* shared life's work. And when

Laura visited, Willamina would make sure to amend her will with the cooperation of Fish and Wildlife and designate this place, their home, as a wildlife sanctuary when she died.

Eleven years later, on the very day that Rudy had passed, Willamina headed out to the walnut tree to nap. Huckleberries were fat on the bush, and nasturtiums bloomed like bolts of colored lights on the forest floor. Willamina, at ninety-one, was quite tired. She eased her old bones onto the moss-covered roots. Birds flew down and landed on her lap. The daughter of Barnaby Junior nestled in her arms as Mrs. Ruddle Wildemore closed her eyes for the very last time.

Her body was never found. Some say the earth swallowed her up. Or that bears or wolves carried her away. But the truth of the matter was that nature wrapped Mrs. Willamina Wildemore within its web while birds, reptiles, amphibians, and animals gathered. They made a crown of chamomile and placed it on Willamina's white-haired head while birds sang *chirp, chirp, chirp, twitter, trill.* They covered her body with earth and leaves as Willamina's spirit crossed to join Rudy's, free and uncontained.

And, once every year during summer, if one is open, if one looks, they'll see them gathered there—all the creatures and nature sharing the fruits of the forest garden in memory of the two who dedicated the better parts of their lives to restoring the wild ones' forest home.

See Mande Matthews's story "For the Love of Wild Things" online at Metaphorosis.
If you liked it, leave a comment. Authors love that!
Remember to subscribe to our e-mail updates so you'll know when new stories are posted.

About the story

The first inkling:
I have long been fascinated with permaculture and food forestry, though, I fear, my thumb is blacker than night. I read once that fairies will help you in your garden, though none have bestowed their blessings on mine. Perhaps they see me as the plant murderess that I am. I'm not giving up, though, and still brave the dry Arizona heat in hopes of one day growing my own food.
The second inkling:

During a Method Writing class, I conjured up a memory. (Method Writing, for those who don't know, was invented by Jack Grapes and is based on Method Acting. It teaches writers how to find their deep voice and often involves writing from your own truths to access authenticity.) The memory that brewed to a boil during a Method Writing session was of my father in the funeral home's austere viewing room under flickering fluorescent lights.

My father passed quietly without pomp or circumstance. No memorial. No mourners lined up to pay respects. Though the entire family would later spread his ashes off Dead Horse Point, only my brother, mother, and I were standing there next to him as he lay on that metal hospital-grade gurney. It was as he wanted it. He was a humble man. Yet, he lived a life of service and good work that benefited hundreds if not thousands.

The two inklings became one:

Food forestry and my father's passing (and processing the grief of his loss) magically merged. I don't know how or why; that's left to the creative subconscious. But they did, and the story was born. For the Love of Wild Things is my tribute to my father and all others who have toiled long and hard, made a difference, yet passed from this big beautiful dance of life without much recognition. I can attest that good work, whether seen or unseen, lives on.

A question for the author

Q: What's your favorite type of pie?

A: I believe all pies are created with equal favorability. That said, I try to stick to a low fat, whole food plant-based, low glycemic diet and have yet to find the perfect pie recipe that fits those criteria. If anyone knows of one, I'd be forever grateful if you'd share it.

About the author

Mande Matthews is a fantasy author and award-winning artist. When Mande is not creating or hunting for fairy rings, she helps her husband with his Native American reservation dog rescue. She lives in the White Mountains of Arizona with her husband and a menagerie of rescued furred, feathered, and special needs animal companions.

MandeMatthews.com, @MandeMatthews

Her Last Will

Karl El-Koura

In the night, the silent robots took away his wife and left a note in her place.

Sensing from his heart rate that he was awake, Toqs' arm band began vibrating with a series of pulses, one for each person wishing to send their condolences. He slapped the band's face to mute the thread without looking at any of the messages.

The note had been printed on a long tent card, placed where his wife had been sleeping. Underneath an access code was the message the robots had printed for him:

HELLO, TOQUER HINGI. WE REGRET TO INFORM YOU THAT **SERENE HINGI**, AGED ONE-HUNDRED-TWENTY-ONE, IS NO LONGER ALIVE. WE INVITE YOU TO WATCH A FIVE-MINUTE CREMATION CEREMONY TODAY AT **09:25** TO COMMEMORATE YOUR WIFE. IF REQUIRED, THE SERVICES OF A GRIEF COUNSELOR ARE AVAILABLE AT NO COST TO YOU FOR THE NEXT TWENTY-FOUR HOURS. HAVE A NICE DAY.

P.S. THIS CODE HAS BEEN PROVIDED TO SERENE HINGI'S FRIENDS AND ACQUAINTANCES.

"No, no, *no!*" Toqs yelled. He looked around the empty bedroom self-consciously. Serene had been catching him talking to himself with increasing frequency over the last few years. But, of course, no one had overheard—the suite was empty except for him.

They'd purchased it once they'd both retired. A place of their own on the outermost ring of the *Adagio*, the space station in orbit around Earth. Toqs loved it. He could sit on the bench of the bay window in their living room and get spectacular views day or night: the moon, the stars, or—his favorite—the spinning Earth, with its daytime blue and green and white, or its pinprick yellow lights of human nocturnal activity. Between that, his books, and his movies, Toqs didn't need much else—except for Serene, who was 'no longer alive', in the gently euphemistic words of the folded piece of plastic paper.

But Serene had become concerned about his mental state.

"You need buddies," she used to say whenever she came home from a power-walk around the ring with friends or a night out to the holos, and caught him talking to himself, or felt sorry for having left him alone.

"I have you," he had always replied. He didn't mind her leaving him for an afternoon or even a night or two; he didn't mind being alone, as he told her repeatedly … because he knew she'd always come back.

"I'm not enough," she'd said, again and again.

He'd never understood that; she had been enough, and she knew it. But had she also known that one day she might be gone, and he'd be left alone, without the expectation of her return to hang on to?

Of course she'd known; everyone dies.

The bed felt colder than normal. His hands dropped to where she'd been sleeping, and he smoothed out the sheet.

It was just after seven-thirty in the morning.

He wouldn't be allowed to grieve his wife, however. Instead, he'd have to deal with what he knew would be a bureaucratic nightmare. That was his definition of a bureaucracy: a complex system where mistakes were easily made but corrected only with great difficulty.

Still clutching the problematic tent card, Toqs pushed his feet into his slippers and shuffled slowly to the galley kitchen, his old muscles needing time—more time every day, it seemed—to loosen up.

They'd set up their terminal on a table in a little nook opposite the fridge, so they could watch the news from Earth and the stations orbiting it while they cooked.

He pulled back the chair and sat down, then dialed the ring's attendant service. "Hello, I received this card," he said, waving it at the camera when the animated face instantly appeared on the screen.

"I'm sorry for your loss." The attendant's head was human-shaped but metallic, so nobody was tricked even subconsciously into thinking they were speaking to a real person. "Would you like to make use of the complimentary services of our grief counselor?"

"I would like to correct an error you've made." He forced himself to take a deep breath, like Serene had taught him, then continued, more calmly: "My wife did not want to be burned."

"That is the default."

"She sent different instructions. Space burial. She made a point of telling me. Please correct it."

The smile on the animated gray face changed by a calculated percentage toward regret. "No such instructions were received—"

"She sent them. Anyway, you're receiving them now. She made a point of telling me. Maybe because of the cost." Cremation was complimentary, which meant included in the cost of living on the *Adagio*; placing your body into a titanium coffin and shooting you toward deep space was extra. "I don't care about the cost. Can you please correct it?"

"Unfortunately not. Since your wife is no longer alive to provide authorization, I cannot change her funeral instructions."

"You said you didn't get any instructions!"

"Correct. The funeral instructions are the default ones, unless new instructions are received."

He leaned back, staring at the metallic face with its eighty percent beatific, twenty percent regretful smile.

In many ways, Toqs felt, this world had been custom-built for him. Almost all of his interactions were automated or with automata, such as the wheeled robots who delivered their groceries or other shopping from the inner rings. When he'd retired after seventy-five years in home systems repair, Serene said that the mental mechanism that allowed him to endure interaction with other people, under so much strain for a century, had finally broken, and he'd sworn off the whole human project. People judged, robots didn't. Neither did animals, like the German Shepherd who'd passed before Toqs had met Serene (a dog he could never bring himself to replace). Robots and dogs were safe, because they didn't make him feel, as clients or acquaintances or even 'friends' did much of the time, as if their eyes were microscopes and he a specimen coming up short.

Occasionally, though, dealing with the rigidity of software could elicit a sense of frustration beyond anything in the power of even the most obtuse person.

Toqs took another deep breath to calm himself; unlike human beings, bots weren't affected by the loss of one's temper. Working himself up with anger would raise his already high blood pressure, and waste his time, and do nothing at all to the equanimous attendant, who was likely having several or maybe even hundreds of simultaneous conversations.

It was quarter to eight.

Toqs began to feel a knot in his stomach and a familiar constriction in his throat, as if his subconscious knew what he'd decided before *he* did. Because he knew enough about the way the software worked to understand that he didn't have time to sort this out with a computer program.

With forced calmness he said, "Can you put me in touch with a human supervisor responsible for burials in this ring?"

He got up and shuffled to the fridge, ordering a glass of cold water for his suddenly very dry mouth.

The animated face blinked a few times, then informed him he was being transferred, and now a harried human face appeared on the screen, a man with drooping eyes and a grizzle of patchwork gray-black stubble along his neck and cheeks.

Always harried, always forcing Toqs to rush through what he needed to say. Which, inevitably, meant nothing came out quite right, and he ended up sounding like an idiot.

"Yes?" the man said without looking at him. The name at the bottom of the screen said ALBUR DRIGIT.

Toqs suddenly didn't know what to do with the glass of water. He took another sip, then set it on the counter.

"Are you there?" Albur Drigit said. "Can you hear me?"

"Hi, yes. I can hear you." He returned to his chair. "The thing is—my wife. She died this morning. Last night, I should say. They took her away. The card said she's to be cremated, okay? But she didn't want that. She wanted—"

"I'm sorry for your loss." He spoke perfunctorily, but Albur's tired eyes flicked over to Toqs to emphasize his sympathy, then flicked away again to one of his other screens. "Name and ID?"

"Toquer Hingi, one-four-nine-eight-oh."

Type, type, type, eyes flick back, half-shut with annoyance and long-suffering. "Not yours, sir—your wife's."

"Oh, sorry," Toqs said, then swallowed again, half-smiled.

Albur stared at him, waiting.

Toqs gave Serene's full name and number.

Type, type, type—pause, scanning, reading. But reading what? Then Albur turned completely away from his other screen and faced Toqs.

For a moment, the professional veneer seemed to have fallen away from Albur's face. He stared at Toqs—but not impatiently like before. His cheeks drooped, as if sadness were weighing down his face. The borrowed confidence from carrying out his duty, the mask of a stressed and harried official, had hidden that sadness.

The moment passed as Albur tried to lift his face with a twitch of a smile. "I see the problem, Mr. Hingi." He spoke hesitantly. "Your—uhm, your wife did provide new funeral instructions about seven months ago—"

"Yes, correct! Around then. Yes!" Toqs was too excited to contain himself. Would it be this easy?

"She didn't complete the form, though. The instructions are still in draft."

"So? It confirms her intentions."

Albur's lips turned up in a skeptical look that seemed much more natural to them than the attempt at a smile. "Maybe her intentions were to think about it more."

"No, no, no." It wasn't going to be easy at all, was it? "She was very clear with me."

"Strictly speaking," Albur said, now fully returned to his efficient bureaucrat persona, "I'm not even supposed to tell you as much as I did."

"I'm trying to make sure she has the burial she wanted. Please."

"Maybe I can help, if you'll speak to a grief counselor. You'd get priority—I could have someone at your place in half an hour."

"What—why?"

Albur rubbed his stubbled chin with his palm. "Grief does strange things to people. It makes them focus on minor things. Emphasize something that wasn't that important to the deceased." He took a long breath and let it out slowly. "I can override her instructions. Submit the form on her behalf. Change everything around. But before doing that, I want to make sure those were really her wishes. Not just your grief talking."

"Yes—I understand. I'll talk to them. But you said at my place. Why does it need to be in person?"

"That's the way they do it now." Albur shrugged. "Maybe they realized they can't hand you a tissue through a screen."

"I don't need to talk to anyone," Toqs said, a little desperately, like a trapped rabbit that knows it's not getting free. But he tried anyway: "I'm fine. I haven't even grieved yet—you people haven't let me. Right now I just want to make sure my wife's wishes are honored."

Albur took another long-suffering breath, then said, "I'm trying to help you, sir. It's your choice. Give me a call back if you change your mind."

"All right. But they can call me here. I won't need tissues."

Toqs spent the next twenty-five minutes pacing his kitchen, his glance bouncing onto and away from the screen, anticipating the call.

The grief counselor didn't ring his terminal, however; she knocked on his door.

"Seriously?" he said out loud.

"We prefer in-person meetings," a woman's voice replied through the door. "I'm Doctor Glazer," she added helpfully.

For a long few moments, he stood rooted to the floor. What kind of grief counselor ignored your wishes and increased your anxiety and already high blood pressure? Weren't they supposed to help calm you?

"Everything okay?" she asked.

He already felt exhausted from his conversation with the unhelpful Albur Drigit. He would've liked to go back to bed for a rest, but the efficient system that processed the deceased as soon as possible—because no one liked to face death these days, or because someone somewhere had determined a quick funeral accelerated the grieving process—wouldn't wait for him.

"Hello?" Dr. Glazer said, a note of concern entering her voice.

In his mind, he could hear Serene say, in that reproachful but kind, understanding, even loving tone: "You're not going to let that poor woman stand out there, are you?"

No, he wouldn't. And not because it was arguably less awkward to let the doctor in than to wait for her to go away. He wouldn't let that poor woman stand out there because he couldn't let Serene down—in this last service he could offer her—due to a temporary social discomfort.

He walked to the front of their home and opened the door. A woman half to a third his age (but, at this stage in his life, almost everyone he encountered was that much younger than him), Dr. Glazer's hair was pulled back in a tight ponytail, and the gentle wrinkles around her lips and green eyes indicated a face, unlike Albur Drigit's, accustomed to smiling.

The echo of Serene's voice played in his mind: "Maybe invite her in?"

He moved out of the way. "Can I get you a drink or something?" When Serene hosted house parties, he had appointed himself on drinks duty—it gave him a chance to escape to the kitchen and recharge every time a new person arrived or when a guest finished their drink. Her friends used to comment to Serene about how helpful and considerate Toqs was, swooping in as soon as he spied an empty glass. She always agreed with them.

"Coffee would be very kind." Dr. Glazer stood in the foyer. She looked around, then back at him, gently smiling.

"I just want my wife buried properly," Toqs said.

"Let's talk about it. Over here?" She indicated the couch in their living room.

"We can go in the kitchen," he said.

"Wherever you're most comfortable."

He turned around to close the door. When she had been especially frustrated with his excuses to get out of socializing, Serene used to call him the human equivalent of a 'wannabe neutrino', trying to minimize his social interactions. She'd made it her project to 'help' him, after he'd retired and his need or desire for isolation had become more prominent. The more he'd resisted, the harder she'd pushed. She'd gone as far as tricking him into social situations, like when she'd convinced him to go to a fancy restaurant with her to celebrate his one-hundred-and-twentieth birthday (he'd long claimed birthday parties were for children only). Of course, once they'd arrived, he'd realized she'd invited everyone they'd ever met on the *Adagio*. ("I never said it would be just the two of us," she'd whispered, smiling innocently, when he shot her a disapproving look at the doors to the restaurant.)

It had been hard to get mad at her; she'd done those things because she loved him. And she'd made him her mission because he'd refused her suggestion of seeking professional help—because he didn't feel there was a problem for a professional to solve. Toqs had been lucky enough to be less neutrino-like when he'd met Serene, and Serene had provided all the social interaction he needed, even setting aside the times she'd forced him to go out and socialize, to have people over to their home, to engage in human interaction. And he did have friends, real friends, although it was true that most of them had by now died and been carried off, burned or buried.

"Mr. Hingi?" Dr. Glazer called.

He closed the door and went to the kitchen.

Dr. Glazer had set herself up at their table, having placed a small tablet in the middle beside their terminal. She asked for permission to transcribe their conversation.

He nodded, then instructed the refrigerator to brew two coffees.

"Tell me about her."

So, slowly and hesitantly at first, he did. Over coffee with a stranger, sitting at the kitchen table where every morning for the last quarter-century he and his wife had had breakfast together, and lunch most days, if she wasn't out, and almost always dinner.

Dr. Glazer was a good listener. Too good. She had a way of nodding and saying "hmm, mhmm" and a warm, Rogerian smile that elicited more words, more stories, more self-revelation.

When he stopped for a moment and realized everything he'd said about the woman he loved and the life they'd shared, he felt stripped naked in front of this stranger. More than naked. He'd once told Serene that he'd only go see a therapist who revealed something about themselves for everything you revealed about yourself. She'd said, "That's not a therapist, Toqs. That's called a friend."

He sat up straighter. "Is that enough, Doctor? Do you have what you need? I'm not beside myself with grief—I'm beside myself with frustration. My wife gave very specific instructions for her burial, but made a mistake and forgot to submit a form. And I just need you to call this guy in charge—this Albur Drigit—and allow me to honor her wishes before it's too late."

He checked his band. 08:58.

After a few moments of staring at him, Dr. Glazer leaned back in the chair and crossed her legs. "I'll send the message," she said. "I'll do it right now, while we finish up. I would like you to answer one last question, Mr. Hingi. What will you do now that your wife has passed?"

He opened his mouth to give a glib response, but closed it again quickly; in that moment, he realized he didn't trust himself to answer. He felt that saying *anything* would cause him to burst into tears in front of this stranger. Because he knew exactly what the rest of his life would be like: here, in this apartment, his world consisting of the four rooms of the suite, spending morning to night sitting on the bench by the window, endlessly watching or waiting for the spinning day-night of the planet where he'd made so many memories with Serene.

"I don't know," he said finally. "Right now I'm focused on burying my wife."

Dr. Glazer nodded, closed her tablet. She stood.

Toqs cleared the empty cups from the table, breathing more freely. That was it; it was done. Serene would be launched into deep space, like she wanted.

He walked Dr. Glazer to the door. She told him about a support group she ran for people who'd lost their spouse, but he nodded without taking in any of the details. As soon as she was gone, he returned to the bedroom and sat on the bed gently, then let himself fall back onto the mattress. He could've slept for hours, but Serene's ceremony was in fifteen minutes.

He pushed his exhausted body out of the bed and into the kitchen. He hesitated at the refrigerator—he was tempted to order a long island iced tea, Serene's favorite drink. But alcohol, especially on an empty stomach, messed up his digestion. He settled on a second cup of coffee instead.

Toqs looked at the tent card's code and wished Dr. Glazer had offered to stay, so he wouldn't have to watch by himself as his wife was buried.

Grabbing the cup of brewed coffee, he lowered himself into the chair and showed the tent card to the screen. The view changed to a black background with white lettering:

FUNERAL CEREMONY OF SERENE HINGI
(CREMATION)
COMMENCING IN—

—with a timer counting down from thirteen minutes.

Toqs stabbed his finger into the attendant call button. "It's not supposed to be a cremation," he said to the animated face. But there was no time to waste. "Put me in touch with Albur Drigit, please."

The animated eyes rolled in their sockets for a few moments, then their gaze resettled on Toqs. "Albur Drigit's terminal is not responding," the bot said. "Would you like me to try again in five minutes and notify you?" There was a shift in the bot's voice, as if reading a new set of instructions. "Alternatively, Albur Drigit is available for in-person meetings while his terminal is malfunctioning."

"Where is he?"

The address was on the other side of the ring ... *thirty* minutes away if Toqs ran at his top speed from fifty or sixty years ago. He had only one viable option: the supersonic carriages that spun around the ring. Normally he would've done anything to avoid being trapped in a small sphere with a dozen or more strangers. Today was abnormal, however. He was already out of his apartment and shuffling toward the stop, where a carriage was boarding. He only just made it inside as it spun up and took off, full with morning commuters.

Toqs hardly noticed the ride, he was so focused on getting to Albur Drigit and fixing the instructions before it was too late. If it wasn't already. At one point, though, he became aware that a small child, maybe six or seven, was staring at him from across the carriage. Toqs stuck out his tongue and she giggled; then she returned the favor, sticking out her little tongue and making him smile. Like robots and German Shepherds, children were all right.

A few stops later, Toqs unclipped himself and stepped off, eyes scanning the directions on the walls. He walked quickly, pushing his aching legs, unused to this kind of activity, until he reached Albur Drigit's door. One more minute until the ceremony. Too late?

Albur answered his furious knocking.

"You've made a huge—" Toqs began breathlessly.

"It's all right," Albur said, then hesitantly reached out a hand and placed it on Toqs' shoulder. Even hunched over, he towered over Toqs. "Come in."

Inside, a projection wall faced a couch, a small plastic table between them. Toqs stared at the couch; one side, which Albur clearly preferred, had a deep impression. The original black of the fabric, evident in the rest of the couch, had turned almost gray in that favored spot.

Albur asked him to sit down, then instructed the screen to turn on.

On the wall, a view of Serene appeared. She lay in a titanium casket, her head resting on a white pillow, while a soft sound—the chanting of many people in low voices—seemed to reach out and envelop her and Toqs in their separate rooms.

He glanced over at Albur, upset that circumstances had led him to experience such an intimate event in the presence of a stranger. Immediately he remembered that, less than thirty minutes earlier, he'd wished he wouldn't have to be alone as his wife was buried—so which one was it?

Albur's eyes were fixed on the screen.

Toqs turned his attention back to the ceremony. The soft sound of the harmonious chanters filled his heart with a strange mixture of hope and sadness. He stared at his wife's resting face— her closed eyes—as if this were a morning like any other and he could lean over and wake her with a kiss.

When the chant was finished, a metallic hand closed the top of the casket and sealed it; her name, number, birth date and today's date were marked in gold lettering on the silver lid. The robot picked up the casket as if it weighed nothing and walked it across the white-walled circular room to an open port in the wall. The port accepted the casket, then accelerated it down the airlock tube, faster and faster, and fired it out the external side. The view followed as the casket sailed through the blackness of space, then the same information—her name and number and dates— appeared at the bottom of the screen as the titanium coffin receded from view.

Toqs swallowed hard. Turning to look at Albur, he said, "Thank you for arranging that. But why didn't you update the description? I wouldn't have come barging over here."

"You're not bothering me," Albur said, rubbing the stubble on his cheek nervously as he met Toqs' gaze. "Would you like something to drink? I've taken the rest of the day off."

"It's nine-thirty in the morning."

"I thought maybe you could use a drink." And suddenly, in the other's sad, lonely eyes, Toqs saw that this man half his age wanted him to stay. For his own or for Albur's benefit, Toqs didn't know.

With effort he pushed himself to his throbbing legs. A drink didn't sound so bad, actually; keeping off his feet for a little longer sounded even better. But best to go home. The last thing he needed, on this day more than any other, was to involve himself with another person's problems.

Albur kept sitting. "I think your wife didn't submit the form on purpose."

The tall man's tone was quiet, conspiratorial. Was he accusing Serene of something? "What?" Toqs snapped.

"She left a note in the form." Albur spoke calmly. "There's prompts, you know—any other instructions, any concerns, words you want said at the ceremony. But she wrote, 'My only concern is that my husband will bury himself instead of me when I die. If you can find a way to get him out of our apartment, on this day at least, I'd sure appreciate it and think kindly of you.'"

Toqs was shaking his head. How could she? Saying that—about *him*—to *strangers*!

"That upsets you?" Albur said, watching him as if studying a fascinating specimen.

"You didn't know her," Toqs said defensively.

"I wish I had," Albur said, rising to his feet. "Let me get you a drink and you can tell me about her."

"She wanted to *fix* me. She couldn't just leave it alone."

"Leave what alone? You?"

"Not me." Toqs shook his head in impatience, frustrated by his inability to convey to this stranger the complex relationship he and Serene had shared. "I just want to be left alone!" he blurted out.

The man towering over him said in a quiet voice, "Maybe she understood you enough to know that you don't want that? Not really."

"Don't speak to me like you know me."

Albur's face remained calm, still.

"And you went along with her plan?" Toqs went on, speaking more coldly. All morning he'd been holding at bay a deep anger toward his wife. Not because she'd forced him out into the world—she'd been doing that ever since they'd met—but for leaving him once and for all. And now, being able to redirect it at Albur allowed him to set that anger loose. "You manipulated me, too? You lied to me? How do you think your supervisors are going to feel about that?”

A dark cloud had formed on Albur’s broad face. But when he spoke, his voice was still calm and soft. “How do you think people feel about the guy responsible for burying their loved ones? How do *you* feel about me? You want me to do my job, then you want to forget about me as quickly as possible, right? Hold up your band. I’ll send you my supervisor’s identification number so you can report me.”

Toqs didn’t move.

“Your wife seems like a very sweet person,” Albur said, dropping his arm. “I was happy to do something nice for her.” He continued to stare down at Toqs. “You can take what she did in a bad way if you want. Probably being angry is easier than being sad. But I’ll tell you this: I wish I had someone in my life who cares about me the way your wife cared about you.”

Toqs returned the stare but refused to speak. He wouldn’t validate anything this stranger, who knew nothing about Serene or the relationship they’d shared for almost ninety years, had to say about her. After a few moments of silence, he turned and left the sad, lonely man in his sad, lonely apartment.

It would be a long walk back. Briefly he considered taking the carriage. It hadn’t been too bad earlier, and the little girl had put a smile on his face. But maybe not today.

He leaned against the wall to gather his strength, then remembered that he’d muted the thread related to Serene. He brought up his arm and glanced through the many messages that had come in that morning, as well as newer ones that continued to pop up, telling him how beautiful her ceremony had been. Serene was gone—and her body receding further away by the minute—but even the quick glance through the things her friends had written made her feel present again.

He allowed his arm to drop. He would read the messages more carefully later. He’d also have to write everyone back. Some people he hadn’t spoken to in a long, long while. He wondered how they were doing.

Slowly he made his way down the hallway, toward his own part of the ring. Albur Drigit *was* a sad man, wasn’t he? What kind of person took the day off of work to … what? Listen to an old man’s stories about his deceased wife?

And Albur really had no idea, did he? Serene had been a complex person, with good and great and bad and terrible qualities and quirks, with her own issues that Toqs had tried to help her work through. And maybe Serene had been able to see past Toqs’ fears and worries; maybe she had understood that he needed a push out into the world. But on this day? As her last act? *Selfless,* Albur would probably say; but Toqs could equally say: stubborn and determined to accomplish her mission. Toqs knew his wife and Albur didn't.

He stopped walking. His breathing had become shallower as he'd worked himself up with these thoughts. He wanted to march back to Albur's door and tell him all of it, explain why it wasn't as simple as Albur had it figured in his head.

But it wasn't worth the effort. Albur wouldn't understand. He couldn't.

Toqs pushed his feet forward.

Maybe Dr. Glazer's group of widows and widowers could understand. If only Toqs had bothered to listen to any of the details.

Someone like Albur could never understand. Even if the sad, lonely man had seen something in Serene's last wish that had inspired him to play along. And if he thought *that* had been selfless, Albur should hear about all the other things Serene had done for Toqs and many others throughout her life.

Albur wouldn't hear those stories, though. Because Toqs wanted to go home to his own apartment. An empty apartment that wasn't going anywhere.

In his mind, he heard Serene's voice again: "You're not going to let that poor man think you're mad at him, are you? Or, even worse"—her voice rose an octave when she pretended to be offended—"that you're mad at *me!*"

He stopped, let out a long sigh.

No, he wouldn't let that poor man think those things—especially not that Toqs was anything but still madly in love with his wife. Not because of a temporary social discomfort.

He turned around, shuffled back to Albur's door.

When the tall man answered, Toqs said, "I'll have that drink now. Long island iced tea." Before Albur could respond, Toqs added quickly, "If the offer still stands—I can tell you about that wonderful woman you just buried."

The heavy, stubbled cheeks lifted. "I'd like that very much," Albur said, stepping out of the doorway to let Toqs in.

See Karl El-Koura's story "Her Last Will" online at Metaphorosis.
If you liked it, leave a comment. Authors love that!

Remember to subscribe to our e-mail updates so you'll know when new stories are posted.

About the story

Hello, my name is Karl El-Koura, and I'm an introvert.

Do they have support groups for introverts, or does no one show up?

I suspect most writers are on the introversion end of the spectrum. Who else would voluntarily lock themselves up alone in a room for hours on end?

Many of my stories, like "Her Last Will", turn out to be about people needing to step outside their comfort zones to connect with other human beings.

This isn't a conscious decision most of the time, but emerges as I think about or write the story and get to know the characters. Perhaps, in the absence of a support group, I use writing to push back against my introverted tendencies.

A question for the author

Q: What is your favorite word?

A: The word that immediately comes to mind is "onomatopoeia". Boom! (When I first learned the word in high school, I thought it was the neatest thing—the way it looked, the way it sounded, even that there was a word to describe words that sound like themselves. Its only drawback is I always have to look up how to spell it.)

About the author

Karl El-Koura lives with his family in Canada's capital city, holds a second-degree black belt in Okinawan Goju Ryu karate, and works a regular job in daylight while writing fiction at night. "Her Last Will" is his second appearance in *Metaphorosis*. His fantasy short story "The Azurian Shield" was published in October 2021.

Portals and Other Lost Things

Elizabeth Rankin

There was no indication that the holes Sylvie accidentally knitted into her first scarf would be portals in space and time.

Her grief counselor had practically insisted she find something to do, now that she'd had three years to grieve over Doug, even if she didn't leave the house to do it. The counselor had meant watercolors or soap making — not breaking the laws of physics.

Outside of a little gardening and cooking for Doug, Sylvie had never pursued a form of artistic expression. The day-to-day was enough. Working, taking care of the girls' homework or practices, and the yearly vacations with Doug at the wheel of the minivan. Sylvie's heart clenched. She didn't cry every time she thought about the past, and that was progress.

A twelfth hole appeared while she wasn't paying close attention to the pattern and Sylvie sighed. Out of habit she looked around for support, someone to laugh with, and saw the smiling faces on the mantle. Framed photos of goofy grins from summer vacations to House on the Rock and Mystery Hole, fully immersed in the kitsch. At the end of the row was an empty frame from the last trip she and Doug had taken, to the Corn Palace. She'd never gotten the photo printed out, never gotten around to checking it off their travel bucket list.

Sylvie got up to take the yawning black hole of the frame away. It reminded her of the last time things had been normal. Of Doug. Of the fact she hadn't left the city in the three years since the funeral. Learning how to do things on her own was challenge enough. Mowing the grass. Dealing with plumbers. Remembering what TV shows she'd always meant to go back and watch, since Doug wasn't interested. It took a year and a half before she got through a day without crying. Planning a trip on her own was far outside her comfort zone. She'd never done it. Trips could go a million different ways she'd never had to think about and wasn't sure she wanted to start.

Her daughters checked in on her, but they had their own lives. Emma lived six hours away. Madelyn had two kids of her own now. They went camping or on bike tours, active excursions to keep the kids entertained. Too much for her, they said, but they'd invite her when they did a different type of vacation. Better for her to stay safe at home.

She returned to the recliner, determined to ignore the holes in her lovely variegated blue yarn and finish the damned scarf. She wasn't sure how the holes had gotten there and couldn't figure out a way to fix them. Nothing in the book she'd bought online talked about it, so it could be an advanced technique. This last one was right in the middle, where it couldn't be ignored. A black gap where yarn should be, small as the tip of her ring finger.

Sylvie squinted at the hole. It was too dark. Had it always been like that? A matte black with no shine, no hint of light. She jabbed a finger through.

Something cold and wet nuzzled her fingertip. Like a nose. She pulled back with a yelp. Sylvie didn't have a pet. Hadn't for a long time.

She tried again, tentative. Soft fur brushed her skin. Sylvie checked her lap for anything that could be mistaken for an animal. She might have been letting the house go a little, but surely not enough to have animals crawling into the furniture. There was nothing but yarn and her stretchiest sweatpants.

She shook all nine inches of scarf she'd managed to complete so far, pulled it taut, and held it out in front of her. All the holes remained black no matter what she held them against, even when she brought her eye up to stare through. No beige carpet. No oversized picture of the family at Dinosaur World, Kentucky. No light. Sylvie turned the scarf over, pushed her finger through the same hole from the other side, and again fur moved under her finger.

Her phone chirped and she jumped. It kept chirping until she fumbled with the swipe to accept the call.

"Hello?" Her voice cracked and she cleared her throat.

"Mom? Are you ok?"

Maddie, her eldest daughter, lived in town and was the worrier now that Sylvie lived alone. The first year without Doug, Sylvie had broken a bone in her hand and not gotten it looked at. At her age, everything hurt anyway. Doug would have bundled her to the ER. Now that he wasn't here, Maddie-the-nurse felt it was her duty to manage her mother's health. Sylvie just wanted to ignore it.

"Oh, I'm fine," Sylvie said. "Doing some knitting."

She eyed the holes and weighed whether to say anything to her daughter. Would she believe it without seeing it? Sylvie wasn't sure she'd believe it herself, and knowing her daughter, Maddie would schedule a barrage of psychiatric visits and CT scans.

"Ok, you sounded surprised," Maddie said. "We're still on for tea tomorrow at three?"

"Oh." Sylvie stroked the lumps in her scarf and tried desperately to think of an excuse to put off the visit. "I forgot tomorrow was Thursday."

It wasn't that she didn't love her daughter, but the visits with just the two of them were strained with Maddie's worry. She would do all the work, bustling around the kitchen like she owned it, not Sylvie. Saying things like 'you rest' and 'you take it easy'.

"Are you not feeling well again?" Maddie's voice sharpened. "I knew the doctor was being lazy. I can make an appointment for this afternoon. Dr. Runyon has openings."

"No, no," Sylvie said. "I just forgot what day it was. They all blend together."

She winced, knowing it was the wrong thing to say. The silence on the other end of the phone confirmed it. Maddie would be on guard tomorrow, looking for signs of deterioration. Sylvie dropped the scarf. Maybe she'd been too long inside after all.

"For tomorrow," Maddie said, neutral, "I'm whipping up a few types of sandwiches. I found watercress, and I'll have ham, egg, and chicken salad. It'll be a fancy tea, just like that show you like."

"Downton Abbey. I finished watching that a few months ago," Sylvie said, a bit too sharp. She tried again, "I've already made the brownies. And I'll make the deviled eggs tomorrow."

One of her greatest disappointments was that her daughters loved Doug's mother's deviled egg recipe instead of her version. Probably because the secret ingredient Doug's family added was sugar, which Sylvie privately thought was disgusting. She could have bought vinegar and capers to make them her way this time, but she didn't want to disappoint Maddie.

Maddie made small talk, then said her goodbyes. The house fell silent. Its emptiness gaped from the hallways and doors, threatening to swallow Sylvie. In her lap, the scarf was a puddle of warmth. More warmth than was natural. A hole leading to a dog was one thing. What was in the others? Would she poke a finger into an acid volcano or a killer plant?

She set the scarf on the arm of the recliner and went to make herself a drink. A good scotch solved many ills.

Glass in hand, Sylvie lay the scarf on the kitchen table. The unnatural blackness of the holes was still there. Light from the fluorescent bulbs illuminated the fabric like it was on an operating table. Nothing about the uneven lines or broken pattern seemed unusual. There weren't any strange symbols accidentally formed by her novice stitches. The yarn had come from the craft store, not an old fortune-teller or mysterious box found in the attic. All appearances said it was a totally ordinary, badly knitted scarf. Something called a straight stockinette pattern, more or less.

Could she have made something magic, without knowing? Or was it some kind of *Twilight Zone* thing, with forces in the universe at work far beyond her understanding? Sylvie wasn't sure what to do next. Doug would have tested the holes. He probably would have made a game of it, rolling dice to decide which he'd poke next. He'd have made sure it was safe first, then invited her to try it, like when they'd gone on the hot sauce factory tour. No one was here to do that for her now.

She swore and knocked back the rest of the scotch. How many more adventures did she have left?

The atmosphere on the other side of the second hole washed her skin with baking heat. When she wiggled her finger, it touched sand. A strong gust of wind pelted grains against her skin. She pulled the opening to her nose and tried to breathe in, hoping for the brine of ocean water, to help tell her where it was. There was nothing, like no air came through at all. Did the holes lead to places on earth, or somewhere else? Calling them 'holes' seemed wrong. They were doorways. Portals that could go anywhere.

She licked her finger and tried to get sand to stick, imagining tiny spots of amethyst and ruby, but the granules fell in the wind or were pushed off by the yarn before she could pull them through. Even stretching the scarf, the clumsy weave was too tight to get more than a single finger through. Sylvie picked at the knit to widen the opening. Energy flickered, like a dying fluorescent bulb. Flashes of the wood veneer underneath the scarf blinked through the blackness. When she stopped plucking, the dark oval stabilized. Delicate things, these portals, if all it took to destroy them was breaking the weave. Which might be good to know.

Snowflakes melted on her body heat in the third portal, and in the fourth something smooth and lush as rose petals flowed against her finger. Each time, she turned the scarf over to be sure they went to the same place from both sides, and they always seemed to. In the fifth hole she felt nothing. Then a tiny pinch, and more, a swarm of miniscule creatures with teeth testing her flesh. Sylvie yelped and yanked her finger back, slapping her palm over the opening.

Could they get through? She waited. Nothing bit into her hand and when she raised it no murderous gnats escaped.

She'd been lucky so far. There were seven holes left that could hold anything. Sylvie folded the scarf to cover all the openings. This was not her imagination. It was dangerous. And impossible.

Someone should know about it. She picked up her phone and looked up the number for NASA. Or was this a national security issue? If nothing could come through, it couldn't cause a problem. Could it? A scientist would want to study this, that was certain. They'd take it away from her, run a lot of tests, and send her on her way.

It could be worth money, she considered, as she eyed the scarf over another, very small, drink. She could sell tickets. To what, though? It was like one of the old attractions, where you stuck your hand into a box and guessed what was inside. No one did that anymore. Who'd want to pay to have their finger chewed on by bugs?

Energy drained out of her. She should mail it to NASA anonymously. If they didn't find anything they'd just think she was a weird lady who liked to knit scarves for astronauts.

What would Doug do?

Throw it out, probably. Once those gnats started biting, he'd say it wasn't worth the risk. He was very practical and usually right. Like when she'd kept raw chicken too long and they'd gotten food poisoning. This could be worse. If those bugs were toxic, like a rattlesnake, she could have died right there on the kitchen floor.

Sylvie opened the drawer to the trash and stared at the paper towels and wrinkled tea bags. The scarf, for all its failings, she'd made on her own. That was what everyone said she should be doing now. Making her own choices. She'd picked out the yarn and the pattern and learned the method. Then she'd made something amazing, something no one else had ever done. It didn't belong in the garbage. Sylvie tucked the scarf into the refrigerator, on the foil covering the pan of cheesecake brownies. It was the best place she could think of for an unidentified and possibly magic object. Between the sturdy doors, the cold, and the delicious baked goods, anything that got out of those holes might stop there.

It took her a long time to go to sleep. She stared at the picture on her nightstand. Their honeymoon, at Wigwam Village in Arizona. Doug had taken a shot of her from behind, steps away.

His hand got into the frame, wrist and fingers blocking the top of one of the wigwams as he reached for her. She stared at that hand every night, though lately she'd also started staring at the back of her head. Back then, her hair had been long, and streamed in the wind as she stood on the hood of the car. It had probably been their best trip, driving Route 66, stopping at every roadside attraction that caught their eye.

The back of the frame held a list of all the places they'd wanted to go. Some crossed off. Some, like the Bonnie Springs wild west resort, had closed. What was left would be enough to fill her time for the rest of her life, if she ever left the city again.

Her finger rubbed back and forth against her palm, still feeling the hard edges of the portal sand, from a beach she'd never seen.

As soon as she woke up enough to remember, Sylvie hurried to the refrigerator and pulled the door open enough to peer inside. The scarf sat on the tinfoil, undisturbed, as far as she could tell. Sylvie unfolded its length and touched the holes, in that just-roused state where the previous day's memories could have been a dream.

No animal nudged her finger in the first hole, but the others blew snow and sand like she remembered.

This was beyond her. She needed some advice, and Maddie would be a good place to start. Sylvie rolled up the scarf and put it back into the refrigerator. After a piece of toast and a shower, she took out all the materials for the eggs. The scarf sat there, waiting, each time she opened the refrigerator door, until Sylvie had to do something with it.

While the eggs boiled, she got paper and a pencil and started a list of portals, numbering 1-12. Those last seven blanks gaped at her until the timer went off. If there was some way to reduce the risk of exploring, they could do it together without Maddie fretting. Sylvie fished the eggs out of the water with a spoon and put them aside to cool. She stared at the spoon, then set it down with a clatter and ran to get the scarf.

The spoon wouldn't fit in any of the holes, but other things might. The end of a knife. A pencil. Tweezers. She gathered them all and used one at a time to try to pull sand from the hole, which seemed the safest option. If she had proof, Maddie couldn't try to say she was losing her mind. The knife and pencil brought back nothing. The tweezers, though — when Sylvie opened them above her hand, tiny sparkles fell from them and brushed against her skin. She closed her fist and laughed. It was real.

She pulled out sand until there was enough to see. Things could come back through if they were attached to her side, it seemed. Against the white of a paper towel, it glinted not red or purple, but green. A search revealed there were beaches on Earth with green sand, including in Hawaii and the Galapagos Islands and a lake in Norway she couldn't pronounce. Hawaii had the only animatronic teddy bear museum in the US, and a life-size whale statue, which would be fun, although the sand could have just as easily have been from Mars for all she knew.

Her phone buzzed with a message from Maddie: "On my way!"

Sylvie folded the paper towel and slid it under her saucer at the table with the unfinished list and set of tweezers. She'd have to wait for the right time to bring it up, test the waters to see how Maddie would react. Sylvie made the eggs, automatically tipping in sugar and mashing up the yolks. Like she'd done a hundred times, or a thousand. She still didn't like them this way. They needed vinegar, and a pinch of dill. A spoonful of pickle relish would be about right. Maddie might be angry, but Sylvie couldn't resist.

She chuckled when she thought of Doug's face, appalled, but the laugh choked in her throat as it flipped to grief. That's how it went. Things seemed fine, until they weren't.

When Maddie arrived, Sylvie returned her daughter's hug with vigor. It felt almost like Christmas, like a secret she'd kept was about to be revealed. There would be wide eyes, but then if she'd done it right, excited smiles.

"You're in a good mood," Maddie said, holding out a set of plastic boxes, heavy with food. "Are you hungry? I brought way more than we need."

"Starving!" Sylvie took the two containers and set them on the counter with a flourish.

Maddie beamed, but her eyes flicked over Sylvie, who tried to tone down her enthusiasm. She didn't want to get Maddie worked up before she had a chance to tell her what was going on.

Maddie set sandwiches on plates while Sylvie prepared the tea.

"What's in these eggs?" Maddie asked after popping one in her mouth.

"Pickle relish," Sylvie said as she brought over the tea caddy.

"You used a different recipe?"

Sylvie couldn't quite tell if the reproach she expected was present in her daughter's tone.

"Well, the kind you've always had were your father's version, not mine." Sylvie sat, not sure why she was talking about this now. "I never liked them. Not with sugar."

"Really?" Maddie's eyebrows were up practically in her bangs. Then she put another on her plate. "I never knew that. Brandon's family puts butter in theirs."

Sylvie braced for more, for admonitions about betraying Doug's traditions — the family traditions — but Maddie patted her mother's arm.

"You can have the eggs any way you want them," Maddie said.

Sylvie tried a smile, but it came out watery. They loaded plates and chatted about everything the grandkids were doing. In the back of Sylvie's mind was the green sand, the fur, and the unknown. Tweezers wouldn't tell them much about the other side. A camera of some kind would be better. Not a selfie stick, that would be too big. She needed one of those cameras they used in surgeries. Like her yearly colonoscopy.

"Can you get a surgical camera at home?" Sylvie realized after she stared into her daughter's surprised face that she had interrupted whatever they were supposed to be talking about.

"A surgical camera?" Maddie's brows furrowed. Sylvie cleared her throat, trying to act casual.

"You know, like the ones they use in going down your throat and looking into your stomach."

"Laparoscopic cameras? Why would you want one of those?" Maddie frowned and straightened her back, eyes narrowed. "You're not going to look in your own stomach, are you?"

"What? No. Don't be ridiculous. How could you think that?"

"I'm just making sure, Mom. You've been cooped up in here by yourself for a couple years, who knows what stuff you've been listening to."

Sylvie felt a scowl drawing her mouth down and took a sip of tea to rearrange her thoughts.

"It's not that. For cleaning." The lie slipped off Sylvie's tongue. This wasn't the right way to start. "I can't remember the last time I cleared out the vents and want to check what's down there."

"Oh, you can get them online," Maddie said, taking a packet of artificial sweetener. Not a sugar cube, like she used to. "Just promise if you are thinking about any medical procedures, you ask me first, ok?"

She smiled like she was joking, but the vigilance in her eyes remained.

"So, what are you doing this summer?" Sylvie changed the subject to travel, something fun and relaxing, that might make Maddie more receptive. "I know you said you were thinking about going out to the Grand Canyon."

"Yep, we're going in the beginning of June. It's going to be hot, but you've got to go when the kids are off, you know?"

The Grand Canyon was close to the giant Lumberjacks at Northern Arizona University. They'd talked many times about crossing them off the list and seeing the Grand Canyon at once, but Maddie didn't mention the statues or the list. The taste of tea lingered in bitter edges on Sylvie's tongue.

"Mom, you look weird," Maddie said. "What's wrong?"

"It's just — are you going to see the Lumberjacks?"

Maddie paused, took a sip of tea, "Are those on your list?"

Sylvie winced at the 'your'. She counted to ten like she had when the girls were small.

"Number 59," Sylvie said.

"Oh." Maddie made her smile gentle. It wasn't her real smile. Sylvie would know; she was still Maddie's mother, after all. "I don't think we'll make it. The kids want to do more hiking."

Did kids like to hike that young? Maddie's boys were just eleven and nine.

"We took you girls all over the country. We had fun." Sylvie's voice quavered at the last, unexpectedly. She found herself looking into her daughter's eyes, searching them for confirmation. Maddie's face crinkled into genuine smile lines.

"Yes, of course we did. But that was your thing, you and Dad."

She didn't say 'and not ours', but she didn't need to. Sylvie understood. The normal places were enough for Maddie. Seeing it so clearly knocked something loose in her. Sylvie felt curiously balanced, on the edge of grief and determination.

"There are a lot of places to cross off," Sylvie said. "I still want to go."

That's why she'd stuck her fingers in those holes.

"Mom." Maddie put her hand over her mother's. It was slightly sticky from the brownie. "You can't go on those trips by yourself, it's not safe. But that's ok. You can do other things. Make your own list, just for you."

Sylvie looked down and swirled her tea. It made sense and was even what her grief counselor had said. Why she'd taken up knitting in the first place. She blinked and saw herself in the recliner, hunched over her knitting and watching old TV shows until she died. The balanced scales inside her tipped to determination.

"Actually," Sylvie said, "I've already started one. I haven't gotten very far yet."

She tapped the paper under her saucer, the one she was going to show Maddie with the portals listed on it.

"That's great, Mom." She patted her hand and pulled away. "You can try out different deviled egg recipes."

Maddie laughed and Sylvie managed a chuckle. Her daughter didn't ask to see the list, as Sylvie had expected. Instead she rose and excused herself to go to the bathroom.

Sylvie half-heartedly gathered courage to tell her daughter about the portals when she got back. Then Maddie strode in and started cleaning the dishes. Sylvie scrambled to her feet, unprepared.

"That's okay, Mom, you take it easy," Maddie said. Just like Sylvie should have known she would.

The confession stuck in her throat as she brought plates to the sink for her daughter to clean. They finished up over idle chatter and hugged their good-byes. Maddie suggested that Sylvie knit everyone scarves for Christmas, left half the food behind 'to make sure you've got enough to eat, Mom', and hurried out the door to pick the kids up from after-school activities.

Sylvie let her go. The paper still sat folded on the table. Grief still tugged at her, for what was, and what wouldn't be. Maddie would never let her do anything with the portals, that was clear. She went to the fridge and took the scarf out, unsure of what to do alone. The fabric didn't feel as cold as she thought it should, just bumpy from her uneven progress. She lay the scarf amongst the salad plates and crumpled napkins on the table, as if it belonged there with the rest of her things.

Careful not to spill the sand, she pulled the tweezers free from her folded list and slid them into hole number six. They skidded across a smooth surface before encountering soft resistance. She snapped them open and closed until they grabbed on to something, and then she pulled. What came out was a white paper square, crimped around the edges. A cocktail napkin.

"Bonnie Springs Steak House now open." Sylvie read the words the second time out loud, because they didn't make sense at first.

She turned the napkin over in her hands. The words didn't change. Written in a wild west type popular in the midcentury, the ink crisp and the paper as clean as if they'd been delivered yesterday. Tears clouded her vision.

Bonnie Springs, number 11 on the list she and Doug had made, had closed five years ago. Not on enough people's travel plans, apparently. It certainly wasn't on Maddie's. Her daughter's mantle full of photos would be different, and no amount of waiting for the right time was going to change that.

Sylvie took out her list and wrote out 'Bonnie Springs' as the destination of portal six. Her heart thrummed. It wasn't too late for her to go on her own.

She turned the paper over and took Maddie's advice to make her own list. There was a lot to do. First, she'd get a camera to explore the other portals. Then learn to make her own and see if she could control where they went. The last step would be finding a way to make a hole big enough to climb through. Once she figured out how she'd done the smaller ones, Sylvie could try using some of that giant, novelty yarn they used to make those puffy knit blankets. She chuckled at the idea of squeezing through one of those. Doug would have gone, and so could she.

Sylvie put the final action item of making a portal for herself at the very bottom. There would be more challenges along the way to add in. She might never get through everything, but she had to try. If she'd made holes in the fabric of the universe on accident, Sylvie could only imagine what she could do on purpose.

*See Elizabeth Rankin's story "Portals and Other Lost Things" online
at Metaphorosis.
If you liked it, leave a comment. Authors love that!
Remember to subscribe to our e-mail updates so you'll know when
new stories are posted.*

About the story

"Portals and Other Lost Things" started from a writing prompt during "Story a Day May" in 2020, although I can't remember the original prompt. Like so many people, I was feeling stuck inside and longing to visit other places, hoping they'd still be around after the pandemic. I was also trying out new hobbies, although knitting (as featured in my story) wasn't one of them.

The first version was as a flash-length revenge story, where my protagonist decides to make her ex disappear through the portals in her scarf. I felt that version was too safe, and my critique group agreed. What I really wanted to do was to explore what would make someone want to take a leap and go through the unknown.

There's a sense of general expectation that after you hit mid-life, you retire from being interesting. This is particularly true for women in our culture. I just hit that stage in my own life, so I might be a little sensitive about it! I wanted to write something that shows that strange things can happen to anyone, and maybe your later years are your most dynamic.

I rewrote the story as a more thoughtful internal narrative to take the reader from where Sylvie is stuck in the expectations of others to how she shakes loose from them. I also wanted to create a little bit of mystery with the portals so some things remain unknown, like how they work and where they go. My beta readers wanted to know more, and that was the point. There's still plenty of life left to explore, even if you're not sure how you're going to get there.

A question for the author

Q: Do you live near where you were born? Have you traveled much?

A: I actually live right down the road from the hospital where I was born! Not on purpose. I left the area for about 10 years, and didn't intend to come back, but fate (a.k.a. the need for a job) intervened. I enjoy traveling and have been to Europe a few times, as well as Mexico and Canada. One of my life goals is to visit every National Park. I've been to 13 so far, out of 63, so that should keep my vacations full for a very long time. Especially because they keep adding them! I'd like to see more of the world, and more of the U.S. as well. There are more fascinating places to go than I'll ever have time for, but I can try!

About the author

Elizabeth Rankin is the daughter of a librarian and grew up telling stories in the stacks. She worked in publishing before transitioning to marketing, where she strictly enforces use of the Oxford comma. When not writing, she might be trying out new recipes, volunteering for more than she should, or playing with her dogs. She lives with her husband in their eventual dream house in Cleveland, Ohio, USA.

@rankin_writes

Infinite Possibilities I

Michael Gardner

1

Adrian's name is typed across the front of the white envelope, but there's no address and no stamp. This was hand delivered.

He stands by his mailbox, raises a hand to shield his eyes from the sinking sun, peers up the road, turns and looks back down toward the corner. No one else is about. A couple of parrots chatter away as they fly overhead.

He lives in a neat suburban cul-de-sac. Quiet. New brick houses, middle class. Young trees not big enough to provide much shade. Tidy yards, except for number six. Adrian's not much of a gardener, but Candice refuses to be talked about like the owners of that house, so he gets out most weekends, mows, rakes, sprays for weeds. She takes care of the plants.

He looks back at the white envelope in his grease-stained hand. There's a small lump inside.

The sun is warm, bordering on hot, even though it's late in the day. He regrets his choice of tracksuit pants. His legs are sticky, moist beneath the material. A bead of sweat escapes his armpit, runs down his side. He blows hot air up across his nose and brow. It doesn't help.

He tears open the end of the envelope, upends the contents into his hand. A white USB. Unlabelled. Maybe a scam? he thinks. A virus? Malware?

But then why go to the trouble of finding out his name and where he lives? That seems very specific for a phishing scam. Why not just address the letter to the homeowner?

It's too hot, he thinks, wiping his brow. He trudges back to the house, the screen door screeching as he opens it.

It's five degrees cooler inside. The feel of the tiled floor beneath his bare feet is a pleasant relief. He moves down the hall, into the living/dining/kitchen space. It's modern, open, airy.

By the kitchen bench, he opens the bin, then hesitates with the USB in hand.

What did Candice say just the other night? Something about missing the old Adrian. The wild Adrian. He was hurt at the time. As if she'd expressed a desire to be with someone else. Someone he can't compete with. And the old Adrian *is* someone he can't compete with. The old Adrian exhausts him.

Still.

He closes the bin, tosses the USB next to his laptop on the bench. He'll decide later, he thinks.

Adrian was high and drunk when he met Candice.

It was late in the evening when his mates convinced him to try a new night club. It wasn't exactly his sort of place, but he relented, lined up, and forked out an exorbitant cover charge.

Inside was a dizzying assault of bass, lights, sweaty bodies, and the noise of people yelling at each other to be heard over the music. He soon gave up trying to talk to his friends, and they left him at the bar as they hit the dance floor.

Candice was dancing. He doesn't recall what she was wearing exactly, but he remembers her hair. Long, auburn, waves of movement that crashed around her. A halo of silk. He watched her move with abandon as he sipped his rum.

When she ceased whirling, when she turned and approached, he thought it was to him that she came. That's why he spoke. "Adrian."

Like his own name was a password that needed to be stated. Like it unlocked something special. And it did, kind of.

She smirked, veered at the last moment, sidled up next to him at the bar and signalled for the bartender. Then with her best Sylvester Stallone impression: "Adrian. Adrian. Addriannnnnn!"

He didn't know how to respond. She didn't let him. She ordered a couple of gin and tonics.

"Is one of them for me, Rocky?" he eventually asked.

She snorted a laugh, turned, looked him up and down. "No."

"Huh." He sipped again, swilled the liquid around his mouth. "You dance like a typhoon."

She regarded him quizzically. "Is that a good thing?"

"Absolutely. Ferocious. Unencumbered. Nature's force and power."

The bartender slid the drinks to Candice, took her cash, disappeared.

"Good answer," she said, smiling lopsidedly, genuinely. He remembered that through his booze haze. That lopsided smile. He used to get it a lot back then. "And how do you dance?" she asked. The bartender dropped her change on the alcohol sticky counter.

"I'm more like a sinking ship."

"So I'd engulf you?"

"If I'm lucky."

"You're not," she stated, picked up her drinks, and left without her change.

He watched her until she disappeared amongst the crowd, then he glanced at the coins on the bar. They glinted under the flashing lights. He felt like he'd missed something. Something that the alcohol wasn't quite letting him see, or feel. Something important, lost without him ever realising it was there in the first place.

But what was he going to do?

Later, as he stumbled from the bar, and along the wet street —had it rained? He couldn't remember—a taxi slowed next to him and the back window rolled down with an electric buzz.

"Yo, Adrian," came the mock deep voice, and there she was again, leaning out the window.

"You giving me a lift?" he asked, hopeful.

"Uh uh," she said, shaking her head. "You're off your tits, and I'm not that sort of girl."

"Oh." The scent of exhaust was acrid, like burnt plastic. It mixed with the smell of wet bitumen, forming a distinctive aroma that stayed with him long after. Two girlfriends were in the back with this lovely stranger. Two girlfriends giggling, urging her to leave him and close the window.

"I'll be back here next Saturday. Maybe if you bring me some of whatever you're on—"

"I'm not on anything," he lied, and received a disbelieving expression. He relented, shrugged, smiled. She smiled back.

"What then, Rocky?" he asked.

"Don't know. Maybe nothing. Maybe we dance. Let's see how it plays out."

"Next Saturday," he repeated.

She nodded, smiled, slapped the taxi door once on the side and it began to move. As it sped up, she leaned further out, and yelled, "Candice," then she was gone again, pulled back inside the cab by her two friends.

He's tinkering at his work bench in the garage when Candice returns home. He jumps a little as the automatic garage door starts to rise. It emits a mix of clunks and whirs, drowning out the hum of Candice's Corolla as it pulls into the drive, stops. It's dusk out, he sees, the streetlights just starting to warm up.

She steps out of the car, and his eyes are drawn to her legs, still shapely after all these years. She wears a pencil skirt, a white silk blouse. She looks unaffected by the heat. She looks stunning.

"Hi," he says, a grunt as much as a greeting. He refocusses on the dirty parts of the lawnmower carburettor lined up on his bench.

It's a familiar game they play. Distance, coolness. It's better than fighting. At least for him. Candice, she can get mad as hell, yell, and scream, then be over it an hour later. But Adrian holds onto things. Weighs each hurt, collects them until they overwhelm him.

"You didn't work today?" she says. Her tone is flat, neutral. No accusation there. Adrian senses one anyway.

"Rostered day off."

"Didn't you have one last week?"

He picks up the bowl nut, scrubs it with the wire brush. "They cut my shifts back," he says. He feels her watching him, but he refuses to look. She's very still. The street is quiet. If there weren't the whisking sound of the steel brush on the nut, he wonders if he'd hear anything.

He knows what she's thinking. She's thinking, 'I told you so.' When Action buses offered him an incentive to move to casual rates, he took it. More money, fewer shifts. But Candice was irate. Another bad career choice. Like when he dropped out of university and never went back. He sees that in her eyes as they dress for work each morning. Her in her suit, him in his blue uniform.

Finally, Candice moves. Her heels click as she glides across the concrete toward the door separating garage from house.

"I'm going out tonight," she tosses toward him casually, daring him to object. Once she would have asked him to join her, but not anymore. She's given up. Her work colleagues and friends just aren't his people. He's made that clear.

He says nothing. Just keeps cleaning. Candice disappears inside.

After he reassembles the lawnmower, he goes inside to the laundry and washes his hands in the tub. As he scrubs, he hears the automatic garage door closing. He knows he's missed Candice. Suspects she waited till he was cleaning up to leave.

It's been like this for a while. Since her mother died, yes, but probably even before that. Sometimes, Candice surprises Adrian with an offer of peace. Like taking him out to dinner a few weeks back where everything seemed easy, and for one evening it was relaxed between them, just like when they first met. But it was only one evening. Things reverted to normal as soon as he told her about moving to casual rates. She yelled, and he took it, and resented her once again for demanding such a huge say in his life while she excluded him from her decisions. Like when she unilaterally chose to abandon their efforts at a family.

Her car turns over, whines as it reverses out onto the street, then gurgles as she drives away. He listens until the sound fades. He sighs, dries his hands.

Back in the kitchen, on his way to the fridge, he spies his computer and the USB lying next to it. He stops, wonders. Maybe if he's careful he can take a quick peek. He'll disconnect the wifi, avoid execute files. Maybe if he does that there will be no risk of infection. Not that he really knows, but he's curious, and he's working hard to justify opening it up.

"Fuck it," he says. He pulls out one of the kitchen stools, sits at the bench. He starts up the computer, sticks the USB in the drive.

There's one file. A video file. Can a video file contain malware? He doesn't know. Probably. He runs his antivirus software, it comes up clean. He opens the file.

A widescreen shot of a drover's hut. It's made of old, grey wood, solidly built. The sort of cabin he'd expect to find in the middle of a national park, but this one is set on a large block of cleared land, a modern road in the foreground, paddocks surrounding it filled with yellow flowers that he suspects are canola. In the distance, movement. Maybe sheep grazing? He can't quite tell. He watches for a while. Nothing changes. He thinks the hut is enclosed by fencing, but the camera shot is not close and it's difficult to tell.

It takes him a while to realise the video is not silent. There's a low drone, like traffic, but a long way away. He increases the volume, and it comes a little stronger, but he can't place exactly what it is. Occasionally, the drone is usurped by a short song from a bird offscreen. But never for long. Soon enough, that hum is back. And all the while the shot of the hut remains the same. Nothing changes. Nothing happens.

Impatient, he scrolls further forward in the video, moving halfway in. Still no change. Just the hut, the paddocks, the empty black road, the drone. He skips to the end. One hour and thirteen minutes and it's the same scene. Although perhaps the day is a little brighter, a result of the sun rising slowly.

He closes the video, stares at his computer screen, unsure what to make of it. He can't imagine why someone would leave this for him, or what he's supposed to do with it.

He runs the antivirus program again. Nothing. He sighs, closes the laptop, then orders takeout without checking the fridge.

He doesn't hear Candice come in. His laptop is connected to the flat screen television in the lounge room. Adrian sits close, on the soft carpet, peering up. He's about halfway through the video, the fifth time he's watched it. He's staring intently at the small window on the left side of the hut. It's covered by a lace curtain, but soon a shadow will pass behind it. Yes, there.

"What are you watching?" Candice asks. Her words sound dull, diluted, like he's sitting at the bottom of a pool looking up at people talking on the deck.

"Huh," he says, turning to find her standing at the edge of the room in a black dress, her hair tied back, a little eyeshadow, lipstick, no wedding band. He glances back at the screen, and the cabin. The shadow is gone.

He feels like he was on the verge of understanding something. That he could nearly see over the crest, but now it's gone. He blinks. His eyes are sore.

"Someone sent me this video in the mail," he says, as if that explains things.

"Who?" Candice asks. She moves into the room, tosses her handbag onto the coffee table. The thud of it makes Adrian jump. He closes his eyes, enjoys the momentary relief it provides. Opens them, glances at the screen, then Candice.

"Don't know. It was anonymous. But the envelope had my name on it, and this USB inside." He gestures to the laptop, his eyes finding the small white protrusion from its side. He realises how silly it sounds. He expects admonishment, but he should know by now that Candice doesn't do predictable.

"Ooh, I read about something like this on Facebook," she says. She sits next to him, folds her legs to the side, props on an outstretched arm. It's the closest they've been for a while. He can't help but smell her—lavender soap, a dash of musky perfume, something else. Aftershave? Sweat? He frowns.

"Facebook?" he says. There's more he wants to say, to ask, but words escape him.

"Yeah, it's a game. Friends nominate you, and this company sends out these videos. You're supposed to work it out."

"Work what out?" he asks, glancing at the screen. This close it looks pixelated, grainy. The drone from the video is prevalent, setting his teeth on edge.

"I don't know exactly. If I did, it wouldn't be as fun, would it? Maybe where this cabin is, what's important about it? It might be like geocaching. You know, follow the coordinates, find the treasure, take something to prove you found it, leave something for the next person."

"Oh." The shot has definitely gotten brighter and the shadows shorter. Like the sun is directly overhead. Here comes the bird again, wait, yes there. A warble. A measure of music, then silence. "Who'd sign me up for this?"

Candice laughs. "I would have done it if I'd thought of it. This could be good for you. Get you out of the house. You're always stuck in that garage."

He swallows, looks at her watching the TV screen.

"Okay, I need a shower, then I'm going to bed. I've got an early meeting tomorrow," she says.

She places a hand on his shoulder, pushes as she rises to her feet. She kisses him on the top of his head, then disappears from the room and heads toward the back of the house.

She didn't say anything about her night, he realises. She has a knack of asking questions, and yet she gives away very little nowadays. Maybe it's always been like this. Maybe he doesn't know much about her at all. Only what she wants him to know.

He stops the video, stares at the blank TV screen. Candice encouraging him to keep going has suddenly put a damper on the exercise. And yet he doesn't want to go to bed. Not yet. He'd prefer to slip into the sheets when Candice is asleep. Like he has most nights since her mother died.

It's part guilt, part anger that she never talked to him after, that she sank into herself for so long before reappearing as if nothing had changed. Even though she did change. She decided to stop trying for a family. She didn't even ask him if that was okay.

He's afraid if he says anything about how much that hurt, it'll lead to them both telling each other what they really feel. That he'll say the words he'll never be able to take back. He doesn't want that. Doesn't want to risk it all ending. So, he avoids her instead.

He finds himself replaying the video, starting from the beginning again.

They'd been going out for a couple of weeks when they ended up parked down by the main beach late one night (or was it early one morning?) smoking weed in his ancient Ford Escort. Windows down, sea breeze rustling their hair. He was captivated by hers, which undulated like the dark waves he couldn't see, but could hear, and that he imagined were pounding the sand relentlessly somewhere in that darkness beyond his front windshield.

He was too stoned to drive. He might have said something to that effect, because she offered. Demanded it, even. Like it was a dare.

"Nuh, you'll wreck my pride and joy," he'd said, grinning around the blunt. He suddenly wondered what he'd do if a cop rolled by and shone a torch on the rust bucket with the windows down, smoke wafting out.

"Come on, don't be a wuss." She liked to needle him. He liked to let her. A vaccination from boredom.

He passed her the last of the joint, and she sucked it down to the nib, the flame glowing orange in the dark, lighting just enough of her lips for him to imagine kissing her again.

She tossed the butt, held the smoke in her lungs, motioned for the keys. He relented. Searched his pockets for them, couldn't find them. Looked on the floor. She exhaled with a rush, coughed, regained composure.

"They're in the ignition, you half-baked fuckwit," she said, laughing. His eyes fell to the steering column, saw the glint of metal. He laughed too.

"Come on. Scooch."

"You'll be careful?" he asked.

"Hell no," she said. The look in her eyes both excited and terrified him. He opened the door, got out and circled around the back as she slid across the console into the driver's seat.

He'd barely got his seatbelt on when she jammed the car into reverse and gunned it backward, braking late.

"Jesus," he yelped.

"Oh, you ain't seen nothing yet." She put it in drive, hit the accelerator.

The car wasn't powerful, but she extracted all of what it had, careering up and down hilly streets, the wind rushing inside, her manic laughter surrounding him. He held onto the dash, white fingertips boring marks into the vinyl.

He must have told her to slow down twenty times, moving from requests to pleading. She didn't listen.

At some point, the car rocketed past the city limits, down a road he didn't know, trees close and leaning in. The weak lights on his car did little to illuminate the dark countryside.

"Candice, stop. Stop now," he ordered. She didn't listen. Just kept going. "Now, or I stop us. This is crazy," he implored. She never even glanced at him, just kept grinning, driving into the dark tunnel of trees.

He later blamed the pot for the rash decision. She did too. But there was something else there too. He didn't like losing control.

He wrenched hard on the parking brake.

The car screamed; Candice might have as well. The back tyres locked and sent smoke into the air, as the car fishtailed across the bitumen. It must have put Candice off her game because at the last moment she jerked the wheel, and the car spun, slid off the road, and ended up facing back the way they'd come. They'd been lucky. It had pulled up a few feet shy of a large gum tree, angled up on an embankment. Adrian could smell sap, eucalyptus, burnt rubber.

In the aftermath, the world was silent outside, harsh breathing inside. Candice still gripped the wheel tightly, hunched, staring out the windscreen into the sickly yellow beams of the headlights.

She turned slowly, looked at him. He felt his face grow hot. He shrugged, his effort at an apology.

"You crazy son of a bitch," she said, so quietly he almost didn't hear her. To his surprise she grabbed his shirt and pulled him hard into a kiss. Then her hands were on his chest, his stomach, undoing the zip of his pants.

He knew that, whatever this was, it was dangerous. He let it happen anyway.

He tells himself he no longer needs Candice's approval, but he's not sure that's true. Would he have really volunteered to take the new number thirty-three bus route if she hadn't judged him the other day? Passively of course, nothing said directly. But he had a toe in the water, felt the temperature change, and now he's reacted.

No one else wanted the route because it meanders through the new estates on the outskirts of the city. Which are a long way from his home, and the depot. A long way from everything, really. Nevertheless, he finds the drive pleasant.

This far out, most people use cars, so passengers are few, and mostly polite elderly people making trips to the shops. The bus is new. It has that new-car smell, laced with a hint of diesel. It's cool, the air conditioner cranked high.

The bus groans as he slows for a roundabout (they're everywhere in these new suburbs). He leans in his seat as he swings out onto it. The bus roars as he exits, as he accelerates again, moves up through the gears.

His only passenger hits the stop button, which dings, and he drifts to a stop beside the next bus shelter. The old man steps off. No one boards. He drives the empty bus away.

He turns onto Peterman Drive, which runs along the edge of the new estates. A long, double lane road with half-built houses on the left, and paddocks marked for future subdivision on the right. He speeds up to 80, the limit out here, enjoys the feel of the heavy machine powering over the bitumen.

That's when he sees it: the hut from the USB, alone amongst a field of yellow canola.

A cool sweat emerges upon his forehead. He feels weak, and anxious. He can't help but stop.

He doesn't screech on the brakes or swing the steering wheel wildly; he's an experienced bus driver. He checks his mirrors, signals, pulls to the left, gently riding the brakes until he rolls to a smooth stop. The doors open with a hiss, hot air spilling into the cab momentarily neutralising the effects of the air conditioner. He sits in his seat for a beat, thinking, then he puts the hazard lights on, jumps out.

He walks around the back of the bus. A burst of hot air rushes over him as a car races by. Then it's just him, the bus still idling, gurgling away, and the hut in the middle of the paddock.

It's a couple of hundred metres back from the road, surrounded by a high, chain-link fence. Weeds have grown up around it, a few stray canola plants mixed in. There're no power lines, no telephone lines. The hut doesn't look like it belongs in its current location. It must have been moved. He wonders if it has heritage status. That might explain the fencing.

He removes his phone, takes a couple of photos, then, on a whim, he records a short video. About thirty seconds. When he's done, he plays it back. It's the sound that strikes him. The sound of his bus. It comes through his phone speakers tinny, small, but so familiar it sets the hairs on his arms on end. The gurgle of his bus through his phone sounds like the low drone that soundtracks the video on the USB.

He swallows, appraises the hut again. He glances at the bus, at his phone, sees the time. He's been here ten minutes. He'll be in the shit if he doesn't get back on his route soon.

He takes one last look, puts his phone away and climbs back on board. He's suddenly certain he's not alone, that a passenger, way up back, has been watching him. He glances in the mirror hurriedly, but there's no one there. He shudders, checks his side mirrors, eases the bus back out onto the road. As he drives, he can't shake the feeling that he's being watched.

Adrian sits at the kitchen bench, hunched over his computer. He doesn't realise Candice is close until he feels her hand caress his shoulder. He jerks upright, feels her breath against his cheek.

"This again. It's really got you in, hasn't it? Any luck?"

He half turns, and she's right there. He can smell her, feel her warmth. If she notices his discomfort, she doesn't let on. She's focussed on the video.

"This isn't from the USB. I took it this afternoon with my phone," he says.

"Your phone?" She turns toward him. They're close. Their lips barely a couple of inches apart. An instinct directs him to close the distance, kiss her. Another makes him turn away. He looks at the screen again without really seeing it. His other senses are focussed on her, where his eyes want to be. Her heat, the feel of her hand resting on his shoulder, the scent of lavender soap, the soft sound of her breathing. He doesn't know why she makes him nervous these days. He's a school kid with a first crush. A girl he likes, but says he doesn't.

"I'm driving a new route—"

"Really," she interrupts. "Good for you." She doesn't seem afflicted with his hesitancy. She kisses him on the cheek, casually throws an arm around him. He tries not to recoil—they've barely touched in God knows how long. His fault, mostly. Because he's worried he's not good enough. Because he didn't live up to her expectations. Because he stopped her seeing her dying mother and how do you forgive something like that? He's punishing himself, he knows. But if he doesn't, wouldn't she?

"It's out on the other side of the city where Sunder Estates is going up. Right toward the backend of the route, I find this hut. I had to stop and take a couple of shots."

"And a video."

"Yeah."

She releases him, sits on the stool next to him, leans into his space to get a closer look. The video is paused, but she hits play. He watches with her. The hut. His eyes focus on the left window. He wonders if she sees it. The subtle movement in the curtain. Not brushed aside, but pressed, like someone has leaned on it, pushed it up against the window. And all the while there's the gurgling drone of his idling bus, transformed somehow into something that burrows into his teeth.

"It looks so similar to what you were watching the other night."

And sounds the same, he thinks, but doesn't say.

"Did you go in? What's inside?" she asks.

"I was working. I couldn't." He glances at her and is pleased when she doesn't shoot him a disapproving glare.

"Okay. Well, when are we going to check it out?" she asks, regarding him with a cocked eyebrow and a smirk.

"We?"

"Why not? Can't let you have all the fun."

He suddenly feels young again. An adventure. They used to go everywhere together and say it was an adventure. Even when it wasn't. Shopping. The beach. A day trip to nowhere. A weekend away. She made it adventurous. She'd make something up, do something stupid, bring along some dope or grog, and he enjoyed it, mostly. And the little part of him that didn't, the times she made him nervous or fearful, well, he felt alive, at least. Unlike this novocaine existence he's leading now.

"Okay. Yes," he says, like he's just made up his mind. "Let's do it together. Find out what the hell this thing is all about. How about tomorrow?"

She makes a clicking sound with her tongue and teeth. An 'I'd like to but can't', sound, and instantly he feels the adrenaline leak from his system, his shoulders slump.

"Tomorrow is packed with client meetings," she says.

"I understand," he jumps in quickly. "They're more important." Always are, he thinks. "Maybe some other time."

The short video has ended. He reaches out and closes the laptop, rises from the stool.

"Where are you going?"

"Garage," he says. He sees that she knows that he's getting up to leave her. To be by himself, where he can keep his hands and mind busy over nothing important.

"Fuck it," she says stopping him. He looks back. "No, I'm in. I'll blow off my four o'clock appointment. But be ready to go as soon as I get home, okay? I want to check it out before it gets dark."

He finds himself grinning like a kid who's been told it's Christmas tomorrow. He nods. "Four it is."

They went to Thailand after Candice graduated. A last hurrah before she started work as an accountant.

Ostensibly, he was still studying, but he couldn't settle. He moved through a variety of unrelated subjects hoping something would stick. He quite enjoyed astrophysics, but Candice convinced him there was no future in it. So, he enrolled in marketing. A future she could see herself in when they got back to Australia.

For the first week in Thailand, they holed up in a backpacker dive on Khao San Road, Bangkok. Each day seemed hotter than the last. Smog and sweat, the stench of baked bitumen, exhaust, and ripe, tropical fruit. Head in a constant haze, hungover from the night before, the smell of alcohol sweating from his pores. Of a night they'd walk the strip, drink and eat at little plastic tables that appeared on the street at dusk. Drink some more.

They'd find somewhere to dance, make chit chat with fellow backpackers, drink. Finish the night with a feed of cheap street food, a bottle of water from the 24 hour Seven Eleven, fuck, pass out.

On the second to last day in Bangkok, they spent the day on the roof of the hostel. There was a pool up there, umbrellas, an outdoor bar. It was no tropical oasis. Mostly baking cement, thick smog that obscured the view of the city. The pool water was more soup warm than refreshing.

They were both laying on deck chairs, two large bottles of Singha beer on the table between them. Candice might have been reading something, but he wasn't. He was staring up into that half gloom that obscured the sun. A shadow passed over him, and when he looked, he found a pale, red headed girl looking at them both.

"Hi," she said, an Australian accent. "This seat taken?" she asked, gesturing to the empty chair beside Candice.

"Nope, all yours," Candice answered, looking up from her book.

"Thanks so much," she said. She spread a towel over the hot plastic surface, then lay down. She removed a cotton top to expose green swimmers and freckled, white skin. "My boyfriend and I just got in, and I'm excited. You guys been here long?" she asked. She began to lather sunscreen on her arms and neck. Adrian didn't really want to chat. He felt like shit from the night before, hence the beer. His thinking was that if he could get drunk again, his body would be tricked into forgetting his hangover.

"Nearly a week," Candice said. She placed her book face down. "We're heading to Ko Tao tomorrow evening. We're going to do some diving."

"That sounds amazing," the girl said, genuine excitement in her voice. "I haven't heard of Ko Tao. Is it nice?"

"Hope so," Candice responded. She hesitated, then rose a little and extended a hand. "I'm Candice, and this is my partner, Adrian."

Adrian took the signal, half rose, waved. "Hey," he mumbled, before slumping back onto his chair.

"Nice to meet you both. I'm Taylor."

Taylor and Candice quickly eased into a conversation as if they'd known each other for years. Adrian was glad they didn't try to involve him. He followed for a little while, but then allowed their words to dissolve into meaningless sounds. They washed over him like waves until he dozed in the chair.

When he woke it was dusk, and there was a big guy perched on the end of Taylor's deck chair. Tall, well built, crewcut, like an army brat.

"Rise and shine," Candice said. "This is Mike."

Adrian reached for his beer, took a sip, found it hot. Mike leaned across Candice, extended a meaty hand. Adrian took it, uncomfortable with the way he veered into Candice's space, skin touching skin.

"Hey," Adrian said, pumping his hand once, releasing him. He was glad to watch Mike pull away from Candice again.

"Mike and Taylor were going to check out Soi Cowboy. Want to go?"

Adrian snorted a laugh. "The stripper district?"

"Yeah, it'll be fun," Candice said.

Adrian didn't think it sounded much fun. It sounded odd. But he wasn't going to argue in front of Candice's new friends. "I guess," he said.

When they went later that evening, he was surprised to find it wasn't as bad as he thought it would be. Mike ended up being pretty decent. The bar they chose was topless, but it was too early in the evening for any of the crazy shit that Adrian was worried would make everyone feel uncomfortable. And most importantly, the place was air conditioned, which was a huge relief after six days of suffocating heat.

Out on the streets he'd seen and fed a baby elephant. With traditional music blaring from speakers around him, he'd bought bananas from the handler. He couldn't help but wonder if the elephant was maltreated. Probably. And he felt guilty. Yet he enjoyed giving them to the calf, hoping they provided some joy for it, at least in that moment.

Candice sidled up to him, drawing his attention from Mike, who'd been talking about football.

"You having fun?"

"Yeah," he said, grinning. "I am, actually. They're nice people. Sorry about earlier, I—"

"Was hungover, I understand. We're all good now, right?"

"Of course."

"You know I love you," she whispered, and while it wasn't the first time she'd said it, it made him tingle in his belly, his chest, his balls.

"I love you too," he said, leaning in. She kissed him on the cheek, then the mouth, pulled back, leaned into his ear again.

"Taylor suggested we swap partners tonight. What do you think?"

Adrian jerked back like he'd been slapped. He felt a smirk on his lips, but then it fell as he saw the serious look on Candice's face. He glanced at Mike, his arm around Taylor, watching him and Candice. They were waiting for him, he saw.

"What? I..." His head was spinning. He licked his lips, but couldn't seem to wet them. He felt trapped, lost. He suddenly wanted to go home.

Candice draped two arms around his neck, pulled him close. "We don't have to," she whispered into his ear. "Of course we don't. But... I've never done anything like that. I don't think you have either. We're young. We have our whole lives together..." she left the thought hanging.

He regarded Taylor again. It was like he was seeing her through fresh eyes. She was attractive, in her way. Lithe, athletic. Yet did that matter? He didn't know. He looked at Mike. He didn't like the thought of that huge body held up over Candice.

"You can say no," she said, as if reading his mind. "I won't mind."

But was that true?

Before he could answer, the bargirl arrived with the tequila shots Mike had ordered. He grabbed one quickly and threw it back, grimacing as it burned his throat.

"And after?" he said.

"After, we go back to normal. This is an overseas thing. A Thailand thing."

"What stays in Thailand," he muttered, and she chuckled, nodded. He sighed. "I'll need a few more of these," he said, holding up the empty shot glass, waggling it.

She kissed him again. Long, passionate. But he felt something leak from him. Something he wasn't sure he'd get back.

He sits in the passenger seat staring out the window as the city falls away behind them. He knows where to go, but Candice insists on following the GPS.

He wonders who all of these people are that have decided to pitch houses on flat ground miles from the city. He realises his house was probably like this once. Until suburbs grew around it, leaving him feeling entitled to judge others who had to settle further out.

The car slows, and he shakes himself from his stupor. Candice has turned onto Peterman Drive, houses on the left, paddocks on the right. She accelerates, and soon he sees the cabin nestled amongst the canola crop, the chain link fence around it.

He looked up cabins like this on his computer and found a number of images of huts in the snowy mountains. Alpine cabins used by drovers, or people who'd become lost. A shared, public resource. Temporary protection against cold winter nights, death.

Perhaps this cabin was the same, once. Its odd location only because the forest that once surrounded it has long been cleared, the surrounding country terraformed into arable land. Now, even that has been encroached upon by suburban sprawl.

Gravel crunches under the wheels of the car as Candice eases onto the verge. Adrian feels the seatbelt grip his chest as Candice brakes more harshly than she intended. She cuts the engine, silencing the tick, tick, tick of the indicator and the buzz of the engine. It's abruptly silent. Invasively quiet. Not another car to be seen or heard on this stretch of new road that looks designed for back-to-back traffic. Future planning at work, Adrian thinks.

"Well," Candice says, the edge of her lips turned up in an excited smile. "What now?"

If he's honest, he hasn't thought that through. That chain link fence looks larger than he remembers. "I guess we go check it out."

They exit the car, check the road for non-existent traffic, cross together. Adrian notices a chorus of buzzing that he presumes is locusts in the canola plants.

The first hurdle is easy enough. A wire fence set a few metres back from the road. Star pickets and three strands of wire. He pulls the top wire up taut so that Candice can duck, and slide through the gap he's made. Then he pushes the same wire down hard, so he can step over it and onto the uneven ground of the paddock. There are depressions in the ground like livestock trod through here recently. Depressions hidden amongst the vibrant green plants, the golden canola flowers.

"Watch your step," he says, as he leads the way, pushing a path through the flora, trying not to crush too much of the crop.

It doesn't take long to reach the chain link fence. He places a hand on it, clawing his fingers through the hexagonal holes. He glances back the way he's come, sees Candice with eyes downcast on the path ahead, sees the thin trail they've cut through the canola. It's obvious that they are the first people to come out to this cabin in a while, at least since the crop matured. It makes him wonder if the maker of the video wanted him to come out here after all.

Candice catches up, places a hand on his shoulder. "How do we get in?"

He doesn't know, so he doesn't reply. He should have brought some pliers to cut the fence. Although would he have done that? That's surely a crime. He spies a gate along the east side, points. "Maybe we try that."

"Good work, Sherlock," Candice says. She goes past him toward the gate.

Adrian hesitates, surveys the rest of the boundary. He wonders again about the fence. If this were a heritage site, shouldn't it have a sign? Something advising of the significance of this construction, why it is being protected, how it is being restored? But he sees nothing like that. He shakes the thought, follows Candice.

The gate is chained, padlocked. But when he rattles it, he sees that there is plenty of flex. He pushes until the gate strains against the chain, and Candice gives a little joyous yelp as she drops to hands and knees and, awkwardly, squeezes through the gap at the bottom. Once through, she holds the gate for him. It's a tighter fit for him. A stray piece of wire tears his shirt and draws blood from his arm, but he gets through.

Candice moves toward the front door. Adrian glances back at the road, checks they are alone. They are. No cars in sight, no people. Yet he feels watched. He surveys the hut, no cameras. He's just on edge about trespassing, he thinks. He follows Candice up onto the porch where she waits by the door.

"Shall I do the honours?" she asks. "Or you?"

"You do it," he says. He expects it to be locked, but the old, rusted, metal handle turns smoothly, and the wooden door swings open silently. A waft of stale air hits him. A smell of wood, and dust.

It's darker inside, cooler. It takes a few seconds for Adrian's eyes to adjust. He steps over the threshold.

It's small, one room, and oddly furnished. Adrian's eyes are drawn to the faded pink recliner sitting on a modern, floral rug. An old, portable television, rabbit ears akimbo, is set on a high table in front of the chair. There's something odd about the TV. There's a weird silver box attached to the left side, which looks homemade.

Next to the recliner is a side table, a book set on top at an odd angle, as if someone tossed it there casually after reading.

The rest of the room is more predictable. On the far side is a wood stove made of thick, black metal, and a small woodpile. There's a kitchen bench and metal sink nearby, and a table made from an old, thick stump. On the right, pressed up against the wall, a single bed frame, no mattress, springs rusted.

"Wow," Candice says quietly as she eases past Adrian and moves to the kitchenette. She squats down and opens the stove, which squeaks.

Adrian's eyes are drawn to the recliner, to the television. He moves closer, appraises the book on the table: *Infinite Possibilities: Navigating the Multiverse.* A glance toward Candice shows her still investigating the kitchen. He slumps into the recliner, picks up the book.

There's a clicking sound. He looks up to see the television warming up. The screen clarifies into an image of a person's head and neck. A very familiar head and neck. His head and neck.

Adrian's heart beats harder, and he feels a sensation in his bowels like someone squeezing. He feels like he's falling.

The man on the screen is not exactly like him, he realises. This version wears glasses, is a little thicker around the neck, a little greyer at the temples. And yet the resemblance is uncanny. It's like staring long and hard at your own reflection in the mirror until you begin to really take in the details of your skin, until familiar images begin to appear strange.

Other Adrian, he thinks.

Other Adrian opens his mouth to speak, but then Candice drops an old frypan, which clangs loudly. Other Adrian's eyes behind the thick glasses dart somewhere to Adrian's left as if he can, impossibly, see into this room. As if he has just heard that clang, and has noticed Candice.

Other Adrian looks back at Adrian, scowls, shakes his head ever so slightly, then the image is gone, the screen black again.

Adrian can't move. He stares at the blank screen, can just make out a distorted reflection of himself. He tries to rationalise what he just saw, but can't. It's like when he was a kid and took apart his watch to understand how it worked, but couldn't put it back together again.

He jumps when Candice touches his shoulder. "Are you just chilling out or something?" she says, snorting a laugh. "Find any clues?"

Clues? He's not sure. He found something. "Did you..." he points at the television.

"What?"

"You didn't..." he tries again, still staring at the blank screen. "I saw... I found..."

"What?" she says, confused. He understands that she missed it.

He recalls Other Adrian scowling, the shake of the head, and intuits that the image wasn't meant for her. He did something wrong bringing her here. Perhaps he did something wrong in coming here himself. He tears his eyes from the screen, glances at the book he's holding. It feels heavy in his hands.

Candice takes it from him, looks at it. A smile slowly materialises on her face. "This is neat," she says. "Your next clue, I'd say."

"A clue?"

"You didn't notice?"

"What?"

She holds the book out toward him. He reads the title again. He doesn't understand. His face bunches, and he sees that Candice sees he isn't following.

"You're focusing on the wrong thing," she says, pointing toward the bottom of the book cover. "Apparently, this book was written by you."

"Infinite Possibilities" continues in next month's issue.
See part I of Michael Gardner's story "Infinite Possibilities" online at
Metaphorosis.
If you liked it, leave a comment. Authors love that!
Remember to subscribe to our e-mail updates so you'll know when
new stories are posted.

About the story

Before I wrote "Infinite Possibilities", I'd read a horror short story that told its tale by describing a series of strange videos. While horror involving videos or photos is not new, I thought the way the story had been done was quite fresh. It was set up as a weird, ambiguous mystery. That got me thinking of my own mystery video, and at some point, I settled on the idea that it should be of an old cabin, like those sometimes found in Australia's alpine state forests.

I'm not quite sure when I decided to mix the cabin video with parallel worlds. But my mind does wander to the idea of parallel worlds often, usually to wonder about what unexpected, horrible things they might contain. For this story, I began to like the idea of my protagonist, Adrian, discovering multiple worlds that contained multiple versions of himself—many like him, but some that had ulterior motives.

The part of the story that evolved most as I wrote was the relationship between Candice and Adrian. I didn't start off thinking their relationship would be strained. In fact, close to the first thing I wrote was their first meeting at the night club. I think that scene could just have easily led to a couple that doted on each other and never had any issues. However, something about the scene made me think these people were opposites, which clearly led to the spark between them, but also conflict. This showed up more and more in the story as I went.

This novella is the longest story I've ever written. It merged two ideas that I thought were interesting, but weird, and a couple of characters I really came to love. I'm glad it found a home with Metaphorosis.

A question for the author

Q: What tools do you write with?

A: The obvious tools are my laptop and Microsoft Word. I'm not much of a pen and paper person. For starters, my handwriting is atrocious, so I often can't read what I've written a few days later.

I'm also not much of a plotter. I've met a few plotters recently and have been impressed with the tools they use. Scrivener for detailed outlining and planning, spreadsheets, multiple character summaries, scene descriptions, etc. It's not that I don't plan at all, but it's mostly done in my head. A key concept, an idea of the ending, a character or two. When I have attempted to write down plans or character descriptions in the past, I find I'm writing the story. So, I tend to just keep going and write it.

The downside of being a pantser is I do multiple, extensive edits and re-writes of my first drafts. Well, some might call it a downside, but I weirdly enjoy editing. Add in a bit of internet research, draw on some lived experiences, a grammar and spell check, and that's about it for my writing tools.

About the author

Michael Gardner is a writer of fantasy and horror who masquerades as an economist by day. His work has appeared in *Writers of the Future Volume 36, Aurealis, Bourbon Penn,* and *Metaphorosis*. He is also a three-time finalist for the Aurealis Awards. You can find out more about Michael and his work at: www.michael-s-gardner.com

October

Problems of the Flesh

Hamilton Perez

It was the month of the apocalypse, and I'd come home to a house of shadows and gloom. The curtains and blinds were all shut, barring any light except what leaked through the door. The air smelled like spoiled fast food. No sound came from within—not his labored breath from the recliner, not even his favorite sitcom laughing hysterically at itself.

That was the first time I doubted.

Not that there hadn't been moments before then. Moments that didn't feel right, I guess, despite having every assurance they would be—*they were*—from the one person who really could say definitively. But it was coming home to darkness that made me wonder if things weren't as they should be. Weren't as promised.

"My Lord …?" I called, but I was met with the same silence, the same dark. *That's fine*, I assured myself, arms shaking, chest tight. *Everything's fine* … "Lord Grivvux?" I tried again, my voice thin as prayer.

Something crashed across the living room floor, and *"Dammit! Is that you?"* his voice called from the black.

Only then did I remember to breathe, though it came out in ragged, uncertain laughter.

The Supreme Lord—Maker, Keeper, Destroyer of Worlds—was alright.

"Yes, my Lord!" I said, fumbling with the bags and keys as I stepped inside, grinning with dumb relief. "It is I, your faithful servant—"

"Sam, please," the Lord God cut me off. "You really don't need to go on like that. Once you've helped your god in and out of the tub, I'd say you're on a more familiar basis." The recliner groaned as he rose to meet me.

"Ah! Yes! Of course!" I said awkwardly, kicking the door shut behind me. "Forgive me, King of Kings, Lord Grivvux of the Permafire."

"It's fine, Sam … And again, *Grux* will be fine."

"*Grux* …" I said, trying on the word, but it still didn't feel right. Thousands of years ago, it was Grivvux—not *Grux*—who was worshiped all across Sumer. The fatted calf was venerated and slain at the Altar of Grivvux, not *Grux.* When our priests and acolytes were seduced by other gods, the family order kept faith with Grivvux, not *Grux.* "I, uh, like it."

I shuffled past him, trying not to catch the sour smell of his skin. No matter how hard I scrubbed, he always smelled like unwashed feet. It was just one more thing to deal with since his long-prophesied return. There was no telling the cause of it all—if it was disbelief in the old powers, the unchecked metastasis of sin, or global warming—but the Lord God had taken human form and now he was, well, *too* human, I guess …

"They had fresh lamb today!" I called over my shoulder.

"How fresh?" he asked, following behind me, his rough soles scratching the hardwood.

"Well, it's not still kicking …"

"Ah …"

Was that disappointment? I wondered, making my way to the kitchen blindly and reaching for the light.

"Please don't—"

The world flashed before I heard him. The Lord God shielded himself with his arm, revealing skin littered with sores. I killed the light, and then we just stood there, embarrassed in the dark.

"Is that because of me?" I finally asked.

"It's best you try not to think about it," he said, but I was already tallying up the day's sins. *I flipped off the Mercedes that cut me off. I lied to the beggar asking for change. I snagged the last box of fiber supplements from an old woman.*

"Did you get the ceremonial robes?" he asked.

"Um, yes, *well* …" I began sorting through plastic bags, searching by feel. "Linnamin's was having a sale." I withdrew two neatly-folded robes. They were black, but presently so was everything.

"It doesn't matter where they came from, Sam." The Lord God walked across the kitchen and turned on the patio light, letting in just enough for us to see by. "So long as we take this seriously."

I looked doubtfully at the mass-produced bathrobes.

Lord Grivvux returned to examine one, brushing it softly with his rough hands. "These will do fine …" he said, pressing the robe against his cheek as though some secret magic were sewn into its design, some hope only the righteous and wise could discern.

"They have a three hundred thread count ..." I said.

That night, we knelt before the fireplace in our ceremonial bathrobes, the fire eating the logs with a crackle and spark that sounded like laughter.

"What's this supposed to do again?" I asked, uncertainly.

"It's a minor restoration spell, Sam. Nothing to be apprehensive about. We're simply appealing to the powers beyond to grant me a greater form, one that isn't in need of such maintenance. One that might inspire a bit more *awe* ..."

"Oh."

Lord Grivvux sensed my doubt and clarified, "So I can better guard against the Last End, Sam."

"Yes, of course. The Big Wet One."

"What?"

"Oh, sorry, nothing. That's just what Mom used to call the Final Flood. Sort of a joke, really. I guess that's not appropriate anymore ..."

He said nothing and continued the preparations.

It was Mom who first taught me the old faith: the rituals, spells, and prophecies. She was pretty transparent about it being what soured her marriage, why Dad ran off before I was born. *It's okay, Samuel,* she'd told me, *Lord Grivvux of the Permafire is your true Father, as he is for all.* She always believed the Lord had big plans for me, but I doubt even she dreamed I'd be the Chosen One to herald our Lord before the end.

Granted, it's not like there were a lot of runners-up.

After Mom passed, I became the last of our order—a lonely ember cooling in the ash. The Grivvuxian Acolytes once comprised thousands, but believers dropped off every year the Lord did not return. You could hardly blame them. Some had witnessed the rise of new gods and queer religions, each promising the same things: peace, prosperity, the end of the world.

Me, I waited forty-three years for the one true God to return— to realize my purpose, or learn if I even had one. So I did what most people do while they wait for things to happen.

I got a job. I paid my bills. I did my time.

It was the planetary alignment that changed all that. Before then, the signs were already rolling in, but I was too blind or stubborn to see them. Toads croaked outside my window—*GRIVV-*

ux ... GRIVV-ux ... The words *He doth come* appeared while making dinner, materializing out of noodles, eggs, or ground beef.

But the planets aligning was the promised sign—they told me when Lord Grivvux was coming, and where he would be. I didn't even know it was happening until an overzealous intern cornered me in the breakroom with it, hoping to initiate some early networking through what was surely to him just an interesting fact.

"Pretty neat, huh? I'm Jimmy—Jim—James!" he stammered nervously before thrusting forth a rigid hand.

"I have to go!" I dropped my coffee and ran to check if what he told me was true, and sure enough, the end was nigh.

That was the last time I stepped foot in that office. An eighteen-year corporate climb abandoned for a higher purpose. *For the greater good.* And for all I know my coffee is still puddled on the breakroom floor and *Jimmy-Jim-James* is running the place.

Things didn't turn out quite like I imagined, though.

"It is ready," said the Lord God solemnly. "First, the mustard seeds, for they contain the Kingdoms of Heaven."

Amongst the assorted ingredients, I found a small pouch. I poured the seeds into my palm and cast them into the fire. The flames took the seeds ungratefully, nipping at my hand.

"Next, Wolf's Claw."

I fumbled through bundles of herbs.

"It's the green one ... white hairs ..."

I found the spindly plant and threw it in. A white light flashed, revealing shadowy figures standing all around us, and when the light dissolved, they too were gone.

"Who were they?" I asked.

"The Watchers. Do not fret. Their presence is a good omen. Now the pennyroyal. Purple."

I had questions. I always had questions. I wasn't *supposed* to have questions though, so I kept my mouth shut, and withdrew a long string of purple bulbs and threw it over the blaze. The fire turned a lavender shade and burned so hot that sweat ran down my forehead and cheeks.

"Now for the mandrake, the one that looks like a—"

"Yeah, I'm familiar with this guy." I took the vaguely human-shaped root from the pile of spell components.

Lord Grivvux watched me, dumbfounded. "*You* know the mandrake?"

"Sort of. Just from Harry Potter." The root roused to life in my hand, gently unfurling its limbs like I'd woken it from a long, restful sleep.

Lord Grivvux narrowed his eyes, considering. "Harry Potter ... Is this some sorcerer that you know?"

"Ah, well, he's a wizard actually, but he's not really—"

Amazement washed over my God's face, a confluence of excitement and frustration, and I felt deeply that I'd done something wrong. "Sam, I wish you had spoken sooner! We should absolutely consult with this wizard before performing the ritual! This could be the break we've been waiting for!"

"No, no, he's like, a character," I fumbled. "In a story. Books. Movies. He isn't real ..."

"Oh," said the Lord God, blank-faced.

"Yeah ..."

The mandrake twisted and writhed in my hand.

"Well ..." said the King of Kings.

"Should we not—"

"Please, proceed," he said with a passive gesture.

A crease opened along the mandrake's head, wailing pitifully, *"Noooo ..."*

"Yikes!" I startled. "Is it speaking?"

"Begging," said Lord Grivvux simply, as if this were expected. A mere fact of the world. I thought he might still be bugged about Harry Potter.

"Why now?" I asked.

"Being eaten or burned or thrown away, it can handle. But to be sacrificed, to be turned over to the Darkness, that is another matter entirely."

"Oh."

"Indeed."

I went to toss it on the fire, but Lord Grivvux stopped me.

"No," he said. "The mandrake is blameless, completely without sin. It must choose to enter the flames. Otherwise the Watchers may not accept our offering."

A hundred questions rattled through my mind. Who were these *Watchers*? They couldn't be gods in their own right, for there was only one God, and Grivvux—not *Grux*—was his name. So what did it mean that they could refuse him? Did freewill really extend that far? I couldn't tell if that made my Lord more godly or less, but just then the fire's warmth began to wane. We were running out of time.

"Does it need convincing?" I asked, preparing my best speech about the salvation of many and the greater good.

"Not from you." Lord Grivvux took the mandrake and cradled it in his arms, whispering to it in some language I could not understand—some language soft and beautiful and profound.

Like a tamed infant, the mandrake grew calm. The Lord set it gently onto the hardwood floor, and with quiet dignity, the noble root stood up and marched steadfast into the fire. Fingers of violet flame wrapped around it, guiding it in until it was swallowed by light. My Lord God smiled, all worry wiped from his face. But behind the wisps of flame, shadows swung against smoke and stone. Somewhere in the fire, life crumbled woefully to ash.

Lord Grivvux leaned forward, closed his eyes, and blew out the fire like it was only a birthday candle. Maybe it was, I thought.

In the smoldering ash, small specks now glistened and shone.

"Draw forth a mustard seed," my Lord commanded.

I found a tiny kernel, bright as a star, and pinched it between my fingers.

"Here! Here!" said my Lord anxiously. I dropped the seed in the center of his palm, and he blew on it delicately, causing it to roll about, growing like a snowball until the mustard seed filled his palm. "Yes ... *yes* ..." said the Lord God as thin green shoots twisted out, branching into alien tendrils. "Come to me ..." Once they touched his cheek, they cast a brilliant light through his skin, until golden rays seeped from his every pore.

It's working ... I thought, amazed.

The image reminded me of when Mom would take me camping, how at the end of every ghost story, she'd put the flashlight in her mouth so her cheeks glowed amber, pink, and gold. Now it made me laugh with melancholy joy—the kind of joy that's known loss yet also knows that no one is ever lost forever.

The light spread through my Lord's body, until he positively *glowed* from scalp to toe, and where the tendril rest, the worn skin cracked like it was only a shell, revealing a golden cheek, golden eye, and golden brow hidden just beneath the surface.

It's true, I thought. *It's all true. It's all real* ... And no words can capture the unutterable joy of that moment. The joy of knowing I'd invested my heart well, that I'd been on the right path all along. The joy as full and ineffable as he was.

But my God blinked, or I did.

The tendril faltered, turned black, wilted to the floor. My king diminished, returned to his tired, frail form.

"What happened?" I asked.

Grivvux sighed. "Magic is a living thing, Sam ... and it has too long been neglected in this world."

He rose, defeated.

I was about to ask what was next, but he simply dropped the ceremonial bathrobe to the floor, revealing his scarred and red-cratered body, and walked silently to his room.

"We'll find the answer, my king!" I shouted after him. "Whatever it takes!"

The only response was the sound of his door shutting me out.

When I'd first found God, hunched and frail in an abandoned church, I'd thought: *That's about right. Not what I expected at all. That's what you want in a god.* So I guess I was willing to overlook what he said when I approached:

"Please don't. Just stay back. It's all wrong. Just let me go ..."

Growing up in a religious household, you think the hardest part of faith is wondering if you're wrong. If in those moments of raw need and vulnerability you're just talking to the wind. And if He isn't real, what is? What virtues or beauty have any significance if not handed down from above? The most frightening thing you can imagine is not the seven hells or the final flood, it's a world without value. Then you meet God face to face and know—*really know*—that we're not alone. There's someone out there. Someone listening. Someone giving purpose and meaning to all things.

You'd think it would be easier after that, but sometimes I missed the not knowing.

The morning after the ritual, I came home to find him on the back patio, talking to the birds. There were three of them: a blue jay, a robin, and a lowly pigeon, all perched side by side along the fence. They whistled and chirped, and Grivvux laughed and whistled back.

Soon more birds swooped in. A whole congregation. A murder —or is that only with crows? They lined the fence like springtime decorations. Their songs were no longer sweet melodies, but busy and discordant, too many voices speaking and disagreeing at once.

Then the lowly pigeon that was there all along stepped forward. It purred at Grivvux, who sighed and whistled back. I couldn't begin to guess what they were discussing, but at the end of it, the pigeon flew to his hand, nuzzling affectionately at his thumb and cooing a strange, sad sound. "Thank you, old friend," said Grivvux as he turned and brought the pigeon inside.

He nodded casually in my direction as he entered, and before I could ask how he was feeling, he tossed the pigeon down his throat like it was just a couple of aspirin. I sat there, mouth gaping, wide-eyed and dumb, while Grivvux leaned with one arm against the kitchen counter, gradually composing himself.

"They remember ..." he said at last, and turned to face me. "I think I feel better."

"Maybe that's the answer ..." I said. *"Birds!"*

Grivvux cringed and waved me off. "Sam, do you have any idea how many birds it would take to put me in just *fair* health?"

"It doesn't matter!" I protested. "Whatever it takes! It's for the greater good!"

"I appreciate your fervor. Did you get the pills?"

It was difficult taking a deity to the doctor. He didn't have a social security number, insurance, or credit cards. And he didn't get sick like people. He didn't get cancer or the flu. He got Despair and Disbelief, Exile and Oblivion. The silver lining is that those conditions have a lot of the same symptoms as the stuff people get, which is why I'd started bribing a pharmacist at the drugstore down the street.

"She wasn't working today," I said.

He nodded vaguely before gripping his stomach. "Maybe you should get her number," he said, bracing against the kitchen counter as a sudden wave of Dread doubled him over.

Generally speaking, bribes fall under the wide umbrella of sin. Granted, a lot of things do, but that doesn't warrant a hand wave, no matter who you are. Unless you're God, I guess, and you're really that desperate, and something really has to be done.

I mean, if the Lord gives his blessing, how can it be a sin?

I still don't know.

Early in his convalescence, Grivvux went into an all-night trance to find someone that could help us. I was never too keen on that idea. Wasn't I supposed to be the one to help? Wasn't that why I'd kept my whole life on hold, and then abandoned all I'd worked for once he finally showed? But when God says *Go for help*, you do not say, *My Lord, I'm right here!*

Her name was Arielle. She was working two jobs to afford the medical bills brought on by her husband's sudden diagnosis of stage-4 leukemia. I knew this before she told me, of course. Grivvux had searched for someone in need, someone desperate enough to help other desperate people. I suppose we were lucky that she happened to be a pharmacist.

Over the months, a sort of quiet camaraderie had developed between us. We were both trapped in our situations, unsure how to move forward, doing whatever we could to keep afloat. Sometimes I wondered if she dreamed what I dreamed—just running away, escaping the chains of duty, the chains of being chosen.

"How's he doing today?" she asked the morning after he ate a bird.

"Getting better some," I said, wondering if we'd have to find an ornithologist struggling to make ends meet. "It's hard to say, though ..."

"Ah, I'm sorry, hon. I know how it is." She rubbed at her ring like a nervous tic.

"How are you holding up?" I asked.

"Ah ..." she said wistfully, lost in thought. "When I left this morning he was feeling better. Watching TV on the couch, splayed out in his boxers and ratty t-shirt. *Barbarian.* It felt oddly normal, though. So I guess I'm good."

"Thank God for good days."

She laughed, dryly. "Not sure I'd thank God if I met him, but to each their own."

The hidden truth of this struck like a spear in my side. Made me wonder if there wasn't something we could do to help, if the Lord could heal her husband, or restore their finances with his weight in gold. But without their plight, Arielle would have no need to help us, and then where would the world be?

Suddenly uncomfortable, I cleared my throat and offered the typical folded papers. Arielle looked at them and frowned. She glanced over her shoulder once, then withdrew a bag from under the counter and passed it to me. I thanked her and turned to leave when I remembered my Lord's firm command.

Maybe you should get her number.

"Listen," I said, turning back. "I was thinking maybe it would be a good idea to exchange phone numbers."

Her brow raised skeptically.

"I just mean—no, I was, uh, thinking, that is, given what we're each going through, I don't know. If you ever want to talk with someone that understands ..."

I arrived home still rubbing the waxy receipt paper between my fingers, unsure how I felt about it—how I *should* feel about it. I was nervous and excited and enticed and I was ashamed for feeling nervous and excited and enticed.

I periodically opened the folded note to gaze at the numbers.

Grivvux was in the backyard again, this time gardening in a blue-and-white Hawaiian shirt and brown pants, both covered in smears of dark soil. On his head was a beach hat with a sunflower design. He'd been tending Mom's garden, which had turned pitiful and weed-grown from neglect ever since her death.

He startled to find me watching him. "Sam! I'm glad you're here," he said, composing himself. "I have a new spell for us to try." He turned back to his work and thrust a spade into the soil, withdrawing a dark pile of earth. "I'm feeling very optimistic," he said, and I could hear the smile in his voice.

"I got her number," I said, feeling a strange tug at my cheeks.

Grivvux stopped digging.

"For your pills," I clarified.

"Yes ... But not just."

My cheeks warmed. "She's married," I said, a little too quickly.

He poked at the soil ponderously before looking over his shoulder. "There are hard times ahead, Sam. Much will be demanded in order to bring about this world's salvation." He returned to the dirt, delicately placing a pink amaryllis. "Do not spurn what joy has offered. You both should take what solace you can while it's available."

"I don't know, my Lor—*Grux*. Her husband is *dying* ..."

"I know." Grux brushed the flower's petals, and then turned to face me. "Sam, this world is naught but shadows and wind. A passing thing, an illusion. All that matters—*really matters*—are the lives caught in it, the lives I intend to save. The only groom is I, and the world is my bride. Call her."

He glanced past me. "Oh hello there, Penny!" He walked over to talk to the neighbor on the other side of the fence. "I'm feeling much better today, thank you. I see your petunias are coming in beautifully. Did you use the coffee grounds like I suggested?"

I met with Arielle the following Wednesday. Not exactly date night, which was fine because it wasn't exactly a date. It was just coffee with a friend. Not even a friend really, an acquaintance—an accomplice. But an hour before meeting, she texted to see if we could get drinks at a local bar instead. And she pushed us from a casual four o'clock to half past eight.

The Mariana was all in a nautical theme, with crossed oars and thick, knotted ropes hanging from the walls. Appropriate, I thought, for the end of the world, the flood that would wash away our cities, our cultures, our sins.

Above the entryway hung a rowboat, old and well-used, with chipped paint and warped wood, darkened so that it almost looked wet with sea spray. It was hard not to stare at it, to imagine it undulating gently over the Pacific, with no one to answer to and nothing to be ashamed of, just rowing, rowing, forever …

"Sam?"

I turned absently when her hand brushed my arm and I jumped in surprise, almost spilling the iced water I'd ordered to occupy my hands.

"Oh hey, Arielle!" I blurted uncomfortably, feeling that vast ocean evaporate around me.

She just laughed.

"So, this is going out …" she said with a wry smile, glancing about the bar.

"Yeah," I nodded. "I guess this is something people do now. We'll see if it takes off."

We ordered drinks and clinked our glasses a bit too hard, the sound reverberating like something delicate warning it might break, but we just laughed and sipped.

The conversation was stilted at first, struggling to navigate the standard *get-to-know-you's* when we already knew so much about each other, but only our sad and intimates. Fortunately, Arielle was intent on avoiding these subjects, dismissing her own with a flippant, "We can skip that, we both know everything's fucked." She punctuated it with a boisterous, if nihilistic, laugh.

Instead, we focused on the relief of going out again, and looking back wistfully to the warmth of summers past. Under the counter, our knees brushed occasionally, stirring awkward laughter and fumbled apologies.

Arielle told me how she missed kayaking, missed floating down the American River on hot days with a cooler full of PBR. She missed the sun hanging like a jewel over the water, and the river-smell on her skin when she headed back home.

"I'd be tipsy as hell by the time we reached shore," she said, "so my husband would have to drive home while I napped in the back seat."

She began to laugh but stopped abruptly, seeming on the verge of tears before quietly composing herself, while the mere mention of her husband drew my chest tight, set my heart thundering against my ribs.

Arielle gave me a quizzical look, then appeared to recognize my discomfort. "Don't worry," she said casually, "he knows I'm here. We tell each other everything. Our marriage is like a church, we're open to everybody."

"Oh," I said, trying to conceal my surprise. "Oh," I said again. The faith was pretty old-school in how it defined marriage—and even more so in how it defined infidelity—but then in the 90's there were attempts to modernize, in the vain hope of drawing new believers. Would open marriages not fold into that? Wasn't love *love*, after all? I wondered if Grux knew, if that's why he said the only groom was him. Did that make this a real date? Did that make this okay? Who determines these things?

"What about you?" she asked.

"Me?"

"Yeah, have you always been taking care of your dad or was there some blessed before time you look back to when you wake in a cold sweat in the middle of the night and can't get back to sleep?" She laughed once in playful self-acknowledgment.

I opened my mouth to speak and realized that I had nothing to say. My childhood wasn't full of adventure or play, it was full of prophecy and tales of annihilation. Each day had opened and closed with prayer, and each prayer opened and closed with the pact:

The world forgets You, but we are not the world.
We hold no grand ambitions, no fanciful dreams of conceit.
We live but to die, born to usher in the end.

I was raised to shun the world; I didn't get to float downstream, and even after Mom passed, it never occurred to me that I could.

"Oh, I've always taken care of him," I said, taking a long sip, swallowing it down.

Arielle nodded. "See, I knew you were one of the good ones," she said with a wink, and finished her own beverage.

I blushed, and she teased me for blushing, and I blushed even more, and she laughed all the harder.

We ordered another round, and the night grew late in an instant. We were so engrossed in laughter and conversation that the owners had to come out and ask us to leave. Their employees had already cleared the tables and mopped around us. We snapped from our daze, apologized, tipped generously, apologized again, and headed out. "Sorry!" Arielle shouted back once they locked the doors behind us, and then we stumbled off together.

The night was crisp and cool and occasionally Arielle would lean against me as we walked off our buzz along the quiet midtown streets.

"... Where'd you park?" I asked lamely.

"Oh, I had an Uber drop me off," she said, pulling out her phone and opening the app.

"Arielle, I—"

"Please," she said, "everyone just calls me Ellie."

Ellie ... I thought. *Of course!* Arielle didn't exactly roll off the tongue, but *Ellie* was laid back. *Ellie* was carefree. *Ellie* was inviting and warm.

"I could drive you home, if you like ..."

The smile she gave me could melt the icecaps entire, and flood the earth in a rush of warm spray.

We lingered awhile in the driveway, heads down, eyes fixed on our own laps. Ellie's right hand turned the ring on her left, the diamond going over and under. Like a karmic wheel, I thought, turning endlessly, going nowhere. I wondered if it was a sign of second thoughts, or a prelude to something else.

"Thank you for this," she said, smiling. "I had a really good time tonight. It feels like it's been so long since I've gotten to do ... *anything.*"

Her smile cracked, then shattered, her face scrunching up, tears streaming. "I'm sorry!" She wiped desperately at her eyes, trying to dam the flood. "This has nothing to do with you," she said with a reassuring hand.

I felt tremendous guilt then. Would she even be in this situation if Grivvux hadn't come down? Would it be such a sin to wish he'd stayed up in his ethereal realm? Just let the world keep spinning with its small joys and heavy sins? I knew already the answer, of course, even if I tried to not know it.

"I know ..." I said, wiping my own cheek.

Her hand reached for mine, and I could feel the wet spots of tears on her skin. Our eyes met, vulnerable and aching. It felt like a call. I shifted closer, but she dropped her head and looked away.

Silence filled the car as our walls resurfaced. I withdrew back to my seat.

"Ughhh ..." she groaned, then laughed and wiped the last tears from her eyes. "What are we doing?" she asked, more to herself than to me it seemed.

"Just what we've been doing," I said, more thinking aloud than answering her. "Trying to stay afloat."

When she kissed me, it was as unexpected as the rapture. Her lips tasted like honey and milk and the dreams you thought could never come true. She pressed against me, her fingers sliding through my hair, pulling me closer until it hurt, blissfully.

I came home, body tingling, lips raw and electric. The house was dark and I didn't even mind. "Hello!" I called, but there was no answer. "Grux?" The house remained quiet. A thought pierced me: *What if I killed him with my sins?* I checked in the kitchen, the patio, turning on lights everywhere as I went, but illuminating nothing.

Had the Lord God died in my care? Had I failed him, failed every living soul on the planet? Were we doomed because of me? Because I wasn't prepared enough for his return? Because I wasn't holy enough to make him whole?

Grux said it was okay, didn't he? Was he wrong about that? Can he be wrong? Is that even possible?

I went down the hall to the master bedroom that once belonged to my mother, and then to me, and now belonged to the Lord Supreme. The door was shut. *He probably just went to bed early*, I told myself. But then I heard his voice, faint but animated, on the other side. I pressed my ear to the door, straining to make out what was said: vague promises, pleas, weeping. *He's praying,* I realized. Listening closer, I caught the words, "Lord Grivvux of the Permafire."

He's praying to himself …

Embarrassed, I stepped away, but just then a loud bell chimed from my pocket and the voice beyond went quiet. I shook with shame and cleared my throat. "My lord, I'm, uh, home. *Grux,* I mean … Hi …"

"Hello, Sam," the voice carried through the door. "I'd like to be alone tonight."

"Sure, I, um, things happened with Ellie."

"I know."

I gulped and retreated to my room. On my phone was an urgent bank notification about a suspicious purchase. I ran the numbers in my head—several rounds of drinks at a high end bar, tips.

I went to check the account, worrying over how much I'd spent. Sure, gold was something we could scrounge up, but it required Grux to do back-breaking labor and spirit-heavy spells, which was hard to justify so I could go on a date.

The flagged purchase was a mail order from *Etsy*. Rush delivery. A sacrificial blade crafted by "authentic virginized monks"—whatever those were. The blade itself was long and curved, with elaborate designs etched along the sides. It looked beautiful, but cruel.

I remembered that Grux had mentioned a new ritual, and ignored the warning.

As foreseen in the Grivvuxian prophecies of old, the weather on the last days of Earth was lovely. Maybe the prophets didn't phrase it quite like that—more like, "there will be no hint of cloud, let alone the harbingers of great rains that will wash away the cultures of man." But however you translate the old texts, those last days were indeed *blessed*.

Not that everyone could appreciate them.

A week after Ellie and I first went out, Grux still hadn't brought up the new spell or the sacrificial blade. He remained distant after Ellie and I started seeing each other, and as often as she came over, Grux still wouldn't let me introduce her.

"We'll meet," he told me. "Just not like that."

"You're no fun," I teased, and he said nothing in response for a long while, just watched me sprucing up the house, spraying air-freshener, hiding arcane instruments and ornaments that we'd experimented with to no avail.

"Be sure you don't grow too attached, Sam," he said warily. "We're here to save the world, not fall in love."

"I'm not in love," I said a bit too quickly. He looked at me, unconvinced. "I'm just doing what you told me," I said. "Like I always have. I'm taking joy while it's available. Isn't that what you said? This whole thing was your idea … my Lord God."

"Yes, Sam. Of course. But remember that the key phrase there was *while it's available*. Sacrifices will have to be made, Sam. Some things can only be paid for in blood."

Immediately, the sacrificial blade from Etsy came to mind.

"I won't let any harm come to her," I said firmly. Ellie had paid enough. I wouldn't let her be dragged through more. This wasn't her faith, wasn't her fight, wasn't her price to pay.

Grux just looked confused, then nodded. "Yes," he said. "I understand. We'll discuss the end of the world at another time. Have fun on your date."

That night, when I brought Arielle home, we found roots of gold set on the kitchen counter like fresh pulled carrots. A folded note sat beside them with the address and rates of a nearby motel.

"What are those?" she asked, confused.

"Nothing," I said, quickly wrapping them in paper towels. "Dad likes to garden is all. He finds all sorts of weird things at the farmer's market!" I opened the fridge and tossed them in the crisper. They clanked metallically as vegetables seldom do.

Ellie didn't take well to the motel meetups. She didn't understand why we couldn't go back to my place anymore, or how I could afford a room every few nights.

"I just think it would be easier if we stayed at your place ..." she said.

"I know. But Dad doesn't like people coming over. It's much better this way."

"Maybe if you introduced us, he'd be okay with me." A mischievous grin took her face. "Or you could sneak me into your room like we're two stupid kids in high school."

"No," I told her. "I can't."

That gleeful expression dissolved into the familiar, everyday gloom. "Shouldn't you be with him, though?" she said, pulling away. It wasn't a question, and I knew we weren't talking about the Lord Supreme. It was him. *Her* him. "Doesn't he need you close by?"

Her eyes turned from me, scanning the room as if seeing it for the first time in all its drab lifelessness. There was no love or life in this room. Everything was sterile, but only superficially. Her eyes bloomed with wonder and disgust, and refused to meet mine.

"He's fine," I said, drawing her back. "If there's trouble, he'll call. Trust me." She was unconvinced, feeling further from me now than ever. If only I could tell her that the author of the universe had given his blessing. Or that the motel was his idea.

"There are hard times ahead," I found myself saying. "Don't spurn what joy has offered. We should take what joy we can while it's available."

Her eyes looked into mine, weighing the words uncertainly. "This isn't joy," she said, tossing her purse onto the pleather chair. "This is staying afloat." She sat on the foot of the bed, and began taking off her heels. "Well?" This while gesturing at my pants with a dismissive hand.

It all works out just fine. That's how the world ends, I told myself this as things fell apart, but there was no conviction in that old faith.

Ellie called me in tears while I waited at the motel. Said something had happened, she was on her way to the hospital. "It's over," she said. "I have to go. I'm sorry."

"I'm sorry too," I said, but she was already gone.

The house was dark when I came home. *Of course it's dark*, I thought. *Why would there be any light in the house of the lord?* I threw my jacket toward the ottoman, heard the buttons scrape the floor, and left it. "Grux?" I called, but there was no answer. Something turned in my stomach—a bad feeling. I wondered if Despair had finally caught up with him, if the pills had only put off the inevitable a few weeks. "My lord?"

Nothing.

I switched on the front lights, but the room stayed dark. In the kitchen, it was the same. The power must have gone out. But then I saw the streetlight over the back fence, its amber rays seeping into the kitchen.

And I saw *them.*

Dark figures stood outside, shadows looking in. *The Watchers.* Almost as soon as I spotted them, the streetlight flickered and died, the shadows melting into night. *Their presence is a good omen,* I remembered and tried not to be afraid.

Blindly, I made my way down the hall to the master bedroom. The door hung halfway open. "*Grux?*" I called in, leaning to peer inside. Enough moonlight came in from the open window that I could faintly make out the shape of the bed. Feathers blew across the floor in a haunting dance.

I was too afraid to go in. Too afraid of what I might find.

"My lord, answer me," I demanded, but there was no reply. "Grux! *Grivvux!* My Lord God, please say something, say anything!"

Only the mindless bluster of wind.

The door creaked as I opened it further and urged myself inside, but before I'd reached the bed, someone struck me from behind and the floor came swinging up to meet me, my head thudding painfully against the hardwood.

"I'm sorry, Sam," said his voice as he climbed over me, pinning me down. "This is the only way to save you!"

"What's happening?" I cried, flailing frantically until I managed to turn over. The eyes were all I could make out in the dark, so wide they seemed lidless. He began chanting in the ancient tongue, and the sacrificial blade winked in the moonlight as it rose over my chest. He drove it down, but I caught his wrist and held him off.

"We're out of time, Sam! This has to happen!"

"But I *served* you," I said, trying not to weep.

"Then *serve me,* Sam! This is for the greater good!"

The greater good ... I remembered the mandrake's sacrifice, how Grux couldn't just throw it in the fire. There were rules even he must obey. "You can't do this!" I screamed, feeling my heart pounding in my ears as the knife inched closer. "I don't agree to this! *Watchers!* I'm not a willing sacrifice!"

"Sam ..." he said, pressing down with all his strength, "*You're* not blameless." The knife jolted closer, its tip pressing into my shirt. "It's not your fault—it was never supposed to be you," he added, as if trying to comfort me before my murder. "There was no one else ... No one left."

Suddenly, I understood. I was only the Chosen One because I was the last. I wasn't *special*. Wasn't *holy*. Wasn't anything more than *here*.

I realized then that I hated him. I hated him for his power, and I hated him for his weakness. I hated him for what he gave and what he demanded. I should have known. Our own scripture tells us: *His right hand gives and his left hand takes, but his right hand also takes.*

With a sudden surge of determination, I pushed the knife from my chest and threw him off me. We struggled and writhed there on the floor, our bodies thumping against the hardwood.

"Sam!" he gasped. "*Please!* Think on what you do! Don't you want to save this world?"

He was stronger than I'd expected. I could barely hold him off.

The feathers ...

Grux was stronger than me now, and he had the knife. He had everything he needed to save the world without me. Yet as we fought, he never swung or stabbed at me, but rather kept the blade tucked flat against his forearm, as if he was afraid of hurting me with it. I realized then that it was important to him that he kill me, but not hurt me.

That was his mistake.

I struck him as hard as I could across the cheek and then wrested the blade from his fumbling hand. Stunned, he reached after it wildly, cutting both hands before recoiling in fear. "Think of her!" he pleaded as I guided the blade over him. "You two were never meant to be forever, Sam! *This will be!*"

"I'm not doing this for her," I said through gritted teeth. "This is for me."

Grux gasped when the knife plunged through him. His lips trembled, searching for the words to undo this. "Oh, Sam," he said —not spitefully, but dripping with pity. "My poor lost child. There's no saving you now. There's no saving any of you ..."

Some last words.

It's been three weeks since I killed the one true god. Ellie's husband passed on the same day. I don't know if that's fate or coincidence, bad luck or nothing. Probably nothing, but then isn't everything?

We spoke once more in the days that followed. She's moving out of town, though she didn't say where she's going and I didn't ask. With the apocalypse on the horizon, I didn't think it mattered much.

"I hope you stay afloat," I told her.

She sniffled and cleared her throat. "I always do."

"No, I mean keep your raft handy."

She laughed and said goodbye.

I buried the Lord Most High in the backyard. He always liked to garden there. But now great thorny roses, bigger and brighter than any I've ever seen, have sprouted through the soft earth and spread through the yard. I don't know how they got there—if they were planted beforehand, or if they're the strange result of bird-magic leaving his body.

At first I ignored them, let them flourish like weeds before they finally tapped dry, their ruby petals wilting through the California drought. I had bigger concerns, after all. The crushing responsibility of the world's doom. The unknowable mystery that clung to my every thought: Did I betray God, or did God betray me?

It's not like I could pray about it.

I watched the world's end from my rooftop, the sun setting over an old world full of quiet joys, hidden griefs, petty and monstrous sins.

But the hour marked upon the cosmic calendar came and went unremarked. No rolling tide of judgment. No righteous annihilation. Maybe without God it couldn't happen. Or maybe the end is still coming and we just got the math wrong.

Maybe.

Maybe.

'Maybe' like the wet mortar around every brick of faith, waiting to harden into cold certainty. *It is not ours to know,* say the holy texts, *but to wait and see what God and fate have conspired.*

Wait and see, like a challenge.

Wait and see, like a threat.

I've started watering the roses at night, when it's cooler out. It's helped to break the habit of my evening prayers, the habit of kneeling and reaching out, only to receive the spiritual equivalent of a disconnect tone. And with Grux gone, a thought has been slowly boring into me:

There's no one to help us but us.

No sorrow or joy but us. No righteousness or sin but us.

The flowers have bounced back pretty quickly, their petals blood-bright, their leaves lush as Eden. My neighbor Penny loves them, and demanded to know my secret. I really didn't know what to tell her—I hadn't done anything special, hadn't applied arcane tricks or esoteric skills or a once in a generation green thumb.

"Care," I told her.

"That's usually what it comes down to," she said, and asked if I wouldn't mind helping her plant some in her own garden.

I've been going over every few days, first to plant the roses, then to help with other small tasks around the house. In turn, she's been showing me how to prune the flowers so they don't grow over each other, how to direct them so that they stay healthy and strong, how to water them at the right times to help with the drought.

"How's your father?" she asked the other day.

"Oh," I said awkwardly, "he actually passed a little while ago …"

"I'm sorry to hear that, dear," she said. "He was a sweet man, I'm sure you miss him terribly. He's still with you though. I can feel him in you."

"Okay," I said, eager to drop it, hoping she was wrong, though a part of me hoped in spite of myself that she was right.

With her guidance, I've mulched and fertilized the soil around the rosebushes, even moved a few to keep them from crowding each other (or growing in the silhouette of a buried body). But the roses grow with a mind all their own, creeping with thorny vines across the yard to latch and climb the walls of the house. And each morning, their blushing, crimson faces turn not towards the rising sun but to my bedroom window, as if watching still for the coming of the lord.

See Hamilton Perez's story "Problems of the Flesh" online at Metaphorosis.
If you liked it, leave a comment. Authors love that!
Remember to subscribe to our e-mail updates so you'll know when new stories are posted.

About the story

I started this story around 2015 as a sort of final goodbye to the religious faith of my early adulthood. I thought it would be interesting if the Second Coming occurred, but rather than

Christ returning in glory, he was weak or ill (though still supernatural). I didn't want to make the story about Christianity (or any particular religion), but rather about the challenges of faith, so I invented Grivvux, and Sam became a vehicle for me to explore what faith expects of us and what we expect of it.

A question for the author

Q: Are you an outline or discovery writer?

A: I've always been more of an outliner, but that's just another way to say that outlining is where I discover. Outlining lets me play with ideas freely, and it lets me jump around the story as things come to me. That said, the actual writing/discover phase always changes the outline, so there's a lot of back and forth, which is probably why it takes me so long to finish anything. But it's the outlining that I enjoy most. That's where I get to play. The writing is where I work.

About the author

Hamilton Perez has been writing stories for as long as he can remember, and possibly even longer than that. His earliest known work is a fan-fiction crossover between *Star Wars, Terminator*, and *Jurassic Park*. It has yet to be picked up by a major studio, but Hamilton remains hopeful. When not writing, he can be found rolling 20-sided dice, playing irresponsibly with medieval weaponry, or chasing squirrels with the dog.

hamiltonperez.com, @TheWritingHam

A Xenothanatologist's Guidebook
to Death Practices Among the Sapient Species of the Outer Perseus Arm of the Milky Way Galaxy

P.G. Streeter

Miri, I'm on my way.

My stomach has settled from that initial lurch of low-*g*. I've acclimated to my small cabin, and to the prospect of a long, lingering isolation.

It's quiet, and lonely, but I've nonetheless opted out of the long sleep of induced stasis. The cabin feels too much like a coffin as it is.

Here I am: alone, except for my precious few possessions, my thoughts—

—and *you*: the ghost I conjure from my deepest memories, a trick to keep myself sane.

Even though months will go by before this vessel approaches relativistic speeds, my sense of time's passage is already blurring. Suddenly, I find myself back in those fields, abandoned and overgrown, that stretched out between our childhood homes.

Do you remember them? It was in those tall, tangled grasses that we first met, first got into mischief.

Along the southern edge of that field, there was a river—mild in most seasons, but ferocious after the rainstorms that came in early spring. There, we'd swim.

I can hear your voice now, calling to me, beckoning me to join you where the current was strongest.

But I'm still afraid of those waters. I did not, *do not*, want to be swept away.

So, I refuse to follow the memory further. I grasp this hardbound book. I read.

Of the billions of star systems observed in the Milky Way's Outer Perseus Arm, human starfarers have thus far discovered 83 that contain life-bearing planets or moons. On 27 of these worlds, we have found species whose intelligence rises to levels we can comfortably categorize as sapient.

This distinction is not always a straightforward one to make. Even when communication can be established, it is hard to gauge intelligence, *which frequently manifests in unexpected ways. Often, therefore, a vital factor in making such a determination has been the assessment made by the Terrestrial Guild of Xenothanatologists, whose members study alien species' attitudes toward death, and their treatment of the dead.*

After all, what could better inform us about species' humanity *than how they conceptualize their* mortality?

This guidebook will present a survey of xenothanatologists' initial findings in this region of the galaxy. These findings are not conclusive or all-encompassing, but the Company hopes they will give you, the budding xenothanatologist, a useful primer, here at the start of your promising career.

Do you insist on interrupting me, Miri?

Yes, I can hear your questions—or, rather, I feel them, like vibrations in the cabin's stale air. If I squint, I can almost see your lips parting as you speak, even if it's just a shimmer in my peripheral vision.

You wonder, of course, about the small marvel I'm clasping in my hands. *Hmm.* How can I explain the ways the world has changed since you've been gone?

When you left me, the world was on the cusp. I wonder if you anticipated the ways in which *Renew* would alter things—even as you refused its life-extending treatments.

Maybe you feared that the coming spike in population would outstrip the pace at which we built new habitats off-planet. Perhaps you worried about the *gap*—that rapidly widening gulf between those who had the means to receive the genetic therapy, and those who didn't.

I wish you had confided more in me, in the end—and I wish I could say I would've listened.

But I think some of the ways the world changed might genuinely have surprised you. For instance: technologies of convenience, such as those digital interfaces we'd gotten so accustomed to reading from, have fallen entirely out of fashion. I think this fact would have surprised me, too, if someone had told it to me during the first century or so of my life!

Now, items like physical, bound books, which take so much *time* to manufacture and get a hold of, are favored commodities. The reason for this is simple, really: now that our lives extend so many centuries, we have the luxury of 'taking it slow'. We *relish* those old technologies, precisely *because* they demand our time and patience. I think you would have liked that.

Of course, the Company would tell you that such things are 'wonderful reminders of our victory over death'. This, I suspect, you would have scoffed at.

This particular book—the guidebook I'm holding now—was one of the first readings assigned in my course of xenothanatological study. I've read it countless times, and, even though I've taken my studies far beyond its pages in the years since, it's still one of my favorites. It still reminds me of those first profound moments of inspiration it sparked in me—insights that I hope will lead me back to *you*.

If you read it with me, now, maybe you'll understand what it is I seek.

Countless cultural groups among the species we've observed follow death practices familiar to Earth-born humans. A plurality of xenocultures inter their dead, and nearly as many employ techniques akin to cremation.

On planets where fire is not a practical solution, we have observed the use of corrosives, voracious parasites, nanotechnology, and even mechanical grinding tools as methods for reducing a body to its component particles. Although some of the methodologies described above are somewhat disquieting to the human observer, their goals are clear, even relatable.

Yet some alien cultures we have encountered maintain thanatological practices that might shock, offend, or perplex those born of Earth. For instance, members of the Crustweaver religious sect on 16 Ellander b have an inviolable taboo against touching the deceased, directly or indirectly. Crustweavers use the dexterity of their long, spindly limbs to step over and around their dead, who are invariably left, unperturbed, in the exact spot where they expired.

The atmospheric conditions on 16 Ellander b, along with the physical makeup of the species' bodies, make for a slow decomposition process: it often takes the equivalent of 30-40 Earth years for a body to fully decompose. To compound the issue, this duration is roughly one-and-a-half times the length of the species' average lifespan. As a result, a Crustweaver who died at the moment of another Crustweaver's birth will likely not have fully decomposed by the time the latter deceases.

As can be imagined, the consequences of these practices are monumental. As Crustweaver communities continue to produce offspring faster than prior generations' bodies biodegrade, new generations find themselves among a landscape increasingly littered with their forebears' corpses.

The Crustweavers inhabit an isolated continent, as non-adherents to this sect's faith have long since learned to stay far away. In the Crustweavers' domain, the very shape of the world alters with each generation's passing. Yet, these pious beings manage to sidestep and squeeze past the dead that are scattered about their streets and homes.

They do so without trepidation or fear. In fact, they do not seem in the least perturbed by the slowly rotting remains of strangers and loved ones alike that pervade their world. They simply live their lives in a state of casual reverence to the fallen. Even as the world around them becomes crowded with cadavers, their taboo remains absolute.

In such cases, we are left to wonder how cultural exchange might even be possible between our people and theirs. However, the intrepid xenothanatologist finds a way.

Do you see the beads of sweat forming on my brow?

Yes, I realize it's quite cool in here. It's not heat, but a swell of dread that's causing me to perspire. The seed of a thought is sprouting in my mind. It's familiar, and unwelcome.

No, I don't wish to share it with you. Not now.

Besides, I can see it: the smirk on your face. Yes, Company texts such as this one love to make these sweeping statements. The intrepid xenothanatologist! I can see why you would find this amusing.

But don't give me that look! I understand that this is dripping with propaganda. I hope you don't assume I'm going into this endeavor with the naïve outlook of a younger man. After all, I'm decidedly *not* young. I haven't been for quite a long time.

Hmm. I'm scrambling to justify my actions, it seems. Is that why I've called upon your memory? Why I, the lifelong rationalist, have let myself get drawn into this game of make-believe?

So be it. I want to explain my choices, so explain them I *will.*

Why, after all, have I devoted myself to this Company's mission? Their job is to sell something, to spread *Renew* to other sapient species...at a cost. What does this act of commerce have to do with *me*?

It's simple: they *need* me—someone who can come to grips with these alien creatures' views on death. This is what I've spent the last several years studying for, after all. And I've studied hard.

When I reach that understanding, my further job is to 'engender a dialogue' on the Company's behalf. I'm to build the cultural inroads needed to open up trade—and I'm sure I'll do so admirably.

None of this is the reason my confidence wavers. This isn't what's making me sweat.

What? Do you have to *needle* me like this? I'd almost forgotten how insistent you could be. But fine, *here*. I'll tell you what image has risen to my mind and made my heart start to beat so fast:

It's your hospice room—and you're no longer in it. They've just have wheeled you away. No—not *you*. The husk you left behind.

Do you see your belongings, scattered about the room? Piled clothes, half-unpacked bags, medical equipment that's still flashing as tubes and cords dangle about, untethered? This is the topography of the world you left behind.

The thought of such a world spurs my actions—but it also fills me with dread.

So, when I think about my mission—my *second* mission, the one I won't speak of out loud—I'm positively brimming with doubt. I'm afraid to talk about it even now—afraid even to whisper it to your ghost.

And although I'm still at the outset of my journey, visions of failure are already starting to cloud my thoughts. With each new world I visit, I'm afraid I'll only find one more empty promise. What if the answers I'm searching for never come?

For you, Miri, I'm still going to try. All I ask is that you bear with me.

Although the rationales behind some species' practices are opaque to our eyes, in many cases, attitudes surrounding death are easy to grasp. This is especially true when they are so clearly based on the biological necessities of the species' lives. Take, for instance, the Spin-Gliders of 44 Olivar c. Not unlike certain Earth sharks, these

sky-dwelling creatures are obligate ram ventilators. That is, they must remain in constant motion for their respiratory systems to function.

The flyers spend their waking lives swooping and diving along the gas giant's hydrogen currents, and the species has even mastered a technique by which they can sleep for short stints while caught in a spiraling gust of hot air. It is astonishing that such beings have developed rich culture and technology while living a life constrained by the need for constant motion; yet, they have done so.

Of course, the only way to come to anything like a complete rest on a planet with no solid surface is to descend to the stratum of liquid hydrogen closer to the planet's core.

The majority of the planet's cultural groups therefore honor their dead in this fashion: they carry them to this liquid surface. Rather than simply allowing them to drop, they take great care to lay their dead upon buoyant, gyroscopically stabilized platforms. Here, no winds carry them, no waves buffet them about. So it is that a Spin-Glider comes to a state of rest only upon death.

If life is motion, then how better to acknowledge—and ultimately accept—its absence, than to create a condition of perfect stillness?

Is that what death is for you, Miri? Stillness?

I can close my eyes, clutch this book to my chest, concentrate on breathing, and know that this brief *pause* doesn't mean the end.

But what's your perspective on the matter? No flights of fancy, no phantoms created by my imagination, will ever give me access to *that* knowledge.

If only you could tell me! After all, you've read much of the same old literature that I have. How many times has that phrase appeared—reference to the 'stillness of the grave'? We grew up in a world where that outcome was an inevitability. And, yet, in your final years, even you knew that it didn't have to be. Not anymore.

For a long time, humanity either accepted the idea that one day all we'd come to rest—or hoped against hope that, in some invisible way, life kept going. Those seemed to be the only options.

But when *Renew* became a reality, things changed: we didn't have to resign ourselves to nothingness or place our hopes in some unknown 'hereafter'. We could continue to live, in the here and now! I saw this, saw the gift it offered us. So why couldn't I persuade *you* to embrace that change as well?

It's ironic, I suppose, that this act of persuasion—the *sales pitch*—is my job now. I study how people on faraway worlds conceptualize death, all so that the Company can sell them *life*.

You'd laugh, I think, to hear about the team I'm a part of. I swear, they stick the prefix *xeno* on any and every old job title, any time alien cultures are involved. There are *xenoeconomists* to negotiate the terms of the trade, and *xenobiologists*, who figure out how to adapt *Renew*'s life-extending biotech to other species' physiology.

And then, there's me: the one who is trusted, above all others, to discover the terms under which our product will be most desirable to our strange new friends.

Me, the person who failed so utterly to convince you that a long life was worth living.

Of course, it is not only the handling and disposal of physical corpses with which the xenothanatologist is concerned. She must ask, how do different xenocultures talk about their dead? How do they memorialize them?

Eulogies and obituaries are prevalent among virtually all literate species in this region of the galaxy. Many deliver short orations or produce written tributes after a loved one's passing, much as Earth humans have historically done. However, many have practices that go much further.

Consider the denizens of 6 Aleska e. You have likely read about this species, for their body plan is famously far closer to Earth humans' than any other extraterrestrial life yet discovered. That is, they have an ovoid head, a neck, torso, and limbs both fore and hind. Further, they walk on these hind legs and reserve the fore for tool use.

While these likenesses are truly extraordinary, it is here that their similarities to our kind end. They have no mouths, no visible organs of hearing or olfaction; their eyes, while prominent, do not resemble our own, but instead consist of a complex beehive of chromelike surfaces that stretch around their heads' circumference.

They go about naked, their pale skin exposed at all times, and it is on this blank canvas that their method of communication emerges. Through a shifting set of luminescent cells just under their outer dermis, these Skinwriters communicate. Intricate images in vibrant colors shift across their bodies, allowing for a complex visual language.

When a Skinwriter dies, its flesh returns to neutral pale tones. It is then that the Artists of the Dead set to work: first, preserving the deceased's body, then inscribing a series of fine tattoos over the entirety of their skin's canvas.

Here is the Skinwriter's epitaph: a pictogrammatic account of the deceased's life, told from birth to death. The craftsmanship of this body art, along with the level of detail recollected in its lines and colors, becomes a permanent tribute to the deceased, displayed forever in a glass mausoleum. A hastily tattooed corpse, or one whose pictograms tell a vague or incomplete story, reveals a life unsatisfactorily lived. Yet, if one's preserved corpse becomes a true work of art, such is the ultimate testament to that person's life.

I was asked, of course, to speak at your funeral. I wrote your obituary—*that* was easy enough. There's a formula there, one I didn't need to stray from. Your life, your education, your accomplishments—all of it lined up into easy paragraphs! I let these simple, reductive facts flow onto the page, all the way to the last sentence, the one that lists the people you've left behind.

Of course, with no children, with your parents and brothers already gone, this left only *me*.

So, yes, I composed the necessary words—and several old friends even reached out to tell me how touching my tribute was.

But when they asked me to *speak*, there was only emptiness inside me, in those deep places where I'd expected to find inspiration.

Were you there, Miri? A true ghost, listening intently for the words I would utter in your honor? Were you ashamed, then, when all I could do was stand there and openly weep?

Do I see you turning your eyes away from me, even now?

Stay with me for a while, I'm begging you. We're getting closer and closer to the questions that have led me to this ship—that have led me across the stars in search of you.

Two species should be further noted for the unique roles language takes in referring to the dead. The first, the insectiform Fim of 19 Magna k have a rich spoken language, a series of chirps and clicks that has led to a wealth of literary art. Yet, the language has a surprising gap: there are no names for the living, no way to refer to other Fim at all.

Their language allows for discussion of the self—of their natural world and their interactions with it, of their desires, and of their own past actions. It likewise has a version of the word you—a way to indicate the speaker's direct audience. But, whether because of an evolutionary quirk of neurology or through a deeply ingrained social practice, a Fim cannot, when talking to a compatriot, refer to a third person and her actions.

That is, they cannot do so until a fellow Fim dies. At this point, her deeds are proclaimed loudly and often. The dead Fim is named immediately—and without deliberation—and that name is, by means of some mechanism we do not yet understand, immediately known to all.

In death, a Fim's story, impossible to discuss during her life, becomes a legend widely told.

As improbable as it seems, 23 Argen c contains a population of beings, the aquatic Kell, whose sociolinguistic response to death is precisely the opposite of the Fims': when a Kell dies, it is, to the remainder of this species, as if he never existed at all.

Upon death, the body begins to sink to the bottom of the planet's highly acidic oceans. Though a living Kell's body produces enzymes which protect him from the corrosive waters, this production stops at death. So, as the dead Kell's body sinks, it quickly begins to disintegrate.

Simultaneously, all other Kell begin to act as if their friend or family member never existed. The requisite vocabulary is no longer available.

In the Company's attempts to communicate about this phenomenon, references to the dead Kell by human translators led to consistently perplexed responses.

Do the Kell immediately forget their dead, or do they act out of strict custom? If the latter, what value system led to such a practice? If the former, then what are the implications for the Kell worldview? Though results are preliminary, our initial outreach group has hypothesized that the Kell are not aware of death's existence at all. Those who live, live. That is all they know.

How can I make you understand how it was for me, Miri? Once you were gone, it was like the truth of your life had become utterly inarticulable.

How could I bring your name from my lips into the world, when the empty space you left was so vast? Any feeble vibrations I attempted to speak into that void would be meaningless, incomplete. They would not be *you*, which means they would be an insult to your memory.

It all sounds extreme, doesn't it? But losing you *was* such an extreme thing to experience. You were there, a part of my life—and then you weren't.

And it only got worse. I kept telling people that I wanted to 'honor your memory', but I soon found myself asking what *memory* was even worth. Every day that passed without you in it, I dissociated even further, to the point where I soon found myself disbelieving my own recollections.

In the wake of your loss, I was unmoored from reality. What was real, I wondered, and what was the fiction I'd created to soothe myself, to make the grief easier to bear? This is the spiral I was caught up in, the state of total panic that consumed me: one where memory was a lie, and every word I uttered was a failed attempt to bring you back.

I felt despair, but I never questioned my choice to embrace extended life. I couldn't allow myself to be erased from the world the same way you had been.

Yet, where could I go from there?

The answer, as I'm sure you've guessed, began to take shape when I first read this book.

Do I sound obsessive? I suppose I must. I became fixated on the idea of finding some alien culture whose views on death might offer me reassurance. When presented, for instance, with the discovery of a species who forget their dead entirely, I found myself wondering if *this* was the solution. Could I abandon your memory, washing you clean from my thoughts so that I wouldn't have to keep shouldering the burden of your loss?

Ultimately, I rejected this notion. It was unseemly, perverse even.

I also quickly discarded any answers rooted in superstition— all those traditions proclaiming a spiritual afterlife. These were untestable, un*knowable*. They were a sign of epistemic defeat, acts of faith I could never commit to.

Still, now that I had started along this path, I was determined to discover *something* out there: some creature in the far-flung cosmos who could offer me solace.

So, my choice was made: I would become a xenothanatologist. I would even sell myself to this Company if that's what it took. I would become the human ambassador to the dead of other worlds.

And, perhaps, I started to realize, to worlds like *ours*: ones that had left death *behind*.

A society's practices surrounding death will necessarily change when that society makes the concept of 'natural death' obsolete. Earth humans, of course, encountered this reality upon the invention of Renew. *Unsurprisingly, other species in the cosmos have also discovered a measure of immortality, whether through natural or technological means.*

Still, it's rare to find a species that truly fits the description of biological *immortality. On Earth, non-sapient species such as lobsters, whose production of the enzyme telomerase allows for unending cell regeneration, are close to achieving such a descriptor. In fact,* Renew *is itself partly inspired by such beings: one important component of the treatment is the prevention of telomere shortening as cells regenerate. However, it is worth noting that while such species do not die by aging, their lives, just as ours, might easily be cut short due to violent means.*

On 8 Alma n, a sapient species appears to have achieved such biologically immortal status. The species—whom we call Stonediggers—have nigh-impenetrable rocklike exteriors. They do not require air to breathe, nor any form of sustenance other than exposure to sunlight. Further, they can store an excess of solar energy that lasts for weeks on end, so death due to solar deprivation is an unlikely outcome. In short, they are virtually unkillable. Like lobsters or Renew-*enhanced humans, they do not age in any recognizable sense; the oldest among them, by Company reckoning, has been alive for nearly twelve million Earth years.*

Elsewhere, technological means have extended other species' lifespan greatly. One such example hails from 1 Hemnes d. There, the Bright Ones claim to have developed the means by which to preserve a dying person's conscious mind and transfer it to a new, synthetic host body. The process, they claimed, might be repeated indefinitely, with perfect fidelity—nothing lost in the transfer.

While similar techniques had been attempted on Earth before Renew *was perfected, humankind had concluded that the consciousness could not survive the transfer process.*

Here, though, we found a fully functioning society of techno-organic beings. Upon first contact, Company representatives determined they would need to investigate further: could this technique supplement our existing life-extending biotechnology?

Can you see them, Miri—the thoughts that have begun to take shape in my mind? I picture you leaning in, listening more attentively than before.

These are the stories, you see, that tantalize me above all others, even if all they provide me with are false glimpses of hope. I really am enthusiastic—practically *evangelical*—about *Renew* and the extended life it offers, but the simple fact is that no matter how far we reach across the cosmos, there is one place we will never be able to spread this technology.

We can't bring it to the *past*. We can't offer it to those whose lives ended before it arrived, nor to those who stubbornly refused its miracle.

Again, you smirk. You're shaking your head—yes, I can see it, no matter how subtle you think you are.

But hear me out, please. Ask, as I did, whether there is a solution here. Can the promise of recovering and transferring a conscious mind offer the missing piece? Not for those of us who already have *Renew* coursing through our veins, but for those who are already gone?

What would it take to retrieve a mind that was lost *long ago*? Could such a person's consciousness be pulled from the ether, brought back into existence?

I imagine your eyes getting wide at this—but don't get your hopes up just yet.

With such questions in mind, Company representatives sought to learn how the Bright Ones' transfer process worked. For how long, post-expiry, might a consciousness be retrieved from the deceased's brain? Does the process involve the transfer of brain tissue itself into the new host body, or are memories and perspectives translated to a new medium?

As it turns out, this purported transfer of consciousness was not what the Bright Ones initially advertised.

A look into the species' past reveals the full story. The Bright Ones long ago developed infinitesimally small surveillance devices— quantum drones—that, produced on a massive scale, began to observe all life across their planet, at all times. All was known; no knowledge was kept secret.

Using the vast data gathered, the engineers of 1 Hemnes d were able to create intricately complex models of a deceased Bright One's mind, informed by the full set of objective experiences encountered over a lifetime. The internal *perspective was not* retained—only inferred—but these inferences were made with a nuanced understanding of Bright One psychology, and were therefore arguably quite accurate.

Yet, it cannot be denied that the deceased person's consciousness was not, in fact, preserved. When one of these biological persons died, their mind was merely recreated. No matter how accurate, it was but a replica. As such, the original beings that once inhabited this land slowly died off, only to be replaced by new, synthetic beings. At some point in the distant past, the last biological Bright One expired. All that remains are their algorithmic replacements, the computer-modeled copies of the deceased.

How could a species have allowed this to occur? Was it merely that, in their inability to cope with the absence of departed loved ones, the Bright Ones decided their simulated presence would suffice? Perhaps only a select few knew the process to be fraudulent, and the masses were merely fooled. We do not yet know the answer.

Although the Company has come to recognize artificial intelligence as true life, the fact remains, nonetheless, that these creatures are not genuine continuations of the lives that had come before.

In the meantime, subsequent visits to 8 Alma n revealed that their story, as well, is more complicated than initially perceived. For one, the appellation given—Stonediggers—in truth applies only to one faction of the species. It remains in use by Earth humans due to its widespread early adoption; however, the differences between the two main factions are worth exploring.

For example, when members of that first faction—the true Stonediggers—come of age, they are known to retreat to isolated places, where they build massive stone shelters and spend their endless lives making little contact with others. On rare occasions, Stonediggers seek partners for mating, but any pairings formed for this purpose last only until their offspring reach maturity.

Only when we met the second faction, called Sun-Sailors, did we learn an astonishing truth: the species, no matter the faction, are not solitary by disposition. In fact, many Stonediggers find the condition of isolation to be torturous. What circumstances, then, might have led these virtually invincible giants to take such extreme precautions against harm?

The Sun-Sailors offered us an explanation for their cousins' behavior: since death is so rare, it is vastly more traumatic than it would be in a world where it is commonplace. Therefore, a segment of the species' population began to take hyperbolic measures to prevent death's occurrence.

Sun-Sailors eschew this philosophy. They live their lives freely, knowing that they will likely persist for millennia—or more—but that, against the backdrop of infinity, the mathematical odds of a tragic demise creep ever closer to 1.

The wisest of the Sun-Sailors insist that even those who persist for billions of years will do so only to one day meet their end as the universe collapses into itself.

Asked about their appellation, the Sun-Sailors revealed something even more astonishing: namely, that it is not uncommon, after several hundred millennia of life, for a Sun-Sailor to quietly walk away from their community and seek out the planet's only functional spaceport. The small craft launched from this port are calibrated for a single destination: their system's fiery yellow star.

For such a one, no funeral services are held, no songs sung. But those who perform this act are nonetheless spoken of with quiet respect: they have confronted the one thing in so long a life that remains unknown, that remains unknowable.

Miri, even though my body feels young—and I suppose it *looks* that way to you, too—I've never felt more aware of how *old* I truly am. In fact, I'm the oldest by far aboard this Company ship.

I'm the only one here who remembers a time when human death was something certain, a mundane occurrence.

To the others, it's some improbable, tragic 'maybe' that can be escaped for centuries on end. They're like the Sun-Sailors: death doesn't weigh heavily on their hearts and minds. They don't seek it out—but it also doesn't dwell with them constantly, as it does with me.

They don't whisper in the dark to someone lost to them long ago; they don't play host to ghosts.

They don't have *you.*

So, while they simply try to sell a product, I look into the cracks and crevices of every new society we find. I study their rituals, their stories, their technology, looking for the one thing we haven't been able to create:

The way to bring someone back.

That's why, until we make planetfall, I'm determined to pore over this book's pages, again and again. I'm desperate to uncover something new.

What is it? Is that your hand I feel, resting on mine? It's still a struggle to see you, to perceive your touch. But it feels like you're guiding my hands, compelling me to riffle backward through these pages. Miri, what I have missed?

Here. Two pages stuck together. What will we find hidden between them?

Maybe we can discover it together.

A small number of social groups among the Spin-Gliders of 44 Olivar c take a different tack entirely.

Rather than allowing their dead a final stasis upon the hydrogen seas below, the citizens of these communities carry their lost loved ones to the globe-spanning windstreams found in the upper atmosphere. Released here, the body of a dead Spin-Glider will be pulled into motion perpetually.

Where there is motion, they argue, there is life.

Living Spin-Gliders cannot join their fallen among these winds: the gusts are violent and strong, and they would whip a living soul away from the world he knew in no time at all.

The second life they release their loved ones to is therefore necessarily a mystery to them; they cannot join until their own time comes. But they believe, with every ounce of their being, that it is real—that they have conquered death.

Is this what you would show me, Miri? A 'second life'—a spiritual mystery?

You know me well enough to realize how hard a pill that is for me to swallow. I don't *do* spirituality; I can't wrap my mind around faith.

Please—don't mock me. Yes, I know. Even now, I'm talking to your ghost. But I'm no fool: I know what you are. You're a child's fantasy, conjured from my memories, the product of my brokenness.

Even as I acknowledge this, you fade from me. Don't go!

Stay with me, and remember, Miri. Remember our field, our river—how only you were strong enough to brave those currents.

I can picture it now: the day when, despite my cries and protests, you let it sweep you away, hollering gleefully as it carried you downstream. We both knew what awaited: a steep ledge overlooking a reservoir. You'd argued again and again that the waters were deep, that the waterfall would carry us safely over. The ten-foot freefall would be a momentary thrill, followed by a refreshing *splash*.

You were fully prepared to take that leap.

But you heard my shouts of protest—or perhaps caught a glimpse of my panicked face as I ran alongside the river after you— and you grabbed a tree root that jutted from the bank. You held on.

When I pulled you out, you said, between shivers, that you wouldn't do it again—not if I wouldn't go with you.

Decades later, though, you let time's river pull you away, even though I refused to follow.

What's worse, Miri, is that you didn't *need* to. Yes, I know: *Renew* was still so new when you got sick—but I'd saved enough money for us *both* to begin the treatment. It was *not* too late.

Yet you just smiled and shook your head, refusing without spoken justification, even knowing that I'd already begun to let it rewrite my own genetics.

And then, you were gone.

Now, I swear I will find you again.

Rivers, skies, worlds of rock and sun and blustering gusts of hydrogen. I look for you in these places.

Deep down, I know my motivations are selfish. You've gone somewhere I don't dare follow, and so, a coward to the end, I look for a way to bring *you* back to *me*.

Knowing all of this, I look out my vessel's starboard window, awaiting the light of alien suns…

I'll sail on past them. I'll traverse this void as far as I must go —carried through the infinite cosmos as if caught in a river's current.

See P.G. Streeter's story "A Xenothanatologist's Guidebook to Death Practices Among the Sapient Species of the Outer Perseus Arm of the Milky Way Galaxy" online at Metaphorosis.
If you liked it, leave a comment. Authors love that!
Remember to subscribe to our e-mail updates so you'll know when new stories are posted.

About the story

A friend of mine recently earned a degree in the field of thanatology—the study of death. I was fascinated to learn about this discipline, and I even imagined that if I were to go back in time to repeat my own years in academia, I might choose to study this subject myself. But, as it is, I've made a career of teaching literature and a hobby of dabbling in some writing of my own. So, I asked: how could I take this idea and apply it to a bit of speculative fiction?

Of course I immediately began imagining alien creatures, and how their own views on death might be shaped by the unique circumstances of their physiology and planetary ecology. The textbook sections of this story started coming to me, and I furiously started to put them to paper.

Attempting to make the personal narrative underpinning all of this work just as well was much more difficult. I knew I needed this part to be more emotional, whereas the textbook portions were intellectual. The narrator needed to be grappling with death on a personal level, and that story needed to resonate with those informational passages in a coherent way. Honestly, though, this was really hard! I'm infinitely grateful to B. Morris Allen, whose guidance during the revision process really helped me make that story come to life so much more strongly than it did in earlier drafts.

The universe is big, and I have no doubt that there's other intelligent life out there. I don't know how those beings conceptualize mortality—but I do know that confronting the reality of death can be a harrowing personal journey. The more I look beyond the initial perspectives I learned by rote as a child—the more I turn to the wisdom of people across different disciplines and from different cultures—the more comfortable I get with the ultimate mystery of it all. Years ago, trying to tell this story would have put me into a state of perpetual heebie-jeebies. Somehow, though, I've gotten to a place where this story was exceedingly fun to write. It's the fun that comes from being curious about ideas, from allowing yourself to luxuriate in questions of what if. Art, and especially fiction, have helped me get there. I hope that, among whatever else it made you think and feel, this story invoked a bit of that curiosity in you, too--and that you had a bit of fun staring into the abyss with me.

A question for the author

Q: How often do you think about writing during a day?

A: Some part of my scattered, overactive mind is probably always thinking about writing, but I've worked really hard to reign that in, and to put those thoughts on hold until an appropriate time arises. Because of this, my phone is full of notes with little snippets of ideas—new premises, story titles, character names, and bits of dialogue that I plan to come back to later. The surfaces of my house are littered with sticky notes and scraps of paper that serve the same purpose. Much of it doesn't end up getting used, but most of the stories I've gotten published these last few years owe themselves in part to those notes. The notes are important for another reason: if I simply dropped everything to write whenever the fancy struck me, I'd probably get fired from my dayjob—and my wife and kids would be pretty grumpy, too.

About the author

P.G Streeter lives with his wife and two sons in Maryland, where he teaches high school English and philosophy. He writes speculative fiction because he can't figure out any other way to get all the strange and disturbing dreams out of his head.

pgstreeter.wordpress.com/publications, @p_g_sWrites

Holding On

Justen Russell

I was eight years old when Yuri Zhilin floated away.

Yuri, the first man to orbit Io; the first human to walk on Ganymede. Replacing the lens of the JUVENTAS orbital telescope was supposed to be a routine procedure. Something done a half-dozen times with a half-dozen other telescopes around the closer planets and their moons. It wasn't even the first untethered spacewalk over Jupiter; Mimi Lin had beaten him to that almost a year earlier.

Still, I *had* to watch. It was Yuri.

I'd sucked up to José all week so we could watch the broadcast together on his father's new omniscreen. At that resolution we could count the stitches under Yuri's ROSCOSMOS badge—four: one for each planet he had orbited. Of course, I was more interested in his hair. Six long, straw-blond strands had escaped the bun on the back of Yuri's head and, without gravity to restrain them, they danced. Hairs just like mine.

Before his spacewalk, Yuri gave a tour of the capsule where he and Mimi had spent the past seven years. He showed the workstations filled with experiments, the sleeping harnesses, and what counted as a toilet in zero g. "Study hard, earthlings," he said in his thick Russian accent, "and you can be like us." José and I, we believed him too.

At the cockpit, Mimi Lin waved for the camera and, for perhaps the first time in my life, I understood what it meant to be jealous. I would have given anything to be her then, to have floated next to Yuri just once.

While he suited up, Yuri explained in Russian the purpose of everything he would wear. Gloves, belt, boots, I caught the main words—just not the small ones in between. José and I would use those same words when we played to make it more authentic. Like it was possible for us to work for ROSCOSMOS too.

Yuri's helmet had its own internal camera and when he put it on, his face appeared as a small inset in the bottom right-hand corner of our screen—smiling as always. He blew a kiss to the Earth, then pushed himself towards the airlock.

Ten meters of open space separated their capsule from the orbital telescope. Any closer and the protective magnetic field of their spacecraft would have damaged the satellite's delicate sensors. Ten meters exactly—no give or take. Mimi Lin held them in perfect alignment.

Yuri had one hundred and eighty-nine successful spacewalks on his record. I knew that number by heart. It was twenty-six more than Mimi Lin. It was nearly double the third place. One hundred eighty-nine times, Yuri Zhilin had stepped out into the void, then on the one hundred and ninetieth his mind shut down.

I could tell something was wrong the moment he pushed off, even before his arms started to flail, even before his legs started to kick. His eyes, so clear in that ultra-high definition inset in the bottom right corner of our screen, went blank. Yuri was no longer there.

With a forty-three-minute speed-of-light delay, there was nothing anyone on earth could do except watch. Whatever would happen already had. Mimi Lin had left the cockpit and hesitated at the airlock; she had suited up, calculated trajectories, and then suited back down. Twenty minutes before we watched Yuri kick off, she had concluded what we were about to: Yuri Zhilin was already gone.

'Space Sickness', the TV commentator explained after the 'live' broadcast cut out. It would become the new word of the summer. 'A rare catatonic response to stimulatory overload in high stress situations.' It was nearly unheard of among professional astronauts, but everyone knew they were the minority in space. Among the asteroid miners and orbital laborers—well—no one kept statistics on them, but 'Space Sickness', we would learn, probably claimed more than half. Outer space was littered with the bodies of those who couldn't quite hold on; usually, they were not broadcast for the whole world to see.

My mother named me Laika after the Russian dog that went to space. I think she meant it to be aspirational. *A stray who made it to the stars.* No one ever told her that the dog died on the way up.

No one tells a woman like my mother things that might ruin her smile.

She left Quito for Manta when they started building the elevator. It was a good time to be a woman with a smile like hers. The streets there were full of contractors, astrophysicists, and astronauts, all with good jobs and full pockets. Back before the gated communities went up, and Manta became another Quito on the sea. Even Yuri passed through on his way up.

She said my father was an astronaut named Mudak. She used to tell me he was where I got my blonde hair. There is no way she could have known for sure—there were a lot of blond foreigners in Manta—but if I was going to have a fake father, he might as well have been an astronaut.

I always knew there was a real Mudak—whether he was my father or not. My mother could not have made up a name like that. See, people did not tell my mother things, but they told me. Things like 'Laika died on the way up' and 'a mutt's name suits a *mulatta* like you'. Things like 'you know *mudak* means testicle in Russian, right?'.

Mudak is like calling someone an asshole. *Mudak* is calling someone a jerk. Usually, *mudak* is what you call a person you don't like, but sometimes Mudak is how another *mudak* introduces his friend when they are trying to be funny and don't want to give a real name to the smiling girl.

I don't know if Mudak really was an astronaut, or if he just wanted to see more than a smile. I don't know if he really was my father, or just the best *mudak* around the right time. All the men my mother smiled at were *mudaks*, but if she had any regrets, she never told me. The *mudaks* kept us fed. At least, they used to.

I never had a smile like my mothers, even before I lost three teeth fighting over something silly like my father and his name, but that did not matter, because I was going to space. Sometimes after I fought, I would tell my mother I had tripped; that I wasn't meant for gravity. She liked that too. "Just like your father," she would say, and I think she meant it—not like the other mothers. The ones who say, "Yes darling, someday you will have a mansion on the hill," because they know that the day their child finally understands, she will have grown up and no longer needs her mother.

For my mom, there was always something romantic about the elevator. It was never just another feature along the horizon. The wind turbines, the luxury cruise liners, the mansions on the hill—those were meant for *mudaks* and not for us. The mutt never gets invited inside, but there is room for her on a rocket, if she isn't concerned about coming back.

In the morning, when the sun shone from the east and the sky was clear, you could see the elevator—a thin, silver thread reflecting the light, stretched taut from heaven to horizon. At night, some trait of the filament in the upper atmosphere caused it to glow—the *equatorial aurora*—and a dancing line of green and purple floated in front of the stars. Most of the time, however, the cable itself was too far away and too thin to see.

Only the crawlers were visible when, for José's tenth birthday, his father drove us to San Mateo, where the cliffs overlooked the ocean. Before the elevator, he'd read, astronauts used to train on special parabolic flights. Ones that fly high in the sky then nose-dive straight down so the passengers inside can feel what it is like to be without gravity. They still did, I told him, just as children, not astronauts-to-be. The first time Yuri floated was at a birthday party where the parents had rented a parabolic plane; but our cliffs would be just as good.

"We will float for two whole seconds," José said. He had done the math and knew that part for sure. "Just like Yuri," he added for me.

We raced up the cliffs, each of us eager to be the first to jump, but in the end, it was José's birthday and I let him win. Only, after he leapt, I didn't; I couldn't.

I remember wanting to. I had been excited, even as José's scream echoed off the water below. But then I walked to the edge to make sure the landing was clear. I don't remember if it was. I just remember how much taller that cliff looked from the top, and how very, very far away the ocean seemed.

José hollered for me to jump. Then, he climbed back up and tried to convince me that it would be okay. It wasn't me that needed convincing, it was my legs; they wouldn't co-operate. They wouldn't step. I wanted to jump. At least, I wanted to *have* jumped, but I couldn't make myself approach that void.

When he could wait no longer, José left me there. He jumped again, and again, and again—and I didn't.

Each time, José was fine. It was me, still at the top, who was broken. I had to climb back down the way I had come up.

José didn't yell at me for ruining his birthday. He pretended we had both had fun, but I cried that night because I knew I would never be a Yuri, or a Mimi—or even brave like my mother when she left everything she had known for a new city. I would never be able to jump.

The next morning my mother wiped away my tears and marched me all the way back to the cliffs. It took hours to get there on foot, but she said, "Trust me." And I did.

We climbed the rocks together—slowly this time—and she stood with me at the top, all the way back from the edge. She said, "Sometimes, when you know what you have to do, it is better not to look." Then she grabbed my hand and said, "Close your eyes," and we ran. We didn't look and we didn't stop, we just fell off the edge of the world, and for two full seconds we were weightless in the air.

I jumped off the cliff a second time, and third, and a fourth—until my mother said we had to go back because the sun would soon disappear. It was easier every time. By the end of the day, it no longer mattered if I ran or if I looked. My legs kept working.

My mother laughed the whole way home—about the way I had screamed in the air, about the way my arms and legs had flailed when I fell. It didn't matter; I had jumped. I laughed about my flailing arms too.

Her smile always made everything okay. I wish I could have learned to smile like my mother, to have given that back to her just once before I left.

'Study hard, earthlings,' Yuri had said, 'and you can be like me.' José, maybe; he had it all planned out, every step required for a documented position at the top. Scholarship to a secondary school on the hill, two years of college outside Manta, engineering degree from the University in another three. He would never be an astronaut—ROSCOSMOS didn't scout for people like us—but he could get up the elevator, so long as his father sold their house to afford tuition. It wouldn't be grades that held him back.

My mother didn't have a house to sell. She had a smile, and every year, it seemed, fewer and fewer men smiled back. Maybe it was the whisper of wrinkles around her eyes, or maybe just the way a city changes, but my mother had started smiling at men she would have never smiled at before. Men who were not good to be around when the smiling stopped.

I used to dream that someday she would only need to smile at me. I would come back and look after her the way she had looked after me; we would hold on together. I knew it would never happen. The best I could dream was that she would no longer need to look after me—a girl who would never smile like my mother could.

I started standing at the docks near the unemployed women and men, waiting for my way out. While José was studying, and the children on the hill played, I pretended I was watching the elevator; but I liked to go best when the weather was bad, when even the crawlers were hard to see.

The docks were less crowded when it rained, and I would think, *Maybe if there is no one else, someone will choose me.* If a boat came by looking for workers, I would puff out my chest and stand on my toes to look strong and tall. Then, I would keep staring where the crawlers should be, even as the boat left.

That is why Belen chose me. She was looking at the elevator too.

"We'll get close enough to touch it," she told me. "If that's what you want." She was tall, and far too thin, with dark curly hair and a frown that said she understood.

She told her captain she'd chosen me instead of a big man with arms the size of tree trunks because, "She'll eat less." He shrugged and wiped the rain from his bald head, then told us both to help him unload.

I'd gotten lucky. You have to get lucky to make it to space. Even Yuri was a backup on his first mission, until the main pilot caught the flu. Before that he was just a *mudak* looking up.

From the shore, the wind turbines had always seemed small. Like the yachts and mansions that also decorated the horizon, they were just toys. Simulacra that filled the ocean between the mainland and the Galapagos, sprouting from the water like reeds in a pond. I used to think, *How can those hoist ten-tonne rockets into space?*

On the rusted *Buena Mañana*, as we floated directly beneath one, the sun flickered in the shadows of its whirring blades, each two hundred meters across. I was almost afraid to see the elevator the same way; afraid and excited. It would be real then. Would I still be willing to leap?

"Mussels will grow anywhere," Belen told me, as she zipped the wetsuit up to my neck. "Hanging out here, where there are no starfish or crabs, they get big."

The elevator had dispensed with the need for rocket fuel—at least at launch—but the crawlers that climbed along it needed energy to reach space. Energy supplied by the wind through those turbines and the massive electric cables that stretched out between them under the sea. As Belen explained, there were mussels growing in long, cylindrical nets called *socks* that dangled all along each cable's length.

"Haru buys them as *seed*," she said. That's what you call juvenile mussels, when they are just large enough to start clumping together—about half the length of a fingernail—mussel seed. Any smaller and they would slip right through the mesh of the *socks*.

"Nine months after we hang them, they are big enough to harvest," Belen said. "That's where we come in. Someone needs to dive down and hook the *socks*, so the crane can haul them up. Don't worry; you'll love it. The open ocean is just like outer space."

She had helmets to make me believe her. Tucked in a locker along the side of the fishing trawler were eight flawless, glassy orbs. Space helmets, exactly as I had seen them in countless magazines and low res-feed. Helmets just like Yuri's, save, of course, the ROSCOSMOS lettering.

"They used to make them in Manta," Belen said, "so, we find plenty floating out here. They work the same in zero bar or ten, so might as well use them diving."

"They float?"

"Would you believe that some people try to ride up outside the elevator with just a helmet and an air tank?" Belen said. "I don't know what they think they'll do after they make it to the top." She chose a small helmet for me to try on. "When they are sitting up there in outer space in a t-shirt and shorts, but they never make it that far anyway. Not with a diving regulator connecting the helmet to the tank."

The helmet felt tight around the neck, but Belen seemed happy with that. "A good seal," she said, "will keep the water out. But a diving regulator," she clipped the helmet in place, "that's what puts air there in the first place. It *regulates* how fast air comes out of the tank. It's designed to match the pressure around it. That way you can breathe when the weight of the entire ocean is trying to squeeze you. In higher pressure water, it delivers higher pressure air. Thing is, at least for the people trying to ride on top of a climber, when there is no pressure around it, a diving regulator won't deliver any air at all ... or maybe the valves freeze?" She hesitated, trying to figure out exactly how someone would die in her hypothetical. "Either way, no air. They pass out halfway up and fall. The water around us is littered with their bodies, and their helmets."

"How *do* you make it up then?" I asked.

"That's the silly part," Belen said. "They want us up there— the companies at least. Nothing is locked. If you pick the right crawler, you can seal yourself inside and ride all the way to space. Most of the floaters out here never had a plan, and never had a chance. But us—it'll be different for us."

I didn't miss her choice of words: *us*.

"From up close, we'll be able to read the logos," Belen said, choosing a helmet for herself. "The mining crawlers are the good ones. Anglo American, Ferrobras New Horizon, Objectif Outre-Terre. The last few times it's been NASA and CNSA. Can't stow away with astronauts."

It hadn't occurred to me to be picky about what spaceship I ended up on. "Why not?" I asked.

"Pick the wrong crawler and it's out the airlock," Belen snapped her fingers, "like that!" Then she laughed. I couldn't tell if she was serious or not.

If anything, the ocean was the opposite of space. At least, the opposite of what I expected space would be. Space was open. Space was empty. Whenever Yuri left his capsule, every star had been visible from light-eons away. The ocean was full.

A blue-green haze swallowed everything around me. It took all that I had to stay calm. Less than a meter away, Belen faded into the murk until the shadow of her shadow was all that remained. The boat above us disappeared and then there was nothing. Nothing above; nothing below. Nothing but blue-green.

We descended further, the water getting darker as well as cloudier until I couldn't see my hands, my breathing getting shallower and faster until, as if by magic, the water cleared. There was a line, turbid above, clear beneath. The lower edge of a vast, undersea cloud.

A little further still and the open, empty darkness was not quite so empty. Something was there in the black; the cable, dark and thicker than I could wrap my arms around. It stretched as far as I could see in either direction. All along its length hung the socks, tall, mesh cylinders bulging with fist-sized mussels.

One after another, we harvested and replaced. Belen showed me how to attach the hook of the crane to the loop of a sock, and how to signal to Captain Haru it was ready to be lifted. Then we waited as the sock ascended, pulled up into the undersea cloud. I could imagine, just as easily, that it fell—plummeting into the thick atmosphere of some gassy moon I was orbiting. In the dark, open depths, there was no up or down; I was weightless. Belen had been right, I loved it.

When the replacement sock came, she showed me how to guide it gently to the cable. Since it was mostly empty, with just a smattering of mussel seed, it was easy to pull around. We lined the ends up so that one draped over each side of the cable. Belen let me unhook the crane and connect it to the next sock.

As I floated, waiting, I imagined I was Yuri outside his spaceship for the first time. I exhaled, and the bubbles streamed up from somewhere near the back of my helmet. I watch them dancing their way to the surface, imagining they were stars.

That was all it took. A moment of distraction.

It was just a light bump as I drifted past one of the dangling socks. Something caught. A valve on my tank, or a clasp on my wetsuit. I couldn't swim away. I couldn't turn. I couldn't move.

In that moment I realized just how very, very far I was below the ocean's surface. Underwater, I couldn't have called to Belen if I had thought to, but I didn't think. *If you know what you have to do* ... fighting panic, I put my feet against the sock ... *it is better not to look* ... I kicked off as hard as I could. The only way to get free. Something shifted inside the sock, and for a moment I moved forward. Then it pulled back twice as hard.

I wheezed. The full weight of the sock and all its mussels slammed against me, knocking the air from my lungs. I coughed, trying to find my wind. I coughed on water.

Water!

I hadn't heard my helmet crack, but water was seeping in. A slow, cold trickle. I moved my head. A stream of bubbles ran towards the surface. Water flooded past my chin. There was nothing I could do. My arms flailed. My legs kicked. I tried to lift my head; anything to keep my mouth above the water. It surged past my ears. I gasped and choked on salt.

A firm hand grabbed my shoulder. Belen! I grabbed back and pulled, together we could ... she kicked me, hard. What little air I had left bubbled out of my nose.

Another blow. Belen pinned me with her bodyweight, holding me down. Drowning me. I tried to fight. Tried to push off her. Then, in one, firm motion, she grabbed my helmet and twisted. The water stopped seeping in. Only the seal had broken. She held me as, with the regulator, she purged air back into the helmet. She continued to hold me until I stopped struggling, until my breathing returned to normal. Until I was calm.

With her hand on mine, Belen guided my hand to the single loop of netting that had tangled around a valve of my air tank. She made me work it free from the sock. Then we ascended together slowly, her guiding me firmly the whole way to the top.

"You panicked," Belen said back at the surface, back on the *Buena Mañana.*

"I— I was drowning."

"Divers get tangled. Helmets come loose. But, if you had stayed calm ..." she frowned. "It's panic that kills, down here and up above."

I wanted to cry.

"You're learning," she said, more gently. "Next time you'll do better."

"N— Next time?" I was shivering, even though I wasn't cold.

Belen wrapped her arm around my shoulder. "Do you know why they want us up there—the orbital companies?" She wiped a tear from my cheek. "Truth is, you can't stow away without someone noticing. We'd never even make it onto the crawler of a research ship, but the mining ships, they want us. Not because we'll work hard, because we're disposable. Everything up there is dangerous. They only *hire* people for the safest jobs. A stowaway gets drilled through by a micrometeorite, there is no paperwork. Construction is better than mining. More jobs to transition to inside. But we only get promoted if, when we fall, we get back up."

I dove more times that day because Belen made me, and over the next few because there was work to do, and I wanted to. I never had another problem, but the thought was always there in the back of my head: it only takes one mistake. If I had stayed calm, if I hadn't panicked ... I thought of my fearless mother, and for perhaps the second time in my life I wondered, what if I wasn't meant for space? Maybe I took after my father. Maybe Space Sickness ran in my blood.

When the night sky was clear, Belen and Captain Haru liked to sit out on the roof of the *Buena Mañana* and watch the stars. I lay beside them as we rocked gently in the ocean waves, not a light between us and the horizon. This, at least, was somewhere I belonged. To look, at least, the stars were free.

"When the first explorers sailed across the equator," Belen said, "they found different constellations in a different sky and had to write new stories to make sense of them. It will be the same up in space. When we finally leave the solar system the stars in the sky will move. We will say things like 'Orion is getting fat, we must be moving towards Betelgeuse', or 'Aquarius has sprung a leak, adjust to starboard'."

"I think they will have computers to tell them where to go," I said. Computers with future engineers like José to program them.

"Computers only say what someone told them to say. I will want to know for myself what I am looking at." Belen said.

"Then look," said Haru. "What a view we have from here." He had been silent so long, I hadn't realized he was listening.

"They need us up there," Belen said, "Space will be tamed by its workers, not its astronauts. For every Magellan or Columbus, there were a hundred unnamed sailors—every bit as impressive— just less well known."

"You are already an important part of it." Haru said. "Until someone finds mussels growing on asteroids, they need you here."

"They will, though," said Belen. "Not mussels, but something. They will forget us eventually. Everyone says there is nothing up there to support life, but that is the same way we used to think of the ocean. When the Polynesians first packed their whole families on boats, they set sail without knowing what they would find. For them the ocean was as hostile as space is to our explorers today."

"Space is not an ocean," Haru said.

"Most of the ocean is empty and inhospitable," Belen said, "but those early explorers found ways of telling what was over the horizon to find islands they needed, and ways of telling what was below the waves to find the fish. We will too. They looked for clouds to find islands with freshwater springs; we will use spectroscopy to tell if asteroids have water and oxides to harvest."

"Maybe someday," Haru said, "but not yet."

"Someday," Belen echoed a little more somberly. She, like me, was looking at the elevator—that glowing purple line—and not the stars behind it.

Belen saw it first.

I know because of the way she swore under her breath and shifted in her seat. In hindsight, that was to block my view. I thought she had cut her hand on a mussel, as I had already a half dozen times that morning. Between the waves and the sweeping shadow of a turbine blade, it could have been anything floating out there.

Haru was not so discreet. "*Puta!*" he swore and jumped to his feet.

"Just leave it," Belen tried. "It's already dead."

There was a sinking feeling in my gut.

"Him, not it," Haru said tersely, "*he* will spoil the waters."

By the time Haru returned with a boathook, *he* had drifted close, bumping against the hull of the *Buena Mañana* with each wave; a human body floating in the water.

His eyes were open, staring up at the sky as what remained of his clothes billowed gently in the waves. The skin was bleached of all color, but with that dark, matted hair and those emaciated cheeks he could only have come from Manta.

"Laika," Belen said urgently. "Go grab a tarp."

"No, we need her help first." Haru hooked under the torso with his pole.

"He'll cook in this sun," Belen insisted. She was already half over the side, grabbing at an arm.

"This is not the last corpse she will see out here. She will need to toughen up eventually."

When I did not leave, Belen relented. "Grab a leg."

The stench was unbearable even before we pulled him from the water. As the body flopped onto the deck with the unpleasant sound of a wet sponge hitting wood, seawater and built-up gasses began to gurgle from his throat. I didn't gag—but Belen did.

Haru walked off to grab the tarp himself. Once again, I could not make myself move.

"If *he* couldn't be bothered to figure out the ocean," Belen told me after Haru had left, "I don't know how *he* expected to figure out space."

I did not help them wrap the body. All I could do was stare. I kept thinking, *He is just a boy. Maybe thirteen or fourteen, my age or younger.* I had not expected that.

I had always known there would be bodies around the elevator, everyone did. *They litter the sea.* But when I had imagined dead bodies floating in the ocean, they were always old. It made no sense, I know. Octogenarians did not try to stow away, but dead and old just went together. At least, they had until then.

I felt sick. I don't remember if I made it to the side of the boat before I threw up.

The dead boy needed glasses—when he was alive, that is. There were small divots in the sides of his head, just above his ears, the kind people got from wearing too-small glasses all their life. When he was young, and did not yet have those glasses, I bet he couldn't see the elevator—even when the light was just right. What about the mansions on the hill? If he could, he looked up there and said, like everyone did when they were too young to know better, "One day I will own one of those." Only, the mansions on the hill grew larger, not more numerous.

Manta used to have factories, and I decided that the dead boy's mother worked in one of those. Maybe a factory making space helmets for the astronauts who went up. She even took one home as a souvenir. She set it on a shelf in the starter home she bought on the side of the valley—back when she could afford a starter home and glasses. Back before the factories closed, there were many people like that.

They were already building spaceships in orbit before the elevator was finished, but they were not building helmets there. Not until someone who already had a mansion on the top of a hill realized it was cheaper to send up tightly packed ingots of metal and solid glass than large, empty helmets. I bet that someone bought their neighbor's mansion after thinking up that idea, so they could tear it down and make their own bigger.

The new space helmets were 3D-printed in a workshop at the top of the elevator, and the factories down in Manta were boarded up. After that, things got harder for everyone, except those who owned the elevator or the workshops up in space. The dead boy's mother had to sell her home and did not buy a new one. She should have sold her souvenir helmet too. Maybe then it wouldn't have been so tempting for her son.

Sometimes my mother did not eat so she could keep me fed, and we were better off than most in the valley. I wondered what it had been like for the boy. Had he waited at the docks like I did, hoping the next boat might pick him instead of someone else? Maybe he had tried to work, and stood in line outside one of the few factories left, hoping it would let him in before it closed too. I could not tell from his bloated hands if he had ever tried another way, or if the elevator was his first as well as his last idea. I would never know if he was like me, drawn to a dream, or if he just had nowhere else to turn but up.

People like us would never get factory jobs or starter homes. People like us made our own way or starved. But if even Yuri had floated away, what hope did the rest of us have?

Belen disappeared, leaving Haru and I to pull the rest of the mussels from the socks. He worked quickly, making up for lost time. I was next to useless. My hands would not stop shaking.

When I couldn't take the silence anymore, I asked, "Do they ever make it—the people who try to ride the elevator?"

He looked at me a moment, then out to sea, as though contemplating the question very carefully. The whole time, his hands never stopped sorting. "Have you made it, Laika?" He finally asked.

"I'm trying," I said.

Haru nodded. "Me too." Then he added, seeing my confused look, "*Make it* is a relative term. The Buddha preaches contentment. If one is content with what they have, then they have *made it.* If one always wants more, then it does not matter how much they have. Those who climb, some of them will *make it* up the elevator, but then what? Have they *made it?* They will share a bunk with five others and work more hours than there are in a day. How long do you really think they will last? A month? A season? Of those who *make it* that far, and that's pretty far, most will be dead within a year. But will they have *made it?* A year with a bunk and two meals a day would be *making it* for some of the people I have seen floating out here."

Haru shook his head. "We tell stories because they give us hope. We say that if someone can make it up the elevator, if they can work hard and stay safe, if they have just the right luck, if they get noticed by just the right people, then maybe they can *make it*—whatever that means. And of course, we say, if they can do it, we could too—if we had to, not that we will. There is a certain comfort to that, no?"

"I don't know." It did not seem comforting.

"You come from Manta. Tell me, have you heard about the mansion that is owned by a former stowaway?"

I nodded. "Everyone has."

"If we were closer to the shore," Haru asked, "could you point it out for me?"

I shook my head. The closest I had ever been was when a *mudak* who liked my mother decided to take us both for a drive in his car. Even he, in his fancy car, couldn't get through the community gates.

"I have heard many stories about starship captains who were once stowaways until they worked their way up. They always retire with a mansion of their own. I've heard it a thousand times, but if even a tenth of those stories were true, then almost all of the mansions on Manta's hill must belong to former stowaways by now. I'd think, if that were the case, then you, a local, could point out one or two for sure. *Apocryphal,* that is what we call stories like that.

"The Buddha preaches contentment. That should be easy for us. You'd think fully bellies, a roof to lay on, and a part to play in what we watch going on above would be enough. We do have a part, Laika, all of us, however small. We feed Manta; without Manta, no elevator, no space. But still, we long for more. We dream dreams and say someday it will be us who *make it*, because there is no real harm in that, until there is.

"Truth is, that boy on the deck never had a chance; maybe thinking he did is what kept him going on hungry nights, but it is also what made him think he could make it up the elevator. I'm sure that even the Buddha looked forward to a dry fire when it rained, but he knew the difference between a dream and reality. That the boy died in the end, that is tragic—but maybe he lived first because of his dream. That, in a way, would have been *making it*—would it not? If only he had known when a dream should remain just a dream."

Belen was at the back of the boat leaning against a railing, looking out towards the elevator as though nothing had happened.

We were close enough now that the crawlers had taken form. The colorful squiggles of company logos were almost clear enough to read—perhaps if I knew their designs better. Belen did not look at me as I approached, but her hand wiped something from her cheek.

She took a sharp, deep breath. "It gets easier," she said, but she did not sound like she believed it. "Just know, for every floater we find out here, there are ten stowaways who make it to the top."

That didn't sound right, but neither did arguing.

"Would you have tried swimming?" Belen asked. "Out on the dock, if I hadn't picked you?" She turned with red ringed-eyes. I had never seen her like that. "If I had picked the fat man instead of you. How long would you have waited for another boat before trying on your own?"

The elevator was too far to swim, but with a raft—would I have tried that eventually? Would I have ended up just like the boy under the tarp? "I don't know," I said. "It's a good thing you chose me."

"Is it?" Belen asked. "I always say I'm going to go up there someday, and Haru laughs with me. Like it's a joke we are sharing, like it's a game. But it's not. Not to me. I want to ride the elevator, Laika. I want to be in space, I ..." She shook her head. "I keep pretending that I can. I keep saying, 'soon'. That I am almost ready, that I have it almost planned out, that I have to be smart about it.

Holding On, by Justen Russell

"I *have* planned it, Laika, you know I have planned it all and planned it all again, but there is only so long I can keep planning and keep pretending that it will happen.

"Every time we are near the elevator, I look at the logos on the crawlers and I actually hope it says NASA, because then I will have an excuse. Then, at least, I can live with myself when I don't. They don't like stowaways on research vessels.

"Twice now it has been for a mining firm, and I didn't go. I could have. There was a pressurized crate and I could have just snuck inside. You know I know how. Maybe they would have caught me. Maybe they would have sent me back down. Maybe it wouldn't have resealed, and I would have died on the way up, but I will never know because I didn't even try."

"I'm glad you didn't die." I wasn't sure what else to say.

"I wish I were dying," Belen said. "How sick is that? I wish I were starving. I tell myself that if I were starving, that if I had no other choice, that if I would die if I didn't find a way to stowaway on the next crawler, I would risk it. I would try because I would have nothing left to lose … but that's not true. I will always have a reason to wait. What does that mean, Laika, that even in my dreams I only go out of desperation, only because there was no other way?"

"That you have something to lose," I said. "That's not such a bad thing."

"Is it?" Belen snapped. "I'm what—too lucky?—too fortunate? Too rich to be desperate enough to follow my dreams—yet too poor for there to be another way." She laughed. Not a happy laugh, an unpleasant half a snort, half a sob. "I'm jealous of a corpse, Laika. It's ridiculous. I am being ridiculous. He is dead. He was stupid and now he is dead and under a tarp and still, I want to be him because at least he tried. At least he had the chance to get lucky. At least he got to know. How pathetic is that? How can that make any sense?"

I never really knew the right words to say. That was my mother. I never had her smile. I pulled Belen close for a hug.

"I want to go," she said, "even if it doesn't work out. Even if I end up dead. I just want to know. Was I good enough? Could I have made it? I want to be up there right now looking down on this ocean of *merda*." She sunk into my arms. "Why can't I do that?"

I spoke my mother's words: "When you know what you have to do, it is better not to look. Just go."

"If only it were that easy," Belen said. "I don't know if I am more scared that I will fall, or that I will never even try—but I'm scared, Laika. I'm scared."

"I'm scared too." I said, and I was. As they never used to tire of telling me: the real Laika, the Russian dog, she died on the way up.

"You're just a kid," Belen said. "You still have time." Did I? Or had we both already looked over the edge and seen the rocks below.

In the morning, as the sun shone from the east, I could see the elevator. Not one thread, but several—six parallel lines stretched taut between the sky and a metal island in the middle of the ocean. I made up my mind before we were close enough to read the labels on the crawlers—if they were wrong, I would wait on that island until they were right. When you know what you have to do, it is better not to look.

I laid my equipment out along the deck—like Belen had for diving—and chose from the regulators hidden in the back of the locker. Those designed for altitude, not diving. Belen had planned everything, and then planned again.

I felt a pang of guilt as I set a helmet on the deck, but there wasn't time for that. I would be forgiven; this was why she had brought me here, to show her it was possible. I took one slow, calming breath, then changed my mind. I ran down the stairs into the *Buena Mañana*'s cabin to where Belen was still asleep.

"I'm going," I whispered, nudging Belen awake. "Come with me. Don't think, just come." She didn't understand but sat up, too groggy to resist my pull, at least, at first.

We were halfway up the stairs when she asked about Haru. I shook my head and pulled her harder. There was no time to slow down.

"He'll be fine." He had his contentment. There were plenty of others in Manta who would love to harvest mussels and look up at the stars. "This is the reason you chose me, isn't it?" The big man on the dock would never have pulled Belen up with him, would never have thought to look up at all.

"Objectif." Belen gasped as we stepped into the sun, and I looked—though I shouldn't have, because I truly did not want to know. The colorful squiggles on one crawler's glossy sides had resolved into the square and circle logo of Objectif Outre-Terre—an orbital construction company.

"We have to go now," I said.

I pulled Belen to the equipment and helped her put it on. Gear for the swim to the island, and gear to stay warm on the ride up.

"I can't," she said, then, as I tried to put a helmet on her head, she finally stopped me. "What if …"

"We could die," I agreed, "maybe. Or we could live. Don't you want to know?" The sea may be littered with the bodies of those who did not *make it*, but Manta was choked full of those who never even tried.

"I want to try," I said. Reflected in Belen's helmet, the elevator did not seem so tall. It seemed to bend towards us—bowing. No one kept statistics on stowaways, but I doubt half made it as far as we already had. "Don't think," I said, "jump."

She let me put the helmet on her head.

With it on, Belen could have been Mimi. It was my own reflection, however, that caught me off guard. Even missing three teeth, I had Yuri's smile: bright, infectious, *content*. We were going to space. The mutts were going to fly.

"Hold on," I said, as I took her hand and we jumped.

See Justen Russell's story "Holding On" online at Metaphorosis.
If you liked it, leave a comment. Authors love that!
Remember to subscribe to our e-mail updates so you'll know when new stories are posted.

About the story

At its core, "Holding On" is about coming to terms with what it means to follow your dreams. In our world, very few people will ever be astronauts, or presidents, or best-selling authors. Even among the privileged and connected, who have more opportunities than most, luck can be more important than skill. In the face of abysmal odds, as we grow up, most of us will replace our childhood dreams with the more attainable sort.

I don't think I ever acknowledged giving up on certain dreams. Somewhere between middle school and University I simply relegated the moonshot goals from "someday soon" to "someday." Very purposely, I never pursued them. Despite wanting to write, it was safer to leave it as a dream for the future, "when I had something to say." The reality was, in putting words to the page I would have had to confront the very real risk that I might fail.

The idea for "Holding On" was flushed out during the first lockdown of the COVID-19 pandemic. In Paris, where I was living, we were mostly confined to our homes. One hour of outdoor activity was permitted each day, provided we were alone and stayed within one kilometer of our apartments. Surrounded by tall buildings, there were only a few spaces I could stand to feel the sun on my skin. It was in one of those, looking up at the bright blue sky, that I started to wonder what a space elevator would look like. Would it seem to taper, would it be visible from a distance, would it seem to curve towards a vanishing point in the sky? Europe has no shortage of tall, impressive monuments. There are architectural spaces that play with space to invoke a sense of grandeur. I have stood beneath building meant to humble me and felt incredibly small. I could imagine what a space elevator would feel like to look at, but not what I would actually see. Maybe that is why I kept coming back to it?

Laika, Belen, and Haru all grew out of those imaginings. I could feel what it would be like for them, growing up, working and living in the shadows of a gateway to the stars. What would it be like to have, always on the horizon, a constant reminder of how small your life currently is, and how big it could be. Living in an impressive city of my own, with great monuments visible along the horizon, far outside of my one-kilometer existence, I could empathize at least a little with their plight.

The mussels came from an article I read about mussel farming off deep-sea wind turbines in the Netherlands. Floating away in space was a deep-seated fear of my wife's that she wanted me to share. The parallels between Polynesian- and space- exploration—that is a pet comparison of mine. I think there are many parallels in the past to the transformations of today: space exploration, artificial intelligence, genetic engineering, migration, inequality, even if the specifics are different.

I suppose you could say "Holding On" came from having far too much time to think and far too little to do but dream my own dreams and turn "someday" back into "someday soon." A big thank you to all those who helped me flesh this story out.

A question for the author

Q: Do you live near where you were born? Have you traveled much?

A: While not quite antipodal, France is an ocean and the bulk of a continent away from my hometown in Western Canada. I suppose you could say that is far away—my parents certainly would. The more I travel, however, and the more places I live, the more "near" becomes a relative term.

I spent a lot of my childhood wrapped up in the casual regionalism that a child uses to define who they are. To be Calgarian (my hometown) was to be not Edmontonian (our rival town), then I moved further and learned I was Albertan (the province of both cities). To be Canadian was to be not American. Then I moved to Europe and learned I was North American all along.

Of course, I changed too. I never feel more North American than when I am outside of the continent, and less North American than when I return to visit.

I have lived in eight cities across two continents, and intend to live in many more. I am excited to see how my worldview shifts with wherever I reside next.

I travel a lot, too. As much as I can. Mostly locally (local to wherever I am living at the time) but sometimes further afield. I feel like "being a tourist" is a skill, and one that I am getting better at with each voyage. I've learned what it is that I like to experience and see when I travel. There are a lot of tourist traps in the world, but sometimes tourist hotspots are must-sees for a reason. If you are ever in Istanbul, you should go and see the Hagia Sophia—it is absolutely amazing—but my core memories of Istanbul are from leaving the beaten path, getting lost, and getting to know the locals.

Of course, if you do travel, it is important to be respectful. Tourism can be damaging to a culture and a place. Especially when we treat someone else's home as a commodity we are entitled to 'because we paid'. When done right, however, travel is not just incredibly rewarding but also incredibly important. We need to meet people who think differently from ourselves, and experience different ways of living. A little cross-cultural awareness can go a long way towards solving many of the important problems of our world.

So, do I think of France as far from where I was born? No, not anymore. I did at first, when I first arrived and didn't speak the language. When I didn't know anyone and I just wanted to go back home. Now that I have gotten to know the people and learned to think a little more like a local, France is home. I wonder where home will be next.

About the author

Justen Russell is a scientist and author, with a PhD in the biological sciences. He lives in Paris, France with his partner and their child. He is anachronistic in his athletics, enjoying historical sword-fighting and swing dance

www.justenrussell.com

Infinite Possibilities II

Michael Gardner

Adrian receives a USB drive in the mail that has footage of a cabin, nothing else. His wife, Candice, thinking it a game, encourages him to solve the mystery. It's apparent that Adrian and Candice's relationship is strained, especially since Candice's mother died.

Adrian stumbles across the location of the cabin and agrees to explore it with Candice. Inside, they find a television, a recliner, a book. The television switches on and reveals a man that looks like Adrian. Other Adrian. The television shuts down before Candice notices. But Candice discovers something else. The book—*Infinite Possibilities: Navigating the Multiverse*—is apparently written by Adrian.

2

He reads at his work bench in the garage. His tools are neatly packed away, and he's wiped the surface down, but it carries the familiar scent of oil and grease. That scent comforts him, grounds him, as he tries to make sense of the book from the cabin. The book with his name on the front.

The multiverse gives life to all possibilities simultaneously. Within it we find infinite, parallel worlds. The fundamentals of these worlds may differ markedly from our own, barely at all, or in some cases, replicate our own world almost exactly.

As I write these words, there is another version of me doing the same thing in their world. And another version of me doing something different, perhaps mowing the lawn while the weather remains warm. There also exist versions of me profoundly different: someone that communicates telepathically, someone that exists in a non-physical state, someone with abilities I can't even fathom. In yet other worlds, I do not exist at all.

Adrian stops, closes his eyes and rubs them with his knuckles. The pressure brings flashes of light into the darkness behind his lids, like lightning streaking across a clouded night sky. Something about the writing, the certainty of it is jarring.

He opens his eyes, turns a couple of pages, picks a passage at random.

Identification and observation has shown us much, but to truly advance discovery, we need to make contact with other worlds, and then determine the means to traverse them. While some in my profession have argued that this latter step cannot be supported by the laws of physics and mathematics, I would remind them that the multiverse contains all possibilities, including that other worlds are governed by laws different to our own. These worlds may already possess the technology to move from one world to the next. It may be as simple as opening a door and stepping through.

As such, I would posit that discovering the means to move between worlds is not a question of how, but when. In the meantime, while we wait for the people with the means to find us, we must focus on advances within our power to make. We must meet them halfway.

The garage door begins to rise, breaking Adrian's focus. He stretches his neck, turns to find Candice ducking under the door. Her car is parked out front, as usual. She's carrying a plastic bag.

"You want to take a break for lunch?" she says, raising the bags. He can see the outline of takeaway containers through the plastic. He suddenly realises how hungry he is.

"Lunch?" he says. "Already?" She glides toward him like she's floating across the garage. She stops next to Adrian, places a hand on his shoulder. A casual gesture. A gesture Adrian is beginning to enjoy again.

"Yes, it's after one and I'm starving. I thought you might be too, so I grabbed some Thai. You interested?"

He glances at the open book, then back at Candice. Nods. "Sure," he says. "That sounds nice."

"So, anything interesting? Any clues about what we do next?"

He shakes his head. "No, not yet."

"May I?" she asks, motioning to the book.

He shrugs, and she takes that as agreement. She starts to turn pages with her free hand, rifling them roughly. It makes him wince, but he doesn't say anything. He doesn't like the idea of pages tearing, which he keeps expecting as she flips them so quickly. He can see she's not really reading, just searching for something to stand out. A signpost that says: 'go here next'. But he's less and less convinced that that is what this is. What it is instead, he doesn't know.

He jumps when Candice slaps the book with her open hand. The sound reverberates around the garage. She grins. "What about this?"

He looks at the pages she's found. Schematics. A plan for some kind of electronic device. He hunches closer, studies it. He turns the page and finds further instructions. He goes back, looks at the materials required.

"Well?" she says.

"Well what?"

"You build things. The book has your name on it. Seems like the next step in the game, doesn't it?"

He builds things, he repeats to himself. It suddenly seems hot in the garage. He can feel the blood pulsing in his temples. The next step for someone like him. He studies the diagram again and what strikes him as odd is its relative simplicity. Surely, in a book about complex physics, schematics should also be complex. They shouldn't be understood by bus drivers who like to tinker with lawn mowers. And yet he does understand. Or enough of it to think he could start building, and perhaps fill in any gaps in his knowledge with YouTube. Candice is right, this appears to be made for him.

"Maybe," he says. He closes the book abruptly, stands. His eyes dart to Candice who frowns, but she doesn't say anything. Not yet anyway.

"We don't want to let the food get cold, do we?" he says, forcing a smile. Her frown deepens. "I'll come back to this later," he tries.

She pauses a beat. "Okay," she says. She gives him one last uncertain look, then turns and makes her way into the house.

He doesn't follow straight away. He casts an eye toward the book again. Just seeing it lying on his bench is unsettling. The book, the USB, the cabin, what he may or may not have seen on that TV screen—together they create a cocktail of uneasiness that he suspects might go away if he just let it all be. Yet, as he stares, he realises he'll come back to it, and construct whatever it is he's meant to construct.

He tells himself it's because Candice won't let up. But the truth is something else. It's him. He needs to know where this leads.

Not long after he proposed, Candice told him she wanted to elope.

They were in a public park, lying on a picnic blanket, the sky clear and bright overhead. They'd brought a bottle of wine and some cheese in a picnic basket. The park was mostly green lawns dotted with a few large trees. It was sparsely populated—only a few families chasing kids or giving the dogs a run. From a playground in the distance came the sounds of childish laughter and squeals of delight.

"Why?" he asked.

She shrugged, rolled onto her back, stared up at the sky. He smiled as he watched her. She was beautiful. He found everything about her confident, nonchalant attitude striking.

"You love me, I love you. I couldn't give a shit about all of the phony hangers-on."

"Our parents?"

She made a dismissive 'psst' sound, glanced at him sideways. "As bad as the rest. They're not in it for us. It's about them. Status with their friends, or plain old pride. I don't want to do something for others. I want to do it for us."

"Where?"

"I don't know. Fiji, maybe? Hawaii? God, we could go to the middle of Australia for all I care, if it's just us."

She rolled back onto her side, faced him, reached out and cupped his jaw in her hand. "This is about us, right?

He leaned toward her, kissed her. Her lips were soft. He pulled away, exhaled a long time.

"Of course," he said. "Yes, of course. I'll marry you wherever you want. Alone on a beach, in a small country pub, wherever. I love you."

She smiled. Kissed him again. "I knew my adventurous Adrian was still in there somewhere."

"Always," he whispered.

She smiled like she didn't believe him. He felt a pang of hurt but didn't say anything. Part of him knew she was right. He wasn't the same as he had been. And yet who was? People grew up, right? One of them had to level out. And if he hadn't, he and Candice would likely have fed off each other, added rocket fuel to rocket fuel, exploded.

They married twelve months later, in a church, in front of family and friends. It was a cliché, but it was the happiest day of his life. He knew Candice had only just tolerated it. Had done it for him, which he'd appreciated at the time.

Yet after, he noticed a subtle change in her. Like she'd realised that he wasn't who he purported to be. Like he'd broken a promise. Not just about the wedding, but about who he was.

Adrian shuts the welder off, flips his visor up. His work is rough, but he can see the joins will hold.

He's created a metal cube: one foot, by one foot, by one foot. The top plate is set with hinges so he can access the interior. There are two holes in the casing: one for the antenna, one for the control panel, both to be attached later. The instructions tell him that the machine will be powered by an internal battery. Convenient, he thinks, for operation anywhere, including at the cabin. He's not sure why that thought pops into his head. He has no reason to think he needs to return there again. Yet that is what he thinks.

He's hot in his coveralls. There're large sweat patches under each arm, and sweat is beaded in his hairline where the welding helmet sits. The garage door is wide open, and a gentle breeze pushes hot air around. The scent of ozone and heated metal permeates the air. He removes his helmet and tosses it onto the bench with a thud.

He found the materials for the casing at his local hardware store, but he ordered the electronic components online. Most should arrive in a week or so, although the motherboard and power supply unit are coming from overseas, so they'll take longer.

He wonders what this thing is for, and what it will do if it works. The book is not at all clear on the machine's purpose. It descends into indecipherable jargon that, no matter how many times Adrian has read it, obscures clear meaning and insight. Perhaps it will do nothing. Perhaps something confounding. Adrian has the unrealistic expectation that he will discover its purpose as he continues to piece it together.

The next step is to create the internal frame for the electronics. He has everything ready, and it shouldn't take long for him to construct, yet his eyes feel sore, gritty. When he holds a hand up level with his face, he sees a slight tremor. He's been at this longer than he can recall. He removes a welding glove, checks his watch, and is not entirely surprised to find it's nearly four.

He doesn't want to stop, but he knows he must. Candice doesn't know he skipped work to do this. Even though she wants him to build the machine, he knows she won't approve of him giving up another shift.

He takes one last look at his work, then begins to tidy his materials away.

Even after they were married, he continued the fantasy that bus driving was temporary, because that seemed important to Candice. To her vision of him, and what he could be. Like most secrets bottled up, it came out at the wrong time, hurt them both.

They were having drinks with a couple from Candice's accounting firm—Dan and Gillian. It was a Friday night, and Candice had booked a table at a new bar in the city. They were tucked away at the back of the venue, but they still had to raise their voices to hear each other over the thrum of the music and the crowd.

Gillian seemed pleasant enough, but Dan rubbed Adrian the wrong way. Dan's eyes lingered on Candice, only to slide away when an attractive woman passed their table on the way to the bar. Dan didn't even try to hide his lurid gaze from Gillian, who seemed happy to ignore it.

"What do you do, Adrian?" Dan directed at him, before his gaze moved back to the crowd. It was an inevitable question, but when Dan asked it, Adrian felt Candice bristle beside him.

"I drive buses," he answered, took a sip from his beer, placed it back on the table with a clink. Dan looked back, cocked an eyebrow, and at the corners of his mouth, a smirk.

"Really. How fascinating. Good honest job, eh?" It was said with condescension, but Adrian chose to ignore it.

"Suits me fine."

Which should have been the end of it, except Candice jumped in. "He's going back to university next semester. He's going to study law, right, Adrian? Tell him."

Adrian grimaced, tried not to show his annoyance. Candice didn't seem to notice. She stared at Dan as Dan watched Adrian. Before he could say anything, Dan spoke.

"The law. Now that's an interesting field of study. Plenty of good jobs in law when you're done, and not just as a lawyer. We have a bunch of good people with a law background in our firm, believe it or not."

Candice agreed, started offering a few of her own thoughts on the benefits of a law degree. Adrian had heard it all before. It shouldn't have irked him as much as it did. But it did. In part it was Dan. The guy was a jerk. But he hated that Candice was so eager to please that arsehole. And perhaps worse, that she seemed ashamed of Adrian.

The words spilled out before he could stop them.

"I hate lawyers. And I fucking hate the way people with a degree look down on those without one, like the feudal system still exists and they've just been made a Lord," he said. His outburst brought an abrupt end to Dan and Candice's discussion. Gillian and Dan both turned to look at him strangely, Candice's face frozen in shock.

"I'm sorry, babe. But I like my job. I don't want," he motioned toward Dan, "to be like that." Dan straightened in his seat, glared at Adrian through narrowed eyes. He looked like he was about to say something spiteful, but Gillian took his arm and squeezed gently. He closed his mouth, remained quiet.

"Let's not do this here," Candice said, and shot an awkward smile across the table toward Dan and Gillian. Adrian ignored her.

"Look, I haven't enrolled in university. I know I said I would, but..." he sighed. "I've made up my mind. I just hadn't got around to telling you."

"You what?" she hissed at him, her mouth a thin, angry line.

"Didn't seem to me it really affected you. Unless you can only love me if I become a corporate crony."

"Oh, fuck you," she said.

Gillian coughed, suggested to Dan that they go get another drink from the bar.

"No need," Adrian said as he pushed his chair back and stood. "Time for me to get to bed. I have a big day tomorrow. You know, driving the bus."

He walked out before anyone could stop him.

The truth was he was pissed at Candice. And himself.

He had enjoyed physics when they first met, had done a few undergraduate courses in astrophysics, was thinking seriously about majoring in it. Candice had thought that too niche, too likely to end with a career in academia. Something Adrian had thought sounded okay, but Candice had grander plans. She convinced him he needed to pursue study that led to a job that paid well. That had options for career advancement. At that time, all he wanted to do was impress her, so he tried it her way.

But nothing stuck. He enrolled in the courses she suggested. Tried them and failed them. Hated them. Instead of leading to a career with money at the end, it led to the accumulation of student debt.

He took the bus driving job mostly to avoid studying. He found he liked it. The familiar routes, the resonant drone of the engine, it put him in a relaxed state, helped him think. What he thought was that if he'd done things his way, he might have been happier.

So, without telling Candice, he re enrolled in physics. He was excited when he walked into his first class, but from that first day he realised something was wrong. Something had passed him by. Like his brain had changed with age. He found the lectures incredibly difficult. Yet the kids that surrounded him didn't seem to share his confusion. He felt old, stupid. He wasn't. He understood machines, could pull apart an engine with his eyes closed. That was something, at least. Not the same, but something.

When he dropped out, he knew with a gut punch finality that university was no longer an option. He felt a failure. And he knew he would cop Candice's judgement when he told her. Perhaps that's why he told Candice the way he did. Maybe her anger was better than her pity.

They fought when Candice got home. Fought as hard as they had since they'd married. They made up a few days later anyway, but things changed. Candice talked less and less about her job, about office politics, about annoying clients. She still invited Adrian to drinks with friends and colleagues from time to-time, but Adrian declined more readily, and Candice seemed happy to accept that.

He initially thought the confrontation had been good for them. Helped set some boundaries. But in time he found that being separated from such a large part of Candice's life began to feel as if he were floating in one bubble, and Candice another.

"Oh," Candice says with a start when she walks into the kitchen. She raises a hand to her chest, stops.

Adrian's sitting at the bench, drinking a glass of water. He feels fresh, clean, his hair still wet from his shower.

"I thought you'd still be at work?" she says, appraising him with curiosity.

"Just a short shift today," he lies, keeps his face neutral. She used the front door for once, so he knows she hasn't seen the machine casing. He's both pleased and disappointed.

Candice finally moves again, tosses the mail onto the bench.

"How was your day?" he asks, perfunctorily. He picks up the envelopes, rifles through them.

"Busy." She drops her handbag onto the floor near the fridge, sighs. "But it's good to be finished, and not have to think about work for a couple of days."

He looks at her confused, then realises it's Friday. He forgets sometimes, working shifts. The days tend to blur.

"I was going to head out with Jenny and the girls tonight. I think some of the husbands are coming along. Do you want to join us?"

He shakes his head. "No, I'm good."

She doesn't look surprised, or disappointed. "Next time," she says, moving toward the back of the house.

He refocusses on the mail. Mostly bills. But then... another plain white envelope, his name typed in capital letters, a small bulge. He swallows.

"There's leftover quiche in the fridge," Candice calls out from their bedroom.

"Yeah, thanks," he says, distracted. He tears open the letter, upends it in his hand. Another USB.

His laptop is still where he left it on the bench. He grabs it, powers it up. From down the hall he hears a sliding door open, close. The shower starts to run. He can hear Candice humming over the patter of water.

He plugs in the USB, this time doesn't bother with antivirus or turning off the wifi; he just opens it and plays the video file.

At first it's just the hut again, standing alone amongst the canola, another sunny day. He knows it's not the same sunny day because there's a trail cut through the crop. It runs from the road up to the chain link fence, then around the perimeter toward the padlocked gate. The trail that he and Candice made.

The shot changes. It zooms out, slowly, until the hut appears to be a very long way away. It zooms until the road is prevalent. This is being filmed from the verge, he thinks. Maybe from someone's yard even, from one of the new houses. There's a distant drone, which rises in volume, like a symphony reaching a crescendo. A blur of white fills the screen. A blur that the camera follows until it resolves into the image of a bus. The number thirty-three. His bus. He wonders if he's driving it.

The bus doesn't slow. It eases around the gentle bend without braking, the sound changing pitch as it disappears from view.

The shot ends abruptly, is replaced with an image of an apartment building. It's about eight stories high, not new, but not old. Grey, unexciting architecture. An entrance at street level, glass doors, rows of silver mailboxes just inside, an elevator. The shot holds steady on that entrance. On the street, random people walk into shot, walk past the building entrance, walk out of shot. They crisscross like ants at work. Focussed.

Then Candice steps into frame. He recognises her instantly. She wears a navy pant suit, large beige handbag over her shoulder. Walking with her is a man he doesn't know. Tall, with dark curly hair. They walk in unison, not too close, not too far apart.

They veer toward the entrance of the apartment building, stop. He opens the door, holds it for her as she steps inside. They approach the elevators, she presses a button, they wait. When the doors open, they slip inside, turn, stand close at the back of the elevator. He thinks he sees a smile on her face as the doors close, but he can't be sure.

Then she's gone.

Adrian's stomach is a hard, tight knot. It feels uncomfortably full, like he's been chewing paper, swallowing it down until it's formed a wet, pulpy mass.

The video returns to the hut. An overcast day now. It looks like it could rain at any moment. It's a message, he thinks. An invitation to return.

"What's that, another video for your game?" Candice asks. He jerks upright, turns and sees her walking across the family room. Her head's cocked, her hands at her right ear fixing an earring.

He closes the laptop guiltily. Doesn't know why he should feel guilty. Nods. "Yep. Another USB."

"Can I look?" she says, finishing with her earring.

"No," he says more loudly than he intended. "There's nothing new. Just the hut again. The same video, really."

She stops by the dining table. "Really? That's odd."

"Maybe an error. I think the book's the thing to focus on."

She nods slowly. "Yeah. Sure. Well, let me know how you go? I won't be too late, okay?"

"Okay," he repeats.

She moves toward him, feathers his forehead with a fleeting kiss, grabs her handbag in a sweeping movement, then disappears toward the front of the house.

When he's certain she's gone, he opens the laptop and plays the video again.

They'd been married three years when he asked her about that night in Thailand.

They were renting at the time, an apartment in the city, close to her work. It was too expensive, and very small. The furniture was cheap—Ikea, gumtree seconds, that sort of thing. He was sitting on the couch rubbing his fingertips over the velvety material of the arm. He didn't recall buying the couch, or going with Candice to pick it up from someone's garage. So how did she get this back to the building, let alone up the three flights of stairs to their apartment?

She sat next to him, feet curled under her, watching a movie he recognised, but couldn't place. One with Tom Hanks in it. Something earnest. Weren't they all?

"Do you ever think about Mike?" he'd blurted out.

She turned slowly, looked at him in a way that suggested she'd just woken from a deep sleep. She cocked her head to the left. "Who?"

"Mike. That guy from Thailand. The couple we met and..." Like a car spluttering on an empty tank of fuel, he ran out of words.

She watched him for a moment, bemused. Then she smiled. Or was it a smirk? "Mike," she said, like she was tasting the word on her lips. "Mike. I must admit, I'd forgotten that was even his name."

She returned her attentions to the movie. For a second, he thought that might be it.

"I thought we agreed never to talk about it. That it was a one time thing?" she said, still staring ahead.

"It was," he jumped in quickly. "I mean, we did. I'm sorry. I don't know why I was thinking about it, it just... popped into my head.

"Do you think about her?" she asked, glancing at him. "What was her name again? I can't remember."

He grimaced. "Me neither."

And she laughed. A genuine laugh that rolled through her whole body. She grabbed the cushion from behind her back and hit him playfully with it. "You liar, it was Taylor."

He couldn't help but laugh too. He nodded. "Ah, yes. Now I remember."

She picked up the remote, muted the television, slid across the couch and wiggled her way under his arm. "What's up? Why are you asking about this after all this time?"

"I don't know," he said, as she rested her head on his chest.

"Do you regret it?" she asked.

"Do you?"

"I don't feel that strongly. It was something that happened."

"Oh," he said, squeezing her shoulder. "So... it was okay?"

She stifled a laugh. "Is that what's bugging you. How it was?" She placed her hand on his thigh. He swallowed, felt something stir. "Well, Mister, truth is, he was rubbish."

"Really," he said, his voice a rasp as she began to rub his leg, moving in circles, moving higher.

"Really," she whispered into his chest. "He had no idea what he was doing. So if I regret anything, it was that I wasted myself on him when I could have had the good stuff next door with you."

He smiled at that.

"What about you and Taylor. Was that okay?"

"Nah," he said quickly. "It was awkward as hell. I didn't feel comfortable at all. It was more like a chore then something to enjoy." Which was a lie, but he couldn't tell her the truth now. He wondered if she was lying as well.

"Good," she said. She undid the button on his pants, slipped her hand inside. "I don't know about you, but I think I've seen this movie. What about we go to bed, erase bad memories?"

As they made love, his thoughts strayed to his night with Taylor. When he came, the power of his orgasm surprised him. Just like back then.

He rolled aside, breathing heavily, wracked with guilt. Candice snuggled up close to him and he lay there, unable to say anything or move, still hoping Candice had lied to him earlier. But he had the feeling she hadn't. Which left him where, exactly?

The canola has a kind of bioluminescence under the waning moon. It's like wading through jellyfish. Adrian reaches the chain link fence, hooks his fingers through, squints, but the features of the cabin are unclear in the dark.

When he left the house, he initially decided to go to the city to find Candice. But he quickly realised he didn't know where to look for her. And what would he do if he did find her? Confront her? Probably not. Yet he didn't want to be stuck at home where he could watch that awful video over and over until he drove himself mad.

Instead, he caught a bus, then another, and another. He rode around thinking until he eventually wound up on the thirty three headed back toward the Sunder Estates.

He pulls his phone from his pocket, flicks on the torch, holds it aloft. The light is meagre, and cuts only a thin path through the gloom, but it's enough to give a little solidity to the wooden walls, the heavy door.

It looks uninviting. Maybe he should just go? There'd be no shame in that, he thinks. Yet he moves anyway, around the perimeter of the fence toward the gate.

It's an effort to squeeze through the gap on his own, but he does. When he steps up onto the deck, he raises a fist as if to knock at the cabin door, but he catches himself, lowers his hand slowly.

He has the feeling again that he's not alone. A sense that someone is on the other side of the door, waiting, watching.

The night is quiet. He has to listen hard to pick up the swish of canola plants in the breeze, a few insects buzzing, the soft drone of traffic far away.

He shakes off the jitters. Forces them down so his conscious brain can take control. He places a hand on the door handle, turns and pushes.

The cabin is dark. He raises his phone, shines it inside, first right to reveal the old bed frame and the kitchenette, then left where he finds the recliner, the odd television with the tumorous electronics. He realises he's holding his breath, exhales.

His first step inside feels awkward, heavy. It's like he's wading through something thick, viscous. Not night air, but oil. The second step is a little easier. As is the third.

He runs a hand along the arm of the recliner. The material is softer than he remembers. Well worn, but in a way that is comforting. It reminds him of his grandmother's house growing up, of the velvet bedspread in the spare room that covered the bed he'd stay in when he visited. He eases himself into the chair. The material caresses his back, his neck.

The television screen illuminates. A blue glow that grows steadily brighter.

His heart jumps in his chest, his muscles tense. His instincts tell him this is all too weird. They tell him to get up, run, but he doesn't. Because why else did he come here tonight? If not for this, then what?

The image on the television clarifies into that of the man that resembles Adrian very closely. The man he saw the other day. He's wearing glasses, has a little more grey at the temples than Adrian, and his neck is thickset, jowly. But otherwise, they could be twins.

The camera is jammed in tight on his face. It nearly fills the screen, but Adrian senses a hint of something odd behind him. The image is grainy, so it's hard to make out clearly, but it looks like flesh. Mounds of it, expanding and contracting like the body of a large, panting animal.

The man's voice—Other Adrian's voice—draws his attention. "Good," he says. "You're alone." His voice is gruffer than Adrian's, and his words are clipped. This is a man who has little time to waste on idle conversation and slow-witted people. Adrian swallows. He's not really sure what to say or what to ask. The words that spill from his mouth surprise him. "How did you get the video of my wife?"

Other Adrian frowns. Perhaps he expected Adrian to ask the who's, the what's, the why's.

"You are the three thousand, four hundred and twenty-third viable variant we have identified. But my agent tells me you are unusual. You do not possess a strong understanding of physics and mathematics."

It isn't phrased as a question, so Adrian doesn't answer. Odd words from the non-question ring loud in his head like the reverberation from a gong. Viable variant? Agent? He licks dry lips.

"I don't... don't understand what my education has to do with Candice?"

Other Adrian stares—a cold gaze. It is a foreign expression conveyed through Adrian's own eyes.

"Nevertheless, she indicated you have sufficient skills to build the receiver," he continues as if Adrian had not spoken. "How is your work progressing?"

"I haven't started," Adrian lies.

He sees a smirk at the corner of Other Adrian's lips. His image disappears from the screen, and is replaced with a shot of Adrian's open garage. From inside there comes a bright, pulsating light, the hiss and spit of the welder, the outline of Adrian in his protective coveralls, his welding helmet.

Adrian suspects the person who took this video is the same that took the video of Candice, and the hut. The agent. He glances toward the open door of the cabin as if he might find this agent standing there filming him now, but there's no one there. When he turns back, Other Adrian is on screen again, glaring, as if he is the one that has been slighted, not Adrian who is being tailed, filmed, shown videos of his wife.

"If you already knew, why even ask?" Adrian spits, angry.

His other self grins. An ugly expression that makes Adrian wonder what he looks like when he feels superior. Does he let it show like this man?

"I know what you're feeling. Or close enough. You're feeling lost, devoid of drive, stuck halfway between a decision made, and a decision to make. You're feeling like there's something more to all of this that you're missing. Something important. I'm here to tell you that there is. I can offer it to you."

Adrian licks his lips. Sweat beads on his forehead. "What are you offering exactly?"

"Knowledge and purpose. I'm offering a fractured piece of the picture its rightful place in the jigsaw puzzle. But this is conditional on you building that machine."

"The machine from your book," Adrian says.

"No, not my book. Another Adrian."

"Another?"

"There are as many versions of us as you can imagine. Some, like me, have made it our life's work to track them down."

"Why?"

A snort of laughter. "It's easier to show you, but I sense you are a stubborn one." He sighs. "Do you understand that in a single string of DNA lies all of the code to you? Everything you need to create a replica of yourself, Adrian?"

"I've heard something like that, yes."

"In the beginning, the universe was one. Then came the big bang. In that moment, everything changed. Not only was your universe formed, your stars, your planets, the seeds to human life on Earth, but so was my universe formed, and the universe of the man who wrote that book, and many, many more. The big bang did not just create, it divided. It split the singular into infinite realms. Only by drawing it all back together can we create the code, the DNA if you will, to what this all means."

"Life, the universe, and everything," Adrian says, smiling at his own joke.

Other Adrian frowns. Behind him, the flesh shudders.

"Mock if you wish, but we've already discovered much."

"We?"

"Of the viable variants I have located, six hundred and ninety-four have already joined me here, adding their knowledge to mine. This has given us some staggering insights. Our findings have been shared in my world, and developed into new medicines and treatments, which have allowed us to lengthen natural human lives. In my world, the average person is expected to live well beyond two hundred years."

"Two hundred," Adrian repeats, eyes wide. That seems ludicrous. And yet isn't talking to himself on a television ludicrous?

"That is just one of the discoveries we have made. A modest beginning. There is much more to do."

"But I don't understand how I can help you. You said it yourself, I have no knowledge of physics and mathematics," he says, a hint of sarcasm in his tone.

"Every Adrian is unique. Your experiences will help build our collective knowledge. I can show you how special you are."

Adrian licks his lips, processing. "All I have to do is build the machine?"

Other Adrian nods, tight lipped. Adrian senses something not said. That there is more to it than just a machine. But he doesn't probe.

"And what if I don't want to go further?

Other Adrian sighs. "I can only make an offer. It is up to you whether to accept or not. But I would ask you this: While you think about what I have said, continue to build. When you are done, return with your questions. If you are satisfied with my answers, then we will use your machine to bring you across to my world."

"And if I'm not, I stay here?"

The man gives a curt nod.

Ordinarily, Adrian doesn't think he'd be tempted by such uncertainty. But one thing Other Adrian says is right. He feels lost, stuck between places. And that video of Candice has set him spinning.

"Okay. I'll keep an open mind. I'll continue to build."

"Excellent. My agent will be in touch."

About four years after Adrian married Candice, he started to worry he'd run out of words. At least the meaningful words. He and Candice still talked about shopping lists, chores, how each other's day had been. They talked about renovations, and work colleagues. But none of that was real.

Then Candice surprised him with something that was.

Adrian had been asleep, early morning. It was Candice's perfume that woke him. He was somewhere in that place between light and dark, between dreams and reality, when her scent invaded—spring flowers, musk. Drowsy eyes opened and there she was, close, hair hanging half over her eyes. She was smiling when she kissed his neck, whispered: "What would you think if I stopped taking my pill?"

He swallowed hard, nearly choked on the saliva. Candice, thinking he was shocked, kept talking. "I mean we don't have to. I know we've never really... And things have been..."

Strained, he'd thought.

"Busy at work," she'd said. "But I guess I'm getting to that age and was thinking—"

"You read my mind," he interrupted, grinning. He rolled back so he could look at her more clearly. "Yes. I really want that. I don't know how to explain it, I just—"

"Want to bring something better into the world," Candice finished. He nodded. He felt tears welling, and he blinked rapidly to hold them back.

She made a strange noise in the back of her throat, leant close, kissed him. He apologised for his morning breath. She said she didn't care. They started trying that morning.

Candice told him it would take a few months to get the pill out of her system. Unfortunately, Candice's mother Alexia was diagnosed with cancer before that happened.

They kept trying intermittently, but without luck. And when they did, Adrian couldn't help but notice the change in Candice. The way she took control, rode him hard, aggressively, like she was angry, bitter. When he did ejaculate, which wasn't all the time, it felt weak and apologetic.

When Alexia died, they stopped having sex.

A month after the funeral, he found the new prescription in the medicine cabinet.

As Adrian finishes installing the battery in the machine, he hears Candice's car. He looks up to see it turn into the drive. He takes a deep breath, exhales loudly. He doesn't know what to feel around her at the moment.

The silence when she cuts the engine is deafening. The door groans as it opens, her high heels click on the cement. When she slams the door, it echoes around their suburban cul de-sac. Adrian flinches.

She walks toward him, and he feels himself shrinking, hoping she won't notice him at his bench. He turns and pretends to engross himself in his work. He hears the tenor of her footsteps change as she moves under the cover of the garage. Then she stops. He imagines her looking at the door to the house, then his back. The tension builds until he can't help but break it, like waves on a beach.

"Going out again?" he says. He hears the accusation in his voice, but hopes she doesn't. He doesn't want to start something.

"Yes. How are you going with the build?" He notices she doesn't invite him to join her. He wonders if she's visiting the man from the video. He doesn't even know how recent that was. She could have moved on. She may have multiple lovers. His hands are shaking. He lowers his tools, places them on the bench either side of the machine.

"It's going okay," he says.

"Do you know what it does? Or how it fits in with your game?"

He forgets sometimes that she still thinks he's solving a puzzle. But then again, isn't he?

"I'm not sure," he says, wondering how much he should say. He's been thinking about this a lot. He clears his throat. "I'm starting to wonder if it might be like a homing beacon. Something that identifies my location."

"Oh. So you turn it on, and if it works they know you've finished, and they come find you and give you a prize?"

His face contracts into a frown. Tension in his jaw, his cheeks. "Perhaps. Or they use my signal to contact me, and then they show me how to find them," he says, the thought concrete for the first time. He rises from his stool, steps back from the work bench, takes a couple of deep breaths and turns to face his wife.

She's looking away from him, back at her car. She's backlit by the afternoon sun, and strands of auburn hair drape across her right eye. In profile, she looks hauntingly beautiful. Adrian's heart jolts to see her. He wants to tell her everything.

She turns, smiles to find him looking at her. He feels connected to her in that moment. "Okay then. Well, I won't hold you up. I'm just going to change into some jeans and then I'll get out of your hair," she says, before moving again. He watches her walk toward the door, then she disappears inside. He wants to call after her, but can't. He wants to share his burden with her, but can't.

He follows her inside, hesitates by the kitchen. He can see the hall, but can't will his legs to move him there. He collapses more than sits at the kitchen bench, puts his head in his shaking hands, waits.

When she returns five minutes later, she doesn't really notice his state. She calls out a brusque farewell, and then is gone.

Before he hears her car start, his phone dings. He lifts his head from his hands. It feels heavy, like a bowling ball. His phone is where he left it, just by the box of tissues on the bench. It might be Candice, texting, "I love you". She does that sometimes.

But it's not. It's an email from an address he doesn't recognise. Redhead22@gmail.com. He normally wouldn't open it, but the subject line grabs his attention. "I can give you answers about the cabin."

He reads the email once, twice, then responds.

"Infinite Possibilities" continues in next month's issue.
See parts I and II of Michael Gardner's story "Infinite Possibilities" online at Metaphorosis.
If you liked it, leave a comment. Authors love that!
Remember to subscribe to our e-mail updates so you'll know when new stories are posted.

November

If Gold Runs Red

Gordon Grice

"Thirteen's too old to be scared of a rock," Clay's dad smirked, even though Clay hadn't said he was scared. They'd come to fish beneath a huge outcrop that loomed over the creek like a giant bending to drink. Hollows brimming with bird droppings glared down at them. Flecks of gleaming green mineral pocked its gray face. Fifty feet up, sage grass and brambles jutted from its crown.

"Remember how I told you," Dad said. "The hook goes through three times, but leave enough worm loose to thrash around and draw some attention."

"Yes, sir," Clay said. They settled down on a lichen-crusted boulder. Clay imagined threading a huge hook three times through Dad. *Leave enough of me loose to thrash around and draw some attention*, Dad would no doubt say, as if he ever failed to draw attention to himself.

"What are you giggling about?" Dad barked. "You'll scare the fish."

Clay sat quietly then. His line looked bent where it entered the water. Six feet down, catfish groped dreamily among the water plants.

Something splashed downstream. Clay glimpsed a bulbous form sliding into the creek.

"We'll have to hunt those beavers out," Dad said. "Look at all those lodges." Clay looked. He had seen the unruly stacks of twigs when they hiked in to look over their new farm, but he hadn't realized what they were. Back east, they never saw beavers. "There's half a dozen dams, too," Dad went on. "That's what slows the creek down and makes this whole area swampy. Clear them out and we'll have a good five acres more to farm."

"Oh," Clay said. Farm work didn't interest him much; he would have preferred to look at the catfish in their dreamy depths.

"Well, I'll be!" Dad shouted, pulling in his line. A fish thrashed at the end of it, paused, then thrashed again. Dad landed it on the boulder and crouched over it. "My God!" he whispered. It was ugly as a sock full of mud, with isinglass eyes glaring over a gaping mouth surrounded by wormy tendrils. As it thrashed, it got its legs under it. It had, by Clay's count, five—jointed, wiry legs like a crawdad's. It went scampering toward the water, and Dad yanked the line to bring it back. "Give me your knife," he said, and Clay unfolded it and held it out to him. "Handle first, dumbass," Dad said. It seemed a shame to kill the fish; it might be the only one of its sort in the world. After Dad gutted it, the fish still struggled feebly to remove the hook, grasping at it with tiny fingers on the end of its tendrils. Dad eased the hook out and dropped the fish into the bucket, which Mama had pointlessly scoured before they set out. Clay hoped its misery was over, but then he heard its little hands—there was no other word for them—scratching at the tin walls.

The next fish they caught was a wonder. It had bigger hands, but only a few wispy legs, hardly enough to scamper on.

Half a dozen ugly fish later, they trudged home along the creek. Clay suddenly raised his eyes to a line of elms fussing in the wind. Some other sound had mingled in with the fussing. Listened for, it went unheard. The elms paused as if to show they had nothing to hide. They stood still as the purple hills beyond. Then a breeze rattled them into motion again.

Clay set down his pole and the bucket full of strange fish and went looking. Dad lumbered on ahead, eyes on the ground, lost in his own thoughts. With luck, Clay could catch up before Dad noticed his absence. The strange sound resumed, subsided, leapt forth once more. Maybe it was water shouldering through stubborn reeds. It might almost have been the weeping of a child. Clay ventured onto stones slick with creek-moss. At last, beneath a cottonwood whose leaves winked and glittered in the wind, he glimpsed bright red and, a second later, a yellow brighter than that.

"Looks like an owl nearly got him, or an eagle," said a grizzled man Clay hadn't noticed. The crooked twig of oak in his hand looked too flimsy to fish with, but the legged catfish dangling from its tip said otherwise.

"What kind of a bird is it?" Clay said. The bright shape flipped and shivered. Its feathers were yellow but stained with welling blood.

"I see you caught one of these deformed fish too," Dad said, interrupting the old man's answer. His boots sent river-rocks clattering out of his way.

"Skitterfish, they call them," the old man said. "My name's Hawkins."

"Ours is Brown," Dad said. Clay could see he was trying his trick of squeezing just a little too hard on the handshake 'to let the other fellow know who's boss'. Hawkins winced, but never stopped smiling. "Skitterfish, you say?"

"Good eating," Hawkins said. "A little butter if you have it, a little salt. People catch them all along this stretch."

"That will have to stop," Dad said. "This land is mine now."

"Folks are used to open range around here," Hawkins smiled. "Cattle country, you know."

"That will have to stop," Dad repeated.

The bird shrilled. Kneeling over it, Clay saw brown ants nibbling its wounds. He brushed them away, like sand from silk. It cooed.

"You'll see lots of strange animals along Saxum Creek," Hawkins said to Clay, as if he had lost interest in Dad. "Too many legs, too smart, too hard to kill. I've seen beaver lodges built with labyrinths inside, like some architect had laid them out. I've seen eagles smart enough to pull the hook out of a fish and fly off with it. I've taken the trophy head from a ten-point buck, only to see the body wander off before I could butcher it. They say it's the saxum— that's the mineral that washes out of that Great Saxum Rock where you were fishing." He pulled a nugget from his pocket, like lead peppered with chips of malachite.

Just then they heard a staccato slapping. Again Clay only glimpsed the beavers slipping into the creek—two of them this time, each leaving a wake of ripples to show where it swam below.

"I'll have to hunt those damn beavers out," Dad said.

"Worth a try," Hawkins said, his smile withering almost into a sneer. "You might look up Hal Vinson in town. He's a trapper from way back."

All the way home, with a pole over his shoulder and the handle of the heavy bucket cutting into his right hand, Clay felt the bird softly thrashing in the bib of his overalls, bumping the little nugget of saxum Hawkins had given him.

"Clay and I've plotted the lodges along my whole property, and the dams too," Dad said, leaning over the hand-drawn map he'd spread on the kitchen table.

"That's a pretty good map," Hal Vinson mumbled. He winced shyly as Mama refilled his coffee. He was a taciturn man, more mustache than meat, and his red eyes looked perpetually on the verge of weeping. Dad said that meant he was a drunk.

"My boy's good at drawing," Dad said. Clay was glad he wasn't at the table where he'd have to acknowledge the compliment. He sat on the floor fixing up a box for the bird he'd brought home, pretending not to hear them. "Point is, how to remove them. Dynamite?"

"Ruin your fishing that way," Vinson mumbled, softer than before, as if to mute a criticism. "I'd say hitch a mule to them and pull. But them beavers are mean. Have to shoot them first."

"I never heard of a mean beaver. How much for the whole job?"

Vinson blinked his bleary eyes. Clearly he wanted no part of such a job.

"I'll give you the pelts," Dad said. "Any beaver pelt you take on my land, by gun or trap, is yours."

Vinson twitched visibly. It was clear to Clay that this represented a greater sum than Dad realized, which Vinson nonetheless preferred to decline. But he withered under Dad's gaze.

"I'll do it for the pelts, I guess," he blinked.

In the night, Clay woke to weeping. The helpless bird showed yellow in the moonlight. When he lit a candle he saw mosquitoes crouching to kiss its wounds. Their bellies swelled so full he saw the vermillion within. The bird writhed and cried.

"Shut that damn bird up!" Dad's voice thundered from the other bedroom, and then Mama's said something soothing that Clay couldn't make out.

He brushed the mosquitoes away. One of them came hovering back, too delirious to abandon this nectar. He grabbed it from the air. When he opened his fist to make sure, he found it smudged into blood and delicate filaments of leg. The bird he lifted with cupped hands. Once he'd soothed it, he put it back in the box he'd built. Already in it for weight were his coins and the speckled nugget of saxum Mr. Hawkins had given him. He lay a handkerchief across it to screen out the mosquitoes. The bird breathed within, softer than distant crickets.

"You'll have to keep that bird quiet, or I'll kill the damn thing," Dad said next morning as they trudged to the creek. "I slept so bad I'm all out of temper."

"Is that what did it?" Clay said.

Dad turned and backhanded him. He saw the blow coming. He knew he was better off not to try dodging. For just an instant, the side of his face felt hot and wet, but then that sensation sizzled away into mere pain. Clay felt tears come to his eyes. He wouldn't cry, not if he could help it. He hated the smirk he'd get. It occurred to him, for the first time in his life, that he might hit Dad back. He was nowhere near as thick, but almost as tall. The slap hadn't even knocked him down. He might win.

"That's for having a smart mouth," Dad hissed, and stomped on toward the creek. Clay followed. Not that he hadn't daydreamed it many times—hitting his father—but it had never occurred to him as an actual plan. The thought sent fear thrilling through him. Of course, even if he did it, Mama would try to smooth things over. She'd tell him fathers got impatient sometimes, and now was a bad time with all the pressure Dad was under, that he'd sacrificed so much to move them all west for a better life, and so on, and it would end with her telling Clay to apologize.

Now that Dad's back was turned, he wiped at his tears. The corner of his mouth felt wet. His tongue found a little blood there.

Dad stomped into the shallows of the creek, parting the head-high cattails like a curtain. The water rilled in little braids over the rocks beyond. Further still, in a sluggish pool at the far side of the creek, a messy beaver lodge stood. "Look at this!" Dad bellowed. "I don't believe Vinson's done a thing."

He slogged out of the creek, carefully not looking at Clay. Clay could read the bunching muscles of his back. They meant he was halfway between rage and regret. Later there would be an apology, along with an explanation of how Clay had brought it on himself. This time he actually had. Clay took a sort of comfort in that.

"What's that?" Dad said. They'd come near the Great Saxum Rock, which seemed to leer at them from the corners of hollow eyes. Something was bobbing briskly round the bend before it.

It was a dead body, *plain as the dumb look on your face*, Clay wanted to say. Dad would have said exactly that if anybody else had asked. It rolled over in the current, as if turning in its sleep, except that its red eyes—Vinson's eyes—were wide open. Clay felt grateful when the current gently rolled those eyes out of sight again. By then the body had passed them.

"Good God!" Dad said. "Do you think we can catch him?"

"I don't think so," Clay stammered. For once, Dad took his opinion as gospel.

That night the yellow bird screamed loud enough to rattle the panes.

"Quiet!" Clay whispered as he rolled out of bed. "He'll hear you!"

The match he struck showed the bird shivering under fluffed feathers in the box he'd made. A wound had burst open into a red scribble. He put his match to a candle; the wick brought a calmer kind of light. The bird settled under his petting. Still, it was too loud.

"You have to be quiet!" he whispered. He noticed its nostrils, fine as the eyes of needles, where flecks of blood had dried.

The door slammed open. The candle-flame danced. Dad was almost invisible in the buffeting shadows. Clay never saw the blow that decked him. He was suddenly sprawling on the wood floor, aware of his teeth, his skull, like the stones in overripe fruit.

His coins clinked in the box. "Leave my stuff alone!" he said.

"I told you what I'd do," Dad said, with a sort of triumph. Then he was out the door. No use following, and besides, Clay's head tingled. He wasn't sure of his footing.

It was easy to hear Dad's progress. His bare feet on the stairs. Mama's exclamation of "Jonathan!" as he went past their room, as if she could possibly be shocked. The front door opening, crashing back. Clay scrambled to his window and looked down in time to see Dad lumber forth into the moonlight with the box in his hand. The bird shrilled, and kept shrilling until he had carried it far out into the darkness.

Half a dozen skitterfish mouthed at a carcass where it floated, snagged among the cattails. Clay watched with interest. Was it another beaver, maybe? He'd found half a dozen dead and skinned, no doubt the work of Hal Vinson before whatever happened to him. The bits of fur on the carcass suggested beaver, but its skull seemed round enough to be human. For a horrid moment he imagined it as Vinson. Could his body somehow have traveled upstream all this way to lodge beneath the Great Saxum Rock? A skitterfish took hold of the skull with its delicate little hands and turned it gently, as if to afford Clay a better view. He leaned out as far as he dared. The carcass bobbed. The fish fussed with each other for position and kissed its flanks.

A shot rang out. It echoed from the trees behind Clay, then echoed again from the great rock opposite. He nearly lost his balance.

Dad wouldn't put up with poachers. Clay set out to investigate. In a few minutes he'd picked his way across on a beaver dam. He had only a vague sense that the shot had come from near the Rock. He was almost surprised to find confirmation. The doe must have been drinking from the creek in plain sight of him, if only he'd looked. Now she lay quivering. He could smell singed fur from the buckshot wounds.

But where was the hunter? He looked downstream, where cottonwoods crowded in, and upstream, where the dam made the water pool lazy and deep. No human footprint showed on the muddy bank, though the deer's tracks, like double stabs, were clear.

"I shoot from the heavens!" a voice laughed. Clay couldn't, for a long moment, see who had spoken. Then he looked up. Ten feet high, within the hollow cheek of the Rock, leaned Hawkins, brandishing his shotgun. "Animals never think to look up," he added.

"My dad won't like it if he catches you hunting on our land," Clay said. He regretted his words instantly. He sounded stingy as his father.

"I've watched your father at his work," Hawkins smiled. "He never looks up either."

Clay didn't know how to take that. It sounded like a threat.

"Stick with me, kid, and I'll teach you a few things your father never knew."

It was more than a year later when, over supper, they heard a woman scream.

Clay paused with a spoonful of potatoes in hand. The steam of them writhed as it rose.

"Someone needs help," Mama said—exasperated, it seemed, because no one was moving.

"Shows how much you know," Dad smirked. "That's a panther."

"Are you sure?" she said.

"Good God, woman, haven't you heard it these three nights running?" Dad said. "And I've seen its tracks beside the barn. We'll have to hunt it. Liable to take some cattle."

The thought of Dad on a dangerous hunt reminded Clay of his guilty secret, of all the days he'd stolen away from chores to learn tracking and shooting from Hawkins. Now he imagined the panther lurking in the trees, gathering itself for a leap, while his father lumbered heedless beneath.

Serve him right. Yet Clay quivered at the thought.

Along Saxum Creek, the cat tracks ran thick, going both ways. Clay knelt to look at them. Immediately he sensed a creeping danger. Something must be watching him. He rose, held his rifle waist high. He wondered if he could hit a moving target.

As he scanned for movement, he noticed a beaver lodge in the creek. He'd seen this one before; it was among those Dad had made him sketch for Vinson. Its top had ruptured. Some of its sticks lay dragged along the bank. This might be old destruction; it might be Vinson's work.

He waded out to it. A mottled branch along the top seemed to waver like grease on a griddle. He got close enough to breathe on it before he realized its mobile texture meant ants—one file trailing out from undergrowth on the bank, another coming back laden. He wondered what sort of food they were dismantling, crumb by crumb.

He pulled himself up from the water and onto the lodge. It creaked and shifted under his weight. He paused. He was near enough now to see over the rim of the crater. A meaty smell rose from the darkness. He found a match in his shirt pocket and struck it. The flame faltered in the humid air. It made the medley of bones within seem to wriggle. He'd never thought of beavers eating meat. Apparently, on Saxum Creek, they did.

The broken lodge he stumbled on a week later told a clearer story. The tracks of the panther led down from the shore—the pugs like a letter M with four little toe-smudges in front. Two beaver kits shivered on the inner dome of grass, nestling on their sides to form a circle. They would die if he left them. His hands were reaching in when one of them barked. It was like oatmeal burbling in a pot, but shriller. Now that it had sensed him, it kept up a steady stream of chirps, asking, he supposed, to be fed. Soon its sibling joined in.

Dad wouldn't put up with this noise.

Maybe he could hide them in the tool shed.

Better just to leave them alone. Why prolong their lives, only to see them killed later on?

Just then he spotted something gleaming in the dark. A match showed him a side-pocket woven of grass, and within it a handful of saxum nuggets. Their flecks winked green in the firelight.

The maples shed red leaves and brown ones. The elms became lacy and beetle-bitten before they, too, cast off their clothes. Clay drove their two milch cows through this rattling litter of leaves one evening, lost in thought. "Too many legs, too smart, too hard to kill"—that was what Hawkins had told them about the animals of Saxum Creek. It seemed to him the beavers had been smart enough to scheme, to somehow kill Vinson when he went to work on their lodges.

And yet the beavers were fewer now. The panther must be taking its toll. It had been a presence on their land for weeks now, calling in the night like a woman with a broken heart, crying until Dad cursed. Its tracks, Hawkins said, showed it to be young, yet big enough to take cattle or kill a man. Many a day, Dad set out with his gun, leaving a list of chores for Clay to finish before sundown.

Something interrupted Clay's thoughts. He took two steps back to be sure what he'd seen. Amid the leaves lay a dead bird. He paused. The cattle knew the way to the barn. The gold shape was battered and dusty, but he recognized it.

There were no ants to trouble its body. They had, he supposed, picked the skeleton the morning after Dad killed the yellow bird. The feathers had not interested them; they remained, an empty suit of clothes for its bones. He was off the usual path by only a yard or so. Maybe the bird had lain here all this time. He poked through the weeds nearby and found the box he'd made, now broken, and even one of the silver dollars it had held.

Of course he had already known what happened to the bird, more or less. Yet the proof hurt him. He felt a headachy pressure behind his eyes, but something in him refused to cry. It was only a bird, after all.

He brought a shovel from the tool shed. As he dug, his own hands, thick like Dad's, somehow made him ashamed.

"Bury him deep," Hawkins smiled, coming up the path with his shotgun. By now Clay was used to his sudden appearances. "Bury him deep; things don't rest easy on Saxum Creek. It's the mineral, you know."

That night the panther shredded his sleep with its calls, and Dad raged through the house. At dawn, Clay opened bleary eyes and decided he'd spend the day trailing it. Both cows were restless while he squeezed their tender udders. "You heard it, too?" he asked.

On his way to the creek, the rifle propped on his shoulder, he was startled to a stop by the sight of Dad's eyes. They looked at him imploringly. He could hardly understand what he was seeing. The eyes were low and upside down. It took a long moment for him to see, among the light-brown maple leaves, the identically colored shape of the panther. It lay draped on Dad, partly obscuring his form, and held him in its paws. It glared jealously at Clay. Its eyes were red and familiar. After a moment it seemed to decide he was no threat. It licked Dad on the face, the neck. Until Dad shuddered, Clay had thought him dead. Certainly he was bloody, though the red leaves among the brown ones made that hard to sort out.

"Go home and bolt the door, Son," Dad said with surprising calm. "If you miss from this distance, he might charge you." The panther growled softly, as if offended by the remark.

Clay brought his rifle to his shoulder. His sights lined up— not on the panther's face, but on his father's.

The possibilities dizzied him. People would think it was an accident.

If only Dad hadn't just now said something kind, something to keep him safe.

Yet killing him might be a kindness in itself. Surely his wounds were fatal?

These thoughts transpired like a syrupy dream. He was aware, at the same time, that he'd taken only a second, that he should take even a little longer with his shot. He should sight carefully; then still his breath, as Hawkins had taught him; then squeeze, rather than pull. He would not get another shot. The panther would melt away into the undergrowth, or else charge and end his troubles.

It glanced up with its rheumy red eyes. He sighted between them. Despite everything. The fur was lighter there, almost white, but peppered with fine black hairs. He stilled his breath. The panther turned its full resentful gaze on Clay, but he was already squeezing the trigger.

The shot flipped it end over end. It landed on its feet and dashed to the left, knocking leaves into the air. It crouched, lashed its tail. The tail straightened. Clay wondered whether he should pelt it with rocks to make sure it was dead.

"That was a good shot, son," Dad coughed. Blood bubbled out of his mouth.

He was too big to carry. In the end, Clay brought him home in the wheelbarrow. "Damnedest thing," he said. "What did I ever do to get Vinson mad at me?"

It reeked of lunacy. A dying man's hallucinations. It wasn't Vinson who had hurt him. Yet it was! The eyes had looked right, anyway.

"You sent him out to kill the beavers, and they killed him."

"I figure it's the creek. A cub drinks where that mineral mixes in, and a dead body besides. It grows up wrong."

"Stay still," Clay said, and paused to lift the barrow over a fallen elm branch. "Every time you talk, more blood pumps out." His back crackled under the strain, but the barrow came over, and Dad didn't fall out or even criticize. He only huffed with pain as the barrow hit the ground again.

"You'll have to go back for our rifles, son," Dad said. "I hate for you to risk it, but those cost money."

Going back was the worst part, worse than Mama's crying, worse than the ragged new orifice they found when they cut Dad's shirt away. Clay, unarmed now, expected the panther behind every bush. He paused for a long time to study a forked elm. The shape within it might be a feline face glaring at him. When he finally dared another step, the shape resolved into nothing, into the grain of the bark.

At the bend of the path where he'd shot it, he was surprised to see the panther lying on the bare patch exactly as he'd left it. He noticed now that it had two tails—the one that had lashed so furiously in its death throes, and another curled around a hind leg.

In a dream, Clay found himself small again. Navigating across the kitchen floor in the dark, he passed beneath the table without ducking. Something outside was asking quiet, liquid questions, and he meant to find it. Out on the starlit porch he noticed nothing out of the ordinary, until the noise came again. It was coming from Dad's ladder-back chair. He hadn't seen the owl that sat there like a man, camouflaged in feathers the color of pine bark. He gasped to see what it was doing: caressing live coals, making the feathered hands singe and stink. It looked at Clay with eyes the size of silver dollars. Their irises, however, were not silver, but striations of pale maple, amber, doe's hide. He concluded they'd once been black but were, from gazing at songbirds with predatory intent, rapidly growing lighter and brighter.

"Was that you, talking?" Clay said. His voice rang childish in his own ears.

The owl blinked, thank God; its stare was about to make Clay run.

"Have you seen the finches on the fence?" Clay said, and turned to point. Something cold pinched his spine, the same trick Dad used to play on him when he was little.

"Did you do that?" he said, trying to placate the thing, looking for somewhere to run. This time the owl didn't even blink. By now the black middles of its eyes floated like bullets in molten gold.

As he woke, his fear drained away faster than he could grasp it, leaving a sadness he had rarely known. He thought of the yellow bird, singing helplessly in its box. He'd held it in his overalls next to his heart, had found its blood in the patterns of his palms, had kept it with his treasures, even after its droppings soiled the box. He tried to remember the beauty of its song, but really it had never sung beautifully, not that he had heard. Its every sound was a shriek of pain or the mournful cooing of pain briefly eased. And then its body had turned up just before Dad got hurt, mingling recriminations with his worry.

'That was a good shot, son,' his father had said. 'My boy's good at drawing.'

Downstairs, he found his parents before the fire. On the settee, Mama twitched in a bad dream of her own. Dad sat in the stuffed chair where they'd propped him to keep him from choking on his own blood. The toe of his left boot, the one he hadn't let them remove because of the pain, smoked. Clay knelt before him to shift his leg. It was heavy and cold. Clay looked up into a face flaccid, critical of nothing. The boot let loose one last wisp. Dad must have stretched it too close to the fire in his death-throes.

I'll bury him deep, Clay thought, already knowing he'd see the man with molten eyes again in dreams. Things don't rest easy on Saxum Creek.

See Gordon Grice's story "If Gold Runs Red" online at Metaphorosis. If you liked it, leave a comment. Authors love that! Remember to subscribe to our e-mail updates so you'll know when new stories are posted.

About the story

Somewhere I picked up a warped, water-stained, moldy volume of Chinese folklore called *The Man Who Sold a Ghost*, translated into English by Yan Hsien-Yi and Gladys Yang. It was packed with gruesome tales of were-foxes and greedy specters. I liked the poetic flavor of one from around 500 AD. It's about a boy rescuing an injured bird. The bird turns out to be a god. He helps the boy get good jobs and such. Actually, I only liked the beginning. The divine explanation and the job-advancement didn't do much for me. I decided to warp the premise to suit my own tastes. Early on, I changed the setting to the rural Western landscape I knew. In later drafts, the boy took on a troubled family life, while the landscape got polluted by a meteoric rock with uncanny effects on living things—a science fiction premise to replace the god I'd sent packing. What I enjoyed most was figuring out the effects the meteorite might have on different animals, from birds to beavers. Really, I had too much fun with that; I ended up cutting unnecessary scenes about earthworms, beetles, owls, and finches. I took the scene of a dead man rolling down a river from a real murder case I covered as a reporter. A witness's bizarre description had stuck with me for years, waiting for a suitable story to fit into.

A question for the author

Q: What made you start writing?

A: I got the urge to write as soon as I learned to read, but I was in college before I wrote a story I liked. My attempts before that ended with frustration, pencil-smears, opening lines too dumb to write past. What broke me through was discovering Edgar Allan Poe's "The Facts in the Case of M. Valdemar." The story started in clinical detachment and ended in one of the most disturbing gore scenes I'd ever read—exactly the sort of scene my teachers had told me to quit writing. It wasn't the gore itself that impressed me. It was how much Poe made it mean, how powerful it felt, how seamlessly he led me through reasonable-seeming steps to a monstrous conclusion. He became my model.

About the author

Gordon Grice is freelance magazine writer and wandering college lecturer whose literary course topics have included horror, homicide, science fiction, monsters, Edgar Allan Poe, and man-eating animals. He frequently teaches creative writing for the UCLA Extension Writer's Program. He and his wife have three sons and two pet tarantulas.

GordonGrice.com, @GordonGrice

Bas Relief

Joshua Grasso

Sveta twisted and turned in the mirror, lifting her shirt to inspect her stomach, flattering herself that it looked harder, firmer, than it had last week. But no, she could easily pinch the flesh into an unsightly fat roll as usual. She pulled up her sleeves, inspecting every inch of her arm, hoping against hope to find something rough and scaly. Again, nothing but soft, pale skin, or what the upperclassmen liked to call 'soft serve'. All quivering adolescent flesh and nothing substantial.

The only thing remotely tough on her body was the crusty elbow scab she had scraped with a key out of boredom. There were people she knew—well, they weren't friends, of course—who could file down keys and fingernails against their skin. Even one guy whose head was so rock-hard that you could break a board over it. She had watched him once during third-period gym, and he just laughed, saying he didn't feel a thing and asking his pals to do it again and again.

Out of sheer desperation, she peeled off her socks and inspected her toes and heels, hoping the skin had hardened, dried out. But even they were baby-smooth and without blemish. There were a few girls who couldn't even wear shoes anymore, as their toes were granite-hard and could deflate soccer balls with a single kick. But after all, only those who didn't change played sports after high school, since flexibility was the surest obstacle to upward mobility.

She must have been ignoring her texts, because when her phone rang, she saw Malorie's name flash over the screen—and she never called.

"Bitch, do you ever look at your phone?" Malorie said, with a laugh.

"Sorry, I'm getting ready—running late. I'll see you in a few."

"Not today you won't. I'm sick off my ass. I might miss the entire week, who knows?"

"Maly, not again!" Sveta said, throwing herself on the bed. "You can't keep doing this. You've already missed, what, ten or twelve days? You'll get suspended."

"Whatever. We don't belong there anyway, among those privileged, petrified snobs. I'm sick of pretending I give a shit. What's the point of even graduating at this point?"

"Because otherwise you'll spend the rest of your life delivering take-out in this two-bit town. Come on, it's just a few more months. Get your ass in the car."

"Sorry, I really am coughing my brains out. *Cough, cough.* See, you can't fake that."

"Bullshit."

"Just take the bus and stop bitching. Or go pass the driving exam already. I mean, a lot of people fail it twice."

"I've already missed the bus, and if you don't take me…I have to ask her. Please don't make me ask her!"

"You two need some quality time together; you'll thank me later. Say hi to the clones in Calc!"

She wasted five minutes trying to call Malorie back, but she never answered. That only left her enough time to catch her mother before she left for work and ask her—or in this case, beg her—to take Sveta to school, which would add twenty minutes to her commute. The second she walked downstairs and they locked eyes her mother knew. She only shook her head and muttered, "Three minutes, and I'm leaving with or without you."

The drive to school was more strained than usual. Sveta sat in the passenger seat, clutching her backpack against her chest, watching the traffic lights zoom past. Her mother's eyes kept cutting over to her, as if trying to pry through the clothes and see some tell-tale sign of transformation. Even as a child, her mother's hands would sweep over her flesh, poking here, prodding there, looking for resistance. *There's still time, you're still young,* she always told her, but it never sounded encouraging.

"You know, maybe you should see someone? Like a therapist? They say it's often a mental block, and you used to have those nightmares, remember?"

Used to. Still did. Always did. But it was better for her mother not to know what kept her awake at night.

"Maybe it's just not my time yet, okay?" Sveta replied. "You're a late bloomer. And Malorie, she still isn't showing."

"Knowing her parents, I'm not surprised," her mother said, with a snicker. "But you come from a long line of *rockers*. Okay, it started late for me—and like a lot of women, just one arm—but look at your grandparents: they were planted on the hill in their forties. It's inspiring to see them looking down on us, along with the rest of our family...so many generations of Beckers and Burlatskys."

She interrupted her speech to honk at someone who had cut her off, then continued.

"I'm just saying, you're almost eighteen...some kids are already thinking about where they'll be planted. If you already had a stiff arm or leg, we could reserve a spot somewhere on the hill, maybe just behind the house next to Daddy? You want to settle down before all the good places are taken."

"I mean, I guess...I just wish everyone didn't make such a big deal about it. It'll happen eventually, won't it?"

"For most people, yes, but you have to be a little proactive," she said, thoughtfully. "Not to speak ill of your friend, but Malorie lives in a trailer park. Her parents never settled down, and I doubt she will, either. Can you imagine, spending your entire life running around, never knowing your place? I knew early on where I wanted to be, who I was going to marry, even before this," she said, raising her arm. "And your father—"

"Can we not?" Sveta said, burying her face in her bag.

Her father, the famous *rock star* himself, who was in a wheelchair at eighteen. He had even made the local paper; a miracle of science, they called him. By the time she was six he was immobilized in the bedroom, just a living rock that would greet her and kiss her goodnight. A few years later they moved him to the yard, since the doctors said he was still *there*, still with them, though they couldn't say for how long. It only took a year before they felt it was time, and moved him up with his parents on the hill, another Becker to watch over the generations-yet-unborn.

"Sveta, you should be proud of him. I know it's tough not to have him around, but he did this for the family...he wanted the best for all of us."

Honestly, she barely remembered him as a living, functional parent. He had always been that *thing* in the bedroom, and she used to dread going in there at all, which was mostly reserved for bedtimes and birthdays. She hated that look in his eyes, which always seemed distant, like he didn't even know who she was. There were statues that looked kinder, more alive.

"Does it hurt?" she asked, after a pause.

"Does what? This?" her mother asked, holding up her 'good' arm, the one that was cracked and gray. "No, not at all. It's just heavier, that's all. If anything, it gives me comfort. I feel like I've become whole, like nothing can hurt me."

"Really? But what happens when you can't move? When you just have to sit around all day, having people wait on you? Doesn't that scare you?"

"If I didn't have such a loving daughter in my life, yes, it might," her mother said, with a smile. "But I know you'll take care of me. And then I'll watch over you, along with your father, from the top of the hill. You can bring your own kids up to see me, and they can hug me, climb me, whatever they like. We'll still be one big happy family."

"I guess so," Sveta said, seeing her school swing into view through the window.

"So listen, I made an appointment for you next week...the therapist came highly recommended," her mother said. "Just try it, just for a session or two. It might help. Because there's no reason you can't do it...there's nothing wrong with you. Really."

She said that last *really* as if convincing herself, lest she see her daughter as a failed experiment, someone unworthy of the Becker-Burlatsky line. She gave Sveta an affectionate pat on the shoulder as she pulled into the lot and wished her a good day. Sveta gave a miserable smile and ducked out of the car, feeling that she had survived this conversation mostly intact (unlike last time, when they had stopped talking to each other for a week).

Still, the pressure to conform and change seemed more intense than usual; not just from her mother, but from Malorie, too. It had become their only topic of conversation, and the closer they got to graduation, the more she felt she had made a decision, even without making one. It made her examine everyone with new eyes today, seeing those who *were* and those who *weren't*. All the jocks seemed to lumber about, some dragging stone legs across the floor or with faces almost set, so that you couldn't tell if they were happy or pissed off. Most of the popular kids—probably for this very reason—seemed to be well advanced, a few using crutches to get about, but one with a neck so stiff he had to turn his body simply to look at his friends. There were only a handful of girls like her who seemed normal, who moved around efficiently but seemed to hide in the background, with no infirmities to boast of. Had it always been like this? Or were people changing faster, younger, so they could be as safe and watchful as their parents?

At lunch, instead of sampling the cafeteria fare, she ducked into the library and pulled up the yearbook archive on the school's website. She scrolled through the decades, going as far back as the 1950's, watching long hair and t-shirts gradually fade into sideburns and neckties, until finally everyone became indistinguishable from the teachers: frame after frame of well-coiffed girls with giant glasses, and crew-cut boys with funeral-director suits. At first it seemed depressing, as if every one of those 1950's kids was half-chiseled out of marble.

Yet at second glance she wasn't so sure. The further back she went, the more the students seemed to have eyes. Naturally, they all *had eyes*, but these seemed alive, full of mystery and excitement. As she went forward, the stares seemed to dim, to look away, to die out. In recent years, she could sense a kind of dullness creep in, a sense that the kids had nothing to live for. Almost like the transformation had started from the inside-out.

Was that how she felt, watching everyone else turn to stone like clockwork? Was that why she still had nightmares, why she was secretly terrified of seeing a patch of gray or a finger locked in place? Of course she knew it was a good thing; she had seen all the movies and read all the books, all those glorious couples turning to stone together as the sun set behind them. Her mother called it *going back to the earth*, and said there was nothing more natural, more romantic. How strange that people used to die in wrinkled, useless skin that had to be buried out of sight and forgotten. Why settle for tombstones when you could become a living monument for those you loved?

And yet it terrified her. She still woke up most nights in a cold sweat from dreams where she was mounted like a *bas relief* over the fireplace. Her parents and friends would gather to inspect her, offering toasts, saying how wonderfully she completed the room. No matter how hard she screamed they only shook their heads, assuring her that the feeling would pass as soon as she let it go. And then she saw all the other terrified faces on the wall, all of them frozen in screaming stone.

She became so lost in these thoughts that she missed both bells and was late to Biology. By the time she arrived, students were already working in pairs on their next experiment. Her normal partner wasn't there, so she had to sit awkwardly at her desk, waiting for the teacher to notice. She thought about asking to be a third wheel in someone else's group, but she could see the looks on their faces; she was on her own. Mr. Malkin, largely immobile behind his desk, suddenly noticed her and waved imperiously.

"Miss Becker, don't just sit there. Your partner's out sick. You can pick up the lab when he returns. Here, take this to Study Hall," he said, handing her a pass.

"Study Hall? But Mr. Malkin, I can't go there! I mean, I'm not...can't I just work with someone here?" she asked, panicked.

"If you had come earlier, maybe, but I can't stop everyone just for you. Now here, take the pass. I have a lab to conduct."

"Mr. Malkin, please, you don't understand—"

"You've only got yourself to blame," he said, with a look that suggested he wasn't just talking about class.

Horrified, she took the pass and felt the whispers of mockery behind her. Study Hall was reserved for students who were on the fast-track to immobility. It allowed them a chance to take all their normal classes in a single room, since they couldn't possibly make it across the building, much less to lunch, between bells. If she walked in there like this, on both feet, without crutches or an obvious impairment, the jokes would never end. She almost thought about ditching school entirely, but without a ride she wouldn't get far. The only other choice was to hide in the bathroom until the bell rang, but that's where the druggies hung out, and she wasn't stoned enough for them, either.

She opened the door to Study Hall and the students—a small group of twelve or so—looked up from their desks, students she knew from junior high and grade school. She had watched them grow up, sometimes being friends with them, sometimes not, until they all got lost in a blur of adolescence. Surprisingly, no one laughed or objected to her presence. The teacher gestured for her pass and then went back to his book, similarly indifferent. Sveta scanned the room, trying to think which student she would piss off the least by sitting beside them.

Helen Canevaro. They had been friends for a short space in third or fourth grade, but something had happened, a spat at a birthday party, she didn't remember. She still fondly remembered spending the night at Helen's house once, reading manga and watching old horror movies until three in the morning. Helen looked up at her with a smile and said hello. Gratefully, Sveta slung her backpack over the chair and sat down, smiling back.

"Hey, good to see you," Sveta said, quietly. "Sorry, I know I don't belong here, I'm kind of a loser, but I got kicked out of class. No lab partner."

"No, it's cool, I've only been here for a few weeks," Helen said, gesturing to her foot. "I don't feel like I belong here, either."

Sveta looked down at her right foot, which at first resembled a mud-stained cast. Upon closer inspection, she could see what used to be toes encrusted with a jumble of mottled stone. Otherwise, though, Helen looked completely normal, her bare arms untouched, except for a small bird tattoo near her left elbow. Their eyes met, and Sveta was startled how much Helen looked like that one girl from the crazy Swedish movie where they sacrificed people.

Maybe that was the real reason they'd stopped hanging out all those years ago. Sometimes girls could tell when she looked at them a certain way, or for too long, and didn't like it.

"Is it hard...you know, getting around?" Sveta asked.

"Yeah, it's kind of a drag," she said, nodding. "It goes all the way up to my knee. I woke up one morning and it was like that, no warning. My parents were thrilled. They would have bought me a car if they thought I could drive it."

"Shit," Sveta said, with a laugh. "I don't know whether to say *congratulations* or *I'm sorry*."

"Both, I guess. What about you? Any signs yet?"

"No, nothing. I'm a total failure. The disappointment of my entire clan," she said dramatically.

"I doubt that. You were someone people always looked up to. I remember when...well, never mind, it's silly."

"No, what?" Sveta asked. "Come on, tell me."

"Oh, you probably won't remember...but back in third grade, we went to the county fair together. Your mom took us."

"Oh right, of course," Sveta said, starting to remember.

"Anyway, there was that booth where you had to throw baseballs at bottles. I sucked, couldn't hit even one. But you hit every one, over and over again. There was a crowd of people watching you, cheering you on, and you kept going until the guy kicked you out. Said you were cheating."

"Oh yeah, I forgot all about that! What a dick."

"But you still won that giant rabbit: it was ridiculously big, cotton-candy pink, with these huge floppy ears, remember? And you gave it to me, even though it was yours, even though I begged you to keep it. You even told me—I know, it sounds silly now—that I was your inspiration."

Sveta didn't have a clear vision of winning the rabbit or giving it to Helen, though the general impression rang true. She only remembered a vague, warm sensation in her gut whenever she thought about their brief friendship. It was still one of the happiest times of her life.

"Sorry I made you keep it. Hopefully you got rid of it in the morning."

"No way, I still have her!" Helen said, eyes wide. "She sits right on my bed...sometimes I even use her as a pillow."

"*Her?* Don't tell me you named it?" Sveta said.

"Of course: Anastasia! I think your name inspired me. Whenever I see her, I always remember you, that night we spent together. I hated that we stopped being friends."

"Yeah, I wonder why we did? I guess it doesn't matter anymore, we were just kids. Maybe we can...you know, start over? Especially since we're stuck here together."

"But only here until your lab partner comes back to class, right? Are they really sick?" Helen asked, cautiously.

"I don't know, maybe. I barely even know the guy," she said, with a shrug.

"Good...I don't like competition," Helen replied.

It was only after the bell rang and they went their separate ways that Sveta realized she still had a crush on Helen, and her third-grade game had been smoother than she thought.

As it happened, her lab partner, Sam Dickey, was having unexpected complications from his sudden change. It happened sometimes. They didn't like to talk about it, but a few students were hospitalized when the change was too abrupt, or when it started in the wrong place. She knew at least one kid had died when his heart turned to stone. That was what scared her the most, the Russian roulette of the transformation. It was almost like someone was having a sick joke at their expense, one time choosing something ridiculous, like an ear, and another, an essential organ. She suddenly felt guilty that she didn't even remember what Sam looked like, other than his glasses, which were always slipping off.

However, after a few days of Study Hall, she fell into a comfortable routine with Helen, no longer worried about being witty or stupid or whatever. Mostly she just spent time observing Helen, noticing all the little things hidden in plain view, but which took days and weeks to pick up. Case in point, she realized Helen was filling up page after page with elaborate arabesques, which sometimes coalesced into familiar shapes and faces. Once, without trying to be too sneaky about it, she spied a dreamy portrait emerge on the margins of Helen's homework.

"Damn, did you do that just on the spot?" she asked.

"Oh—yeah, I mean, I'm just scribbling. It helps me think, it always has. It's nothing really."

"If you do that, you must have other stuff, too, like where you're really trying. Can you show me?"

Helen grew a bit red at the suggestion, though it was clear that the scribbles were a subtle invitation to see more. But now she was nervous to go all the way.

"Well, look, don't read too much into this...but I wanted to give you this. I was just worried you would think, *wow, that's weird* or something. But I made it for you."

Helen unzipped her backpack and removed a sketch pad smudged with charcoal on the cover. She opened the cover and flipped past several pages of abstract images, still lives, landscapes, houses. Then she came to one of the last pages, which, after a grin, she nudged over toward Sveta. Sveta could tell what it was even upside-down, even before her eyes really put it together.

It was a portrait of her, a bit idealized, of course, but taken by someone who had paid attention, who caught more than just the shoulder-length hair, the freckles, the little gap in her teeth. She saw her hesitation, her excitement, her awkwardness, her beauty. That was Sveta's first thought when she really took in the portrait: *Jesus, she's gorgeous.* Because she really felt like she was looking at Helen looking at her, and so much of Helen had bled through that it made the portrait feel like a warm embrace that wouldn't let go.

"My God, Helen...this is wonderful. I mean, I wish I looked like that. When did you do this?"

"A few nights ago. I got bored doing my homework...or rather, I couldn't concentrate on my homework. I kept thinking about you."

So there, I said it, her eyes seemed to announce. They were wide-awake eyes, right there, looking to the future. Like those fifties kids in the yearbook, but no longer carved in stone.

"It's wonderful, I love it," Sveta said, stroking it with her hand. "It's perfect."

"Then it was worth doing," Helen said, with a smile. "It's yours, of course. I still have the original."

"Where, in your head?"

Helen gave a little nod that suggested both yes and no. They didn't say another word for the rest of class, allowing Sveta to replay the scene over and over until she knew it by heart.

Sveta waited for Helen after school, saw her coming out of the building on her crutches, her dead leg holding her back, bringing tears of frustration. When she suddenly looked up and saw Sveta, her face went blank, the pain retreating. Then her eyes lit up again. Sveta didn't look at who was watching, what they might think (or what she might think tomorrow). She went right up to Helen and said something, she didn't even remember what, and kissed her. Really quickly, before either of them could think twice. Helen's eyes stayed wide-open in surprise, only closing as she pulled away, drinking it in.

"That's for the drawing," Sveta said, awkwardly.

"I have a few more, if you want to see them. But I keep them at home."

"I want to see everything. I mean, if you'll let me...if I'm not being, you know, too weird or something."

"Whatever...I like weird girls."

A car pulled up just behind them, which Sveta recognized from the general cacophony (shuddering engine, muffled sounds of Black Sabbath) as Malorie's car. She tried to ignore it and steal as much time as she could, but Malorie laid on the horn: a long, impatient blast. Sveta gave a backwards wave in Malorie's direction.

"Shit, I gotta go. My ride. You want to come? We can take you —"

"No, my mom insists on picking me up. But thanks. I'll text you later, okay?"

Another honk. Sveta gave Helen a quick squeeze of the hand and darted into the passenger seat of the 'Gremlin' as they called it, though she had no idea what brand or model it was. Malorie zoomed off and even went between the parked buses with their STOP signs extended. A few kids flipped her off.

"I'd be doing them a favor," she muttered. "So what, are you hanging out with her now?"

"Yeah, I mean, we're friends," Sveta said, cautiously. "I met her in Study Hall. She's funny, you'd like her."

"I heard she was a stuck-up bitch. But, I mean, if *you* like her."

"I do. She's cool. So, you actually came to school today. What's the occasion?"

"Girl, I guess I'm celebrating," she said, accelerating dramatically out of the parking lot. "I tried to text you, but you were too busy with what's-her-face."

"Celebrating? Why, did Steve send you a dick-pic or something?"

"Honestly, they look the same as his selfies, so who knows? But for real, check this shit out," she said, revealing her left hand, which she had kept hidden at her side.

Flashing it in Sveta's face, she revealed four fingers that were completely stone, with only one, the pinky, unscathed. Sveta shrieked and immediately grabbed it, running her fingers over each one, amazed and terrified by the transformation. Only a few days ago Malorie had made fun of all the *stoners*, as she jokingly called them, comparing the stratification of torsos and biceps. But now she seemed almost giddy over her change, having already posted it across social media, where, she explained, it already had hundreds of likes.

"My parents are flipping out," Malorie said, trying unsuccessfully to wiggle her fingers. "You know how they said I was on my own for college? Well, guess who just put up five thousand bucks?"

"You're joking! Really? Just because of this?"

"Hell yeah, because of this. A lot of people say if you get fingers first, that's a good sign. It means you're as good as gold by your twenties. So if I can get into State, or even one of the liberal arts schools, I might jumpstart fingers into an arm and a leg—or hell, even a torso!"

"But weren't you going to take a gap year or something? So you could travel the country, hike all over the Southwest? Remember the postcard I sent you of the giant saguaro? You were even going to get a tattoo."

Malorie frowned at the reminder, clearly from a different time, a different life. The world before she knew she had a future, or a body worth investing in.

"I mean…that would be cool, but I can't just waste an entire year when I could, you know, be getting ahead. And why go to Arizona or wherever when there are so many good colleges here?"

"And that's what you really want?" Sveta said, hesitantly. "You just seemed so happy, like you had everything figured out. This shouldn't change things completely."

"But it does, like a million percent! I never thought I would have a chance to settle down, find a place on the hill where everyone can see me. And who knows, after college I might be solid rock. Think what that would mean to my parents!"

"To be a statue before you're thirty?" she said, unable to hide her disappointment. "You saw what happened to my father; I barely knew him, Maly. What if you have kids? Is that how you want them to remember you? Because they won't remember you at all. You'll just be that thing in the garden, or up on the hill, reminding them to study hard and eat their vegetables."

Malorie abruptly switched lanes and pulled into an abandoned gas station where they used to hang out, where Malorie allegedly made out with some guy who just graduated. The car slammed to a halt and Malorie just glared at her, her soft hand gripping the wheel.

"I thought you would be happy for me," she said, her deep voice cracking. "You're the only person I really wanted to tell, Sveta. Because I knew you would give a shit. Or at least understand. I wasn't supposed to change and you know it. My parents are soft-skinned, trailer-trash rednecks. And I'm trailer-trash, too."

"No, Maly, I do—I get it. I *am* happy for you. I just don't think you should be in such a hurry to be like everyone else. You're different than them, you always said so. That's why we're friends. And we'll still be friends, no matter what."

"What the fuck do you know about me?" Malorie said, giving her a shove. "Maybe I've wanted this my whole life but was too scared to ask? Maybe I didn't want to be disappointed like I always am? People don't give two shits about me around here, Sveta. I don't have parents, a reputation like yours. I'll always be *that girl* to them."

"Who cares? I like *that girl*, don't you? And since when do you need them to like you? It's us against the world, remember?"

Malorie gave a world-weary laugh, as if she had heard this before, many times, in fact, and still didn't buy it. Sveta tried to backtrack, but Malorie cut her off, rolling down the window and yelling "bullshit!" at the top of her lungs. Sveta waited for the moment to pass, for Malorie to realize she was overacting and apologize, but it seemed she was just warming up.

"We were never on the same side," Malorie said, eyes flashing. "You're still the same old Sveta, slumming it with me until you find something better. But you don't know the first thing about me... like the reason I hate your guts."

"Do tell," Sveta muttered.

"You're everything I want to be, everything I tried to believe in. You made me feel that it was okay to be who I was. But then I started to see that you didn't even believe in yourself. People used to look up to you, you know? You were the girl *most likely to succeed* and shit. But now...they talk a lot of shit behind your back. They think you've given up; we all do."

"Why, because I'm not practicing to become a lawn ornament? Is that what little kids really dream of doing when they grow up? Why can't we look around, get lost, not try to be exactly like our parents? Why is everyone in such a rush to do nothing for the rest of their lives?"

"Actually, I'm trying *not* to be like my parents," Malorie said, sucking her teeth. "But I'd like to see how far you get with what's-her-name. You think she really cares about you? Today, maybe, but tomorrow she's going to want something real, something lasting. I know I do."

"Then lucky for me she's not like you," Sveta snapped. "No, she's the person I thought you were, the one I felt safe with, who I trusted more than anyone on earth. But I guess friendship's only skin deep...so you'll need a new friend to go with your fucked-up hand."

They drove home in silence, and when they pulled up to Sveta's house, Malorie just sat there, idling. Sveta just sat there, too, trying to think of whether to salvage their relationship or blow it to hell. Malorie beat her to it.

"I love how no one's supposed to change but you," she said, looking away. "I have to remain the fuck-up, the loser, while you figure it out. And once you do, you sure as hell won't wait for me. You'll leave me in the dust."

"Maly, that's not true. I've always had your back."

"You mean you've *held me* back. When I talked about college, or having kids, or anything you don't agree with, it's always *don't do it, it's not you, you'll regret it*. But what if I don't have the same regrets as you?"

"So your answer is to do what everyone else does, to follow them off the same fucking cliff? That's your idea of finding yourself? No, you're smarter than that."

"Everyone goes there for a reason," Malorie said, coldly. "It's what we all secretly want. Like falling in love, having a family. No one stays in the valley unless they have to, even if they lie to themselves and say they prefer it. Life looks better up on the hill, and you know it. At least, your father did."

"Fuck off, Malorie," she said, and opened the door.

"You first," Malorie returned.

As soon as Sveta got out, Malorie sped away, music blasting. Sveta knew she wouldn't see her again for months, maybe not ever. Now she had no one to talk to, no one to console her for being different, no one to confide in about her feelings for Helen. Of course, that's what choosing your own path was all about: being alone, choosing the road less traveled by. She had to have faith in the destination, in ending up far away in some happily-ever-after, even if it never was. All the same, the conversation hit its mark, and she replayed Malorie's words and her responses far more than she cared to. Even when Helen started texting her after dinner, she was only half-listening, thinking about *who* Helen was talking to: the now-her or the one-to-come? The one who had rock legs like Helen did, or the loser who never would?

After a few days, Sveta had made her decision: she and Helen had to break up. Partly it was everything Malorie had told her; partly it was her own fear of commitment. But what really clinched it was the meme making the rounds of the school, a picture of two people playing Paper-Scissors-Rock, the hands of one opponent forming scissors, the other forming rock. On the 'rock' someone had Photoshopped a picture of Helen's head, and on the 'scissors', Sveta's. Though the words of the meme had a few variations, the most consistent one said *Happy Valentine's Day*, with a copy even making its way to her locker at school. The message was clear: rock always beats scissors, and not even love can change the rules of the game. She shuddered to think how often Helen had seen it, and what she must have thought the first, second, and fiftieth time it swam through her feed.

Sveta had to tell her face-to-face, and it had to be at school, so she wouldn't waver and change her mind at the last minute. Of course, it was harder now that Sveta's bio partner had returned and she was back in class doing make-up. Worse still, without Malorie, her mother had to pick her up from school, and she was always there at 3:15 on the dot. So Sveta had about five minutes to waylay Helen, find somewhere semi-private, and tell her the truth. She spent the entire day planning her route, worried about the distance between their rooms and the congestion in the hallway. When the release bell finally rang, she was the first one out the door, pushing and prodding her way across the building to Study Hall, which was precariously close to the exit. A few minutes late, and Helen would slip through the doors and make it into her mom's car before Sveta could say a word.

She made it in record time, just as people were starting to trickle out of other rooms, though Study Hall seemed comfortably full (it took them much longer to leave, obviously). Sveta flattened herself against the wall, eyes picking out every jock and bonehead who left the room, excited—yet crushed—when it wasn't Helen. Seven or eight people came out, then a few more, then one more... then the teacher himself, who flicked off the lights.

Holy shit, where was she?

She knew Helen was here today, because she had said she had a Calc test and couldn't chat over breakfast. Frantic, Sveta began sweeping up and down the hallways, looking for any sign of her presence. She checked both of their lockers (nope), circled back to her last-hour class (no one), and even checked the bathrooms, trying to match the shoes beneath each of the stalls (Nikes; Helen only wore Converse). After five or six minutes she knew it was too late, that somehow she had missed Helen, even though she had covered all the bases and left nothing to chance.

As her heart stopped racing, she became aware of a steady, pulsating hum just around or behind her. Shit, her phone! In her anxiety she had missed an entire stream of texts from Helen. Pulling them up, they all basically said, *Where are you? Really need to talk! Meet me in the locker room. Are you coming? Sveta? Hello???*

It took her another three or four minutes to make her way to the locker room (the hallways were packed now), but it was a well-chosen spot, completely dead. She found Helen sitting in a dark corner of the room on a bench, hugging her knees while she stared down at her phone, waiting for a reply. Sveta swept in and started apologizing, saying she was sorry but they really had to talk, it wouldn't take a minute...but that's as far as she got.

Even as she was explaining, her mind was processing Helen's face and expression. She had been crying. Her eyes were red and there were tissues all over the floor, so she had obviously been here awhile. She must have skipped out early to come here, which explained why Sveta hadn't seen her in Study Hall. But wait, had Helen figured it out? No way, she had been way too careful—and hell, she hadn't even known it herself until just this morning. Sveta walked over and took her hand, squeezing it.

"My God, Helen. What happened?"

Helen gave a little laugh, her expression more happy-sad than distraught, her eyes burning with some hidden passion she couldn't betray. Helen stood up and pulled her close. They embraced, and Helen whispered something in her ear, which sounded like, *Well, I guess I'm all yours now*. What did that mean? As they embraced, Sveta instinctively reached out to support her, since without her crutches there's no way Helen wouldn't—

"Holy shit, your crutches! Helen, where...?"

She was standing straight on both legs, her eyes brimming with tears.

"Sveta, it's gone. Just like that. I woke up this morning...and it was gone. I was too scared to tell you. I made up the Calc test. I've been working towards it all day."

Open-mouthed, Sveta looked down at Helen's bare feet (she had taken off both shoes and socks) and saw two beautiful feet, painted nails and all. She didn't know what to say or think, so she sputtered with a kind of choking laugh, which made Helen laugh even harder.

"I wanted so badly for it to go away. Every night I begged God or whoever was listening to get rid of it. I didn't want anything to take me away from you. And now...well, I don't know what to think. But I'm happy...I *think*!"

"I don't understand, it's gone, like, really gone?" Sveta said, shaking her head. "So you're not...you're not going to be one of them? You can do that?"

"I mean, it's happened before, you hear stories, but I didn't believe them. I guess it helps if you're really in love," she said, looking up at her. "Sorry if that freaks you out, but that's where we are right now. I'm in love with you, and I want you to know that I gave this up, all of it, for you."

Sveta started crying, and she just stood there, pressing her head against Helen's, feeling happier than she knew what to do with. Sveta realized how stupid she had been to come here, to say what she thought was kindness. It would have been kinder to simply tell her the truth: that she was scared. Scared to fall in love, scared that Helen had made a mistake, scared that she would have to watch Helen figure it out in slow motion.

"But what about your parents? They were so happy...what are you going to tell them?" Sveta asked.

"I don't know; I don't care. They'll just have to deal with it. Because honestly, I was only worried about you."

"You really think I give a shit about what your leg looked like? That I liked you for that?"

"No...but when everyone else does, or would, it's hard to make exceptions. I still can't believe you see me, the real me, rather than...someone else."

"I see you...I look at you every day, and never stop looking," Sveta replied, kissing her. "That's why I'm in love with you, too."

"What if that's not enough? I mean, for now it is, but what if you feel differently later on? That's what I'm scared of. I might never grow it back, Sveta. This might be it. And I'm cool with that... I don't want to be that girl anymore. I want you to love me like this."

"Then good, let's both be over it! Whatever happens, we won't regret what we lost. We're just freaks of nature. The losers left behind to love each other."

Helen laughed, and they kissed each other again and again. She could almost believe they would be happy now, even without the future she once planned, that everyone else in the world expected. She nuzzled against Sveta's cheek, kissed her neck, brushing the hair away so she could nibble her ear.

"Oh God! Sveta!" Helen exclaimed, almost leaping back.

"What? What?" Sveta said, catching her. "What's wrong?"

Helen's eyes were large, alive, frightened. Her hand flew to her mouth as she backed away. Sveta began feeling all over her face, trying to wipe away invisible bugs, when a finger grazed her ear. Or what used to be her ear. Its once-smooth surface was now furrowed and sharp. She felt it again and again, hoping it was just some trick of the moment, excitement and fear running rampant.

But no, it was there, and it had changed. She had changed. Part of her was horrified, wanting to rip off the offending ear. Another part was secretly relieved that she could still do it, after all. That she wasn't a lost cause like everyone (well, her mother) feared. Strangely, she had slept soundly for the past few nights without a single nightmare, as if she had finally made peace with her fear. Of course, she didn't want it for herself, her mother, or because of anything Malorie said; she wanted it for Helen, to prove to her that they could still be together. Maybe that's why her father had been able to do it so young, with so much of his life still ahead of him. Because he had a 'Helen' too.

"But I thought...you couldn't," Helen whispered.

"I can't! I mean, I couldn't! I have no idea how this happened. I guess...I don't know, I was scared to lose you, too."

"So you gave me the one thing I can't return," Helen said, with a laugh. "Well, Merry Christmas, Sveta! I got you the same thing."

"Thanks, it's just what I wanted," Sveta said.

She stumbled forward and fell into Helen's embrace, enveloped in tears and silence. Sveta's phone began vibrating again, a stream of texts from her mom, wondering where the hell she was and if she wanted to start walking home from now on? She returned it to her pocket, didn't care whether she walked home or stayed in this room for the rest of the night. She could only stare at Helen and remember that Keats poem about a lover chasing a nymph for all eternity, never catching her, always in the heat of pursuit. That's where she felt she was with Helen right now, and where they always would be; their fingers almost touching, their happiness real, but not of this earth.

"What do we do now?" Helen asked.

"Just hold me," Sveta said, closing her eyes. "Maybe if we stay here long enough, we'll fossilize into a *bas relief* so some modern-day Keats can write a poem about us. You know that poem...*beauty is truth, truth beauty,—that is all ye know on earth, and all ye need to know.*"

"You're such a show-off," Helen said, smiling. "Yeah, we read it in AP-English. But I think it's about an urn, and not a bas-whatever."

"Same difference. It's old, it's beautiful, it tells the truth."

"What truth?"

"Like Keats, we're going to live forever. And that's all I need to know."

*See Joshua Grasso's story "Bas Relief" online at Metaphorosis.
If you liked it, leave a comment. Authors love that!
Remember to subscribe to our e-mail updates so you'll know when
new stories are posted.*

About the story

"Bas Relief" was inspired by my experience teaching college students, typically those fresh out of high school. So many of them choose the same 2-3 majors, have the same 2-3 goals, and almost all of them want to become their parents (i.e., successful, big house, vacations, etc.) as soon as possible. They don't seem very excited about learning, or growing as a person, or taking changes that might lead to unexpected destinations. I kept thinking of them as young people quickly turning into stone, desperate to plant themselves into a suburban neighborhood as soon as possible and have the accumulated wealth of the world grow over them like moss. The more I thought about it, the basic outline of the story suggested itself, of teenagers who are pushed to 'change' as soon as possible so they can take their places on the hill, forming a man-made mountain of the 'haves' that look down at the unfortunate 'have nots'. I originally meant this to be satire, but as I started playing with the characters, a love story suggested itself, since being young is about finding love as much as finding yourself. Indeed, your initial identity as a person is often formed by how you want others to see you, and how someone convinces you to see yourself (or imagine yourself) because they believe in you. So I wanted this story to be about more than satirizing people who grow up too fast, and a society that makes them; I also wanted it to be about how you decide to open yourself to being in love when you're still at war with yourself, and how trust people to see the real 'you'.

A question for the author

Q: Do you use music for inspiration? If so, what do you listen to?

A: I honestly have trouble writing without music, since the right music unlocks the 'act' of writing itself. It's not that I need a soundtrack to my writing (since the music rarely completely matches what I'm trying to convey), but I need a piece that is sympathetic to either the mood I'm in at the time. Often, when I find the right piece of music, it can influence the writing and attach itself to a specific scene or character in unexpected ways. I'm a classical music nut, and have collected it seriously since I was about 17 (I'm in my 40's now), so I listen to everything from Bach to Mozart to Beethoven to Tchaikovsky to Stravinsky to Shostakovich and beyond. Orchestral music, in particular, seems to complement the act of writing since it's purely visual and emotional, yet without leading you down a specific alley the way music with words often do. You can put a favorite symphony on repeat and hear different stories each time, which is great, since writing requires you to come up with something new each time!

About the author

Joshua Grasso is a professor of English at a small university in Oklahoma, where he teaches classes in British and World Literature, writing, and comics. He holds a PhD from Miami University where he specialized in 18th c. British Literature. When not teaching or writing, he enjoys hanging out with his two boys (one of whom is college bound!), reading everything he can get his hands on, and hunting for old vinyl and cds of classical music.
@JoshuaGrasso

An Hour in the City of Lightning

A.D. Guzman

The match flared orange and momentarily suffused crisp December air with an oddly soothing aroma of sulfur and smoke. Matt touched it to the end of his cigarette and inhaled deeply. Eyes closed, he exhaled a dragon-esque cloud and leaned against the church's brick wall.

"I thought you quit."

Matt cracked an eye and adjusted his glasses. His childhood confidant and cousin Renee stood beside him, one hand pressed to her lower back, the other supporting the weight of her eighth month of pregnancy. Thick, chestnut curls framed wide, impish green eyes and a crooked smile.

"I quit." Matt took another drag of his cigarette and tried to angle the smoke away from her. "But even a condemned man gets a last smoke before facing the firing squad."

"*Grandpa's* dead." Renee snatched the cigarette, then ground it out on the sidewalk. "*You're* just giving the eulogy in front of a bunch of grieving relatives."

Afternoon sun bathed them in a golden glow, though the winter chill worried its way through Matt's thin suit coat and dress slacks with annoying persistence. He rubbed his hands together and blew on them. A faint growl of thunder announced a storm cresting the northern horizon. A jagged line of lightning burned across the dark gray clouds.

"I'd rather face a firing squad," Matt confessed. "And Gran's been after me. Criticizing my hair, my clothes. Even my glasses are too 'hipster'. At least she's talking to me again, after my apparently unforgiveable sin of becoming a teacher instead of a doctor."

"I know Gran kind of pushed you away, but what about the rest of us? We've missed you. *I've* missed you." Renee paused and dropped her gaze to the slope of her belly. "Jim was laid off three months ago and things have been tough. You and Grandpa always knew what to say to make things right. But you practically disappeared. And now Grandpa.”

Matt flinched. When the Gran who used to cut his grilled cheeses into perfect triangles declared his chosen profession a waste, it had stung. But the constant, offhanded digs at him and decreasingly subtle cold shoulder had built a distance between them that made Matt feel like a hostile intruder at family functions. Eventually, he’d stopped coming. Renee was right; he had disappeared on her.

Renee put a hand on his shoulder. “Gran only wants the best for you. You should cut her a little slack. She just lost her anchor of over sixty years. To lose the person that’s been with you through *everything*, to have to handle that grief alone... Besides she wouldn’t have chosen you to give the speech if she didn’t think you’d do him proud.”

“I’m not so sure of that.” Matt pulled the slightly wrinkled print-out from his suit pocket. “She reduced my speech to a résumé of his accomplishments. There’s nothing about the man Grandpa was.”

Renee graciously allowed the change of subject. “Remember how he always hid our Christmas presents and made us follow clues to find them?”

Matt smiled. “I think he used that as an excuse to get us to do his chores.”

They chuckled and watched the brewing storm toss bursts of light back and forth across the sky.

“He had a unique way of putting things,” Matt said. “I remember he called each bolt of lightning a universe, born and extinguished in an instant, and thunder the cry of mourning. Although, get a few beers in him, then Grandpa swore up and down it was angels farting.”

Renee wiped her eyes and choked out a laugh. “Grandpa sure could wax poetic when the mood struck. You’re a lot like him, you know. You both love telling unusual stories.”

“Then maybe I’ll write a book of them.”

“You’d better.” Renee patted her belly. “This kid is going to need to know about his Great-Grandpa.”

Matt threw his arm over her shoulders in a hug. “Well, we’d better get inside before they send a search party.”

A loose nail made the lectern rock beneath Matt's nervous grip as he stood on the church's small stage beside his Grandpa's gleaming coffin. The sea of somber faces stared expectantly at him. Waiting. He ran a sweaty hand through his hair and shoved his glasses up the bridge of his nose. His freshman literature classes averaged over three hundred students, and he'd never had so much as a butterfly until now.

Renee rubbed her belly, discreetly flashing him a thumbs-up sign. Farther down, seated primly between Matt's father and Aunt Patrice, Gran dabbed her eyes with a lace hankie.

Matt looked at Gran's version of his speech, then deliberately folded it and slipped it back into his pocket next to an old velvet earring box Grandpa had given him. Gran's eyes widened behind her glasses and her hankie dropped forgotten to her lap. Her hand flew to the rose pendant she always wore for special occasions.

He cleared his throat and adjusted his tie. "Jeff Walters ... my grandpa. He ... um ... Well, it's hard to sum up a man. Impossible really. I mean, how can you encompass a person and their impact on the world in just a few words?

"We like closure. We like our laces tied, our ducks in a row, a pot of gold at the end of our rainbows. But the truth of the matter is that we're not threads in some cosmic tapestry that can be neatly trimmed and tied off when our part is complete. We're messy, wild, our influences unpredictable and often unintentional.

" 'We're like lightning,' Grandpa used to say. 'Bright, loud, dangerous. Brief but beautiful bursts of raw energy streaking through the world. For good or evil, our very existence alters the universe. And that's a damn big responsibility.'

"Which is exactly how Grandpa lived—though anyone who's ever seen him tinkering with his tractor can attest to that loud and dangerous bit." Matt grinned at the few bold enough to chuckle. "It's no surprise that Grandpa chose lightning as his analogy for life. His passion for the phenomenon is local legend. I don't think any of us will forget the Chicken Fiasco of '89." More laughter, louder this time.

"Grandpa was a man who saw magic in the mundane and potential in the most ordinary people. But what most of you might not know is why. When I was eleven, Grandpa took me camping and fishing for a weekend, just me and him. While we were on the lake, a good twenty minutes from where we'd put in, a storm swept in out of nowhere. A big monster with lots of rain and wind and lightning. I'd never seen Grandpa so excited. Those steel gray eyes mirrored the darkened sky. He tossed our rods into the bottom of the boat, told me to get down by his feet, started the motor and turned us back to shore.

"We bumped across the choppy water. Those twenty minutes it would take to get back seemed more like twenty hours. I stared up into a black, boiling maw with white lightning fangs behind us and knew it was hunting me.

"Grandpa must have noticed my fear, because he put on his story-telling grin and said, 'Awesome sight, ain't it, boy? There's a whole universe in there. In the lightning. That's what lightning is. Whole other worlds that're born, age and die in a split second. But they ain't lost; no energy ever is. It just ... changes. And who knows, maybe we're just a flash of lightning in some other universe too.'

" 'Nuh-uh,' I argued. 'Lightning is just a bunch of static electricity. We learned that in school.'

" 'Hogwash! I've been there, Matt. Spent an hour in the city of lightning. Any of your teachers or your books ever do that?'

"I shook my head. Then Grandpa cleared his throat and told me this story:

It was late summer, hotter'n hell and air so thick you could wring it out. I was seventeen, workin' the field for my Daddy, who'd been laid up by a kick from the mule. A storm blew in outta nowhere, a lot like this'un. I had just one more row to plow and decided to finish it out 'fore heading back to the house.

There was a deafening roar. It was the sound of the world tearin' apart, confusin' the senses. Noise blinded, light deafened. I tasted ozone, smelled 'lectricity. I could feel each'n every molecule of the air around me. I was livin' so hard I was dyin'.

Matt paused. He had a bad habit of speaking too fast when nervous. A baby in the back whimpered, precursor to a full-on wail. Its mother tossed a diaper bag over her shoulder and eased her way to the end of her row, flashing an apologetic smile as everyone turned to watch her go. Once the pair left, Matt took a deep breath and went on, "Grandpa's distraction was working. While I tried to figure out his metaphors, I couldn't focus on the weather chasing our little boat across the lake. I said, 'That doesn't make sense, Grandpa.'

"His tone became grave, and he turned his steely eyes on me. 'You're a dreamer, boy. More like me than your old man.' He touched a finger to my chest. 'Keep lookin' at the world with more'n your eyes, and one day you'll understand.'

"I nodded, wide-eyed. Grandpa continued with his tale:

When I came to my senses, the field was gone. I was standin', naked as a jaybird, in the middle of a crowded street. Like to died of embarrassment 'fore I noticed that these weren't the kind of folks you bump into down at the post office.

Their skin was a shiny black like that there volcano stuff, with pale flecks that sparkled in the purple sunlight. The texture was wrong, too, like they really was made of rock or glass. Their eyes was jewels. They didn't have no noses and not a strand of hair.

Four long, skinny limbs like our arms an' legs sprouted from short, stocky chests. Each hand only had four fingers, two of 'em thumbs. They moved funny, kinda like overgrown chickens 'cause their knee and elbow joints didn't bend like mine.

The city itself…well, looked somethin' like I'd imagine heaven to be. The buildings grew organic-like, more sculpture than architecture. Whatever material they used gave off white light that wiggled up into the violet sunlight like you see in them aurora things up north. I shaded my eyes from instinct more than pain—so much light shoulda blinded me, but I could see just fine.

A woman fell into step beside me. Don't ask me how I knew it was a woman; I just did. I smiled and asked, "Don't suppose you can tell me where I am?"

She brushed her fingertips 'cross the back of my hand. And I knew, like findin' a memory I'd forgot, that I was in Grown on Bay Rock, the capital of The Great Continent, the last settlement of the Children of the Third Sun. I was Visitor from Another Dimension and she wanted to know my name and the name of my Mother Sun.

"Name's Jeff," I told her. "From Texas. That's in the United States. It's a country on Earth."

Again, I knew her question when her fingers touched mine. "Earth is your sun?"

I shook my head. "No, it's my planet. The rock we live on."

She smiled and bluish streaks zigzagged 'cross her skin between them pale flecks, a thunderstorm in miniature. She touched a hand to her torso, then twined her fingers with mine. "I am One Who Comes Third and Brings Happiness. I study the possibility of multiple dimensions and travel between them. Visitor from Another Dimension Jeff, you are proof of my theory. What is your purpose here?"

"My purpose?"

"You are an inter-dimensional envoy, yes? A representative of the Children of your sun?"

"No."

"A researcher like myself, then? A scientist?"

I laughed and slapped my knee. "Whoo-boy, have you got the wrong idea, lady. I'm just a simple farmer. I can read, write and figure well enough, but I don't know nothin' about other dimensions."

That odd skin-lightning returned, but this time it was more purple. "Then how did you come to be here, Visitor from Another Dimension Jeff?"

I shrugged. "Beats me. Best guess, my dang mule kicked me in the head and this is a dream."

"You must come from a less advanced world. I had not considered that possibility." Her skin flashed with mustard yellow streaks. I think she was a mite disappointed. "Well, if you dream, then let it be a good dream. Come, there is much to see before you wake."

It was the strangest sight-seeing tour I'd ever been on. I walked gardens of natural stone, though it don't seem right to call 'em stones, because each was as unique and beautiful as a snowflake. Some towered strong and mighty as oaks, others swept along the path, delicate as honeysuckle bushes, or clustered in little bunches like flowers.

One Who Comes Third and Brings Happiness explained that each stone took generations of gardeners thousands of years to grow. The occasional fountain of inky water filled the air with a pleasant tinkling. I couldn't smell a thing. Like walkin' through a garden in full bloom with a head cold. I guess without noses, they didn't have a sense of smell and didn't need their gardens to smell nice.

She took me to an art museum. Alien landscapes hung beside Picasso-like portraits. Irregular lumps of stone outnumbered the art, though. No painting or designs. Just big, ugly boulders on display. My guide went and put her hands all over one of 'em. Then she pulled me over and made me hug it, too. Now, I've never seen a museum that let you put your paws on the art, so I figured it had to be some kinda good luck charm. She explained that the artist's work was inside, not outside, for me to feel.

That threw me 'til I figured that if we had a sense of smell and they didn't, then maybe they got senses we don't. It embarrassed me, not bein' able to see this thing she was clearly so proud of. I asked if she'd describe it to me, and she touched her hand to mine …

Matt paused to take a sip a from a convenient water bottle the funeral director had placed in the lectern. He was slipping into professor mode, a welcome reprieve from his previous nerves. His trained eye spotted a few people checking phones, but most were paying attention.

"Thunder clapped and the boat's engine sputtered out. We'd finally reached the dock, jostled against it by the waves, but all my attention was on Grandpa. 'What did you see, Grandpa? What was inside the rock?'

"He reached up and wiped his eyes. Rain poured down his face in tiny rivers, but for a second, I thought he might have been crying.

" 'I didn't see nothin'. But what I felt …' His voice faltered. 'I just wish I could tell you, son. Imagine the very best day of your life stuck like a fly in amber, a perfect moment suspended for forever. And then do the same ten years later. It's the same moment, but not the same moment. The way when you're ten what you want most is a new bike, then ten years later it's a new car, then maybe ten years later a new house. The same want, just a different object. It was like that, Matt.'

"We grabbed our gear and scrambled for the cover of our cabin porch. Grandpa fixed us each a mug of cocoa, then continued:

I followed One Who Comes Third and Brings Happiness until my dogs were barkin'. Remember, I'd already been plowin' all day before getting zapped there. We saw their government and their churches to the Third Sun. We visited slums where coal-black bums, eyes milky and cracked, skin as dull and lifeless as real coal, huddled along the sidewalks.

She took me to the top of one of the towers. From the observation deck, I saw the city latticed below. Beyond, a pale, landscape, smooth as polished bone, curved around a harbor of inky water 'til it blended with the indigo horizon. That swollen purple sun shattered into millions of glitterin' shards against the sea. One Who Comes Third and Brings Happiness stood beside me, a melancholy green color sparkin' across her black skin.

She touched her hand to mine. "Our world is dying, Visitor from Another Dimension Jeff. What you see here is the decaying carcass of a once-vibrant society."

"But it's beautiful," I told her.

"Even Death has beauty after a fashion, but I would have you know our world as it once was."

I don't know how she did it, but suddenly I knew that place. I remembered its beginnin' and its histories. I knew its days of innocence, its awkward adolescence, the spectacle of its maturity up to that very moment, when it hobbled along in its final glory, leanin' on Death's tender shoulder. Didn't realize I was cryin' 'til I felt tears on my bare chest.

She touched my cheeks curiously and seemed to draw understandin' from my tears like she done from my hand. "Do not mourn us, Visitor from Another Dimension Jeff. Remember us. Everything ends, as it must, or there would be nothing new in the universe. But nothing is truly lost. It merely changes."

I think I fell in love with her a little, the way a boy falls a little in love with his kindergarten teacher, and I wanted to share somethin' of my world. It dawned on me then that in the entire time I'd been there, I hadn't seen so much as a leaf, a stick or a tuft of grass. So I grabbed her hand and tried to give her what I'd give any girl I wanted to impress—a flower. I thought about the most perfect blossom I'd ever laid eyes on. I thought about the satiny texture of the petals, the fragrance, the color, the shape, and the joy I'd felt after seein' this result of my hard work.

When I opened my eyes, she had one hand pressed over her torso where I guessed her heart was and a steady pulsing rainbow of sparks washed across her black skin. Didn't take much intuition to figure she was cryin', too.

She extended her hand, a flat stone the size of a quarter gripped between both thumbs.

"Even if only as a dream, something of this place will endure. It has been a unique pleasure to spend this hour with you."

Then she took my hand, nestled the stone onto my palm and folded my fingers closed over it, like a mama swaddlin' her babe. I swallowed around a knot in my throat. I might not have been a scientist or explorer, but I was a farmer. And I knew exactly what to do with a seed.

Matt paused. The church was silent; even the sniffling had stopped. Most leaned forward in their seats, attentive; but some resembled the Math and Science majors in his freshman English class. He risked a look at Gran, expecting wrath. Instead, she clutched that rose so hard her knuckles went white, a hint of a smile on her face even as tears and snot dripped freely. She held his gaze, then deliberately mouthed, "Thank you."

Maybe asking him to do the speech had been a kind of olive branch, and changing it was her way of pushing him to do exactly what he'd done: give a spontaneous, heartfelt tribute to the man they all loved. Tears burning his own eyes, Matt dipped his head to her in acceptance of this chance for reconciliation.

"Grandpa had been struck by lightning while working in the field. He came to with his mother wailing over him, but suffered nothing worse than a couple of minor burns. Now, the odds of being struck by lightning are better than your chances of ever meeting another man as wonderful as him. He might not have changed the world, but he changed the way a good number of us perceive it."

Matt stuck his hand in his jacket pocket and grasped the velvet box. "A single story hardly feels adequate to fill the void left by Grandpa's death, but we can take comfort in knowing that even if only as a story, something of him endures. That we *are* a lot like lightning. Our very existence alters the universe. And no one is truly lost when they've changed those left behind."

The graveside service was unpleasantly chilly. A stiff afternoon breeze had kicked up and dropped the temperature close to freezing. Matt stood, huddled in his coat, between Bill the bait shop guy and Grandpa's mechanic as he waited his turn to pay his last respects.

Renee waddled to his side, her chestnut curls bobbing and weaving drunkenly in the wind, a white rose clutched in her hand. "Now you definitely have to write that book. I don't think I've ever seen Gran cry like that. I saw you two hug and make up earlier, too. Does that mean you'll come to the family luncheon?"

She tried to play it casual, but Matt could tell by the way she bit her lip and picked at her fingernails that his answer really mattered to her. Things must have been worse than she'd let on before. He'd noticed her husband Jim's absence. "Wouldn't miss it," he assured her. "We've got a lot of catching up to do."

Renee turned so he wouldn't see her relief, so Matt pretended not to notice. Bill said a quick prayer over the coffin, then Matt and Renee were next. They stepped forward and Renee dropped the rose onto the lid. They shuffled on until they stood a short distance from the gathered mourners.

"So," Renee spoke in a semi-whisper. "Did Grandpa really get struck by lightning?"

Matt nodded.

"Then that story, I mean, he had like brain damage or something, right?" Renee pressed. "A hallucination. Although knowing Grandpa, he might have just made the whole thing up."

"I guess anything's possible, but ..." Matt pulled the box from his pocket and caressed the velvety exterior, the same as he'd done so many years ago out on that lake. "Grandpa told that story and passed this on to a frightened boy who was looking for reassurance in a storm. I think yours is a different kind of storm, but you're scared and looking for reassurance, too." He took Renee's hand and planted the box firmly in her palm, folding her fingers over it.

She gazed up at him, her expression mildly puzzled, then lifted the lid. Matt couldn't see the quarter-sized stone nestled inside from this angle, but he caught the rainbow reflection in Renee's eyes as that mysterious light pulsed across the stone's surface. Renee gasped and clutched the box to her chest. "Is this...? It isn't just some story?"

"It's a reminder. Even if only as a story, something of that place endures. Something of Grandpa endures." With a conspiratorial wink, Matt gestured at her belly, leaned close to her ear and whispered, "And we will always be there to help you through the storm."

See A.D. Guzman's story "An Hour in the City of Lightning" online at Metaphorosis.
If you liked it, leave a comment. Authors love that!
Remember to subscribe to our e-mail updates so you'll know when new stories are posted.

About the story

"An Hour in the City of Lightning" began with my grandmother literally kicking me and my kids and my father out when we showed up at her house to sit a bedside vigil for my dying grandfather because, according to her, we weren't family. And a fascinating documentary about how awesome lightning is! Angry and hurt, I vented those feelings into a story where I could properly say goodbye to my grandfather and transform that hurt into something beautiful and wonderful. Now that time has passed, I was able to purge that initial anger and keep the beautiful celebration of how "no one is truly lost when they've changed those left behind."

The characters are, of course, not my family. My grandfather was a respected lawyer and judge, not a farmer, but he was a loveable, jolly man who slapped tunes for us grandkids on his false leg (he lost it in WWII) and invented funny nicknames for the people in his life. My nickname was Little Mandidty Went to the City and Played a Ditty. My favorite was his proctologist Dr. Roe, or as he called him, Dr. Row, Row, Row Your Bottom. I borrowed his humor and kindness for the grandpa character. In fairness to my grandmother, she adopted my mother as a child so we were only family on paper not by blood. And I've come to think a lot of her traits that I borrowed for Gran were probably the result of being a very ambitious woman living in a time and place with few opportunities for a woman to achieve respect and authority for herself.

The lightning documentary did not imply that there are other worlds inside lightning, but rather, it showed footage of how lightning decides where to strike, following stepped leaders branching and dissipating faster than the eye can see until that perfect connection is made. This reminded me of multiverse theories, of realities branching off, and thus the City of Lightning was born. I've never ventured beyond our universe myself, but I hold out hope that there is a myriad of strange and wonderful worlds out there to be discovered. And that we'll give them the respect they deserve when we do.

A question for the author

Q: If someone wanted to make an animated series out of your work, based on the title or recurring themes, what would it look like?

A: I love this question because I often picture my story as a movie or animation as I'm writing. For "An Hour in the City of Lightning" I totally see something in the style of Miyazaki's *Howl's Moving Castle* or *Castle in the Sky*. Studio Ghibli has a beautiful and honest way of bringing the most mundane and extraordinary characters to life, side by side in the same or parallel universes, so I would love to see my characters represented that way. Also, the worldbuilding in Miyazaki's animation shows a love and respect for nature and depicts strange worlds as places equally as complex, beautiful, dangerous, and real as our own, which I feel aligns with the dual dimensions and themes of my story.

About the author

A.D. Guzman is a writer of speculative fiction and all-around lover of story. She earned a Bachelor of Arts in English from Texas A&M Commerce. She taught adult ESL for fourteen years and preschool Spanish for eight. Now, she coordinates Wills Point Veterinary Clinic's online store, dabbles in payroll and serves as occasional, unofficial IT support. She serves as Membership Chair on the Friends of Riter C. Hulsey Public Library board, proudly producing amusing and informative promotional materials. She's a hobby bird photographer and, if you like birds and/or fantasy, she has some acrylic and watercolor pieces you'll love. She runs, does yoga, bikes, hikes, pretty much anything active and outdoors. She lives in Texas with her husband, two wonderful adult kids, four finches, three parakeets, a cat, and a snake.

adguzmanwrites.com, @AD_Guzman00

Infinite Possibilities III

Michael Gardner

A mystery USB leads Adrian to a cabin where he finds a book written by himself. The book contains schematics for a machine. Adrian, being good with his hands, starts to build.

Adrian receives a second USB. It contains video proof that his wife, Candice, is having an affair. Distraught, Adrian returns to the cabin. The television inside turns on, reveals Other Adrian. Other Adrian explains he is from a parallel world. His life's work is locating other versions of himself, bringing them across to his world where they share knowledge and unlock the mysteries of the universe. Other Adrian needs Adrian to build the machine to bring him across.

Later, Adrian receives an email from Other Adrian's agent asking to meet.

3

He's chosen one of the coffee places in the city that Candice talks about. A place on the corner of a pedestrian mall, and a busy road. It's newly painted, polished concrete floors, a strange assortment of furniture—some old, some new—which Adrian senses is less random and more planned than appears at first glance.

He takes a table outside, in the mall. It isn't the nicest table. The drone of cars from the nearby road is prevalent. As is the scent of tar and exhaust, which overpowers the smell of coffee. But he wants to be outside, to have a view of his contact when they arrive. Deep down, he's also wondering if Candice might drop by, catch him out with someone, realise he's got secrets too. Why else has he picked a cafe that she talks about? But then again, when was the last time she mentioned this place? A month ago? More? He doesn't know. If he's honest, he doesn't really listen anymore. Is that why she looks elsewhere? No, that's on her, not him.

He watches pedestrians approach in twos, in threes, more. Some stop, survey the menu, others walk on. The breeze is picking up, but it's warm out, even as the sun sinks low in the sky.

When the waiter approaches, he orders a cappuccino to get rid of him. That's when he sees her.

Taylor Bradbury. The expat he met in Thailand. That forced herself into his and Candice's world. That convinced Candice to share him. That rocked his world, then left. And even though he didn't want to think of her over the years, he has, often.

Seeing her now, he recalls the feel of her velvet, red hair across his chest. Like a phantom limb. He swallows, shrinks in his chair. He simultaneously wants to talk to her, and to sneak away.

She's talking to the waiter, who turns and points at Adrian, and she looks, catches his eye, and he hers, and it's too late to go. He jerks upright, clears his throat. She smiles, walks toward him. He can't bring himself to smile back.

She slides into the chair across from him, places her handbag on the ground, leans forward, and his eyes are drawn to the shock of red hair that slides half across her left eye, and the pale freckled skin of her cheek. In his mind, he knows those freckles continue down her chest, and her stomach. He swallows again.

"Long time," she says. There's a huskiness in her voice he doesn't remember. Experience, age. A change that makes her more attractive.

"I thought I was getting answers, not more..." He shrugs, gives some sort of weak hand wave.

"Questions? Maybe I bring both," she says, laughs. She leans back into her chair, casual. A shadow tells him someone else is close, and he looks up to see a man backlit by the sun. He blinks twice, and the image resolves into a waiter carrying his coffee. The man places it in front of him.

"Anything else?" the waiter asks.

"You have anything harder than this?" Taylor says.

"We have an assortment of wines and beers. Would you like to see a menu?"

"No. Just bring me a pale ale if you have one?"

Adrian holds up two fingers. "Two, please," he says.

The waiter nods. Then he's gone.

Adrian watches Taylor watch him wrestle with all of this. He forces a smile. "So..." he says.

"I took the videos. I dropped off the USBs. I—"

"You're his agent."

She hesitates a beat. "Your agent."

"No. That's not me. That's..." But how does he finish?

She reaches out and places a hand on his. Electricity sizzles across his skin. Heat. He snatches his hand back.

"I work as a historian for the Council," she says, as if that explain things. He feels his face bunch in confusion. She hurries on. "My team is responsible for documenting, restoring and maintaining local historical sites."

"Like the cabin," he says.

"Like the cabin," she repeats.

The waiter reappears with a tray, two beers—a craft beer that Adrian doesn't recognise—two glasses. Adrian holds his tongue as the waiter places a bottle in front of Taylor, and then another in front of him. They clink pleasantly against the glass-topped table. He deposits the glasses, then dissolves back into the cafe throng without offering to pour their drinks.

Taylor pours her beer into the glass. Adrian grabs the bottle and takes a long draw. It's achingly cold, bitter. When he places the half empty bottle back on the table, Taylor is looking at him with a grin. She raises her glass, "Cheers," she says, takes a sip.

After she swallows, she continues. "The furniture appeared one day. The TV, the rug, the armchair."

"Someone moved it in? Someone else? Another agent maybe?"

She shakes her head, no. She seems certain. "The cabin was being restored. We had the fences in place, and the gate was locked each night. There was no sign that the fence or lock had been tampered with, and yet one day the cabin was empty, the next..."

"Not," he offers.

She takes another sip of beer. It's familiar, he thinks, the way she licks her top lip after. Déjà vu.

"We removed it, paid a company to dispose of it. Then it happened again. I was alone when I found it the second time. I dropped by the site on my way to the office, I can't even remember why. Remeasuring the beam we were repairing, maybe? Anyway, it was back. What looked like the same TV. The same rug. The same armchair and side table and TV stand. As well as a book."

"By me."

"Yes, by you. Then you were there. On the screen. And so was I."

"You were on the screen as well?"

She nods. "Never at the same time. It would switch from you to me."

"Other Adrian."

"Pardon?"

"That's what I call him."

She nods at this, like she approves.

"I've never seen you," he says.

"No, Other Adrian said it wouldn't help. Not when I explained our brief interaction."

"You told him about Thailand?"

"Not in detail, but the gist of it. The brevity of our time together. Have you been reading your book?"

Adrian pauses a beat, nods. "Some. Infinite worlds with infinite possibilities."

She shrugs. "Other Adrian says that is not strictly true. The infinite possibilities part, that is. Some things are always drawn together. It happens over and over again, like electrons orbiting a nucleus. They may stray, but the attraction remains. In this possibility, you've strayed."

Adrian feels hot, sweaty. Taylor seems clearer than clear, realer than real. "What does that mean?" he asks.

"Other Adrian and Other Taylor, they're together in their world, and most others they find. They're doing this together. Bringing other versions of them—of us—together. Joining our experiences to crack open the skull of the universe, to look inside at the grey matter, to learn it all."

Like finding a god and destroying her, he thinks. He shivers despite the heat. She reaches toward him again, hesitates. When he keeps his hand on the table, she lowers hers, places it on his. This time he maintains contact, allows the heat of her skin to spark a fire inside him and send embers into his bloodstream, into his pounding heart, into his brain.

"Thailand was meant to happen," she says, her voice a soft rasp. "This was meant to happen."

His hand is shaking under hers. He feels desire. A want. He doesn't trust himself. He gently untangles his hand from hers, stands.

"I'm sorry," he says. "I can't... I'm sorry."

He turns to leave, but stops when she speaks. "I can show you where Candice is now. Whom she is with. What she is doing."

He swallows. He wills himself to leave. But he can't. He turns back toward Taylor's intense flame, sits. "I'm not sure I want that."

She sighs with sympathy. "I know. But it's necessary."

And he understands that it is. He won't be able to move forward without it. He nods, and Taylor calls for the bill.

He was thirty-six when his appendix burst. The pain had built steadily over several days, a burning sensation that he at first mistook for indigestion. But it became sharper, focused. A throbbing low in his right side that felt like a nail had been hammered into his gut when he applied pressure. In hindsight, he was naive. He thought it was his diet, or drinking too much. He'd continued driving the bus as the pain had built, then the fever, hoping it'd all go away.

It was Candice that twigged to what was going on. Which was odd in hindsight. They weren't talking much at the time. She was grieving her mother and after some clumsy efforts by Adrian to provide comfort, she made clear there was nothing he could do to make it better. So, he gave her space. And at the same time started to resent her for going back on the pill without a discussion.

Despite that, she must have intuited something was wrong with him, because she broke through, and somehow deduced what was happening. When she said the word appendix, it was like watching an old silent film where a lightbulb turns on above the main character's head.

By the time he got to the hospital, he felt better. The pressure in his right side had reached a crescendo and suddenly, like jumping from a plane, he felt weightless, he felt relief. They told him after that that was the moment it ruptured.

He doesn't remember much about going into surgery. An anaesthetist that asked him if he was nervous, his replying no, all the while the heart monitor pinging like a slot machine revealing his lie. He remembers lights, counting backward, then... he was awake.

It was all over, but he didn't realise at first. He didn't realise much of anything, other than that there was a presence next to him, slumped in a hard armchair.

"Mum?" he asked, surprised at how sluggish his words sounded. He could see he was in a hospital, but in those first few moments, he wasn't sure why. "Mum?" he said again.

A hand reached out, grasped his. Young skin. Maybe not as young as it once was, but warm, soft. The first time Candice had touched him in months. Or maybe, if he were honest, the first time he'd allowed her touch to get through the shell he'd erected. And maybe then only because of the morphine that fogged his senses, that made him confused about what was going on.

"It's me, babe," came the weary reply. He forced himself to look her over, to take her in. She'd just woken, but even in his daze, he could see she was exhausted.

"Did you stay here all night?" he asked in that slow, unfamiliar drawl. His mouth felt so dry.

As if intuiting this, she held out a cup for him, helped him sip it. When he was done, he sighed and sat back against his pillows.

"Don't worry about me," she'd said, smiling. "Get some sleep."

And he had. It had been easy to sink back into oblivion, to let the drugs wash his mind clean. But before he went to sleep, a thought struck him. Stuck with him. *Would I have done that for her?* He didn't know. But something about that act, that willingness to put aside her comfort just to make sure he had someone familiar nearby when he woke in a drugged daze, half confused, that struck him as something amazing.

Adrian and Taylor stand across the road from the apartment building that Adrian last saw on video. The apartment building that his wife disappeared into with a strange man.

"She comes here at least once a week, sometimes more," Taylor says. Adrian deduces that she's been following his wife for some time. A conclusion that seems important, but he's too distracted to give it much attention.

"She's there now?" he asks, staring across the road. It's still light out, but only just. The sun has sunk most of the way beneath the horizon, and the sky has faded from blue to grey.

"Yes."

He sees the man again in his mind. The tall man, with dark hair, in the nice suit. A success, unlike him. He swallows, notices the sweat in his armpits spreading like spilt ink on paper.

"His apartment is on the third floor. I know which one," Taylor says. He looks at her, sees a sparkle in her eye. She appears to be enjoying herself. His face tightens into a frown. As he looks back across the road the street lights shimmer to life, one after the other.

"They deserve to be caught, to be screamed at, to..." Taylor leaves the thought hanging. His mind takes it, runs with it. He imagines kicking in a door, yelling. It doesn't feel right. Just as quickly, he imagines stumbling into a bedroom that smells of sweat and sex, losing his words, his anger replaced with embarrassment. He imagines himself apologising, and he feels his face redden. He swallows again. "No," he says, barely a whisper. "No, I don't think so. I don't want to see... I don't—"

"I understand," Taylor interjects, and takes his clammy hand in her soft, dry one. She rubs the back of it, ever so gently, with her thumb. A thumb that is small, and smooth, and sensual. Adrian's eyes are drawn to it, watching it move back and forth.

Slowly, very slowly, his eyes move up her pale arm, to her shoulder, to her face, and her green eyes looking back at him. They sparkle with a want.

She licks her lips. They look so red, ripe. "We could get another drink? Or...?"

His hand tingles, his stomach flutters. He shakes his head, unwinds his hand from hers. "No, not tonight. I just want to go home." He hates the sound of defeat in his voice.

"Not tonight?" she asks.

He's married. He should make clear he means not ever. But he doesn't. He leaves that door open. "I've got more work to do on the machine."

She smiles. "Okay, then. A raincheck."

Adrian stares at the maze of wires and circuits in the machine. His eyesight is strained, his hair is greasy, and he can smell his own body odour. He's exhausted, and he just wants to leave the garage and take a shower, but he can't, not yet.

He's followed the instructions in the book, and yet the machine does nothing. Not that the book really explains what it is supposed to do, but he knows that the nothing it is currently doing is not right. There should be a hum of electricity when he switches it on, a vibration of power, heat. But there's nothing, and he's certain he's made an error in the construction. A loose wire, a faulty connection. Yet he can't seem to locate the problem.

He's so tired he's having trouble seeing straight. But he can't let this go. So he stares into the casing, into the circuitry, into the jungle of wiring. There's something comforting about the trance he's in, as unfathomable and impenetrable as it is.

The loud groan of the garage door rising jerks him from his stupor. He turns, squints as bright sunlight assaults his eyes. Morning already? he thinks. He sees bare feet, legs, a short skirt, shoes held in a slender hand. She's been out all night, he realises, while he has been here working.

She doesn't see him at first. It gives him time to appraise her. A ruffled top, make-up smeared, hair frazzled. He wants to despise her, but instead the usual cocktail of confused emotions emerges. Lust, love, a deep, throbbing pain like an infected tooth.

He clears his throat, and her head jerks toward him, her eyes widen with surprise. "Adrian?" she says. "You're up early."

She stands on the periphery of the garage, frozen.

He blinks. It feels like slow motion. He nods toward the machine as if that explains it.

"Oh," she says. She takes two hesitant steps into the garage, stops. "Have you finished?"

"Where were you?" he asks. His voice sounds strange in his ears, feels strange leaving his mouth. It's like listening to someone else, someone emotionless. A bluff, because his emotions are a pit of seething snakes, constricting, biting, slithering all over one another.

"Out," she says too loudly. Her eyes dart away. "With Jenny and the girls, like I said." She glances back at him.

"All night? Or you slept it off at Jenny's place."

Candice swallows, which sounds loud contrasted with the quiet of the early morning. "I stayed with Jenny, of course."

"Like last weekend," he says.

She straightens, places both hands on her hips, the right still holding her shoes. "Yes, like last weekend. What did you think I was doing?" she says, on the offensive now. His body responds like it always does. His stomach dives down to his toes, his neck warms, his heart beats harder. He's a chastened child, being told off in front of the class. He hates this feeling. Hates that she knows she can do this to him, turn on him and make him feel apologetic for her behaviour.

He licks his lips. They're dry, and his tongue does little to moisten them. He tries to hold her gaze, but he can't. He lowers his eyes, shakes his head in a half apology.

She continues to glower for a few beats, then she moves toward the door into the house, her bare feet padding softly against the cement.

His words surprise him as much as her. "Who is he?"

She freezes. He regards her curiously, waits. He's nervous, and yet he also feels removed from his physical body, watching everything from a safe distance.

She turns slowly, purses her lips, huffs. "So that's what you think of me. A whore? Or are you just jealous, once again, that I have a life? That I refuse to give up, and wallow at home every weekend with you feeling sorry for myself? Is that it?"

He opens his mouth to respond, but she doesn't let him.

"I was out with Jenny. Understood? I keep telling you that you can come out with us anytime you like. It's you that chooses not to. So you don't get the right to start throwing wild accusations around just because you've let your imagination run away with you."

He rises from his seat, the stool screeching as it slides over the concrete.

"No, don't fucking come near me. I'm getting a shower, and having a sleep. You could do with the same. You stink. But do me a favour, take the spare room."

She turns to go, and he's suddenly overwhelmed by the unfairness of it all. His heart turns to fire. His churning belly hardens into stone and he feels his face contort into something bitter. "Twenty-six Charlton Street," Adrian hisses.

She stutters mid-stride, deflates before his eyes. When she looks back her mouth is an 'o', and her eyes are glassy with a hint of tears. Adrian thinks she will continue to deny what he knows. Thinks she will attack him again. But she doesn't. She turns, and rushes into the house.

He wakes with a start, confused, hot, disoriented. Bright sunlight penetrates the room through flimsy curtains. A room that isn't his. This one has pale grey walls, and a musty smell. A linen doona covers him. Then it hits him. His accusation, Candice's reaction, his nap in the spare room.

He throws the covers back, sits up on the edge of the bed. Everything feels different. Like he went to sleep Adrian, and woke up someone else. The room feels on the edge of eruption. A build-up of electricity. A dam holding a torrent of water back. He feels dizzy, and he clings hard to the bed as if this might keep him from falling. He closes his eyes, opens them. The dizziness recedes.

He rises, eases the door open, pokes a head out. It's quiet. The house is steeped in it. Not a silence of emptiness, but something else. A full silence. Filled with words yet to be said. He knows Candice is in their room, sleeping or feigning sleep. Right now, he doesn't care. That she's here, or for her words. He doesn't need to do this her way. He doesn't need to listen. He's shared his knowledge. Now he can act. Move on. But to where? His mind wanders to Taylor, to the machine, to the cabin.

He moves out of the bedroom, walks as quietly as he can into the living/dining/kitchen space. He's still wearing the clothes he worked through the night in. They're crumpled, and smell of stale sweat.

In the kitchen he checks the clock on the microwave, sees that it's just after eleven am. He hasn't slept long. He thinks about turning the kettle on, but then thinks better of it. He doesn't want to rouse her. He wants this moment to himself. The eye of the storm. He removes orange juice from the fridge, quietly pours a glass, and sits at the bench to drink.

He spies his phone on the charger, removes it, checks for messages, none, emails, one. He opens it and there she is. Redhead22. The only thing she's sent is a phone number. He checks the hall again as if he might find Candice lurking there, then dials. As it rings, he gets up and goes to the garage, closes the door behind him. She answers.

"I was wondering when you'd call," she says. Her voice is husky, sensual.

Adrian swallows. "When I'd call? Not if?"

"I'm an optimist." He can hear the smile in her words. She's enjoying this, he thinks. "How did she take it?" she asks.

He wonders how she knew he'd confront her. "Like Candice."

"What's that mean?"

He shakes his head. Like it's my fault, he thinks. He wonders for the briefest moment whether it might be, but then corrects himself. No. It's not. It's hers. What has he ever done but be faithful? And yet there's guilt there. Something that gnaws at him, which he pushes down, ignores for now. "It means she took it badly, but that doesn't matter. I've nearly finished the machine."

"Oh?" she says, both like this is a surprise and expected at the same time. "So you've decided? You'll be brought across? To join him? To join us?" There's an eagerness in her tone.

"I'd like to speak to him again first," he says.

"Of course."

"And I won't do it alone."

"You won't have to. I'll be there."

He swallows again. In his mind he dips into the past and feels, vividly, her soft hands. He sees the pale skin of her arm as it caresses his chest. He can feel the swell of her breasts against him. He shivers. She said they were made for each other. It's inevitable. A repeated attraction across infinite worlds. He feels it.

"Do you have a car?" he asks.

"Yes, of course."

"Will you come get me when I'm finished?"

"Yes," she whispers into the phone. "I will."

"Taylor?"

"Yes, Adrian." He wants to thank her for finding him. He wants to explain his excitement, his curiosity, his fear, his guilt. Yet the words avoid his grasp. "I'll call again soon."

She hangs up. He stares at the dormant phone in his hand for a moment, then he goes to his workbench, and feeling fresher, he begins to recheck the wiring.

He finishes soldering, places the iron on the bench, stretches his neck left, right. It clicks loudly, he grimaces, rolls his shoulders.

He takes a breath, switches the machine on, waits for a hum of electricity, waits for something, anything to happen.

Nothing.

His shoulders slump. He flips the power switch off, then on. Nothing. Off again.

The door to the house opens. He looks and finds Candice standing in the doorframe, hands on hips, pouting. "Okay, I'm sorry. You caught me, and I'm sorry."

He stares, wants to say something, can't.

She steps into the garage, continues. "It didn't mean anything. Nothing. It... I..." As he watches, she appears to shrink into herself. She takes a couple more hesitant steps, stops. Her voice is softer when she speaks. "I didn't want this. Not really. It's just... We..."

He sees tears in her eyes. One spills onto her cheek, and leaves a silvery trail as it runs toward her chin. Part of him feels sorry for her. Another part observes from afar, detached.

"It's been so long," she whispers, and yet he hears her voice clearly across the garage. "So long since you looked at me like I was... new. Lovely."

She sniffs. He feels the pull of the machine, the temptation to turn and work again on its faults, and yet her gravity also draws him.

"His name is John. He made me feel special. I haven't felt like that since we met. And... it's no excuse, I know, but I wanted to recapture what we had once. Just for a time."

She falls into a deep silence, looks at her feet. Waits. He can't help but stare at her. She's pitiful and untrustworthy, he tells himself. From outside comes the sounds of birdsong, and a dog barking a few streets away.

"Okay. Fine," he mutters. "Now leave me alone."

She looks at him then as if he's a bug she'd like to bring her boot down on. She looks at him as if he's the one that's been caught fucking someone else. He should be angry, but he's not. He's tired of this one-sided discussion. But he can see there's more.

"You get what I'm saying, don't you?" she asks, her voice rising. "This is your fault. Your fucking fault." She glowers. "I married someone else. Someone exciting. Then he changed. Into you. I just want my Adrian back. Not this fucking tranquilized, no ambition, emotionally bereft person you've become. I wanted to feel something, Adrian. Anything. That's why I cheated, you bastard." She's screaming now. Red faced, arms gesticulating, breathing hard.

Adrian sighs, turns away and refocuses on the machine. He flinches when Candice screams. A wail that rises until his ears hurt, and he has to cover them with both hands. After, silence. He drops his hands, and hears only Candice's harsh breathing.

He turns to her. Looks at her purple, angry face. "I have work to do," he says quietly.

She looks like she will explode. Opens her mouth, closes it. Opens it again. "With that machine?" she screeches. "With that fucking game. Why? What's so important?"

"You told me I needed something like this in my life," he says, knowing that she doesn't know that the game is real, that something big is at stake. He stares at her, and she at him. He doesn't feel the guilt anymore, or the obligation. She's broken all of that. He turns back to the machine and picks up the soldering iron. He waits for her to yell again, but she doesn't. Instead, he hears her footsteps as she moves back into the house. It makes him feel larger, bolder. If he can just find this faulty wire, he thinks. He resumes his work.

Twelve months back, Adrian relented and went out with Candice and her friends. They all met up at an Italian restaurant in the city with nice food, and nicer wine. He doesn't recall the name of the place, but he remembers the exposed brick, the smoky scent of the wood fired pizza oven, the buzz of wait staff floating between patrons.

They were given a large table along one wall of the restaurant. He sat on the bench against the wall next to Candice.

He was struck that night by her people. In a few short years, they'd all changed. He didn't know any of them. The only topics they talked about were the office, difficult clients, and clever solutions. They used jargon that made discussions hard to follow. Whole sentences floated by him.

He presumed most of them worked with Candice—colleagues, bosses, and managers once removed. Important people, comfortable in their own spheres. People who'd shrunk the world down to a bubble small enough to understand and beat. A bubble that contained accounting, a firm of a few hundred people, and a list of clients. Beyond that, nothing of importance.

The thing was, from the perspective of an outsider—and a lowly bus driver who didn't define himself by his meagre contribution to society at that—the stream of words was both impressive and thin. Like discovering the new town you've entered is actually a movie set with nothing but scaffolding behind the colourful facade.

These people only seemed to have two settings: talk, or wait to talk. And for all of the fancy words, the topics were always about whomever was the speaker at the time.

Yet that night sticks in his mind. On one level, Candice mimicked them, and he listened to her with the same detached and horrified fascination as he did the others. But when someone else took centre stage, she'd place her hand on his knee under the table, lean close to him until her hair ticked his ear, the side of his neck. Sometimes she'd sneak a kiss. A quick peck on his cheek, occasionally something that lingered longer, a nibble at the corner of his mouth. She'd lean in and whisper real words to him. She thanked him a lot. Told him she loved him. Told him she couldn't have got where she was without him.

That night he saw her. Not the pantomime she produced for work. Not the judgement at home. Her. The girl he'd first met and fallen for. It was like she'd lifted the window a crack to let in fresh air, and through it he'd caught the scent of her, a flash of the real her walking by.

That night he realised that behind their difficulties, if he could just peel back the layers enough, he'd find her still there. Someone pure and familiar. He just had to try.

But it was easy to fall back into old habits, and familiar patterns. Adrian promised to try, but he put it off to next week, then the week after, then eventually he stopped promising. And she didn't reveal herself again.

It's hot in the garage. Adrian's sweating, beads running freely down his back, his chest. His armpits are dark, wet, and the heady stink of him is in his nostrils. There's also the scent of solder in the air, sharp and biting. One more try, he thinks. He turns on the power.

At first, nothing changes. But then he notices a subtle increase in heat, and hears the soft, resonant hum of electricity coursing through wires. He smiles so broadly his cheeks hurt. He's finally done it.

Carefully, he swings the top steel panel back into place. As it clicks together, he feels the machine vibrate under his hands, so subtly he might not have noticed if he weren't touching the casing. The hairs on his arm rise. He feels something in his spine do the same, then his brain. He suddenly feels naked. Like a monstrous eye has opened and turned toward him. He feels small, inconsequential under that gaze. He pulls his hands away like he's been stung, flips the power off. The hum dies, the vibrations cease, and he feels himself again. He puts it down to working too hard without enough sleep.

He takes out his phone, calls Taylor.

"Did you fix it?" she asks, excitedly.

"I fixed it," he says.

She makes a sound that makes him think of sex and sweat. A sound she might have made in bed with him all those years ago. He swallows hard.

"I'll be there in twenty minutes."

"Wait," he says, and for a moment he's not sure if he's caught her before she's hung up. Then he hears her breathing.

"For what?"

"You're really sure about this? You're ready to just leave this world behind on the promises of a stranger? What if it's a trick? What if it's not what he promised?" He can't shake the feeling that this is all too big, too crazy, and important. He doesn't seem to have enough information to make an informed decision. He feels his emotions are running too high. That someone may be coercing him into something that he shouldn't do.

"I didn't talk to a stranger," she says matter-of-factly. "I spoke to me. Then I spoke to you."

Other Adrian isn't him, he thinks.

"If you can't trust yourself, whom can you trust?" she says. "And besides, what's here for me that's so great?"

He hesitates, thinking. "Okay," he says eventually. "But give me half an hour. I desperately need a shower."

"Half an hour it is." He can hear the smile in her voice.

Candice is waiting when he steps out of the bathroom, hair wet, a towel wrapped around his waist. She looks like she's been crying, and her arms are crossed defensively across her chest.

He stops, stares, waits.

"Can we talk?" she says. Her voice is soft, raspy. He feels for her briefly, until he recalls what she did. This isn't his fault.

"I don't have time," he says. He steps past her, and walks to their bedroom. He doesn't know what he should wear, or what he should bring. Candice follows him into the room. He ignores her, removes clean underwear from his drawer, puts them on without removing the towel.

"I want to explain," she says, watching him as he opens the wardrobe. He rifles through his shirts, eventually picks a plain, white tee, throws it over his head.

"I miss you," she says.

He regards her quizzically, turns back to the wardrobe, finds a pair of black chinos. "Well, I'm always here," he says, not looking.

"But you're not," she says.

He hesitates, drops the towel and steps into his pants.

"You haven't been for a long time," she continues. "I feel like you've disappeared into yourself. You've anesthetised the vibrant parts of you."

He shoots her a glare, opens his mouth to say something, but then can't bring himself to fight. He swings the wardrobe door open wider. There's a mirror affixed to the inside. He runs a hand through his wet hair. He can see her in the reflection, eyes on his back. Sad eyes.

"This can't all be my fault," he says.

"I know, I'm not saying it is, I'm just trying to explain why—"

"Why you fucked a stranger?" he says, glancing at her reflection. He watches her cheeks redden, tears well in her eyes.

"You were such hard work."

He barks a laugh. "I'm hard work. I don't argue, I clean up after myself, I fucking encourage you every time you go after a promotion at work, even if it means I don't see you for weeks while you work ridiculous hours."

"Yes." She exhales for a long time. "And that's how you float by. Remember when we first went out? The arguments we'd have, the ideas we'd discuss, the way we fucked?"

He does remember it. Familiar, and foreign. Like a place he can't find his way back to. He turns, tries to step past her. She blocks him.

"What I did was wrong. Horrible even. But it was a cry for help. Please, Adrian." She grabs his hands with hers, squeezes until they hurt. He can feel her pain, feel her anguish, her desire. "Please, come back to me. Fight for me. For the us that once was. Please?"

He stares into her eyes. Big, brown eyes. He can't remember the last time he looked into them. Saw how much lay behind them. The honesty. He opens his mouth to respond when a car horn sounds. Candice's head jerks around like she might be able to see the car through the walls of their house. Without eye contact, it's easier. He pulls his hands free. "That's my ride," he says.

"Your ride?"

He nods. "I'm sorry, Candice. I've got to go." He eases past her, moves quickly to the garage. She doesn't follow.

When he raises the garage door, Taylor is waiting, parked in his driveway, the back of her hatchback open. It's still light out, but not for much longer.

He carries the machine to her car, manoeuvres it into the back, closes the hatch. He climbs into the passenger seat, and Taylor reaches across, places a hand on his knee, squeezes.

"Ready?" she asks. He nods. She starts the car, eases out of the driveway.

As they gain speed, he turns and looks back at the house. He sees Candice standing in the open garage, watching. He watches her until they turn out of the street, until he can't see Candice or his house anymore.

Something has been set in motion. Something that he can't stop now even if he wanted to.

"Infinite Possibilities" continues in next month's issue.
See Parts I, II, and III of Michael Gardner's story "Infinite Possibilities" online at Metaphorosis.
If you liked it, leave a comment. Authors love that!
Remember to subscribe to our e-mail updates so you'll know when new stories are posted.

December

The Dragon's Due

Christopher Warden

The dragon dove out of the sky, claws extended, ready to strike. Its scales flashed so brightly in the morning sun that it hurt my eyes. As it landed, claws still out, jaws agape, I wondered if it might grab me. Pinned by its claws, its fangs would rip me in two with ease. Or perhaps it would roast me alive, the smoke hopefully suffocating me before the flames blistered my skin off. Either way, it would be a serious violation of the rules.

The dragon had size and strength, fangs and claws, fire and flight. I had the rules. That and my brains. It hardly seemed enough.

Fortunately, dragons are not fools (unlike many of the people I work for). True, it wanted to eat me, but one human cannot feed a dragon. One human is an appetizer. Dragons need lots of people, a whole kingdom of people, or in this case, a duchy.

But even a duchy is not enough. If a dragon hunts any area at will, it will deplete the human population in a matter of months. After that, it must move on, often into another dragon's territory, which means they fight. That causes huge fires and massive destruction. It's a nightmare, with towns and farmland destroyed: chaos, exodus, and plague — things that neither dragons nor people want.

Hunter and prey both need a more stable solution. That's where I come in.

The dragon settled down on the hillside slightly above me. It had claimed the higher ground, always a shrewd tactic. It stretched its great wings once, almost like a yawn, then curled its tail around its massive frame and settled its head upon the ground. It peered at me, and I could see my reflection in its eyes.

I smiled, took a breath, and began my spiel.

"An honor to make your acquaintance," I said, bowing. I always bow at the start. Dragons, like nobles, like it. "As you know," I said, trying to appear calm, "I am here representing the local Duke to negotiate a four-year contract regarding your food supply."

I've personally never liked the term 'food supply', but the other options are even less appetizing: 'human death toll' is too prejudicial, 'deliveries' too commercial, 'bounty' too bucolic, 'morsels' too light-hearted, and 'quota' too antiseptic.

The dragon said nothing to my opening; it was still eyeing me, making me feel like a leg of juicy spit-roasted lamb. Had I misjudged the situation? Would it just eat me? Yes, there would be repercussions for such an act, but that would be little comfort to me as I was being digested in its stomach. I swallowed hard. The dragon was intimidating me, trying to unnerve me. Best to just continue.

"Like all contracts, the agreement we reach will require both parties to make certain…sacrifices." I always like to get that word in: *sacrifice*. It reminds the dragon that lives are at stake. Dragons don't care about human lives, except in terms of quantity, but there's no harm in reminding the dragon that our side does not share its point of view.

It spoke then; its voice was distinctive. Most dragons have unpleasant voices: harsh, gravel-filled growls. Maybe it's all the fire coming out of their throats. This dragon had the voice of a tenor.

"Virgins," it said. "I want virgins."

"Virgins? You're a dragon, not a vampire." I said. "How could virginity make a difference to you?"

"Sex makes human flesh taste sour," it said in its beautiful voice. It almost sounded like a castrato. I wondered if that had something to do with its request, but I wasn't about to ask. *Never piss off the dragon* is the first unwritten rule of my guild.

Then it dawned on me. It didn't want virgins. It wanted young people: tender and succulent like veal. But it knew that would look bad, would cause an uproar — hence the virgin request. Because for some insane reason, that was actually more…palatable?

I almost smiled, but I didn't want to tip my hand.

"You know," I said in an innocent tone, "there's a convent nearby — lots of nuns. I'm sure they are all virgins, probably eager to be martyrs. I can arrange for a good number of them to come to you."

The dragon growled at that, and I allowed myself a smile at the growl. We both knew that most of the nuns were crones — not the tender meat it was hoping for. And so it was struck by its own lance. Or perhaps burned by its own breath? More importantly, it was something I could leverage.

The dragon glowered at me for a bit, then hissed out two words: "No nuns."

"Well," I said. "If you insist on excluding nuns, it means the total number of victims will have to go down — fair's fair," I said.

I think it almost sighed then.

"How much?" it asked.

And so, we began to haggle over the nun exclusion. The negotiations had begun. An hour later, I had scored my first victory and saved a dozen lives, which not only felt good, but also netted me as many gold coins.

That's how I make my money. Every life I save garners me a coin. The guild determines each territory's projected human-dragon consumption cost, and the assigned negotiator tries to beat that estimate.

I know it sounds cold-blooded, but in my line of work you have to be willing to sell lives to save lives. It's like being a general who needs to take a hill; you know it will cost a certain number of soldiers. You want to make it the smallest number, but it's still going to cost.

"I have yet to see your credentials," the dragon said. It was trying to change the subject and get on a new footing — always a good idea when you've had a setback.

I bowed again and showed my letters of accreditation. My name, Edwin Skein, was emblazoned upon a long vellum scroll in gold ink. The appendices showed a record I was proud of: negotiated settlements with a dozen dragons. My Curriculum Vitae listed my publications in the Journal of Dragon Dealings. I wondered if this dragon had (perhaps in preparation) read any of my writings. Though the guild frowned upon it, it was well known that dragons read the journal; some were so bold as to subscribe.

The negotiations with this dragon, who was named Blood-Wind, (yes, they always have names like that), were grueling. Throughout, its belly rumbled louder and louder. Near the end, it was like a kettle drum beating a march. That was good; it made Blood-Wind eager to conclude the deal. It made me fairly eager also. We had left the hillside and were working in its lair: a many-chambered cave it called Dire-Skull (and yes, they always name their lairs like that too).

After three weeks of haggling, we were ready to lock it up: one thousand eight hundred souls, many taken from local orphanages, to be delivered monthly over four years. The orphanage was a brilliant stroke on my part: young people no one minded parting with. Their inclusion let me shave almost five hundred lives off the deal. I told myself that many of those orphans would have died anyway. The fate of orphans in our modern age is, at best perilous. At least this way, their deaths would save lives. A rationalization, I suppose, but in my line of work, there's a lot of that.

As I tallied the final numbers, I realized this negotiation was a great success. Of course, I would get no thanks.

When a general wins a battle, he's praised. In my case, I'd be called 'ghoul', 'parasite', 'leech', 'traitor', not to my face but behind my back. I would be lumped with the dragon as another monster. It doesn't bother me. Like the dragon, I've grown a tough hide. I'm used to the looks of anger and resentment when I ride into a town. I'm used to eating alone and being served at the back of a hall. I knew what the locals thought about my kind.

But I also knew that this deal was saving lives. In terms of the greater good, this was an excellent arrangement. Between the nuns and the orphans, Nurbleville was getting off light, So I was pleased, even proud of this contract. Then disaster showed up.

Disaster was six foot ten, clad in heavy armor, sitting on the biggest horse imaginable. Disaster was named Sir Granger Goodwin of the Strong Arm. He was blond and blue-eyed and handsome, and he was here to slay the dragon. Just one look at him, and I knew that half the duchy would think he could do it, too.

I was sitting outside at a tavern (alone as usual) enjoying a well-earned celebratory ale when the knight rode in. He went straight to the town square, followed by his squire, a skinny kid on a mule. Sir Goodwin stood up in his stirrups. It made him look like a giant. The squire pulled out a bugle and blew it until a crowd had formed.

"People of Nurble," Sir Goodwin shouted. "I have come to deliver you from evil. I have come to slay the dragon!"

He swung up his lance. I smiled at that; the symbolism was too much.

"My Lance will pierce the dragon's heart. My aim will be guided by God; all I ask in return are your prayers. Strengthened by your faith, I cannot fail." He was either a terrific liar, a lunatic, or both.

As the crowd grew thicker, Goodwin's description of the slaying of Blood-Wind grew more and more ludicrous. I grew more and more nervous. Fortunately, Duke Nurble arrived. I was relieved to see that Nurble also looked nervous. Nurble was a pragmatic politician. He'd gained his title not by war, but by deft scheming: buying land and shaving coins. He was of the breed of nobility who lived by trade, not sword. Nurble's father had been a pig farmer. The Duke was so modern as to be proud of his father's lowly past: a sow decorated his coat arms. Goodwin, on the other hand, was clearly from an ancient line of warriors.

Despite their differences, the two nobles, astride their horses, leaned towards each other and began to quietly murmur to one another. After a brief exchange, Sir Goodwin turned back to the crowd.

"People of Nurble, I go now to take council with your Duke. Soon, the dragon shall be destroyed; soon, we shall all be rejoicing! Have faith." Then the whole lot of them, knight, Duke, squire, and guards, rode off to the castle.

I followed.

I was on foot, so getting to the Duke's castle took me much longer. Don't imagine some grey fortress when I say castle. The Duke had built a chateau. On arrival, I was taken to the Duke's library: a sad collection of worm-eaten books. It had only three pristine sections: one on pig farming, one on pastry making, and the third (hidden by a false shelf) was made up of cheap erotica mixed with well-thumbed manuals on poisons and soporifics. I'd heard rumors of local maidens disappearing, only to reappear days later with no memory of what had happened to them. The peasants said it was vampires. My contacts in the Undead Umbrage Union had assured me Nurbleville was vampire-free. Here was the actual answer. Despite my regular dealings with the horrors of my trade, I shuddered. To help take my mind off the matter and help pass the time, I took out one of the pig books.

I did not have to wait long. The Duke came in both smiling and sweating. He looked like a combination of the types of books he kept: a pig eating an eclair stuffed with a filling of hidden toxic obscenity.

"Good news!" he said with an enthusiasm that might have been directed at a piglet about to be slaughtered, a cream puff devoured, or a maiden…well, you get the idea.

"What news, my lord?" I said in as neutral a tone as I could muster.

"Sir Goodwin will slay the dragon in the morning."

I nearly laughed, but instead coughed hard. *Never piss off the nobles* is the second rule of my guild. I stood up and bowed. I had to be careful here. As with dragons, noblemen must be dealt with gingerly. The two have much in common: power, irritability, not to mention terrible breath. This was certainly the case with Duke Nurble. Especially the breath.

"In that case, my services are no longer required," I said.

The Duke looked surprised.

"Sir Goodwin thought you might object," he said.

"Object? What would be the point? I will, however, leave your duchy immediately."

"But you'll miss the victory feast," the Duke said.

"Victory feast?" I asked.

"Yes," he said. "I am told dragon meat is a fine repast: wonderful in meat pies."

I wanted to point out that the business at hand was less like baking pastries and more like making sausage, but I doubted he would get my point.

"No one actually knows what dragon tastes like, my lord," I said. "No one has ever slain a dragon."

"So, you do doubt Sir Goodwin! He told me you would cast doubt upon his valor."

"I am sure he is most valorous, but the dragon is large, fierce, and scaled; it breathes fire and flies. I am not sure that valor will win over all that. And after the battle, the dragon's wrath will be great."

"You assume Sir Goodwin will fail," the Duke said.

"A safe assumption," I said.

"It was Sir Goodwin who defeated that giant to the North," the Duke said.

This took me aback a bit. I had heard through my friends in the Behemoth Bargainer's Brotherhood that the Giant of Bungbole had been slain. So it had been Sir Goodwin who'd (literally) killed Robert Red-Nose's negotiations.

Was it possible? I wondered.

"A giant, while formidable, is no dragon," I said.

"Sir Goodwin has slain a dragon," the Duke said triumphantly.

"Well, he claims he has. My guild keeps close ties regarding all draconic matters. The consequences of such a deed would have reverberated throughout the kingdom."

"It did not happen in the kingdom," a new voice interjected. Hunched in the doorway, looking more giant than ever, was Sir Goodwin. He strode in, his spurs chinking, and threw a gauntlet down on the table. For a moment, I thought he was challenging me to a duel, but then I looked more closely at the gauntlet. It was greenish and scaled: dragon skin.

To my credit, I did not gasp.

"I was on crusade in the East when I came upon the beast," Sir Goodwin said. His face lost all expression, his voice distant and hushed as if he were telling a holy parable, though one involving massive bloodshed.

"Go on," the Duke said. "Tell him!"

The knight nodded; he needed no encouragement.

"To be fair," Sir Goodwin said, "it was old, old even for a dragon, so perhaps not as formidable as the beast I will slay tomorrow, but it was a dragon. I rode away at first, then spun and charged. Before it could react, I struck. My lance found its heart. No doubt God was with me that day. I skinned it and made these gloves and a gambeson for myself and my steed; they resist all fire. The flames of dragons cannot touch me."

"Tell him about the blood!" the Duke blurted.

Sir Goodwin smiled. "After I slew the dragon, I cut out its heart and drank its lifeblood. Since then, I have been blessed with remarkable strength of limb."

The Duke tittered. Nurble was like a love-smitten maiden or a bully's toady. The Duke pulled out a piece of twisted metal from his purse and threw it down next to the gauntlet. It was, or rather had been, a horseshoe; it was now nearly straight. Sir Goodwin picked it up and twisted it back into a U-shape. It was like watching a child bend a green willow reed. The Duke clapped his hands in delight.

My blood ran cold. It was worse than I had thought. Sir Goodwin wasn't just some oversized lunatic. He was the authentic item, an actual slayer of dragons, a figure from legend, a hero. There is nothing, and I mean nothing, more dangerous than a hero. They bring ruin and disaster. There are whole guild treatises written about how to deal with heroes, all of them useless. I had been fearful before; now, I was near panic, but I kept my face motionless.

"Remarkable," I said. "You are to be commended, good sir knight."

Sir Goodwin beamed. "I go now to pray in the Duke's chapel. I will keep vigil there and take midnight mass. On the morrow, with my soul refreshed, I will kill the dragon." He turned and left, spurs still clinking.

When I could no longer hear the jingling of his spurs, I turned to the Duke.

Before I could speak, the Duke cut me off.

"I will not hear any attacks against that man," he said.

I paused. I couldn't stop Sir Goodwin by myself. Dragons I could handle, but a hero? I would need help. I would need the Duke.

I smiled and again bowed.

"Well, I had best be on my way then; I need to be far away from here," I said.

"You still think he will lose!" the Duke exclaimed.

"No, he will win, but it doesn't matter. It will not be safe here," I said.

"But once the dragon is dead, all will be safe."

"Do you recall a certain peasant uprising in Marco?" I asked.

"Yes. Some serfs killed their lord Marco and declared themselves free," the Duke snorted.

"What happened?" I asked.

"The king called us to action. I sent a hundred men."

"And the peasants?"

"Hung from trees, drawn and quartered," the Duke said with a warm smile.

"An example was made."

"Of course," the Duke said. "What's this to do with Goodwin?"

"Not Goodwin, rather your realm and the realms around you. To the South is the Duchy of Rubabar. My guild-sister Olga Oakenboard negotiated a contract between Duke Rubabar and Bone-Melter seven years ago."

"Bone-Melter?" the Duke asked.

"The dragon that occupies Rubabar's lands," I said.

"What is it about these dragons and their names!" the Duke exclaimed.

"I know, I know," I said.

"Does it actually melt bones?"

"Frequently and with great relish," I replied.

"Why?"

"Something about the marrow..."

"Egads!" the Duke said. He looked at me with disgust, as if I were the one melting bones.

"Why are you bringing up Rubabar's dragon?" Nurble asked.

"For the same reason, I bring up your Eastern neighbor Baron Horegirth and his dragon, Skull-Spitter."

"Skull-Spitter?" the Duke said. "Does it actually spit out...?" the Duke pointed to his own head rather than finish the question.

"With great accuracy," I replied. "Can you guess what lies to the West?"

"I would hazard another dragon," he replied smartly.

"Two actually," I said, "a mated pair: Fire-Fart and its mate, Spiff the Sun Blocker."

"Well, I know there's no dragon to the North!" the Duke said as if this proved something.

"It's too cold; that is why a giant was there," I said.

"So that's why the Baron Bungbole never has to hire your lot. Seems unfair."

"Indeed, he is blessed," I said, not bothering to point out that the Baron could barely grow enough crops to feed himself or his people, let alone giants.

"Why are you telling me about all these other dragons? They are not my concern. Blood-Wind is the problem."

"They are not your concern now," I said. "But what happens when these other dragons learn that Blood-Wind's been killed? Just like you did with the peasants, they'll set an example. Can Sir Goodwin slay four dragons? They will fly here and destroy everything," I said.

The Duke's lower lip quivered a bit, but he swallowed hard. "Nonsense," he said, "you talk as if they were men; they are beasts."

"Beasts who can negotiate a contract, sign one with a tail dipped in ink, tally peasants delivered, read a manifest; beasts with long, long memories."

"You're trying to frighten me," the Duke said.

"You should be frightened," I said.

"Piffle! They are beasts; nothing will happen."

I sighed. It was clear the Duke would never come around. The idea of killing the dragon was too appealing. I made a quick calculation. I should be safe if I bought a horse and rode to the North immediately. It would be tight but manageable.

I did not move.

At first, I thought that my pride kept me there, or perhaps fear of the damage to my reputation. What else could it be? Why should I care about the people of Nurble? They didn't care about me. All I got from them were looks of suspicion, even hate. They called me 'Dragon-lover', 'ghoul', 'flesh-trader'.

But that didn't mean they deserved death. I've seen what happens when you rebel against a dragon: burned bodies and wrecked buildings, stones cracked and iron melted, ash stretching for miles, pools of poison and acid where once lay fields and ponds.

I looked at the Duke. He didn't know; he didn't understand dragons; he only understood his world, the world of nobles. Perhaps that was the answer...

"Fine," I said. "Let's speak of more practical matters. How was Sir Goodwin rewarded for slaying that giant?"

"Betrothed to the Bungbole's daughter," the Duke replied.

"Isn't there a rivalry between you and Bungbole, a dispute over farmland?"

"What of it?" the Duke asked.

"Why would the future son-in-law of your rival aid you?"

"He seeks glory," the Duke said.

"Indeed, after he slays the dragon, your peasants will cheer him. How do you feel about the next Baron of Bungbole being idolized by your subjects?" I asked.

Finally, the Duke looked afraid.

"You think Sir Goodwin plans to overthrow me?" he asked.

"Sir Goodwin is a genuinely noble soul, but his future father-in-law, the good Baron? You know him well. What kind of man is he?" I knew the answer: a treacherous bastard, just like Nurble.

The Duke sank into his chair. He resembled a deflated pig bladder.

"I am lost," he said.

I smiled.

"We must stop Goodwin," I said.

"How?" the Duke asked.

"Poison?" I asked.

The Duke's eye glanced toward the hidden bookshelf.

"Such an act would be ignoble," the Duke said softly.

"Agreed," I said. "And with that dragon blood in him, he might resist the poison. Besides, he is fasting. The only medium would be the holy wine he takes at mass."

"To poison sacramental wine would be a grave sin," the Duke said; his tone was more thoughtful than shocked.

"An unthinkable act," I replied. I looked down at the table, where the glove still rested.

I picked up the glove and waved it triumphantly.

"I have the answer," I said.

"What? The glove? Can we use it against Goodwin somehow?" the Duke asked. He snatched the glove from me and began examining it.

"You misunderstand. I can show the glove to the dragon. Explain the danger. If the dragon knows beforehand that the knight is fire-proof and preternaturally strong, it can fight him on its own terms. Fly up and drop boulders on him or something. True, Goodwin will die, but at least he'll die a hero's death, and my warning will allow me to ask for a further reduction in our offering."

"And you will reap even more gold," the Duke said, giving me a speculative look.

"I am willing to refund the addition to you," I said.

The Duke looked skeptical.

"A dragon negotiator willing to take a cut in commission? It's unheard of," the Duke said.

Like everyone, the Duke assumed I was only in it for the money. Never mind the burned bodies and wrecked towers that would come if we didn't stop the knight. No one ever understands until it's too late.

"Consider it a further incentive. I prefer to continue dealing with you rather than Baron Bungbole," I lied. "He's a Northern bumpkin; you are sophisticated. Besides, after this, I'll have such a good rapport with Blood-Wind that future dealings will be much easier, far more lucrative. I'm willing to set aside profit today for greater profit tomorrow." The Duke smiled at the explanation. With an overly formal gesture, as if he were bestowing a medal, he handed the glove back to me.

"Go and keep an eye on the knight," I said. "Keep him occupied in prayer, and I will go to the dragon."

Duke Nurble sighed.

"Ah well, I suppose we have no choice. Such a shame," the Duke said, shaking his head.

"A ruler must make difficult choices," I said, "You must protect yourself and your kingdom above all else. It's for the greater good — for your subjects and heirs."

"Yes. I must think of my heirs," the Duke answered. Again, his tone was thoughtful, which should have alerted me. Sighing one last time, he heaved himself up and departed.

I waited, collecting my thoughts, formulating how I should approach the dragon. Then I made my way out of the library and towards the courtyard and the gate.

It was evening. The castle walls cast long shadows. In the shadows, I saw movement. Lank, helmeted figures were following me. I picked up my pace; my companions did also. Ahead, two came into view, crossing their halberds to make a barricade. Behind me, I heard movement. I spun and saw one of the Duke's guards lunging for me, a club in hand. I dodged one blow, but another guard came forward, then another. They raised their clubs. I tried to run, but they had me surrounded. The clubs came down. Darkness engulfed me.

I woke in a dungeon, my head aching. I was in chains, and I could hear the slow drip of water. The Duke stood before me.

"I take it you changed your mind," I said.

"You were most convincing, especially regarding how my vassals would view Sir Goodwin. That's really what persuaded me that you were on to something," he said.

"I am," I said. "It's not too late."

"It was what you said about him being a hero. You see, Sir Goodwin is already a hero in the Count's land. He has already slain a giant there. So I suggested to Sir Goodwin that he break his engagement to the Count's daughter and marry my daughter instead: she is prettier and her dowry larger. The good knight agreed. So now I, and not the Count, will have a hero as a son-in-law. A double hero once he kills the dragon."

"The other dragons will not stand for it," I warned.

"Tush, I doubt they will care, and if they do, then you can negotiate an agreement. You will stay here a few days so as not to interfere, and then I will release you."

I thought of arguing, but realized it was pointless. I looked around: the walls were damp, the air cold. I felt a glimmer of hope, not for the Duke or his realm but for myself.

"This is a deep dungeon," I said.

"Yes, we are far underground. Once, there was a tower above. I had it torn down for my chateau, but I kept the underpinnings. I knew this dungeon would be useful. Make no trouble, or this place will be your tomb."

Smiling, the Duke departed. I wondered how long he would be smiling. Carefully, I sat down. My head was still reeling from the clubs. I felt nauseous. Was it from my battered skull or my predicament, or both? I couldn't tell. My mind went round in circles. I had misjudged the Duke. I had underestimated the knight. I was bad at reading people. Perhaps it was due to all my time dealing with dragons. Maybe it was because so many people viewed me as being on par with dragons: another creature feeding off human sacrifice. It had hardened me. I had spent too much time drinking in taverns alone, celebrating my victories alone. Instead of sharing what I had done with others, convincing them that what I did was for the best (despite how ugly and monstrous it seemed), I'd wallowed in self-pity. And now I would pay the price. I would die down here, unless this dungeon really was as deep and damp as I hoped it was.

My guard was named Grugney. He was a dim-witted soul who thought nobles were on par with angels. Grugney told me that Sir Goodwin had triumphed. A great feast was taking place above, and the Duke, with tremendous largess, had sent down a plate of roasted dragon meat. Out of professional courtesy, I did not eat it. Grugney thought me a fool and ate it himself. I am not sure how much time passed, but after what seemed like days, I was awakened by the sound of rumbling. The ground shook. I heard distant screams. I knew that above me, a great fire raged. Fortunately, the air down here was clean. Smoke rises and I was underground.

Eventually, Grugney came to my cell. His face was covered in tear-stained soot.

"Dragons!" he cried. "The sky is full of dragons!"

"Perhaps the Duke should send Sir Goodwin out," I said.

"Goodwin is dead! They picked him up and dropped him from up high. Everything is on fire. You must come. You must stop them!"

I shook my head.

"There is no stopping them. Do you want to live, Grugney?"

"Yes! Save me!" Grugney cried. Finally, someone had said something sensible.

"Open the door," I said.

He did so.

"Unchain me," I said.

He did so.

"Are there stores down here? Water and food?" I asked.

"Yes."

"Then we will wait it out," I said.

Grugney stared at me in horror, but a look of resignation came to his face. He nodded in agreement and sat down on the floor in a hunch, hiding his face.

Over the next two days, we heard many screams, explosions, and roars. They must have been very loud to reach down here. It was rough on poor Grugney. He cowered in a corner of the cell, crying for much of the time.

I tried to shut the sound out. I spent as much time as I could recalling all the details I knew about the four dragons above. Skull-Spitter would be playfully spitting heads at various targets. Bone-Melter would be eating hot marrow, and Fire-Fart? Well, he had that name for a reason. As to his mate, she would probably be judiciously comparing her current paramour to the other two males. I recalled a report that Silas Strenk had written about Skull-Spitter. It noted Spitter as highly intelligent and judicious, even for a dragon. The report described him as copper in color. As for Bone-Melter, I had heard that he was scarred from fights with other dragons; he had a bad reputation in the guild. There was little information on the mated pair. Hopefully, all four would be gone when we emerged.

Eventually, there was silence.

Was it over?

We crawled up and out.

Ruin greeted us.

Grugney fell to his knees. The look on his face was a microcosm of horror. Tears streamed down his cheeks, and his mouth trembled: all his angels were dead. Then he fainted, which was probably for the best. If he was anything like me, he'd be over the worst of it when he woke. I had been about his age when my village had tried to rebel.

I scouted ahead; it was as I expected. The Duchy of Nurble was no more. The town, the farms, the Duke's castle were destroyed. Sir Goodwin's lance was sticking upright atop a pile of rubble like a pole. Stuck upon it, like a flag at half-mast, was Sir Goodwin. I suspect the dragons had dropped him multiple times from the sky. His armor stopped fire; falling was another matter. At the base of the lance was the Duke's body, burned to a crisp. He looked like a roasted pig.

All around, I heard moans and cries. It was difficult to tell where the sounds came from until one realized they were coming from everywhere. Above, the sun was obscured, the sky full of smoke. I stumbled forward, making my way to a tall, smoke-obscured tower that was somehow still standing. Then the tower moved.

A low, rumbling noise, like a huge Catherine wheel being turned on chains, echoed around me.

Wings emerged from the side of the 'tower', and I realized that the dragons had not left. An immense, fanged face, eyes shining with cunning and confidence, emerged from the smoke. To my left, I heard the padding of enormous feet; another head appeared, peering down at me with dispassionate contempt. To my right, two more heads, necks tenderly intertwined, growled both amorously and hungrily.

Like the Duke's lands, I was surrounded by dragons. The one ahead stared at me for a moment more, then began to open its mouth.

I nearly froze but willed myself to move; I bowed as best I could, flourishing my hands in supplication.

"It is an honor to meet you, oh illustrious Spitter of Skulls," I said, keeping my voice calm. Inwardly, I prayed that the report I had read on Skull-Spitter's coloration was accurate.

The dragon ahead, copper in color, paused in mid-breath, then cocked its head to one side.

"Guild?" it growled.

"Yes, I am Edwin of the Negotiators Guild at your service."

"I would think that a member of the guild would know better than to have allowed this," the dragon said. It *was* Skull-Spitter.

"Rest assured, I tried to prevent it. I was locked in the dungeon below this former keep by its owner." I pointed to the roasted pig. "The Duke would not listen to reason. He was going to have me executed for attempting to warn Blood-Wind."

"For that, your death will be swift," Skull-Spitter said.

I wanted to run. I wanted to scream. I even wanted to fight (how, I don't know), but I knew none of that would save me. I had to think and think quickly.

"Thank you," I said, bowing again. "I, of course, understand. It is a shame that the guild will not. They will view all of you with great distrust when they hear of this tragic incident. The circumstance will look most suspect. It appears you decided to carve up Blood-Wind's territory for yourselves."

"Nonsense," Skull-Spitter said.

"Of course," I replied quickly, "but consider how ludicrous it will seem that a knight slew a dragon. No one will believe that a man," I pointed to Sir Goodwin's half-mast corpse, "slew the great Blood-Wind."

This gave Skull-Spitter pause.

"It's stalling," the one to my right said. "Kill it and be done with it."

"As a trusted guild member, I could write a report explaining what happened; it would only be circulated among the upper leadership. This could all be kept quiet — something we all want. No one wants more incidents like this."

To my left, Fire-Fart spoke. "Aren't you that Edwin who wrote that piece on Dragon Counting systems in the quarterly?"

"I am, oh great scaled one," I said.

"I quite liked that," the dragon said.

"I've always thought the draconic use of base eight rather than ten to be superior," I said.

"Of course. After all…"

"Eight is a power of two," I interjected hastily.

"Exactly," Fire-Fart said, nodding. Dragons love maths. They love gold and eating people more, but mathematics is a close third.

"You should do a study on egg combinatorics," Fire-Fart said speculatively.

"I am planning one, actually," I lied. "Should I survive."

Ahead of me, Skull-Spitter's head lowered and came close to me.

"Now, I remember you. You negotiated a contract for my niece a few years ago. She said you were quite good."

"Your niece is as nearly discerning as you, oh great spitter of heads." I bowed my own head as I spoke.

"She is clever," Skull-Spitter said proudly. Male dragons are often more fond of their nieces and nephews than their own (supposed) offspring. This is due no doubt to the overly amorous nature of female dragons, but I did not say this. *Never piss off the dragon.*

"Well, what do the rest of you think?" Skull-Spitter asked.

"Remember, my lord, you will need to negotiate this new territory between you, not to mention new contracts with the respective humans in your expanded territories. There will also need to be a master contract with the guild," I said. With each tedious item I listed, I could see the dragons almost wince. They hate such details.

"Oh, spare him. Fire-Fart will be mopey if he doesn't get that piece on egg maths," this came from Spiff, Fire-Fart's mate.

"Well, I want to melt his bones," Bone-Melter said, not surprisingly.

"You've been melting bones all day," Skull-Spitter said. "I'm with Sun Blocker. He'll be useful."

"I agree," Fire-Fart said.

"Very well," Bone-Melter growled. With a great leap, he flew into the sky. The gust nearly knocked me over.

"Remember to cover combinatorics of first-ordered egg pairs," Fire-Fart said.

"Farewell," Spiff said, more to Skull-Spitter than to me.

"Well, little human, you're quite clever for one of your kind," Spitter said.

I said nothing: compliments from dragons are not always a welcome thing. The dragon continued.

"You have your work cut out for you. Of course, you'll make quite a killing off this." A low chuckle came from Skull-Spitter's mouth. It was the first time I had ever heard a dragon laugh.

"The only ones killing here are you and your kind," I said hotly. It simply leapt out of me.

Skull-Spitter growled. I had violated the first rule. I had pissed off the dragon. Was I to die after all?

Instead, the dragon raised his head high and roared. I nearly shat myself from the sound. My head, still recovering from those mace blows, was instantly splitting.

"Even you don't understand," Spitter said. "You humans need us. You may hate us, but trust me, the world would be a real horror show without us dragons around to keep your kind in check. These warrens of yours would get bigger and bigger. Pretty soon, you'd be living like rats, and you'd ruin the land, breeding like crazy. You think this is bad?" It swept one wing over the surrounding ruin. "This is nothing to what the world would look like if your kind was in charge. No, you're far too dangerous to go unchecked. Without us, you'd become real monsters."

Then he laughed again, and with a great leap, he flew straight up and disappeared into the smoke. I knew he would be home soon, curled up and dreaming dragon dreams in his warren, which was undoubtedly called Death-Cap or Fear-Spike or some other ridiculous name.

I sat down on a pile of rocks and began to plan. There was a lot to do: reports to write, proposals to draft. I wanted to get started, but I stopped. I could hear the cries of the survivors. Someone would have to find the able-bodied, organize them, gather food and water, build shelters. The convent had probably been spared. I could get word to the nuns. It was work that would be profitless, maybe even thankless, but it would have to come first. After all, they were my people. Anything else was too monstrous to consider.

See Christopher Warden's story "The Dragon's Due" online at Metaphorosis.
If you liked it, leave a comment. Authors love that!
Remember to subscribe to our e-mail updates so you'll know when new stories are posted.

About the story

Beyond an ever-present desire to turn things upside down, this story was inspired by the "Fable of the Dragon Tyrant" metaphor tale made popular by Oxford philosopher Nick Bostrom and the you-tuber personality CGP Grey. The argument was that we should try and get rid of aging; it was presented as a fable about people paying tribute to a dragon. I found the whole thing naive, misguided, and, frankly, destructive. It actually made me angry. I think this story is my act of rebellion against the notion of fighting against things that we should be wise enough to accept. It's not always reasonable or even safe to tilt at windmills; sometimes, the results can be disastrous.

That initial impulse then grew as I thought about the notion of "heroes" and crusaders: both the big macho type and the righteous do-gooders who have no self-doubt and can't be made to question their purpose. I liked the idea of a narrator who wasn't charismatic or well-liked but who was cursed with being right.

A question for the author

Q: What's a genre you'd like to write, but don't or can't?

A: I would love to write a heist story. I think this goes back to my childhood dream of being a cat burglar. Nailing down all the details has discouraged me from pursuing it.

About the author

Chris Warden is a native of California. He is married to Jane Warden; they have two adult children. Chris graduated from U.C. Berkeley with a degree in philosophy. He has worked as a web developer, computer programmer, game designer, and UX developer.

He enjoys body surfing, body boarding, and ocean swimming. He spends an inordinate amount of time in the ocean but has still not figured out how to breathe underwater.

www.criswar.com/write

Through the Middle

J.B. Kish

There's a woman driving slowly down highway 27 in their direction, and every couple of miles, she opens her window and lets a handful of something human-tasting scatter in the wind. Ashes, Rory suspects. She misses the man who's now dust and cries a little as she goes, singing Bill Withers because the radio doesn't play much more than static and gospel out this far. Bump thinks the powdered man must have liked Bill Withers very much.

At the speed she's going, she'll reach the diner in about thirty minutes. Rory presses a finger into the countertop and thanks Bump for the heads up. Then he puts on a fresh pot of coffee. Coffee's a good start for sadness like this, Rory thinks, and he should know. He's only just found happiness again.

Rory sits behind the counter, shaped like a farm egg. He's put on weight that rounds him. Muscular legs stick out beneath his body like a pair of clearance sale limbs not intended for him, and he wears the rest of his skin like thick diving dress, rich with small folds that retreat from his ribs and neck. His body is a game of hide and seek: American traditional appearing around each corner. There's a woman in a bathing suit diving down his forearm. A faded anchor on his bicep. Twin sparrows on his chest that no longer fly straight.

Half an hour passes, and her Civic pulls up to the far-flung roadside diner. Rory plays "Grandma's Hands" on the jukebox and pours a fresh cup of coffee. The woman walks in with a newborn puppy, and he greets her warmly. When she hears Bill Withers, she buckles a little, and Rory helps her to a nearby booth. "Here," he says, placing a ceramic mug in front of her. "This will make you feel better."

Rory disappears into the kitchen and fixes the woman—her name is Aliyah—something to eat. For a long time, Aliyah reclines in the booth and stares at the sunset with the puppy in her lap. Her t-shirt is cotton-white, floating elegantly above a pair of cut off shorts and some skateboard sneakers. The skin of her cheek is pocked with dark acne scars that she's not covered up. She looks like the subject in a Rockwell painting.

Bump asks who Rockwell is and Rory places a finger on the wall like he's using a walkie talkie. Silently, he explains Norman Rockwell was an artist who used to paint restaurants like theirs. Then Rory slides a turkey sandwich in front of Aliyah and asks if she'd appreciate company. She accepts politely, and he wonders for one terrifying moment what he—an old man in his seventies—can offer this woman, if anything. He knows nothing about being young or black or growing up in these times. But he has an ear, which is all she seems to need, and Aliyah explains she's wandering southern Oregon, spreading her father's ashes. He was one of the west coast's most celebrated archeologists, and he died peacefully of old age a month ago. After an hour, Aliyah makes an embarrassed face. She's been talking this whole time and hasn't asked Rory one question about himself.

Rory prefers it this way. He doesn't like talking about his father or the Navy; he's not the kind of discarded thing that complains. Anyway, nothing before matters because this is where he matters most. Of course, Aliyah doesn't understand that at all and surprises him by asking, *What's next.*

Rory laughs through his nose. "The only way this diner shuts down is because I've died and there's no one left to open it."

"Suppose you win the lottery."

He sips his coffee too quickly and wets his mustache; Aliyah grins as he dabs his mouth dry. "I grew this thing in the Navy because I had a baby face. My commanding officer said it would make me look smart."

"Did it?"

Rory nods and sits back. "In the Navy, you know exactly where you matter most. They tell you where to be and what to do. How to shave, how to dress. After I got out, I spent a long time searching for value again. When I found this restaurant and its customers, I *did* win the lottery. I don't think I could ever walk away from that."

Aliyah ponders his words a while before dismissing them with the wave of a hand; he can't help but fall in love with her a little. *Aliyah's* value, she explains, chases her like the puppy on her lap. She gets job offers because her father had important friends and they think her trowel was destined to continue his legacy. But she doesn't want a life in the dirt. She wants to start a vegan bakery. "But is that a terrible idea?"

It's not, and Rory envies how clearly she sees herself.

"You know, I've heard of you," Aliyah says. He points to his breast, and she nods. "They say there's a hermit in the desert that helps people. That's you, I think."

He shrugs. "Most folks know what they need. Sometimes they have to hear it a specific way."

On the way out the door, she thanks him for good company and happy coincidences. "Bill Withers was my father's favorite, you know."

Rory holds up a finger and fetches a cup of coffee to-go. "For the road," he explains, and then he grabs a handful of sugar packets from the table. "And for the bakery."

Aliyah chuckles at the gift and gives Rory a squeezing hug. "We'll see."

His heart beats like a young man's as she heads down the road. It was a nice cup of shared coffee, he thinks. Coffee's always a good start for sadness like that. Then Bump asks if Norman Rockwell can come paint their restaurant, and Rory laughs before turning in for the night.

Bump came through the middle.

That's the only way he's able to tell it. One day, he 'passed through the middle and surfaced here', just about the same as most customers. He could be extraterrestrial, but Bump didn't come from the great above. He came from deep, deep below, 'through the middle', and burst up against the ground like a pimple on the cheek of southern Oregon's desert.

Rory never tries to dig him up because it wouldn't be polite, and Bump seems satisfied enough to exist under the asphalt bloom behind the diner, which houses him like a geodesic dome. Besides, Bump says the asphalt is what connects him to the road and the people traveling their way. It's through this that he can feel the vibration of human emotions, touch palms through cracked leather steering wheels, and read Rory the prologue of their customers. It's what makes the pair a uniquely wonderful team, and why Rory is truly happy for the first time in a long while.

This is why Rory's stomach drops when Bump says someone is coming, but he can't sense anything about them. Bump can perceive the subtle weight of their body through the driver's side tires, but the rest feels eerie and quiet. It's almost as if there's no one there at all. *Can Mustangs drive themselves on this planet?* he asks Rory realizes he's not breathing and tries to inhale casually.

Anyway, says Bump. *They should be here tomorrow afternoon.*

But first, there's a man and a woman—a college couple in their twenties—coming down the highway, and whenever she brings up his temper, he wrings the steering wheel in a way she can't see. His little outbursts are growing more frequent, and even though he apologizes, they seem to be dancing around an incident— something like a *push* or maybe a *fall*, Bump says. They can't agree on which. The woman is assertive, but occasionally her voice is nervous around the edge. Rory thanks Bump for the heads up. With a frown, he puts on a fresh pot of coffee. Coffee's a good start when dealing with men like this. As it drips, he can't help his mind wandering to his tools out back and finds himself asking how hard it might be to dig a man-sized hole.

You'll not stick him down here with me, Bump jokes.

A while later, the bell rings, and without asking, Rory pours two fresh cups of coffee.

A tattooed woman appears at his counter, looks down with a smile, and dubs him a saint. She holds the ceramic mug under her nose with both hands and breathes deep. She's brunette and diamond shaped, with as much life as a fresh battery. When the boyfriend appears over her shoulder, he has a square head and practiced neutrality. A chameleon: Rory spots it right away. Polite. Jovial. Makes pleasant conversation all the way up until he leaves for the bathroom, which is outside around back. Rory forgets to mention the very specific jimmy required to unlock its door from inside, and that buys him a while to chat.

He places a pastrami sandwich in front of the tattooed woman with a roll of silverware. Her jaw drops playfully, and she asks why Rory owns a diner in the absolute middle of nowhere.

"Pills," he says candidly because she needs to hear this a specific way. She doesn't follow. "When I got out of the Navy, I took a job as a line cook and spent thirty years making people happy. And then we got bought out; I was fired by a hot shot celebrity for not understanding molecular gastronomy. No one in Portland wants to hire an old cook with bad knees, so when I hit the bottom, I drove down here to eat enough Oxycodone to put me in the ground."

Her eyes grow wide, and she has the packed cheek of a squirrel.

Rory smiles, easing a bit of this uninvited tension, "I found this restaurant instead."

The woman smiles uncomfortably. "Good for you." She tries to end the conversation on a high note. "So many five-star ratings online, you must be doing something right."

Suddenly Bump is there, in Rory's mind. *The mustang is going much faster. It will be here sooner*, he says.

Rory's heart skips a beat. What *is* all this nonsense about self-driving cars and phantom drivers? He discretely presses his right fingertip into the counter. The entire finger has vibrated with heat since the day he met Bump, when he pressed down on the asphalt dome curiously, and their connection was calcified. He theorizes it's a kind of foreign energy that comes from the other side—through the middle. When he presses down, he can sense its vein-like release, connecting him from the counter to the floor below, which joins with the building's foundation, the earth around, and ultimately allows him to project thoughts to his friend out back. *You're imagining things*, he tells Bump, and then he lifts his finger, ending the conversation.

Rory returns to the woman, distracted. "The point is," he continues, "it wasn't good enough to keep telling my family I'd change. People tell themselves they can just wake up tomorrow and *do better*. But I had to work at it. Leave an unhealthy environment, change my life. Otherwise, all those good intentions were just smoke and vapor."

The woman's eyes narrow slightly.

He makes a noise in the back of his throat, then nods toward the bathroom. "What I'm saying is, people don't magically wake up and *do better*. Unless he does the work, his apologies are just smoke and vapor." Then Rory tops off her coffee. "Understand?"

The blood drains from the woman's face and the bell rings over her shoulder. "Old man," her boyfriend growls. He walks up to the counter and throws the key into Rory's chest. It lands against the floor with a jingle. "Bathroom door is broken as hell." Then he nudges the woman with his elbow. "Hurry up and pay."

The whole interaction was a bit heavier handed than Rory prefers. When they've left, he walks out to the road and stares into the distance. He envisions a Mustang blowing fire from its tailpipe, riding a cloud of smog. And then, for reasons he cannot explain, he thinks of constructing a white tower for the first time in years.

What would you do if I passed back through the middle? Bump asks.

The sun is tangerine-orange and quickly fading. Rory flips a chicken breast on the charcoal grill he's rolled out back. With an elderly groan, he touches a finger to the ground. *You know it's rather unfair that I must speak through my finger, but* you *can project your thoughts directly into me.*

Humans are surprisingly complex, Bump answers. *Would you stay at the diner?*

Rory is annoyed and tense. *I'd climb the white tower and throw myself off,* he snips.

Bump is quiet a while, then says, *The mustang will be here soon.*

"Lord!" Rory shouts with his actual voice. "What is all this about?"

When Bump doesn't respond, Rory splays his fingers in frustration. "Fine," he says, "Let it come," and he walks inside. He grabs a large piece of parchment paper and writes 'PERMANENTLY CLOSED', then tapes it to the front door and kills the lights. There's not a single glowing bulb in the entire dining room. Out back, he waves a dismissive hand at bump and takes his dinner to bed.

He's here, Bump whispers.

Rory opens his eyes with a start, then sticks his head out the trailer door and spots a light in the restaurant. "He?"

The one driving the Mustang. He's waiting for you inside.

"It's nearly five in the morning."

You should go in, is all Bump says.

Inside, there's a handsome man sitting at the counter eating a bag of potato chips. He looks like he stepped off a Hollywood movie set, but Rory can't decide why. His features are elusive: Latin American one moment, Eastern European the next. There is a fresh pot of coffee on the counter, and he invites Rory to join him.

"Who are you?" Rory whispers, looking down at his parchment paper sign, which has been folded into a perfect square on the counter.

"Name's *Very Hungry,*" the man says with a punchline smile. It's a joke, but Rory's not laughing. The stranger reaches into his pocket and pulls out three one-hundred-dollar bills. "Can you make the perfect burger?"

Well now, just what in the hell is this? Rory wonders. *And why are you suddenly so damned quiet?* he asks Bump through the countertop. Bump doesn't answer.

"Every time I come here, I can't wait to get my hands on a real American cheeseburger." The stranger makes two fists. "But you can't go to a drive thru. What's the point of anticipation if the food's no good?" He slides the money forward. "Three hundred dollars for the best burger you can make."

Rory scowls. Breaking into his diner—scaring his friend—that's one thing. Questioning his ability on the grill is another entirely! He takes the money and draws up his torso. "I'll make it to-go."

Rory returns with possibly the greatest hamburger he's ever made. Carefully sculpted. Cooked to perfection. Golden French fries that could usher in the seventh trumpet! Lettuce so crisp it looked plastic!

And what does he find waiting for him? Nothing.

The Mustang is still parked outside, but there's no one sitting behind the counter.

Rory, says Bump.

He closes his eyes. *Shit*, he thinks, keeping this particular thought to himself. Cautiously, he walks out back and finds the handsome man standing above Bump, looking down at the asphalt dome with a mouth full of potato chips. Rory licks his lips and presses a finger into a wooden railing. "What is this?" he asks.

Rory, says Bump, *this is Hadrian. Hadrian, this is Rory.*

Hadrian waves and smiles. It's not unkind, and Rory hates him for that.

Hadrian is my grandchild, adds Bump.

Inside, the to-go box is empty. Rory is three hundred dollars richer, and he's never felt worse.

Hadrian is here to take Bump home. Bump left without telling anyone, and at his age, he really needs to be looked after. A depression drapes over Rory like a series of blankets, one after the other. He feels heavier the longer Hadrian talks.

"But," Rory whispers. "We're quite good friends."

"That's a funny pair," suggests Hadrian. The sun illuminates the diner with a warm glow. Dust floats along the rays of light like sad poetry.

"I've come to care for your grandfather very deeply," explains Rory. He finds himself appealing to the man's sense of empathy, but who's to say if Hadrian has any to begin with. His kind comes through the middle and takes on a form that emulates the planet's inhabitants. That didn't necessarily mean they possess the same emotional capacity. "Perhaps he could stay here with me?" Rory's smile is desperate.

Hadrian shakes his head. "Grandfather got stuck trying to emerge. It happens occasionally. I'm here to help." He takes a long sip of coffee and sighs gratefully. "Have you considered what you'll do when Bump passes back through the middle?"

Rory's too scared of the white tower to answer, so Hadrian adds, "Would you like to pass through the middle with us instead?"

Through the middle—it's a terrifying notion! Timid, he whispers, "Your grandfather's never told me much about where you come from. And this is my home."

"So, you wish to stay here?"

"I wish for things to stay as they are!"

"They cannot," Hadrian says in a way that's not unkind. "We leave tonight."

Tears gallop down Rory's cheek. It's just like life to do this to him again. The bell over the door rings, and Rory jumps. Quickly, he dries his cheeks and waves hello to a pair of men with a young boy. Farmers perhaps? "Be right with you," he calls. "Grab a seat anywhere."

Rory plucks his apron from the counter, pausing long enough to ask Bump why he didn't give a heads up on their new customers.

"'I've suspended your connection to my grandfather," Hadrian whispers. "Only temporarily."

Suspended their connect—how dare he! What kind of game was he playing? Rory's face is beet read. He opens his mouth to shout when—

"Hey fella," one of the men calls. "Coffees and a juice."

Rory is shaking. Gradually, his expression lifts upward and he fetches their order. Standing above them, he withdraws a pad of paper and a pencil, clears his throat, and wonders why he's so uneasy.

"Y'all from around here?"

Neither man looks up from their menus. They're vaguely like one another. Brother's maybe? Or perhaps it's just coincidence. The youngest, a boy of ten or eleven, stares out the window thoughtfully. He has a book on his lap—*The Spectator Bird*—but never opens it. The eldest, a leathery man with ruddy cheeks, looks down at his wristwatch and speaks in a way that's not intended for Rory. "Two hours," he whispers.

The other nods and looks up from his menu. "Three omelets, bacon, white toast all around."

Rory notes the order and retrieves the menus. "Beautiful day out there."

The younger man slides his cup forward. "Top off, please."

As Rory steps back into the kitchen, Hadrian raises a polite finger. "I'd love one of those omelets, if it's not a complete bother."

The kitchen door swings shut, and for a long while, Rory stares at the range. Slowly, he begins making the order. It's easy. It's muscle memory. He could make omelets in his sleep, and without meaning it, his mind drifts to the white tower. He makes sure his index finger isn't touching anything that connects him to Bump, and he's ashamed of it. *How much is left?* he wonders. He is pulled from the question by the distinct smell of eggs starting to burn. He saves the omelets just in time. Again, it's muscle memory. He really could do this in his sleep.

After breakfast, the man with ruddy cheeks pays and Rory asks how everything was. "Sure," the man answers. "Good enough."

The blood drains from Rory's face as their truck pulls out the lot and disappears down the road. Hadrian picks at the men's leftovers while Rory dumbly removes his apron and floats outside, into his trailer, and opens the closet door. He pushes aside a few shirts and finds a shoebox tucked all the way in the back. Inside is an orange prescription bottle with ten tablets that make a maraca sound when he shakes them. His heart pounds as if it means to crack his ribs, and suddenly Rory can't breathe. He races outside for air.

Hadrian sits on a folding chair next to Bump, finishing a side of potatoes. After Rory's caught his breath, he drags a chair next to them and squeezes the plastic bottle between both hands.

Were you able to serve those men? Bump asks.

Hadrian nods; he's allowed them to speak again.

"I was able to feed them," Rory answers. "If that's what you mean."

Quietly, he opens the plastic bottle and slides half the contents into his palm. They're heavier than he remembers, like they have somewhere important to be. He imagines them pecking through his skin and dropping out the back of his hand, so he stacks them one by one on his armrest before they can get away. Carefully, he constructs a beautiful white tower and envisions himself standing atop it, leaning out over a smooth, granite edge. The vast Oregon desert yawns beneath him, and his heart flutters at the brush of an old friend. An adrenaline he hasn't felt in years.

Rory's only closed his eyes for a moment when his chair nudges strangely, and when he looks back down, the tower is missing, and Hadrian is making a childish face. "These aren't good at all."

"You ate that?" Rory sits up as Hadrian dry swallows a white paste.

Hadrian's eyes widen. "The mints?"

"You can't have."

"Hadrian," Bump says. "Those were Rory's mints."

Rory presses a finger into his armrest. "They're not mints." Then to Hadrian, "You need to vomit."

"You mean on command?"

"Quickly."

"What happens if I don't?"

Rory doesn't answer, which is answer enough. "Oh." says Hadrian, sitting back. "Interesting."

"How exactly?"

"Well, if I don't, then my grandfather stays here, and you get what you want."

Rory's blood thickens with pressure. "I don't want your grandfather to be stuck here."

"But you don't want him to leave either."

"I don't want things to change." He's about to stand and force Hadrian to vomit himself. "What about our customers?"

"Will they stop coming?"

"How do you propose I help them without your grandfather here? Look what happened in there."

Hadrian makes a face like he finally understands the riddle in front of him. "My grandfather gives you value."

Rory draws himself upright. "Of course not."

"Is there someone else who does that?"

"His commanding officer," Bump says brightly.

Rory twists his hands anxiously. "My what?"

"You told the dust-man's daughter that your commanding officer made you grow that mustache and now you're smarter. He has given you value."

"No."

"You're not smart?"

"I was always smart."

"The mustache doesn't make you smart?"

"You need to throw up right now."

Hadrian holds out both palms like he didn't read that part of the human manual. "Do I punch myself?"

"Who then?" Bump asks.

"No one *gives* me value," Rory barks. "Stick your finger all the way down your throat until something happens."

Hadrian does as he's told.

Rory twist the cap onto the prescription bottle and stuffs the remaining pills into his pocket. "What would you have me do?" he growls. "Leave the diner tonight? Abandon my customers?"

"The diner gives you value," Bump clarifies.

"No." Rory pinches his brow and then points at Hadrian. "*Deeper.*" Hadrian grunts in acknowledgment and his finger descends another inch.

"Then what?"

"*I* do," Rory shouts. "I'm good at this. I'm good at helping people!" He stands and grabs Hadrian's elbow. He pushes upward and the man's finger disappears another inch. Hadrian gags fantastically; he vomits white bile onto Rory's clothes. It's unclear if he's disposed of all five pills, but Rory suspects it's enough. He's about to stumble backward when a small voice clears its throat: "Sir?"

They turn in surprise. The boy from breakfast peeks around the corner with a cautious expression. Rory let's go of Hadrian, who wipes his mouth and waves.

Bravely, the child asks, "You seen my book?"

"Book?" Then Rory understands. He waves the boy inside and searches the booth where they ate. He gets down on his hands and knees, hoping to find it under the table.

"What were you two fighting about?" the boy asks from behind.

"If I told you my mustache," Rory mutters, "would you believe me?"

Rory cranes his neck and spots the book wedged between the wall and booth. He reaches out and can nearly touch it with the tip of his finger, but Bump is idling there. Instead, Rory uses his ring finger to paddle at the book's spine until it falls to the floor.

Grunting, he shuffles backward and feels every vertebrae of his back unfurl. "Here." The boy takes the book and nods in thanks.

"Those men." Rory motions to the truck outside.

"My uncles."

"They don't talk much, do they?"

"Sure they do."

Sure they do. Rory's about to ask what terrible things they've been saying about breakfast when the boy turns and heads for the door.

"Wait—" Rory calls out and the child stops to look over his shoulder. Rory wants to ask; he's desperate to know, but a thick feeling of shame coats his throat. Frankly, the words are so dull in shape that even his mouth is bored with them, on top of which he's just realized how badly he stinks. The truth is, he's so insecure that this entire moment feels perfectly normal, and he hates himself for that.

The boy startles him by going first. "It doesn't matter if he doesn't like it."

Rory stops. He doesn't understand.

"Your mustache." The boy draws himself upward and walks across the checkered floor with raw, adolescent confidence. He places a companionable hand on Rory's bicep and says firmly, "I think it only matters if *you* like the mustache."

There's an inaudible *crack* of ivory-white granite.

With a radiant clap on his arm, the boy turns and jogs out. Rory opens and closes his mouth like a fish. His eyes have gently doubled in size, and there's a tangible warmth in his bicep. He floats to the window, and as the boy climbs up into the truck, he spots Rory. The boy waves and then reaches backward, withdrawing a plastic comb from his pocket. He holds it horizontally beneath his nose and smiles through the prongs.

Nothing here is as she remembers it. Aliyah sits in her Civic, staring up at the diner which is no longer the diner. It's *Dot's*, and Dot is a woman who doesn't allow dogs in her restaurant, so Koda waits in the car. Aliyah sits at a booth craning her neck, waiting for the hermit to round a corner.

Dot is a short Thai woman in her fifties who can carry more plates than seems possible. She tends to a busy dining room before dropping a cup of coffee in front of Aliyah. "Morning. Need some time or are you ready?"

"The man who worked here, an older gentleman."

Dot doesn't follow.

"He was the owner just a few months ago. Did he..." Aliyah tilts her head morbidly.

Dot shakes her chin no. "He sold."

Aliyah's stomach pirouettes. "He what?"

Dot smiles politely while scanning the restaurant from the corner of her eye. "If you need a little time with the menu..."

Aliyah nods and falls back into the booth, struggling to understand. She's driven all this way so he could talk her out of it.

What's she supposed to do now? Take the job and play secretary for a department of PhDs obsessed with her last name? How could this have happened?

The hermit *sold* his lottery?

Aliyah sips her coffee and stares at a caddy of sugar packets and room temperature creamer. Dot returns a while later and refills her cup.

"Did he say anything?" Aliyah asks. "Or where he was going?"

"Were you friends?" When Aliyah doesn't answer, Dot nods. "He sold quickly."

Aliyah knits her brow and chews the inside of her cheek. She can feel herself sinking inward.

"He left something." Dot speaks softly as if telling a secret. "A funny note taped out front with a couple urns of coffee." Then she turns and points to a bulletin board near the door. "I couldn't bring myself to throw it away."

When she spots the note, Aliyah's skin prickles. She climbs out of the booth and walks to the board.

Passed through the middle, she reads. *Help yourself to some coffee. No matter the problem, I've always found coffee is a good start.*

"Hon?" Dot's voice appears over her shoulder. "Do you need more time with the menu?"

Rubbing her thumb over the note, Aliyah shakes her head. She pays for a coffee to-go and Dot fetches her a paper cup. As she turns to leave, Aliyah plucks a few sugar packets from a nearby caddy. She pictures the old hermit in the desert who used to help people. Who told people things they knew, just said a specific way. Without thinking, she grabs a handful more. She stuffs her jacket pockets with little white packets until they are full. Pretty soon, she's emptying another caddy over a table and scooping them into her saddle bag.

"Hey!" Dot shouts from the register, her eyes wide.

Aliyah smiles apologetically as she empties a third caddy directly into her bag. Then a fourth.

"I said stop!" calls Dot, but the bell above the door is already ringing. Aliyah is racing to her car, shouting an apology through the window. She's got to get going!

Bill Withers glides into place as she and Koda soar down the highway toward home. Aliyah's turning down the job; she was never meant for a life in the dirt. She's decided to take her sugar packets and build something brand new.

See J.B. Kish's story "Through the Middle" online at Metaphorosis.
If you liked it, leave a comment. Authors love that!
Remember to subscribe to our e-mail updates so you'll know when
new stories are posted.

About the story

A few years ago, I drove past a restaurant and found myself jotting down the concept for a new story: Guy pays $300 for the best hamburger someone can make. It didn't mean much to me at the time. I actually had no idea why someone would pay so much for a hamburger of all things. But I liked the imagery, and even though the idea would spend years collecting dust in my notes folder, it stuck with me.

This is how most of my stories come together. I capture small vignettes like that until I begin to see connective tissue. In the case of Through the Middle, the three notes that acted as the story's foundation were:

- Guy pays $300 for the best hamburger someone can make
- Diner in the middle of nowhere
- What if aliens didn't come from above, what if they came from below

I spent days mashing these ideas together, writing various outlines for how they might work. Sometimes the ideas just won't gel, no matter how hard I try. But "Through the Middle" was one of those wonderful, rare occasions where the story quickly began to tell itself.

A question for the author

Q: Do you have a garden? Have you ever grown your own food?

A: My wife is a hobbit of a woman. She spends most of her free time in our garden. While I've dabbled with a vegetable or two, she's got the green thumb in our family. During the summer, we spend a lot of time outside. I'm usually focused on a woodworking project while she's digging around in the dirt somewhere.

About the author

Originally from the Southwest, J.B. Kish moved to Portland, Oregon, in 2012. He is currently working on his second novel.

www.jbkish.com, @JohnBoyKish

Love, Death, and the Electric Soul

Alexandra Peel

"HushCabs. What's your location?"

"9 Trinity Heights. Quick as you can!"

"On our way, sir. Serina, you got this one?" The operator, Boyd, made it sound like a confirmation, rather than an ask.

Serina pulled a microfilament from her forearm port. The minute tube retreated into the Memory Loop device. The words, *'Of c-c-course I'm real, honey'*, settled on top of the pile of memories. The ML was playing up, again. She pocketed the gadget, irritated.

"I was just about to sign off." Serina sighed. Popped her neck left then right. Checked the holowatch on the dash. She'd been on since half six this morning. Ten hours, fifteen minutes.

"Tel and Brandy are mid-run. Kal's got a flyer. Trace and Pete called in sick. You're all I got."

She rolled her eyes at the two-way radio, "Aw shit. Got no one waiting for me, so may as well."

Brief pause. Faint hum before the radio crackled with Boyd's voice. Curt, though concerned. *"Don't go there, Serina. Just keep your shit together and grab the punter."*

She eased the cab out into traffic. Silent. The air-con wafted 'pine-scented' breeze across her face and exposed collar bones. She didn't have a clue what pine was. Something from the old times. Flowers, maybe? Checked the mirror, and glimpsed blue eyes underlined in blue shadows.

It took less than five minutes to skilfully navigate the early evening traffic; ducking between Old Hall, Roberts, and Paisley streets. She tapped a control. The driver's seat sighed as it expanded just enough to relieve the pressure on her backside and thighs. HushCabs could afford top tech, because they were exclusive, and charged more than most companies in the city. HushCabs weren't just quiet vehicles, they specialised in taking fares to places they didn't want colleagues, friends, or family to find out about. For whatever reason. It wasn't the company's business. They never asked. She had the door open as soon as she pulled into the pick-up zone. The customer easy to spot, practically dancing from one foot to the other in anticipation. Before he was even in, he blurted,

"Festival Gardens!" Just under six kilometres. Fifteen, maybe twenty minutes on clear roads. "You took your time. Hurry!" Serina glanced at the dash holowatch. It had taken her three minutes. She didn't argue. Never did. "I'll give you extra if you floor it!" his voice panicky.

She chuckled, "This isn't a movie, sir. We don't 'floor it'. There's lights, and crossings, not to mention a speed limit."

"Double!" he squeaked. Tempting, was the instant notion. But she didn't want to get pulled over and lose her license. Good jobs were not easy to come by these days.

Wow, this guy was seriously rattled. She watched him in her rear-view mirror. Not sitting back, sitting forward. Gripping the headrest of the front passenger seat with one hand. Glancing out the window, at his watch, her dash watch, and something in his other hand.

"I gotta get it back in time."

"Hmm hmm."

"Never been late before. Forgot the time. This once." She saw he had tears on his face. Started to feel uncomfortable. "God, I miss her so much when she's in there," he looked down at whatever was in his palm. "I love you, Laura honey."

She tried to concentrate on driving. Tried to block out her passenger's personal pain. Put her foot down on Sefton and Riverside. No lights along here. Back in the twenty-first century, the Advisory Council had turned off everything outside the prime cities. Save energy. Stop pollution. All that. Long after the space-based solar relays and Oceanic Energy Grid were operational, suburbs and abandoned industrial sites weren't fully reconnected — especially in towns and cities in the north. Halfway along Riverside, he gave her further directions. Past the old festival grounds — Pete had told her that there used to be actual gardens here. With trees. She supposed it must be true, otherwise, why would it have that name? Through some disused industrial site, finally coming to a halt outside a single isolated building.

"Want me to wait?" she asked as he dashed from the vehicle. Thought she caught a 'yeah'.

She plugged a microfilament from the dash into her forearm port. A syrupy voice inside her head — *Virtual cigarettes — for that healthier life choice.* She inhaled; habitual behaviour in response to pseudo stimulus, and looked at the place her ride had dashed into. Weeds occupied cracks in the paving. Single-storey building. Looked like a cross between a retro-style diner and a bunch of shipping containers. Polished chrome, once — hints glinting between rust and painted and cracked facade. Above the door, she could just make out part of a faded sign — Museum. She lowered the driver's window. A museum? Out here? Museum of what? Warm air hurried into the cool interior. The smell of dust. A hint of the not-too-distant river. If loneliness had an odour, this was it. She removed the dash port jack, pulled the small, black box from her pants pocket, and transferred to her Memory Loop. *'Just ch-ch-checking you're still real.' 'Of course, I'm real, ho-neeeee—'* the voices stretched into distorted bass. Her ride came walking out just then. Relieved. Like someone who had visited the bathroom. She whipped the jack out.

"Everything okay?" she asked as he settled back onto the rear seat. He nodded. His face was dry now. Looked like he'd washed it. "Back to Trinity Heights?" She started the cab.

"A drink. Anywhere. Any bar," he said.

He was silent the whole trip back. It took longer, the traffic heavier as more workers left at the end of their daily shifts. She pulled up outside The Furnace, a place she frequented, assuming he would want somewhere quiet.

"Join me." His request surprised her. "Come on, you must take a break some time."

You never fraternised with customers. You didn't want that sort of relationship, where they later used your 'friendship' as a bargaining tool for fare reductions. Plus, it was just weird. She shook her head. She'd go home. Alone. Jack in. Lie awake all night. Remembering.

"Listen," he said. "I got an eye for people. Y'know, facial tics, body language. Pardon me if I'm prying, but you look like someone who could do with a drink yourself. I sure as hell do. Drinking alone is crap. I promise I won't ask you to reduce my fare."

He must have read her mind, she thought. Her eyes went to the holowatch. Six-ten. Been on shift eleven hours, forty minutes. Fuck it. She parked the cab around the corner in an overnight bay. Followed him into the bar. Low-hanging light over each table. Gave the place an intimate feel despite its size. They took a two-seater next to the window. Ordered drinks. Sat in silence until the waiter returned.

"Cheers," he raised his glass and swallowed half before she had sipped hers. He let out a satisfied sigh. "Needed that."

For two hours, she and Frake; *first name Albert, don't like it, call me Frake,* consumed two bottles of house wine along with a selection of ales and liquors. As though each was trying to outdo the other. Very few words had been exchanged. But now, she stared at his blurred face as he said,

"I was returning my wife."

She thought she had misheard. Didn't respond. Frake took it as a sign to continue. Words slurring, hiccoughing intermittently, wiping tears. He was a PR man. Widowed. Told her the museum was a front for something else. It was a secret place where souls were stored. She spurted ale when she laughed. If she hadn't had a cavernous evening of sleeplessness before her, and if he'd been dressed like one of those Neo Dropout freaks, she'd have left. Souls! What a load of bollocks. We live, we die, and that's the end of it.

"Seriously." Hurt expression. "It's real," insistent. "They keep the souls of the dead. You can rent them out for a limited time. I heard about it from a colleague whose kid had died. Be with them again. Feel their company." He glanced up warily, "Talk to them." He spoke of Laura's smile. Laura's laughter. The way her nose wrinkled across the bridge when she giggled. She'd been killed in a hit and run. Sudden. Shocking. So young.

"Bull. Shit." He was having a joke at her expense. But he promised it was true. Outside the bar, he repeated something he'd said earlier.

"I can tell, y'know. When you've lost someone, you learn to see it in other people's faces. You lost someone too. Didn't you?"

She dismissed him. Angry. Caught the loop-train home. Lay on the rumpled bed. Plugged in her microfilament.

'Just ch-checking you're still real,' her own recorded voice said.

'Of course, I'm real, honey.'

Imagined the touch of his fingers on her cheek. She closed her eyes. He smiled and leaned in to kiss her. No contact. Loops were made from collected recordings, simulations, and holopics. You couldn't replicate physicality. His image flickered. This generally indicated a display driver issue. Or prolonged use.

'Remember … … on that river cruise last summer?' he smiled.

'Of course, I do.' "Of course, I do." She spoke the words over her own.

Creating the Memory Loop had been a costly and time-consuming endeavour. She couldn't afford the fees of the ML Corp, so she'd paid a Street Looper. Guys who had the skills, but not all the swanky tech of MLC. It was still pricey. Black-market tech didn't come cheap; the Loopers, Docs and Modders had overheads too, y'know. She and the engineer had sat through hours of fragmented voice recordings; from Michael's workplace, submitted by friends, and family — at least those sympathetic to Serina's request. Original video and audio recordings worked the best. But some people had False Memories, FMs, created. The pitch, rhythm and cadence of the deceased's voice were easily copied using old deep fake tech. She had requested a couple of alterations; nothing much. When Michael had knelt to propose at a friend's dinner party, she'd spluttered, 'Are you for real?' The friend had recorded it. His response only needed the 'for' removed to give her a starter to her 'Memory'. It was a patchwork substitute at best. Her responses were then recorded. The editing was tedious. If you were lucky enough to have enough data, a whole day's worth of conversations could be reconstructed. She'd had her Memory Loop designed so that her voice was quieter than Michael's. Speaking the words out loud just felt more real. At the time, it was all she had wanted — the memories.

'*You wore that....*' Laugh. Blip. '*And then you bloody well jumped in the river. Wearing it!*'

'*It was...*'

'*... dress.*'

'*Who cares?*'

Blip. '*Of course, I'm real, honey.*' Back to the bloody beginning.

She yanked the jack free. Sat up, quick. Sobbing uncontrollably. God, she missed him so much, it hurt like physical pain. Shitty fucking technology. In two years, it had fragmented horribly. He's gone, gone, gone. Shitty waste. "It's not fucking fair!" she wailed at the unadorned walls.

It played on her mind. She continued her twelve-hour shifts. *Keep busy. That's the thing.* Was on her way to get her Memory Loop upgraded when she saw Frake again. She was drinking coffee outside one of the generic multi-national corporation outlets. Maybe she should go for the Physical Interactive Hologram? That way, she'd get to see him with her eyes open. Be able to interact with him, to a limited degree. But the prices were horrendous. A shadow fell across her pad. Glancing up, she saw a vaguely familiar face. Vaguely, because her memory of it was wobbly and distorted through an alcohol-fuelled haze.

"Hi," Frake raised a hand hesitantly. "Remember me?"

She nodded. He seemed relieved. They exchanged pleasantries. Small talk. And then, before she knew what was coming out of her mouth, she asked him about the museum. He told her that he had been visiting for six months. Since Laura had passed. He did it fortnightly. Was looking forward to his next one.

"What's it like?" she asked.

"Like nothing else."

"What d'you mean?"

"You know those Memory Loops?" he gestured to her forearm. "And those Interactive Holos? Better than that."

"Better? How?"

"Because they're *real*. It's *them*. Not a memory, or a copy. It *is* Laura." His excitement was evident. Infectious.

"Can't be. They're…" she couldn't say it.

"Dead," he whispered. She winced. "I know. I'm sorry. But believe me. I know my Laura. They found a way to contain the human soul."

It preoccupied her for days. *They found a way to contain the human soul.* She tried to keep busy. Worked more hours. Sought distraction. Visited late-night cinema shows to keep her from lying in bed — *their* bed. Drank too much. Paced her room, eyes darting to the holoportrait of him on her dressing table. *They found a way to contain the human soul.*

Finally, she drove out there.

The inside matched the exterior. Run-down, ill-lit. Cases lining the walls displayed bits and pieces from a bygone age. Radio parts. Components from digital devices. Part of a satellite dish. Gateway switches, faster than light transmission relays, and a 'multi-port power amplifier', whatever that was. One glass display stand held a torpedo-shaped thing. Sleek, silver, shaped like a dolphin without fins or tail. About the size of her forearm from elbow to wrist. 'Primary Connection', the exhibit label read. The impression was that someone had created an amateur exhibit of their private collection of junk. No wonder it was neglected. About to leave — what a waste of time, Frake had been screwing with her — she noticed a man sitting on a chair with his back against one wall, reading. No one else was in the museum.

Feeling nervous, stupid, she asked, "What is all this?" He told her it was all about communication.

"How marvellous," he said, "and baffling, that humans were able to create some of the most sophisticated communication hardware, and yet were unable to actually listen to one another. Let alone visitors." He waffled on about this piece and that to the point that she became irritable and bored.

"And this is it? I thought..." gesturing around the small room. He gave her an odd look. His eyes were the colour of moss in the dim lighting. Why had she come? he asked. Told him someone had recommended it. Was she disappointed? To be honest, yes. She had hoped for more. Maybe she was interested in their 'special' collection? She nodded solemnly.

A heavy door in the back wall. He keyed into a pad beside it. It slid open on well-maintained hinges. He ushered her through. Pleasantly cool, the lighting muted. The walls were painted a relaxing shade of deep blue. An unfamiliar sense of calm came upon her.

"Hello, can I help you?" A woman with vibrant green eyes smiled warmly.

There was nothing on the walls to indicate what the interior held, simply the words *Found Souls*, in a white, flourishing font above the slick reception desk. The smell of the previous room, the river and the dust were missing. In fact, there seemed an absence of odour. Reminded her of the ICU. She swallowed back the tears.

Still staring at the white words, said "Hi." What was she supposed to say? Felt like she'd been given access to a secret club; maybe this was true. Was she meant to offer a codeword?

"Please, take your time." The woman indicated a chair. Serena sat. "I'm the Museum custodian, and we aim to keep our customers, both parties, content." What the hell did she mean by that? Serina suddenly felt she had made a mistake. Looked around for hidden cameras. Was it an elaborate joke after all? The custodian continued, "I understand that, on your first time, you might be nervous. It's a tricky thing to get to grips with, isn't it?" She sat beside Serina. "Most people first come because it was recommended."

"I never heard of you before a couple of weeks ago," Serina said, guarded.

"We don't exactly advertise. We're a relatively new enterprise. Doctors Landro and Foyle wanted to be certain everything worked."

"Worked?"

"Of course. One wouldn't want to have contact with the deceased without assurances."

"Of course." Serina glanced around again.

"And we need to ensure everyone's safety."

"Safety? You mean it's dangerous?"

The woman smiled amiably. "No. Not if instructions are followed."

Alanna, the custodian, asked a huge list of questions, checking off responses on some hi-tech data device unfamiliar to

Serina. Who had told her about the museum? Had she any medical conditions? Did she believe in an afterlife? How many friends did she have? Any living family members? Did she get on with her neighbours? Her age. Her weight. Her daily habits. How long ago had Michael been killed?

Once Serina had recovered and wiped her eyes with the proffered towelette, she was taken through a set of doors that whispered open, quiet as HushCabs seating. Down a short flight of steps, and into a large room of slim display cabinets. There were three other people in here, talking to whatever the cabinets held. Alanna left her alone, giving her time to reach a definite decision. Serina walked slowly to the nearest case. Inside was a holograph of a girl. About six years old, with short reddish hair and wearing silver dungarees. Serina watched her wave and then hopscotch forward, before jumping back to the start. Wave. Hop. Inside the locked glass door, a discrete plaque displayed the name, *Rebekka Wilmot*. Attached to it was a small, silver fish-shaped object about the size of her little finger. Two of the three other visitors sat at a different display and waved to an elderly man sitting on a riverbank, fishing. They each had a tiny 'fish' stuck to their right temple. They were having a conversation — this was *not* a hologram. At least if it was, Serina thought, it was a bloody brilliant one.

On one of the cases, she pressed a button on the plinth. Serina listened to a woman's voice describe how her life had changed since her brother had come back into her life. How the museum had helped the pain to go. She couldn't praise the staff enough. The third person spoke to her as he was leaving. He was the father of the soul over there — he indicated a young man, waving. The father's overjoyed words at receiving his son back struck her hard. The accident had destroyed the family, he told her, but the museum had healed it. He sang the praises of the doctors. Of the technology. Couldn't thank them enough for allowing him more time with his son. He seemed genuinely happy as he bade her farewell and left.

"The families kindly allowed us to exhibit their loved ones so that others can see the potential. Get a feel for what one will experience. They really don't mind if you interact with them." Alanna walked back into the room. "But most want to keep things private, understandably. Not everyone wants to share their discovery or join with their loved ones. Or they don't want to *yet*."

"You mean," Serina didn't know how to pose her question. "The souls of these people are, where? In those little things stuck on their temples? How? I don't understand. Haven't they gone to

Heaven?" aware that she sounded like a kid. Felt the blush flare across her face and chest. Heaven. When did she, Serina Esther Cosgrove, ever believe in Heaven, or life after death in any form for that matter? *We live, we die, and that's the end. Isn't it?*

Alanna explained, in plain language. One's loved one's souls did go to the next place beyond here, wherever that was. Doctors Landro and Foyle had developed ways to tap into the *ethereal realm*, as she put it. Serina thought it sounded like bullshit. Communication technology had advanced beyond anything anyone could have suspected. Contact had been made accidentally, originally. And when the first souls came willingly, they saw it as a way to alleviate much loneliness and suffering in the world. *A way to make a fortune, more like,* Serina imagined.

"Think of it as an advanced Memory Loop," Alanna said. "Except they are with you, in real-time. Because the souls of the dead are untethered to a geographic location, they can actualise where we are."

"Like a hologram?"

"A thousand times better," Alanna affirmed. "Because they're with you like they were in life."

She didn't understand a lot of what the custodian spoke about. Serina swung from scathing scepticism to wanting to believe. Souls weren't real, she kept telling herself. But what if I'm wrong? What if it's true? What if she could have some 'real' time with Michael? Found herself babbling about the terrible assault. Attackers never identified.

"At the funeral, I just sat there thinking, 'It's not real. He can't be dead…' "

She felt strangely unburdened afterwards. The whole business seemed crazy. The custodian suggested a trial run. Free. *It's probably a new holo-tech,* Serina theorised. But decided, as it was a free offer, to see what it was all about. She went ahead and gave Michael's details to Alanna. She was given a Soul Relay Coil or SRC, as it was called, and instructions. Signed a contract that her eyes skimmed but her brain barely registered.

She was given a private room. Where she could 'meet', her Soul Mate again. Tastefully and simply decorated, it contained only two chairs and a short sofa. She took out the 'coil'. It came in two parts. Less coil, more fishlike, it was definitely metal, but it lay soft and light in her palm. Its outer surface was articulated so that it moved fluidly when she flexed her hand. The other side flat and a little slick to the touch. The second part, which went into her ear, was a pea-sized ball on a kind of rubber silicone earpiece. She reread the instructions and attached the earpiece. The other adhered to her temple, forming itself to the contours. How the hell was this supposed to even create a hologram? She was still fairly certain that the whole thing was a hoax perpetrated to cash in on the bereaved.

"Hello?" She waited. "Are you there, Michael?"

Something whacked the side of her head. It went dark. When she opened her eyes, he was sitting on the sofa.

"Oh!" Was all she could manage.

"Hi, sugar."

Despite her incredulity, her uncertainty, Serina approached the image of Michael. He looked as he always had. Tentatively, half hopeful, half expecting her suspicion that it was all fake to be proved true, and readying herself for disappointment, she reached out. Her hand made contact. She snatched it back. Frightened and incredulous. He remained composed, waiting. Serina swallowed down the lump in her throat. Bit her thumb, hard. She was awake, they hadn't drugged her, as she'd begun to suspect. He tilted his head and raised his eyebrows. She dived forward, expecting him to vanish in a puff. Imagined. A dream. Her arms closed around his neck. She smelt his cologne. His hair was slightly musky from labouring at the factory. He was solid.

"Oh," her breath stilted, gasping. Thought she might faint. "Michael. It's really you?"

He embraced her the way he used to. Kissed the tip of her ear. "It's me, Serina. What took you so long?"

She cried in his arms for an age. They sat on the sofa, she awkwardly curled on his lap, her knees almost touching her chin, and talked. Not the Memory Loop conversation, but actual words. Remember that summer in Scotland? What a beautiful island. That terrible meal she cooked. Their first autonomous drive car, second-hand junk of course. The time they tried a stasis pod. She laughed until she cried.

"What's it like?" she finally asked.

Michael gave a little shake of the head. "That's something we can't do. Can't tell the living about the other side."

"There are rules in Heaven?" she laughed despite herself.

"Not exactly," he ran his thumb along her cheek, "I can't remember."

"Oh."

Serina had prepared herself for a short visitation — that's what Alanna called the connections to the souls. So, when it ended, she experienced sadness that Michael was not with her anymore, elation that such a thing was possible, but anticipation for next time. Deliriously happy, she returned the SRC and thanked Alanna. The custodian seemed delighted for her, pleased it had worked and that it had eased Serina's pain.

After her first 'freebie', she had hesitated about trying again. After the initial exhilaration had worn off, she had begun to question whether what she had experienced was an illusion. The logical portion of her brain argued that it was not real. The soul isn't real. It was simply super advanced technology. It happens all of the time. Scientists and engineers are always producing new things. *We live, we die, and that's the end.* But her heart said different. So, it was a while before she returned. Partly, she didn't care because this was definitely way better than the Memory Loop or any hologram she had experienced. It was time with Michael.

She visited every last Friday of the month, for four months. The next time she saw Frake, she thanked him for introducing her to the Museum. He was delighted at her newly rekindled relationship. Told her he was 'seeing' Laura twice a week. "You can feel their heart beating, can't you?" Expression animated. When she asked how come she never saw him at the Museum, he told her that he took Laura home. Serina remembered the cab drive; of course! he'd been holding his SRC then.

"How?" she exclaimed. Desperate.

He told her about the rental system. He said clients were encouraged to take their SRCs home. Gave you a longer connection. Of course, one had to pay more for it — like being a Platinum member of a club. How could he afford it? she asked. He had taken out a loan, several it turned out. Initially wary, she approached Alanna at the end of one of her museum visits and discovered that indeed Frake spoke the truth. Alanna said that Serina and Michael seemed to have made a positive and effective connection. That they were compatible. She did not elaborate, nor did Serina ask what she meant — of course she and Michael were compatible. They had been engaged to be married before his passing. Alanna suggested Serina put in a rental request. This would be reviewed, and a decision reached within the month.

The response was quicker than she expected. "It's to be back by five o'clock the day following use," Alanna said. Serina couldn't wait. It cost her three months' wages. But long hours for two years and no holidays had ensured her funds were sound.

Frake introduced her to a small, discreet group of people who were all soul users. Mostly 'Platinum' members of the museum. They explained how practice had extended the time spent with their loved ones. For seven months, she had returned her SRC on time. How did they manage it? Some had been users since the Museum began operation three years ago. They brushed her concerns aside. What could the custodian do about it once you had the coil? They paid for them, didn't they? Would the Museum send out the reclamation guys, or its version of them? Ha! At a later meeting, Serina was thrilled to learn that some of the group were able to spend whole nights or days with their dearly departed. Their enthusiasm was infectious. Their neurosis and edginess ignored. Moments of disillusion were explained away. Like when three of the members said that their dead spouses had been pressing them for more time together.

It took a few meetings to realise that the group was growing smaller. The long-term users no longer turned up. Then Frake heard that Samuel, the longest user, had been found in a coma in his apartment. It was sad, they agreed, but hadn't he looked ill for a while? Another had completely blanked Frake when he'd waved to her on the street. Like she didn't recognise him, he said.

The times spent with Michael were the best. Better than before, she told herself. How could this be? How could a soul be here, really? Ultimately, it didn't matter. It felt like they had been given a fresh start. It bore absolutely no comparison to the ML or a hologram. She could touch him, smell him. This was not a recording. This was Michael in the flesh. Often, he couldn't remember events she reminisced about. Sometimes his eyes seemed to look through, not at, her. But she did not care. She could hold him again. Kiss him. Properly. Not like the stupid Memory Loop. Warm and heart-meltingly romantic in a way he had never been in life. He was, she believed, more amorous than when he had been alive. It was to be expected, she supposed, that someone who had experienced death and Heaven would have peculiarities. She ignored them all. She was more in love with Michael than she ever had been. She told herself it was because it was his soul she was with, the body thrown aside had left the best of him. He wanted to be with her more than ever. Talked of them staying together.

Serina seldom used the HushCabs canteen. A tiny room to the rear of the basement office in a multi-storey complex. Work had lost what little attraction it previously held. But she needed the money now. She poured coffee.

"Hasn't been seen for weeks." Kal leaned back on his chair. "Probably in a mental health lockup by now."

"You talk a lot of hooey," Pete said.

"It's true. They get addicted." Kal said.

"What's that?" Serina said, sitting next to Pete.

Pete shoved his pad into a pocket. Reached for his cab keycard, "Kal says a bloke he knows was communing with his dead missus. Claims he got some device or other from a shady customer, who said he could actually see her again. Can you believe that?" Pete guffawed and headed out.

Kal studied Serina over the rim of his mug. She avoided his gaze. "You know what I'm on about, don't you?" He placed the mug on the table, both hands wrapped around it.

"What d'you mean?"

"You didn't bat an eye when Pete told you. You didn't laugh."

"So?"

Kal regarded her some more. "Don't tell me you're onto it too. Serina! Please don't tell me you're 'in touch' with Michael," making air quotes. His expression slid from exasperation to concern.

She claimed not to know what Kal was talking about. Denied knowledge of the *fucking Soul device*, as he put it. Finally admitted that she had been in touch with her dead fiancé. Kal was furious. Called her stupid. Said she was meddling in things that she didn't understand. The bastards touting the idea couldn't understand.

"How can we," he gestured, all-encompassing, "have an inkling of the afterlife? How do we know where souls go, or what they are? We know nothing. And we shouldn't be meddling in their affairs, Serina!"

"But, Kal," she felt tears welling.

"It's some crackpot con by some bloody quack! Or worse."

"No. It's him. It really is. I didn't believe it at first, but —"

"Serina, listen to me, honey." He took one of her hands in his large, calloused ones. "I know it's terribly hard, especially for a young one like you. I know what it's like. I lost my Gina ten years back. Do I miss her? Every single day. Does it hurt? Absolutely. Would I like to see her again? Of course, I bloody would. But alive, honey. Not this mockery of a human soul, or whatever it is they're fobbing you off with."

"It is him. It's Michael. He remembers everything from his life, from our life together. It's not a mockery." She knew it wasn't true as she said it. Michael didn't remember everything. But wasn't that to be expected when a person had been dead two years?

Kal sighed and stood. "If you know what's good for you, you'll stay away from whoever deals with this tripe and try to carry on without him. It's what's natural."

After a whole intoxicating evening with Michael, Serina thought about what Kal had said to her. Nonsense. She and Michael were better than ever. Happier than before. His memory returned with each reminder. Michael had assisted her efforts to extend the time they spent together. Alanna had, surprisingly, been understanding about the late returns of the SRC. Of course, there was a surcharge, but she seemed remarkably flexible. Kal warned Serina it was addictive. Michael called Serina his addiction. Kal accused her of living in a fantasy. Michael confessed he believed they had been given a new chance. Kal talked about living with the pain of loss. Michael said they could be together forever. Kal told her there was no such thing as forever.

Michael said,

"I love you." He was perfect. "Don't return me tomorrow," he said.

Serina considered his suggestion as she sat outside the Museum, engine ticking over, the device in the palm of her hand. Hadn't seen Frake for months. The members of the group had dwindled to two; Serina and a bloke called Douglas. He said that the others had succeeded in permanently uniting with their loved ones. She recalled Kal's words in the canteen: 'Probably in the mental health lockup by now.'

She lay on her bed. Attached the Soul Relay Coil. Michael arrived instantly. Quicker each time, she noticed. His beautiful lips curved in a smile. His blue eyes shone green from the neon sign across the street.

"My love."

"Darling."

"Have you decided?" he whispered, lips brushing her ear.

Serina sighed. "I have. I will."

"You're sure? You want us to stay together forever?"

She kissed him passionately. "I do!" Michael lay down beside her. "Will it hurt?"

She closed her eyes and felt a sensation of something passing over her. Felt Michael's presence more intensely, growing, encompassing. Like he had lain on top of her and was sinking through her skin, her muscle, her bones. Deliciously intoxicating. She half opened her eyes. His face close above her. Concentrating. *Relax*, she heard his voice in her head. I*t's easier if you just let go.* She shuddered as if jarred on a bumpy road. He was inside all of her, and she was being squeezed into a smaller and smaller part of herself. Could feel Michael's soul pressing hers down. A hint of panic. *Is this death?* she wondered. Soothing overtures. An invisible finger on her lips. *I'm disappearing.* Smaller and smaller. Saw blue sparks ahead, pulsing gently.

For some reason, she thought about the arcane communication debris she'd seen at the museum. The weird silver

'Primary Connection' exhibit. It was all about communication, the attendant said. *Or lack of.* She saw Alanna's green eyes as she said that they were compatible. Soul Relay Coil — the word Relay repeating in her dwindling mind. What did they mean by 'relay'? What was being relayed?

Michael's infiltrating tones. She hadn't listened. *We* hadn't listened. Relay. To pass on, to receive. All those things in space. All those unanswered signals that people said were stuff and nonsense. We just didn't listen properly.

Tendrils reached forth, tickling inside her head, making a connection. Momentarily, she and he were harnessed together. Two in one. *Relax, it's easier if you just let go.* But suddenly, felt like she was sliding down a water park slide. Corkscrewing into ever tighter circles. *Easier for whom?* came the thought. Realising, too late that Michael — no, not Michael, an interloper, a liar, *an other*, occupied her body. *They found a way to contain the human soul.* Who, the thought slipped like silk into her mind, were *They?* Green eyes passed before her; the attendant, the custodian. Michael. And her conscious mind, her soul, was entering the SRC.

She didn't even have a mouth with which to cry out.

See Alexandra Peel's story "Love, Death, and the Electric Soul"
online at Metaphorosis.
If you liked it, leave a comment. Authors love that!
Remember to subscribe to our e-mail updates so you'll know when
new stories are posted.

About the story

Love makes the world go around, or so they say. Love connects. Romantic love combined with pragma binds us. Death is common to us all, and yet can isolate individuals. The existence of a soul is still debated, in some circles.

I initially responded to the call for something about a museum. What — I wondered; would be the oddest thing a museum would house? What do we never see in museums and galleries? What, in fact, do we never see? The human soul. I knew it was going to be a futuristic piece immediately.

Then, I thought, but how can we see this elusive thing? Why on earth would anyone want to 'capture' it, display it, rent it out? There had to be an ulterior motive. I saw this clapped-out building in my mind. Nothing exciting — but what lay inside was going to change the lives of those who entered it in a way they could barely imagine. Then I imagined a person who does not believe in the soul, but they're in so much emotional pain, that they will grab onto anything to ease it.

Serina came fully formed, sitting in her taxi. Her fiancé is dead. She is alone in the world. Holograms and electronic memories don't cut it anymore for her. She desperately wants her fiancé back — and a chance meeting provides her with access to the museum's secret. I saw a photograph of the Allen Telescope Array in California, of the SETI institute and wondered what if 'they' have made contact — and we simply didn't understand? And decided to combine it with the very human — what would happen to someone who does not believe in an afterlife, or a soul, 'We live, we die and that's the end.' Serina says, who then encounters one — or does she?

A question for the author

Q: Is there a specific environment you find most conducive to writing, and is it different for different kinds of scenes?

A: These days I like silence. It's hard to come by what with the neighbours' dogs, shouting, music and so on. I often wear headphones and have some music playing very quietly to try and drown out extraneous noise. The music is always relevant to the story I am working on, so I research and make a short playlist each time. I have collections of film scores, sci-fi sounds, 17th century lute music, protest songs and Elizabethan pieces. I'm working in my daughter's old bedroom at the moment, which is painted white. The wall before me contains maps of the world I invented for a historical fantasy novel. Sketches of towns, an inset map, showing a detailed part of the map at a larger scale. And lots of sticky post-it notes. The from the window view is an uninspiring one of other people's houses — so I look at the sky above the roofs.

About the author

Alexandra is a visual artist turned author. She has a degree in Fine Art: Sculpture. She has been a freelance artist, community artist, graphics tutor and bookseller. She currently works as a Learning Support practitioner in a F.E/H.E college. She hails from the sunny island of Britain!

www.sticksandstonesbooks.com, @AlexandraPeel

Snowman

Han Whiteoak

Meltwater dripped from the snowman's carrot nose as he boarded the train. A soggy red scarf hung around his neck as he slid down the aisle like a melting glacier, leaving a glistening wet trail.

Alma elbowed her dad. "Look!"

Dad was skimming the headlines on his tablet. She knew without looking that they were bad — fires here or floods there. Gran, whom they were going to visit, would have been ranting about the state of the world, but Dad read quietly, giving only a little nasal sigh every now and again.

He sighed now as he glanced up. "Don't point, Alma. It's rude."

As the snowman slid past Alma, she gave him an encouraging smile. With one twiggy hand, he stiffly raised his bobble hat at her. It settled back on his head as he headed for a seat behind them on the shady side of the train.

Alma, who had twisted around in her seat to watch, turned back to Dad. "Where's he going?"

"North, I guess."

"Why?"

"It still snows up there."

That morning, a freak snowstorm had delayed their train leaving the city. The passengers, stamping their feet on the platform, had complained. *Snow like the olden days*, they'd said. *So much for global warming.*

The train clunked back into motion. Outside the window, the snow was already melting, dripping from the early-budding trees. Alma pulled off her jumper and stuffed it under her seat. It was the first time they'd been to visit Gran since coastal flooding had damaged the railway line. There had been a lot of debate, which they'd followed closely through the TV, over whether the damage was worth repairing, as the same thing was likely to happen again. Dad had fretted, phoned Gran, fretted some more. "She's raging herself into an early grave over all this," he'd said. Finally, the track had been fixed, new defenses had been erected, and now they were on their way.

Alma kept sneaking glances at the snowman. She could remember only one winter where it had snowed enough to build one. Gran had tutted at Alma's inexperience and shown her how to roll the snow into a ball almost as big as herself. Gran had lifted a smaller ball on top to make the snowman's head, and hoisted Alma up so she could give him eyes and mouth and nose. Draping her favourite red scarf around his neck, Alma had whispered a promise to the snowman that they'd be friends forever. But by the following morning, he had melted to a pile of slush.

The snowman on the train quietly dripped. He pushed and pulled at the window, trying to open it. One twiggy arm splintered with the effort, leaving his hand dangling by a strip of bark. Half-melted, his mouth sagged to one side, like Gran after she'd fallen from the roof of the town hall, protesting for cleaner air.

The snowman needed help. And yet no one did anything. Dad was engrossed in the latest tragic news story, sighing and shaking his head. When she said, "Dad, do you think we should..." he put a finger to his lips without looking up.

Alma had promised to be good today. When Dad said be good, he meant she should be quiet and not trigger one of his headaches. But Gran said goodness was more than that. It was about helping people who needed it. Alma wasn't sure whether a snowman counted as people, but that part didn't seem as important as the part about the helping. Pulling a band from her plaited hair, she slid off her seat and approached the snowman, who turned to her with sad coal eyes.

"It's alright," she said. "I want to help."

He stared at her blankly. She pointed at his broken arm. He held it out. It was covered in scaly lichen, which scratched her fingers as she took his dangling hand and bound it as best she could.

A murmur hummed through the carriage. When Alma looked up, Dad was standing over her. "Leave it alone, love. Come and sit down."

She looked at the snowman, beads of water running down his head, and back at her father. "He's melting."

"I know, but there's nothing we can do."

Alma knew she shouldn't make a scene. But she couldn't ignore the snowman. With lots of help from her medical team, Gran had recovered, so that now her face was nearly symmetrical again. Surely the snowman could get better too?

She pulled herself up to her full height, the top of her head level with Dad's chest. "Gran says I should always help when I can."

Dad looked tired. When he opened his mouth, Alma was sure he was about to order her to sit down, but then he said gently, "That's true. She does say that." He sighed. "Well, then. What should we do?"

Alma reached past the snowman and pulled open the window. The breeze sent the melted drops on the snowman's cheeks streaming back towards the seat. He didn't look any colder.

She thought for a moment. "We can get the train staff to turn the heating down!"

Newspapers rustled. Whispers hissed. Dad looked embarrassed.

"Excuse me," an old woman protested. "I've just taken off my coat."

"Can't you put it back on?" Alma said. "Look!"

The snowman's nose drooped. As his face softened, hollows opened around his eyes, which threatened to topple from their sockets. His hat slid from his head and landed soggily in the aisle. The other passengers pretended to be absorbed in phones or books.

"Very sad." The woman barely glanced at the snowman. "But what can I do?"

Alma glared and crossed her arms.

"Well, now," said an old man, whose dog had snatched up the snowman's hat and started chewing on it. "Perhaps we could take a vote."

Grown-ups never did anything without a lot of talking. Each person gave their opinion on the temperature in the carriage, and then repeated it, louder, when someone else disagreed. Frustrated, Alma fanned the snowman with her book. It didn't help.

"What's the point in talking about this?" said one passenger.

"We'd have to get all the other carriages to agree," said another. "It'll never happen."

"I don't think it's warm, anyway," said the old woman. She pulled her fur coat across her like a blanket and glowered over it, red-faced.

The discussion went round in circles. Every time the passengers neared agreement, someone piped up that the snowman didn't look so bad.

"It was dribbly when it boarded," said the old woman. "You can't blame us for that."

"Snowmen have always melted," said the dog owner. "It's natural."

"That's not true," said Alma.

But no one listened.

The snowman slumped against the window. He looked smaller than before. Couldn't they see this was urgent?

"Come on," Dad said. "This is our stop."

Alma looked out at the slushy platform. "Wait!" Gently, she cradled what was left of the snowman and carried him out. He was so shrunken that he weighed barely anything. She had to support his head so it didn't topple off his shoulders. His meltwater soaked her gloves.

They stepped onto the platform and made their way towards the station exit. Dad had his hand firmly on Alma's shoulder. He was looking around for Gran. Arms full of the snowman, Alma wiped her tears on her opposite shoulder.

The snowman was dripping through her fingers. She laid him on a drift beside the station entrance. Travellers stamped past, not caring.

"What's that?" said a voice. "You can't leave that there. It's littering."

Dad stepped between Alma and the station worker. "It's a snowman that was on the train. My daughter wanted to help."

"Aye, my kids are into all that too," the man said.

Alma ignored him. She straightened the snowman's buttons and dug his carrot nose into the snow so it stood upright. She took off her hat and laid it where the top of his head should be. He was so melted it was hard to tell, but she thought she saw a smile ripple across his face.

"Looks like he's had it," the man said. He sounded almost gleeful about it. "If you don't want to keep the bits as a souvenir, there's a bin over there."

Alma's hands balled into fists. She whirled around, ready to tell the man he was a heartless idiot, but caught sight of a hunched figure making her way across the car park, leaning on her stick.

"Gran!"

She ran over, wrapped her arms around the old woman's waist and, in sniffling sobs, told her the whole story. The station worker backed away as Gran turned her steely gaze on him.

"Now then," she said, once he'd gone. "Who have we here?"

The snowman was no more than a carrot, a blood-red scarf, and a few discarded lumps of coal.

"I'm sorry," Alma said. "I tried to help, but I failed."

"No," said Gran. "You didn't fail. You let him know someone cares. That counts for a lot."

"But he died. I couldn't even make the people on the train listen."

"Well," Gran said, straightening up to her full height. "Getting people to listen is harder than saving even one snowman. But that doesn't mean it's not worth a try."

"Mother..." Dad said.

"Hush," she said. "By the sound of it, you've been no use."

"I didn't stop her," Dad protested.

"Never mind not stopping her. What were you doing to help?" She took Alma's hand and started to lead her across the car park. "Now, I know a thing or two about making people listen."

Dad trailed along behind them, carrying their heavy bag. Alma snuggled into her grandmother's side, wiping her tears on the old lady's coat. She had the feeling they were about to start something important.

See Han Whiteoak's story "Snowman" online at Metaphorosis.
If you liked it, leave a comment. Authors love that!
Remember to subscribe to our e-mail updates so you'll know when
new stories are posted.

About the story

When asked to write about the origins of "Snowman", I actually couldn't remember how the story started. After looking back through an old notebook, I realized that the original idea came from a *Furious Fiction* prompt:

- Your story must take place on a TRAIN.
- Your story must include something FROZEN.
- Your story must include three 3-word sentences in a row.

Furious Fiction accepts entries of up to 500 words which must be submitted two days after the prompts are released. The version I entered was much shorter and less well developed than the final story that appears in *Metaphorosis*. Alma, Dad, and Gran didn't appear at all. Instead, unnamed train passengers talked about the snowman but refused to help him.

Around the same time, I was taking a short story course taught by Emily Devane through the organisation Comma Press. Emily set a homework exercise to write about "an unexpected thing in a normal setting." I chose to keep working on this story, adding Alma and her father and bringing it up to around 900 words.

After a bit more reworking, I submitted Snowman to *Metaphorosis*. Editor B. Morris Allen liked it but pointed out that it was more of a mood piece than a story. During edits, Gran's role became much stronger. I realised she had a potential as a mentor and could be the catalyst to turn this emotional encounter with a snowman into a life-changing event for Alma.

I'd always thought of this story as a climate change metaphor, with the snowman as the "elephant in the room" that everyone was determined to ignore. One goal during edits was to make this theme more obvious.

A question for the author

Q: How do pets/children/significant others help/hinder your process?

A: Not having a partner, children or pets frees up time for writing, although I often give in to the urge to take a break and go to the park where I can watch other people's dogs run around happily. My best friend, who is a big fan of the *Metaphorosis* podcast, is always happy to read my stories and discuss them in detail. However, as he knows me so well, he often predicts plot twists or understands what I mean even when I've explained it badly. I'm in a couple of writing groups so I can get a range of feedback.

About the author

Han Whiteoak is a speculative fiction writer living in Sheffield, England. They have a degree in physics, a passion for the Peak District, and an incurable habit of borrowing more library books than it is possible to read during the loan period.

www.hanwhiteoak.me, @hanwhiteoak

Infinite Possibilities IV

Michael Gardner

A mystery USB leads Adrian to a cabin, where Other Adrian appears on an old television. Other Adrian is a version of himself from a parallel world. He encourages Adrian to build a machine that will facilitate travel to Other Adrian's world. Other Adrian informs him that his agent will be in contact.

Adrian has just found out his wife, Candice, is having an affair. He meets Other Adrian's agent, who turns out to be a woman, Taylor, that Adrian had a brief relationship with years ago. Taylor convinces him to confront Candice about her affair, and to go with Taylor to Other Adrian's world.

Adrian fights with Candice. He completes the machine, and with Taylor, leaves Candice to return to the cabin.

4

As Taylor inserts her key into the padlock, Adrian glances back over the canola toward the housing estate, and Taylor's car parked on the verge of the empty road. Night has fallen, but the moon is full, and casts the scene in a soft, silvery glow. There is no wind. It's almost as if the world is holding its breath with anticipation. It makes Adrian nervous. Hairs raise on his arms, his heart quickens.

He turns back to see Taylor slide the chain from the gate and drop it to the ground. She pushes the gate inward, waits for Adrian to enter.

The machine is deceptively heavy, seemingly getting heavier the longer he carries it. His forearms burn. He moves with quick, stuttering steps up onto the deck. He has to wait again for Taylor to catch up, to open the cabin door. Inside, nothing has changed. Thick wooden walls, the old kitchenette, the metal bed frame at one end. In the middle of the room is the television on the stand, the rug, the armchair. A slice of suburbia in a nineteenth century cabin.

He can't hold the machine any longer. His arms are numb. He lurches inside, half places, half drops his creation onto the rug.

"Careful," Taylor exclaims. She's quickly at his shoulder, running a hand over the casing like it's a wounded pup. He rises, steps back from it.

"Sorry," he says, wondering why he's apologising.

Taylor's face softens, and she opens her mouth to say something, but the words remain unsaid as her eyes dart toward the television screen. Adrian follows her gaze, and finds it warming up. What was black is now blue and backlit. Shadows resolve into recognisable forms. A thick neck, glasses, pursed lips—Other Adrian's face. And filling the background, strange fleshy protrusions that rise and fall rhythmically, like a sick animal breathing raggedly, but no animal Adrian has ever seen. The room is filled with them. Veined, monstrous masses, shuddering. It makes Adrian feel sick. What the fuck are they? His mind can't process the images.

"You're both here, good," Other Adrian says, commanding Adrian's focus. He swallows. The image on the television zooms, and Other Adrian's face fills the screen.

Taylor takes his hand, and he looks down to see his calloused hand wrapped in her slender fingers. His mouth is dry.

"I see you've completed the machine. Not far from the tree, Adrian," he says, the hint of a smirk on his lips. "Is it operational?"

Before Adrian can answer, Taylor jumps in. "Yes. He's tested the receiver."

Adrian's brow furrows. Her tone is sharp, the husk gone, replaced with an authority he doesn't recognise.

"Show me," Other Adrian says, and Taylor reaches for the machine, but Adrian shakes himself from his fugue and grabs at her wrist, stopping her.

"No, wait. I have more questions. I... I..." What? he thinks. "I'd like to hear again what you are offering."

Other Adrian's eyes move from Taylor to Adrian. He sighs—a disappointed school principal. "We've been through that," he says. Then silence.

Adrian tries again. "Well, what about where you are taking us? What is your world like?" he asks, his eyes darting to the flesh behind Other Adrian. "And how does bringing us there help you discover more about the universe? I'm not a scientist, I'm not smart. And Taylor? You said nothing of her last time—"

"I told you my agent would be in contact."

"Yes, but how did you contact her?"

"We don't have time for this." Then, to Taylor. "Start the receiver."

Taylor pulls free of Adrian. "Don't worry," she says. She looks certain, calm. But why would she be? She leans over and switches the machine on. It starts to hum, and he feels the vibrations of it in his skin, in his bones, his brain. His legs go weak.

"But how do you know?" he croaks, his voice not sounding like his own. Is it happening already? Taylor places hands on his shoulders, guides him backward. He wants to resist, but his legs won't obey. They move of their own accord. His heart feels like it's pumping gelatine. He bumps up against the armchair, his knees go, and he slumps into the chair.

"There you go," Taylor says, placing his useless arms in his lap. She holds two fingers against his wrist, and Adrian realises she's taking his pulse.

"What are you doing?" he drawls. His tongue is fat, useless. The saliva's gone, but his eyes water. There's pressure behind them. He looks from Taylor to the television, where Other Adrian grins. Behind him, the tissue is throbbing. It seems to be synchronised with the vibrations of Adrian's machine.

"Why did you need me to build the receiver?" he asks. He wrestles for control of his head, his eyes, he forces them to move to Taylor. "You said Other Adrian sent the television, this chair, the book. So why not just send a receiver?"

He hears a wet, gurgling sound from Other Adrian that he first mistakes as coughing, but realises is laughter. "Oh, finally. You're putting it together. Not as stupid as I suspected."

"The field doesn't support complex machinery," Taylor says. "Only organic matter and inanimate objects." And then, to Other Adrian, "His pulse is steady, breathing normal. Proceed."

Normal, he thinks. His breathing sounds like a jet engine in his ears. His heartbeat is erratic. The air in the room is hot. It's crushing him. Yet none of that is the odd thing, his mind says through the ooze. Why is she reporting to Other Adrian? And then he understands.

"He sent you. You made the modifications to the television once you arrived."

She turns, looks at him coldly. "Yes. And you made the receiver to bring us back."

"You said you were a local historian. You knew about our past."

"Yes."

"You lied?"

"No. Taylor, your Taylor, was a local historian. I found her here. She was… generally cooperative."

"Where is she now then?" he asks.

"With me," she says, tapping her temple.

He doesn't understand. None of this makes sense. He can hear something else now. A squelching. Like the sound of fish slapping against the bottom of a boat. But large fish. Many of them.

And then he feels pressure everywhere, like he's been encircled by the coils of a monstrous python, which squeezes. But the flesh of this snake is warm, not cold. It has fine hairs that tickle his neck and arms, and it is slick with a rancid-scented sweat that makes him want to retch.

He cranes as far as his uncooperative neck allows, but there's nothing behind him. The sensation of something squeezing him remains, though.

There's a jolt, and suddenly he feels like he's in two places at once. The cabin, as well as the room on the other side of the television screen.

"I don't want this," he moans.

There is that phlegmy sound again, Other Adrian's laughter. "Buyer's remorse, that is all. But I promise you, you will be better off here with us."

And as afraid as he is, he wonders. Maybe he's right. Without Candice, what's left? Drifting through life, driving the bus, ignoring a wife that fucks other men?

He sees Candice. She's crying, she's guilty, she's angry. She's trying to get him to pursue university, to find a better career, to take more shifts at work. She's trying to get him to have a little fun, to solve a puzzle that arrived in the post. A puzzle that she thought was a simple game, something that he might enjoy, which turned out to be much more. And yet as he relives that day again, the day he held the USB in his hands, he sees her anew, like he's floating out of body watching them both. She encouraged him. She's always encouraged him. If she doesn't love him, why do that? Why bother? To assuage her guilt? He doesn't buy that.

He hears her voice in his head. No, not in his head. He wrenches his gaze toward the door. Candice is there, eyes wide, pale in the moonlight, her mouth agape.

"What the fuck is…" but she doesn't finish.

"What's she doing here?" Other Adrian growls onscreen. Taylor lunges, and Adrian tries to get his swollen tongue to cooperate long enough to warn her.

But he doesn't need to. She's never really needed him, he realises, and this is no different. While he's still forming the words, Candice steps toward Taylor, not away. He sees her pull her arm back, and then she swings what appears to be one of his shifter spanners hard into Taylor's face. There's a sickening crack, and Taylor's head snaps back, and she collapses at Candice's feet with a heavy thud.

Candice, still brandishing the shifter, shakes. She's looking at Taylor's prone form, then at the screen, then Adrian pinned to the armchair. Her whole body shivers like a mirage.

"It's you," she says so quiet that Adrian almost doesn't hear her. "It's you there... but also..."

"That's not me," are the words he forces from his throat.

She stares at him, her face a ball of worry and confusion. "Adrian?" she asks.

And he's never been so glad to hear his wife say his name. He tries to smile, hopes it doesn't look grotesque. Suddenly their problems seem non-existent. A trifle that he turned into something insurmountable. He's never felt such relief.

From the television screen comes a grunt of annoyance. "Enough," says Other Adrian. There is motion there. Adrian feels a sharp jolt like he's riding a rollercoaster into a vertical loop, g-forces slamming his head against the headrest. It's hard to keep his eyes open.

From Candice, he hears his name again, but it's garbled. He tries to tell her to switch the receiver off. He's not sure he's successful. He feels hands on his shoulders shaking him. He hopes it's her. There's a slap to his face, but it feels distant, and oddly cold, which is nice given the humidity in the air, and the fever heat of the flesh that enfolds him.

He hears Candice's voice once more. Then everything goes black.

The worst thing Adrian ever did was stop Candice seeing her mother the night she died. It wasn't intentional, yet intention didn't change the end result.

He thought Alexia had been getting better. The chemo seemed to have halted the spread of the cancer, and Alexia, over those last few days, had a little more energy. It was Alexia that suggested that he take Candice away for the weekend. A break from work. A break from sickness.

Candice didn't want to go. She wanted to stay close to her mother, just in case. Truth was, Adrian had grown jealous of Alexia over the course of her illness. The majority of Candice's time was allocated to her, not him. It made him wonder how she would be if they had a child. Yet he comforted himself that that would be different. That would be investing time in life, not death. A terrible thought, he knew. But that was what he thought.

He spent more than they could afford to rent an apartment by the beach. He wanted to take Candice near the water so they could try for that kid with the sound of the waves in their ears. A throwback to their first years dating at university, their make-out spot in a mostly empty carpark right on the far end of the main beach. He couldn't recreate it exactly, but he wanted the sound.

The car was packed, ready to go, when Alexia called. Candice picked up after one ring and smiled as she said hello. But as Adrian watched, that smile became a straight line, then a frown. She listened for a long time, then offered to come over, which shouldn't have irritated Adrian as much as it did. But it did. He swallowed, turned away and rapped his fingers on top of the car. Candice glanced at him, shrugged apologetically, listened.

"Okay, Mum. Love you. Bye."

She'd barely hung up the phone when he jumped in, impatient. "What's up?" he asked, staring across the roof of the car.

Candice shook her head, bit her bottom lip, sighed. "She's having nose bleeds, and she's dizzy."

"Oh," he said. He couldn't think of what else to say.

"She says she's okay, she just couldn't find her painkillers…" Candice said, trailing off.

"Well, if she's okay—"

"I don't think she is. She sounded… a little spacey. Her painkillers are in the cupboard over the sink, like they always have been." Candice stepped toward the car, stopped, looked at Adrian. "I think something's wrong. I think we should cancel. We can go next week—"

"Honey," Adrian said. He regretted his tone, but continued anyway. "Alexia's a grown woman. She knows how she feels. I know she's sick, but you're jumping at shadows."

Candice cleared her throat, opened her mouth to say something, but then closed it again without speaking.

"It was her idea, remember? She wants you to have some time to relax. Plus, we're only two hour's drive away. Not far, really. You deserve this. Stop feeling guilty."

She hesitated, then nodded. "You're right. She'd tell me, wouldn't she?"

"Of course, honey." He desperately wanted to get going before it got dark. But he didn't risk pushing her more than he had. He watched her thinking.

"Okay. But I might give her a call in an hour, if you don't mind."

"Of course not. In fact, why don't you call her when we get there, as well?"

She smiled, a sad smile, but a smile nonetheless. She opened the car door and slipped inside. He felt a pang of guilt, a tightness in his belly that gripped him for a moment, but then passed. He wasn't being selfish, he told himself. This was about more than just his enjoyment. It was about their chance to create a family. He slid into the driver's seat, reached over and squeezed Candice's leg. She held her phone tightly in both hands. She looked at him, smiled again. He closed the door with a bang, started the engine, and headed off.

An hour later, when Candice tried to call, they'd hit the mountains and couldn't get reception. So she had to wait until they arrived in the seaside town.

It wasn't Alexia who answered. It was a nurse. She explained that Alexia had called the ambulance, and she'd been admitted to hospital. Her nosebleeds hadn't stopped, and she'd taken a turn. They were doing tests.

Candice was frantic, insisting that they return that night. To his eternal shame, Adrian argued against it, which resulted in her screaming at him.

He relented, eventually, and the trip was conducted in silence. Hers in fear, his in anger.

Alexia passed before they got home.

Adrian wakes to a sensory assault unlike anything he's ever experienced before. Blinding white light. The din of a thousand people talking simultaneously. The scent of ozone, burnt hair. The taste of metal. Cold, and heat. The sharp pain of tiny cuts, followed by tender caresses.

For a time all he can do is freeze, grit his teeth, sweat and hope the feelings disperse. He's a cat encircled in a towel; he doesn't know which way is up, down, or where to head for relief.

Slowly, the cacophony of stimuli dulls. It's still there, but manageable. Which allows him to assess his environment more thoroughly. He quickly identifies greater problems.

What he thinks of as light, he realises he can't actually see. What he thinks of as sound is beyond audible, a presence in his mind, a radio signal through the airwaves, and him the receiver. Taste, touch, scent—all of these things feel intensely familiar, yet different. Non-physical. It's like he's floating in amniotic fluid, inside a giant womb. Yet everything is floating, his insides, his outsides, his thoughts.

He tries to run his hands over his body to soothe his panic, but finds nothing. No body, no hands. He tries to scream, but no sound comes forth. Something creeps into his mind. A whisper: "Adrian."

More panic. He gags on the taste of copper. It recedes, and he back-pedals from the brink of insanity.

"Who... who is that? Where am I? What..." he was going to ask what happened to Candice, but then he remembers. He recalls Other Adrian on the screen, the receiver messing with his head, his body. He felt squeezed, drawn away. But where to? This isn't the other world he was expecting.

"You're in his realm, like all of us," says a voice that feels like his own, but isn't. "Physically subsumed, mentally joined. Part of a hive mind now, but controlled by—"

"—ourselves—" interrupts a second voice.

"—not ourselves. Nothing like ourselves. He's—" comes a third.

"—evil—"

"—manipulative—"

"Other Adrian," Adrian projects.

There's a chorus of voices then, murmuring agreement reflecting back at Adrian the rightness of his description. The voices all sound like him, he thinks: the cadence, the tone, the feel of them.

"You said subsumed," Adrian interjects. The throng hushes slowly, like a crowd at the theatre as the curtains open.

"Yes, bodily subsumed. You can feel it if you concentrate. Reach out and we'll guide you." The voice pauses, waits. Adrian complies, and searches for his physical body; he reaches out with his mind for his hands, his feet, his chest and...

He falls into his body and is instantly crushed by a huge weight. He's damp, hot, surrounded by darkness. He feels intense pressure, then relief, then pressure, like his body is being gummed by a toothless giant. There's no pain as such, but even in his anesthetised state he knows his bones are breaking, and his organs are turning to jelly.

He jerks back hard, finds himself in the white space again. "What the hell?" he hisses.

"Yes, unpleasant."

"But that's impossible, I..."

"Impossible in your world. Impossible in mine as well."

Many more murmur agreement.

"But there are infinite worlds and infinite possibilities. Not all follow the same laws as each other."

Another Adrian chimes in. "In this world, it is better to think of Other Adrian as a large amoeba. An amorphous, creature, able to subsume others into itself. To grow stronger, larger, to learn."

"To feed. On the flesh—"

"—and our minds."

The Adrians allow Adrian a moment to process this. Instead, he pictures Candice coming home from work, finding him at his workbench. She always engaged him first. With small talk, a touch on his shoulder, something. Always first. He'll never have that again.

He's hit by the weight of his stalemate life. Neither moving forward, nor back. Floating. Resenting Candice for pushing him. Pushing him, he sees now, just to live a little more. He could have chosen to do so many things. He thought he'd chosen her. He thought she'd failed him, finding someone else. But it was him, he realises. He begrudged her for changing, for trying new things, for going after her career, for meeting new people, for trying to drag him with her. He begrudged her for mourning her mother. And for putting her grief before his desire for a family. How hadn't he understood this before? He wonders why she stayed.

All of this rushes through his mind like a man given news of a terminal diagnosis. A man forced to reassess his life, knowing it will end soon, and the time to fix his mistakes is insufficient.

"Candice," he thinks, and it's so plaintive, so quiet, he wonders if they even hear. But their murmuring suggests they do. And that they understand.

"Most of us lost her. Nearly all of us."

"But Other Adrian said Taylor was our soulmate."

"Lies," hisses another.

"But don't give up."

"No, don't give up."

"Infinite worlds with infinite love stories better than our own."

Adrian hopes that is true.

"And with your arrival, a final hope."

Adrian's attention is honed, he focusses in on the presence that said those words. "Hope?"

"Yes, hope. But we must act fast. He'll return soon."

"Act? To do what?"

"To overwhelm Other Adrian."

"I don't understand. How?"

"Some of us have been with him for a very long time. Studying, watching, waiting."

"We have found a chink. When he feeds, he exhibits—"

"—weakness. He becomes distracted. When he brings a new Adrian across, for a few moments only, he loosens the tight hold on us, focusses instead on the consummation."

"We've waited."

"Building our forces."

"He's been too powerful for us, as many of us as there are."

"Until now."

"Until now."

"We think."

"We hope."

"We're sure."

"If we all work together."

"We can wrest back control from him, and—"

"Candice. Can I see Candice again?" Adrian asks, desperate.

There is a swell of voices, and hurried discussions.

"Perhaps. But we must act now. Are you ready?"

"I don't even know—"

But he doesn't finish. The light is suddenly rushing by like he's riding the nose of a bullet train tearing through a white-lit tunnel. He's pushed flat against a surge of movement behind him. Screaming in his ears, a roar. He screams himself.

He slams hard into something that feels like a solid wall of steel. He disintegrates.

Adrian blinks, and is shocked to find he has eyelids again. The physical sensation of them feels strange after a period of having nothing.

But this body is not his own.

It's bulky, monstrous. He fills the room, each part of him pressing against the floor and the walls. There's humid air on his naked skin, and sweat oozes from his pores. The floor is slippery beneath his mass.

He's slumped over a bank of machinery, hands caressing a keyboard marked with odd symbols. His arms are stunted, a contrast to the rest of him. Intuitively, like being fed answers through an earphone, he knows that the machine before him controls the receiver that he built back home. But it also controls numerous other receivers in numerous other worlds.

Something hits him hard from behind like a truck mowing down a deer. There are voices in his head, screeching. Then Other Adrian speaks, his voice close and angry: "You ungrateful vermin, get out of my—" but the threat is cut short, the pressure eases. Adrian is in control again.

He pushes his monstrous torso upright. It's hard work. He can feel Other Adrian just behind a thin veil, fighting, but being held for the time being by Adrian's brethren. Yet Other Adrian still seems to retain enough will to make control difficult. Adrian feels like he's pushing a laden shopping trolley with a broken wheel. It won't let him go straight; it pulls him into displays of food, passing shoppers.

"What have you done with him?" demands Candice. Her voice sounds crackly, far away. He stares at a monitor affixed to the wall, and sees her on the screen, in the cabin, an empty armchair behind her.

He smiles at the sight of her.

"Don't grin at me, you smug prick. Answer me."

"Candice," he says, but the voice is not his own. It's deeper, gruffer. "It's me. This thing I'm in, this version of me, he brought me to his world, but I'm fighting back. I'm in him, but it's me."

Candice steps toward the screen, grimaces. She brandishes the large spanner still. Behind her he sees Taylor motionless on the floor. He wonders if she is still alive. Knowledge falls into his mind like rain on parched earth. He understands that Other Adrian was in the process of using the receiver to bring Taylor back next. The machinery has locked on, and will soon pull her into this world.

"Is this a joke?" Candice hisses. "Is this a fucking joke?"

There's not enough time to explain properly or convince her of who he is. He tries anyway.

"We used to go to the beach. The car park at the south end, late at night, where we'd smoke weed and talk about our futures. We both had huge dreams, but only one of us followed through. I broke our bargain, Candice. I never realised till now. But I did, and I'm sorry."

He watches her face waver, uncertain. The angry thin line that is her mouth falls into a frown. "How do you know this?"

"It's me, baby. I'm sorry. I know why you did what you did. I drove you to it through my selfishness. My inactivity. I should have done more to keep us close. I should have worked harder, at least on that one, important thing. I should have worked at us."

He feels on the brink of tears. He sees Candice's eyes moisten too. She opens her mouth, closes it. He doesn't know if she really believes it's him. But after a moment, the words flow from her like a torrent.

"I'm so sorry. I'm so, so sorry. I had no right. I know it doesn't matter, but I didn't love him. I never did. It was always you, I..." she starts to sob.

"I know, Candice. I do. It's just I've been too stupid to return the love you deserve."

A jolt forces him into blackness. He feels hundreds of presences slithering over each other like snakes, one larger, and more powerful than the rest—a python hissing, biting, writhing. But then the masses prevail, and overwhelm it once more. He opens his eyes to see Candice's worried expression.

"I don't have much time," Adrian says.

"Come home. Please come home, for me."

He taps into the collective minds of all the Adrians and confirms his suspicion. His shoulders slump. He feels an aching emptiness in the pit of his huge belly, like an icy vacuum. He shakes his head slowly. "I can't," he says, his voice a rasp. Candice sobs louder.

He wipes roughly at the tears that have fallen on his cheeks, then runs his hands over the keyboard, knowing instinctively what controls to issue.

There is a dull thumping sound, and Taylor is suddenly in the room, unconscious, face down on the wet floor.

"I'm glad of the time we had," he says to Candice. She's still crying, but watches him intently. "Even though I wasted so much of it, you were what made life worthwhile."

He feels the sea breeze as she holds his hand. Their feet are up on the dash of his car as they look out at the clear night sky and listen to the rhythmic sound of waves crashing.

"Please don't go," she whispers.

"I wish I didn't have to. But I do. There's more of us out there, Candice. Infinite versions of us, in different states of being. Some yet to meet, some deeply in love, some just starting out, like we did once, with all the promise of a lifetime to come. I can't let him take that from all of them."

"What about us?" she implores.

The cold in his stomach spreads through his limbs. He can barely choke out the words: "I love you."

He sees her next to him in the hospital when he wakes. He feels the ache as he sits with her at her mother's funeral, unable to take the hurt away. He sees the glint in her eye, the devilish smile on her lips as they make love. He sees her watching him as he works at his bench. Just watching, trying to decipher his thoughts.

The Adrians feed him what he needs.

His hands work quickly. Practiced hands flipping switches, typing instructions. He tunes out Candice's anguish as he works, but glances toward her occasionally, trying to keep her in his mind.

He engages all the receivers at his disposal. There are so many, in so many worlds. He doesn't need to wait for any of them to lock onto targets. Not for this task. He just needs them open. He initiates the dimensional transporter, the device Other Adrian used to send Taylor, the armchair, and the rug to him. He refocusses it, and along with the receivers creates a lengthy, complex loop.

"Goodbye, Candice," he says.

Other Adrian smashes through the defences of the Adrians, slams into him and squeezes. "What the fuck have you done?" he cries into Adrian's head, and out loud. "What the fuck—"

But it's too late.

The transporter makes a sound. A tick, tick, tick, then it pauses a beat. Whoosh.

Adrian can still feel Other Adrian's monstrous body. He feels the agony as its fat leg is sucked from the room, wrenched from its body, spat out in another world, only to be returned a second later, reduced to gore and splatter.

A slice of his shoulder and arm are gone, exposing bone. Other Adrian screams. Part of its stomach next, viscera slithering to the floor.

The receivers continue to send the parts back—shredded flesh, the stink of broken insides, shards of bone and blood raining down like a thunderstorm of red.

Adrian senses relief all around. He senses elation and celebration. He's not alone here at the end. And while he can't see Candice anymore, he has her firmly in mind.

Their vessel shudders, jerks. Torn and shredded. Crunched and diminished. Other Adrian wails like a spoilt child, but it's too late for him.

Adrian binds with the others, and they comfort him, and he them. They each share memories of their lives, recollections of love, and Candice.

He shares one memory. A memory of him and Candice locked in each other's arms, their whole lives ahead.
And then it ends.

See all the installments of Michael Gardner's story "Infinite Possibilities" online at Metaphorosis.
If you liked it, leave a comment. Authors love that!
Remember to subscribe to our e-mail updates so you'll know when new stories are posted.

Copyright

"The Eye of the Goddess" © 2022, Samuel Parr
"The Lost Library" © 2022, Mahmud El Sayed
"By the Scars Shall You Know" © 2022, Daniel Ausema
"The Girl Who Drew the World" © 2022, L.D. Oxford
"The Heebie-Jeebie Beam" © 2022, E.C. Fuller

"Queen of Crows" © 2022, Rachel Ayers
"The Hissing Trees" © 2022, Ian Donnell Arbuckle
"The Crystal Pyramid" © 2022, Mia Ram
"Frozen in Glass" © 2022, Hope Davies

"To the Wild Sea" © 2022, B. Morris Allen
"For the Love of Wild Things" © 2022, Mande Matthews
"Her Last Will" © 2022, Karl El-Koura
"Portals and Other Lost Things" © 2022, Elizabeth Rankin
"Infinite Possibilities I" © 2022, Michael Gardner

"Problems of the Flesh" © 2022, Hamilton Perez
"A Xenothanatologist's Guidebook to Death Practices Among the Sapient Species of the Outer
     Perseus Arm of the Milky Way Galaxy" © 2022, P.G. Streeter
"Holding On" © 2022, Justen Russell
"Infinite Possibilities II" © 2022, Michael Gardner

"If Gold Runs Red" © 2022, Gordon Grice
"Bas Relief" © 2022, Joshua Grasso
"An Hour in the City of Lightning" © 2022, A.D. Guzman
"Infinite Possibilities III" © 2022, Michael Gardner

"The Dragon's Due" © 2022, Christopher Warden
"Through the Middle" © 2022, J.B. Kish
"Love, Death, and the Electric Soul" © 2022, Alexandra Peel
"Snowman" © 2022, Han Whiteoak
"Infinite Possibilities IV" © 2022, Michael Gardner

Moral rights asserted

Each author whose work is included in this book has asserted their moral rights, including the right to be identified as the author of their respective work(s).

Publisher

Metaphorosis Magazine is an imprint of
Metaphorosis Publishing
Neskowin, OR, USA

www.metaphorosis.com

"Metaphorosis" is a registered trademark.

Discounts available

Substantial discounts are available for educational institutions, including writing workshops. Discounts are also available for quantity purchases. For details, contact Metaphorosis at metaphorosis.com/about

Metaphorosis Publishing

Metaphorosis offers beautifully written science fiction and fantasy. Our imprints include:

Metaphorosis Magazine

Plant Based Press

Verdage

Vestige

Joyful Heave

You can also find us:
@MetaphorosisMag
writing.exchange/@metaphorosis
www.facebook.com/metaphorosis

Help keep Metaphorosis running at
Patreon.com/metaphorosis

See more about some of our books on the following pages.

Metaphorosis
a magazine of speculative fiction

Metaphorosis is an online speculative fiction magazine dedicated to quality writing. We publish an original story every week, along with author bios, interviews, and notes on story origins.

We also publish monthly print and e-book issues, as well as yearly Best of and Complete anthologies.

Come and see us online at magazine.Metaphorosis.com.

Plant Based Press

Vegan-friendly science fiction and fantasy, including anthologies of the year's best SFF stories, from 2016-2020.

Chambers of the Heart
speculative stories
by
B. Morris Allen

A heart that's a building, a dog that's a program, a woman sinking irretrievably — stories about love, loss, and movement.

Susurrus

A darkly romantic story of magic, love, and suffering.

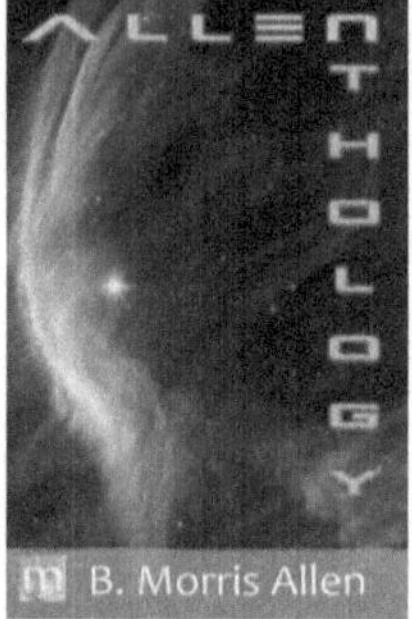

Allenthology: Volume I

Including three full collections of SFF stories.

Verdage

Science fiction and fantasy books for writers – full of great stories, often with an additional focus on the craft of speculative fiction writing.

Reading 5X5 x3

Changes

How do stories move from 'maybe' to published?

Here are 15 case studies of stories published in *Metaphorosis* magazine.

Reading 5X5 x2

Duets

How do authors' voices change when they collaborate?

A round-robin of five talented science fiction and fantasy authors collaborating with each other and writing solo.

Including stories by Evan Marcroft, David Gallay, J. Tynan Burke, L'Erin Ogle, and Douglas Anstruther.

Score

an SFF symphony

An anthology with an emotional score from the heights of joy to the depths of despair – but always with a little hope shining through.

Reading 5X5

Five stories, five times

See how different writers take on the same material.

Reading 5X5

Writers' Edition

Two extra stories, the story seed, and authors' notes on writing.

Vestige

Novelettes, novellas, and novels by Metaphorosis authors.

The Nocturnals
Mariah Montoya

Night is Dangerous. Day is deadly.
Where day and night last thirty years, humans move constantly stay ahead of the night and cruel Nocturnals that call it home. But a boy is lost out there.